THE LAKE GENEVA CHRONICLES

THE
LAKE GENEVA
CHRONICLES

A TRIBUTE TO THE
AMERICAN SPIRIT

Beverly Horvath DiMare

BLUE DOLPHIN PUBLISHING

Published by Blue Dolphin Publishing, Inc.
Fine Books for all Ages

For inquiries or orders, address
Blue Dolphin Publishing, Inc.
P.O. Box 8, Nevada City, CA 95959
Orders: 1-800-643-0765
Web: www.bluedolphinpublishing.com

ISBN: 978-1-57733-120-9 (hardcover)
ISBN: 978-1-57733-236-7 (paperback)
ISBN: 978-1-57733-326-5 (e-book)

First printing, February, 2006
Second printing, August 2008
Third printing, March 2011

Library of Congress Cataloging-in-Publication Data

DiMare, Beverly Horvath, 1946-
  The Lake Geneva chronicles : a tribute to the great power and beauty
of love / Beverly Horvath DiMare.
      p. cm.
   ISBN 1-57733-120-6 (alk. paper)
   1. Fontana (Wis.)—Fiction. 2. Rural families—Fiction. 3. Immigrants—
Fiction. 4. Wisconsin—Fiction. 5. Farm life—Fiction. I. Title.

  PS3604.I464L35 2004
  813'.6—dc22

                                                              2004008656

Cover Art: Beverly Horvath DiMare

Printed in the United States of America

10   9   8   7   6   5   4   3

To honor both the concept and the reality of "family."
Wheresoever true respect and love abide,
There one will consistently find its essence.

PREFACE

TO LIVE UPON THIS BEAUTIFUL EARTH without having firmly established some sort of meaningful "credo" for living, or essential philosophy which engenders one's more noble beliefs, would be akin to being a sailor navigating through the vast oceans of this world without benefit of compass, or map, or trusty star by which to sail. Traveling through the years devoid of the basic comfort of some "master plan," as it were, is to be sadly remiss in one's responsibilities. This truth becomes especially poignant whenever a person becomes a parent. Children naturally live by the example—or lack of example—characteristically proffered by this traditionally vital caregiver. Therefore, the intrinsic principles originally set forth by parents ultimately become that same critical "guiding light" for the child.

Although *THE LAKE GENEVA CHRONICLES* may be properly described as a work of fiction, the story is based very much upon fact. It is the story of the history of my paternal grandparents who immigrated to America during the early part of this past century from their former home in Central Europe. As with countless other citizens who were arriving daily from other lands, their own early lives were fraught with numerous challenges.

For example, somehow my young grandparents managed to barely escape a bloody revolution where Pancho Villa and his fellow insurgents vengefully occupied Mexico City back in the winter of 1914-1915. Later on they were forced to gingerly side-step the highly destructive antics of Capone's mob in Chicago, as well as survive as best they could the inevitable loss of a highly lucrative business enterprise during that infamous autumn of 1929. This, of course, proved to be the significant prelude to those anguished years of untold suffering known as the Great Depression. By then Louis and Wilma Horvath and their many children eventually retreated to a small farming community in Wisconsin to live, and to work, and to find a bit of much-needed sanity in those rather insane years of our more turbulent World History.

During my own earliest infancy which began in the autumn of 1946, a portion of many a happy summer, thereafter, was spent in the Lake Geneva area. The large, well-manicured farmstead still located across the street from the German Settlement Cemetery there on highway "D," did, indeed, once belong to my father's parents. But sometime in 1931, because of a second mortgage which appeared unannounced a year or so after the family took up residence there—a factor which, because of insufficient funds on their part, led to the inevitable "bank foreclosure"— everyone was forced to leave behind the comfort of this welcome haven, and to take up temporary lodging instead within the tiny hamlet referred to, back then, as "Peck's Station." And so it was here, behind a general store more or less similar to the one described in this story, that my grandparents and their eleven children lived for a brief time. This included my own father, Frederick—or "Fritz" for the sake of our story, who was barely five years old at the time.

Following yet two more necessary moves over the next several years, a more permanent home was established in William's Bay. This, then, is the modest but wonderful farmstead which lives on in my cherished memories. It is this same environment, I might add, which I have chosen to share with the reader in this story. However, because of the highly sentimental proximity of that former original farmstead, which lies directly across from that special "little cemetery there on the hill" and where three generations of "our people" are now buried, I purposely chose to tell this most personal of tales just as I have.

My grandfather was an accomplished artist. During those financially desperate years from 1930 to the start of the Second World War he was occasionally able to sell his sketches and paintings to members of the wealthier and more influential families who owned summer homes around the lake. These same modest funds generally helped to supplement the family income.

Although many of the various details of my story actually happened, during those more rare moments where I have chosen to purposely depart from the hallowed truth of any given situation, only to "artistically embellish" upon the known facts, as it were, this near-sacred liberty was taken with characteristic humility, and only in deference to some overriding and far more critical philosophical truth which begged to be shared. In light of this, I lovingly recall that my grandmother embraced a life-long passion for gardening. As a toddler and youth I observed how she lavished such care upon the many potted oleander trees which lined the gravel driveway of our family home. And in July there was the famous strawberry patch which lingers still, with such clarity, within my memory. Finally, too, with respect to my Uncle Eddie, the brief letter paraphrased within one of the latter chapters of this book—the same personal correspondence sent by him to his brother, Willy, from North Africa during the early spring of 1943 only days before his P-40 was shot down by an enemy aircraft and he was killed—remains a personal treasure whose significance gently reaches forward from that moment in time to firmly touch the present, and helps to greatly personalize the overall historic perspective of the times.

Looking back upon my childhood, as I tend to do more and more these days, I frequently imagine that I must have been a most unusual child. As my parents would undoubtedly concur, while other youngsters were occupied in busily collecting toy dolls and the like, I remained ever-busy collecting "real people." This was not in the literal sense, certainly, but rather in the figurative sense, for the functioning of the minds and the hearts of others—the overall condition of their souls—has forever fascinated me.

In an effort to remain true to myself, as well as to the reader, it shall also be important for the reader to note that the character of "Adam Bodray" is intended to represent a vehicle for the telling of this special tale. For the greater portion of my adult life I have relentlessly fought against the abject tyranny of child abuse. With this in mind, then, this particular young boy is the personification of that innocent and vulnerable child within each of us. Moreover, with regard to the story's several other colorful fictional representations in the form of Cornelia Grimsley, "Doc" Owens, Harry Hopkins, and Henry Bodray, these characterizations are basically the encapsulation of the various people which have been painstakingly "collected" by me throughout my life travels. They represent the very same "types of individuals," I might add, whom all readers have surely encountered to some degree or another upon their own interesting journey.

Sometime during the early summer of 1958 my father was assigned to Montgomery, Alabama to attend a year-long course offered by the Air War College. Subsequently my young brother and I were enrolled for the autumn semester in a small public school that was located across town. Those following months of fall and winter and spring, which comprised the remainder of that particular year and part of the next, naturally constituted my formal sixth-grade education. This same critical time period became for me a pivotal point in my intellectual and emotional growth. I learned many important truths regarding human nature, as well as the often irrational ways of the world, which were not being openly taught in any classroom.

Day in and day out I quietly observed the children of our local African American citizens being forced to walk to their own designated schools, and in all sorts of weather, while my fellow students and I comfortably rode our busses to our own prescribed schools. Likewise by law, and with arrogant impunity, all public facilities such as lavatories and drinking fountains were systematically marked with highly offensive signs denoting "for colored only" or "for whites only," and the degrading truth of it all left me wondering why this obvious lack of justice was being tolerated by anyone.

In my child-like naiveté I never imagined that such sobering matters as these, indicative of such gross injustice on the part of society as a whole, were actually only the tip of a most unsavory "iceberg," and that, truly, far worse sins than these were being committed against members of this segment of our population on an on-going basis. How could the child I was back then ever have guessed that the instinctive craving for justice which I was experiencing for the first time—that same fundamental craving which all good people endlessly carry within their hearts—would eventually be evolving into a much-longed-for reality for our nation as a whole—and in the not too distant future?

Just as Time has surely proven, those sacred and haunting chords from the then only tentative music of Truth and Justice, which a large body of our citizens was already beginning to softly hum in unison, would be growing louder, and still louder, to finally develop into our present-day indisputably hard-won and unquenchable symphony of voices known as the Civil Rights Movement. Undoubtedly it was these same strong and indelible impressions which were so firmly imprinted upon my twelve-year-old heart and mind. The impressions have not only survived all these many years, but have actually grown stronger in order to have "given birth," so to speak, to the special characters represented by the members of the Earl Ketchum family whom the reader ultimately meets later on in this story.

With further regard to this premier literary attempt on my part, I have chosen to speak in those more "universally human terms" which embrace such powerful issues as the sacredness of family, and the incalculable value of genuine friendship. My story also seeks to adequately address the utter baseness of child abuse, in any form, which continues to plague our world society.

I speak of the love of one's God and one's country. Likewise, the growing fragility of America's democratic process which, although held in reverent esteem by so many of our citizens, is being consistently taken for granted, little by little, by just as many more. The dedicated reader shall similarly discover the timeless scenario of those bitterly warring factions of "Truth, and Justice, and Goodness," versus "Profound Ignorance, and Injustice, and Evil" more or less underpinning each and every consecutive chapter. Lastly, but not least of all, the story's philosophy acknowledges that undeniable seed of emotional hunger with which every human soul is born—the same hearty seed that, in time, manages first to expand, and then to faithfully germinate and grow, only to finally live on quite often to severely chafe the spirit as one travels the entire distance from cradle to grave....

Serious work upon the manuscript for this story began in earnest in January of 1996. Needless to say so much has happened to our world since then. As Time has surely proven, ignorance and hatred remain mankind's great destroyers. Because of this sobering reality our priceless treasures of Freedom and Democracy still come at such a substantially high price.

Recently we as a country were poignantly reminded that true patriotism and true courage have forevermore lived, not only within the hearts of our great men and women of every generation, but so significantly within the minds and hearts of this great country's average citizens. Throughout our relatively short history as a nation our enemies have consistently underestimated our resolve.

As a country we are now slowly relearning the inescapable reality that it is the strong and resilient family which continuously remains the critical foundation of every strong society. We must lovingly teach our children this important truth, just as our children must also teach their own children. For far too many years now this country's statisticians, poll-takers, and political pundits have all too readily been assuring us that the "traditional family" is fast becoming extinct. Although there is significant factual evidence to support this foreboding statement, my own optimistic nature wants so much to believe that that notoriously predictable pendulum of change is about to begin to swing the other way. I also hold to the belief that anywhere true respect and love are present, there one will also find the true concept of "family." This story is a tribute to such sacred things as these.

Although my heart is forever destined to remain American through and through, my soul is obliged to remain a truly caring citizen of this world. Perhaps it is because of this innate and unusually strong "spiritual duality" that I have always thoroughly appreciated the gloriously fascinating amalgamation inherent within this nation's cultural diversification. For generation upon generation hopeful representatives from every conceivable corner of our vast and frequently troubled world continue to arrive at our bright and shining shores avidly seeking the many freedoms that our Democracy faithfully promises, thereby ultimately enriching the entire body of our citizens in the process. With these highly significant sentiments foremost in mind, be it known that this carefully crafted treatise stands as a tangible expression of the great love and deep respect this writer continues to nurture for this same wonderful country of her birth. It represents nothing less than a proud tribute to the "indomitable" American Spirit which not only built this amazing land we all love so much, but that same ever-vigilant collective spirit which has forsworn to endlessly guard and protect our special way of life.

BHD
September 19, 2001
North Palm Beach, Florida

"*Do not be deceived in men, for it is the worst, and the easiest of deceptions; far better to be cheated in price, than in the goods; nothing is more important than to look within: only there is a difference between knowing merchandise and knowing men; a great science to understand the minds of men, and to discern their humors: just as important to have studied men, as to have studied books.*"

—Baltasar Gracian

"*...As long as Kindness,*
The Pure, still stays with his heart, man
Not unhappily measures himself
Against the Godhead...."

—Friedrich Holderline

PROLOGUE

F ELIX LAUDER WAS AN UNUSUALLY COMPLEX MAN. Early in life he grew to abhor the abuse of power—the abuse of power in any form. Early on, too, as the story goes, he was forced to heed several painful lessons dealing with this very issue which automatically negated the abiding faith and deep regard he once held for the Profession of Law. Eventually he came to believe that, although there is a great deal of Law being practiced everywhere in the world, there is precious little Justice for all available in the end.

More than anything else this gross irregularity was blamed upon those decidedly corrupt individuals living and thriving among the more honest few; those well-educated subversives, in other words, who willfully taint the noble concepts of Truth and Justice by defiling the very laws which they help to create in the first place, in order to be able to further their own interests in some way or another. With a slightly melancholy smile that only helped to thoroughly captivate the keen attention of this listener, my friend would go on to quietly state his view that: Truth is a beggar! And Justice, if it can be found at all, frequently comes in unexpected forms....

After learning all of this about the man, the reader might naturally be tempted to judge him from the start as some sort of jaded Utopian. Or, still yet, along similarly negative lines, perhaps one of society's more disgruntled and thin-skinned misfits, but in actual fact this would be the farthest thing from the truth.

Because of a particularly distasteful incident, which had marked him early on in his youth, for the remainder of his life Felix Lauder waged a private war upon the Catholic Church. In doing so his long marriage eventually suffered real casualties from this on-going conflict. Thinking back I surmise that inwardly he harbored great disdain for all organized religions, believing that the unavoidable human aspect of each acted as a fertile subterfuge to harbor real disease and corruption, thereby giving license to those who would go about gravely distorting that which is

innately good in the human soul. And yet, even though to my knowledge this remarkable man had never once set foot within any formal
house of worship, nor recanted in the least that strongly held position
of his by eventually invoking a truce of any sort with that great bastion
of formidable power there in Rome, he became for me the epitome of
what a truly religious person should be.

My friend was a self-educated man. He remained an "armchair philosopher," as he himself once modestly put it. Often he would openly
lament, in that reserved yet still quietly passionate manner of his: "What
would life be like, Adam, without all my cherished books? My music?
My canvases, paint brushes, and oils...?" Then, as if to mentally gather
together those things which he surely felt were life's more significant
gifts, in order to duly categorize them within this same vital grouping for
safekeeping, after a brief but thoughtful pause he went on to add, "What
indeed, my young friend, would life be like—without love?"

Early on in our relationship I quickly learned that these sorts of
questions he habitually posed were basically rhetorical in nature and,
therefore, required no real response on my part. Philosophers, you see,
are like this. Now and then they will openly proffer some sort of tantalizing question merely for the question's sake and nothing more than this.
Much as if by putting that reasonable thought into actual words was a
way of formalizing that logic, thereby helping to assure its future legitimacy. The entire process, I quickly came to realize, could be compared to
a chess game where one competent player chooses to utilize both sides of
the board at the same time. So it is, then, within the active minds of both
the chess master, as well as the very able philosopher. One's mind simply
divides itself, so to speak, for the task at hand. Each worthy participant
plays his or her respective role where a splendid dialogue for two is taking place, and all within the confines of one solitary active mind.

During his full and indisputably well-lived lifetime Felix Lauder
was neither a stranger to success, nor to failure. Through the good times
and, particularly, through the bad he managed to forever maintain the
great dignity of spirit for which I shall always remember and admire
him. What remains so incredibly sad, however, is the fact that he was
never quite the same person after what happened to the members of the
Ketchum family. After that brutal and wholly unnecessary tragedy occurred something critical within the extreme core of his being lay badly
broken never to be mended again. Needless to say, it literally broke my
heart to have been a witness to it all.

Even with the deaths of several of his own beloved children which
had occurred one after the other over a period of several years; and,

subsequently, with the indescribable heartache that forever accompanies such unnatural events as these where doting parents are forced to outlive their progeny, I watched him and his wife struggle greatly with their mutual loss. I watched them fight on each occasion to master that overwhelming sorrow and, eventually, to be able to reach a point where all their terrible sadness could be placed within its more proper perspective with the passing of the years. But for Felix it would not prove to be so with that particular other incident....

Over the years my great friend developed some rather interesting notions regarding many of life's more intriguing issues. Even from the beginning of our relationship I came to savor the manner in which his mind worked. Towards the end of his lifetime, for instance, during a particularly dramatic encounter between the two of us when he felt a profound need to reveal many of his innermost secrets, I recall how he told me that, "The Gods are forever predisposed to playing games with our lives, Adam. They so generously give to us only to take back those same precious gifts somewhere down the road, causing us tremendous pain and sorrow in the process. But," he also added, as if somehow he felt obliged to further explain and defend these dire actions of the Gods, "as all wise and compassionate mortals know, and in complete fairness to these same omnipotent beings, one must not judge them too harshly in the end. For you see the Gods tend to behave as they do, not out of any sense of cruelty on their parts, but rather out of a sense of ignorance. After all, how could these near-perfect beings ever know what it is like to be thoroughly mortal—thoroughly human in every sense of the word, with each of us possessing our numerous vulnerabilities, as well as our many ever-fragile strengths? What becomes intolerable, however, and what may never be forgiven in the least, is the extreme cruelty one human being willfully inflicts upon another. Nowhere is there a more ruthless form of betrayal than that which comes from the hand, and from the heart, of one's own!"

How I miss the man. Those few years we were privileged to share with each other remain a consummate gift. To this day no one else has ever made so significant an impression upon my life as he. Although Felix Lauder died years ago at the relatively young age of seventy when I was but a young man myself, not a single day has ever come or gone when I have not paused to faithfully recall something meaningful he once said or did. After all, he was my great teacher.... With immense pride I shall further state that he was my truest friend. And from the moment of our very first meeting, from that special day of days which is destined to live forevermore within my heart as the day of "the strawberries and the storm," he became for me the loving father that I might have other-wise never known....

With my dear friend's passing back in the early autumn of 1947, followed by his wife's death some seventeen years after that, I rarely found any reason to return to the Lake Geneva area. However during numerous periods throughout these past many years of my adult life, before the Lauder family farmstead was actually sold to the current owners and then renovated at considerable cost from top to bottom, I nursed a serious obsession to spend a complete summer or autumn there at Peck's Station.... Indeed, how very great was my secret longing to return to this once familiar place in order to write, and to paint, and to attempt—more than anything else, to respectfully conjure up those familial ghosts of the past.

This same dear little house of my childhood and youth remained unoccupied for decades, and, therefore, had naturally fallen into a rather sad state of ill-repair. Nevertheless with the considerable attributes of some rare and gifted shaman I might have happily summoned forth tiny fragments of what used to be. Commiserating to my heart's content with those special people I grew to love so much, I should have happily wandered from room to room, all the while eagerly searching out and emotionally soaking up all the sacred sights, and sounds, and smells of long ago.

Regrettably, though, it is said that the spirits of our dearly departed never return to places which have become unfamiliar to them. Perhaps, too, this simple wisdom is as it ought to be. Instead I find that I am forced to content myself in merely remembering as I do. After all, is it not in continually remembering those we have loved, and lost, that we continue to honor them still?

"Felix, do you believe in the reality of heaven and hell? Life after death?", I once asked my dear teacher. Some of our more enlightening talks would often start off this way. They happened at times when he and I worked side-by-side—or head-to-head, which was more the case on that particular day. The year was 1935 ... and within a few weeks' time I would more or less be celebrating my fourteenth birthday.

I clearly remember that it was in the early spring of that very year when together Felix and I finally climbed atop the roof of the old farm-house. We sat perched securely along the apex of the roof line, just above one of the dormers, diligently repairing numerous imperfections which were discovered long before within the wooden base covering of the roof itself.

Problems with the leaky roof had been developing for quite some time, judging from the overall damage. But during those incredibly trying years of the Great Depression era, when it proved a noteworthy task for most people just to be able to keep body and soul forged together by regularly supplying food for the table and clothing for the back, precious funds for necessities such as roof repairs were a luxury few could justify. Still, the on-going deterioration of this long-neglected task had finally reached a critical point where matters could no longer be ignored.

Buckets and deep cooking pots of every imaginable size and description had been readily enlisted and strategically placed in various areas all around the wooden flooring of the upstairs bedrooms and bathroom. They were carefully positioned in such a manner so as to be certain to catch the endless succession of drops of dirty water that were a natural result of the recently melting snow. As we lay in bed at night listening to the endless cacophony of music which was being orchestrated by these droplets of moisture as they tumbled into their respective containers at various speeds, a horribly restless slumber was produced, especially during those first several evenings. Mercifully, however, that entire maddening sound which the evening hours somehow only tended to magnify became less and less offensive with the passing of time. So much so, in fact, that towards the end the total effect was no longer noticed very much at all. I suppose that one might compare this sensation to the loud annoying ticking sound that an unfamiliar clock makes upon the ear from the start. With this similarly continuous assault of noise upon the mind, for sanity sake, one eventually decides to "tune out" or muffle the rude unpleasantness.

That winter was an especially harsh one. It was a season of record-breaking statistics, as blizzard upon blizzard continued to bombard the region without mercy. Man and beast, alike, suffered through the interminable weather with scant relief that year. Because of this each passing day seemed to automatically produce a new container or two that was hastily added to the army already assembled there in the Lauder home. At one point, before the repair work had actually commenced in earnest, the now bare floor of our communal sleeping area upstairs was littered with such a wild assortment of containers that it reminded me of a three-dimensional mosaic which had been haphazardly displayed by some wild artist of obvious ill repute.

To arrive without incident from one corner of a room to another a person was forced to remember to carefully negotiate this maze of debris upon the floor. This ongoing maneuver was no easy task, be assured, especially when one was in a hurry, or whenever it grew dark outside and one failed to turn on the wall switch. I confess that in the beginning all of this seemed an interesting diversion from our more normal way of living. However, in no time at all, what began easily enough as a minor inconvenience with a pot here and a bucket over there soon grew into a real nuisance. This fact was especially so for Emma Lauder, since it was she who always insisted upon personally overseeing any cleanup effort on the part of an offender whenever one of us every now and then chanced to miscalculate that rather unforgiving course.

For those youngest members among the Lauder's many children this temporary arrangement in the family's lifestyle proved fruitful for the daily invention of wonderful games. Healthy children seem to possess an enviable knack for making the best out of even the most difficult situations. When the inclement winter weather was at its worst and the adults and older children found themselves generally at odds with one another over one small thing or another—due primarily to their collective boredom and to the subsequent irritation that being "housebound" for such long stretches of time naturally engendered, it became those happy games of "hop-scotch" or "blind man's bluff" played with abandon throughout the entire upstairs area of the old house that inevitably resulted in some minor accident. In retrospect, though, all this seemed such a small price to pay for the endless hours of laughter and good-natured fun that these occasions always managed to afford the youngsters....

The well-worn collar of my hand-me-down jacket which had originally belonged to my beloved George, and to young Lewis long before that, was pulled up snugly about my neck to help ward off the brisk March breeze. Spring's stingy warmth from the sun's weak rays barely made any impression upon my back, as I labored. Early on I chose to remove my warm mittens, in order to spare them the indignity of becoming permanently ruined by the sticky foul-smelling tar which I was being entrusted to apply correctly to the needy patches of the roof that had been painstakingly scraped and cleaned by Felix the week before.

Felix Lauder remained the consummate perfectionist in every project that he ever undertook. This was a natural part of the unwritten code by which he lived. He believed unequivocally that the quality of the outcome of one's endeavor, no matter how large or how small the undertaking might be, was a direct reflection upon the basic quality of the individual. His children and I lived by his example. With this in mind deep down I recognized how it must have galled him to have been made to succumb to this far less desirable method of repairing the roof. Had there been money enough available to do the job properly he surely would have opted to replace the entire structure of the slowly rotting roof by erecting healthy new trusses, followed then by a sturdy new plywood covering. Instead, because of the family's financially difficult circumstances, we were being forced to merely apply this more temporary dressing of "piecemeal work" as Felix, with rancor, more than once referred to what we were now doing.

The meager funds, in fact, which were dutifully solicited in order to purchase the several pounds of roofing nails, tar, and asphalt shingles for the job at hand came into being the way so much of the family's emergency funds came into being. One particular morning when Felix, several of the Lauder children, and I were preparing to drive into town to secure those necessary items from Otto Grimsley's general store, I was in the process of hurriedly finishing my breakfast alone in the dining room. It was Saturday and for some unexplainable reason I had overslept.

So as not to keep the others waiting unnecessarily I remained speedily spooning generous portions of warm oatmeal into my mouth when my eyes eventually wandered to a familiar spot on the wall directly across the large round table before me. Much to my unexpected amazement, however, instead of finding the familiar oil painting which I had long admired, in its place I soon discovered a rather telling two-foot square patch of slightly more pristine wall paint whose clarity and freshness stood out ever so slightly in contrast to the rest of the wall covering which had naturally grown more faded with the passing of the years.

My unexpected discovery that morning was akin to a rude slap in the face, since I had grown especially fond of that particular painting. During those first years when I originally came to live with the Lauder family, and with every meal of each day thereafter which I was privileged to either share with them as a group—or with those more infrequent meals which I, for one reason or another, ended up taking alone, my eyes would invariably make their way to that special place on the otherwise undecorated wall before me.

Long since had I memorized the painting's every nuance; its every shadow and line. Although the rendering consisted of what to my untrained eye seemed to be a mere handful of brush strokes from the master's tools, the overall composition held the power to continually mesmerize me each time I studied it. Indeed, the more I contemplated the painting, the more meaning I was able to discern in the work's amazing play of light against darkness.

The relatively small canvas was one of Felix's earliest compositions. It clearly hailed from a time when he still resided as a young man in his native Hungary. In the right hand bottom corner, partially hidden by several brush strokes which insinuated more than anything else the presence of dried grasses and weeds, one could find the initial of the artist's first name, a period, and then his last name clearly defined in thin lines of black paint. Upon the line immediately underneath was etched within thicker paint which had been applied with a pallet knife the word: "Beled"; and, directly beside this, the date 1897....

For me the hypnotic beauty of this special scene lay in its lesson of utter simplicity. Pleasing combinations of muted hues of gray against black, with the warmer colors of raw umber and burnt sienna mingled upon cream and white, merely hinted at movement as several large black ravens sparred with each other upon a steep snow bank of soft newly fallen snow. How clever was the artist! How haunting was his ability to say so much in such an unfettered and forthright manner.

Staring forlornly at the naked wall that day momentarily invoked a spontaneous feeling of great loss, and, quite frankly, a mood of equally stark betrayal. Naturally my first impulse was to have run to my benefactor, and to have respectfully chided him for what I originally perceived as disloyalty on his part, for it soon became quite clear to me what had happened. How could my friend have chosen this particular work of his to sell? My wonderful painting! And with all the other oils and watercolors of his from which to choose? And yet in fairness to this good man I had never actually declared to anyone—least of all to him—just what the painting had grown to mean to me.

So in the end while I sat staring at that empty spot on the wall, my unfinished breakfast before me having since grown quite cold and wholly unappetizing, and my earlier morning spirit of lightheartedness at the prospect of accompanying Felix and the others into town that day to fetch the roofing material now somewhat dampened, I finally began to feel twinges of guilt. Perhaps it was I who needed chiding, after all. Knowing Felix, as I did, I was quite certain that, had he been given even the slightest inkling of my deep regard for this particular work of his, he surely would never have chosen to part with it as he had. Instead, he might have chosen something else to sell. But the roof needed repairing. This was the long and the short of the situation. Finally, with a certain amount of reluctant graciousness, I made myself accept this fact.

Back on the roof that day my fingers were growing painfully numb from the cold. Upon Felix's command, however, which was usually just a nod of his slightly bowed head since he habitually kept several roofing nails clenched expertly between his front teeth until he needed them, making it impossible for him to communicate with me in any other fashion, I would confidently spring into action by deftly applying a generous glob of sticky tar exactly where it was required.

We always worked exceedingly well together, Felix and I—very much like well-calibrated machines. This time my job basically amounted to generously smearing that highly ignoble substance with an unusual looking brush which was always kept in its special tin bucket. Then that same warm waterproof adhesive would be quickly spread around to properly cover every trace of the exposed wood. After this, and almost as if he were taking his queue from me, Felix would promptly set an asphalt shingle directly over the tarry spot. Finally raising the notably heavy iron hammer up over his head, he would bring the indispensable object back down in a graceful arc as the long squarish nails were firmly driven into place one by one. To better assure my safety the weighty metal container containing the tar was conveniently secured by a generous length of sturdy clothes line that, in turn, was prudently hooked through a makeshift pulley there upon one corner of the roof, and then extended even further in order to be finally attached around my waist.

Naturally Felix was concentrating on our task, all the while wearing a slightly pensive frown upon his face. Since youngsters possess a fascinating propensity for introducing topics of a sublime nature in a relatively simple and straightforward manner—and, quite often, without the slightest warning, with my somewhat casual and unexpected delivery of that timeless question regarding one of life's more poignant dilemmas, my dear friend immediately halted what he was doing and quickly glanced up over his bifocals to stare at me for a brief second or two.

Then just as quickly, as if he had not even heard the profoundly serious question I posed only seconds before, he became absorbed once again in what he was attempting to finish. With a certain sense of admiration I watched intently as his left hand retrieved the last nail from its trusty holding place there between his tightly pursed lips. Soon, just as he was doing all morning long, he also removed the large hammer from its designated compartment there within his leather carpenter's apron. Raising the tool into the air, yet one more time, Felix expertly brought it down as contact was being made between the two entities over and over again, until at long last the hearty nail was properly driven into place.

None of my questions ever went unanswered. Even on those rare occasions when Felix Lauder did not know the answer to a particular question, he always said so. Eventually, time permitting, as if he felt a keen obligation to investigate and secure the truth not only for my benefit alone, but for his own benefit as well, we would purposefully wander off together to one of the many books on one of the many shelves of that immense bookcase in the parlor—or to the local library, if that is what it finally took, to satisfy our needs.

My friend held the firm belief that natural curiosity was vital to real learning and should be perpetually encouraged and stimulated whenever possible, especially in young children. This "congenital curiosity," as he liked to refer to it, remains an invaluable trait with which most healthy minds are born; the vital bedrock, as it were, for higher learning.

"Nearly everyone possesses the ability to memorize a page of information and then spew it out upon command," the Lauder children and I more than once heard Felix say whenever we happened upon the subject. "Memorization, after all, is merely a mental exercise intended to help keep the brain fit, just as walking benefits the body," he patiently insisted. "But when these mental exercises become chronic in their use, much to the exclusion of the more desirable obsession to search out and secure the facts, then ultimately real learning is negated due to the reality that more often than not information that is collected in this fashion soon becomes forgotten over time. It is, instead, that innocent and most fervent compulsion to know the truth of any situation, and the ensuing effort put forth to this end, that tends the most to leave a lasting impression upon the human mind!"

Relative to questions his children and I frequently posed to Felix, no matter how complex or how trivial the subject matter of our inquiry might seem, in time each and every topic would be patiently addressed. With regard to this fine person, this special habit of his was just one of the many things upon which one could steadfastly rely. He made a habit of treating others—their person, as well as their feelings and ideas—with the greatest respect. Keeping this in mind, I continued to wait very patiently for the answer which I believed wholeheartedly would eventually be forthcoming; the answer to the bothersome question which had plagued me for such a long time already.

The pinnacle of that familiar landmark which was the William's Bay water tower could barely be discerned there to the far southwest, floating, more or less, just above the subtle line of giant maple and oak trees in the far distance. Beyond that point, and out of sight, was the lake.

Felix sat up straight. Cupping the small of his back with both hands, he stretched a little. The tedious work which we both enthusiastically undertook just after dawn that morning was growing hard on him.

Presently, as he had taken to doing all morning long, he began to rub his gloveless hands together rather vigorously and then to blow upon them several times in order to help inspire the necessary circulation of blood. Our combined efforts to restore the roof were paying off. Critically we judged that we had finally reached the halfway mark. Three or four hours more of seriously concentrated effort after lunch, if we were lucky, would surely finish the job. I became fairly elated as I contemplated this fact.

Puffs of cloud-like vapor from our steady breathing served to remind us that the real season of spring, with its much-coveted promise of more dependable warmth, was not yet upon us. From this prized vantage point of ours where we were now both resting atop the roof, the panoramic view was really quite impressive in its own special sort of way. Stretches of barren fields, for example, continued to slumber on below us and gently fanned out for miles in nearly every direction. Although it was practically midday already, there lingered still a hint of latent frost aptly tucked away in many of the secret hiding places there among the vast sea of upturned clumps of frozen earth. Like fragile crystallized wisps of powder sugar it was. Likewise, within the pasture nearest the pump house, a dozen cows snuggled together as closely as they possibly could in the welcomed familiarity that served to help keep them all warm.

Even the large twisted bundle of dry honeysuckle vine, too, seemed determined to huddle even closer than usual to the north side of the barn for better protection against the scourge of frequent gusts of frigid air. Its deceptively lifeless looking form betrayed not the slightest hint of the amazing transformation of which it was capable. Soon it would be bursting forth in all its glory to herald the miracle that is spring, all the while having ceremoniously exchanged its somber wintry robes of muted browns and grays for that more elegant finery of bright beryline green, with an endless profusion of tiny white fragrant flowers to follow not far behind.

The only point of real interest that managed to break the vast flatness of the stark landscape that encircled us was a gentle rise to the immediate southeast of us, upon which sat a small Gothic style chapel. Nestled here and there around the solid base of this strong stone edifice, in no particularly discernible pattern, was scattered some twenty or thirty graves. A narrow paved road separated the churchyard from the Lauder's property line, the very roof of the farmhouse upon which we were presently sitting being some three hundred yards, or so, away. Surrounding the entire perimeter of this hallowed ground was an ancient-looking yet relatively well-maintained black wrought-iron fence. Its evenly spaced succession of massive ten-foot-high spires reached towards heaven in an unbroken line, save for a short span in one far back corner where two of the long rods were missing. In the foreground a wide double gate opened and closed to the road.

Local history holds that in the winter of 1836 the first settlers came from Europe to make their homes in this beautiful region of Wisconsin. Families were predominately German, although not exclusively. Since there was as yet no official church or cemetery in the area at that time, many generous residents opened their own homes to serve as community gathering places in order to be able to celebrate the weekly Sabbath, as well as the traditional holidays that naturally occurred throughout the rest of the year. Although the graveyard has existed since around this time, the present chapel was not brought into existence until sometime in 1853.

Located at one furthermost point within this same small cemetery, familiarly nestled in that ever protective corner beneath the fragile limbs of a newly planted red maple tree, lay buried two of Felix and Emma Lauder's eleven children. On the side closest to the iron fence rests the mortal remains of our beloved George who died four years ago—four years ago that past January. Nearby, within a mere arm's length of his younger brother, lays buried young Lewis who was the family's first-born.

Even at a glance the twin graves stood apart from all the rest in two distinct ways, the first being the obvious fact that they were both relatively new. Many a pioneer resident of this same cemetery whose own loved ones had once assumed responsibility for the care of their respective graves, by dutifully trimming the unruly grass in the summer months, for example, in order that the more robust and highly overbearing tufts might not eventually overtake the grave marker; or by planting ivy or flowering perennials that would continuously beautify the area throughout the growing season, had themselves in time also passed from this life.

Understandably at this point, and often with no one else left behind to continue their upkeep, the solitary care of several of these same unfortunate family shrines ultimately was left to the ravages of Mother Nature—and to Time. As if to prove this very point many a badly weathered headstone stood cocked at an unnatural angle, its once proud straight head now leaning more and more precariously towards the ground with every passing decade, and its noble inscription so badly worn in a few instances—or completely illegible in others, that in the end the identity of the grave's poor occupant was rendered a mystery for all time.

For ages the very positioning of the tiny cemetery there upon the hill made it vulnerable to attack. Each season called forth its own specific brand of interminable insults which for the most part went unnoticed and unchallenged. For example, during those seemingly endless months of many a rough winter where everything that remained exposed to the rigors of those unkind elements were literally frozen diamond-hard, the infamously bitter Arctic wind would unceasingly whip up and down the gentle slope of hill with a vengeance to batter with unbelievable harshness all that stood within its path. Likewise during many a robust spring when those characteristically healthy streams of cold rain so often grew into wild torrents, they too continued to faithfully erode earth and stone alike. And certainly when, without mercy, the scorching summer sun predictably baked everything within its powerful reach, day after day, and month after month, then Time—inevitable Time, eventually claimed its due.

The second way the two newer graves stood apart from the others was in the fact that neither of them as yet possessed what Felix referred to as a "substantial marker" of the more typical granite or marble type. Such things, needless to say, were very costly and consequently financially out of reach for the family during these difficult years. On both occasions, however, when the need for a temporary marker arose, Felix, two of his remaining older sons, and I traveled to the outskirts of town where together we methodically felled a large oak tree. It became this same noble tree's superior hard white wood which so generously provided the necessary material for the small crosses that were eventually hand-crafted and then hand-carved by the proud patriarch of this special family.

I recall that both markers were noticeably simple in design. They stood devoid of the more exemplary decorations, save for the appropriate letters and numerals which made up the names and the dates of each. Painstakingly this very personal information was carved deep into the obliging wood. In clean bold script the markers read: George Lauder; 1911–1931, and Lewis Lauder; 1909–1933.

Any sensitive individual, especially someone who was familiar with the art of woodworking, could readily appreciate the profound attention to detail which was lavished upon these articles. The two separate components of both crosses had been structurally melded and finally secured in such an excellent manner that each finished piece seemed as though it had been brought forth from its massive tree trunk whole, and complete unto itself—without seam, or metal brace, or any other visible contrivance of any sort. I often marveled at the craftsmanship. Those grave markers represented, especially to me, the tangible tribute of a good father's deep and abiding love.

Regrettably I was never really given the opportunity of getting to know young Lewis the way that I got to know the other Lauder children. As the eldest son of this remarkable family he had some years prior to my own arrival within their lives already left their former home in Chicago so that he could make his way in the world. He telephoned home on a regular basis though and made efforts to return to the family whenever possible, especially in late December as everyone made ready to gather together to celebrate the traditional holiday of Christmas.

Although Felix Lauder for deeply personal reasons had fiercely defended against the baptism of each one of his children, his strong-willed wife was left with no other recourse but to go behind his back. Indeed, with the consecutive births of each of their children, Emma Lauder was forced to literally sneak off with their precious bundle in order to participate in one of her faith's most fundamental precepts. Yet, oddly enough, the yearly celebration of Christmas had been a concession easily won by this lady from the very beginning of their relationship.

That first holiday which I was to miraculously share with the family as a whole would always live on in my mind as the most special of all. Naturally after George's death nothing would ever be quite the same for any of us again. That enviable spontaneity and joy which each of us experienced in great abundance, and which we foolishly imagined would surely last forever, all but disappeared—almost as if that same beautiful emotion had been buried alive with him.

Later there would be the compounding of this tragedy with the untimely death of young Lewis two summers later. The horrible incident occurred while this beloved son was in the process of piloting one of the bombers that was part of the growing fleet of aircraft belonging to America's fledgling Army Air Corps. That day as his craft descended over the James River on its appointed route towards Langley Field a malfunction occurred within the engine of the plane, causing Lewis and his crew of three to perish in the subsequent crash-landing. Needless to say it would prove to be many a year gone by before a holiday of any sort made its welcome appearance within the Lauder household.

However, during that very first truly remarkable Christmas of which I was destined to become an integral part, days before young Lewis arrived home on one of his customary holiday "passes" his mother busied herself planning one of those elaborate meals of hers. These memorable feasts were elaborate only in the sense of those "little extras," as she liked to call them, which gloriously appeared only at this special time of year. For example there would be the wonderful Christmas sweet bread that would be generously filled to near bursting with nuts and candied fruit … and roasted wild turkey, or pheasant, that was properly dressed and then soaked for many hours in cold milk to help tame the often strong taste of the meat. Those well-secured prizes were generally part of the bounty from hunting season and it was for Christmas Eve supper, especially, that the birds would be stuffed with apples, bread, and spices and then basted for hours with a marvelous sauce that was laced with a special brand of strong "spirits" which was used exclusively for this special purpose.

In fact I learned that each late autumn, for numerous years during the time before Prohibition actually became law in this country, a small bottle of some rare cognac, along with several bars of much-treasured chocolate, would arrive in the mail from Vienna—by way of Mrs. Lauder's much-adored brother, Uncle Rudy. After the law was passed, however, and with the advent of those cruel Depression years that followed, these luxury articles became nearly impossible to come by and so were jealously hoarded by the lady of the house. Later they were sparingly used only for very special celebrations like Christmas.

One highly treasured bottle of rare cognac in particular, which had been a gift to the family years before when they resided in Mexico City, up to a certain point in time remained conspicuously displayed on a lower glass shelf in the cupboard located within the dining room. This same ornately-cut crystal bottle was clearly a work of art in its own right. It served to marvelously highlight the thick amber liquid within, especially after the item had been carefully polished and then managed to catch the late afternoon sunlight just so. I recall, too, that the fragile carafe remained properly sealed by a generous length of gold filigree thread which encircled its thick squat neck many times over. Nobly displayed at its center was a blood-red wax impression that was heavily embossed with the manufacturer's coat of arms.

Perhaps this treasured gift was originally intended as a keepsake to remind certain members of the Lauder family of happier times gone by, I really cannot say for sure. But I do distinctly recall that anytime one of the children asked Mrs. Lauder why she never made use of the contents of this particularly special bottle for her cooking, she habitually shrugged her little shrug, and then smiled ever so wistfully only to exclaim with a heavy accent which betrayed her proud Austrian-Czech heritage, "Oh, it's for saving, don't you know?! No doubt, some day it will be used for something very special—something very special, indeed!"

Although many a Christmas, and birthday, and wedding anniversary had surely come and gone from the day that bottle first arrived in the Lauder family household, still this elegant keepsake was being held in reserve for whatever would prove to be its final destiny. And, even though to my unbiased way of thinking the alternative liquid used in the delicious gravy that particular year really did not seem to do much to the taste—either way, really, still I came to understand that this ritual of hers was just a way in which this much-adored member of the family, who resided somewhere far across the wide Atlantic, could be with us during those more cherished moments.

In keeping with the best holiday culinary traditions that year Emma Lauder made her famous dumplings with caraway seed, along with a side dish of homemade sauerkraut. In order to thoroughly please Felix she also added her amazing sweet and sour red cabbage to the already extensive holiday menu. That same vegetable had earlier been born from the ample bounty taken from the family's garden the previous year. And as a grand finale to appropriately top off this marvelous fare, not unlike a bejeweled crown sitting atop the proud brow of some Austrian-Hungarian head of state, for dessert we excitedly anticipated the cutting of the Yule log.

Since I have endlessly suffered the pangs of the proverbial "sweet tooth" for as long as I can remember, I particularly recall that this sinfully rich concoction was made with a dozen or more eggs. After the thick rich golden batter was properly baked and then the light spongy cake properly cooled following that, this masterpiece would be generously spread with a slightly tart apricot or raspberry jam before being rolled up and completely iced from top to bottom, and from end to end, with a heavenly rich whipped cream that stood in dense little peaks in response to having been so rigorously beaten. Finally, heavy curls of dark semisweet chocolate garnished its entire length. At the very center of this festive creation a fresh holly sprig was thoughtfully placed with great ceremony by our proud chef to remind us, as if any of us could possibly forget, that a truly special time of the year had once again descended upon the world.

Days in advance of that remarkable Christmas Eve all the younger children and I were requested by Felix to gather around the large round table in the dining room, in the early evening hours just before bedtime, it was, to help make decorative ropes for the Christmas tree. Since I was still quite young myself during this time, and although I had been residing only a short while with these more than pleasant people, I was naturally invited to join in the fun despite my initial shyness and reserve.

How I came to relish that particular moment in time. Using long needles and extra-long lengths of sturdy string we pierced each firm red cranberry through its center and then properly secured them one by one so that the festive ropes might be used when finished to gracefully loop around the outer branches of our tree. And, lest I forget, there were the truly marvelous cookie treats which would soon be tied to the outer branches of the freshly cut young pine tree. These delightful homemade honey biscuits were cleverly created in the shape of each of the children's hands, left and right, with our names cleverly spelled out in dark raisins on both sides.

I remember so well, too, how on that first Christmas Eve morning with nearly the entire family present that it was Mrs. Lauder who went about happily placing fresh holly sprigs and pine branches throughout the little house to help add to the festive spirit of things. Previously I had never heard of anyone ever doing such a thing. Consequently, though, the healthy and exhilarating scent of the great outdoors would naturally find its way inside every room of the house, often lingering there for days.

The overall effect of all of this was really quite wonderful. While the lady of the house went about accomplishing this rather simple task, she took to absentmindedly humming some sort of cheerful little song. In the end a tiny bouquet of pine branches, and holly berries, and cheerful mistletoe was lovingly placed within a favorite vase of hers and then set atop a small table next to the bed where our cherished visitor would soon be sleeping upon his long-awaited return home that particular year. For me, especially, that simple gesture was highly indicative of the gracious spirit inherent in this particular mother's attention to the smallest detail. How much these tiny inexpensive extravagances managed to add to our lives.

Just before that heart-warming scene of young Lewis Lauder's much-anticipated arrival actually took place, this same proud and exceedingly happy woman could be seen quickly waltzing through the rooms of our small simple abode, critically checking to see whether or not any improvement might be made relative to her having created a proper "homecoming" for her first-born son. Fondly I recall how Emma Lauder became a bit flustered with excitement when, at the very last moment—just seconds, in fact, before the sound of Lewis' footsteps could be heard there on the front porch and all the eager family members loudly shouted out their collective greeting in unison—she seemed obliged to rush into her room in order to put on one of her two good dresses. I further observed her gaze critically at herself in the full-length mirror in the hallway downstairs, by turning first one way, and then the other. Soon enough, and apparently without a second more of deliberation, once again she sprinted back into the bedroom, seemingly a bit exasperated with herself at this point, in order to hurriedly change into her alternate article of clothing.

After that first Christmas Eve supper, apparently in keeping with what had long become a Lauder family tradition, the eldest child in the family enthusiastically lifted one of the younger members overhead to finally place the "Christmas angel" at the top of the tree. This having been done, everyone took their turn to light a small white candle on the tree. Then, as part of the prescribed finale, all of us remained behind within the little parlor to enjoy each other's company as we dallied over our own individual cup of hot apple cider.

When young Lewis was away somewhere, which was most of the time, often out of the clear blue we received some sort of parcel from him or merely a note reminding us that the family remained ever in his thoughts. But it was more or less through the countless stories concerning his more memorable escapades as a young boy, especially during those first years of his early life when the family resided in Mexico City— and, likewise, those highly prized tales of his later heroics as a young fighter pilot, that I happened upon my overall knowledge of him. Until that overwhelming sadness of great loss eventually invaded the Lauder home those priceless sagas were told and then retold with great enthusiasm during many a family gathering throughout the year—especially at supper time. And so these same precious moments of open sharing were the main source that provided me with any sort of accurate perspective with reference to him.

It was, however, the Lauder family's second son, George, whom I came especially to know and to love. Shortly after he and I met, this special son of theirs quickly became my much-longed-for "soul mate" who in the few short months of our brief time together was to touch my young life in such a manner that I would remain enriched for all my years to come. More than any of the other children he remained unequaled in his ability to bring cheer and sunlight into the lives of other people, and for making any difficult situation far more bearable.

I confess, too, after all these years and without even an ounce of shame, that I secretly envied George. In every sense he was everything that I longed to be. Although he had been a number of years older than I, he managed nonetheless to make me feel that I was his equal in everything we did together. In no time at all I enthusiastically became his ever-present shadow, so to speak, but he never seemed to mind. This fact still continues to amaze me. What really amazes me still was the confidence he always showed in me. Naturally in my ongoing effort to live up to his rather elevated opinion of me I found myself rising to the occasion and accomplishing things that I might not have otherwise even considered attempting under the tutelage of anyone else. Within that protective mantle of his treasured friendship in which I was so proudly cloaked, he naturally became my hero—my great hero, utterly and completely.

Some years after George's death, during the bittersweet process of my ever-frequent reminiscing about those years of my childhood when my dear friend and I had become so much a part of each other's lives, I finally formulated a theory that George was one of those rare and wholly fortunate individuals who instinctively lives their life in a heightened state of awareness. He lived in a more or less "chronic state of being," as though from the very second of his conception onward throughout the duration of his too brief existence in this world he somehow pre-resolved in the very core of his being the fact that for him the continuous movement of the hands on the "clock of Time" moved far more swiftly for him than it did for others. I also surmise that subconsciously for him the element of Time was perceived as neither a friend, nor as a dreaded enemy, but rather as an acknowledged key factor in the miraculous equation called Life which he embraced unconditionally. Armed as my friend was with this valuable intrinsic knowledge his spirit automatically resolved to make the most of each and every day, staunchly refusing to squander even the smallest fraction of any hour of any day that was his.

George's spirit had been a "human comet" whose vitality and brilliance streaked across the heavens and lighted up our lives. He lived so fully in that brief time that his family and I were privileged to know him that by the time he was finally summoned from us, in terms of total energy expounded, I carefully calculated that he had by then lived more than one full lifetime already.

How the many members of his family and I missed him. With his untimely leave-taking, especially during those first truly dismal weeks immediately following his funeral when the sheer reality of the finality of it all quickly set in for most of us, the daily laughter and the atmosphere of joy for living which we associated primarily with him, and which we all somehow believed would go on and on forever, abruptly vanished. I recall that the county coroner's official notation on George's certificate of death stated coldly and succinctly that he died from "complications of pneumonia," but I know that there was far more to the story than this. Yes, I know the truth. I know for certain that with all that had transpired during those many weeks just prior to his death that in the end he really died of a broken heart….

After having become momentarily lost in these many thoughts of mine my attention finally wandered from the cemetery back to the man who was still quietly seated beside me on the roof. Prudently Felix and I chose to move from our former positions, there at the very top of the roof, downwards to a place farther below and close beside a protective wall of one of the dormers. This contrivance of ours, just as we hoped, proved to better shelter us from the healthy wind. Removing the clean linen handkerchief which he habitually carried in the deep right-hand pocket of his loosely constructed work trousers, my dear friend began polishing the highly besmudged lenses of his wire-rimmed glasses, just as I observed him do on countless other occasions in the past.

Now and then the brisk wind would play with the tiny tufts of his sparse salt and pepper colored hair. Those same bits of renegade hair, which somehow managed to successfully remain free from the confines of the tight-fitting woolen cap his wife knitted for him several Christmases ago, were being blown out away from his head and neck and then back in again....

Nearby a goshawk could be seen skillfully riding the currents of turbulent air. From where we continued to sit upon the roof she glided past our heads in a seemingly effortless display of her aerial talents. Soon we could make out, in amazing detail, the subtle pattern of her impressive plumage. Then in a blink of an eye she abruptly changed course to glide over a portion of the sleeping fields that lay to our immediate right, most probably searching for a rodent, or a hare, that might eventually come out of hiding in search of its own afternoon meal that day.

Although Felix was already a man of some fifty-eight years of age his overall appearance had remained remarkably the same over the decades, judging from the succession of various family photographs which had begun to be collected some thirty or forty years before. At the moment, however, the taut skin of his face was nearly translucent from our hours of exposure to the cold. Its normally pink and warm glow had been temporarily replaced by a fine porcelain hue of fragile whiteness that was tinged with pale blue. And after those long oppressive hours upon the roof both of us were now suffering with lips which were painfully dry, and cracked, and very unpleasant to the touch.

After my friend's glasses were cleaned sufficiently enough to please him, and after they were replaced on the familiar spot there upon the bridge of his long straight nose, he took a moment more to blow the protuberance with the same trusty cloth before ceremoniously folding it and returning it to his pocket. Pausing to silently scan the horizon, just as I had been doing only moments before, his gaze came at last to rest upon the little chapel with its cemetery grounds and he sighed. This particular sigh of his, it seemed to me, had not issued forth from any sense of mere physical tiredness on his part, but rather from a much deeper source. Indeed, this far more sacred little sound seemed to have escaped from somewhere else. It was an indication of the kind of profound weariness with which only the soul may become familiar....

Now his attention turned to me. Presently he was studying my face, and my eyes, in the highly intense and wholly familiar manner to which his wife and his children and I had long grown accustomed. Much like a "geologist of the heart" he would painlessly take a reading from his subject using the infallible instruments of his own spirituality. It was his nature to probe the heart and the soul of others. This I felt about him from our very first meeting. With the complete trust which naturally evolved as our friendship had grown, our eyes continued to hold one another. Then as if he guessed all along the reason for the urgency of my question regarding the subject of "heaven and hell," and "life after death"—and, of course, the true context in which it had been asked—he solemnly said, "I miss him, too, Adam.... I miss them both so terribly much!"

Soon Felix was silently contemplating his hands. They lay motionless in his lap at the moment. After a little while, however, during which time neither of us had chosen to speak a word, I watched as he slowly placed them inside the deep pockets of his ever-faithful old plaid workjacket for warmth. Because of the diabetes which had manifested itself when he was a much younger man, he remained conscious always of the fact that he was naturally more susceptible to the cold than were other more hearty individuals. This is why he had not fought the idea when his wife called him back into the kitchen that morning, just as we started out the door to begin the day's work on the roof. In his preoccupation with the challenge that lay ahead his forgetting to take his hat along had merely been a careless oversight on his part. Eventually he would have surely realized that on such a day as today something important was missing. And then in his quiet and wholly polite manner that was as much a part of this amazing man as was the charm of his melodic Magyar accent, with a sense of chagrin he might have asked me the small favor of returning to the cloak room that was situated between the downstairs bedroom and the kitchen, naturally in order to bring him what he required.

We continued to sit together without speaking for a few moments more that day, just resting for a bit. Then as if having sufficiently formulated his thoughts relative to the subject of my much earlier inquiry, and finally putting them into terms that he now felt comfortable enough to share with me, he paused to declare, "Your question earlier on, Adam, was whether or not I believe in the reality of heaven and hell.... Whether or not I believe in life after death, is this not so?"

I nodded in affirmation, as I comically croaked, "Yes sir, that was, and still is, my question!" These days the relatively strange sound of my own voice had the ability to confound me. With puberty having firmly descended upon me at long last, and in full measure—and with the reality that I was now standing, more or less, at the exhilarating threshold of manhood, the necessary hormonal changes were beginning to do phenomenal things to my entire person. Because of this, naturally, my normally pleasant sounding voice would often betray me. Lately it did not even seem to belong to me at all. Usually at the most inappropriate times I would suffer some minor embarrassment whenever my words or phrases made their wary appearance.

In what seemed to me to be a slightly distracted manner, Felix slowly repeated the phrases, "heaven and hell" ... "life after death." Then without the slightest trace of mockery in his voice or in his manner, while he chose once more to gaze out across the frozen fields that surrounded us, he offered in a rather somber mood perhaps more to himself than to me, "Lofty subjects, to be sure ... lofty subjects for lofty places such as these!"

After a bit more introspection on his part Felix finally turned to me and proceeded to answer my question by posing several serious questions of his own, as he respectfully asked, "Need one pass from this life in order to experience what is commonly referred to as 'heaven' and 'hell'? Aren't these things found in this world already, and in overwhelming abundance?!" Shortly, after yet another pause my friend went on to patiently confide to me, once again in the form of a question, "And, as far as the subject of 'life after death' is concerned, Adam, what would you say if I were to assure you that it is possible to live, and to die, and then to be reborn again many times over in the course of a single lifetime?!"

"Doc" Owens was the only person I knew who could ever hold his own with Felix Lauder in matters of philosophical discussions of this nature. The two of them were the best of friends and I simply could not imagine it being any other way than this. Over the years "Doc" made it a habit to stop at our home, whenever he was free to do so, in order to "look in on us" as he would always say with a sincere and thoroughly contagious smile. This quiet-spoken gentleman from West Virginia rarely ever announced his arrival. It remains my belief that because he and Felix were so very comfortable in their regard for each other, none of us—Emma Lauder included, ever considered it necessary for him to behave in any other way.

Upon some unexpected visit of his to the Lauder home, happily we would rush about to set an extra place for our good friend there at our already crowded table. It would be after these special meals, generally, while these two excellent men sat outside on the porch on a pleasant evening, or underneath one of the huge shade trees in the back yard, or in the parlor, instead, whenever the weather was inhospitable for one reason or another, that I silently observed with considerable awe the two of them happily interacting.

Like powerful eagles, together they soared high over the tallest mountains, intellectually speaking, upon those endless currents of robust thoughts and ideas. Occasionally I watched as the two scholars, not unlike major athletes participating in some rigorous physical endeavor, would become literally flushed with excitement at being able to present some unusual theory or new idea. Next, they would follow through to see the entire process to its inevitable conclusion—from beginning to end—by plausibly substantiating everything, step by logical step.

By admission both were avid students of metaphysics. And it proved to be poetry—the wonderful poetry of Walt Whitman and William Carlos Williams, especially—that was responsible for having initially brought them together as lifelong friends. With a single notion that would be casually thrown out in the open by one or the other, sometimes just in passing, or during those times when they might be occupied with something else—like the time Felix helped his best friend clean the carburetor of his old Ford—soon they would be off and running with their ideas, eagerly pursuing and investigating one tangent, then another, quite often to the apparent neglect of the important job at hand.

I came to believe that this rare friendship of theirs which was based early on upon their common intellectual pursuits served to help alleviate, in great part, the basic loneliness that is fairly common in those who possess the ability to communicate on uncommonly high levels of thought. They were genuine "soul mates" of the first order and this reality pleased me very much indeed.

But at that tender age of fourteen, as I continued to sit next to Felix high atop the roof of the farmhouse on that brisk March day, I, myself, was admittedly no match for my dear mentor in this way. My simple need at the moment for a comprehensible answer to what was bothering me arose from a poignant dream I had had concerning George many weeks after his death. Although I did not go into the exact reason for my inquiry with Felix, at this point, he undoubtedly understood none-theless that the issue was of great importance to me. With his typical compassion to share his thoughts on this fascinating subject, he soon took pity upon me as he began to say, "Perhaps the elusive answer to the important question you're asking, Adam, lies in the more traditional vein of thinking."

Once again Felix was thoughtfully studying me as he went on to carefully state: "As I find myself all too quickly approaching the prover-bial 'deep autumn of my existence,' throughout my many rich years of living—and loving—more so now than ever I have become painfully aware that there are certain questions of universally monumental impor-tance that seem destined to go on, and on, without the welcome benefit of any concrete resolution.... These profoundly disturbing questions, actually, are the same ones far wiser men than you and I have been wrestling with since the dawn of time!

"Perhaps it is exactly this unsolvable aspect of the mystery of 'heaven and hell'—and 'life after death,' that rests at the very core of its entice-ment for many of us—the reason, I might add, why this enticement steadfastly remains the essence of the mystery's overwhelming beauty! Although these twin enigmas appear basically opposed to one another by their very nature—similar, in effect, to the opposites of 'light and dark' and 'good and evil'—it seems to me that they really serve in the end to compliment each other.... Don't you agree? Could one entity possibly exist without its counterpart? For example, consider an artist's rendering of a particular subject in oil or in watercolor.... Does not the work itself come into focus—into being, in the real sense, with that same play of opposites? That marvelous play of light against darkness?!"

After a brief pause my friend continued what he was telling me, by adding, "That alluring relationship between these twin enigmas of 'life' and 'death' remain enveloped in such mystery that one continues to endlessly perplex oneself in one's best efforts to understand everything in the only terms, and with the only tools, with which one has long accustomed oneself to using. Is it conceivable, then, that there exist worlds other than the only one with which we have become so familiar? Other plateaus or realms of thought, perhaps? Other dimensions of being? Why should one choose to limit oneself by not imagining, at the very least, such astonishing possibilities?!

Felix immediately fell silent. Soon he was smiling the smile I loved so well. I was beginning to be caught up in this special vision he was painting for me. Somehow, too, these ideas were having a reassuring and comforting effect upon me. Then, as if to sum up this particular aspect of his philosophy, he went on to say, "A concept to which I personally ascribe is one which wholeheartedly embraces these twin miracles of 'life and death' as part and parcel of a 'much greater vision,' a 'divine plan,' if you will, whose immense scope and overall significance shall one day undoubtedly be revealed to each of us in its entirety!"

"Are you afraid of dying?" I found myself asking my dear friend. My honest inquiry had escaped my mouth even before I had taken the appropriate time to debate with myself whether or not I should have asked it. Somehow it just seemed natural that our discussion should inevitably lead us to this important point.

Once more Felix took a moment to study the open vista that spread before us, as if the answer to my bold question might be discovered in those similarly wide open places within his heart. This time without looking my way he quietly responded by assuring me, "I have little doubt that I shall be ready, when my time finally arrives."

As we sat contemplating the huge significance of the issue at hand, he went on to further explain his thoughts on the subject by saying, "Adam, I am often struck by the fact that one's life naturally evolves in the manner of a circle. You see, as a youngster growing up in Hungary I was privileged to have been raised amongst those who toiled the land. While I eventually grew to manhood and traveled this vast world, following my dreams and attempting to make a success of my life, I ultimately discovered with great appreciation that that amazing circle of my life—that evolutionary process, in essence—has returned me to a fairly similar place relative to my origin. Once again at this much later time in my life, I find myself toiling the land and still loving it! As I see it, the circle of my life has nearly completed itself by having returned me to my beginning, in a manner of speaking.

"It is my sincere belief that those of us whose existence intimately coincides with the passing of the seasons are eventually forced to acknowledge that we are born with an infinitely special time-piece within our souls that beats to the timeless rhythm of nature. As a farmer or other great lover of the land who covets all that this life holds dear, we quickly come to know that life and death are inseparable…. We come to realize that one entity simply cannot exist without the other. In a way there is a certain reassurance in this knowledge, too, for in our wisdom we come to recognize that death has the potential of becoming one's dear friend. Indeed, without the mercy of death, in time life would become unimaginably intolerable. Naturally, with the acceptance of this rational reality comes the basic alleviation of the terror that death holds over so many.

"Yes…" Felix was respectfully assuring me, "I shall be ready when death finally comes to call for me at my window. I shall be ready, and I shan't be afraid!" With this, we both fell silent. In a little bit, however, I was following my friend's gaze. It slowly continued to scan the great openness all around us, only once again to finally catch sight of the small chapel and graveyard across the way. As my friend's interest came to rest solidly there upon that special place, he sighed, as he softly confided to me, "What life never quite prepares one for, however, is the death of one's children…. Somehow an intrinsic injustice is forever perpetrated, when one is made to outlive one's progeny!"

Felix turned now to regard me, and in doing this simple thing he removed his hands from their pockets. After inching a little more closer to where I was sitting, he casually laced one arm through mine and then returned his hands, once again, to where they would continue to benefit from the warmth of these felt-lined conveniences. From that very first day when he and I had chanced to meet, I sensed that here was a man whose essential well-being, emotionally speaking, required some form of even the most subtle physical contact with others. For him it was as if to reach out to casually touch the hand, or the shoulder, or, now and then, the cheek of another, was to ground himself more firmly to this world.

This frequent behavior of being compelled to make that brief contact with others was a quintessential part of his basic confident nature, as if somewhere deep down within himself he understood that the other person required this contact, too. These overtures, mind you, were never made in any manner that could ever be considered even the least bit offensive, but, rather, in a manner that was basically human in the most profound sense. As we sat together on the roof that day, huddled together more closely now than before, after a moment more of seemingly great reflection on his part he went on to confide to me with noticeable feeling in his voice, "I choose to believe, more than anything else, Adam, that genuine love is a miracle. And, based pretty much upon my own personal experience, I have also come to understand that real love has the ability to conquer death!"

With this unusual revelation of his, Felix took to concentrating his gaze upon me. Behind the shiny prisms of his wire-rimmed glasses his eyes were literally swimming like jewels. I honestly could not tell whether this was from the wind which had recently changed directions, or, rather, from the apparent emotion which seemed to be at the base of what my dear teacher and friend was currently thinking and feeling. Soon he went on to repeat the phrase, almost as if he were repeating a long familiar prayer, "Love is stronger than death!"

In a little while, when he seemed more in control of his emotions, he went on to say, "People I have loved and lost in this life have occasionally appeared to me over the years in dreams. These dreams seem so very real at times, as if the highly significant regard which that special person felt for me while he or she lived has not diminished in the least, and continues to flow back to me from wherever their spirit may now be! Naturally, the overwhelming effect that this always produces is most uncanny.... It is as though the power of this mutual love is so tenacious that it is able to reach backward, somehow, through that heavy and oppressively dark curtain of death in order to gently stroke the soul in pain, and to bring with that amazing moment of grace some small measure of comfort in the process....

"Great scientific minds would naturally have a field day with all this," Felix was musing. "These same learned thinkers would characteristically challenge the statements I just made. In a highly warranted effort to uphold the traditions of rational thought with regard to such noble subjects as science and mathematics, particularly, these same good folks might feel duty-bound to hold my feet to the fire and to rightfully demand full disclosure of conclusive data to support this seductive idea of mine!

"Standing before them without the slightest sense of embarrassment, I would be forced to confess that I did not have the facts they required. Nor, for that matter, even an iota of tangible evidence that might help lead to the conclusive proof they were seeking.... And yet, I would feel an obligation to state, quite emphatically, that I have come to believe that there are just some miracles that are destined to defy knowledge gathering in those more familiar terms. These powerful images that come to me in dream sequences seem, rather, to be based on a language entirely their own; a profoundly moving language of the spirit, unlike the spoken or written word, where their messages effortlessly transverse the reality of time and space as we have traditionally come to understand it."

Suddenly there was a lump in my throat. I found this uncommon information which my dear friend was now sharing with me of tremendous interest. I longed to tell him of my dream of George and how that sublime moment both comforted me—and, at the very same time, troubled my spirit greatly. Somehow, though, I was beginning to understand that Felix Lauder from this rather poignant description of his own experiences already understood everything quite well. I was listening with continued interest, as he went on to say, "I take pride in being a realist in my thinking, Adam—but you already know this about me!"

Now he was smiling, as he went on to further admit, "I also plead guilty to being a hopeless romantic, as well! And yet does the philosophy of being a 'true realist,' while at the same time remaining a 'hopeless romantic,' automatically conflict with one another?"

"I don't know," I answered. Soon, in an impetuous moment of playfulness, I went on to inquire with a small laugh, "Would you then be referred to as a 'romantic realist'? Or a 'realistic romantic'?"

Presently, we both were laughing. We were cold, and hungry, and exceedingly tired from that morning's work, but somehow this meaningful discussion and this bit of laughter we were both enjoying together at the moment made everything seem better. As if to pick up the fragile thread of an idea that would conclude what Felix had been previously saying, he went on to tell me, "I suppose the underlying question remains: Since I strive my whole life through to relate to all that life encompasses in terms of basic 'realism' and 'truth'—does, then, a mind which functions in this manner necessarily undergo some semblance of privation by allowing the 'romantic side' of its nature to possibly cloud the issue of what is truly 'real'? In other words, with respect to these beautiful dreams which I frequently experience, am I actually feeling this profound feeling of love which seems somehow to be miraculously transmitted back to me from somewhere beyond the grave? Or am I merely allowing myself to believe this, because I wish so much to believe that such miracles are possible!?"

With Felix Lauder's totally open and honest revelations about the very things which had occupied my own mind since George's death four years ago, it occurred to me that day as we sat upon the roof, speaking at length about those profoundly important issues which we both seemed to hold in common, that what my dear teacher had previously said before—about there being certain questions relevant to the subject of "life and death," and, more specifically, "life after death" that were destined to go unanswered in the real sense—was true. I was learning, too, and with great respect, that even the most gifted philosophers do not always have the answers. I was beginning to appreciate that all of us, more or less, travel down the same road in search of those elusive answers to the same troubling questions. It becomes one's entire journey that ultimately lends the necessary perspective. Perhaps it becomes that cumulative process of learning all one can about life and one's individual place in the world during whatever brief time we are given that is the major goal, as well as accepting the fact that it is perfectly natural that there will always be mysteries in this life that will continue to endlessly perplex us.

These were my thoughts that day, as the two of us sat silently mulling over the many things our conversation had brought to light. Soon, as if finally choosing to stray from the original topic, Felix began to gracefully wave his right hand out across the wide panoramic view that encircled us to ask with marked feeling, "Do you feel the miracles happening all around us, Adam?! To the average person who lacks a certain sensitivity and imagination, what we are witnessing here at the moment might seem relatively uninspiring—boring, most probably! Others would look at the leafless trees down there, and the equally naked bushes whose fragile branches and twigs still remain tightly wrapped to protect themselves from the cold—and, too, the frozen earth with its precious animal life slumbering on in peaceful hibernation far below the surface—and not see anything miraculous in all of it!

"But living close to this wondrous earth, as we do—working it and loving it as we do, we know that it continues to pulsate with the beauty of life endlessly throughout each and every season of the year, just as with the very heartbeat of the earth itself. This wonderful land, along with the coming season of spring, holds the perennial promise of hope!

"This spiritual time, I feel, may be compared to a grand orchestra whose very able Conductor is in the process of making everything ready for the first performance of the year.... Everyone is 'tuning up,' as they say in the music profession! Those well-trained participants have vowed to make certain that each plays splendidly together as a group, in tempo to the timeless rhythm of life renewing itself.

"Can you hear the music?! For example, do you hear the string section—over there?" Suddenly Felix began gesturing with his slim graceful left hand towards the left as he spoke these words. "And the percussionists and woodwind section—over here?" Of course now he was gesturing once again to the right, with his right hand, as he was telling me all this.

How I loved to see him when an inspirational mood took hold of him—as now. George had been like this, only more so. Like a magician or some particularly gifted visionary who was not ashamed to allow the playful child within him to become openly inspired, Felix would be moved to paint marvelous scenes with his words. "Soon," he was telling me, "all of the enchanting music shall begin to be played in earnest, and all the beauty of this glorious life as it slowly renews itself—with its superb colors, and intoxicating fragrances, and rich, rich extravagances, will surely be blessing our lives once more!"

As the artist he was, and, too, the soulful humanist, his children and I remained the welcomed beneficiaries of all he shared in this way. In a little while, as if choosing to return once more to our original subject, he said to me, "As you see, my dear young friend, I do not have all the answers. I wish I did... Needless to say, it is with absolute humility that I frequently remind myself of this significant fact!

"However, I shall also confess that very early in my life, during my earliest childhood, in fact, I came to embrace a particularly important 'credo for living' which I feel has served me rather well during all these many years. One manages, you see, if one is intelligent, to learn from the past. The future, too, continually beckons with its tantalizing promises and dreams.... But, truly, the past is past—and the future, if it is meant to be, is off in the distance somewhere. So what is vastly important to grasp and cling to is the present—the precious here and now! One should strive to remember this. To do otherwise is to cheat one's self in the worse possible way, and in the process to cheat those who love us and share our lives!

"You see, Adam, quite simply it remains our daily acts of kindness—be they grand in size or minuscule, that are destined to live on in a keen sense of immortality. After all, one arrives in this world a mere traveler of sorts—a visitor, in effect, who by virtue of the gift of life is obliged to live that life in order to make a positive difference in the world. This represents the ideal, of course—for to live only to take is a great sin! To live without returning something noble in the process is really the most selfish quality of all. The emptiest sort of existence!

"Since time immemorial countless people have come to believe that there is some sort of complicated or magical formula to achieving lasting happiness in this life. But if the simple truth were presented to them, handed to them on a 'silver platter,' as it were, they would remain fairly astonished to learn that the elusive happiness which they seek is, and has always been, just within their reach all the while....

"Do you recall what happens when you toss a rock or stone into the lake?" Felix was asking me.

I thought for a moment and then answered, "Ripples form, naturally...."

"Yes, exactly," Felix agreed.

"And the larger the stone...?"

"The bigger the splash, and the more pronounced the rippling effect," I confidently responded.

"Yes! And those ripples tend to gently play one upon the next—and on, and on, and on—isn't this so?"

I silently nodded in agreement.

"Well, our kindness to others is very much like those smooth, flat stones," he was telling me softly. "We toss them out into the world, quite often with abandon, and usually without expecting anything in return, really.... It all boils down to the relatively simple matter of kindness for kindness sake! Kindness that is based upon nothing less than one's deeply-rooted spiritual integrity. That simple action, then, commonly sets the ripple effect into motion, the very same way that goodness generally begets goodness, with one kind deed playing upon the next, until positive things begin to happen in the world!"

"Then," I was surmising, as I picked up his train of thought, "the converse must also be true. By this I mean that bad deeds produce ripples that affect the world in the negative sense."

"Yes! Quite so. Quite so!"

After a moment's contemplation, Felix went on to say, "In the emotional sense I have always remained profoundly touched by the unexpected kindness of others—by the unexpected kindness of strangers, especially.... For during those times when life seems so unkind—so utterly inhospitable, and hope seems but a distant memory or some unreachable dream, someone whom I never met before, some special someone whom I am unlikely to ever meet again, unexpectedly touches my life with some gentle kindness and instantly my usually strong faith in human nature, and the world as a whole, is instantly rekindled!"

How poignant were these words of his. Tears of understanding and approval had begun to well up in my own eyes. Surely my dear friend could never forget what a stranger's unprecedented kindness had done for me.

There were distinct moments, like these, in my relationship with Felix when I felt especially privileged in that he cared enough to be able to open his heart to me, as he was doing at this moment. It had long occurred to me that many fortunate people are born into stations of privilege—and reference now is not being made in terms of financial wealth, at all, but rather in the far more important sense of having been born into a loving family where kindness, and respect, and a daily sharing of feelings and ideas are so commonplace that this much preferred interaction is basically taken for granted by those intimately involved.

On that blessed day when Fate made me its supreme gift by bringing the Lauder family and me together, my young life up to then had known only the most cruel sort of deprivation with regard to body and spirit. The shabbiness of my former existence became all the more contrasted when shaded against my new life which, in this dear family's wonderful kindness, they had openly invited me to share.

From that very first instant I was never once guilty of allowing a single solitary aspect of our mutual caring, and sharing, to be taken for granted. Felix, and our beloved George, and all the others, perhaps without having truly comprehended my desperate situation in the beginning, had quite literally saved the child that I once was from perishing.

I confess, too, that back then I lived in a more or less continuous state of anxiety. I greatly feared that this precious gift, which had been so magnanimously bestowed upon me in such a wholly unexpected fashion, would eventually be taken from me just as quickly. I agonized that certainly one day, against my most fervent wishes, I would be uprooted from this protective haven of abundant love and security, to be made to make my way again, alone, in the unkind world which I had come to know so very well. I feared with certainty that the dreaded process would begin all over again where I would continue to be helplessly passed from one foster home to the next.... And so, as if to better deal with this coming psychological pain of eventual abandonment, early on I secretly vowed to absorb all the goodness, and all the sanity, that my limited time with this special family would allow. I attempted to stoically fortify my young spirit against the inevitable coming solitude of deepest winter. By doing this I imagined that perhaps my forced leave-taking might become slightly more tolerable in the end.

From my earliest recollections, which began not terribly long after the time of my birth and extended up to very nearly my ninth year of living when Felix Lauder finally found me, I had always been alone. No one belonged to me. Equally as sad, I belonged to no one. It was that same little boy I once was—with his enduringly fierce sense of natural curiosity, as well as his insatiable hunger for love and acceptance; and now, this same far more confident young man who consistently sought out facts by merely asking, just exactly as I had done on this very day, that was responsible for my having made this unsolicited overture regarding the subject of "heaven and hell," and "life after death," to my dear teacher and friend. Being true once again to himself, as well as to me, it was Felix who rose to the occasion by taking the time to share these priceless moments and these equally precious thoughts with me....

From somewhere down below us we could hear a young voice ask with considerable petulance, "Aren't you two 'ever' coming down from there?!" Before we had a chance to answer this first question, another was immediately hurled our way, as the same wee voice inquired further, "Aren't you both cold enough—and hungry enough, by now?!"

Felix was chuckling at the moment. Together we both leaned over a badly rusted length of gutter to look down into the bright and shining face of the Lauder's ten-year-old daughter, Maria Christina. Lately she had taken to wearing her mother's apron over her play clothes. That brightly colored piece of cotton fabric was generally rolled at the waist to shorten it when she walked, with the longer than usual ties wound a couple of times around her tiny waist and then secured in the front with a neat bow. I could not help but notice that she was standing with her hands upon her hips precisely in the manner in which I witnessed her mother do a thousand times already. Silently stationed right beside her was five-year-old baby, Anna Allegra—the youngest member of the family, tightly pressing her ever-present blanket to her heart and avidly sucking her thumb as usual. "Well, my 'Mary Contrary' and 'Anna Banana,'..." their father was cheerfully saying, "not only are we quite frozen at this very moment, we are completely famished, as well!"

Felix adored his daughters. These nicknames for them had naturally evolved not so long after their births, the way most nicknames tend to do, as each personality began to take shape and form itself. But the girls staunchly refused to allow anyone else, family member and friend alike, to refer to them in this way. Indeed, once when I was in an exceedingly playful mood myself, and teasingly called little Annie by the nickname her father had bestowed upon her early on, she quickly walked away from me without answering. When I purposely followed after her and unwisely continued to try to illicit some sort of a response by addressing her in this same manner of familiarity, over and over again, she promptly halted in her tracks and immediately spun around to face me. Taking a fairly menacing step towards me and by now literally glaring at me with an intensity that was both amusing and a little bit frightening at the same time, she ceremoniously removed her thumb from her mouth to soundly inform me, with a "lisping lilt" due to the fact her front teeth were still missing, "My name to everyone is 'A-n-n-a'! For your information, Adam, Father is the only one allowed to call me by my pet name. Kindly remember this from now on!"

Felix and I were already in the process of beginning to gingerly make our way towards the corner of the roof where earlier we had left the ladder leaning against the house. We decided to leave the materials and tools where they were for our eventual return after lunch. I did, however, carry the tar bucket down with me in order that I might refill it later.

Young William Lauder and I were nearly the same age and it had been his designated job that morning to fill the bucket with hot tar when the supply ran low, or whenever the substance solidified too quickly because of the cold weather. Our mutual agreement that day had been that whenever I tapped three times loudly upon the roof, which was his signal to leave the kitchen table where he was busy finishing a geography project for school, the sticky bucket would be lowered to the ground by its long rope for him to fill. Then having done his part Willy would tug firmly on the rope which was my signal from him for me to carefully pull the bucket back up again. It was Felix who devised this simple plan. Of course, it seemed to work out just fine.

"Please go tell your mother that Adam and I are on our way down to wash up for lunch," Felix was urging the girls. Long before we left the kitchen that morning the tantalizing smell of baking bread had already filled the air, both inside and outside the house. Naturally this far more desirable fragrance had had to compete all this while with the ruthlessly pungent odor of the hot tar which remained cooking on the fire down below.

How I adored Emma Lauder's cooking—especially her marvelous bread. As was usually the case, twice a week preparations were made for creating the indispensable six or eight loaves which helped fill the bellies of all her growing children. Anything left of these "day-old loaves," and such occasions tended to be rather rare, would be prudently put aside to make bread crumbs to thicken soups and stews—or for this lady's scrumptious bread pudding made with apples and raisins and cinnamon.

This especially "savvy" homemaker possessed a significant gift for "stretching the dollar," as she proudly called her unfaltering sense of frugality. For example, as a family during this particular lunch period we would undoubtedly be sharing the small quantity of leftovers from our supper last evening which had already been thoughtfully augmented by now with plenty of tasty vegetables to help "extend" the meal. This virtual feast eventually developed into a rather marvelous "new goulash," since it was born from an original recipe that had been much altered over the years, solely in order to accommodate the hard times and also to properly satisfy all the physically active, and, consequently, very hungry members of this large tribe.

Mrs. Lauder once matter-of-factly explained to me as she was in the very process of preparing the ingredients for this same meal that "real goulash" consisted primarily of meat, but that she had some time ago out of necessity altered the classic Hungarian version to one that was basically her own creation. It had more or less evolved into a sort of stew instead. Although a small portion of beef, or veal, or mutton, always continued to be the foundation for this glorious tasting meal, with the abundance of paprika which she had managed to "stockpile" whenever her brother still managed to send it from Vienna, and with the sweet onions and other spices which were added and then carefully blended along with the large amount of vegetables, it was impossible for me to imagine the original recipe being any better than what she already served us.

Last season's abundant harvest of green beans, carrots, peas, russet potatoes, cabbage, and corn from our own plentiful vegetable garden, had been painstakingly "put up" as the process was known. This time-honored method called for skillfully cleaning the fruits and vegetables and then carefully placing measured portions into large, clean, glass quart-size jars which were eventually properly sealed. Finally the containers would be cooked or steamed at a high temperature to kill any hazardous bacteria. After proper cooling, the precious produce would be labeled, dated, and then duly placed within some designated area within the large walk-in pantry just off the kitchen.

This wonderful method of keeping fruits and vegetables available throughout the year was actually quite common among those who lived in rural society. It was both an art as well as a science to be able to preserve the quality of this life-sustaining nourishment that would see a family through the bleakest winter and, if one planned well enough, long past early spring when such things were otherwise unavailable.

In a way this marvelous food which we planted and carefully tended throughout the growing season of each year, and then harvested as a family with particular pride, was akin to "communion" in the most religious sense. At every stage of the entire process we labored with our hands and hearts, close to the those we loved, and close, also, to the earth we respected and loved so much.

It was with this same underlying feeling of participating in an important celebration that Emma Lauder would always urge us all to respectfully bow our heads and to ask for God's blessing at lunch time, and, once again, at supper time. As the remarkably close-knit group that we already were we came to readily acknowledge that it was with the help of good weather—the necessary rain and sunshine, as well as our own honest sweat and often backbreaking labor—which always managed to provide these wonderful foods for our table.

We toiled together as a group all through the planting season of late spring and then well into the growing season of summertime. Harvest time occurred throughout the duration of all those months, depending upon what was being grown at the time. By early or mid-October, just as the colorful leaves were at their best—but just prior to their having entirely fallen from the trees in their timeless, breathtaking ritual; and after the screens on all the windows and doors of our farmhouse were dutifully replaced by sturdy storm windows that naturally helped to better insulate our little abode from the cold weather that was fast approaching, there in the deep pantry off the kitchen sat manifest proof that good things come with hard work.

Every shelf of the sumptuous walk-in pantry proudly bore jar upon magnificent jar of the sweet fruit of apple, plum, apricot, peach, and cherry—and, too, dozens of containers of several different vegetables. This prized bounty, whose vibrant colors and mouth-watering taste never diminished in the least with the passing of the many months ahead, literally "glittered" in their shining jars whenever the small overhead light in this small room was turned on. Like precious gems in a jeweler's proud showcase, they endlessly beckoned each observer to partake of the lush goodness that was truly the cumulative fruits of this family's labor.

In terms of food, or clothing—or anything else for that matter, which the family required—nothing was ever wasted. Absolutely nothing. Poignant reflections of the truth of the times were imprinted upon our minds and hearts on a daily basis. It became crystal clear to each and every member of our large body that the frightening deprivation and daily suffering of so many others—good people no different from ourselves—lay just within reach outside our very own front door. Felix used to say, in a mood of general seriousness, that to be thoughtless of this ever present truth—or, worse yet, to be uncaring—was viewed as contemptible at the very least. Perpetual callousness of this nature was viewed as criminal.

As Felix and I entered the little house that afternoon, we immediately removed our soiled boots and heavy outer clothing within the little vestibule just off the kitchen. As was always the family custom, too, we were obliged to neatly hang our belongings upon the wooden wall pegs that were provided for this purpose. Then, as was also our habit, we would carefully line up our shoes or boots right underneath these articles of clothing—in a straight line, upon the brightly polished floor beneath.

Judging from the mass of clothing and shoes that were already assembled there, Felix and I quickly realized that we were the last ones to arrive. Opening the inner door which led from the enclosed back porch area of the house into the cheerful kitchen, we were both greeted by the excellent warmth of the little room with its fragrant smells of wonderful food. There was also the ever-familiar and ever-reassuring hum of all the other family members as they were speaking and laughing. Several of the older children were arguing a bit, as children often do, and jostling one another in their collective attempt to hurriedly wash their hands at the sink. What inexpressible joy was mine at being able to be part of it all.... Life in this wonderfully busy household often seemed like a typical day at Grand Central Station, and I truly grew to love it.

Emma Lauder had already taken her place at the large table with the younger children. Felix and I remained standing momentarily at the tail end of that impressive line of healthy young people—indeed, behind the family's six strapping sons who were nearly finished sharing the soap bar and towels in what had become a ritualistic and noisy process of making ourselves "presentable enough," as the cook would unfailingly remark, in order for all of us to be worthy to seat ourselves at the family table.

Every single one of the older Lauder children were responsible individuals. Amazingly enough even the youngest children, at the earliest age, displayed impressive signs of already being this way, too. Customarily upon each early Saturday morning, after the designated chores around the farm were properly discharged, the older boys would busy themselves for the rest of that day by involving themselves in odd jobs around the community. This, their father strongly contended, helped supplement the family income and, just as importantly, instilled within each of the children a real appreciation for what it took to earn a dollar.

During those difficult years jobs of any kind where nearly impossible to come by, both for grown-ups, as well as for young adults alike. But with much concentrated effort, a little "Yankee ingenuity," and a whole lot of luck, several of the Lauder boys had eventually managed to succeed in this area. A great part of the luck factor in being able to find this much-coveted employment, it must be admitted, was due to the fact that many wealthy families from Chicago's elite owned grand summer homes around the lake. Consequently some of us were able to make ourselves indispensable as gardeners and house-boys, as well as caddies and greens-keeper's assistants during the busy seasons of late spring through autumn for the local golf and country club. Now and then it also proved highly fortuitous that a handful of these same well-to-do families would purchase Felix Lauder's paintings—his fine watercolors, oils, or pencil sketches, whenever our family circumstances turned difficult and necessity dictated a need for such things.

That particular year twelve-year-old Fritz, the clan's ninth child and the second youngest son, worked on Saturdays as a gardener's assistant for a retired University of Chicago professor by the name of Downing. Later on, when he was a good deal older, during the years more towards the end of those economically oppressive times and just prior to America's involvement in World War II, I remember that this same young man managed to work evenings as a draftsman for an engineering firm in Delavan. Sometime during these challenging years, as well, he found part-time employment in the infamous Chicago stock yards....

Here—in this unforgettable place, any sense of childhood innocence was quickly and forever banished, as one was required to stand knee-deep in the blood and entrails of all the slaughtered animals, all the while the brutalized flesh went through a specific process in order to make its way finally to the table for human consumption. Once in a mood of sharing Fritz reluctantly recounted to me—with entirely far too much detail, those brief yet difficult months he spent in that highly ignoble atmosphere. After hearing what he had to say that day I could very easily understand why he developed such a strong aversion to the sight and to the taste of meat in any form.

Eighteen-year-old Albert and twenty-year-old Robert, on the other hand, during that particular year of 1935 when the badly needed repairs on the roof were finally taking place, worked together in shifts at a local gas station. Since each of them had a real romance going as far as the automobile was concerned, the work they naturally accomplished in the form of minor car repairs, or in oil changes and the like, proved to be somewhat of a pleasure for them. And during the busy months of summer, with heavy traffic coming and going from the city on nearly an hourly basis, a fairly unbroken chain of interesting seasonal visitors also brought along with it those attractive young daughters from Chicago's more prosperous families. Consequently, daily work at the well-situated little convenience ultimately became even more exciting for these two healthy, hot-blooded young brothers.

On those busy Saturdays—and frequently after school, too, brother Willy who was fourteen that year, like me, usually helped out at Dunbar's Drug Store, stocking items on the numerous shelves there. Although the pay was minimal, Everett Dunbar, the proprietor, thoughtfully made up for this reality. Whenever Felix went to purchase his insulin, he was provided with a hefty discount. But, as was already mentioned, for Willy on this particular weekend time had been reserved for putting the finishing touches on an important geography project. I remember that even as a youth this special member of the family possessed a significantly quick mind, a rather dry sense of humor, and a real passion for learning. And, very much like his father, he commanded a true gift for patiently imparting to others those various gems of knowledge which he had summarily acquired. Looking back it seems inevitable that one day he should eventually have become a much respected Professor of Economics at one of this country's premiere universities. That day, in advance of this necessary change in Willy's work schedule, a prearrangement was made with Mr. Dunbar which allowed for make-up time somewhere in the future.

Furthermore, during that same period, sixteen-year-old Charley found employment at the local country club as a busboy. And as luck would certainly have it, he charmed the devil out of the management and finally talked the club's owner into hiring his fifteen-year-old younger brother, Eddie, for similar work there in the establishment's busy kitchen.

As for me, I was hired on a full-time basis by Mr. Dunbar to help deliver the newspapers that were deposited on a regular basis there at his drug store. A portion of this same daily publication was naturally kept there with "Old Man Dunbar," as we affectionately used to refer to him, upon the bottom shelf of his little newsstand directly behind the front counter of the store, while the rest were delivered to various homes in the neighboring communities by a handful of eager young workers like myself. I found that I had little trouble recruiting someone else to take my place, temporarily speaking, until the work on the roof was completed. Although I greatly valued working for the newspaper—for it was the Tribune which indirectly paid my salary, and learned to quickly rouse myself from my warm bed long before the "crack of dawn" each day in order to properly meet my responsibilities, I greatly welcomed this chance to help Felix as I was doing.

The youngest children which included Stephan, who was eight years old that year—and Maria and Annie, who were introduced earlier, finally completed this large and impressive family portrait. Because of the three younger children's ages and "inexperience"—as little Stevie himself would always chime in to say whenever there was table talk concerning family jobs outside the home—it was Emma Lauder who dutifully kept them busy, and therefore out of trouble, with small chores around the house.

The scent of the marvelous "goulash," which was mingling rather powerfully with the tantalizing fragrance of freshly baked rye bread, was nearly more than I could manage. Likewise that much welcomed warmth of the little room was just beginning to help thaw out my face, and hands, and feet. While I respectfully took my appointed place at the large crowded table, I remained pleasantly mindful of the happy chattering of these same beloved family members. Consciously I paused to allow this wholly nourishing atmosphere to envelope me body and spirit. It became my fervent wish to absorb every detail of the moment in order to be able to make it mine forever.

Then, as was Emma Lauder's habit, she graciously nodded to Felix as a signal between them. Right away each of us finally fell silent to respect-fully bow our head in prayer. No one at the table could have been more thankful to God for these enormous blessings than I. While Felix spoke the familiar words to a short prayer his wife always requested that he offer at times like these—the same words to a short benediction which always floated so effortlessly to the surface of my consciousness from somewhere deep within that personal repository of mine where all of my special memories and dreams are kept; that very same acknowledg-ment, mind you, that I had heard for the first time somewhere long, long ago in the now distant world of my earliest childhood, I silently offered my own fervent prayer of thanks.... With all my heart I thanked God for the plentiful food which we were all about to share. I thanked Him, too, for the sheltering roof above our heads whose necessary repair work would soon be completed by Felix and me. But most of all I was thankful, beyond words, for this family's strong constitution of ever-healing love and acceptance of which I had become a most grateful part.

1.

Grown-ups who comfortably theorize that the innocence of very young children acts as a natural protection against the great trials and tribulations of a difficult life, do not know very much about children. These same obtuse individuals really do not know very much about life either. It is plain enough to see that somehow they fail miserably in remembering what life can be like when viewed through the guileless eyes of any vulnerable young child. After all, a child's dreams shine no less brightly, nor any less beautifully, than those of any grown-up. They do, however, remain far more fragile in every way.

Generally speaking, it is true that most children are born with a certain natural resilience—a physical and spiritual pliability which mercifully acts to help buffer them against the many hazards of survival. However, it also remains a noteworthy reality that because this same innocence remains the fulcrum of the child's uncompromising trust, with a continuous barrage of wanton physical cruelty and/or grave spiritual debasement which lasts for any extended period of time, the child's innate trust soon becomes irreparably damaged. Eventually trust is replaced by a thoroughly deep-seated fear and mistrust of others that could conceivably last an entire lifetime.

The basic need for love and acceptance within each of us is unquestionably primordial. Indeed, that same vital force is the essential ingredient responsible for helping to make a human being thoroughly human. To continually thwart this psychologically inborn proclivity which is so openly and so honestly sought causes the infant or young child to soon recoil with confusion and horror as it eventually learns to seek shelter within itself for its own basic emotional needs. Because of one's fundamental instinct to seek genuine warmth and nurturing, which remains the birthright of every living thing—particularly every human child, anyone who out of gross ignorance, or basic moral debauchery, purposely destroys or defiles that sacred innocence is truly evil.... Without question, such people are evil beyond description.

I was born Adam Henry Bodray in Pittsburgh, Pennsylvania, in the early spring of 1921. So states my birth certificate. My father was Henry "Hank" Bodray. According to official file data that was registered by authorities who were responsible for eventually placing me in several foster homes one after the other, beginning shortly after my birth, he was listed as a part-time carpenter, as well as a full-time alcoholic.

With regard to those same penurious documents my mother had been Dealya Tillman Bodray who was originally from New Orleans. At the time of my birth she was merely sixteen years of age. From the moment I made my entrance into this world, and through all the many years that have followed, I have been unable to learn anything else that was significant about her. Nowhere could a solitary photograph of her be located, nor the tiniest memento purposely left behind as proof that she existed; nor anyone, for that matter, who might have even known her in the slightest way and could have better helped me understand who she was—and, in so doing, finally helped me better understand who I am.... All my life a meaningful part of me has mourned this very sad fact.

It would seem that my mother abandoned me not long after my birth to the sole care of my father, who then, himself, very soon after that gave up custody of me. It was not until several years later, during that critical time just before my father's death, that Fate had for the best of reasons decided to officially introduce my father and me.

My earliest recollection as a very young child is being cared for by a special woman whose kind and gentle nature prompted her to rock me in her arms while she sang me to sleep. Who had this kind soul been? My own mother, by chance? Or someone instead who might have been related to me in some other way? Both mentally and emotionally speaking, how far back in memory is it possible for any of us to travel, in order to be able to remember something significant about our earliest past?

I also clearly recall the fragments of a prayer which must have been repeated over and over again during this early time as well, for, in a wonderful sense, a solitary phrase has managed to linger, still, within the complex labyrinth of my mind. For whatever reason the words have left their imprint upon my life. These same distant tissue-fragile memories have survived within a half-mist world, though—within a vague sort of enchanted half dream.

Actually, there have been times throughout my life when I have sincerely questioned their validity. Their wholesome beauty somehow seems so out of place—so contrary and totally out of character, in the truest sense, when measured against the years that followed.

During those lonely and often brutal years to which I privately refer as "my incarceration," when I was systematically passed from home to home and from family to family, I came to think of myself as a small fragile leaf whose destiny it was to be carried down a perilous, fast-moving river. Without having any say in the matter at all that same hapless entity always sought to cling so desperately to the passage's steep canyon walls, or some friendly rock, or perhaps a well-placed branch throughout its tumultuous journey downstream, in an ever-fervent attempt to help save itself from ultimately drowning.

In order to remain true to my history, as I proceed to openly relay these many intimate facts, I feel obliged to honestly state that when I was placed in these numerous foster homes to live briefly among those various strangers, there were naturally some families that were understandably much better than others. But because my placement anywhere guaranteed that each family who accepted me was granted a small stipend as a monthly reward for looking after me, my basic presence within their lives, for the most part, seemed to be emotionally lacking in so many ways.

Slowly I began to see myself as the hopeless outsider forever peering within. I was the hungry soul forced to remain outside the "circle of light." At no time during those years did I ever feel truly welcomed or wanted. My overall impression was that I was little more than a piece of furniture or a minor appliance, perhaps, which was basically expendable save for the little extra money that always traveled with me.

Because of this on-going emotionally destructive situation it seems to me that I purposely allowed myself to grow a little hardened with the passing of time. I know now that this behavior was merely a mechanism to help me better cope with this profound sense of alienation that I was being made to feel with the rest of the world. Attempting to go against my basic nature which passionately desired to be involved with others in a wholesome emotional sense, I found myself, instead, striving hard to develop an overall feeling of emotional detachment to my surroundings, as well as to the various people who had been paid to feed and clothe me.

Alas, the reader must not think me ungrateful in the slightest sense for any small kindness I might have received during those early years. As with most people I was born an individual who, more than anything else, longed for love—and at the very same time wished just as much to be given a chance to be able to love in return. For, truly, the human spirit remains persistent as it comes into this world ready to celebrate life. But with those highly disturbing circumstances of my first years, and with the day-to-day emotional disappointments that began to collect over time and then to weigh so heavily upon my vulnerable spirit, I confess that a grave internal conflict began to arise that I had great difficulty resolving.

Sometime during this same tenuous period of my young life, too, I found an overwhelming need to invent a friend. This childhood method of better contending with great loneliness and despair is not uncommon in situations of this sort. Certainly this relatively benign behavior is not an example of having the psyche fragment in some frantic and unhealthy attempt to escape reality by creating multiple personalities. No. It is, rather, a desperate but wholly innocent and healthy endeavor to invoke a necessary fantasy at will that would duly incorporate into a painful daily reality a little sanity in order to make life bearable.

This imaginary playmate and most trusted confidant of mine was named Jake. Still to this day I am unable to say for certain from whence the name appeared. Up to that point in time I had never before met anyone with that name, nor had I found this particular appellation in a book, since I had not as yet learned to read. I am quite certain that not once in all those tender formative years of mine had I ever even seen a copy of anything that was printed in any fashion, save for a copy of the Bible. And for reasons which I shall soon relate this good book eventually came to signify to my exceedingly tender spirit an example of extreme cruelty and gross perversion whose longtime presence within my life pushed me to a point of profound despair.

It remains highly significant that it was during this most challenging time in my young life when my dear friend "Jake" first made his welcomed appearance. My imaginary friend, or alter ego as some might choose to refer to this persona of the mind, was there for me through "thick and thin." This same gentle friend, whom I had so brilliantly yet effortlessly conjured up, was like a large safe rock to which I chose to firmly attach myself upon my long perilous journey downstream.

It was not until sometime after those first many months when Felix Lauder and his family had so kindly taken me in without pay, and without anything but a sincere desire to help the needy child I was, that I felt comfortable enough to finally bid my make-believe friend farewell. One fine day he simply vanished for good—quietly and unobtrusively tiptoeing out of my life, very much the way he first arrived.

During the early autumn of what I calculate must have been my fifth year of life, I was placed in the home of one Reverend James Pouley and his family. Up to that day my basic existence remained only relatively difficult. However in a matter of a few hours after I initially made this man's acquaintance my life eventually became a living hell—a living hell, pure and simple.

Reverend Pouley was an ecclesiastic minister and a much respected public figure within the small suburb of Pittsburgh in which we lived.... I recall that he made a point of often telling me this. Throughout any given weekday he and I had relatively little association with one another. It was during each and every Sunday afternoon, however, after this man's professional commitments at the local church or hospital had been met, and after we as a family—which included his wife and two daughters—all returned home, that this terrible personal abuse would regularly commence.

To study the exterior of this two-faced and black-hearted man one was apt to come away with the strong impression that he was predisposed to genuine kindness towards all. He seemed outwardly most genial in his interaction with everyone. After Sunday service, he stood outside the doors of his church, drawing languidly on his strangely shaped pipe that was filled with an awful Turkish tobacco. Its acrid smelling smoke not only tended to permeate the air all around, but managed to befoul everything else that it touched as well.

There Reverend Pouley always stood, this cheerful and overtly charming pinnacle of local society. There he was, with his ever-gracious smile which to everyone—everyone but me, that is—tended to exude great warmth of spirit, eagerly shaking the hands of his parishioners as they were enthusiastically offered to him in passing. Often I studied him as he pleasantly kissed or exuberantly hugged one of the newborn infants or youngest children belonging to the numerous members of his trusting "flock," as those innocents were proudly presented to him for his official blessing. Indeed, outwardly he gave off the wholesome fragrance of being a truly excellent soul who remained beyond reproach for any reason.

After we as a family returned to the Pouley's home on those early Sunday afternoons, however, all the while his wife and daughters innocently busied themselves with their own interests downstairs, I was automatically sent to my room upstairs in order that this "educator" could privately "instruct me in matters pertaining to the salvation of my almighty soul..." as he invariably put it. His unique method for attempting to accomplish this end never wavered in the least in its delivery, week, after week, after week. Predictably I trembled through and through to hear him slowly make his way up the creaking wooden steps of the staircase. Then, sure of foot and walking with a sense of great purpose, I could hear as he slowly and deliberately proceeded down the narrow hall towards the small room which I occupied....

As he entered the well-appointed space where I awaited my fate, this awful man would place a small cylindrical shaped tin upon the intricately-carved wooden clothing chest nearby. Taking up a copy of the Bible which was always left in the same place near my bed, he opened the thick book to search randomly for an appropriate passage. Finally finding the Scripture of his choice for that particular week, he then lay the open book near the edge of the bed as he reached for the small tin. Automatically stripping me of my knickers and underclothing, which usually lay in a disheveled pile around my ankles, at this point, I was forced around and bent hard against the bed.

With an obscene rhythmic lunging motion my cruel guardian would stand directly behind me, making contact with my body, over and over again, all the while the sickening stench and greasy feel of the cold white lard from the tin coated his large hand which now tightly covered my mouth in order that I might not be able to cry out in any manner. All these powerful sensations came together to form a large, solid, putrid mass that firmly lodged itself within my small chest and throat, threatening to properly suffocate me in the end.

As he huskily whispered the words from the passage he was reading into my ear from behind, in between the terrible rhythmical grunts and groans caused from his extreme physical exertion, the nauseating smell of the cold lard mixed with the horrible scent of his awful tobacco continued to mercilessly assault me. When this seemingly endless episode of unspeakable abuse was finally over, he matter-of-factly wiped clean his hand upon the back of my shirt, as he stood tall once more to further secure the fly of his trousers. Immediately following this, with a hollow metallic clicking sound the lid belonging to the little tin was snapped shut again, after which the trusty cylinder was finally slid back down into the pocket of his pants. Lastly, just as he unfailingly remembered to do each week, this same evil rapist would casually close the thick book from which he had been reading. After returning it to its regular place there upon the chest nearby, he wordlessly left the room, promptly locking the door behind him.

After his departure each week—after I could hear his resounding footsteps there upon the stairs once more as he proceeded to make his descent into the parlor below—only then would I allow myself to slide down upon the floor, while my hands and face sought refuge in the scratchy fabric of the bed covering. With the violent convulsions that racked my small body I tightly clenched my jaws together in a supreme effort to keep from biting my tongue or damaging my teeth....

Hypocrite! Pious fraud! Evil despoiler of innocent young children! Be well-advised that nowhere within the entire universe shall there be a dark enough hole of refuge in which you might ultimately hide yourself! Both God and I know the truth! Naturally these are the thoughts that come to my mind—even now, after all these many years. What others might not properly ascertain as I so openly offer this most personal confession is the sobering reality that such inexcusable actions on the part of my antagonist had doubly wounded the innocent and vulnerable child that I once had been. The insidiousness of that repetitively cruel act not only brutalized me in the obvious physical and emotional manner, but it began to slowly sabotage my spiritual well-being as well by firmly convincing me that I must indeed be an evil person myself in order for another to continuously treat me this way. My rudimentary confidence and basic sense of self-worth as a human being were being systematically negated—slowly being dismantled brick by sacred brick, in effect, with this ongoing abuse. So much so, in fact, that I actually reached a point in time where I actively questioned why I was ever born....

Oddly enough, though, even with my having been immersed as I was in the total helplessness of the situation, I never once cried. Never. Never, with all of that unspeakable abuse, did I ever allow my assailant to break me in this manner. Something deep within me—some sacred fragment of a tiny seed of my basic dignity managed to survive, along with a good deal of childish stubbornness, too, no doubt, miraculously preventing me from allowing this horrible man to completely destroy me. By not allowing myself to openly weep this simple resolve of mine consistently remained my small private victory of the spirit!

Laying there in a crumpled heap amongst my child's clothing, physically and emotionally bruised and bloodied from this ritualistic encounter with the devil himself, my grievously wounded spirit had once again been literally ground into the dirt by the heel of this man's oppressive boot. Over and over again I would tell myself how much I thoroughly detested him....

Raising my bowed head, ultimately I would catch sight of the thick book which remained reposing on the wooden chest only a few feet away, dutifully awaiting that inevitable "next time" to occur. That very same book, mind you, which continued to bear silent witness to my extreme degradation of body and soul. Needless to say it was during these seemingly hopeless times that I sincerely pondered the existence of God. I vowed that if there was a God, as I was led to believe, then certainly during times like these I was being forced to admit that I hated Him, too, for having thus abandoned me.

2.

THOSE HAUNTING SOUNDS from any distant train whistle, especially when heard during the course of a long lonely night, have always held an indescribably special place in my heart. That same bittersweet, moody music—not unlike the effect of a soulful harmonica piece well played—remains part of the fabric of my spirit and shall forevermore tend to call forth those distinctly personal memories from my long ago past....

During that interminable time when I was forced to live at the mercy of Reverend Pouley, I eventually developed a real need to express my utter unhappiness. I was not born to be a troublemaker—on the contrary—but with the extremely vulnerable circumstances in which I helplessly found myself week after week, I began to invent small ways in which to lash out in order to get even. But just as the reader may well imagine, with these rare and highly uncharacteristic outbursts of mine, I eventually only created more problems for myself in the end.

How I detested school. From the very beginning I felt that it was a thoroughly uncomfortable environment in which I just did not belong. Since I could neither read nor even write my name, as the other children apparently seemed to be able to do quite easily enough when Mrs. Pouley subjected me to the ridicule of my classmates on that first encounter I had ever had with formal education of any kind, I vowed to myself that this brand new abuse would definitely be short-lived.

When the wife of my supreme antagonist dutifully presented her daughters and me to our new teacher, each of us was dressed in our brand new and rather expensive clothing. After I was instructed where to sit, and where to find the clothes closet and lavatory, I politely excused myself under the pretext of needing to use the toilet and quickly made my escape.

Something deep down within me simply "snapped" that day. So on my way out the front door of that little school house and down the tree-lined street on that warm early autumn morning, I felt not the slightest twinge of guilt as I solemnly promised myself to make the most of that entire day—and possibly the next. Having promised not to return to the Pouley household by choice I vaguely contemplated the grave punishment which would undoubtedly be waiting for me there upon my inevitable return.

My loyal partner-in-crime, Jake, cheerfully accompanied me as I journeyed quite some distance out to an old stone quarry which was located somewhere on the outskirts of town. As soon as we arrived at this pleasant place, we instantly removed our clothing to swim in its cold crystal clear water. Essentially the experience was very much like a holiday for our spirits, for the water, and the sun, and the gloriously fresh air had the ability to cheer us from head to toe.

We managed for this brief while, at least, to crawl from the dark and ever frightening box which the Pouley household represented to me. Our innocent souls had been trapped for such a long time already. Now that we had successfully made our escape and had wandered out into this non-threatening atmosphere where we could finally breathe so much more freely, I was prepared to pay any price that would be required of me in the long run, just for this brief taste of sweet freedom.

For lunch and again for supper on that hot September day, Jake and I dined quite happily on the plentiful blackberries which we picked from the nearby bushes. That night we entertained ourselves for long hours by blissfully languishing beneath the comforting blanket of the deep velvet sky, counting stars and enthusiastically sharing our most fervent wishes and dreams for the future.

There, too, amongst the soothing night sounds of the tuneful crickets and the haunting calls of the great horned owl, I finally bowed to that much delayed great release that comes with weeping. In the sacred solitude that surrounded me, I consented to allow the flood gates of my young heart to be opened and at long last to weep as I never wept before.

Nearby there was a train track whose twin rails incorporated themselves for some distance over a wide precarious chasm which was the deep quarry itself, creating an unusual bridge in effect. Two times that day—actually two times each and every day—once in the early afternoon and then again long after dark, a train's scheduled approach could be detected in the far distance. The tranquilizing and pleasantly muffled sound of its whistle would first be heard way off in the distance, long before the powerful and noisy conveyance actually arrived within sight to eventually cross the bridge.

It was after the evening train's passing on that second night when my make-believe friend and I managed to climb to the top of that unique structure. There in the moonlight, with a multitude of stars flickering overhead in our private protective canopy, we sat together upon a narrow portion of the track. Our bare feet remained freely dangling over that great open abyss, between the sturdy bridge upon which we were both sitting and the deep cold crystalline water far, far below....

In our heart of hearts we devised a desperate plan. It became a secret covenant in the truest sense where, should our lives become even more unbearable than they already were, we would climb upon these very tracks one day—upon this very spot, in fact, and wait for a coming train. We promised to be brave together. This, we firmly decided, was essential.... We would be obliged to faithfully rely upon each other for the necessary courage and fortitude that these future actions of ours would naturally require. Because of our seemingly endless despair, we would consciously be choosing this permanent way out of our great misery by ending our lives together in this rather uncomplicated and straightforward manner.

After all it takes a great deal of unhappiness, on a rather large scale, and over a fairly long period of time, to finally bring a human being to a point of profound despair—especially a child who by their very nature is born happy and optimistic, and continues to remain so given the slightest encouragement. But that weekly anguish which I was being forced to endure, without there being any end in sight, could not be allowed to go on for much longer. And so this desperate plan which my little companion and I devised together on that late evening, as we sat all alone together high above the rest of the world, was to be our "insurance card" for the future.

Although I could never have guessed it, those two remarkable days and nights of complete freedom, which had fundamentally come about from my own desperate initiative to escape my cruel confinement, were to be the blessed precursor that would very shortly be heralding a dramatic new change in my young life. Because of this poignant reality, from that time onward I have always associated the sound of a train's music with this same miraculous "turning point" in my life.

Indeed, this sweetest of symbols was soon to herald the beginning of a personal journey which would eventually lead me to that long awaited peace and sanity for which I endlessly yearned. Throughout my entire life—through the good times, as well as through the bad—this experience has somehow managed to endure and to shine ever so brightly in any given night, whenever I chance to hear the distant haunting sound of some train going anywhere....

Needless to say, my truancy—even for that brief while, profoundly embarrassed my evil care-giver, Reverend Pouley. Consequently, he quite naturally became greatly angered. To the highly misinformed collective minds of his unsuspecting parishioners his having taken me in, as he had, was viewed as a kind gesture of immense proportions. After all, how could any of those good people have ever guessed the truth of the real situation?

It was the local constable and his very able assistant who first discovered my whereabouts. With undue ceremony they literally dragged me back to the place where I least wished to be. After the officers returned me to the custody of that terrible man, apologizing rather profusely for their delay in having located me, the second the front door was closed behind them Reverend Pouley managed to grab me by the hair at the back of my head. With a vice-like grip that involuntarily brought tears to my eyes, I was immediately marched upstairs. Once again, on that early Wednesday morning, the day became just another shameful Sunday afternoon—only this time the betrayal came in conjunction with a very sound thrashing from the good reverend's belt.

The following day, I was not asked to attend school. Likewise I received nothing to eat since my disgraceful return, either. While the Pouley girls were both dutifully taken off to class, I remained locked away in my room upstairs, lying across my bed and nursing the welts and bruises which covered my body's torso and thighs.

Sometime later on that morning I heard the distinct sound of a car stopping at the front of the house. After that, a car door opened and closed, and one could hear muffled voices slowly progressing towards the house from somewhere down below. As I made my way to the window to observe the visitors in an attempt to discover their identity, I could hear yet another more familiar sound which was my bedroom door being hastily unlocked, and then opened....

There in the doorway stood Reverend Pouley. Directly behind him and peering at me with notable interest from around one of his shoulders was a gentleman and a lady whom I did not know. In a thoroughly suspicious and kindly sounding voice that made my blood run cold, my jailer invited me downstairs. One of the visitors, I noted, who preceded us on our descent from the second floor to the ground floor, was carrying a briefcase, and so my immediate impression was that I was being reassigned to a new foster home.

Everything began happening so quickly. I was not addressed in any manner during the entire meeting that followed in the parlor. At one point I heard Reverend Pouley tell these strangers, as he removed his ever-present and ever-stinking pipe from his mouth, "There simply is no other solution, my good people! As you can imagine, my family and I have for a long time now lavished real love and attention upon this 'ungrateful brat,' and presently we have finally approached a point where we unanimously decided that we can no longer put up with the unkind abuse which this awful child consistently chooses to dole out to us in return!"

There was an unpretentious-looking valise sitting by a large comfortable chair as one entered the parlor by way of the front door. From this rather surreptitious-looking bag the woman visitor removed a pair of knickers which seemed badly worn. The jacket, too, was very small, as were a pair of shoes that had certainly seen better days. While I stood in the center of the room, in front of everyone, I was promptly searched by my awful host for anything that I may have "stolen." After this minor indignity was performed, the good quality clothing which had been provided me by the Pouley family was duly removed from my person and then promptly taken away.... Soon I found myself being quickly dressed in these other things which some kind soul had thoughtfully provided for me instead.

In this unfamiliar attire the visiting couple walked with me to the front door, and as they were saying their polite good-byes to their congenial host and hostess, I stubbornly chose not to turn and acknowledge the family whose home I was escaping. Neither did any one of them make an attempt to bid me farewell in any way. All I fervently wished to do was to leave behind this horrible place—this horrible part of my life, for whatever was now waiting ahead for me.

As the rear car door was held open for me and the gentleman politely helped me step into the back to find my seat, I looked up just in time to see Reverend Pouley in the process of closing the front door to his house. I well recall that the ensuing loud thud had a certain firm finality about it. Suddenly the huge oppressiveness of those past many, many months upon my young life seemed to be miraculously lifted from my small shoulders. It was as if the minor event of that door being soundly shut upon me signaled one chapter of my life being permanently closed, while another waited just ahead to be miraculously opened....

Very slowly the automobile began to move forward. As I sat on the right hand side of the wide seat in the rear all by myself, I could not help noticing how long my new knickers were. There was also the obvious fact that the cuffs of the sleeves of the cotton shirt I was currently wearing were at least a couple of inches above where they might have been. My new shoes, too, which really were not new in the real sense, were already beginning to pinch my toes. Even with all this, though—with the early afternoon sunlight filtering into the side window of the moving car, I became acutely mindful of its pleasant warmth playing upon my face and chest, and immediately began to feel deeply comforted. Suddenly the new world into which I was being escorted by these two beautiful strangers began to look better and better, and I sat back to enjoy the ride.

3.

M Y HOUR OF DELIVERANCE WAS AT HAND. Of this important reality I was becoming more and more certain. While I continued to sit uncomfortably upon the rear seat of the shiny, black, early model Packard automobile, which vaguely reminded me of the one the Pouley family owned, all I could see was the back portion of the heads of the man and the woman sitting in the front seat. Resting there with my legs stretched out before me in a fairly unnatural position, my head was subsequently being rigidly pushed back against the car's smooth seat cushion. With a sense of frustration I was rediscovering that I was not even tall enough yet to be able to see out of the side window of the car as it sped along to wherever it was that the three of us were going.

Instead a mesmerizing kaleidoscopic parade of tree tops, and telephone poles with wires, and the pinnacles of many of the taller buildings as we passed them by managed to firmly hold my attention. From where I was currently sitting, too, within the more open places I could see the pearly white clouds as they spread their fragile wings of cirrus curls across the bright blue background of the sky.

At the tender age of seven and a half I recognized that I was still quite small for my age. In all my early years of growing up I came to regard my ever present hunger for food as normal. Rarely had I ever found myself in any other position, so consequently I really had no other perspective upon which to base any comparison. I was quite certain, though, that at no time had I ever eaten a meal and felt truly satisfied that I had eaten my fill. Naturally, with this chronic nutritional deprivation, I most probably was not thriving as I could and should have been.

The kindly gentleman and lady who were now my traveling companions spoke little since our journey began. There was so much I would have asked them, if only I could have found the courage to speak. In a little while the car, after numerous turns and an erratic pattern of stopping and starting, finally came to a standstill in a noisy place. Presently I could clearly hear the sound of other car horns blaring, and several people shouting at the same time as well. I also detected someone blowing a shrill whistle at various intervals—the same sort of whistle a policeman might use. Shortly our car's motor fell silent. The gentleman slid from his place there behind the wheel and walked around the car to assist the woman, and together they opened my car door and proceeded to help me out.

Each of them politely took up one of my hands—and so, with my small slightly moist hands entwined within their drier and far larger ones, we proceeded to walk hastily across a huge parking lot and from there into a very large building. Everywhere there was a great deal of movement and noise. Throngs of people were scurrying about with suitcases and other paraphernalia in tow—including children of various ages, and pets, stopping now and then to glance at their watches or up at a large board whose entire face bore much writing all over it.

"Are we going somewhere?" I asked with a bit of hesitation, as the three of us finally found a little alcove near a wall that was out of the mainstream of traffic. The nice lady was kneeling down in front of me now. She took a comb from her purse and quickly ran it through my hair. In a moment more she was also wiping my face with a clean white handkerchief which had also been thoughtfully extracted from her carry-all.

Then, before she answered my question, from that same leather bag she unexpectedly produced a small piece of cardboard that had two long strings attached to it. Upon this sturdy sign and in small black letters was written several lines of neatly presented script. As she attached this item to one of the top buttons of my shirt by carefully winding the stings around and around several times, she finally tied the remaining extra little ends in a tight knot to further secure the placard.

After all this had been done she paused a few seconds to critically study me. I was also carefully studying her and I readily recall that she was young and extremely pretty. I also could not help but notice that she smelled quite wonderful, too, as she smiled at me and said, "No, young Adam, we won't be traveling on with you from here. As you see I have attached this important information to your shirt, in order that you won't become lost on your train ride to Chicago."

It is impossible for me to say for certain how my countenance must have appeared at that precise moment, but I can assure the reader that I felt genuinely stunned. Somehow things seemed to be happening to me at a lightening speed, as if the small leaf I perceived myself to be had finally wrenched itself free from the huge impediment which had held it captive for such a long, long time. Now it was being unexpectedly swept up, and out, into a fast moving current within the vast "river of life" to be carried heaven knows where.

I began to feel a twinge of panic. Sensing this the pretty woman instinctively placed her hands upon my narrow shoulders in an attempt to comfort me, as she said, "You'll enjoy the ride ... I promise! Chicago used to be my home when I was a little girl of about your age. There's so much to see along the way.... And when you arrive at the station there someone from the station master's office has promised to meet you, and to wait with you until your father comes to fetch you."

I felt now, for certain, that I was going to faint. Had I heard correctly? Had this woman actually said "my father"? Suddenly a thousand questions flooded my poor dazed mind, but all I could do was to stand there, in complete silence, much beset with high mental and emotional confusion.

"Please don't worry! Don't be frightened..." I barely heard her say. This kind lady's words were traveling from some great distance away to reach me, very much as though each of us were standing at the opposite ends of an incredibly long tunnel. Then from somewhere nearby I heard the familiar sound of a train's whistle as it now began insistently calling to me....

Presently, with considerable haste these same good people—again, each having taken up one of my hands—were rushing with me down a long high-covered corridor where an immense silver train was waiting upon one of the many sets of silver tracks. The gentleman with whom I was traveling, after having stopped at one of the train's many sets of doors in order to speak briefly with a uniformed man, received a nod from this person in answer to whatever had been asked.

With a broad grin the friendly conductor gestured to the door immediately beside him and then proceeded to help the three of us up the three steep steps into the waiting car. After walking just a little way we promptly located what I was told was to be my seat for the entire journey. Other passengers, I could not help but notice, were placing their personal belongings high above their seats in special compartments—and underneath their seats as well. But I had nothing to put anywhere, since all I owned in the entire world was only what I was presently wearing.

A loud sharp whistle from somewhere within the vicinity sounded twice, and as the lady made me comfortable, the gentleman handed me a large brown paper bag, as he told me, "We thought you might be hungry, Adam.... Inside you'll find a sandwich, some fruit, and cookies—enough for the entire journey, I should imagine! Also, here's some change in case you might wish to purchase something from the conductor's assistant when he makes his rounds later."

As this extraordinarily kind stranger was telling me all this, he simultaneously dipped into one of his trouser pockets. Soon his hand came out clutching a wide variety of several different sized coins. Quickly searching through the change, and then thoughtfully extracting the money he wished to give me, he proceeded to gently press the unexpected gift into my hand.

Just as the last set of whistles blew these two fine people each quickly bid me good-bye and I helplessly watched as they hurried back up the aisle towards the train's door. In order to be able to see outside I promptly decided to pull myself up upon my knees. As I knelt there upon the seat, I eagerly pressed my warm face against the cool smooth glass of the window in hopes of seeing my generous benefactors one last time.

Just as I fervently imagined, I found them both standing there below my window, as the train in which I was to journey slowly began to pull away from that spot. Wearing remarkably similar expressions on their already rather serious-looking countenances, together they each raised a hand to wave to me.... Had I imagined it? Were there tears in the lovely eyes of this kind lady as I instinctively raised my right hand in a spontaneous salute of farewell?

For a good while I rode in this same kneeling position of mine in order to be able to see the many interesting sights, all the while my silver chariot sped along its polished tracks. Initially we traveled past old dingy buildings, and dozens of solitary links of abandoned train cars whose own tracks converged and then crisscrossed within a wide congested public area. In a little while the stark dirtiness of this great industrial city began to change, and then to completely recede, little by little.

Later at a high speed the other passengers and I were gliding past neatly kept homes with small gardens and yards that were speckled with children's swings and other playthings. Dogs, too, would frequently traverse the boundaries of the given parameters of these same yards. I watched with mild amusement as they madly chased after us barking rather aggressively, albeit quite soundlessly, all the while. Much later on, still, as if by sheer magic the scenery changed yet again, as our marvelous train snaked its way through cool green forests, and lovely open countryside with its shining lakes and rich farmland, imparting to this hungry young traveler the intoxicating freedom of spirit which only such wide open places have the ability to bring.

This was my very first real trip anywhere. I also confess that the endless rocking motion of the vehicle in which I was traveling pleased me very much. That slightly hypnotic and melodic sound of the train's heavy metal wheels, too, as they continuously glided over the closely fitted joints of the tracks—where one segment of rail was expertly welded to the next, added to the experience in a memorable way. In time, however, I discovered that the bottom portion of my legs had gone completely numb from the fact that I had been kneeling for ever so long in that one fixed position. To gain relief from this odd sensation I finally turned around and quickly seated myself facing forward.

With a spark of keen interest I soon remembered the lunch bag that was patiently waiting for me upon the nearby seat. At the sight of that generous offering I suddenly recalled how very hungry I was. Opening the crisp paper wrapper which held the sandwich I discovered two generous slices of thick heavy bread, and in between the bread were traces of creamy butter and rich yellow mustard, as well as several slices of heavenly bologna. As if this had not already been enough, there was also a large red apple. In fact, it was the biggest apple I had ever seen in my life. Wrapped separately from all the rest of these items were three gigantic oatmeal cookies that were each nearly as large as the sandwich itself.

When the conductor's assistant finally made his rounds down the long aisle to service the needs of his passengers by offering them drinks and "smokes" and newspapers, I happily remembered the money that earlier was pressed into my small hand. Since I had no idea on earth how to deal with even the most basic transaction of money, I now remained at the mercy of the young man who was handing me my container of milk. With a modest air of feigned confidence, however, pretending all the while as if I knew exactly what I was doing, I reached over and handed him two of the larger coins which were part of that significant gift to me. Glancing down at what I had just bestowed upon him, the man merely smiled a little.

Almost immediately, without bothering to say anything to me, the railroad official proceeded to return the larger silver piece. Reaching underneath the metal coin-changer that he wore at the front of his wide belt, he swiftly and expertly clicked the interesting apparatus in two places, instantly producing the amount that was to be my change. Finally handing me what I could only assume was my just due, he then politely tipped his hat as if to finalize our business transaction.

That entire process of having purchased something all by myself, and for the very first time, fascinated me. That same man, too, who was instrumental in having made it all possible, had also greatly interested me. Watching him move on ahead to assist another passenger I decided, then and there, that that was what I wished to be when I grew up. After all, I simply could not imagine anything more grand than traveling around the countryside, seeing to the needs of polite travelers, and making change for them all day long by wearing a marvelous belt similar to his in every way.

With this bright and shiny new idea firmly planted within my mind, I sighed with satisfaction and sat back at once to eat my meal. It was quite a long while since I had eaten anything substantial, if one did not bother to count the blackberries, or my Monday morning breakfast that awful day when I was depressingly whisked off to school by Mrs. Pouley. Without a doubt it must have been all the highly unusual excitement of those past many hours that became responsible for my not having called this important fact more to the forefront of my mind. But now, with this virtual feast waiting invitingly at my fingertips, I hungrily dove into its goodness.

As I began to eat, I decided that it would be prudent to save half the sandwich for later, since I could never be sure when I might find food again. Reverend Pouley frequently withheld meals as a means to further punish me, so I learned to more or less hoard food. But this time, because of my extreme hunger, my well-intended promise to myself that day eventually fell by the wayside—or track side, which might be more appropriate to say in this case.

In no time at all I managed to polish off the huge sandwich, and the crisp red apple, as well as two of the gigantic cookies, with milk, without having made the slightest apology to myself. Carefully I wrapped the remaining cookie within its original paper for safekeeping and then finally slid it into my jacket pocket which was laying across the vacant seat next to me.

Not long after all this the food's extraordinary spell, along with the gentle rocking motion of the train, produced in me a real need for sleep. For me, at least, this most unusual day of days seemed to be slowly coming to an end. Outside a soft golden glow from the setting sun was bathing everything in a rich and subtle warmth. With someone's open window nearby and with the play of that sporadic breeze which continued to caress my face, I remained powerless against sleep's overwhelming seduction.

As my ever-faithful transport made progress on its appointed northwest route from the "Smoky City" of Pittsburgh, steadily onward towards the equally large and impressive city of Chicago, I was overcome by a profound obligation to close my heavy eyelids, while at the same time I barely recall resting my head against the padded cushion of my seat back. Vaguely, little by little, I became conscious of finally being able to let go of the many disturbing events of those past many hours. Even the sharp reality of my present circumstances, with the nagging feeling of not knowing what Fate really had in store for me, softened and receded and finally began to melt away....

As the powerful God Morpheus gently enfolded the sleeping child within his ever-compassionate arms, there briefly floated somewhere in the light fluffiness of my peaceful mind several questions. For instance: Who was my father, after all? And why on earth had it taken him so long to find me? Where could he have possibly been during all these incredibly lonely years? Would he be able to recognize me, as I waited for him in that place called Chicago? And how was I to know him? Finally, just before I completely surrendered to that blessed oblivion of deepest slumber; just before that kindly nether world completely enveloped my body and soul, as I made my slow and effortless descent through and then down well past the highly instructive world of dreams, I fervently prayed that my mother would be waiting somewhere there for me, too.

4.

QUITE NATURALLY the ever abiding concepts of time, and place, and distance, are perceived far more differently by small children than they are by adults. When I finally awoke from my intense sleep in a somewhat confounded state, I found myself unexpectedly lying across both seats now. My head was resting comfortably upon my jacket which had been carefully folded underneath me. Having absolutely no idea how long I had been sleeping, nor exactly how I arrived in my present position, I slowly drew myself up into a sitting position there upon the seat nearest the window to thoroughly contemplate the matter. As if sluggishly ambling its way through a sort of heavy fog my poor mind attempted to recall the events of the recent past. Soon I was noticing that someone had taken the trouble to cover me with a loosely woven pale blue shawl that smelled pleasantly of summer flowers....

After rubbing my eyes with the back of my loosely clenched fists, I instinctively began to run my fingers through my sleep-tousled hair. As I was doing this, a woman who seemed much advanced in years appeared from somewhere behind me. As she slowly bent towards me to collect the article of clothing which had served so well as my blanket while I slept, she smiled warmly at me and said, "You've slept for such a long time… You must have been extremely tired!" While she carefully folded that small treasure that reminded me of what a cloud might feel like, she graciously leaned over to whisper to me that I would find the lavatory towards the rear of our compartment, should I feel a need to do so.

Perhaps it was the power of her timely suggestion that lent a real urgency to my present situation. I began to fidget uncomfortably in my seat. As my distress increased, I promptly excused myself to hurriedly brush past her. Using the commode in that tiny space that endlessly shifted and lurched to one side, and then to the other, was no easy task I was to discover. After I finished, however, and dutifully washed and dried my hands, I returned to my place to find an impressive container of orange juice and a large thick sweet roll—with plump little raisins on top—sitting upon a white napkin on the very seat I had just recently vacated. Right away I searched around for the conductor's assistant but found no one.

Instead that same "angel of kindness"—the very woman who had earlier shown such solicitude in looking after me, was standing in the aisle now, placing a neat wide-brimmed straw hat atop her finely chiseled head of silver gray hair. With admirable dexterity she took a moment more to use a long hat pin to better secure that obviously well-worn ornament. As a voice with considerable authority loudly announced our train's arrival into the town of South Bend, Indiana, my special traveling companion took a moment more to don a pair of snow-white cotton gloves.

After this she reached down towards the floor to collect a large traveling case, along with her fine blue shawl which was waiting there carefully draped over the back of the seat which she must have earlier occupied. I watched as she began walking towards me. Pausing a moment next to the double seat where I remained steadfastly observing her every movement, in the same warm voice which seemed to exactly match the suppleness of her lovely shawl, she said somewhat apologetically, "I couldn't finish my breakfast, as you see. My children and grandchildren often tell me that I eat like a little bird!" With this down-to-earth comment of hers, the elderly woman chuckled good-naturedly. In a moment she continued on to say, "I'd be so pleased if you'd do me the great favor of finishing the food for me instead!"

With this generous remark the sweet woman smiled her charming smile and began to quickly move up the aisle in the direction of the door. Again she paused, however, and as if there was still something more that she had wished to tell me, she turned around and quickly returned to the same place to further address me by saying, "I wish you well, young man.... I sincerely hope that you'll be happy, wherever life takes you!"

Her unexpected words on that fine day were nothing less than a benediction. A lovely prayer, in effect. My relentless gaze followed her back up the aisle and as she reached the door I anxiously waited for her to turn around to look at me one last time, and perhaps even to wave to me, but she chose not to do this. Watching her disappear through the doorway, as I did, it was all I could do to keep from jumping up and running after her, the urge was so strong. Somehow she had profoundly touched my heart. Sitting back within my seat, once more, I contemplated the reality of how different people can be. How, for example, some individuals seem so naturally inclined to be calculating and cruel;

while others are motivated to be so utterly thoughtful and kind, each no doubt acting upon some deep inner predisposition.

Something about this remarkable woman's overall demeanor made a lasting impression upon me. There was a certain undeniable regality of spirit which she exuded, so similar to her finely knitted shawl that effused the delicate and highly pleasing fragrance of flowers. Does the quality of one's soul, in a manner similar to this, have the power to give off an essence of goodness or evil? To hint, perhaps, at the intangible makeup of those basic critical things which lay deep within each of us? Are such things possible?

Even with this kindly stranger no longer physically present, I still chose to thoughtfully contemplate her small, strong, compact physique. Likewise her proud head of thick silver hair, her suntanned face and neck, and her small rough hands that were most certainly no stranger to hard work over a long lifetime already. I recall that she wore sensible shoes and clothing that, although well worn like that marvelous hat, were decidedly well polished and wholly immaculate in their overall presentation. Yes! This combination of small relevant details concerning her person were hints into the circumstances of her life. Tiny privileged secrets, I might add, that had the ability to reveal the quality of her very character. Like priceless seashells on a beach these particulars were there for the taking. There to be gently scooped up and respectfully analyzed, and then, if one were so inclined, carefully slipped, piece by piece, into one of the many compartments of one's heart for safe keeping.

Having finally taken all these things into account, I confess that it was that wonderful perky little straw hat which had helped tie the entire package together so perfectly. That same glorious little bonnet had seen many seasons come and go, not unlike its dignified owner herself. That item's far newer moss-green grosgrain ribbon and solitary yellow daisy, which bobbed ever so slightly as the old woman walked along, managed to infuse her crowning ornament with new life, just as all of this had so proudly betrayed her unmistakable sense of femininity. These significant things were the personification of that sacred and timeless essence of womanliness which forever holds the indisputable power to touch the hearts of all men—all men, both young and old.

Was it not the consummate German poet and philosopher Goethe, himself, who proclaimed so poignantly in terms of the "Eternal Feminine"? In reference to this most beloved tale of "Faustian" truths was he not, in fact, referring to that same revered feminine elixir reminiscent of "home and hearth"? That profoundly sacred primordial soul of every "earth mother" whose caring, and loving, and nurturing ways can never be underestimated since they hold the indisputable power to forever civilize the cruel tendencies of society by fearlessly reaching out to gently stroke, and then to eventually win over, those coldest hearts among men?

The ever-faithful train which bore me steadily onward towards my new life in Chicago departed from this last station in a timely fashion. With a loud whistle from its impressive horn the other passengers and I were on our way once more. As I knelt upon the seat to look from my window a second time, again I became thoroughly entranced with all that we were passing.

Our indubitable arrival into the vastly complex city of Chicago, itself, was now becoming somewhat slow and tedious business. Not unlike our departure from the city of Pittsburgh had been, the slow progress we were currently making was marked by a seemingly endless procession of neighborhood upon neighborhood comprised of a consortium of similarly constructed houses, churches of various descriptions, and small businesses and schools, which all seemed to blend together to form one continuous and amazingly immense town.

After traveling some distance through the depressing dinginess of warehouse upon warehouse, and tiny ill-kept shanties whose grimy and frequently damaged windows every now and then mirrored our own reflection as we passed, our train entered a large busy train yard to responsibly navigate through a maze of abandoned cars and train engines that littered both sides of our pathway. The vehicle's once powerful speed had been steadily reduced long before it finally made its way into the huge terminal into which it slowly glided to a full stop.

After I claimed my crumpled jacket, I stood up in front of my seat to stretch my legs a bit and then to wait patiently for nearly everyone else in the compartment to disembark before I actually made my way to the door. This time a new man in uniform was waiting there to greet me as I carefully moved from my compartment's interior platform to descend the waiting stairs. Pausing a moment to study his cheerful face, out of sheer necessity I finally found the courage to ask him the favor of reading the small cardboard notice which had been securely tied to my shirt upon the start of my long journey.

"It says here, sonny, that your name is Adam Bodray, and that you belong to a Mr. Henry Bodray who lives off Highway 'D' just north of Lake Geneva, Wisconsin...." After a slight pause where this elderly man felt obliged to gaze from the document he was thoughtfully deciphering, only to quickly fasten his stare directly upon me, he asked as his eyes held mine, "I presume that this would be your father, is this correct?"

I nodded but said nothing. Then the helpful gentleman went on to tell me, "Although this card goes on to give your father's address, there's clearly no telephone number. However there's a little notation on the very bottom of this card which indicates that your father will be here at this station to meet this train on the afternoon of September 19th, which is today!"

"Is it afternoon, yet?" I politely inquired.

"Oh yes, indeed!" my new acquaintance was quick to assure me. Then, as if to actually verify this fact, he proceeded to gently tug upon one end of a golden chain which was gracefully looped across a portion of his pin stripped vest. Methodically retrieving a small exquisite pocket watch from its well-concealed slit in the article of clothing he was wearing, he promptly clicked open the timepiece. While the charming reliance played a few notes of some sort of cheerful tune, he went on to helpfully announce, "Why it's exactly three thirty-five in the afternoon, already!"

Thanking him for his help I quickly moved away from both the train and the man, for fear that he might be inclined to ask me something more about my father. For some reason it just seemed natural that this outgoing person's next question might relate to some basic random information regarding my father's appearance, for example, and I surely would have been far too embarrassed to have been placed in this uncomfortable situation and eventually be forced to admit that I never actually met my father.

I automatically claimed a spot against a far wall where I could still see the door of the same train in which I had traveled so far. Waiting and waiting all the while I continued earnestly searching every male passerby to see whether he might be searching for someone, too.

After what seemed like a very long time my feet and my legs were beginning to ache. My shoes undoubtedly were helping to contribute to this unhappy state of affairs, since they had grown so abominably tight. Eventually I found myself regarding those wretched necessities as Reverend Pouley's final insult towards me.

Right away in an attempt to temporarily solve this fairly minor problem of mine I took the liberty of folding my jacket inside out and, as I was in the process of doing this, I happily remembered the large cookie which was earlier placed inside one interior pocket. In no time at all I was sitting far more comfortably upon the concrete floor, on top of my jacket, and off and out of the mainstream of traffic. But I still made sure that I was quite able to view the comings and goings of other people as they traveled past me. Soon I indulged myself further by hungrily devouring that last large treat which had by this time broken up into several smaller pieces within its wax paper....

A long time must have passed. The remainder of the ornate light fixtures which were systematically placed upon the various walls throughout the massive building had finally been turned on to help ward off the growing dimness all around. I was becoming a bit worried now. By chance had my father forgotten about me? If so, how was I to notify him of my arrival here in Chicago if he had no telephone? Suddenly I felt compelled to reach into the deep pocket of my ill-fitting knickers to reassuringly finger the several loose coins which still remained the tangible proof of great kindness received from those two good people back in Pittsburgh. Would this money be enough for a phone call? And, should it prove to be so, whom was I to call in the end?

Slowly, and quite deliberately, I began to pace about the area. I was beginning to realize that I needed to formulate some sort of plan, if I did not wish to spend the rest of my childhood in this place. What was it the young woman said to me as she was preparing me for my journey? Was not someone supposed to be here to wait with me? And then I remembered. Yes, it was to have been someone from the station master's office.

After prudently shaking out my jacket, I tried in vain to put the darn thing on—primarily in order to spare myself the tedious business of carrying it around with me, but quickly found that it was far too small for this. With the obstinate article of clothing not cooperating in the least in my valiant attempt to wear it, I folded it up instead and proceeded to carry it with me as I vowed to boldly venture forth in search of this person called the "station master." With the continuously moving throngs of people from that afternoon's various incoming and outgoing trains having already long ago dispersed and vacated the premises, I found that I was now completely alone....

I was alone. Certainly it was this oppressive feeling of total insularity within this strange new place, combined with the swiftly growing apprehension of what the future might bring—or, rather, might not bring, that began to weigh so heavily upon me. After all, this was not a very encouraging start to any future relationship between my father and me. At this point I was on the verge of beginning to feel extremely sorry for myself.

I began to walk a little way in one direction to see if I could locate someone who might be able to help me. With the back of one hand I began to wipe away the tears that were just now spilling over my lashes and beginning to run down my cheeks in a steady stream. With the hollow echoing sound my footsteps were producing as I moved on, I soon found myself thinking: Why was I so foolishly placing so much hope upon this reunion with my father? Why in the world was I doing this to myself? Those perpetual evergreen hopes of mine, along with my endless belief in my dreams, always led to such heart wrenching disappointment in the end! When would I finally learn not to keep sabotaging whatever small amount of dignity that I had left?!

Not long after this, yet from quite a distance away, I watched with growing interest as a small solitary figure slowly began to move my way. At this seemingly late hour this other person and I seemed to be the only people in this immense fortress. I stopped for a moment, holding my breath. Then, just as if my heart were in control of my feet, instinctively my own pace began to quicken as I, in turn, began to move towards the approaching figure. All the while I began hoping—hoping with all my being, that it might really be he. Please, I was telling myself under my breath, please let it be my father.... Please. Please! And please let him be as happy to finally see me, as I shall be to see him.

Although the space that continued to separate me from this gradually approaching figure was steadily growing more and more narrow, I could see that the man was still a good distance away from me. But as we continued to make progress towards each other his overall presence naturally became increasingly more real, as well as were the various details of his person which were slowly unfolding—like a mystery, before my very eyes. This is when I first detected something rather odd—something acutely troubling, to be perfectly honest. And the more keenly I studied the situation the more it became apparent to me that it was indeed the extremely odd manner in which this person was maneuvering towards me that seemed radically different somehow....

Was the man crippled in some major way? From where I stood, at least, it surely appeared that his left foot was cocked outwardly at a really queer angle, making it necessary for him to literally drag it along beside him. It was as though the appendage basically was unrelated to him, save for the fact that it seemed to help him maintain a certain basic balance. Furthermore the torso of this daunting vision, as it menacingly lumbered towards me, commanded the most unusual posture which obliged it to lean forward with its head pointing more towards the ground in its pathetic struggle to gain progressive forward momentum in this way. Decidedly the approaching phantom moved not at all with a smooth and natural human gait.

I waited, now, quite literally frozen to the very spot where I originally stopped only moments before. My heart was beating so quickly that I feared for certain that it was going to escape the confines of my small chest and fly away. Soon, within the middle of that vast emptiness of the train station, the highly disturbing figure approached even closer to finally halt some twenty feet away.

With obvious difficulty the man slowly straightened himself a little and then ever so slowly began to cock his head towards me in a noticeably quizzical fashion, causing this entire exaggerated movement on his part to resemble the stiff and highly animated maneuver a store mannequin might be forced to make when being manipulated into place. Apparently this was all being done in order to allow the visitor to properly gage the progress he was making in my direction. At the moment, with the man more or less stooping before me as he was, I thoughtfully imagined that had he been able to stand perfectly tall he certainly might have been as tall as he seemed thin.

Even the heavy-looking, faded green woolen coat that he was wearing at the present time—the same great coat which naturally swept along the ground as he traveled along—could not hide this fact. I observed, too, that both of his hands were missing. They were lost somewhere within the deep cavernous pockets of that immense coat. Likewise I could see that this unusual visitor wore heavy black leather boots that were badly worn. The left one was quite tattered, actually, and both were extremely dusty judging from a portion of each which went peeking out from underneath the same voluminous fabric of his outer gear. During all this time, while I remained dutifully occupied in studying him, he, in turn, was silently appraising me....

Although it was the social custom of the day for men and women to wear a hat whenever they went out in public, the man standing before me now was not wearing a hat of any kind. With mild interest, too, I could see plainly enough that his long and rather ill-kept hair was dark red like mine. Naturally all this vital information was gathered in a few fleeting moments only, and as I carefully studied his face I noticed that he was not clean-shaven at all but had a substantial growth of reddish colored beard which, along with his hair, acted as a frame to better highlight his eyes.

Very soon, while I remained transfixed where I was, the man once again began to wend his way towards me. He finally came to rest not more than five feet or so away. Although I was fairly short for my age, with the visitor's badly stooped posture, his eyes and mine were some-what level with one another. While I continued to helplessly gaze at him he seemed to waver a bit unsteadily before me. Concentrating on him now, as closely as I was, I must confess that it was his eyes that were the most disturbing aspect of his person....

They were dark green in color—very similar to my own, I was re-flecting. But unlike mine they floated rather lifelessly in a troubled sea of yellow film that was finely interwoven all over with tiny red threads. Indeed, it would be this same highly disturbing aspect of his features from which there would be no escaping. These same pain-ridden eyes were destined to haunt my dreams long after his death. Certainly, and probably without the slightest premeditation on his part, those myste-rious windows of his soul were now openly assaulting me! They were grievously wounding my exceedingly tender spirit and I could not, for the life of me, fathom why this should be so.

In truth, if I were pressed to adequately describe the impression which this initial encounter of ours was making upon me, I should say that it was as if my father's eyes were the eyes of a mortally wounded sparrow who somehow understood its inevitable fate—and, perhaps, even secretly longed for it. His basic demeanor, along with those blood-shot and flat-looking eyes, were mirroring a lifetime of pain and suffer-ing. More suffering, I imagined, than any one person had the right to ever know.

Suddenly my petty childish hurt feelings, which I had been nurs-ing so solicitously only moments before, promptly faded away. Those same insignificant wounds of mine had arisen from a self-inflicted insult which was genuinely inspired by my original perception that my father had forgotten me. Instead, as I helplessly stood before this man whom I now instinctively believed was part of me, I groped around in my mind for something appropriate to say. In the end, however, I discovered that I was cursed with muteness.

With extreme awkwardness and seemingly major discomfort of movement on his part my father dragged himself that short distance towards me, finally closing the narrow gap that had up to this point separated us. He then drew a long pale hand from the confines of his great coat and as he reached towards me I responded in kind by instantly taking a step backwards, naturally in order to remain out of his reach. I confess that this natural reaction of mine was wholly unplanned. From my cultivated mistrust of the basic intentions of others, I rarely welcomed the touch of others—the overtly familiar touch of certain strangers, especially. My response had been so quick, and even to my-self seemed so negative and unfriendly, that I immediately felt my face growing warm with embarrassment.

However the tall gaunt man standing before me acted as though he had not even noticed this tactless behavior of mine. Soon he managed to close the space between us, yet once again, by merely taking another step in my direction. At this point he reached towards me a second time in order to take up the card which I was wearing.

Watching him with feigned indifference I could literally feel his breath upon my face. It smelled unpleasantly of strong drink. And, as he slowly read the information which the little card contained, I could not help but notice, too, that his long thin hand was trembling rather severely....

Hastily perusing the small piece of cardboard my father finally al-lowed it to casually drop from his hand. It fell as gently as a dried autumn leaf might fall, and just as soundlessly, there against my shirt. Very nearly within the same motion I watched as he replaced his long colorless hand back within its pocket. And, before he turned to drag himself back in the direction from whence he had just arrived, he spoke to me in a voice that was noticeably hesitant and quite hoarse, as he finally informed me, "We're a good distance from the house… We'd best be on our way."

Without looking back at me and without saying anything else my father began to move himself forward and away from me. Wordlessly, myself, I continued to watch his every movement. With a sense of acute fascination I could not decide whether or not I wished to follow him. Al-though by now this most unusual man had receded quite some distance away from me, all the while I continued to wrestle with so many things that I was feeling at the moment, I observed him pause and then finally turn around to regard me with an extremely tired look. His overall body language seemed to be telling me that it was with an overwhelming ef-fort that he had finally made it this far to fetch me, and that if I were truly wise I should surely hurry along and not keep him waiting any longer.

Continuing to weigh the situation most carefully, I discovered that a great part of me wanted to resist going with this man. And yet, if I did not consent to go with him, where else was I to go? It was rare, indeed, whenever I behaved really foolishly. I learned early in life that survival was an important game to be played—and played as well as one possibly could. Although I felt firmly rooted to that particular spot, there in the cavernous building that was the train station—for indeed, after these long hours of waiting all alone, the place had become a haven for me of sorts, where I felt that I was relatively safe from harm—I was presently being forced to make a decision.

As I continued to observe the intimidating figure of my father receding little by little, to become smaller and smaller, I finally freed myself from my stupor to quickly hurry after him. In no time at all I was currently walking just a few paces behind him, stubbornly choosing not to walk by his side as I might have otherwise done merely as a matter of principle. After all it was as if this minor personal gesture of mine signified my ability to retain some semblance of mastery over my life, at least with regard to decision making. This is where I remained, as man and boy eventually left the train station together.

How I longed to take off my horrible shoes. By now they had become a virtual bane to my existence. Actually, I found it quite easy to loath these poor inanimate objects, as if in an aspect of transference they served quite well to embody all that was wrong with my young life up to this point. A large blister had formed upon the back of each of my heels making this long trek excruciatingly painful. In the end I decided against removing the offenders, there in the middle of that desolate parking lot, for fear that I might lose sight of the man I was shadowing—lose him for good, and this possibility frightened me more than anything else. After walking across several deserted streets and yet another large parking lot, we finally arrived at an old beat-up truck that was parked under a street lamp, well beyond the outer perimeter of what had seemed to mark the confines of the train station's property.

My father dragged himself around to the driver's side of the truck. Having eventually opened the badly creaking door, with even more difficulty he managed to slide in behind the vehicle's steering wheel. All the while he remained in the process of accomplishing this, I was unhappily discovering that my initial attempt at opening my passenger side door was also proving to be a real challenge. Forced to push and pull with undue enthusiasm from the very start I just was not having much luck. Then with my father leaning over at one point to firmly smack the door several times with his clenched fist from the inside, and with me perched precariously upon the truck's running board attempting to pull on the stubborn door handle, together we eventually managed to pry it open. Following this and without having uttered a single word I quickly climbed up next to him to sit upon the well-worn seat. From there, I proceeded to slam shut the door.

Where I was currently sitting I unexpectedly discovered that the large window before me was either lower than usual, or the seat was unusually high, for I found myself benefiting from a splendidly unimpeded view of the darkened street ahead that was lined on both sides with lamps similar to the one that was located directly overhead. With a firm click the truck's headlights were turned on. After the ancient rusty vehicle was put into gear, noisily we moved away from the curb and out onto the road. Finally, at long last, father and son were on their way together, heading ever onward into that foreboding night.... They were heading to wherever it was that Fate decreed they should be going.

A short time after we left the lights of the great city of Chicago far behind us a gentle rain began to fall. Both windows of the truck were partially rolled down at the moment to prevent the windshield from fogging up. Consequently the rich smell of the early autumn rain, along with the little musical duet that the truck's smooth tires were playing upon the wet shiny road as we traveled on, lifted my spirits just a fraction.

The healthy breeze, too, which was coursing in through the slightly opened windows, was pleasantly cool and fresh in spite of its dampness. Those twin swishing and humming sounds from the windshield wipers as they rhythmically cut their wide arc across the glass in front of us was trying its best to hypnotize me. I was so tired.... I was so incredibly weary that I was well beyond the point of feeling any more disappointment regarding the unusual events of the past few hours.

Despite this overriding fact, however, the winding course which my father and I were traveling still left something to the imagination. Because of the overwhelming darkness all around us nothing much could be discerned on either side of the road. The uneven headlights of the old truck seemed to be carving a lighted tunnel effect through the wet gloom of the night as we traveled ever onward.

With the rain growing heavy at one point on our journey to Lake Geneva, I was obliged to roll up my window. Directly ahead the healthy rain's slanted lines were visually bisecting the diffused light being thrown forward by the truck's twin orbs. With the thick patches of ground fog that settled here and there over the hilly road we were slowly traversing, the scene became for me a study in surrealism. I could not help wondering if this unusual scenario through which I was living at the moment was some sort of omen—some sort of prophetic portent of what the future eventually had in store for me.

My father had not uttered a solitary word since the few he spoke to me back at the train station. Every now and then out of a sense of deep and abiding curiosity I would quietly steal a glance at him. I did not wish to run the risk of offending him by appearing to stare at him so openly.

But in the end, really, it was as though I were not sitting there beside him at all. He appeared to be completely engrossed in his own thoughts—lost within his own world, and therefore it was truly as though I did not exist for him in any sense. I recall that he drove the truck in a slightly hunched over position—close to the wheel, all the while straining hard to see the road that was winding on before us in the pouring rain. Naturally his head remained in profile, and not once in all this time had he even turned to look in my direction.

Indeed, the stranger beside me was a study in grave concentration. Both of his hands continued to grip the wheel of the truck and I noticed that little by little the tremors which had afflicted him back at the station were becoming even more pronounced. As this was happening he seemed committed to taking an even firmer hold of the wheel than before, in order to better control this unpleasant shaking sensation.

By the dim illumination which was being reflected back at us from the headlights of the truck, as it bounced off the curtain of thick fog outside, the accentuated knuckles of both of my companion's long slender hands stood out white in bold relief against the grayness of the sparse flesh that covered the rest of his hands. At one point he slowed down the forward movement of our transport long enough to wipe away the perspiration which had formed prominent droplets across that portion of his face that remained exposed to me. And in an ongoing fashion, he ardently wet his lips with his tongue, as if they and his mouth might be very dry.

In a few moments more our truck went literally careening off the smooth surface of the road upon which we were traveling. It rambled noisily on down a pathway that seemed rough and unfinished, judging from the way the vehicle bounced and jerked along. This little annex road led to a small hideaway, of sorts—a "honky-tonk" or "speakeasy," to be more precise, within whose interior a reddish light dimly glowed through several heavily veiled windows. A fairly muted and grating music, too, issued forth from within this same shanty of a building, along with the sound of people yelling, and laughing—and arguing some, too.

Soon enough my father was busy haphazardly parking the truck to one far side of this building, away from the numerous other vehicles. After that, and with what seemed to me to be an extraordinary example of unbridled emotional enthusiasm on his part, he quickly opened the door to his side of the truck in order to carefully extract himself from behind the wheel. Before he slammed the door shut, however, he paused to look in at me and to casually say in a thick voice, "Wait here for me. I won't be long."

With the insistent rain that was now being continuously blown at the truck from the left side mostly, a healthy profusion of droplets of water already began to be collected upon the torn cracked seat and the badly battered steering wheel, as well as the distinctly weathered dashboard in front of me. Promptly I reached over to quickly roll up the window.

Sitting back in the company of myself, once more, I became somewhat absentmindedly absorbed in watching all the large drops of rain as they began to evenly disperse themselves across the entire field of the badly cracked old windshield. Studying them, now, in a growing stupor of complete exhaustion, I decided that they reminded me of a multitude of teardrops. The heaviness of each droplet naturally grew as the salubrious rain continued to baptize our old truck. Wondrously highlighted against what had become a proper background of pale rose-colored light, which was being filtered into the cab of our vehicle through the nearby windows of the adjacent building, many of those lovely crystalline pearls soon began to silently glide down the glass in an unbroken procession and to finally meld with other pearls, creating a grand vicissitude of enchantment....

This, of course, was the very last thought of any significance that my mind entertained that night. Sometime shortly after this I fell into a deep sleep. Without a doubt, I had already reached a point of physical and emotional saturation where I no longer cared anymore about anything.

Alas! Once again that small fragile leaf was on the move.... Currently it remained floating, or so it certainly seemed, off from the more adventurous freedom of that swiftly moving current of yesterday and into a silent and thoroughly ominous world of the present. In a real sense it lay temporarily reposing within a profound state of limbo, where it would be insufferably detained one last time, before it would be finally allowed to journey into that blessed world of genuine kindness—and a far more dependable state of sanity, for which it had forever longed.

5.

WHAT AN INTRIGUING PATHWAY does each individual's journey fashion through that glorious stuff called Life. Looking back now upon my own long history, and, indeed, upon my own unique pathway which naturally curves and meanders for a while, and then frequently undulates without the slightest warning to some comical or tragic rhythm all its own, I poignantly acknowledge the reality that I continue to mark my steady progress towards the inevitable end of that entire miraculous process, seemingly at times as if somehow all of it had been preordained for me in some manner.

Without a doubt, Fate works in mysterious ways. Throughout my life's long and incredibly interesting journey quite often I have pondered the provocative notion that it may well have been the notorious gangster Al Capone who was indirectly responsible for having brought the Lauder family and me together. Yes, as thoroughly unlikely as it might seem to the reader—and certainly without bestowing the least bit of excess credit where it is unwarranted in any way, I should be forced to honestly admit that it was that same totally unsympathetic character who ultimately, and quite innocently, played such an important role in my life....

Those amazingly fruitful years, which extended from the latter half of the nineteenth century onward, embodied for Europe and for America, too, a steady stream of highly significant growth and change. Growth and change, both in the positive sense as well as in the negative. Slowly the world was freeing itself from the highly restrictive social and emotional constraints which had been placed upon it by the Victorian era. With this fact and with all the important contributions that naturally continued to be brought about by the Industrial Revolution the world was being quickly ushered into a new and promising time.

More so now than ever, women were beginning to find their voices. With Elizabeth Stanton, Susan B. Anthony, Lucretia Mott, and others who initially proposed and then bitterly fought for the rights of women in America, a shock wave would soon be felt around the world. Brave women and their compatriots, both near and far, would finally be banding together to help escort each other into a bright new phase of their common history. No longer would they be made to suffer under the remorseless yoke of a male dominated universe. Men, in general, were being put on notice.... This fact remains highly significant for never again would the proverbial "genie" be forced back into her bottle.

Now man's silent and far too frequently Stoic counterpart—represented in the substantial figures of wife, mother, sister, daughter, lover and friend, would be joining with other sisters and together finally rise united to claim their far more-honored and far more well-deserved place in society. With this long-awaited solidarity would naturally also come a new hard-won self respect. Never again would the world be quite the same as it had been.

During this same period of time highly impressive examples of America's indisputable creativity in the various realms of achievement could readily be found in the highly significant work of such giants as Frank Lloyd Wright whose innovative design of the Imperial Hotel in Tokyo, Japan, in 1922, had just completed its metamorphosis from paper and pen into the more tangible reality of concrete, and steel, and glass. During these fertile years, too, Alfred Stieglitz compelled the recognition of photography as a fine art. Later in his life after having teamed with the passionate artist, Georgia O'Keeffe—both in the sense of his photography, as well as having personally joined forces as husband and wife—for years the duo managed to celebrate together the splendid "art of living."

These were unbelievably exciting times. In September 1901, after the assassination of President William McKinley, the dynamic and thoroughly irrepressible Theodore Roosevelt became our 26th president. Not long after that on December 17, 1903, near Kitty Hawk, North Carolina, the brothers Orville and Wilbur Wright successfully achieved their first controlled and sustained flights in a power-driven airplane. Side by side from their modest bicycle shop in Dayton, Ohio, these two adventurers significantly changed the world forever by turning man's ageless dream of flight into a glorious reality.

Naturally not to be outdone by those highly innovative men from Ohio, with respect to advancing the new century with his own astounding inventions, in 1908, Henry Ford presented the world with his own gift of the Model T. Later it was to be his substantial contribution to both great wars in the mass production of ambulances, airplanes, munitions, tanks and submarines chasers that was to help overwhelmingly influence the outcome of each of those major world conflicts.

In 1894, a French army officer by the name of Captain Alfred Dreyfus was unjustly convicted of treason, court-martialed, and subsequently sent to Devil's Island for years of solitary confinement. For well over a decade his ever-faithful supporters rallied continuously to clear his name of that unfair charge of espionage. These believers in Truth and Justice, of course, included his dear wife, Colonel Georges Picquart, and the writer Emile Zola. Naturally amid this daunting colossal uproar where violent partisanship literally dominated French life, and where newspapers on both continents faithfully chronicled each and every detail of what had become known as "The Dreyfus Affair," it was not until 1906 that the supreme court of appeals exonerated the poor man of any wrongdoing. Some years later from his safe haven there in England, where he had earlier fled to avoid prosecution, Major Ferdinand Walsin Esterhazy finally admitted to being the traitor.

Sometime in 1914, America's legendary Babe Ruth was sold by the Baltimore Orioles as a pitcher to the Boston Red Socks. And, as the saying goes, the rest is sport's history. During that same year back in Martinez, California, "Joltin' Joe" DiMaggio, who was also destined to become another one of the greatest baseball players of all time, was actually then only a mere babe in diapers.

With regard to the wonderful subject of music, too, Scott Joplin's cheerful toe-tapping tunes, which were first composed around the turn of the century and onward until his death in 1917, could still be heard being played and enjoyed throughout the following decades nearly everywhere on both continents. Then as all of us recall there was the great Louis "Satchmo" Armstrong's innovative Jazz improvisations. Even years before he joined Chicago's King Oliver's group in 1922, which ultimately helped to further distinguish his already lengthy career, it would not be long before he permanently ascended to his rightful place as the music legend he has become.

During those highly inspirational years, as well, the ever talented brothers George and Ira Gershwin touched and forever transformed the world of popular music by composing what quickly became some of this country's most original and highly acclaimed work. The unforgettable "Rhapsody in Blue" and "An American in Paris" stand justly elevated within the musical consciousness of the world. These particular pieces splendidly combine the more traditional music forms with those of the indisputably "soulful" American sounds of jazz that was proudly born of Negro folk music and rhythms.

There was a theatrical producer of lavish stage productions by the name of Florenz Ziegfeld who single-handedly took Chicago and the rest of the world by storm. Many notable stars under his tutelage, some whom later went on to create lasting names for themselves in films, were the incomparable Fannie Brice, Eddie Cantor, Will Rogers, and W.C. Fields.

Likewise the magnificent music of the Russian-born pianist, composer, and conductor, Sergei Rachmaninoff, had already by now left its indelible mark upon the world of classical music. With the second of his four piano concertos, his Prelude in C Sharp Minor, and his Rhapsody on a Theme of Paganini, he became immortalized. Although this superb artist twice refused permanent conductorship of the Boston Symphony Orchestra, in 1935, not long before his death, he chose to honor America by becoming one of its citizens.

In Europe, interestingly enough, during those very years the notable Swiss painter Paul Klee recently discovered new theories in the use of color which were rendered thereafter in his whimsical and often fascinating images. Although his many works embody sophisticated theories in abstract thought, they remain clothed, nonetheless, in a certain charming child-like finery which lent an appearance of great innocence to his art. Often it is this same play of opposites that lends his work its uniqueness. Similarly the highly prolific Spanish artist Pablo Picasso had taken up residence in Paris. With his cubist concepts, which evolved during this particular phase of his long and prodigious career, he firmly established the rationale that a work of art may exist as a significant object well beyond any attempt to represent reality in its more familiar sense.

On both continents, at the moment—in Europe, as well as here in America—the preeminently controversial names of Sigmund Freud and Carl Jung had already for quite some time become household words. They, like their progressive counterpart Nietzsche, stood in open defiance of the pervasive emotional illness which continued to saturate the nineteenth century. Gross ill-health due primarily as Jung himself writes: "to illusions perpetrated by the times: hypocrisy, half-truths, faked emotions, sickly morality, bogus and sapless religiosity." Needless to say, the intrepid excursions by both these uncommon men into the heretofore uncharted regions of the human psyche were to firmly establish the rational basis for psychoanalysis. Freud's "Interpretations of Dreams" had recently been published. And the once taboo subject of human sexuality, which was all too rarely addressed openly by society in any manner, was now being placed by him, particularly, at the center of the operating table. For the sake of advancing clinical medicine, and under a bright lamp for all the world to see, this ever-fascinating subject would be sensitively probed, expertly dissected, and then critically analyzed, in order for all of us to be able to gain a far more tolerant perspective relative to its importance as a key factor whose understanding and appreciation contribute greatly to a more healthy and happy individual.

With the popularity of the Temperance Movements which began in Kansas shortly after the Civil War, Prohibition become a heated national political issue, especially in the latter part of the 19th century. This movement gained further impetus in World War I when conservative policies limited liquor output. After the war national prohibition became the law with the Eighteenth Amendment to the Constitution and forbade the manufacture, sale, import, or export of intoxicating beverages.

But what amounted to little more than a zealous experiment to legislate society's morals ended in dismal failure. This law naturally gave rise to an illicit entrepreneurship in the form of smuggling and bootlegging and on an unprecedented scale. So much so, in fact, that federal agents sworn to uphold law and order in this country were forced to swim upstream against the dangerous current that spawned such vicious social piranhas as Al Capone and his mob.

Likewise during this same tumultuous time in American history film makers, and quite often journalists, too, fell under the thumb of the mob bosses who also controlled corrupt politicians and magistrates. And if these same people were not "on the take," as so many were, for fear of brutal reprisals somewhere down the road others often tended to purposely neglect their responsibilities by sidestepping the truth. Instead these misguided folks painted pictures for public consumption that endlessly glorified the exploits of these twentieth-century "desperadoes." By failing to properly address the facts, and crusading to realistically expose the issues of prostitution, bootlegging, political corruption—and murder—for the tragically serious issues that they were, Justice was thwarted at nearly every turn, making it impotent against the demoralization of the times.... Like a huge menacing cancer which was destined to ally itself with the immensity of the numerous other social problems that were to later manifest themselves within those harrowing years of the Great Depression era, this vast unwholesomeness grew and spread throughout the land threatening to ruin this nation in the process.

More often than not it was the scores of victims resulting from this all pervasive ruthlessness—and their loved ones, too—who suffered either directly or indirectly from the brutality of these same lawless years. Speaking on behalf of the subject of "victims" and in complete fairness to portraying the situation's many facets, there was the huge population of Italian immigrants who, in their daily ongoing attempt to live exemplary lives relative to being fine, proud, contributing citizens of this wonderful country, were forced to live in the damning shadow of that foul corruption and debauchery. Society far too often is guilty of unkind generalizations that deeply wound the innocent among us. One ethnic group automatically becomes guilty by association. With this same evidential ignorance and lack of compassion the already lengthy list of unfortunates only increased.

During these same volatile years, America remained a busy place.... Indeed the world as a whole remained an active caldron of growing agitation where forces both positive and negative continued to pull at the very fabric of daily existence. Perhaps this restless time between the great wars, particularly here in America, was best portrayed by F. Scott Fitzgerald in his 1925 novel, *The Great Gatsby*. As the popular literary spokesman of the "jazz age," Fitzgerald painted the disturbing portrait of the painful disintegration of the "American Dream" from more or less the perspective of the upper classes. Similarly the famous film producer and actor Charlie Chaplin took the responsibility of speaking so eloquently on behalf of the dignity of the working class and the extreme poor through his poignant humor on film. All in all, what was being reflected was a proud nation which little by little was losing its equilibrium and slowly teetering upon the brink of self-destruction.

Something significant seemed to be happening to the world during these years of its more fast-paced history. It was as if the cruel and sobering reality of death and destruction—which occurred on such a huge scale during the first great war, had severely jolted all of humanity, thereafter creating an uncomfortable atmosphere where many individuals felt a desperate obligation to seek answers to important questions concerning the very meaning of Life itself.

In effect this same generation of people had become lost—lost in the emotional sense—by having misplaced an important part of their souls. Numerous individuals who fought in World War I, and had survived; as well as those others who had lived abroad before, during, and after the conflict, seemed compelled now to remain behind in Europe, diligently searching for that significant part of themselves which they felt was missing.

These same people included writers, and poets, and artists, many of whom became members of the infamous "expatriate circle." This social club embraced such luminaries as James Joyce, Hemingway, Gertrude Stein, and Ezra Pound. Beautiful black artists like Josephine Baker whose artistic individuality was enthusiastically accepted in Europe quickly discovered that her work here in the land of her birth was originally shunned. Likewise the renowned dancer Isadora Duncan, who was also a creative innovator of expressionism, found relatively little early success here in America. But having proceeded on to Budapest, Berlin, and London, in 1903, she was finally able to establish what would eventually become her worldwide triumphs.

John Steinbeck's immortal story entitled *The Grapes of Wrath* remains a disturbing "looking glass" into the great suffering of this proud nation and its equally proud people. Essentially it speaks very eloquently of the common man's noble spirit. And in 1939 this endearing American writer won the Pulitzer Prize for this particular masterpiece of his.

Sometime within the autumn of 1924, in yet another part of the world, Russia's much beloved poet Boris Leonidovich Pasternak wrote and published his collection of five short stories which included, *"Detstvo Lyuvers"* (The Childhood of Lovers). This fairly complex work is a highly perceptive portrayal of a young girl's coming of age. As the consummate humanist that he naturally remains, his entire body of truly memorable works continually personify his passionate philosophy of life and serve to make him one of the more outstanding international symbols representative of the incorruptible moral courage of an artist in conflict with his political environment.

Both in Europe, as well as here in America, the silent suffering of so many continued long after the bombing and the gunfire of the first Great War was stilled. Seemingly in a fervent attempt to help blot out the truth of the situation lost souls everywhere climbed aboard a brightly painted merry-go-round whose already fast paced, hedonistic music was accelerating more and more to a wild and feverish pitch.

Around this time, too, as if to add gasoline to that already healthy fire of discontent which was slowly growing out of control, a young Austrian citizen from the town of Braunau named Adolf Hitler moved to Munich, Germany. As History would have it, he further enlisted in the Bavarian army in order to fight in that same world conflict. Later, after a failed coup to overthrow the existing political party in 1923, he was jailed in the Landsberg Fortress. Amid the growing tension and acute political unrest which was spawned by the social depression that now was slowly engulfing the entire world, it was here that he penned his infamous *Mein Kampf,* a rabid self-portrait of extreme madness which embodied his anti-Semitic outpourings, worship of power, disdain for morality, and strategy for world domination.

Charles A. Lindbergh—or "Lucky Lindy" as he was affectionately dubbed, properly astounded the world by landing in Paris to a hero's welcome during that famous spring of 1927, after a nonstop solo flight from New York across the wide Atlantic in his now renowned aircraft called *The Spirit of St. Louis.* Not long after this some enterprising person named a highly energetic jitterbug dance after him, naturally in order to personally honor the famous aviator. And lest we be inclined to forget, during these very same exciting years a sprightly young woman from Atchison, Kansas, by the name of Amelia Earhart, was also proudly beginning to make a name for herself in what had been up to that point in time a rather dangerous occupation designed formerly for men.

As with all the other prospective citizens who first arrived at these bright and ever promising shores of America, Felix and Emma Lauder had traveled from central Europe around the turn of the century in search of the "American dream." Their rich heritage, along with their ever passionate hope for a happy and productive life for themselves and for their children, would eventually come to be played out, quietly noted, and then forever absorbed by this ever-hungry land.... With the fervent repetition of this same evolutionary process our country continues to greatly enhance itself with respect to its growing ethnic diversity—that diversity, indeed, which continues to be responsible for creating the famous "melting pot" concept which is still the proud basis of American life today.

From the start these same good people grew to fiercely love this adopted country of theirs. They taught their many children and me to love it, too. I remember how Felix always likened our beloved Republic to "a beautiful quilt of many colors and many equally glorious textures representative of all peoples everywhere!" He believed unequivocally that it was a rare privilege to become even a small part of such an amazing land. Those who continue to arrive here from other places around the world continue to create a vast wealth from which all of us eventually partake in the marvelous blending and re-blending of customs, and philosophies, and astounding abilities relative to art, music, literature, science, mathematics, and so much more.

Although a good portion of Felix Lauder's soul was destined to remain Hungarian, his heart nonetheless became essentially American through and through. Because of this fact he earnestly professed his passionate belief that each and every citizen of this great nation has an all-encompassing obligation which morally dictates a creed to faithfully honor our nation's "democratic process." By remaining an integral and active part of this laudable phenomenon we as its citizens assure that the continuation of those priceless freedoms we so naturally enjoy, but so often take for granted, shall be forever upheld.

To illustrate this important point Felix carefully instilled within each of us an unshakable belief that voting, and serving on jury duty, as well as yielding to military service in some form whenever the necessity arose, are public positions of trust that remain nothing less than consummate privileges of the highest order. Needless to say he and his family had been prepared utterly to back up this stringent philosophy of theirs. With characteristic distinction, and in the most personal way imaginable, nearly every one of the Lauder sons would in time be proudly stepping forth to serve this country. Eventually they would also all be placing their very lives upon the line. And in so doing two of these same beloved sons of theirs would ultimately die in the service of our country.... They would die, as have so many other valiant men and women throughout our relatively brief history, in order to help secure this nation's most sacred of beliefs.

Bela Kornitzer, the renowned writer and historian, himself having become a deeply devout champion of Democracy after courageously fleeing Hungary's Communist oppression, proudly became an American citizen by a special act of Congress. In his highly acclaimed 1955 historical "time capsule" entitled: "THE GREAT AMERICAN HERITAGE," he so convincingly conveys to the reader that it is the average American family which traditionally remains the profound nucleus of our strong society, and it is from this noble center that society's truly great people are born. To quote from his work, he strongly felt that "the essence of democracy is reflected in the tolerant democratic attitude that prevails in the typical American family, and in the moral strength handed down by their forebears." This historical document has been crafted for each of us, as the author says in his own words, "with a deep reverence for the essential values of democracy, and with anxiety over the sinister forces that are trying to undermine it."

Karl Marx's once noble-sounding philosophy was initially wholeheartedly embraced by many within our world community. Later it was implemented at a terrible cost of many millions of lives by Lenin, and, too, his ruthless disciple Stalin, in that ongoing social revolution whose impetus was initially conceived and eventually born from centuries of cruel suppression by Czarist Russia. Unhappily what amounted to a social experiment gone horribly wrong ultimately proved to be nothing more than a greatly flawed fairy-tale for grown-ups. Without question, although it remains each and every person's supreme moral obligation to seek a better world for all men that is founded upon genuine Goodness, and Truth, and Justice for all, when the founders of that initially attractive-sounding new mandate failed to take into account those more base realities of human nature which tend to grossly taint those truly noble concepts through use of subversion, violence, and cruelty, is it any wonder that even from its inception onward that this totally wayward endeavor was justly doomed to become a dismal failure? When the rule of law for any society becomes so significantly corrupted by insuring the cruelest sort of spiritual subjugation of its masses, the heroic yet vulnerable individual is perversely stripped of his or her personal rights and dignity as a human being. In the end what positive progress does World History make when one tyrannical system merely replaces another?

Little more than a mere decade ago, although a great part of our world body exuberantly presided over the funeral services held to commemorate the death of Communism in the former Soviet Union—and, too, its tyrannical subjugation that was consistently inflicted upon its unwilling subjects during all of that time, please remain well-advised that that same formidable beast is yet alive and well. It continues still to insidiously prowl about among us. In fact, Tyranny in a variety of forms continues to remain exceedingly alive and well within our world. Consequently, proud Russia's relatively new-found freedom, along with that promising albeit somewhat elusive pathway to stability and greater prosperity for all its citizens—including all the hopeful citizens belonging to the former USSR's satellitic countries of Hungary, Czechoslovakia, Poland, Rumania, etc.—remains an extremely fragile entity worthy of great worldwide respect.

America, with all the goodness she traditionally embodies, remains a bright shining island locked within a turbulent sea filled with ever-pervasive pockets of decadent radicalism that help feed and sustain the madness inherent in every tyrant, and despot, and nihilist. Democracy, in truth, is a slow process of "becoming." The necessary time required to enact a stable transformation from the dark oppressive tragedy of the past, into the healthy life-promoting light of the future, must therefore be assiduously learned and absorbed as quickly as possible. Seemingly we have frittered away so much time already.

Needless to say, without the faithful commitment and continuous support of those collective well-wishing outsiders among us who desire so much to nurture this current situation, as a concerned and responsible world-body we must strive to help assure victory for all concerned. This entire "molting process," which naturally renders these same coura-geous souls so vulnerable at the moment, could inevitably cause their thoroughly challenging undertaking to collapse under its own consid-erable weight. If we, as the genuine well-wishers that we are, do not remain vigilant, the noble experiment shall ultimately be doomed, and in the process what shall eventually be promoted are colossal waves of unimaginable chaos throughout the world.

So with regard to the indisputably critical issue of human society's more civilized forms of government—namely Democracy, in its truest form, History has proven in the past, and on more than one occasion already, that what any successful society fails to continue to cherish, it eventually loses. Should the guiding principles upon which our own truly noble society was originally founded come to be consistently taken for granted and therefore woefully neglected to be properly safe-guarded, subversive forces shall certainly step in to use the opportunity to work their terrible mischief. One must strive forever to remember this truth. Those pathetically misinformed souls among us who remain disinterested neophytes in the realm of human nature as it pertains to world history—and world politics, particularly, tend to underplay or basically ignore the seriousness of the current situation. Ours remains a dangerously explosive world. We live day-to-day with a hair-trigger detonator.... Perhaps this regrettably troubling reality is far more true now, than at any other time in our world's chaotic history.

Those precious gifts of "life, liberty, and the pursuit of happiness" which are inherent in our beloved Constitution come at the price of eternal vigilance. Those "sinister forces" to which Bela Kornitzer so pas-sionately alluded are indeed very much alive and well. And contrary to growing public opinion it continues to be this important issue, as well as the tremendously dangerous malaise which tears at the very fabric of our daily experiences as citizens, that ultimately may prove to be our world's ultimate downfall.

Consider for a moment the slow and painful desolation of our more traditional values of American family life which have been sired, in great part, by the overall pervasive degradation of women and children within our current culture. Consider, too, what amounts to a significant and growing wave of anti-law and antigovernment sentiment which causti-cally pervades our daily lives as citizens. Likewise, there exists a rare and potent sort of spiritual alienation which openly threatens to devour

our children. This nation's acute drug abuse, too, not only substantially decimates the individual, but profoundly contributes to the destruction of family life in general, as well as the weakening of our institutions of learning, and before our very eyes is turning each of our cities and suburbs into war zones of crime and decay....

Moreover, and most notably within the last decade of the past century, there has undeniably existed such a staggering degree of unprecedented disease and moral corruption of elected officials throughout our nation's government. Because of this as citizens of this justifiably proud nation all of us have been brought exceedingly low by the experience. These same corruptible and corrupting elected officials might very well have permanently compromised the glory of all that we as Americans hold dear. Seemingly, and at long last, we as a body have finally been forced to recall the poignant reality that personal integrity does indeed matter.

Without such critically important things as moral integrity in our leaders this sacred way of life, which was once firmly founded upon the thoroughly sound principles of Democracy for all its citizens, shall one day perish. Should this calamitous day every come about History shall ultimately be forced to sadly glance back in order to recall its pale and lifeless form.... In light of this overwhelming tragedy it would be faithfully recorded somewhere in all the history books to come that this beautiful ideal of ours was soundly murdered. Murdered, not necessarily from the overt actions of those sinister outside forces as soothsayers throughout our fairly short history have so often predicted, but destroyed more notably from the many years of abject apathy which somehow was allowed to ferment deep within the hearts of the majority of our citizens.

With these important things in mind let us also find the necessary courage to address the all-encompassing sense of radical world change which is currently rearing its ugly head upon the not-so-distant horizon. These highly negative changes smack dangerously of an all-too-familiar disease and corruption that is spawned by pervasive worldwide instability reminiscent of former times. Indeed, I am alluding here to those unspeakably chaotic times within this most recently past century that conjure up horrific ghost-like phantoms of the past. Is it merely this writer's paranoia speaking, or is it conceivable that once again similar lawless proponents of yet another perceived "New World Order" are presently attempting to assert their "familiar old religion" upon the world as a whole, and without the slightest regard for lessons learned from the past? Just as before, with a truly ruthless thirst for power do these same criminals embrace within their tragic death grip the reckless philosophy that "the end always justifies the means"?

Let us not forget that Cuba's Fidel Castro eventually won his bitter revolution decades ago which was initially predicated upon his openly professed love for freedom and democracy. World History has since unfavorably recorded the real truth, instead. It might behoove each and every legitimate society, henceforth, to endlessly question that proverbial "banner" behind which its citizens are occasionally required to march. Beware, good and wise people! Beware of those dangerous wolves who so cunningly dress themselves in sheep's clothing. Beware, as well, that hypnotic carousel's ever-haunting music which unceasingly plays on, and on, and on....

Democracy! Oh sweet, and ever-sacred, Democracy! With all your laudable strengths, as well as all your acknowledged weaknesses, you alone remain that small vulnerable island within a vast sea of endless flux and chaos. You alone are that beautiful lighthouse whose precious beacon of purest light leads the weary and spent traveler to safety! Is it, then, merely the intuitive poet and sensitive artist among us, as well as those astute and notoriously loyal children of Herodotus, who instinctively place their ear to the ground and strain hard to listen for the approaching hoof beats of those dreaded Horsemen of the Apocalypse? Within the far wider picture, at this very moment, do they alone suffer that repetitive nightmare where humanity's subversive legions unite en masse in order to reek their cataclysmic horror upon an unsuspecting world—yet one more time? Surely sane men everywhere have been driven quite mad with this painful vision!

Who then shall rouse the multitude of our own society's more complacent citizens, as they so foolishly sleep on? Where is that noble "gatekeeper" who from the very beginning had so faithfully sworn to uphold this most sacred of Trusts? And to loudly, and ever so clearly, sound the warning alarm in defiance of such future tragedy? Where is the vast throng of people which not so long ago had always been willing to stand strong against this ever-growing and ever-frightening wave of negative change—to stamp it out, thus furthering the magnificent cause of all that our beloved Constitution holds dear?

Since virtually all immigrants arriving from other places were obliged to enter legally through the port of Ellis Island, the Lauder family eventually traveled on from there to the mid-west... The family headed onward to Chicago where they were to live for a number of years. With great enthusiasm, and a steely commitment to succeed in the highly competitive world of business, Felix Lauder eventually set up a manufacturing venture which designed and produced stylish hats for both men and women. Later the bounty of his craft was openly displayed in an elegant store on Michigan Avenue which he owned and managed. Since this particular article of clothing was in ever popular demand throughout this country, as well as in Europe, with seemingly endless hours of hard work for many years the struggle and sacrifice eventually began to pay handsome dividends.

In time the monetary success of this enterprise was multiplied many times over when the business was extended to include the manufacturing of wigs. Naturally with the ongoing tremendous popularity being gained by filmmakers in Hollywood, props of this sort were becoming a staple of the wardrobe departments there and also within the theater and opera departments throughout this land, as well as throughout the rest of the world, too. Opening a firm in Mexico City sometime around 1908, where attention to the finest details was inherent in the manufacturing of these items, proved to be a stroke of genius. There within the lush semitropical environment of Mexico, one was not forced to contend with the growing shadiness of the labor unions whose often corrupt dealings often led directly to the mob. With the locally talented seamstresses and equally superb craftsmen living in that interesting part of the world, great pride was taken in hand-tying the individual strands of hair and then painstakingly sewing them into a skull cap made of washable good quality cotton fabric. Consequently the finished product became a work of art, in a real sense, and the name of Felix Lauder's firm soon became synonymous with excellent quality which eventually became second to none.

With the growing success of both companies, the young family—which by now included young Lewis and George—prudently decided to move from their residence in Chicago to a small comfortable "hacienda" located within a quiet district of Mexico City. One may only speculate how wonderful it must have been for the family to gain even a brief respite from the rigors of those harsh northern winters.

Later on as an adopted member of their group I was frequently captivated by family photographs which were taken during those seemingly more tranquil and happy times. One picture, especially, bestowed upon the viewer the feeling that these same magnificent world travelers would be able to make their happy home nearly anywhere in the universe, for the truly important ingredient which was solely responsible for the success of the family unit always seemed to travel with them. This critical ingredient, of course, was love. And within that muted sepia tinted photograph, which often absorbed my youthful thoughts and fantasies, the radiant smiles of the proud parents and the apparent playfulness of their two young sons as the group proudly posed before a lovely tiled-roof bungalow where bougainvillea, and cactus, and oleander grew all around in healthy profusion, one could thoughtfully contemplate their obvious happiness and the enviable security that forever embodied for me the words "family" and "home."

As it happened, though, sometime around the late autumn of 1914, during one of Mexico's more major revolutionary upheavals that was led this time by Doroteo Arango—or Pancho Villa, as he has become better known throughout the pages of history—the young family was finally forced to leave behind this other home of theirs. In so doing they also left behind a thriving business in that capital city and were forced to flee back to America. In December of that very year, in his ongoing bid for social justice, Villa and his notoriously menacing forces marched on Mexico City. With the indisputable complexity of all this violent social unrest and political intrigue within this particular region of the world—and, with the first great war which was now beginning to rage in Europe, history's stage was being set for the continuation of more years of bitter, bloody fighting that would eventually result in the death of many, many people.

With the Lauder family's hasty return to Chicago during this harrowing time in their lives this part of the business was to have remained permanently lost to them. Felix and his young wife just barely managed to escape from the bullet ridden scourge of this violent episode in their lives with their two young sons in their arms, and a few meager funds sewn into the hem of Emma Lauder's skirt for safekeeping. Likewise a handful of important travel documents, as well as several much-prized family photos—not to mention one terribly unlikely bottle of rare cognac that was carefully wrapped within the pages of a local Spanish newspaper, traveled with them only to arrive home again to the familiar streets of the city they still called "home," but which all too soon would be mercilessly plagued by Capone and his henchmen.

Felix Lauder's hat manufacturing business did manage to continue to thrive there in Chicago, until that fateful autumn day in 1929 when he like countless others lost everything—everything, except a certain amount of reserve cash which had been prudently put aside and not banked with all his other assets. The stock market crash officially marked the beginning of those long years of social malaise and unrequited suffering known as the Great Depression. Not many families remained unscathed by this unprecedented phenomenon.

This, indeed, was the beginning of many remarkably dark years for family life, in general. In sociological terms during all the previous decades of the world's history, it was traditionally the man who remained the family "bread winner." This, in essence, is how the majority of men established their identities—just as their fathers, and grandfathers, and great-grandfathers had done before them; while women remained at home providing the internal stability that traditionally comes with homemaking, and the "hands-on" nurturing of the couple's children. It became the combined efforts of these two highly significant roles that lent dignity and strength and meaning to marriage, and further helped to assure the overall preservation of the family unit itself.

With the stock market crash on that October day, however, powerful negative forces began to be set into motion. Jobs, financial security, human dignity—all were lost over night, quite literally. It was this strong, pervasive, ongoing negative force which helped to undermine relationships, and further burden society with its uncontrollable rise in alcoholism that so often spawns domestic violence, and street violence, and other such crimes....

In a mood of utter despair many men chose to end their lives rather than face the frightening and humiliating future. Sick jokes, too, which graphically alluded to these same despondent souls jumping from buildings, or shooting themselves in order to escape the unkind reality of the situation, began to make their way into society's vernacular.

With respect to the issue of human nature, difficult times tend to bring out the best in some people, as well as the worst in others. I readily recall that it was with astounding accuracy that one of the more poignant contemporary visual accounts of those times powerfully portrayed the unfortunate social malaise of this period in our American History. This stunning work remains an important book of photographs entitled: *A Vision Shared: A Classic Portrait of America and Its People, 1935–1943.*

Initially this extraordinary collaborative effort was the "brain child" of Columbia University Historian Roy Stryker, who, finally, with F.D.R's blessing, thoughtfully gathered together several of this country's outstanding photographers, and painters, and filmmakers. These courageous people, in turn, pledged to thoroughly scan this country of ours with their cameras and "flashes of inspiration" in tow in order to be able to bring forth what each unflinchingly believed remained their moral obligation. Together these same bold visionaries sought to bring forth that much-needed albeit highly embarrassing evidence of the sorry truth of the current state of affairs.

Eventually it became this haunting authenticity which helped to orientate our sluggish government into realizing the horrible seriousness of the plight of over one-third of this nation's ill-fed, ill-housed, and ill-clad citizens. If a good picture is indeed worth "a thousand words," as the familiar saying goes, than this highly significant and totally unprecedented effort inspired by a number of fine people such as Walker Evans, Dorothea Lange, Ben Shahn and Pare Lorenz, finally managed to clarify that reality. In no uncertain terms this stunning "truth" ultimately helped lead America towards its much welcomed salvation.

Back then, as far as most things went—real estate included, it was a buyers market. But unfortunately as a sort of maddening "Catch 22" so few people had any money at all. However, with the modest funds which had not been lost to the Lauder family during this time, at a remarkably low price Felix managed to purchase a small delicatessen not far from where his former showroom on Michigan Avenue was once located.

It must also be mentioned that one of the more highly successful ploys of Capone during those years, which was cunningly calculated to help him gain a more ruthless stranglehold on the business interests there in Chicago, was by forcibly demanding "tribute." In other words, the mob would see to it that a successful business enterprise was "protected" from the mob, when the owner of the business paid up front for this ongoing service. Plain and simple it was blackmail and extortion personified.

Felix Lauder bore nothing but contempt for the likes of Capone and his feral disciples. He grew to abhor what he referred to as the "unabashed and well-orchestrated mutilation of the American Dream" by thugs employed by the Jewish, Irish, and Italian elements of the mob that were eventually all to be unified under Capone's rule. My dear friend felt that he certainly had not labored as hard as he had, and for so many years, to be made to bow to this corruption. Openly he refused to negotiate with these "parasites" on any terms when such funds were initially solicited from him. However, after a truly frightening personal experience that was obviously meant to represent a stern warning to him, he eventually was forced to plot some sort of hurried alternative.

Basically he wished to rid himself of the business, rather than be made to stoop to the unsavory practices of these very corrupt individuals.

"Cash was king," as the saying went. But for the multitude of citizens who had no such thing the barter system was re-implemented on a huge scale. Soon this became the only option for obtaining what one required in order to be able to live and to provide for one's family. With the total of the Lauder family's remaining assets now having been secured within the modest little restaurant, Felix desperately devised a plan where the family home on Wilson Avenue, along with the newly-acquired restaurant which up to that point had remained in business for only a few short weeks, were traded quite literally for a farm and acreage in Wisconsin.

So it was towards the end of that fateful year of 1929 that Felix, his wife, and their many children, finally decided to leave behind the grievously wounded city of Chicago—along with a handful of badly broken dreams, to travel onward to Lake Geneva, Wisconsin. As one may readily imagine this became their worthy attempt to safeguard all which was deemed most sacred to them. Without becoming unduly immersed in self-pity, nor chronic bitterness either, I suspect, these strong and wholly determined people ventured forward together to optimistically begin what they sincerely hoped would prove to be a new and far more promising chapter in their already tempestuous lives.

Just as benevolent Fate would also have it, they, as well as my father and I—at least up to this point in time, remained the unsuspecting characters in a real life drama whose paths would finally one fine day be intersecting, only to later become inextricably entwined together within one of the very pleasant little farming communities in that region. After all it was Felix Lauder's fervent and uncompromising commitment to protect his family, by dutifully escaping the likes of Capone and his sordid philosophy, that ultimately was responsible for our becoming neighbors in the end.

Strangely enough, too, my own father had originally come to this same small farming town a few years after the first great war ended, in order to help oversee a fragment of Capone's far reaching bootlegging empire. Indeed, this was his sole occupation for quite some time, until he finally became too ill from the very substance which he was making available—against the law—to others. Long before I was miraculously summoned from the home of Reverend Pouley my father had already claimed "squatter's rights" and moved into a small abandoned house on "Highway D," located on the outskirts of town. This same ramshackle building, which was legally condemned years before he managed to take up residence there, was situated next door to the very farmhouse into which the Lauder family would eventually be moving.

In a manner of speaking the entire world was becoming smaller and more compact, as well as far more dangerously complex. Life for the individual seemed to be growing more and more ephemeral—more fragile, somehow, with the passing of each day. It was rumored that at any given hour one could actually feel the tension in the air. One could feel the spontaneous friction and worrisome heat which was slowly being generated by the electricity of the times....

Yes, little by little, the world was becoming a far more dangerous place. The irrational doctrine of isolationism would no longer prove to be a viable alternative for any nation's survival. History, it would surely seem, is forever damned to repeating its mistakes over and over again. Regrettably enough Humanity seems forever destined to reproduce those same troubling sins of the most base and utterly irredeemable nature. For, without a doubt, the common denominator of each and every miserable plot that has occurred throughout the ages continues to be human nature—human nature, with all of its multiple facets and varying degrees, of good, and evil, and indifference.

Likewise, as it has always been, and shall continue to always be, the counterweight which tends to help offset this sobering reality shall forevermore be found in the divine gifts of music, and art, and literature. These precious necessities are the life-sustaining "fingerprints" of the more sensitive and imaginative human spirit. These vital things continue to remain nothing less than that supremely worthwhile moral compass upon which other sensitive souls often rely for guidance. Along with the ever-noble concepts of brotherhood, and genuine friendship, and kindness—oh yes, those simple daily acts of real kindness, above all else, these were, and still are, and shall forevermore continue to remain, the vital stabilizing forces which help keep the scales of our collective lives from tipping themselves permanently towards complete and total annihilation.

Actions, whether positive or negative, which occur even in the most isolated or remote regions of our planet, have the potential to profoundly affect the world as a whole. Each of us, in essence, remains a member of this large and all-encompassing "family of man." Needless to say, since no man is able to live happily alone unto himself, countries of men, too, naturally require the respect and decent fellowship of other countries. Our actions, quite simply—whether those of an individual, or those of a multitude of individuals, become relevant no matter how seemingly insignificant they might appear at first, since they tend more often than not to impact in some way upon the entire world body as a whole.

And so as the ever-merciful Gods consented to finally smile down upon me, at long last, the characters within my noble little story—these same minor yet still relatively important actors who had each taken their special place upon their own tiny stage which naturally dwelled within the much larger scope of that far greater world stage, were all in the process of slowly coming together.... Quite miraculously they were slowly gravitating towards one another, in order that they might one day profoundly touch each other's lives in the most meaningful manner. Soon the real happiness I was to know in my life would be beginning in earnest. Soon, all my fragile hopes, and all of my worthwhile dreams, would finally be coming true.

6.

EVENTUALLY I AWOKE FROM MY INTENSE SLEEP to the unfriendly sound of birds chirping loudly all around the truck. While I sat up straight and stretched a bit, after being contorted in a rather uncomfortable position there upon the short lumpy seat of my father's truck for an undetermined period of time, I gazed out my side window to witness several grackle vocalizing in a nearby tree. The unpleasant group's attention was focused upon two of their comrades who were noisily fighting over a small shiny object upon the ground, not far from where I was sitting. I noticed immediately, too, that the hours of rain during the night had brought with it much cooler weather. I shivered as I quickly took up my jacket and wrapped it as tightly as I could around my shoulders, in a vain attempt to help warm myself a little.

My wretched shoes were lying on the floor of the truck's cab, directly in front of me, now—actually mocking me. I could further see by the early morning light that my socks were soiled with dry blood in the back from the wounds which had been incurred by my having worn them for far too long. As I remained sitting there the many events of the previous day came flooding back to me. Just as I made up my mind to leave the truck in search of my father, the sound of nearby footsteps upon the driveway could be heard coming in my direction.

Right away I turned to see my father staggering towards me. This unfortunate sight did not please me at all. He was carrying something wrapped in a brown paper bag, and I noted with mild interest that the object was being firmly clutched to his chest with one arm in an obvious subterfuge to protect it as if the item were dearer to him than anything else in the world....

Fumbling with the ignition key with his free hand, as he was, he inadvertently dropped the item upon the ground. After mumbling something incoherent to himself, I further watched him retrieve the key with difficulty. Finally my father made his way to the driver's side of the vehicle. Carefully sliding the packaged object he was carrying into one of the ample side pockets of his huge green coat, with a couple of firm tugs on the old rusted door it eventually creaked open....

Standing just a bit more erect in order to be able to climb into the vehicle's cab, this same drunken individual grasped the wheel with both hands to help steady himself.... Matter-of-factly glancing in my direction, and, having finally caught my eye, I watched further as he seemed thoroughly perplexed at finding me sitting there. In this fairly impeded state of his it was obvious that mentally he was groping for an explanation of who I might be, and why in the world I was sitting there, plain as day, inside the cab of his truck.

In a spontaneous effort to help him out, and with all the dignity and respect that I could muster—under the circumstances, I quickly sought to remind him, as I said, "I'm your son, Adam—remember?" And then, as an afterthought, to help make things a bit more clear to him, I quickly added, "I arrived from Pittsburgh yesterday."

Grunting something inaudible as the dim light of recognition finally dawned in his glazed-over eyes, the man climbed awkwardly into the truck and went to place the key in the ignition, but managed to drop it yet again. To spare him any unnecessary physical discomfort, as well as any possible embarrassment that might naturally have arisen had he tried to discover the item's whereabouts all by himself, I quickly bent down to effortlessly retrieve it. Then, nearly within the same movement, I proceeded to hand the valuable object to him without saying a word.

We eventually made our way to the main road with some difficulty that morning. In my father's drunken state, the vehicle in which we traveled wove dangerously from one side of the parking lot to the other. Soon I held my breath as we picked up speed and literally bolted out from the gravel pathway onto the blacktopped road ahead—much like a cork from its bottle, completely ignoring the stop sign located at the end and to the right of this annex road upon which we had been briefly traveling. This insane maneuver caused us to very nearly miss the blacktopped road altogether. We went careening across it and almost ended up in a deep ditch which was located on the far side of the two-lane thoroughfare.

My father fought briefly to gain control of the wheel, all the while slurring an unbroken chain of wild obscenities. Openly studying him, now, I worried how in the world we were going to make it safely to where ever it was that we were supposed to be going. His highly irresponsible antics caused my heart to beat much faster than normal, and the palms of both my hands were perspiring. I discovered, too, at that precise moment, that I was no longer cold.

Not long after we left the speakeasy we found ourselves traveling through softly rolling hills of rich farmland. In a short while my father chose to slow down the truck's forward momentum a bit, and just before he turned off the main road I noticed that on the right hand side, just ahead, was a lovely hill with a small chapel perched sturdily upon its crest. Directly across the street from this same noble looking edifice was a large farmstead which, upon first glance, seemed extremely well tended....

Our old beat-up truck slowed down just barely enough to make a sharp left turn on this same road. Then we bolted rather wildly across an ill-kept yard, bouncing all the while due to the terrain's many ruts and uneven areas, only to stop abruptly in front of a dwelling. With obvious difficulty the man behind the wheel, still without having said anything to me, sluggishly extracted himself from the vehicle. With even greater difficulty he began to slowly weave his way towards the structure sitting before us.... From where I continued to observe, he somewhat tentatively negotiated the several steps that led to the front door. Eventually he entered the place through this same opening and just as quickly finally disappeared from view.

For some moments more I just sat where I was, dubiously taking in my new surroundings. That wretched house, if one could really refer to it as such, was in a state of even poorer shape than either the man or his truck. The two-story shack which had only seconds before swallowed my father whole was decidedly lopsided, to say the least. One simply could not ignore its strangely shaped old roof, either, which was grotesquely sunken and misaligned with the entire rest of the dingy abode. All around the place, as well, in what was surely meant to represent a yard, grew tall weeds of every possible size and description.... Overall, they looked thoroughly dry in spite of the recent rain. An ancient looking and completely rusted out oil drum was lying upon its side, not far from the front wheels of the truck, partially buried within the soil....

Having retrieved my horrible shoes from their former resting place there on the tattered flooring of the battered truck, I decided to tie the laces tightly together. Belligerently slinging them over my left shoulder I firmly vowed to myself that never again would I put them upon my feet. Since I was unable to open either of the doors of the truck from the inside all by myself, I cleverly rolled my passenger side window all the way down. After carefully crawling out of the vehicle, I first began to tentatively feel around for the rubber grips of the running board with one stockinged foot. Once safely there, I finally managed to land securely upon the ground.

Quite frankly, I was hungry, dirty, and still quite tired—not to mention terribly depressed at the moment. Leaning back against the door of the truck, I contemplated whether or not I wished to enter that God forsaken place. Even to the young child that I was at the time, this habitat, along with my presently dire circumstances, hinted loudly at some intangible danger. I found myself wondering when I might awaken from this ongoing nightmare of mine.

Eventually it proved to be my dependable curiosity, and, too, the somber fact that I really had no other options at this point in time, that finally made me venture forward. Bravely yet rather slowly, I headed towards the house in which I was to dwell for several months to come.

By the time I made it across that short span of yard with the intention of reaching the front area of the house, my already soiled socks, and indeed every speck of the bottom portion of my extra-long knickers, were literally dotted with burrs and nettles whose tenacious little rapier-like teeth refused to strike a truce of any kind. Even when I was standing perfectly still, searching in vain for a safe surface upon which to place my foot next, those vicious assailants which were already firmly attached to me would continue without relief to bite their way through the worn fabric of my socks and even deeper into the vulnerable flesh of my tender feet....

I finally arrived at the front staircase which ultimately led upwards to the sorry little shack. Immediately I noticed that the bottom two unusually steep wooden steps were clearly rotted away. Within these twin rectangular-shaped open areas, which basically formed the aperture within each frame of these same woefully neglected spaces, grew more of the same type of hearty weeds which had just attacked me. So that I might make my way safely to the porch area above I was forced to gingerly negotiate around to the far left side of the damage where the footing seemed more secure. Furthermore, what was apparently left of the stair's banister on either side was presently laying strewn upon the ground in badly fragmented pieces of several assorted sizes.

The porch area itself, once I arrived, seemed sound enough. Finding that I could not wait a second longer to relieve myself from those pesky annoyances from which I was now actually suffering, I promptly took a seat on the wooden landing at the top of the stairs and slowly, piece by feisty piece, began to painstakingly remove each clump of the tenacious burrs. Little by little everything reluctantly but mercifully released its hold upon me, and I quickly tossed the debris over the nearby hand-railing of the porch.

After this was done I stood up and began to walk around. Right away I noticed that there was a modest looking two-seater wooden swing that was hanging from two giant rusty hooks which were deeply lodged within one of the heavy structural beams of the roof.... Upon my critical inspection all somehow seemed intact.

On either side of the front door, however, were two long dirty windows which were each missing several panes of glass. The shards of broken material lay scattered directly beneath each casement in a telltale sign of terrible neglect, while those once gaping holes within the windows themselves were haphazardly stuffed with old yellowed newspaper.

The front door, as I hesitantly approached, had been conveniently left ajar. Eventually I was to discover that its top hinge was missing causing the heavy weight of the thick wood to consistently be dragged across the flooring, consequently etching deep scratch marks within the immediate interior of the entranceway.

Alas, there was no sign of my father. While I began to quietly me-ander around the ground floor of the dilapidated house, thoughtfully taking in every detail, I came to suspect that in order for him to have gained his much needed respite from the rest of the world he must have chosen to go upstairs to be alone.

Shortly I could not avoid noticing that the entire place smelled strongly of a particular mustiness that only comes with old age and with slowly rotting wet wood. There was also an unmistakable scent of some-thing else which immediately accosted my sensitive nose—something even more offensive in nature.... Sometime in the near future I would be correctly associating this same unpleasant phenomenon with the decomposition of animal matter—more precisely, a dead and decaying rodent.

Presently, though, as I moved about the sparsely appointed little area that I imagined was meant to represent a parlor, a multitude of dry colorless leaves which long ago had been blown in from outside softly crumbled into tiny fragments beneath the weight of my now shoeless feet. In no time at all I happened upon the first of only two pieces of fur-niture to be found in this part of the house. It was the badly weathered frame of a single high-back wooden chair whose seat was missing. Those several nails whose faithful duty it once had been to hold this necessary item in place stuck out helplessly in midair like the sharp quills of a circular porcupine. Across the room and pushed up against a far wall whose paint was badly flaking, as well as hopelessly stained in many areas due to years of water damage, a heavy-looking wooden roll-top desk mutely greeted my arrival.

Opening this poor old relic all the way by carefully rolling back its tambour-style cover proved impossible. I did, however, manage to open it halfway. Nothing of great and abiding interest lay within except for a long box which contained four lonely wooden matches. Directly beside the desk, and sitting all by itself there upon the warped flooring, was a dusty old lamp whose entire presence was heavily encrusted with cobwebs. Ever so slowly with the index finger of my right hand I gingerly removed the sticky substance, only to eventually discover that the lamp was empty and also missing its wick.

Not far from this desk and located along a wall more towards the center of the room—between another window, and the front door area, itself—I was pleased to discover an old potbellied, wood-burning stove.... Its magnificent black wrought iron presence, there in the tiny room, would eventually prove to be a lifesaver in the cold winter months to come. I took further note that the smoke stack—or vent—which protruded out from above this valuable heating element and then curved back upon itself to ultimately disappear into the wall directly behind it, seemed undamaged. There was a sort of baritonal clicking sound as I carefully unlatched the stove's heavy door to peer inside. I found it completely empty of either wood, or coal—or even ashes, for that matter.

In no time at all I finished tracing the entire perimeter of this little place. Once again I arrived in front of the staircase, exactly where this fact-finding journey of mine had originally begun. Standing there at the moment, at the bottom of the first step of the many stairs that led to the second floor, I was trying to decide whether I felt brave enough to extend my investigation to include the upper story of the house. Finally, though, after careful deliberation, it was my keen sense of foreboding that was ultimately responsible for my having decided to pass up this particular opportunity. I decided that for now, at least, without further ado it might prove far wiser for me to walk on towards what I imagined was the kitchen....

A bit of relief from the unpleasant atmosphere of the previous room was eventually obtained here. The offensive odors, at least, had lost their initial impact. As I slowly but ever so silently passed through the wooden portal off the main entryway of the house and into the even more sterile environment of what represented a kitchen, I noticed that this room, too, like the other, was completely bare—totally inhospitable, in every sense. What usually represented an important part of any home showed not the slightest hint of having been used for quite some time.

There in one corner space against the far wall, near a door which led out back, sat a rickety old ice box. Like the front door it also had been left ajar to disclose to view nothing of great importance—except for a clear empty bottle that apparently had been laying undisturbed on its side at the bottom of this old appliance for ages. Next to the bottle were the fragments of what once had been either a bird's nest or the long ago abode of some ingenious rodent.

The short counter top and sink area located right beneath a single grime-covered window were empty, as were the twin cabinets located above it and on either side. A hand pump that was normally used for retrieving water was appropriately situated over at one end of the ancient porcelain sink which itself was obviously badly cracked and severely rusted, creating an interesting pattern effect worthy of mild interest. Oddly enough, too, in a small pantry located directly beneath the sink was the telltale vestige of what once must have been a large and healthy bar of soap. No doubt this mere modicum of its former impressive self—this simple cleansing agent—sat forlornly and totally isolated within a cracked and badly chipped teacup inside an otherwise empty cabinet. Poignantly it whispered to me of tales reminiscent of times when wonderful life—and lovely living things, inhabited the place. And in sad understanding, as well as complete sympathy, I acknowledged the deep painful furrows that had long ago been etched within its firm contours of lye solution....

Through the dirty glass window of the back kitchen door a promise of refreshing sunlight—and even more glorious fresh air—beckoned to me. With considerable difficulty I managed to turn the old rusty key within its old rusty lock. Pulling upon the door with all the physical strength I could muster, the barrier finally gave way. It literally flew open to loudly strike the back interior wall behind it with a firmly resounding thud. Before me was a screened door—or, rather, a mere frame of a door whose tattered strips of discolored screening began to gently float and flutter towards me in answer to the unexpected movement of clean fresh autumn air. Immediately that blessed oxygen began to course through the small room, and, of course, to graciously fill my much-relieved nostrils and lungs in the process.

Leaving the kitchen behind, I soon found myself out back upon the tiny wooden porch that was located just off the kitchen. Standing there upon that small perch—not unlike a young sojourner standing atop the decking of a forlorn and abandoned old ship, I took in the view of an old outhouse in one far corner of the same ill-kept yard. Upon the ground below and not far from where I was standing a large partially damaged wooden tub was sitting amongst the thick weeds and yellow dandelions.... Much to my growing interest the still sturdy basin was nearly filled to its brim with water—the same rich bounty, no doubt, that was collected from the recent rains of last night.

Suddenly the exquisite vision of a bath danced and played within my mind's eye, while I stood contemplating the sun's rays as they twinkled and played upon the stillness of the water. Even though the ancient house had no plumbing or electricity, I firmly resolved—then and there, to remain undaunted at having been denied these somewhat minor conveniences of life. Merely upon some healthy impulse, I quickly retrieved the paper-thin bar of soap from its secret resting place there in the little pantry. Now, with a growing sense of pride at becoming more self-sufficient in being able to look after my basic need to wash myself, at least, I cleverly decided to also make good use of the rain water in the wooden tub that had been generously provided for me.

So there on the small well-weathered rear porch, amid the late morning chatter of birds and the enthusiastic song of the katydid, I removed my clothing piece by piece. In a way I felt morally obligated to embrace this simple task as a special ceremony of sorts—a minor ritual intended to celebrate the restoration of my mind, as well as the cleansing of my body. Emotionally speaking, more than anything else at that particular moment I longed to burn those old worn articles of clothing which, in effect, were acting all along as a "second skin" to me. They were to my very sensitive spirit pitiful remnants that were constantly reminding me of my not-so-distant painful past. But naturally, having nothing else to wear, my small ceremony of simply washing and renewing myself would live on in the end to represent the same thing.

In this uncomplicated fashion I was instinctively craving a much required closure to all that I had heretofore previously endured during those difficult seven and a half years of my life. Deep within the very core of me I willed that this moment in time remain a marker; something of an extremely personal nature whose knowledge, and vital acceptance, would somehow help to place me upon the path to self-healing....

Standing before the old damaged tub, now, I carefully tossed my too-short shirt and my too-long knickers onto a dry step nearby. Next, I proceeded to remove my underclothes. Taking off my socks, however, would prove to be the biggest challenge of all for the tight cotton fabric of each sock had more or less laminated itself to the bloody wounds of the heels of each of my sore feet. Patiently sitting upon the side of the wooden basin I scooped up a handful of the gentle rainwater and slowly and most carefully began saturating my socks—first one, then the other, until they both finally agreed to relinquish their power over me.

The water was so cold. Large goose pimples suddenly covered every inch of me. Soon enough, as well, my teeth began to chatter as the unkind temperature of the cold clear substance continued to make contact with my skin. The mild mental and physical sluggishness from which I had earlier been so significantly suffering now began to melt away….

After thoroughly cleansing my hair, and face, and body, I also diligently scrubbed my underpants and socks and finally laid them upon one step to the already warm autumn sun for drying. Standing in the cheerful morning sunlight, with my thin cotton undershirt I quickly dried myself and once again forced myself to put on my shirt and my knickers.

Eventually challenging those awful shoes, which by now had grown to become my hated enemy, I finally made a long overdue decision regarding their future. With an immense sense of unwholesome glee that surely must have bordered upon the obscene, I took a moment to carefully wrap the long laces of each around those two pieces of worn leather as tightly as I possibly could, thus forming a single more compact projectile. Thoughtfully studying the item that I was holding for a few seconds longer I generously bestowed upon the little bundle a sort of personal "farewell benediction" which I actually made up on the spot in order to help celebrate the occasion. With a sense of unparalleled joy rising strong within my vindictive young heart, I then took the bold initiative and properly hurled the shoes far out into the weeds. I remember that they quickly landed within one particularly nasty-looking corner of the messy lot. No sooner had this important deed been expertly accomplished when I staunchly committed myself to going barefooted from that point forward.

Still, after all this time, there was no sign of my father. Being so very hungry, I carefully collected the pieces of change that had been earlier placed near my dry clothing there on the porch step. After that I quickly set out across the open fields, which lay just beyond our homestead, in search of something to eat. The large cookie of yesterday afternoon had been my last meal, and I was becoming noticeably light-headed from lack of nourishment.

Walking barefooted through the weed and burr infested ground cover that was growing all around this more densely infested back yard was time-consuming work. Just as with my earlier trek from the truck to the front porch area of the house, the sharp claws from those pesky little nettles would once again bite into the soft flesh of my soles and ankles, slowing my progress considerably. Eventually, though, as I steadily made my way past the outhouse and well beyond the perimeter of what represented our property line, I came upon the pleasantness of cultured farmland whose acre upon acre of rich soft earth most gratefully began to soothe my sore and aching feet.

Deep crisscross impressions from the wheels of some sort of heavy farming equipment used to harvest that season's grain previously had softened and lifted the dirt in some places, while in others instances compressed it rather tightly, all-in-all creating an interesting patterned effect down the pathway I was traveling. That near sensual sensation of the large clods of fresh rich black earth squishing up between my little toes as I walked managed to lift my spirits in spite of my hunger.

I was beginning to glory in the mild sense of euphoria that was sweeping through my being. How good it made me feel to finally imagine, even in the smallest respect, that I was becoming "captain of my ship," so to speak. Although I was completely unsure of what life held in store for me, with the late September sun warming me all over, as it was; and, too, with the light cool breeze which bore with it the unmistakable sensation that a real change was in the air—that same familiar change, I might add, which subtly marks the dependable cyclical movement of one season slowly passing into another, I found myself hurrying along to see what might lay up ahead.

In many respects I was beginning to think myself a wealthy young man. Not only had I just enjoyed a much-needed bath, but very recently I even managed to properly rid myself of those terrible shoes. And, as I continued to confidently walk on across those vast connecting acres of field after field, within my pocket jingled a few coins which I believed whole-wholeheartedly would surely buy me something substantial to eat. All in all my world was beginning to look a little brighter and I happily smiled to myself.

Soon I approached a cornfield which also had been recently worked. The telltale remnants of what must have been a bountiful harvest lay strewn all about the good earth in several different directions. Cheerfully I made my way onward, traveling one of the long furrows between what once surely must have contained countless rows of green and gold stalks of rich grain growing far taller than myself.

I continued to walk for what seemed an extremely long while. Eventually, however, the path I was traveling led to a single lane dirt road and on the opposite side of this country trail lay a small well-maintained farmstead. Near this same road, too, beneath a large oak tree whose leaves were just now hinting at the slowly beginning process which would turn them all their various shades of brilliant gold, and red, and orange, sat a rough-hewn wooden table that held several wire baskets filled with marvelous looking apples. This fruit represented to me, quite literally, "manna from heaven." And, as I approached the long sturdy table in order to carefully study this unexpected vision more closely, I noticed a sign with some writing upon it, which, naturally, I could not decipher.

Just beyond where I was now standing was a similarly constructed fence of unplaned wood which resembled the table that held the fruit, with a man diligently laboring in a flower garden nearby. Normally I would never have openly sought anyone's company. I was prone to be a bit leery of strangers, in general. However, with my ever-growing hunger literally gnawing at my insides—very much the way great loneliness has the ability to chew at one's heart, shortly it was out of a real sense of desperation that I made my way up the narrow driveway that led to where the man remained totally engrossed in his work....

Truthfully, it never occurred to me to just take the fruit. I could never be a thief, no matter how difficult my situation might be. And so as the man with the large straw hat bent solicitously over the hoe he was using, obviously to help clear away the various strands of renegade grass which had entrenched themselves in his nearly pristine garden, he did not hear me approach him from behind.

All along the fence and directly to my left, now, was growing a multitude of gigantic sunflowers. Their noble crowns were bowing low in response to the heaviness of their well-seeded headdress. Within a period of two or three weeks their nutritious bounty would be carefully harvested, as I would be privileged to learn first-hand one day....

Indeed, for many years already this simple yet highly pleasing habit of their owner brought real pleasure every year to himself, as well as to his many friends and neighbors. I well recall that after the shiny smooth seeds were collected, washed, sufficiently dried, properly buttered, and then carefully roasted within a wood-burning oven, they would be set aside to cool in small individual containers. Sometime later on these same receptacles were carefully sealed and decorated with cheerful red paper ribbon. When the holidays of December eventually came around, with obvious affection these personalized gifts would be proudly presented to others.

During many a long wintry evening, as members of local families warmed themselves by an open hearth or potbellied stove, those tasty crunchy morsels would be readily enjoyed. This marvelous fare, in fact, would quietly speak to us of the many weeks beforehand when, before their completed metamorphosis had actually taken place to this edible stage, the little seeds remained an essential part of those amazing flowers which grew in such happy abundance....

Respectfully standing five or six feet directly behind the man, at the moment, I loudly cleared my throat in an attempt to win his attention—but my simple strategy failed me, since the stranger could not seem to hear this clever overture of mine above the rhythmic pulses that his garden tool was making against the ground. Instead of remaining where I was, however, I decided to use a new approach by promptly moving several feet to one side of this avid gardener, now placing myself more within his peripheral field of vision.... Finally, at long last, having witnessed this modest movement of mine, the worker abruptly ceased what he was doing and immediately stood up to visually acknowledge my presence. Upon seeing me he smiled warmly and somehow actually seemed genuinely pleased to find this young stranger standing before him.

"G-g-ood afternoon, to y-you, y-young f-fella," he stammered. After quickly and rather smoothly taking in the features of my person, he went further to cheerfully inquire, "I t-take pride in kn-knowing everyone who l-lives in these parts, b-but I know that I've never s-seen or m-met you before.... Tell m-me, then, whom m-might you be?"

The gentle undulation of his speech pattern seemed similar, in effect, to the hesitant intonations that had been present in the man's hoeing effort. Presently he was extracting a large red handkerchief from the rear pocket of his overalls with one hand, and, as he removed his hat with the other, he began to enthusiastically wipe away the perspiration from his moist face.

His full cheeks, I was noticing, were the exact rosy color of the fall dahlias which were growing in neat little rows—everywhere, all around our feet. I judged the gentleman to be elderly—but not old. There was a quality about him that instantly put me at ease, and as he continued to smile warmly at me, out of politeness I stepped towards him and extended my hand, as I told him, "My name is Adam."

Without the slightest hesitation on his part, he quickly offered his own larger hand in response to my gesture. His handshake was firm and strong.... I liked that. And, as we stood greeting each other in this polite age-old tradition of friendship, he made a memorable attempt to further inquire about my last name, as he said, "Adam...."

Since I should have been thoroughly mortified, at this point, to have to admit to anyone that my father was Henry Bodray and that we lived not far from this man's lovely farm in that terrible place of ours, I abruptly put him off by stating quite simply, but firmly, "Adam! Just call me—Adam."

As the man went about cheerfully shaking my right hand he continued to thoughtfully study me in a wholly inoffensive manner. Very soon he properly introduced himself, by telling me, "I'm H-harry Hopkins, A-adam. I was b-born in this c-community long a-ago.... In f-fact, I've l-lived here all m-my life!"

With this genuinely friendly and nonthreatening sort of demeanor which was being exuded by this cheerful man I decided, right then and there, that I liked him. He really was not all that much taller than myself in stature. However unlike me he seemed to be a bit overweight in spite of his loosely fitting work clothes. In retrospect I guess he possessed the sort of pleasant plumpness that comes with many people in their later years. In this case, particularly, the situation hinted strongly of a once vigorous physical constitution in the man's far younger days which, either out of unconscious neglect, or a basic lack of interest, had by now waned to a greater degree.

"What m-may I d-do for y-you, young A-adam?"

At this point my mouth was fairly watering in hungry anticipation as I thought of those picture-perfect apples sitting upon the table just beyond the fence, so I asked, "How much would one of your baskets of apples cost?" In my heart I was greatly hoping for a favorable reply and so I held my breath as I continued to finger the coins that jingled a little in the right hand pocket of my knickers. With this initial question of mine, I rather impetuously leapt ahead of myself by presenting the open palm of my hand in order to eagerly show this fine stranger the change I was carrying with me. Then, before he actually had a chance to even consider my first inquiry, I went ahead to further barrage him with a second point at issue as I quickly asked whether or not he felt that there were enough funds to buy those already much coveted items.

"Oh, the a-apples!" he half shouted with a bit of merriment. Actually the truth of the situation which was responsible for this same cheerful lightheartedness on his part was about to make itself known to me, as he said, "M-my apples are a-always free to wh-whomever wishes to t-take them. You s-see at the e-end of each w-week when I'm r-raking up the l-leaves in the y-yard I find all the a-apples which haven't y-yet been p-pilfered by the squirrels, or b-birds, or deer. R-rather than see them r-rot a-away I p-place them o-out by the f-fence for passersby to t-take. Everyone in these p-parts has long b-been familiar w-with this little habit of m-mine," he said happily. Then while he replaced his handkerchief in its rear pocket and playfully patted his well-worn straw hat back upon his head, he further informed me as he gently took my elbow to help guide me back down the driveway towards the table, "There is o-only a modest p-portion of m-my b-best crop of W-winesap apples left. C-come and we'll f-find s-several p-perfect specimens for y-you to take with y-you!"

I watched with great interest as this kind and generous soul carefully went about critically inspecting each of the pieces of fruit, within each one of the many baskets, there upon the long table. My brand-new friend was carefully putting aside the several which in his estimation were worthy of my having. His utterly solicitous manner in doing this simple thing for me really touched my heart. I could see that he was definitely a person who enjoyed other people; a man, I further surmised, who not only felt comfortable in their presence but also had the ability to make others feel comfortable by being around him. In my heart of hearts I found myself wishing that I could be more like him in this way.

For quite some time now I became aware of a faintly annoying squeaking sound—something to which I could not as yet put a name. But as I waited patiently for Mr. Hopkins to finish doing what he was doing from across the far back side of his yard, more or less hugging a high hedge of well-manicured pine trees in the distance, an elderly woman dressed in a nightgown, and robe, and slippers was slowly making prog-ress as she shuffled along, heading in the direction of the house....

She was diligently pulling a child's wagon back along what seemed to be some sort of prescribed pathway. In any event, it was the turn-ing movement of the wheels of that wagon—specifically their urgent need for oil or some other lubricant, that was making this high-pitched squeaking noise that continued on and on without pause. Speechlessly I gazed from the man standing there beside me, back to the woman who was slowly plodding along pulling this child's simple play toy. I was trying to imagine whether the two people might be related in some way—and attempting to guess, more than anything else, just why this person was behaving as she was.

In a moment more, I heard Mr. Hopkins tell me, "Well, h-here is the b-best of the lot!" Stepping away to admire the pile of lovely fruit for a second or two, he then promptly turned away from me and started up the driveway as he called back to tell me, "W-wait there for m-me! I'll b-be right b-back."

While I dutifully waited for him, I quickly reached for one of the apples which had been tempting me ever since my arrival there. I was so hungry. Having randomly made my selection from the generous pile of fruit Mr. Hopkins put aside for me, I raised the treasure first to my nose in order that I might enjoy its wonderful scent. Then without wasting another second I bit soundly into the sphere's crunchy outer covering and began to lustily devour every bit of its sweet, firm pulp; then its seeds and core—and finally its everything.

Just as I was about to take up a second apple, I watched as my bene-factor came back down the driveway towards me happily whistling as he walked. In one hand he carried a cloth sack which was light brown in color—and which, I soon discovered, could be opened and closed by its drawstring. Pausing before me at the moment my enthusiastic new acquaintance reached out to show me the small gift, as he explained, "Thought y-you could u-use this nifty pouch to c-carry all your a-apples. C-comes in mighty h-handy for all s-sorts of things, actually!" As he opened the marvelous little invention to show me exactly how it worked, he extracted something wrapped carefully in paper. Glancing from the object to me, he also went on to tell me, "A-also th-thought you m-might enjoy s-some ch-cheese. I m-made it m-myself several m-months b-back. R-recipe's been in m-my family for g-generations!"

Once again Mr. Hopkins was openly studying the features of my face. With a certain profundity which managed to leave its lasting impression upon me, he further remarked, as if he felt an urgent need to further explain the reason for this kind gesture of his, "F-for s-some reason, a-apples and ch-cheese just n-naturally seem to g-go together, very m-much like fr-friendship and sh-sharing always s-seem to go t-together!"

My rather keen instincts were telling me that here was a man who was a kindred spirit in the sense that he was also no stranger to loneli-ness. I could feel this important truth even though he had not openly spoken of it. "Thank you for your kindness to me," I found myself say-ing to him.

At the moment he was in the process of carefully placing the apples he had chosen for me into the cloth sack. As I made ready to leave behind his pleasant company in order to dutifully travel onward to find a quiet out-of-the-way place to enjoy more of my lunch, it was he this time who offered his hand to me as he bid me good-bye. While I was in the process of enthusiastically returning this simple gesture, I distinctly felt a certain reluctance on his part in letting me go.

Then, for a second time that day, from over this good man's right shoulder I witnessed the old woman pulling the wagon along a shorter length of hedge which was all that was exposed to my view at this point. Soon, if she continued to remain true to her behavior, she would eventually be reaching the end of that delimitation, only to turn around and slowly plod back again in the direction from which she had just come, all the while trailing the noisy little wagon behind her.... While Mr. Hopkins momentarily busied himself by rearranging the fruit that remained behind on the wooden table, I continued to observe the lone figure as she did eventually disappear behind a portion of the house. Although I could no longer visually follow her progress, with the ongoing squeaking sound the wagon was continuously making the general proximity of her whereabouts remained known to both Mr. Hopkins and to me, as she, no doubt, went about with her perpetual movement back and forth across the wide span of yard.

People who share small towns together do not have any secrets from one another. This, I discovered, is just one of those indisputable facts of life. For better, or for worse, this truth remains the intrinsic unadorned nature of all small rural communities. Here, probably more than anywhere else, the proverbial "grapevine" sinks its sturdy and highly proliferous roots deep and manages to consistently thrive on the shared joys, as well as the heart-wrenching sorrows, of all its many inhabitants.

Unbeknownst to me at the moment, without having yet "tipped his hand," so to speak, Mr. Hopkins already knew far more about me than I did about him. But because he was by nature a sensitive man, he followed my initial lead that day by not having insisted upon bringing forth the embarrassing truth about my situation.

As it happened this kindly man continued to hold the distinguished position of very ably running the small post office there at Peck's Station which also boasted for some years of having a Western Union branch. Naturally, and more or less because of this, he quickly came to know everybody—both visitor and resident alike, just as everyone eventually came to know and to like him. Actually, it was he who originally received the urgent telegram sent to my father from the Children's Home Society in Pittsburgh, stressing a need for the officials there to make contact with my father.

Many months before that fateful day in mid-October, when this country suffered the tremendous economic jolt from the stock market's crash that was responsible for propelling it headlong into those dark and demented years, this same organization which had placed me, as well as many other children, in our various foster homes over the years had already fallen on hard times financially speaking. Before the home was obliged to close its doors for good, in a challenging and timely effort to place its many wards in responsible environments, desperate attempts were even being made to locate parents who had previously altogether neglected care of their own children.

Keenly attuned to my emotional needs, as he obviously was, Mr. Hopkins in his abundant kindness chose not to harass me in the slightest manner by openly addressing these unhappy facts of my life which he was already privileged to know. Instead he simply offered to help me in his own highly effective manner by providing this wonderful food, and this equally healthy social interaction, both of which I was in such great need.

In the years to come he and I would eventually be standing upon far more level ground, relative to our mutual understanding of the circumstances of each other's lives. I would learn, for example, that my new friend had not always suffered from the speech impediment with which he was forced to live these days. Likewise, the old woman who endless pulled the child's wagon back and forth across the yard, seemingly without stopping to rest at all, was his beloved wife, Ugenia, of some forty years.

In the future, too, this extraordinarily supportive individual and I would be forming an even stronger bond of friendship with Felix Lauder and his family. Certainly with regard to this mutually valued friendship of ours, which was to ultimately form between the three of us, especially, I would finally come to know the truth of the Hopkins family's interesting life. I would come to learn of the great tragedy which was responsible for Mr. Hopkins loneliness, as well as the reason why his dear wife had long ago completely lost her ability to relate to the real world in any rational manner.

I was also to learn the astonishing truth that everyone in these parts also knew my father—by reputation, mostly. Although he remained a loner by choice, his longtime and not so clandestine history of dealing with the mob had by now become legendary in these parts. Certainly because of this highly distasteful fact, he automatically became ostracized from the very beginning; permanently set apart, in a real sense, by all the more decent folks who made up our community.

After I bid Mr. Hopkins good-bye and faithfully promised to visit him again, I returned once more to the dirt road which ran past his home. Pausing for just a second, I was attempting to decide in which direction I should go—for, really, it made little difference to me that day. Adventure of some sort beckoned from nearly every direction and so I decided to travel onward, just the same, towards the left to see where the remainder of the day would be taking me.

There were distinct moments in my young life when I managed to put aside the heaviness of my personal circumstances and consciously remembered to be the inventive child at play. Having spied an old tin can hiding in the dense weeds by the side of the road, with my excellent cloth sack now slung carelessly over one shoulder—all the while I began munching a second apple, I proceeded to entertain myself for quite some time by kicking the hollow object back and forth across the pathway I trod. It became a simple game for one whose rules, I arbitrarily decided, would be to intentionally miss the occasional potholes and ruts which were filled with the fresh rain water from last evening's storm.

Soon my pleasant travels brought me to a set of railroad tracks. What normally would have represented far more well-groomed grav-eled spaces between its rails were presently filled, instead, with spindly grasses and a variety of common wild flower which had managed to miraculously take seed. Somehow this unexpected beauty looked strangely out of place growing where it was, but seemed to be thriving undisturbed just the same, giving proof to my initial theory that this por-tion of this particular line had for some time been abandoned. Nearby was a tall and rather spindly old oak tree. In a spirit of true child-like impetuousness, which was founded upon my insatiably natural curios-ity, I took the liberty of hanging my heavy knapsack there upon one of the "old-timers" more sturdy lower limbs, and I set about climbing the tree to have a better look around....

By thoughtfully scanning the area from where I remained clinging to a fairly secure branch at the very top of this immense tree, I readily spotted several buildings to the far left. One, in particular, looked like a small train station—just up ahead. After scurrying back down the tree, I quickly collected my carry-all with its abundance of precious food inside and promptly headed off to investigate the town there in the distance.

Making good progress in that general direction now, by agilely stepping upon the unevenly spaced wooden ties located there between those same ill-kept tracks, as well as balancing myself every now and then upon the system's slowly deteriorating rails, I could not help but notice that a number of the ties were actually missing. The obvious neglect of this minor tributary, which had once been a proud link to the vast network of greater railroad lines that crisscrossed over every part of our great land, somehow greatly saddened me. Neglect in any form brought about this same involuntary feeling.

As I continued slowly to make my way towards the little station, even from a good distance away I noticed a large sign posted at the top far right of the ticket office and later a similar looking one displayed between two posts out front, indicating, I was to later learn, the name of the tiny hamlet of "Fayetteville"—or "Peck's Station." Once, as the story goes, the Peck family operated a popular creamery at what for many years had been the last stop for the local Eagle Line branch. Because of this fact the railroad men who serviced the community somehow took to referring to it in this manner. Upon further inspection I soon realized that this hut, too, which functioned some time ago as a stationmaster's office, was naturally also abandoned.

There seemed to be no one else around at the moment. After walking across the slightly raised wooden platform upon which the modest looking building was constructed, I tried the badly tarnished brass door knob in an attempt to gain access to the room within, but found it properly locked instead. Respectfully peering through one dust-covered pane of glass, with my nose and cheek pressed ever so close, I tried hard to see what I could see....

Scattered all around for the sensitive soul to find were telltale hints of a once busy bustling history of the place. Across the room, for instance, was a long desk which supported above it a tall glass window whose circular opening was designed specifically for business transactions between the employees of the company and its patrons. Here, no doubt, countless travel accommodations were made over a period of many years. One imagines, too, what eager anticipation children and their parents—or grandparents, might have felt while boarding a train to travel to visit family members living elsewhere. Local businessmen who owned and operated successful farms that produced grain or animal stock might also have conceivably been traveling on from here to Milwaukee—or Chicago, perhaps, to make provisions for the sale of their riches. And then, of course, there would be those invaluable mail bags filled with important messages, or packages, all which naturally impacted upon the lives of so many people and in such a significant manner. Such things were part and parcel of the very lifeline which the railroads represented. In effect, it was these minor railroad tributaries that eventually became responsible for helping to people rural communities in the beginning; while at the same time allowed the growing number of these community's inhabitants to remain physically and emotionally connected to the far busier pace of the outlying world, should they choose to do so.

Behind the counter and posted upon the back wall was a calendar displaying a photograph of the American flag. To the immediate right of this tabular arrangement of days gone by was a large vacant billboard which formerly offered indispensable advice to each and every traveler regarding important destinations and times.

Nearby, within that same space, I could see a large wooden wall clock. Its shiny brass pendulum once faithfully ticked back and forth to the ever comforting rhythm of the passing of time but had long ago fallen silent. Likewise, upon the otherwise cleanly swept unpolished gray wooden slates of the flooring, a tiny portion of a lone ticket stub protruded out from underneath its secret hiding place, there beneath a long empty bench, completely filling my heart to near bursting with a deeply felt longing to travel somewhere—anywhere, at the moment....

Directly across from this particular little station, along a dirt road, was located a handful of well-kept wooden buildings. The one on the far left was a post office which I eventually detected was not in operation at the moment; the very same little branch office, actually, with its Western Union office where my new-found friend, Mr. Hopkins, worked. There was also a modest-looking little drug store located in the middle of the block which the Everett Dunbar family owned and managed. Directly next door to this, on the right, was Angelo Balducci's barbershop that displayed its fanciful red and white candy-striped cylinder out front, next to a cheerful looking sign printed in bold red, white, and green letters. Finally taking up the rest of that entire block was a rather impressive-looking general store which instantly seized and then fervently held my growing interest.

Naturally, with the approach of winter coming our way, the days were now growing noticeably shorter and shorter. Although I had not the faintest idea of what time it might already be, I could tell, nonetheless, that the day was quickly waning.... Far too soon the warm butter-yellow and vermilion colored sun would be comfortably sliding back down into its distant envelope—there upon the far horizon, to finally disappear with the coming of evening. Before long it would be necessary for me to find my way back to the house where my father lived. But first I so wished to investigate this interesting place which, unlike either the train station, the post office, the drug store, or the barber shop, still seemed open for business.

For several moments I remained standing out in front of the place, totally absorbed in thoughtfully studying all of the various wares that were attractively displayed there in the front window, before I finally decided to have a look inside. Very soon my hungry eyes did not know where to gaze first.... There were so many amazing things to see.

With Mr. Hopkins' new gift still comfortably slung over my left shoulder, and with both my hands tucked confidently within the pockets of my well-worn and too-long knickers, my shoeless feet made nary a sound upon the smooth boards of the flooring as I entered the large room. Truly, never before had I been inside a store quite like this one. I became literally fascinated by all there was to see....

Seemingly every speck of available space was being used for some purpose. Even from the open rafters overhead, for instance, there hung such things as laundry baskets, wheelbarrows, and various sorts of leather accessories used for harnessing farm animals to wagons or plows. Again, upon one entire wall to my immediate right as I entered the place, there was being neatly displayed a variety of garden tools such as shovels, rakes, and pitchforks; as well as those more familiar household utensils which ranged from kitchen measuring cups, and hot water bottles, to the basic toilet plunger.

To my far left, now, near a window which looked out onto the tranquility of the surrounding fields, and which was rather masterly situated not so very far from a formidable-looking potbellied stove, was nestled a modestly designed circular wooden table with chairs to accommodate four people. More or less residing at the table's center was an open checker board whose well-worn pieces for the game were already neatly set in place for use. Close by and upon the floor next to this friendly grouping of furniture sat an indispensable brass cuspidor.

Continuing to aimlessly meander about the charming place, I noticed, too, that behind a long counter which extended almost the entire length of most of the back wall; and which, I would eventually discover, usually served perfectly well as a convenient work table to trim fabric, was an equally long chest which contained a multitude of fascinating little polished drawers.... Each intimate little storage place held its own prescribed articles for sale, such as needles and threads, and different sorts of screws and nuts and bolts.

Directly above this treasure-trove of indispensable objects were located several open shelves that reached up to the ceiling of the room and displayed bolt upon bolt of cheerful cotton and gingham fabric, along with generous rolls of muslin used as an interfacing for tailoring various articles of clothing. Standing nearby and ready for use during any given day of any busy work week, to the far side of this long well-stocked wall was a sturdy wooden ladder. This same handy device reached nearly to the ceiling itself and could faithfully be rolled along the floor on metal casters in order that a salesperson might be able to secure any one of those higher and otherwise impossible to reach articles on the shelves whenever necessary.

For generation upon generation talented women of rural society proudly made clothing for themselves, as well as for the members of their families. This was pretty much a given. Rarely would anyone think to buy "store-bought" apparel, except perhaps through the Montgomery Ward Catalog....

The Montgomery Ward & Co., Inc., in fact, was founded in Chicago by Aaron Montgomery Ward in 1872, as the world's first general-merchandise mail-order catalog business. Its fetching history is a true American success story. As the official account goes, Aaron Ward was a young traveling salesman concerned by the high prices rural Americans were paying for shoddy goods. Eventually he conceived the idea of selling quality merchandise by direct mail. His original company modestly began by distributing a single sheet catalog listing 163 items which included small appliances such as irons, and scrubbing boards; dress shoes, and work boots, and other various apparel for adults and children alike. Later on the company sold those much appreciated "time-savers" for America's busy homemakers, including such modern marvels as washing machines and hot water heaters.

That now famous slogan: "Your Satisfaction Guaranteed or Your Money Back," quickly became a strict policy first advertised in this young entrepreneur's 1875 catalog. The company's innovative promise to refund the purchase price to any dissatisfied customer remained its central promise to patrons and a vital part of its upbeat philosophy which always wisely placed the customer's needs first. Indeed, until recently, this very sound thinking continued to be the reasoning that had long assured the company's huge success. Next to the Bible, as a matter of fact—which could be found in some form within nearly every home, and place of worship, and hotel, and library, here in America—the annual edition of the Montgomery Ward Catalog eventually became just as familiar.

As I continued to explore my interesting surroundings, the titillating combination of various interesting scents from here and there began to invade my consciousness. Standing more or less at the center of the huge well-stocked room I took a moment to try and properly decipher the various components that were being blended together to form this overall pleasant wave of fragrances which was permeating every corner of the room. Besides the pleasingly warm smell of all the leather objects dangling overhead, and the hint of coffee beans mingled with the unusual scent of raw unshelled peanuts that were being openly displayed in twin gunny sacks at the end of the protracted counter, there also appeared to be the fairly distinct odor of dill pickles that was definitely coming from somewhere in the room....

In no time at all, as I passed a door that led out back to where tall stacks of roofing shingles, huge barrels of various types of heavy-duty nails, sturdy drums of semi-solidified tar, along with various sizes of machine cut planks for building construction and repair work were carefully stored, I privately congratulated myself for my rather keen detective work. Finally locating an impressive wooden barrel that was sitting in one corner of the large room, within its rotund interior I soon discovered—as I gingerly lifted its wooden lid—that it was filled to the brim with a briny solution where a multitude of large healthy cucumbers were silently residing almost completely submerged.

Upon the counter top, being invitingly displayed just above this huge barrel of fermented vegetables, sat a single row of a half-dozen glass apothecary jars. Each contained a different brand of penny candy—small glorious pieces of hard colorful sweets—that interested me far more than the pickles ever could. As I slowly filed past these same enchanting vessels, trying to determine what sort of confection each might be holding, a stern voice from somewhere behind the counter demanded, "What business do you have here?!"

Upon hearing the question—for, truly, I had become so happily lost in my own private world of thoughts and imaginings that for some odd reason I believed myself to be alone amongst all these interesting things—the reader may well imagine how startled I instantly became when I finally found myself looking up to unexpectedly behold the countenance of a woman whose face and eyes exactly matched the unfriendliness of her tone. Indeed her undeniably disquieting eyes were exuding such extreme displeasure, as she continued to glare at me over her spectacles, that I actually forgot to answer her. Once again she felt a need to repeat her question, only this time as if there must have been something seriously wrong with me the first time around.

"How much is the candy?" I quickly retorted, trying hard to compose myself after this unwarranted verbal attack of hers. Thinking back upon that day when Cornelia Grimsley and I met for the first time, I well imagine that that seven-and-a-half-year-old urchin standing before her on that late afternoon surely had not made much of an impression. With my small undernourished presence, my somewhat comical and ill-fitting clothing—not to mention my presently bare, and dirty, and wounded feet—how could either of us have known, at that point, just how involved we would eventually be becoming in each other's lives? How could I have possibly realized that I was standing before the unkind soul who would eventually become Felix Lauder's nemesis—in all her dark and wicked glory....

This decidedly nasty woman, with her deeply entrenched preju-dicial ideas and her cruel tendencies, wore more than one face. Most children and certain animals, too, tend to be relatively excellent judges of character, even at a young age. So it was during this first encounter of ours which spontaneously produced in me such a thoroughly uncom-fortable feeling of grave mistrust and acute foreboding that whenever possible I managed to go to unusual lengths in order to avoid her com-pany. Furthermore I sincerely regret to say that even with the passing of all the years to come those initial impressions of mine, where this particular woman was concerned, would eventually prove to be all too well founded.

Veritably, over the years I was to reside in this small picturesque town, Cornelia Grimsley inevitably came to represent to me the antith-esis of all that Felix Lauder was not. According to George, as well as to other highly reputable local sources, being the consummate gossip and busybody that she just naturally tended to be, she had already become responsible for much unkind mischief.... Most certainly as day follows night, she would be living on in the future to forever mark many lives within this small community of ours—and in the most profoundly nega-tive sense.

Poor Otto Grimsley, her meek and rather mild-mannered husband, had for ages held the coveted position of mayor of the tiny hamlet of Peck's Station. However, it was a long accepted fact by everybody who lived in these parts that he acted merely as a convenient figurehead, since it was his pushy and highly domineering wife who really ran every show.

Basically, I really liked Mr. Grimsley—even from the very beginning. Whenever his wife remained absent for any length of time, it became a real cause for celebration, much as if that hour or two represented an honest to goodness holiday. During those far too infrequent times, too, when Mrs. Grimsley was committed somewhere else for a whole morning, or even just part of an afternoon, her husband naturally assumed responsibility for running the store. On such occasions I could not help but notice the stunning fact that from the moment this occurred Otto Grimsley immediately adopted a far more comfortable and pleasing posture. Actually everyone else in the store—including other patrons and each of their employees, too, would seem noticeably relieved in this same sort of endearing way—due, exclusively, to this abominable woman's absence.

Quite often I felt truly sympathetic towards this hopelessly downtrodden man who was required to live day-in and day-out with that same overbearing wife of his. In my worthy opinion, this poor henpecked individual automatically symbolized what it might be like to be a hermit crab. It became his natural inclination to forever protect himself by silently retreating within his shell when threatened in the least, and every now and then making a wary appearance whenever the coast might be clear, naturally to happily venture forth and claim for himself a bit of sunshine.

I remember particularly well, too, that there was a charming game that Otto Grimsley and I would often play together when I was still quite young. Whenever I visited the general store during those infrequent times when Otto Grimsley was alone with only his helpers present, he always took it upon himself to personally assist me. Usually George and I would go there on a fairly regular basis each early Sunday afternoon, directly after completing our chores around the farm, in order to purchase our necessary fishing supplies and to shop for my penny's worth of candy with the small coin George always slipped me.

Like a gifted comedian released upon his little stage, who spontaneously wished to entertain the young child that I once was, I never could keep from smiling as this good soul purposely affected a charming attitude of feigned wariness and pretended to stealthily scan the entire room with his open hand cupped Indian scout fashion across his now slightly wrinkled brow. He was perfectly mimicking his thorough, yet bogus, search for his indomitable wife.... Then, predictably not having discovered her whereabouts anywhere within our immediate vicinity, in a grand exaggerated manner he would wipe his forehead as he correspondingly sighed with relief. Finally, with an impish wink that literally spoke volumes, he proceeded to add yet another partial scoopful of those delectable sweets to the correct amount that had already been weighed up, just for the heck of it.

After the tiny bag was dutifully sealed, I continued to watch with immense pleasure as he chose to end this same magical game of ours by immediately holding up an index finger to his lips. Of course I automatically did the same, as if to signify our mutual acknowledgment that this simple gesture of generosity on his part was strictly forbidden. I further declare that it was in being able to occasionally overstep those unreasonable boundaries which had long ago been written in stone by his difficult wife that helped to feed this fine man's gentle and fun-loving nature, and in doing so occasionally allowed him to share with a kindred spirit such as myself that more generous and playful side of his personality.

Indeed, it must have been during special times like these that his poor soul would momentarily escape the cruel confines of the shameful box in which it was forced to dwell so much of the time. Naturally this unspoken yet mutually understood truth, which consequently inspired this remarkable interaction between adult and child, was really the key to the game's wonderful allure for both of us and with a sense of exhilaration we played it whenever possible.

Throughout the succeeding years, as I came to better understand people and also came to more fully understand life itself, I have often thought back upon this decent individual and the bitter circumstances of his life. How difficult and unfair it must have been to live most of his life with such an uncompromising and castrating partner. Yes, whenever I chance to think back upon this time in my life, I occasionally remember this good man and just as frequently continue to feel sorry for him. Certainly, too, and on more than one occasion, I have also grieved for the couple's younger son Ugo.

Cornelia and Otto Grimsley had three children. During the time of my arrival within the community of "Peck's Station," young Ugo was barely four years old. Although I cannot remember his having uttered a single word in all the years I knew him, out of all the people within that highly dysfunctional family of theirs, he and his father were the only two people whom I could ever abide in the least.

Once when the boy was older and Felix felt compelled to take the youngster under his wing—secretly, of course, in an effort to bring a little stability and happiness into the child's lonely life, he thoughtfully included him in a woodworking shop. Although the original project began casually enough as a distinctly personal family affair by involving several of my dear mentor's own children and me, it eventually also included a smattering of other interested local children.

Right away I was particularly pleased to witness an overwhelming change in our dear little Ugo. Even though he utterly refused to speak a single word to any of us during all the sessions in which we worked so patiently with him, Felix sincerely believed that at one point he actually came very close to doing so. Had we been given just a little more time with him, perhaps he might have eventually chosen to honor us by uttering his very first coherent sound.

During several of those productive albeit gloomy winter Sunday afternoons, before our harmless little ruse was finally discovered by Cornelia Grimsley and our happy and indisputably healthy interaction with the boy was permanently terminated, everyone present had a chance to briefly observe young Ugo Grimsley actually begin to blossom in the emotional sense. Truly, during those bimonthly group meetings of ours, bright rosy color seemed to magically appear in his naturally pale little cheeks. Felix and I would happily watch him lose himself to the project in which our thoughtful and caring teacher had so generously involved him. I can hardly forget, either, how he smiled so proudly every now and then as he lifted the precious object of a simply designed bird high into the air for all of us to admire; that same small piece of soft balsa wood upon which he and Felix were so diligently working.

After the would-be article was initially cut away from its originally far larger piece of scrap material and whittled down into a much more manageable size, it was soon expertly polished into shape for use as a humble paperweight. As a most professional finishing touch, too, this same wee work of art was covered on the bottom by soft green felt which remained a rather poignant reminder of the Lauder family's former hat manufacturing business. "Doc" Owens eventually concluded, after having once thoroughly examined little Ugo, that the child's inability to speak had not stemmed from a physical impairment of any kind but rather more than likely from the day-to-day stress under which the poor sweet fellow was forced to live at home.

Latisha Grimsley, on the other hand, was the couple's only daughter and their middle child. She turned sixteen sometime after I arrived in the community. If it is possible for a mother to be drawn more to one of her children than to any of the others, I was forced to conclude that this young woman remained the apple of her mother's eye in every possible sense, much to the exclusion and to the bitter emotional neglect of not only her two brothers, but to her father as well.

To this very day I shall honestly state that never again have I met anyone who suffered more from narcissism than that poor child-woman. It remains my worthy opinion that eventually she became so wrapped up in her looks and more notably within her unhealthy preoccupation with Hollywood's celluloid world of film, not to mention the more unwholesome make-believe world which the film's famous stars came to engender, that I truly believe she had significant difficulty discerning where her make-believe world ended and where the real world began.

During those fairly frequent times when George and I would briefly visit the Grimsley's store to buy fishing hooks or a length of fishing line before we headed over to the lake on any given Sunday afternoon to catch up on our fishing, there the two of us would generally find Latisha.... Invariably we would spot her sitting all by herself at one far end of the long counter of the store overtly preening in an undisguised attempt to mimic that month's outlandish clothing, or hair style, or make-up that she discovered in a recent magazine. It became her ongoing effort to consciously adopt for herself a particular attitude being openly exhibited by any one of those several much-adored sirens of Hollywood's silver screen.

When she was not fully occupied in doing this, instead she would be intently pouring over some other sort of current publication that chronicled every detail of the doings of this same particular crowd. Becoming practically obsessed to devour every bit of gossip contained within the pages of the text, all the while critically consulting the many glossy photographs therein, she would very often stop to glance at her likeness within a small hand-held mirror that she always carried on her person.

With immense fondness I readily recall a humorous incident which so adequately highlights the basic differences between the personalities of two interesting people.... On one particular Sunday visit to the Grimsley's store, merely days after I went to live with the Lauder family, in fact, George and I remained standing to one far side of the long counter there, thoroughly engrossed in threading a new lure my dear friend had just purchased. For many weeks during that entire past summer George managed to save a fragment of his earnings that came from his work as a lifeguard down by the lake, naturally in order to possess this same "jewel of a lure" as he called it. Latisha Grimsley, on the other hand, was busy doing something in another part of the store when we initially arrived that day. However, as soon as she caught sight of George, she immediately dropped what she was doing and quickly sauntered our way....

Within the Lauder family it was no secret that Latisha Grimsley had had a profound crush on this special member of their group. And, true to form, as usual George always managed to graciously take everything in stride. That special morning I watched with growing fascination as this mere wisp of a girl promptly went about initiating a truly amazing transformation, by instantly affecting the unmistakable attitude of one of Hollywood's preeminent "vamps." Coming towards us now, and in a low and comically sultry voice that seemed totally contrary to her basically underdeveloped and still quite innocent girlish nature, she automatically proceeded to quite literally drape herself over that same end of the counter very near to where we both were still standing at this point. Overtly batting her eyes at George, all the while crooning in a wholly suggestive manner that even I could not have possibly misinterpreted, she said, "You Lauder men sure are a handsome bunch!"

Having been initially unaware of Latisha's approach, George was at first only a little distracted by what she said. However, merely seconds after she uttered these rather engaging words of hers, I continued to observe their interaction as my best friend quickly glanced up from what he was attempting to accomplish at the moment, only to finally catch and firmly hold Latisha's eye. Without missing so much as a beat, he then answered her in his exquisitely pleasant manner, by quietly stating for the record, "Ah! Yes.... Well, my dear parents, as well as my equally dear grandparents, thank you very much for your kind words, young lady!" After taking another second or two more to pull tight a length of the fishing line with which he had been struggling all this while, he promptly went on to expound a bit more, as he quickly announced, "But you see, quite honestly, these same marvelous people have always had to accept either the credit or the blame for what you now see before you—mostly, I suppose, because I absolutely refuse to claim responsibility for any of it myself!" With this he smiled that ever-beguiling smile of his, both at Latisha and then at me. Having just completed tying the last knot in the long series of knots that were required to secure the new lure, he firmly grasped his well-used fishing pole in his left hand, as with his right he playfully slapped me across my shoulders to exclaim, "Well, sport ... if we don't hurry down to the lake, we'll surely end up coming home empty-handed!"

Right after this, as the two of us quickly made ready to part company with the now rather speechless young woman who continued to wear somewhat of a truly perplexed expression, George politely saluted to her with his free hand in a lighthearted gesture of farewell that had already become a habit with him whenever he parted company with anyone. This, of course, on that memorable day of days was also followed with a cheerful, "Good day to you, Miss Grimsley!"

Frequently studying Latisha Grimsley, as I chose to do, whenever she assisted her mother or father in assisting other customers who forever frequented their general store to purchase one thing or another, time and time again I became somewhat fascinated by the fact that she was incapable of passing any one of the various department's several large glass cases without pausing to unduly admire her reflection therein. One day two of the younger Lauder brothers and I decided to play a truly unkind trick on her, basically in order to prove the point that this obsession of hers was slowly getting out of hand.

During one exceedingly fine afternoon when Latisha was summoned by either her mother or her father to make a delivery to Mr. Balducci's barber shop next door, which was usually on a fairly regular basis to return his professional scissors that had been expertly sharpened by Otto Grimsley there in the rear of the store, my highly enthusiastic partners-in-crime and I placed a remarkably generous pile of dog poop directly along the trail that this young woman would naturally be forced to take to accomplish this end. Thinking back I actually believe that we had bets going between ourselves with respect to just how it would all end up. We bet that as always Latisha would become so preoccupied with admiring herself in the spotless plate glass store windows that she passed all along the way that eventually she simply could not fail to miss stepping into the stinky mess which we carefully arranged upon the sidewalk solely for her benefit.

Clustered secretly to one side of the abandoned station master's hut, there across the street, those other criminals and I watched and waited with bated breath as our innocent victim cheerfully departed through the front door of her parents' store that day. We continued to observe with even greater interest as she proceeded to turn right, and then to head down towards the barber shop. Wobbling slightly now upon a pair of brand-new high heels which she and her mother recently received from the mail-order catalog, true to form—and just as the others and I faithfully predicted—the proud young woman barely even made it past the windows of her family's own shop before pausing to rearrange her hair, check her lipstick, fluff up the collar of her stylish-looking dress, and finally check to see if her petticoat was at all peeking out from underneath the bottom portion of her long skirt....

What a splendid howl she gave off, only seconds later. One rather elegant-looking new shoe all but disappeared within the sumptuous mound of droppings that we cunningly left for her on the sidewalk that day. Without bothering to travel the rest of the way down the block to make her delivery, she managed instead to clutch the irregular-looking package she was carrying even closer than usual to her chest for moral support, as she hurriedly hobbled back to the general store soiled shoe in hand and loudly wailing all the way.

Children can often be wantonly cruel. True compassion and true kindness—those highly desirable character traits that tend to act as a civilizing force upon every society, are learned for the most part. Likewise, there is also much to be said in favor of the Golden Rule. Whenever I look back upon that colorful yet relatively minor event, I sometimes feel pangs of contrition with respect to my part in the meanness which transpired on that summer's day. After all it was I, more than the other two, who basically engineered the entire episode. As my guilty cohorts and I remained literally doubled over with laughter for quite some time, in fact, we were still hiding there behind the abandoned railroad station. Eventually taking turns to enthusiastically pantomime Latisha's fall from grace, by endlessly recounting every detail of the rude little farce we had perpetrated, I soon began to realize that our great mirth had come at the price of ruining someone else's pleasure.

In an attempt to partially redeem myself I could rationalize the situation by choosing to believe that my friends and I behaved as we did with the girl's welfare in mind. For example, I could state that we did it in order to teach her a lesson with respect to the importance of watching where she walked, lest she fall into a manhole one day, or perhaps experience something equally as terrible as this. But, as they say, this would be coloring the truth. The simple, rotten, unvarnished truth of the matter still remains that we were all being extremely unkind that day, and, furthermore, we thoroughly enjoyed being so. Although this negative behavior did not change the course of the world in any major way that day, for me it became a valuable lesson in my needing to develop a more mature and sensitive outlook in dealing with others.

I imagine that had we been older, and wiser, and far more amicable than we were at the time, my friends and I might have looked upon Latisha Grimsley's situation in a far more compassionate light. We might have realized that this behavior of hers, which so often tended to irritate us because it leaned so excessively towards complete self-absorption in a "comedy of manners" sense, was in fact just a way for her to escape the chronically unpleasant situation at home, very similar to the way her younger brother chose to control his own situation, and in the only way he knew how—by refusing to speak.

In a way our rather disgusting joke was responsible for having doubly wounded that day. In retrospect, and most probably in a wholly unconscious sense, I speculate that that same behavior of ours was conceived to not only punish the daughter, but also to indirectly punish the mother as well. Indeed, when I think back upon those years with the true compassion that generally comes with growing older, I occasionally find myself wondering what became of this young woman. I wonder, most of all, whether or not she ever lived to broaden her perspective of life and, in so doing, managed to ultimately discover who she really was in the end.

Without a doubt the most wholly despicable person within the entire Grimsley's family, whom I literally came to fiercely disdain in every possible way, was their older son, Shamus. For me this overbearing individual was the epitome of a bully in its worst form. Physically speaking, he was huge in stature. As a vulnerable young child and an equally vulnerable young adult, I was forever given the impression that he towered over me—and somehow always would.

Shamus was also as strong as an ox. Each spring he managed without the slightest difficulty to win every contest of strength initiated at the annual county fair. This daunting combination of tremendous physical size and strength, coupled with the fact that he possessed a notoriously brutal temper, not to mention a distinctly cruel disposition very similar to his mother's in a certain way, was essentially the basis for that abnormal fear which I endlessly harbored for him.

By far what made this whole situation even worse was that, unlike his mother, Shamus Grimsley was mentally deficient in the most ordinary sense. Actually, when you come right down to it, he was amazingly dull-witted. Having taken all this into account very early in our relationship, it was frequently this same odious figure lumbering towards me as I made my way down a street, or across a field, or anywhere else for that matter, especially when I was alone, that brought real terror to my heart. With the rudimentary instincts present within some sort of wild carnivore, somehow it always seemed within his power to actually sense my basic fear of him; to actually smell it out, in effect, thereby giving him a distinct advantage and all the more pleasure in terrorizing me whenever possible.

In an attempt to adequately sum up my perception of Shamus Grimsley, which was properly grasped immediately during our initial meeting and which had never faltered in the least during all the years I was to know him, I should further state for the record that I knew him to be the sort of mindless brute who would sit behind a barn somewhere to slowly and deliberately dismantle the wings off some helpless but-

terfly.... Indeed, I am absolutely certain that he would have greatly relished this simple accomplishment for the sake of the perverse pleasure
it endlessly gave him in being able to cruelly obliterate that which would
never be within his power to fully respect, and therefore to fully appreciate. So similar to his mother was he as a destroyer by nature that from
the moment I first laid eyes upon him, until the occasion of his abrupt
demise, I lived in continuous fear that somehow I should come to a bad
end—solely because of him.

I remember that Cornelia Grimsley showed little patience with her
elder son. Sometimes quite savagely, and far too often in the presence of
others, she would criticize and demean him. Or when in his predictable
dullness, he did not respond as quickly as she felt he should, she cuffed
him hard against his cheek with her fist, or otherwise reached for some
handy object there in the store to mercilessly clobber him repeatedly
across the shoulders and over the top of his head. This, in turn, would
naturally arouse Shamus Grimsley's substantial predilection towards
antisocial behavior. In order to get even for these reoccurring insults,
he often became obsessed to search for creative ways to vent his own
considerable frustration. Naturally in so doing he ultimately managed
to make life exceedingly difficult for others which, more or less, always
tended to include all the local butterflies, as well as young Ugo and
me.

Studying Mrs. Grimsley for the first time that day, studying her eyes,
especially, which were the mirror of her soul, and which were to remind
me always of some cunning bird of prey, I never imagined the part that
she would be indirectly playing in one thoroughly tragic scenario that
would end with the deaths of three members of our community. Those
same three special people who eventually would become so very dear
to the Lauder family and to me....

"We're getting ready to close for the day," Cornelia Grimsley was impatiently telling me. Then to answer my question she went on to inform
me, "All the confection in the jars is five cents for a quarter pound." Next,
as if to clarify the matter even further, she rudely added, "Five cents....
Five cents, mixed or not!"

As this unsavory character was speaking to me, standing there and
leaning to one side of the counter with one short squatty hand poised
matter-of-factly upon one ample hip, my right hand nervously fingered
the several coins which I was presently carrying in my deep pocket.
These meager funds were all I had to my name. They were meant to last
me and to surely be spent on more important things than candy. But for

some reason, perhaps out of a need to prove to this unfriendly individual that I was not loitering nor intentionally being any sort of a nuisance to her, I eventually withdrew the money from my pocket. Shortly after having randomly selected a coin, I reached up as far as I could and then politely placed it upon the counter that separated the two of us.

Upon witnessing this action of mine Mrs. Grimsley promptly reached down behind the counter and brought forth a small white cone-shaped paper bag. While she held a sturdy glass scooper in the air, she addressed me further by asking, "Which will it be, then?! Mixed? Or would you prefer to have all the same variety?"

"The lemon drops only, if you please," I found myself respectfully answering. Lemon drops were my favorite candy. However, had this uncommonly rude proprietress of that interesting establishment been even the slightest bit more genial, or at least more patient with me that day, I would have naturally felt brave enough to inquire about what sort of candy the other five containers held, since it was only the lemon drops with which I was familiar. Acutely studying this middle-aged woman, now, with her mousy brown hair drawn back tightly into its meager little bun there at the base of her scrawny neck, and, too, with the indelible furrows superficially etched into the corners of her thin colorless lips, adding greatly to the overall unsociable effect her frown was making upon me that day while she went about methodically retrieving a small amount of the pale yellow almond-shaped confection from its crystal jar, I realized then and there that the two of us would never be friends. And, as I silently continued to observe her, as she in turn painstakingly shook those last few pieces of the candy from the scooper into the bag frowning even more in the process, I prudently felt that it would be best for me to make my modest purchase as quickly as possible and then to just leave the premises.

After the opportunity was taken to weigh my small purchase yet one last time, no doubt to make certain that she was giving me the exact measure, and not a smidgen more, she matter-of-factly folded under the top of the bag and reached across the counter to hand it to me. With this, I thanked her and promptly turned to leave.

"Don't forget your change!" she yelled after me. Then just as I returned to the counter to hear the sound of the cash register's bell loudly calling out—and just before the machine's drawer was pushed shut, instead of politely handing the change to me, which would have been the normal thing to do under the circumstances, this highly unpleasant woman went and set the coins on the counter somewhere just out of my reach. Even with me standing there upon tip toes and blindly feeling around to properly ascertain the whereabouts of what she had returned to me, for at the time I remained far too short to be able to view the top of the counter at all, I was becoming a little embarrassed at not being able to locate those thin pieces of precious metal. During all of this prolonged effort of mine, Cornelia Grimsley merely stood by watching my difficulty with what may only be described as mild amusement. Eventually tiring of this unfair one-sided game of hers, not unlike some malicious cat toying with a helpless little mouse, she finally consented to take up the coins herself and then to literally toss them in my direction.

Frantically I scurried about searching for my valuable assets. The change initially bounced off my chest and shoulders and then quickly fell onto the wooden flooring to roll away in several different directions at the same time. No sooner did I manage to collect everything and then quickly stand up straight in order to replace the funds within my pocket for safekeeping, when I unhappily discovered this unkind soul standing directly behind me.... Quick as a flash, before I even had time to realize what was happening to me, the proprietress of that establishment actually grabbed hold of the back of the collar of my shirt. Now with my bare feet hardly touching the floor, at this point, and while the two of us were presently in the graceless process of quickly moving forward together, I found myself being hastily escorted towards the front door.

Eventually exiting the shop, I discovered that I was still clinging steadfastly to the strong cords of the sturdy cloth bag which Harry Hopkins, in his supreme kindness, had bequeathed to me earlier that day. Clutched now within my moist right hand was the smooth white paper bag filled with the sweet tartness of the lemon drops that somehow properly symbolized for me the remarkable contrast between that earlier meeting with my dear benefactor, and this more recent and far less civilized interaction inspired by this newest acquaintance of mine. It occurred to me that for a second time within a relatively short period the front door of a building was once again being promptly closed behind me and just as firmly being bolted with a loud clicking thud. And, once again, with a sense of basic dignity, I began walking away without looking back.

Normally I was not afraid of the dark. However, with the depressing reality of my needing to return to that truly dreadful house where my father was undoubtedly waiting for me, I was becoming terribly afraid. On my long walk home, while mindfully retracing the route which had taken me to Peck's Station in the first place, it finally dawned on me that I may well have something serious for which to answer. The fact remained that I had so selfishly involved myself in my lighthearted and carefree travels that day, without notifying my father of my whereabouts.

With my late arrival home like this, I tried to imagine what my father might say to me. Would he be thoroughly disappointed, or even angry, that I was so completely heedless of the time? If so, was it wise of me to be the one to set forth this sort of negative precedence so soon in our relationship? With growing apprehension I finally set my sights for home. Once again it was as though my poor heart was being weighted with a heavy stone.

That glorious and formerly friendly sun was quickly setting there to my left. Forlornly I proceeded to make my way across the growing darkness of the surrounding fields and I could see that twilight was fast approaching. A silver slit of a new moon hung ever so lightly in the clear sky above me.... Soon enough, too, a stiff brisk breeze similar to the one I experienced earlier on was rudely finding its way through the thin woven fabric of my cotton shirt and pants causing me to shiver from the cold.

While I marched along, thoughtfully contemplating my dirty bare feet that had once been happily plodding these same furrows of warmer earth, I felt myself recoiling from the unpleasant realities of what was taking place. How in the world was I going to make it through the winter without warm clothing of any kind? Without shoes, either? In a worthwhile attempt to briefly mollify my growing apprehensions, I finally reminded myself that at least I would not be going hungry for several days to come, thanks to my excellent fortune of having made a really good friend.

Standing at the moment only a short distance from the side of my father's house, emotionally taking in the sorry sight that loomed before me and trying hard to decide whether to enter through the front door or the back, I noticed that our truck remained parked exactly where we had left it. Soon I was again slowly making my way across the burr-infested lot in order to reach the front porch. Before I began negotiating the broken steps to arrive safely on the porch area above, for a few long moments more I stood staring up at the dark and forbidding place, solemnly contemplating my fate.

I actually remember thinking, quite passionately, as a matter of fact, that if a bolt of lightening were to miraculously descend from that cloudless deep velvet sky overhead and to mercifully strike me dead upon the spot—inevitably sparing me the horrible ordeal of having to endure re-entering that awful place—I should have gladly welcomed it. But such amazing things rarely occur upon demand. And so, with as much fortitude as I could possibly muster, I gingerly climbed the rickety steps out front to eventually land once again upon the more sound boards of the porch decking.

Just as before the main entrance to the house stood partially ajar. From within that otherwise totally darkened house I soon became aware of a faint glow of pale light that was shining forth from some as yet unknown source. While I ever so cautiously crossed the threshold, nearly forgetting to breathe at this point, the mystery of the light finally managed to solve itself. There, poised at the top of the stairs and mutely observing my entrance, was my father. He remained hunched over in the way I remembered him from before, with an eerie light from the glass lamp that he was holding throwing his immensely contorted shadow all along the stairwell wall....

Like a lone gargoyle, he was, precariously perched in silent greeting. Solicitously cradling the base of the object that he was holding more to his chest, no doubt in order to help stop the container of flammable liquid from vibrating so dangerously, I could plainly see that his violent tremors were beginning to re-emerge.

I continued to observe the man, fairly spellbound, as with noted difficulty he slowly began to make his descent. All the while he uttered not a solitary word. Since there was no banister on either side of the staircase to which he might cling for support, my father made his way down the dangerous passageway using his own unique method of locomotion. He accomplished this by first leaning against one wall with his right shoulder and then by more or less sliding along as he made a point to avoid certain areas of the badly rotting stairs. After he safely arrived at the landing where I still remained carefully studying him, he chose to slowly drag himself past me and promptly headed off in the direction of the kitchen....

Apparently this time he remembered who I was. Although he did not seem angry in the least that I remained absent for the entire day, I could sense that a certain irritability was quickly surfacing. Undoubtedly this negative feeling was related to his need for strong drink, since his hands, as well as the rest of him, were slowly beginning to shake rather alarmingly. Not long after he disappeared to my right, from somewhere in the darkness just beyond where the circle of light ended and the darkness began, I distinctly heard him say with a gratingly hoarse voice, "Come here, quickly!"

In response to this staunch edict of his, I hurriedly placed the sack Mr. Hopkins had given me upon the bottom step, along with the small paper bag containing the candy that I recently purchased. Following now in the direction of my father's voice, I could not help wondering all the while whether this was part of what Fate had destined for me; basically, to always to be trailing after this man, whenever he saw fit to command me as he was again doing.

Directly behind the door which separated the foyer from the tiny kitchen area, and superbly well-hidden within the supportive wall which was part of the staircase itself, was located a small walk-in cabinet. This clever hiding place would have nearly been impossible to detect had one not been specifically looking for it. Without delay my father opened the interesting little door and entered. I further speculated that had any other adult attempted to do this same thing the person would naturally have been obliged to stoop low in order to accomplish this end. However, owing to my father's peculiar physical handicap, as he preceded me into this little out-of-the-way place, I noticed that his already stooped shoulders nary grazed the top of the short entryway.

With the growing familiarity that came with the sound of my companion's scratchy and impatient voice, I heard him say, "Hold the lamp here for me.... Take care that you don't touch the globe—it's hot!" Then, with my having done exactly as my father requested, he went on to further command, "Bring the light lower, damn you!"

Soon I was dutifully squatting beside him, lamp in hand, silently watching him take out a small pocket knife. As he exposed the clean blade which shown brightly by the light of the glass container that I was presently holding, he promptly wedged the sharp tip of the weapon into a thin slit in between two wide wooden boards within the flooring. Without much resistance one short board finally gave way and ended up in his hand. Then as my father directed me to bring the light even closer, in order to see within the vacant space below, right away he reached down and withdrew a badly rusted and much battered old coffee can.

With me continuing to do my part, my extremely irritable companion went on to quickly pry off the container's lid, finally exposing a large wad of some sort of folded paper. His hands were shaking rather pathetically now, as he soon withdrew the entire contents of the can. Being displayed before my amazed eyes was more money than I had ever seen. More money, in fact, than I imagined any one person ever had the right to possess.

"This is to be our secret," my father was cautiously warning me. As usual his large hatless head was cocked abnormally to one side, in that decidedly odd manner of his, in order for his eyes to be able to find mine. Soon he went on to tell me, "Never speak about this to anyone else! Nor show to another living soul what I'm showing you here tonight… Swear to it!"

"I swear." I found myself loudly whispering.

I could see that my father was growing more and more agitated with every passing moment. As before—in the truck, heavy telltale drops of perspiration had already formed upon his brow. While he quickly withdrew several limp worn bills from the massive amount still being clutched within his firm grasp, he handed them to me, telling me in that same highly cautious tone, "Spend only what you need. Don't ever waste what I give you, do you understand?!"

My eyes continued to hold his with an unwavering stare, but all I could do at this point was to nod my head in mute acknowledgment of these simple rules to the special pact we were now forming between us. My troubled companion went on to further state, with a noticeably solemn sense of profound conviction that undoubtedly was the result of firsthand knowledge gained with respect to the subject, "There are people in this world who'd kill for just a fraction of what I've shown you here tonight—do you understand me!?" Next, in order to enlighten me as to what he further expected of me, he went on to say, "I stay out late every night, and eventually come home to sleep most mornings. You must learn to look after yourself! Never depend on me for anything—do you understand?"

"I understand," I whispered back, just as the taut muscles within my small neck and throat slowly began to contract rather painfully.

Quickly the lid was replaced upon the battered container that held all this treasure. However, before it was actually put back into the opening within the floor, the man standing next to me cautioned me even further by stressing, "Always remember to replace the lid tightly on the can…. Always! Rats will eat anything—even paper, if you let them!"

As the unobtrusive little cabinet door was finally closed off once more, my father noticed that I was not holding the lamp that he had entrusted to me in a properly level manner. Reaching over to abruptly right the base for me, he finally declared in a wholly angry manner, "Take care, too, that you don't upset the lamp! This old place would burn like a tinderbox with any sort of mishap like that."…

With these dire words of warning echoing within my brain, my father was gone from my side. While I stood momentarily planted where he left me, still holding the glass object whose soft glow and warmth was still bathing my face, I could hear the unnatural sound that this most unusual man was making as he proceeded to negotiate his way down the front steps of the house. By the time I safely stowed the money that was given to me deep within one pocket of my knickers and began walking towards the front door, I heard the truck's motor being noisily cranked up as the vehicle was eventually put into gear.

Motionlessly standing there upon the front porch now, all the while still clinging to the fragile warmth of the lamp, I noticed that the heavily weathered wooden swing began to creak ever so slightly there upon its rusted hooks just behind me in answer to the healthy breeze as it continued to endlessly play about the exterior of our old house. Against my will I was being rendered a mere distant spectator, as I thoughtfully watched my father drive off towards the right. After he reached the black topped road that ran past our place, he quickly sped up and continued on his way at a wholly reckless pace. In what surely seemed like less than a moment, I rather dispassionately witnessed the old vehicle's single tail light finally disappear from view.

Having grown weary of standing in that one place I took the initiative to safely stow the valuable lamp upon the floor, adjacent to the wall of the house, and promptly climbed upon the wooden swing to merely sit for a while. With the ever-present movement of the cool autumn wind as it continued to playfully whiffle my hair to and fro, an indescribably formidable depression began to slowly descend upon me. This wholly unhealthy feeling began to literally permeate every pore of my entire being. It was true that no one was hurting me, at least in any overt sense these days. For this, naturally, I was most grateful. But the currently oppressive loneliness which I was feeling at the moment, not to mention all the terrible loneliness which I wholeheartedly believed would be mine in the future, began to rest so heavily upon my young heart that I finally began to weep.

After a time, however, I remembered all the valuable treasure that I hastily left behind on the bottom step in the foyer. The pleasurable thought of the marvelous apples and cheese was making me hungry again. Drying my moist eyes with one ragged cuff from the sleeve of my thin cotton shirt, I gingerly stepped down from the swing and very carefully collected the lamp to re-enter the house.

Even before I chanced to lift the glass and metal fixture that I was carefully cradling to one side, naturally to benefit my being able to better see the sack that I trusted still remained sitting where I left it, my keen eye caught the slight movement of something on the nearby step.

Instinctively raising the trusty globe ever higher to allow the radius of beneficial light to more helpfully expand to a point where the entire portion of half a dozen lower steps might be more clearly exposed to view, I unexpectedly happened upon the presence of a huge gray rat....

I confess that although I was greatly startled at first to find the impressive rodent sitting there atop my much prized possessions, after the initial shock quickly wore off I could actually feel myself growing hot with increasing anger at his offensive intrusion. Now, with the menacing presence of that impudent little beast, somehow the fragile equation of how I was to survive from day to day seemed threatened. Abruptly I realized that there was a distinct possibility that I might soon lose the only things in the world that definitely belonged to me.

My mind literally raced on in a desperate effort to formulate a plan to rid myself of the nuisance. Not unlike a criminal being caught red-handed in the act of stealing, with my bright interrogation lamp poised overhead, the cunning rascal's jet black beady eyes literally glowed by the light I was holding. Furthermore he seemed to be telling me that he was as fond of apples and cheese as I was.

Currently the unfortunate cone-shaped paper bag, which earlier had protectively enveloped my lemon drops, lay badly ruptured nearby. The majority of its contents was haphazardly scattered along the surface of the bottom step, as well as upon the floor directly below. Undoubtedly not the sort of fellow that suffered the pangs of a sweet tooth like me, this crafty usurper had obviously moved on to claim the substantial booty inside my bag instead.

Mentally and emotionally I was preparing myself for the ensuing fight which was not going to be easy. As I remained steadfastly observing this unannounced guest of ours, I noticed right away that he was already far more well-fed than I. And, as my worthy challenger and I briefly remained in a state of suspended animation—both of us critically appraising one another while at the same time carefully plotting our next move, I could just tell that it was going to be a long standoff for both of us, unless I could somehow manage to obtain and then keep the upper hand.

After all, that keen and highly laudable process of evolution whose unwavering doctrine maintains the survival of the fittest had definitely prepared my adversary for the battle at hand. With our having initially startled each other, the visitor soon seemed to lose any sense of fear of me whatsoever. In a way, I had to admire his cleverness and his cunning—his splendid ability at being able to look after himself in his daily attempt to survive. Perhaps the two of us had more in common than I was willing to admit. As the intelligent rat finally grew tired of this very minor nonthreatening sort of confrontation which was taking place at the moment, he soon began to busy himself by attacking my cloth bag with his razor-sharp teeth.

With this totally unforgivable behavior of his, I instantly became furious. In a state of real panic now, not knowing what else to do, I carefully set the lamp to one side of the front door. This more or less allowed the somewhat sparse light to be continuously projected upon the intruder. Properly seized with a highly original plan, I promptly flew into a frenzied little dance step—hopping up and down, and then from side to side, all the while making loud hooting noises in a desperate attempt to buy a little more time....

In the end, however, my quick spastic movements, along with my rather savage elocutionary technique, were basically received in a noticeably unimpressed manner, judging from the fact that the formidable-looking rodent only managed to briefly cease his biting effort to casually glance my way before returning to his pilfering efforts. Naturally without shoes upon my feet this same routine, which was earnestly calculated to frighten the pest away, ended up being far less than it should have been.

Suddenly I became heroically inspired by the remembrance of that seatless chair waiting nearby within the parlor. While I left the lamp where it was, I swiftly turned the corner to grope around for what I perceived would eventually aid me in my forthcoming battle. Returning to the steps with the frame of the chair soundly in hand, I began to wildly gesture with it in a continuous back and forth lunging motion, each time nearly rapping the little beast upon its head on numerous occasions. Then at long last, with a begrudging air of defeat, my worthy opponent jumped from the step and raced around the corner to disappear somewhere in the next room.

Hurriedly I took the necessary time to thoroughly examine my special present which my new friend had given me. I would be obliged to throw away the spoiled candy that lay all about my feet—this, of course, was a given. Certainly, too, from my critical point of view, this particular minor loss was not really something I would have any trouble living with, owing to the reality that such unpleasant memories still lingered from its purchase. Without a doubt, though, I should have become literally heartbroken if my precious sack, along with its contents of valuable food, had been ruined as well.

Carefully passing my hands all over the cotton fabric, and then taking a brief moment more to thoroughly consult the long cords which
were an important part of the handy little object, I could see that no real
damage was done in the end. Thankfully, everything remained pretty
much in tack. Of course, from now on I would be forced to consider the
presence of this other house guest in the future, and not court disaster
again by being so careless with my things.

I reclaimed my precious sack and promptly draped it comfortably
over my left shoulder for safekeeping. Carefully collecting each and every piece of the brightly-colored candy that had been wantonly spread
about the place, and therefore ruined in the process, I momentarily
stepped outside to properly discard it. Then I wadded up what was
left of the little paper bag and picking up the lamp walked over to the
potbellied stove in the parlor to place the refuse inside. Perhaps with a
bit of kindling this same trash might one day help to engage a superior
fire that would eventually warm this part of the house when the real
scourge of winter finally arrived.

My supper that night consisted of more apples and cheese. Feast-
ing upon these welcome gifts I remained contentedly swinging back
and forth upon the comfortable two-seater there on the front porch.
Eventually finishing enough food to properly satisfy myself I once again
claimed the glass lamp to enter the house. Since my father had already
departed for the evening, I felt that here was a chance to salve my curiosity by finally concluding that morning's expedition which earlier I was
not brave enough to continue.

In climbing the stairs that led to the second floor, I followed my father's prudent example and walked along the far left side of each step,
essentially hugging the supporting wall—much as the rat had done
when making its escape into the parlor. Naturally this was a conscious
effort on my part to keep from injuring myself, since along the way there
were four broken fragments of wood which now merely hinted at the
steps that once must have existed. The sparse covering of these far lesser
boards had evolved into sharp rotting protrusions of dank wood instead,
and flared out indiscriminately to barely cover the blackness below.

After arriving at the top landing I realized with moderate interest
that the second floor of this rickety old house consisted merely of a single
sparsely-appointed room. Remembering back to that time I imagine that
it closely resembled what could have passed for a monk's retreat—or, on
a far less positive note, perhaps a prison cell....

There between two windows whose soiled and tattered shades were each drawn down as far as they could reach, in order to keep out the rest of the world, I suspected, stood an old makeshift bed—a cot, really, exactly the sort a soldier might sleep upon. Directly across from this sat an old chest of drawers that was unusually short and squatty in design. The top of this piece of furniture was totally clean in appearance; completely devoid of any of the normal articles that one might conceivably find under the circumstances, save for a large looking glass whose mirror was cracked in several places thereby gravely distorting the image of my face as I peered into it.

However, tucked securely into one bottom corner of this damaged looking glass, I quickly spied a solitary black and white photograph. Like a magnet, I felt powerfully drawn to it.... While I allowed myself the liberty of respectfully removing the article from its resting place, there by the soft light of the lamp that I was dutifully carrying I made it my primary business to carefully study every aspect of this personal memento which continued to totally engross my attention for quite some time.

One day, years from that time, this same snapshot would prove to be of great significance to me. Posing for the camera as they stood knee-deep in snow were five young soldiers leaning against a badly battered tank which loomed rather ominously behind them. It was plain enough to see that this particular vehicle of war was hopelessly damaged and that each young man looked uncomfortably cold, in spite of the fact that they were all dressed in identical helmets and long woolen coats....

I was fascinated, as well, to observe that four of the boyish-looking men were huddled more closely together, smiling in spite of their apparent discomfort. Each of them was brandishing an impressive weapon which incorporated a sharp dagger-like protrusion attached to the end of the gun's muzzle. Standing slightly apart from them, however, more off to himself with his hands in his pockets, was the fifth infantryman who wore a far more serious expression than did the others and who I could now see bore a striking resemblance to my father.

Although all the men were bundled up and wearing their heavy garb to protect themselves from the inclement weather, I could still tell that each of them was standing tall and proud, with my father more or less towering a good head above everyone else. It was my father—of this I was certain. I would know those enigmatic eyes anywhere. Indeed, not only were they the same unfathomable eyes which seemed so serious for the young man that he was at the time, but in many ways they seemed to match the same distant eyes which now had grown even more breath-takingly sad and even more lost in such deep personal pain....

Was my father wounded sometime later on during this same conflict? Continuing to meticulously study each and every detail of the photograph, it was obvious to me that during this particular time of his life, at least, his body looked remarkably strong and healthy and did not at all resemble the grotesquely contorted figure that he eventually became.

Could such a thing have been the cause of his troublesome physical infirmity? And what might have become of these same companions of his; these same youthfully handsome lads in the picture who, like him, seemed to have had everything for which to live? These same brave young men, who obviously chose to place their individual lives upon the line and, in the process, found themselves dutifully bowing to their nation's most sacred of causes, had they ultimately left behind heartbroken family members and friends to grieve for them? Or, like my father, had these equally noble comrades-in-arms all managed to survive in the end?

With these significant thoughts of mine which were naturally being inspired by that single photograph, there arose in me many other questions which I had so wished to ask my father. For example, would there perhaps ever come a time when the two of us would feel comfortable enough to share these important thoughts? Undoubtedly my father was a man filled with many secrets. Would he inevitably be able to learn to trust me enough and to care for me enough to one day be able to help me put together the various pieces of the obviously complex puzzle of his life; and in so doing not only help me eventually learn who he really is, but one day also allow me to more easily come to know who I am?

Long ago I learned that one cannot truly love that which one does not in great part truly comprehend. True regard for another, true respect for their person, as well as for their ideas, is based upon a sound and on-going process of patient understanding. Likewise, true understanding is based upon one's fundamental willingness to openly share the truth. It was with these important thoughts that I reluctantly replaced the special item which I only temporarily borrowed. In the end I carefully wedged the small picture back between the damaged glass and the badly flaking wooden frame of the mirror, exactly where I found it. Somehow the moment had profoundly touched me, as if my having accidentally stumbled upon this bit of critical information—this small fragment of truth, in other words, had already helped clarify certain things about my father in my own mind.

Even at this early point in our relationship to only be able to speculate upon the personal drama of my father's earlier life, which had undoubtedly helped mold him into the man he eventually became, was a real start in the right direction. Having deeply pondered this rather poignant reality, I soon found myself slowly growing less afraid of this person with whom I was at least biologically connected. Suddenly the unusual man who sired me no longer seemed merely a malformed phantom whose dire presence caused me great discomfort and dread. Fortuitously happening upon that small unexpected treasure, as I had, became for me a tiny privileged window into his past. Indeed, that rare moment ultimately lent me a wholly new and far more positive prospective with regard to him. This significantly reassuring fact somehow both pleased and comforted me a good deal.

Beside the antique chest was a closet. As I cautiously opened it and then stepped within, I initially thought it to be empty, save for an extremely dust-ridden uniform which was hanging to one far side upon a long metal bar. Close by my feet, however, and scattered all around the flooring of this small storage place was also an impressive array of empty liquor bottles which had obviously been haphazardly discarded. Beyond all this I eventually discovered a narrow straw-stuffed mattress that was loosely rolled up and covered with a thick pea-soup colored blanket.

Upon closer inspection the bedding seemed clean enough but incredibly dusty. Located directly within its center was inscribed some sort of an insignia. The old mattress, too, after I carefully rolled it open, looked a bit moth-eaten. A pesky rat, or perhaps merely a squadron of hungry moths, chewed little holes here and there within the heavy cotton seersucker material of its covering. Because of this small fragments of telltale threads of dry straw stuck out from various places. I further speculated that the mat's stuffing must have made an excellent nest for some cleaver usurper in the past.

Having not wished to intrude in any manner upon my father's need for privacy, I decided instead to make my own comfy spot downstairs in the parlor. Besides with winter coming I just could not imagine a more choice spot than lying upon this new-found mat, as well as one day in the not-too-distant future basking comfortably next to the much coveted warmth of the stove.

After I safely anchored the glass lamp at the top of the stairs, in order to throw the light where I most required it, I attempted first to carry the substantially heavy blanket down below where it would eventually service my needs. Then, as well, I struggled even more to carefully manipulate the cumbersome mattress down past the dangerous areas of the stairway, only to finally arrive safely with it upon the landing in the foyer below. All through my laborious efforts that evening, as I huffed and puffed along, I promised myself that I should be prepared to fight any number of rats in order to be able to establish a viable space for myself in this house.

Before I knew it I found myself spreading the old mattress over a portion of the porch railing out front. I then soundly beat it upon both sides, trying hard to rid it of all the dust.

In no time, I managed to create a substantially comfortable little haven for myself there upon the wide open porch. I simply refused to be shut away in that horrible house, at least for the time being. Certainly when the weather finally changed for the worse and the stove was eventually brought into working condition, and above all after I finally reckoned with my acquaintance—the rat—by eventually discovering where he managed to enter our house, then I should naturally feel happier to claim the parlor as my future living quarters.

Cleverly, though, so as not to run the risk of attracting more four-legged opponents which might raid my traveling sack, causing me to possibly lose everything for good, I decided to place my precious possessions within the potbellied stove for safekeeping. Opting to keep the paper money which my father had recently given to me within one deep pocket, along with the scant remaining change from my trip, I eventually reclined upon the lumpy mattress and promptly covered myself with the heavy green blanket.

How exhausted I soon discovered I was. With that rather pleasant creaking sound that the nearby swing continued to make while it sang me its unusual lullaby, and with the cool refreshing wind blowing all around me, I turned to briefly glance up at the moon and the stars as they in turn continued to smile down upon me from the heavens above. Shortly I closed my eyes and began to remember all that had been accomplished that day....

All in all I sincerely felt that it had been a good day, as days go. Not only had I made a valuable new friend, but I managed to win a small victory over a very large rat. Having recalled all this to mind with a healthy yawn I was beginning to feel rather proud of myself.

And, as I restlessly dreamed a dream that night, I was to have been forever marked by the astonishingly memorable vision of Cornelia Grimsley as she rode atop an impressive military tank, traveling helter-skelter fashion across a vast barren wasteland that stretched endlessly on, and on, for as far as the eye could see.... In one hand, like some larger-than-life Wagnerian characterization, she was vaingloriously brandishing a bloodied bayonet, all the while being pursued by legion upon loyal legion of squeaking, jumping, biting rodents.

7.

DURING THE NIGHT a gentle frost came to decorate the wild weeds that were growing all around our yard. Yesterday's brisk wind, too, had turned even more unfriendly, as I was about to immediately discover upon awaking from my camp-out on the front porch. Right away I could tell that bathing was not going to be a pleasure.

Sprinting through the downstairs of the house with the keen thought of making my way out back to relieve myself, and then possibly washing up for the day, I discovered that the back kitchen door remained unlocked just as I left it on the previous morning. As I struggled yet again to open this partition and then to jauntily step through the screenless outer door, I instantly spied a large cardboard box sitting in plain view. As a matter of fact, the huge mysterious object was positioned in such a manner, there directly upon the top step, it practically blocked my way down into the yard below. I was thinking: How can this be? I knew for certain that the thing had not been there yesterday....

Slowly approaching the unexpected vision, as if by touching it I might prove conclusively that it was real and not just an extension of my unusual dream of last night, I initially attempted to push it a fraction with the toes of one foot but found right off that it was far too heavy for this. Fairly overcome with a tremendous sense of curiosity, and completely forgetting about what had originally brought me out back in the first place, I eventually grasped the top panels of this beguiling entity and slowly proceeded to open it....

Suddenly it became a thousand Fourth of July evenings, all bunched into one. Within this miraculous package I eventually discovered piece upon incredible piece, and item upon incredible item, of all the marvelous clothing that any needy child could ever desire. With a sense of genuine awe, or rather more in a mild state of shock, really, I proceeded to carefully unpack all that I could only suppose had been left there for me at the back of our house on that extraordinary morning.

Carefully wrapped in coarse brown paper and then solicitously tied up with a large bow of red paper ribbon were thick bulky hand-knit sweaters—half a dozen, at least. And two pairs of corduroy knickers where someone had purposely sewn neat little leather patches onto the knees.... How delighted I was to find that they looked as though they might actually fit for a change.

And there were shoes! Goodness, gracious.... Wondrous shoes that must have been worn before for several deep scuff marks could still be detected along their front and sides, even though the minor defects had been carefully polished over. Thank God each pair seemed far roomier than my previous pair. Their relatively unusual design, basically, was one where the vamp continued up beneath the top and then lapped over it from the sides in what was referred to as a modified "blucher" style. Certainly by doubling my socks, which were also being so thoughtfully provided for me, these critical articles of attire might prove to work out quite well. Naturally, with all this more than comforting knowledge, the reader can just imagine how ecstatically happy I was at the moment.

More towards the bottom of the box, now, there was an amazing woolen jacket. It was the sort which incorporated a high collar, as well as a luxuriously thick lamb's wool lining. Eventually I discovered several pairs of gloves. And, too, a brightly colored woolen cap that bore leather panels cleverly designed to cover one's ears for warmth. Wrapped separately in heavy tissue paper at the very bottom of the sumptuous container were several sets of heavy long johns that would undoubtedly be put to good use right away. Lastly, believe it or not, I discovered a pair of bright yellow rubber galoshes into which I immediately stepped and proudly began to march around the decking in an exhilarating surge of playfulness.

Goodness! Who in the world was I to thank for this overwhelming act of generosity?! Perplexed now beyond belief, while I slowly dressed myself for the day in several items carefully selected from the substantial pile of clothing that lay strewn all around the deck, a genuine feeling of inner-warmth and real happiness enveloped me with every layer of clothing I applied.

Thoughtfully reviewing in my mind every conceivable possibility of who might have been responsible for my new wardrobe, in a short time I easily narrowed it down to three people: my father, Mr. Hopkins, and the exceedingly rude woman I met at the general store late yesterday afternoon.... After all these were the only people I knew here in town.

Right off the bat, however, without even a second thought I immediately discounted the proprietress of the local emporium. At any rate
there was absolutely no need to think for a moment that she might be
capable of such kind behavior. Then, of course, there was my father, but
I felt strongly that this just was not the sort of thing he would think to
do. What was it he told me last night, before he left? Something about
not counting on him for anything?

Finally owing to the more or less infallible process of elimination,
I came to think hard upon my new friend, Mr. Hopkins.... Although I
sincerely believed that he was certainly someone who was generous
enough for a major gift like this, for some unexplainable reason I automatically tended to negate this initial theory of mine by having chosen
instead to erroneously believe that he was childless. Accepting the basic
premise that he might well have had children, or grandchildren, for that
matter, who were in essence my real benefactors where the clothing was
concerned, had not as yet congealed within my brain. I did feel obliged,
however, to some day make it my business to finally discover the answer
to this puzzling question of how my splendid box came to be.

But standing at the moment upon the decking of the back porch, and
presently being far well-dressed enough to venture forth into that brand
new day, I was enthusiastically acknowledging that once again the day
belonged entirely to me. Yesterday proved to be most interesting. I had
not the slightest regret about anything that ultimately happened. So,
with this thought acting as a sort of guiding light, in effect, I decided to
proceed onward to systematically discover even more about the interesting little community in which I had come to live.

The quaint yet deserted cemetery across the way sparked my curiosity next. Fitted now with the grand warmth of my excellent new clothing,
and taking up my cloth bag upon my shoulder, as before, I headed out
into the brisk windy sunlit morning, pledging all the while to experience
all that I could that day.

However, before I crossed the road to explore the small burial
ground with its tiny chapel that was situated at its center, I stood for a
few moments at the end of the long gravel driveway that led up to the
attractive farmhouse nearby. Neither yesterday nor today did anyone
seem to be about the place. I noticed, too, with genuine admiration, how
well-kept everything seemed to be. Something deep within me was
urging me to have a look around, but I fought the idea. Although I was
an extremely curious person by nature, I was not a snoop in any sense
of the word, so I decided in the end to forego any hint of impropriety

with regard to the subject of trespassing and headed directly across the road instead.

Standing before the huge black wrought-iron double doors of the cemetery gate which remained closed at the moment, I felt a bit intimidated at the prospect of having to wrestle with their sheer size and weight. In order that I might enter the place and be able to have a proper look around, I opted to walk around the outside perimeter of the grounds to merely explore a little, feeling that this is where I might be forced to remain. Presently though, and much to my pleasant surprise, as I arrived at the southwest side of the small compound, I found an open spot there in the fence where a couple of the tall spires were missing. And so, without further ado, I took the bold initiative and stepped inside....

Covering the entire area of this most peaceful of places did not take very long. As I continued to respectfully meander about the various graves that were placed here and there in no particular pattern, I stopped every now and then to gently trace with my fingers some of the deeply etched letters and numerals of the more interesting headstones.... Very soon I found myself standing upon tiptoe at the base of one of the deeply recessed windows of the chapel attempting to have a peek at what lay within, but found that the design of the little church was such that the windows were placed fairly high off the ground. Rounding the building, next, I came at last upon a set of wooden double doors. Trying the appropriate one in hopes of entering the building, with much satisfaction I found it unlocked and finally went inside.

During these earlier years of our country's history, it was a reassuring fact that folks who lived in the more rural regions rarely found a need to secure their homes, or automobiles, or other personal possessions in any manner. Neighbor knew neighbor; and each stranger one chanced to meet was perceived as one's perspective friend. Somehow all this was extremely comforting.

It was not such an outlandish occurrence either, back in those days, after one found oneself in a position of selling a home or farmstead that at the very last moment when the time came to ceremoniously hand over the front door key to the new owner, it suddenly became necessary to make a hasty unscheduled trip to the local hardware store. Owing to the fact that the original set of keys had rarely ever been used during a period of some thirty or forty years, a replacement set of new keys and new locks were consequently purchased and installed if the new owners so desired.

During those previously far more gentle decades, too, most citizens everywhere took great pride in possessing a basic integrity which was carefully handed down from generation to generation. Immense pleasure was taken in one's family name, for instance, an extremely valuable concept where an individual not only honored himself in the present, but consciously continued to honor all the previous generations of members of the same group that had come before him. For the sake of posterity, no less, it remained one's overt intention to keep the ball rolling by carefully instructing one's offspring in this same identical manner, in order that family honor might survive and perhaps even flourish way into the future.

Naturally this particular mind set helped to create a far more positive behavior pattern in general. On a daily basis decent treatment was due to each and every individual. With regard to these mutually important issues, more often than not it became the custom to conduct one's daily business on a promise sincerely made followed by a firm handshake to seal any bargain.

When a neighbor's barn or home accidentally burned to the ground, there was always dependable help on the way. Or when a farmer was cursed, as so often happened, with unseasonably bad weather that decimated a season's crops and therefore unexpectedly plunged that family into a state of economic hardship where its members would be sufficiently denied adequate means to financially make it through the year, naturally it would be the consistently loyal commitment of one's neighbor that would eventually see this man and his family through the hard times.

People possessed a particular empathy for others that so sadly seems to be missing these days. Friend could forever count upon their friend. Frequently one found that one could even count on those individuals who were in the beginning mere acquaintances. So often, too, stranger would frequently aid stranger in a gesture that enriched both parties in the end, since most individuals had relatively little difficulty placing themselves in their neighbor's circumstances. Because of this it naturally became rather easy to become morally bound to that other person in the name of compassion.

The interior of the small chapel, I was soon to discover, was incredibly stark in design. Because of this it immediately became very beautiful to me. Only half a dozen simple wooden benches had been constructed to accommodate visitors. Quietly I took my place at the very rear of the room, in order to sit and to meditate upon the impressions that were forming from all the stimuli around me....

Early morning sunlight was pouring through the undecorated window at the very front of the chapel, softly bathing everything in clarity and brightness and lending a certain beatific quality to the moment. Normally I was not particularly fond of churches. As the reader might surely imagine, Reverend Pouley had thoroughly ruined any interest for me in this area.

But on that particularly beautiful day, as I remained sitting there by myself in the tiny chapel, I began to feel genuinely comforted and at peace. Of course it would be much later on with the great benefit of hindsight that I would come to relive this moment in time. Likewise, I would be arriving at the conclusion that that same starkness, as well as the perception of quiet strength which this same spiritual fortress exuded, were surely representative of the strength and basic fervor for living that was endlessly engendered within the hearts and the minds of many generations of noble citizens who had peopled this rural community. Looking back what was being felt that day was surely the genuine no-nonsense, non-artificial aspect synonymous with the pioneering spirit of European immigrants who deeply valued religion and found that by incorporating it into their daily lives, from cradle to grave, essentially, that they were providing for themselves and their families the necessary sustenance and meaningful meaning which would help guide them through the rigors and challenges that living forever demands.

Eventually rising to leave the tiny chapel, I turned and walked directly towards the back of the building and out through the double doors to finally secure them behind me. I decided to sit for a little while upon one of the steps out front and to seriously contemplate with a growing reverence the unfathomable milieu of the present. Soon the playful wind began cavorting with several newly fallen leaves, slowly blowing them across an area of vacant ground not far from where I was sitting.... At this point in time how could I have ever imagined just how important this small plot of sacred ground would eventually become to me? How could I have possibly guessed that several of those special people whom I would come to truly love and revere with all my heart would one day be buried here?

There the innocent child sat, knowing not what life held in store for him; not comprehending, in the slightest manner, the significant fact that real joy and real sorrow remain the twin sides of that same amazing coin of Life.... And unbeknownst to him, as well, very soon he should be experiencing both in very great measure.

After I left the small cemetery behind, I purposely chose to walk in the opposite direction that I took yesterday by following along the blacktopped road that ran between the burial ground and the attractive farm across the way. Back then Wisconsin, as well as the entire rest of our country for that matter, had a whole lot of wide open spaces. As I continued to plod happily along, I slowly began to think that maybe I made an error in judgment by having chosen to travel this way, for already I had been walking for an amazingly long time without having run into another living soul, or farmstead, or anything else.

Shortly, though, I began to hear the distinct sound of some sort of noisy vehicle; noisier, in fact, than my father's own truck, as it was making progress towards me on the same road. That highly unusual sound was coming from behind me, so I prudently stopped, and turned, and stepped off the road, in order that I might not be run over.

A-ooo-gah! A-ooo-gah! was the unforgettable sound that I was now hearing, as if someone was thoughtfully heralding their own arrival in this rather unique manner. In the nick of time, as I quickly removed myself from the road, an early model Ford Coupe came sputtering along over the crest of the hill which I had just negotiated. As the driver of this little vehicle unexpectedly spotted me quietly standing there, he soon cruised to a full stop, just a few paces directly in front of me.

Both windows of the funny-looking little car were rolled down. An elderly man who was wearing a formal-looking black suit which was noticeably worn and rather crumpled at the moment leaned over to address me in his easygoing West Virginia drawl, as he politely inquired, "Where ya headed, son?" Seeing my thoroughly perplexed expression when I chanced to see a chicken sitting in the car's snug back seat, there directly behind him, the driver went on to ask in a totally nonplused manner, "Could I give ya a lift into town?"

The antique car itself seemed to be held together by nothing more than a hope and a prayer. Although I distinctly remember hearing the polite questions being asked of me, I still could not seem to take my eyes off the small Rhode Island red as she sat rather comfortably in the rear of the automobile. Rest assured that this was one of the strangest sights I had ever seen. Every now and then this unusually composed little bird would give off a modest little clucking sound, and although I noticed right away that she did not seem the least bit bothered that I was standing there completely amazed by her presence, she in turn was beginning to eye me just as suspiciously as I undoubtedly must have remained eyeing her....

In truth I was not the least bit fond of chickens—or roosters, either, for that matter. Actually it would be fair to state that I harbored a genuine fear of those diminutive feathered creatures. During one of my previous stints, where one of the families with whom I was briefly placed as an even younger child owned an immense chicken raising operation, there occurred a frightening incident which I believed at the time had marked me for life—and in more ways than one.

As it happened at the highly impressionable young age of about three, or possibly four, one day I wandered unattended into one of the many pens searching for eggs, just the way I observed several of the grown-ups doing time and time again. No sooner had I entered the confines of the large roost where a number of fat and fairly contented looking hens were dutifully sitting about, doing what chickens naturally seem to do best, from out of nowhere a pesky and highly irritated rooster decided to fly at me and to brazenly attack my head over and over again with its sharp beak and talons.

Instinctively I valiantly strove to protect myself with one arm, as with the other I vainly attempted to fend off the nasty beast all the while slowly backtracking in a rather desperate effort to make my way back across the yard towards the wire gate through which only moments earlier I had so foolishly entered. I just managed to literally stumble out of the difficult situation and then to swiftly bolt the rickety door behind me. Finally, as if to add insult to injury, my caregivers at the time offered little condolences on my behalf as they were obliged to wash and dress my multiple scratches and scrapes, severely admonishing me all the while.

"Oh, that's my traveling companion, Zelda,..." the driver of the car was matter-of-factly telling me. "She won't hurt you. Just ignore her, and climb into the front seat, here, with me!"

This is how "Doc" Owens and I initially met. When I remember back to that day I still cannot help smiling from ear to ear. What a marvelous man he was. And it must also be readily admitted, in actual fact, that I even ended up liking his little friend, Zelda, who really turned out to be a clever and thoroughly entertaining little clown.

As I sat beside this friendly person who had taken the trouble to offer me a ride, I suddenly realized that I had absolutely no idea where I was going myself. So looking for suggestions at this point, I simply asked in response to his initial query, "Where are you headed?"

"Oh, I'm on my way to William's Bay to see one of my patients," "Doc" was explaining. "It's Mrs. Rozario.... Her baby's due any moment now!"

"William's Bay will be just fine," I was assuring him, as I uncomfortably continued to keep one wary eye on the suspicious little passenger in the back seat. All this while I sincerely hoped that my having detained the driver as I had would not prove to be a problem for his patient in the end.

Soon the noisy, dusty, dent-ridden vehicle was on the move again. We traveled only a short distance when I finally felt obliged to state, more in the form of a question, "Having a chicken for a traveling companion is pretty unusual, don't you agree?!"

"Doc" Owens was smiling, now, as he answered, "I've often speculated that my particular circumstances may well be unique in all the world!"

"How'd you manage to hook up with her, in the first place?"

"It's a rather interesting story, actually," he was confiding to me. "My Zelda was a gift last Easter from little Netty Nolan, one of the children I helped bring into the world three years ago..." Our car bumped and chugged along, every so often giving off a soft backfiring noise which naturally upset the bird in the back seat.

"I've attended the births of two generations of citizens living within the three surrounding communities," I was hearing him quietly state with a touch of real pride in his voice. "Naturally when that sweet little girl made me the offer of owning one of her most prized possessions, I found I just couldn't disappoint her by not accepting the baby chick that she so lovingly presented to me that morning. Right away I foolishly imagined that I'd be giving it away to someone who was far better qualified to care for it than I—but, as Fate would have it, not long after the present had become mine, a funny thing began to happen.... Ya see, as time went by, I actually found that I'd developed a fondness for the wee bird. Originally I kept her in a cardboard box here on the front seat. But chickens grow fast, and before long she just naturally took to riding there on the back seat instead.

"Each time I visit the Nolan family not only does the family always inquire about my health, but everyone always inquires about the health and happiness of our mutual little friend sitting back there—especially Netty.... It didn't take me long to realize that the two of us—the bird and I, that is, are destined to remain together 'till death us do part.'"

"How do you manage to keep the car clean?" I couldn't help but ask. I knew very well just how filthy chickens could be. In the past I would be forever cleaning their "handiwork" off the bottom of my shoes.

"Well, she's pretty much trained herself to defecate outside the vehicle. Thought it was going to be a real problem, at first, but she seems to appreciate a clean car as much as I do. The only thing I must always remain mindful of, however, is where she lays her eggs.... She's taken to hiding them in the most gawl dern places! I still manage to create an accident for myself every now and then, especially whenever I'm in too much of a hurry and fail to check the seat—or the floor, as I climb into the car!"

In front of me now, upon the feather-littered floor, I spotted an old well-worn black leather bag. Right next to it was a dusty black fedora which had been turned upside down and where, I could readily see, were safely snuggling several small white eggs. Again, I inquired, "Do you eat the eggs she provides?"

"Sometimes. Quite often, though, I manage to give them away. For instance, whenever I stop to visit a patient around breakfast time—or supper time, and I'm kindly invited to share a meal with these fine people as I so often am, well then as a kind gesture of gratitude in return, I'm often able to offer my host or hostess a hat-full of fresh eggs, which always seems to be appreciated!"

"Zelda sort of earns her keep, then...."

"Oh, yes," I was being assured. "She earns her keep many times over by being a good traveling companion, too! Ya see, my profession always keeps me on the road at all times of the day and night and I've come to welcome the decent company of my little fine feathered friend back there."

Perhaps as a noteworthy point of interest to the reader I feel obliged to state that around eighty different makes of cars and trucks have been manufactured in Wisconsin since 1900. The first auto race in the world, in fact, was held in 1878 between two steam wagons that raced from Green Bay to Madison. In what was considered a highly impressive speed at the time the vehicles traveled at a "breakneck velocity" of six miles per hour. And first prize consisted of a purse of $10,000 which was undoubtedly worth many more times what it is today.

In 1889, too, the first practical gasoline-powered automobile was built in Milwaukee by Gottfried Schloemer. By 1914 there were approximately 1,258,000 registered autos in the United States, with Henry Ford manufacturing 300,000 per year. During that same year a Scripps-Booth, for example, which was manufactured in Detroit, sold for $775—new. And Herbert Hoover's 1932 plea to his fellow Americans to "Buy an automobile and help restore prosperity" became a familiar everyday catch-phrase, as did the more poignant little jingle which tended to offset this more pragmatic philosophy:

> "My auto, tis of thee,
> Short cut to poverty—
> Of thee I chant.
> I blew a pile of dough
> On you three years ago,
> Now you refuse to go—
> Or won't or can't!"

As a matter of fact the vintage automobile in which "Doc" Owens and I were presently traveling had been a wedding gift in the late spring of 1910, from Daniel Evingston Daily IV, to Dr. Chester Owens and his new wife, the former Elizabeth Farnsworth Daily of Boston. Once "Doc" confided to Felix and me, during one of those more rare moments of sharing this particular topic of his more painful past, that this union of theirs was doomed from the start.

Being the well-known socialite daughter and the only child of a wealthy man whose rather impressive lineage dated back to the "founding fathers" of this great nation helped to account for the spoiled willfulness that was, in overwhelming measure, partially responsible for the trials and tribulations which occurred very early on in the couple's marriage. This same negative experience, I might add, was to have forever marked the good doctor's mind and heart for life. It would also prove responsible for having made him forego even the slightest inclination in future years of abandoning his most treasured state of reclaimed bachelorhood.

According to the story, no sooner had the ink dried upon the couple's marriage license when that rather unkind and uncompromising bride went about in earnest trying quite literally to make her husband over—"from attic to basement, and from inside-out," was exactly how the good doctor phrased it. Elizabeth Daily and her family had actually expected this much respected and much beloved country doctor to give up his ever-demanding practice in Lake Geneva. They professed to be more than willing to reinstate him, instead, within his new father-in-law's far more prestigious and far better paying practice on New York's Fifth Avenue. Although "Doc" truly loved this woman in the beginning when he courted and won her, it was not until immediately after the ceremony that her true character traits began to emerge in all their greedy selfishness, ultimately rendering him quite brokenhearted and also understandably bitter in the end.

"Had I not the courage to nip our immense problem in the bud, right away," I heard him calmly confide to Felix as the three of us sat on the

Lauder's porch one early evening in June, a number of years after all of us had become good friends, "my life simply would never have belonged to me. Indeed, my dear little wife would have gone about systematically destroying all that I hold dear!

"When Elizabeth and I met, as far as women were concerned, I shall admit that I was a mere 'babe in the woods.' However, it did not take me very long after the ceremony to reach the frightening conclusion that I was 'had' from the start! Elizabeth and I were total opposites, as far as our having possessed the slightest similarities regarding our mutual outlook on life. More specifically, we lacked any sort of similar values with regard to concrete principles of ethics!

"My perennial belief that good people should only come together in marriage with the honorable intention of enriching each other's lives—and in several truly profound ways, including the spiritual sense, immediately fell by the wayside. In the end, had I chosen to sacrifice myself upon that ever-demanding alter of matrimony merely to adhere to a basic sense of loyalty which is an intrinsic part of my nature, we would have grown to despise each other, Elizabeth and I. We would have ruthlessly negated whatever faint shadow of any pleasantness that might have ever existed between us in the beginning.... So inevitably it was far better for me to end the relationship as I eventually was forced to do. Anyway, I should never have consented to becoming anyone's 'lap dog'—and that, as they say, is that!"

According to this same poignant account, during that first and only year of their marriage "Doc" somehow persuaded his stubborn young bride to travel to Lake Geneva to live. He had long grown extremely fond of the uncomplicated way of life there and the basic sense of honesty and sacrifice that being a dedicated country doctor naturally engendered, just as he surely grew to love her. Mistakenly, however, he believed that with time Elizabeth Daily would learn to share this important vision of his and to eventually learn to be happy with him there. A modest little room—or "love nest", as he initially referred to it, in Samantha Park's boarding house was dutifully secured for them until such a time when he felt that the couple would finally be able to afford to build a place of their own. But this was not to be....

"Doc" and his Elizabeth were as chemically different, and as highly incompatible, as oil and water. With a deeply abiding sense of great loss and perhaps an even greater sense of personal failure on his part that understandably accompanied the ensuing annulment of their union, those few meager possessions of his that amounted to little more than half a dozen medical books from his student years, several intimate love letters between the two of them, and one particularly telling photograph taken sometime just after the two initially met, were eventually packed away in boxes and then finally stored in one small corner of a room in Mrs. Park's residence.

In time that faithful little Ford motor car became in great part the living quarters of this fine man. Whenever he was not briefly napping at the home of one of his more gracious patients, there upon some familiar sofa which always tended to serve so well as a makeshift bed for him, because of the rather selfless life he always led, citizens of the surrounding communities frequently found him grabbing his much-needed "forty winks" there behind the wheel of his little automobile that was usually unobtrusively parked somewhere off by the side of some lonely country road.

In a truly loving sense "Doc" Owens reminded me of a gentle turtle who was forever traveling about from place to place, all the while happily carrying with him the few important things he always required. For him these vital things consisted of his trusty black leather bag, along with several volumes of choice poetry that he openly acknowledged were "food for his ever-hungry soul" and, consequently, remained highly indispensable items that he "simply couldn't live without."

Frequently a patient's family would offer our dear friend a home-cooked meal, or a daily shower to help keep him going. These simple acts of kindness often represented payment to him, since people in those parts rarely had funds enough to pay for medical care in the more traditional manner. In the end it was this same noble practice of medicine, along with "Doc's" much-beloved patients, which eventually became the wife, and the children, as well as the warm and loving home that were earlier denied him.

Without a doubt "Doc's" patients adored him, just as he in turn seemed to live for their general welfare. Of course it goes without saying, too, that the ever-demanding practice of his art was something that was held in the highest esteem by all of us. I recall that once Felix reminded his many children and me, when this particular subject arose concerning the issue of the innate responsibilities that are inherent in the profession of medicine, about the wisdom of the sixteenth-century Swiss physician and alchemist Paracelsus.... Indeed, contained within the ancient pages of this learned man's own published thesis entitled *Liber De Caducis,* he endeavors to explain his own personal views on the worthiness of any good physician, as he so eloquently tells the reader: "First of all it is very necessary to tell of the compassion that must be innate in a physician.... Where there is no love, there is no art! And the practice of this art lies in the heart; if the heart is true, the physician within you will also be true. Physician and Medicine are essentially nothing less than a mercy conferred upon the needy by God!"

When I grew older, I was to think that this country gentleman, with his high cheekbones and rather tall, gaunt, slightly stooped shoulders, as well as his thoroughly engaging hazel-colored eyes, reminded me of a particularly attractive likeness of Abraham Lincoln which I eventually came across in one of my high school studies. For as long as I knew him, "Doc" Owens always looked physically older in years than he actually was, probably due in great part to the fact that he was forever being deprived of any quality rest.

In hindsight I am unable to recall him ever taking a vacation, either. However, he naturally possessed such an enviable love of life. This seemed to supply him with the necessary energy that always tended to help him surmount this particularly difficult circumstance of his profession; this "given," in other words, that forever remains an ever-abiding part of the difficult life of any conscientious physician.

I discovered, too, from our very first meeting on that remarkable day, that his interesting accent was exceedingly smooth upon the ear, exactly the way his marvelous easygoing manner was so incredibly smooth upon one's heart. And as I listened attentively to what he was sharing with me, regarding his little "Zelda," I was beginning to suspect that this community in which I recently came to live was obviously blessed with more than one good person.

The lovely country road upon which we were both presently traveling eventually descended rather rapidly down a modest little hill and there, directly to our left, I was immediately treated to my very first glimpse of Lake Geneva. Involuntarily I must have given off some sort of gleeful sound which basically indicated my pleasurable surprise at seeing it as we were. "Doc" found himself agreeing with me, as he said, "It is beautiful, isn't it?! I'm forever struck by the very same feeling whenever I see it, even though I've lived in these parts for so many years already.

"For me the lake is a living thing. As any day progresses, numerous changes in the water's mood will make itself apparent, if one is paying attention," he was telling me. "The seasons, too, naturally bring the most dramatic changes. Soon the frigid winter weather will be freezing the water of the entire lake solid and in the coming months one may actually drive, or walk, across the lake from one end to the other. It's undoubtedly the closest thing any of us mortals will ever experience, when it comes to being able to 'walk on water'!"

"Doc" Owens was finally bringing his noisy little car to a stop, just in front of several rows of boats that had already been pulled up upon the shore. They were turned over and essentially being "dry docked" for the winter. This necessary habit of covering the boats with thick waterproof oil cloth tarps always remained a significant sign that summer, with all its hustling and bustling visitors, was more or less behind us. Before too long the ice boats would be soundlessly skimming across this frozen terrain....

At impressive speeds those daredevil sportsmen who piloted these specially designed crafts would endlessly beguile both our local inhabitants, as well as those heartier winter visitors among us, by frequently defying the laws of known physics. Likewise, those similarly "hearty souls" within our community would also soon be in the process of setting up their uniquely designed little "houses," there upon the lake's frozen surface, in order to be able to ice fish.

"Mind if I let ya off here?" the good doctor was asking me. "I'll have to hurry if I plan to be of any assistance to my patient. I discovered early in my practice that babies make a habit of coming whenever they choose to come, not necessarily when they're expected to come.... This fact always manages to keep me on my toes!" He was smiling at me as I thanked him for the ride. As I quickly closed the car door, he sped off down the street, briefly waving at me from out the window with his left hand. His small traveling companion Zelda fluttered just once before settling back down to quietly enjoy the rest of the ride.

As I stood there watching the old car disappear from view, it occurred to me that neither this fine man nor I had actually taken the opportunity to properly introduce ourselves. Eventually I came to realize that the reason for this was very simple. Basically this exceptionally kind gentleman had automatically included me within his all-encompassing "extended family" which this community represented and over which he faithfully stood guard. Because of this, and because of the fact that he was also in a hurry that day, our not having taken the appropriate time to formally introduce ourselves apparently was of little significance to either of us. Both of us behaved as though we were already friends, and that we were surely destined to meet again. This, of course, remained a subtle compliment that had not gone unnoticed nor unappreciated by me.

I spent the better part of the rest of the day walking around that wonderful sleepy little town of Williams Bay. Upon our entrance into the community I noticed that we had passed several shops. More or less towards the top of a modest incline, which stood directly behind me now, I was soon to rediscover a series of small family-owned businesses which included a hardware store. With only a small portion of those same significant funds which my father had so fortuitously bestowed upon me the evening before, I was able to finally purchase a generous length of rope for a special project that I earlier had taken pains to carefully hatch within my mind. Around that same block, but located on another street which ran parallel to this one, I later unexpectedly discovered a terrific bakery where I simply could not resist buying a long loaf of freshly baked raisin bread and nothing less than a dozen sugar cookies.

At the top of a nearby rise in the terrain, onwards just a ways towards the far left, I located a most impressive building known as the Yerkes Observatory. I eventually learned from the Lauder family that in 1892 the American financier Charles Tyson generously furnished to the University of Chicago substantial funds to help establish this astronomical structure that was specifically designed to safely house its principal instrument which at the time was a forty-inch refracting telescope, and which was hailed as the largest of its type in the world.

George once referred to this same wonder as "the home of the giant eye" whose shameless nocturnal wanderings shared with all of us the ever-enticing secrets of the universe. This is where the two of us— George and I, that is, would always go fishing on Sunday, not far from this wonderful building itself. In fact, located within a particular spot on these very grounds one might conceivably still be able to discover our secret entrance. Back all those years ago, through the thick ground cover of fern and aspen saplings growing all around, a narrow hard-to-find path led us to an especially beautiful spot down by the lake where we would usually catch pan fish and large-mouthed bass if we were really lucky.

Before George's death this was where so much of our free time was spent together. After his death, this was were I usually came to be alone with my great sadness. Indeed, it was on this very day of my first visit to William's Bay that I accidentally discovered this choice spot and promptly claimed it for my very own. Enjoying beyond measure my lunch of apples and cheese, with a side-order of newly acquired bread and cookies, I listened attentively to the insistent wind as it endlessly sang through the aspen leaves. Shortly I found myself concentrating on the soothing sound the ripples from the waves were making as they continuously lapped the smooth stones that haphazardly decorated the lake's ongoing curvature of the long irregular shore-line. Out more towards the center of this deep glacier lake, the healthy wind was working its magic by whipping up the dark emerald green waters. So much so that modest little "white caps" could be seen playing there amongst the waves.

During one particularly memorable summer, of all the many summers past, with particular fondness I recall that several of the older Lauder boys bartered their way into ownership of a secondhand boat that initially needed extensive repairs. With everyone's very able assistance, though, in time we finally managed as a family to make the needy vessel "sea-worthy" once again.

In my free time I accepted the important task of helping to sand down the badly rotting craft. Since this particular job ultimately proved to be significantly tedious, our collective daily work together ended up taking us several weeks to accomplish.

After the multitude of holes within the boat were properly plugged with hot tar and its entire body received a double coat of durable paint, a sorely neglected gasoline-powered motor was somehow secured and then miraculously rebuilt by Albert Lauder. This makeshift marine engine was payment more or less for some extensive car repairs he made for one of the visitors from Chicago the previous summer, and was eventually fitted on to the small two-person craft. After this since buying a pair of water skis was totally out of the question, financially speaking, someone in the family came up with the clever idea of using the family's old winter toboggan for a similar purpose instead.

As a necessary prelude to this major event the sturdy wood of this heavy sled was generously waxed all over to help waterproof it, and also to help make it glide through the water with a minimal amount of resistance. Right before we hauled the well-weathered coaster over to the lake to try out our nifty experiment, a small piece of old carpeting was securely tacked to the top flat surface. This way each rider, when standing upon its normally too-slick surface, would naturally fare far better in trying to keep their footing as soon as our little craft began to pull rider and sled along behind itself....

What glorious summer days those were. With the bulk of our group of eight or so people forced to remain on a small stretch of beach at one more deserted end of the lake, until their individual time to compete came around, two of us at a time proceeded to take turns to meet the thrilling challenge of this new game. Basically the object of the game, which sounded deceptively simple enough, was to be able to withstand the rigorous zigzag motion any "crazed driver" of our boat would naturally attempt to impose upon any one of the riders whenever it became their turn to be dragged behind the boat. Since by basic design our newly refurbished "skiing" device had no rudder, each participant was naturally obliged to fight every step of the way in order to be able to keep the large board steady and not fall off.

By the end of any given summer Sunday afternoon the much-coveted prize of a rather rusty old plaque which one of the younger children discovered and claimed for himself somewhere at a local garage sale was always ceremoniously bestowed upon that particular person who had proven able enough to stay on board the longest. I well recall that even on those hottest summer days the water of our beautiful lake remained extremely cold. Frequently it took a long hot bath, as well as a cup or two of hot homemade soup waiting there in the kitchen, before any of us would finally consider ourselves thoroughly warm enough.

If necessity is the mother of invention and mimicry remains the most sincere form of flattery, then much to our pleasant surprise that summer—as well as numerous summers thereafter, several children whose families lived around the lake decided to forego the use of their more traditional water skis and ended up putting their winter toboggans to good use, just as we had done.

It was a well-known fact that Al Capone owned a large estate on the lake. Thinking back it was almost as though poor Felix and his family would never be completely free from those long and ever-pervasive tentacles of this awful man's far reaching influence, no matter how hard they might try. During many an evening throughout the year, as George and I sometimes discovered whenever we went night fishing, the numerous windows of this gangster's huge mansion, that very grand property by which he had come into ownership through the wholesale suffering of so many others, would always glow brightly with party lights....

Parked along the wide and protracted driveway, as well as within the expansive courtyard of this same immense house, one would invariably observe a multitude of shiny Cadillacs, and Duesenbergs, and Rolls Royce limousines as they and their faithful chauffeurs awaited their various owners. Often, too, the more refined music of some popular band of the day, coupled with the happy chattering and laughter of all the merrymaking guests, would endlessly fan out across the lake, causing—at least for some of us—a highly disturbing contrast when critically viewed against the backdrop of the pain and misery of the times.

Despite this particularly unflattering portrait of debauchery, I would still come to earnestly cherish this marvelous lake. This wonderful body of water would ultimately become for me the focal point of so many wholesome memories; fond memories happily created during the many years I was to live in this lovely spot. As an adult, long after I was to leave this part of my life behind in the physical sense, it eventually became these same poignant photographs taken with my ever-greedy mind and heart that somehow still manage to sustain me.

Leaving town on foot that day by following the same route "Doc" Owens and I had initially taken to arrive in Williams Bay, I finally ended up hitching a ride with a helpful man who was transporting hay within his horse-drawn wagon. Although this considerate soul was unable to take me to the front doorstep of my father's house—a wholly insignificant fact for which he seemed compelled to apologize, but which I never really expected, he did instead drop me off not too far from where I could just see in the far distance the recognizable steeple of our small chapel securely perched upon the little hill. Once I spotted this place of growing familiarity, I knew for certain that I was already home.

My father was absent when I arrived back at the house on this particular day. It remained unclear to me whether he had left early before my return or whether he just never made it home after his drinking bout of the previous evening. In order to make the most of what remained of that late afternoon, I busied myself cleaning out the old icebox in the kitchen. After this was done I carefully placed all my food inside, and then with the generous length of rope which was purchased earlier that day at the hardware store, I properly secured the door of the appliance so that the cunning rat would not be able to steal from me again.

The following days were uneventful for the most part. The weather had warmed again, and so it was no longer necessary for me to wear such heavy clothing as before. I managed, also, to work with the pump in the kitchen. After tinkering with it long enough, and after having pumped it endlessly until the foul-smelling, orange-colored water from the well outside finally ran clean, I acknowledged with a real sense of satisfaction that my father and I would be able to live a bit easier now by finally having the great luxury of running water.

Before the extremely cold winter weather finally began to settle in upon us more permanently, I continued to take my daily excursions around the community just as before. However, these days my father's health was beginning to fail quite noticeably.... His complexion, in fact, had presently taken on the same yellowish hue as the whites of his eyes and with his not feeling well enough to go out very much any more, I felt an obligation to remain nearby in case he should ever need me.

I remember that there was a silver flask he always kept hidden under one side of the mattress of his bed. Without the slightest regard for his progressively failing health, nearly every other day now he had me walk to the speakeasy which was located not so far from our place to purchase on his behalf a desperately needed refill of booze. Generally after my breakfast, and always upon his request, I learned to take a shortcut across several fields which I discovered significantly cut my travel time to this colorful establishment by quite a fair amount. Just as importantly this strategy allowed me to arrive unnoticed at the building's back entrance which was stressed, more than once, as an extraordinarily critical issue by my father.

With his meticulous prepping I was carefully instructed to knock three times upon that same thick back door.... When a small square-cut peephole was eventually opened to me and only someone's eye could be seen, as well as the usual woman's coarse voice calling out, "Whatcha want?"—I was told to always respond by saying, "Hank sends his regards!"

I recall that the same older woman always stood in the doorway to greet me. Wearing a wholly unflattering low-cut dress and plenty of white face paint that gave her sagging flesh the appearance that she was at least partially embalmed, she would squint critically at me, almost as if the fresh air and gentle daylight that came flooding in upon her at times like these somehow deeply offended her.

Upon seeing me standing there the woman would invariably poke her head outside to suspiciously have a quick look around. Naturally always finding me alone, she seemed much relieved by this fact. Likewise she invariably made it her business to invite me to step inside while she went about filling my father's flask. Instead, however, my polite answer would always remain pretty much the same, as I said in reply, "Thanks, but I'll wait out here, if it's just the same to you."

"Suit yourself, kid," the woman would matter-of-factly answer, as both she and I played this same orchestrated little number often several times a week. Since bootlegging was illegal, naturally no quality control was ever placed on the illicit manufacturing of this more low-grade liquor. Consequently, to extend the ever available supply even further, thereby making an even greater profit for the greedy lawbreakers who were selling it, much of this "bathtub gin"—or "rot gut" as it was appropriately named—would be cut with highly poisonous additives that would eventually cause blindness, severe liver and brain damage and the like, and would all too frequently hasten the miserable death of many people who indulged in the awful stuff.

Once in a desperate effort to find some real help for my father, after he seemed near death at one particular point in time, I made the great mistake of asking him whether I might travel into town to try and find a doctor for him. Naturally my first thought along these lines immediately flowed back to the good man with whom I traveled to Williams Bay many days earlier.

But with this simple overture of mine which had been so sincerely made in order that help might be secured for him, I well remember how my father swiftly grabbed the front of my shirt as I stood close to his cot that day. Bringing my face nearer to his own he openly raged at me, as he said between clenched teeth, "Don't you ever do anything like that, do you hear me?! I don't need anyone.... I've never needed anyone! And don't you ever forget it!"

For me this complex individual had already evolved into a lone "wolf of the steppes."... Indeed, in my later years whenever I looked back upon this difficult time for both of us, my father came to represent the flesh and blood personification of Hesse's character of Harry Haller in *Steppenwolf.* Within that self-inflicted isolation of his and over a period of many years, no doubt, my father continued to search for whatever redemption he might find inside a liquor bottle. On the one hand he felt rigidly compelled to outwardly shun the world of men; while on the other, by allowing his dire spiritual craving for some sort of healthy interaction with another soul to be consistently thwarted, he obviously caused himself untold suffering.

From that point in time the long lonely days merely came and went for me. With the arrival of the intensely cold weather I rarely went out anymore except to run that particular errand for my father, and, of course, to supply myself with the basic food whenever the situation arose.

My father would never eat anything. Even from the beginning whenever I prepared food for him—even the simplest of meals, all would end up untouched and therefore wasted. He seemed instead to exclusively prefer his "liquid nourishment," as he liked to refer to it.

More and more I noticed that the previous light and happy mood which I had earlier been in the process of carefully cultivating began to slowly wane away and to take on the depressingly somber colors of the winter terrain outside. More and more, too, I spent the better part of every day sleeping; hibernating, in effect, in an uncomplicated effort to better deal with the growing darkness in which my soul was slowly becoming immersed once more.

Sometime after winter began in earnest the same "guardian angel" who most probably was responsible for providing the generous box of clothing weeks before also took to so thoughtfully leaving a cord of neatly cut firewood piled high upon the decking of the back porch. Quite amazingly enough, too, the stubborn old front door to my father's house was finally repaired, no doubt during one afternoon when I left the house for only an hour or two. There at the top one could find a brand new shiny brass fitting which replaced the old broken and badly rusted one, thus enabling me to close the large opening against the bitter cold.

Every now and then I was certainly tempted to believe in miracles. And as I continuously warmed myself by the wonderful heat that was pulsating from our black wrought-iron stove, there in the dingy parlor, throughout all those many difficult months ahead when I remained endlessly worrying about my father and his failing health, I fought hard to focus upon the positive effects such small miracles were making upon my life.

8.

WHEN THE ROMANS first familiarized themselves with the western part of Hungary in 14 BC, it was called Pannonia and was inhabited by Illyrians and Celts. Not long after this time—speaking now, of course, in terms of history's clock, the land was duly incorporated into the Holy Roman Empire as a province. The area east of the Danube was never a part of Rome, however, and was largely occupied by various Germanic and Asiatic peoples.

Similarly the Avars held this region for more than 200 years, but were finally displaced by Charlemagne around 800 AD. Then sometime in the fifth century, a nomadic Finno-Ugrian people known as the Magyars began a westward march from their former home within the Eurasian Steppe. The Roman Emperor Arnulf, in 892, invited these same hearty people to help him subdue the Moravians and, under the elected leadership of the great Magyar chieftain Arpad, thus began the tempestuous settlement of the Great Hungarian Plain....

Magyars were notoriously fierce fighters. History actually tells us that early on they were the "scourge of Europe," as their original body of seven tribes eventually grew in number to repeatedly overrun and subjugate the resident Slavs and Huns in order to expand their territories. Our own English word "ogre," a corruption of "Hungar," attests to their notoriety. It is also a noteworthy fact that these same nomadic people placed tremendous importance on the strength of the individual family unit, thereby giving due respect to the relevance women and children naturally played in their close-knit society....

Now and then when the Lauder children and I were old enough to better appreciate the subject matter of this particular topic, Felix always took pleasure in pointing out this particular fact concerning the Magyar people. Once he even went on to openly declare, with a slightly impish gleam in his eye, that "Magyars were notoriously fierce warriors and equally passionate lovers!" All this while he seemed actively engaged in attempting to elicit some sort of a response from his seemingly disinterested wife who, I recall, was sitting somewhere just within earshot. Then, having waited in vain for some slight hint from Emma Lauder that she either agreed or disagreed with this characteristically playful comment of his, he comically scratched his head in a feigned manner of extreme thoughtfulness to further state, "Or could that possibly have been notoriously passionate warriors and equally fierce lovers?!"

During those first many weeks when I continued to reside with my father in his house, curiously enough I never became aware of any significant movement from anyone living next door. In fact the general daily whereabouts of these phantom operatives continued to remain somewhat of a mystery to me.

Since my arrival the only person I ever rarely chanced to see from the privacy of my father's bedroom windows upstairs, or from the dingy kitchen window downstairs—both which afforded me an excellent view of our neighbor's driveway and part of their home, was an elderly man who came every day with a wagon of hay. Once while returning home from one of my usual errands I quite literally nearly ran into this individual as he was leaving the place. Purely out of curiosity I felt compelled to ask him whether he was the owner of that fine place.

"Oh, no," he answered matter-of-factly, "I'm Carl Reading from down the road a piece.... I've been hired to look after things around here, at least until the new owners arrive. Most of all I'm expected to feed the animals out back—especially old Zechariah!"

I remained pensive for a moment before my curiosity got the better of me. In the end I found myself enthusiastically inquiring, "Who is Zechariah?"

"Old Zech is a prized bull that was naturally sold with the other livestock, when this place was recently purchased by a family from Chicago."

"When will the new people be coming?"

"Any day now.... Sometime just before Christmas, I expect. Then this place should really start hopping—with all those children!"

"What do you mean," I could not help but ask.

"Haven't you heard? I figured everybody around these parts knows that the new owners have eleven children. I believe their family name is Lauder...."

As I watched the caretaker drive away, I stood there thoughtfully contemplating the interesting news that was just shared with me. Eleven children! Thirteen people?! Why that makes enough people for an entire baseball team! Next I found myself foolishly wondering whether this family's arrival, as was promised, would have any impact at all upon my unusually quiet and totally uneventful life.

Since I possessed no accurate way to record the passing of time, I virtually lost track of how long I had already been residing where I was. Most probably the holiday of Christmas would have also come and gone without the slightest notice, just as Thanksgiving already did, had it not been for Mr. Reading's offhanded reference to the approaching holiday.

Not long after this brief yet highly informative conversation of ours took place, it was upon my late morning return from the speakeasy to oblige my father's needs that I wandered out back to bring in more firewood for the stove.... There, sitting almost out of reach upon the generous pile of neatly stacked fuel, was a relatively small object carefully swaddled in coarse brown paper and tied up with a bright red paper ribbon. The offering was very similar, in fact, to the manner in which my box of wonderful clothing had been presented to me some time ago.

With growing pleasure I carefully unwrapped the item to eventually discover a glass jar filled with flavorful sunflower seeds. It was my first real Christmas present ever. As I sat by the warmth of the friendly stove later on that evening, immensely enjoying this rare treat, I was discovering that a small precious seed of hope had already been planted within my fertile heart that very day. With the astonishing news of the large family that was planning to move in next door, sometime in the not too distant future; and, of course, with my amazingly kind "guardian angel" who somehow always managed to secretly visit me whenever I needed him the most, there appeared upon the horizon of my young life a bright ray of much needed sunshine… Indeed, I found myself frequently wondering at all of it, as I began to humbly bask in the simple pleasure of its fragile existence.

Then exactly two days before the Christmas of 1929, and sometime during the late afternoon hours as the sparsely filtered daylight of winter slowly began to fade away, a light snow began to fall.... I was busy in the kitchen attempting to engage the kerosene lamp in a worthy effort to help ward off the growing dimness in the room so that I might prepare myself a little supper. Suddenly I was forced to cease what I was doing in deference to the unusual sound of a cheerful harmonica tune that I realized was coming to me from somewhere off in the distance....

Yes, without a doubt, it was the sound of glorious harmonica music! Straining at the moment with all my might to better hear the happy-sounding melody, I impetuously climbed upon the kitchen counter to gaze through the grimy film of the window's glass. Very soon I became fairly captivated by what was happening next door....

Coming up the long curved driveway at the moment was an impressive black automobile carrying many people. Arriving close behind this vehicle was a secondhand truck whose open rear section was obviously crammed full of many of the personal household items belonging to this sizable family. I could also readily see that the tires of both the car and the truck were carving slight impressions into the newly fallen snow which was already beginning to lightly dust the gravel passageway these people were traversing.

And the person who was responsible for creating all that wondrously cheerful harmonica music was none other than George Lauder—my very own soon-to-be-friend! While George sat in the passenger side of the truck, I seem to recall that it was his older brother Lewis who continued to expertly maneuver their vehicle behind the family sedan that Felix was driving....

From an open window of the car a young voice enthusiastically called forth into the stillness of the approaching evening, just as the vehicles' motors were simultaneously turned off and that happy acoustical phenomenon of the lovely music abruptly ceased, "Are we finally here? Is this the place?! Is this to be our new home, Papa?"

With this passionate entreaty the doors of both vehicles were immediately thrust open, and out stepped all the various members of this exuberant group. The youngest member, of course—tiny baby Anna, was being carried in her mother's arms, all the while being solicitously sheltered from the robust flakes of snow which were beginning to fall quite heavily by now.

This is how they all came, those amazing people from Chicago. Those wonderful people whom I would surely come to know so well, and to love so much. They arrived in a softly falling snow two days before Christmas, to the glorious sound of happy music being played upon a harmonica....

Each and every precious detail of that magical scene was indelibly imprinted upon my heart that very moment. Everything became deeply embedded in the most profound sense, just as are all those other more integral silver and gold threads of one's happier moments in life which, all-in-all, help to comprise the rather ornate and highly unique pattern that ultimately becomes the very fabric of one's being.

While the mother and younger children quickly entered the protective confines of their new home, there occurred a frenetic display of rather organized movement as the father of this formidable tribe, along with all of his older sons, hurriedly wrestled with all of their personal items on the truck. With a sense of urgency they managed to bring everything inside the house in order to keep what they owned from becoming wet, and perhaps even ruined, with the coming storm. Next, from the rear of the automobile, a large cumbersome phonograph was being carefully removed and just as hurriedly taken into the house.

After this several traveling cases of various sizes and a number of decorative lamps were also being hastily ushered into the warmth and security of the farmhouse. Towards the bottom of all that had already been quickly removed from the rear of the truck several medium-sized boxes still remained, causing their owners some difficulty judging from the fact that each one seemed remarkably heavy thus requiring more than one person at a time to carry them.

As I watched every single bit of this robust action that was taking place outside from my self-prescribed secret post there at the window of our little kitchen, I was actually setting a pattern for the coming months ahead. This harmless behavior of mine would be serving me quite well over time by allowing me to vicariously become a small part of this family's healthy interaction between its many members. In a way it was as though I were being engaged on a dependable daily basis in carefully watching a real-life film, or rather one of those Saturday morning silent movie "cliff-hanger" series, whose calculating aim it was to remain endlessly action-packed, thereby leaving the movie-goer thoroughly enraptured. So much so, in fact, that one would actually count the days of the following week in eager anticipation of the coming weekend and another segment of that exciting movie.

After the automobile and truck were depleted of their considerable cargo and properly bedded down for the night inside the barn; and when the men of the family, themselves, finally disappeared within the sanctuary of the little house, I observed with continued interest that the formerly darkened and far more reserved-looking abode across the way was in the process of slowly coming to life. Each one of its many windows began to glow softly with every light that was now being turned on within its every room.... How splendid it all was!

With a growing sense of painful nostalgia it seemed to me that the happy scene across the way was akin to a beautiful study one might find upon the front of a friendly Christmas card. For there, with the large pristine flakes of virgin snow falling continuously all about the place, I could actually feel that emanating from this same sacred core within the powerful surrounding storm an excellent new warmth was beginning to spread my way. Already this lovely scene was tugging at the heart-strings of this hungriest of onlookers; this soul-weary traveler who was presently being so helplessly, and so hopelessly, inspired by the wholesome promises of happier times to come. That night I went to bed deeply pondering what the morning might bring....

It is a fairly well-known fact, especially by people living in rural communities, in particular, that farm life can often be a very dangerous way to earn a living. This seems to be especially so for unsuspecting city folk who possess little or no experience in the day-to-day running of such things. It was not uncommon in agrestic America to occasionally find members within one's own community who were maimed in some manner. Someone ended up missing fingers, or arms, or feet even, from a tragic accident where a moment's lack of strict discipline in using some sort of dangerous machinery ended up costing them dearly.

Early that next morning I awoke to the unusual sound of numerous children spontaneously laughing and shouting outside. That momentary effect in my semiconscious state, of course, had unwittingly transported me back to my first and only day of school. As I made my way to my secret place at the kitchen window, I was treated to watching several of the younger members of the Lauder clan as they were in the process of harvesting a bevy of tightly-packed snowballs to throw at one another.

Having wandered off more to themselves, at the moment, two of the older boys from this original group were now breaking off long twigs from a nearby leafless maple tree. In time they commenced to playfully duel with each other at one far side of the house, just as one of the youngest children promptly took to comically collapsing into a modest snow bank—face up, naturally, there near the back rear porch area. Energetically moving both his little arms up and down in the snow, all the while keeping the rest of his body quite still, he proceeded to loudly call out, "Look at the angel I'm making! Look, everybody! For heaven sake, somebody go get Mother—so she may see the angel I'm making!"

Later on that day from my covert post there at one of my father's bedroom windows I happened to witness the patriarch of this beguiling group helping Mr. Reading unload hay from Mr. Reading's truck. Not long after this he and his reliable neighbor were both using a pulley located just above an open window at the very top of the barn to hoist numerous heavy bales of feed through this same cavity for storage sake. While this particular project was firmly underway, a bloodcurdling scream from one of the children issued forth from somewhere behind the barn area. The unnatural sound quite literally hung there in the cold brittle winter air. Shortly, in what seemed like little more than a heartbeat, a child was seen running around the side of that same building to frantically declare, "Father! Father! Come quick! Eddie is going to die! Eddie is going to die!"

With each man not having even bothered to put down his pitchfork, together both of them went bounding around the structure to investigate the trouble. From my secret place of disadvantage there behind one torn window shade, while my father continued to restlessly sleep off the alcohol he recently consumed, I could see nothing of the real drama which was undoubtedly unfolding next door....

Eventually as I dutifully held my post, all the while fervently hoping that no one in the family was hurt in any way, I watched with great interest as Felix Lauder finally reappeared from around the barn. He was being followed somewhat ceremoniously by a modest procession of several of his younger children. Each was wearing a similar expression of pensive sobriety at the moment. Continuing to personally escort his son Eddie back in the direction of the farmhouse, with one of his hands firmly planted across the shoulders of this nine-year-old youngster, and with his other hand carrying what appeared to be an empty milking pail, he, himself, was wearing a look of extreme exasperation. At one point I finally heard him patiently tell the lucky child, "Please remember from now on, Edward, that it is only the cow which gives the milk.... And it is the bull who will certainly give you plenty more trouble, should you ever again mistake him for a cow!"

For quite a few years after I became an adopted member of this extraordinary family, Old Zechariah seemed to continue to bear a real grudge towards Eddie. Every time the two of them beheld each other, usually at a safe distance from that moment onward, the bull would stare directly at the boy and then slowly lower his impressive head to enthusiastically paw the ground as if he were challenging Eddie. Indeed, it was as if he remembered the incident quite well and was not quite yet disposed to forgiving the grievance.

By the time young Annie had grown to be nine years old, however, Old Zech had properly buried the hatchet, so to speak. With time the old fellow had at long last reached a point where he consented to behave towards everyone—including our dear Eddie, much like a lamb would behave by docilely allowing himself to be led around his pen by the large brass ring in his nose.

On Christmas Eve of that same special year, shortly after lunch time it was, several of the older members of the Lauder clan took the truck and quickly disappeared for quite a long while. When they returned, I observed that tied to the back section of the vehicle was a medium-sized tree. Eventually the entire family gathered outside that day to watch as the lovely blue spruce was trimmed of its lower branches. Of course the lady of the house immediately claimed these remnants for herself.... Shortly after this occurred a bottom two inch segment of the tree's trunk was cleanly sawed off, in order that the remaining piece might be carefully scored in several places. This more common strategy would soon allow the evergreen to continue to drink when it was placed in its usual container of sugar-water there within one corner of the Lauder family's little parlor. Fondly remembering back to that special day and all of those interesting family activities that were so jubilantly taking place across the way, not in a million years could I ever have believed that during the following Christmas Eve I should actually become very much a part of this same undeniably happy life of these very fine people. But genuine miracles do actually occur—of this I remain unquestionably certain.

That winter was particularly difficult, as far as bad weather was concerned. From the time shortly after the beginning of the New Year, onward until the very earliest weeks of that more tentative spring, I rarely had any occasion to see our neighbors either coming or going. They, like most of the rest of us within the community, wisely took to keeping indoors for comfort sake. However, with the arrival of the much-welcomed slightly warmer weather, much as if the world were awakening from its long slumber and naturally stretching and yawning to signal the event, more interesting things began to happen next door....

For example during every other weekend or so, when the lady of the house was able to induct into service a couple of willing and able bodies to assist her, several rolled-up carpets were carried to the side of the little house. After being systematically unrolled, they were each heaved onto the clothesline to be soundly beaten clean with a special wooden paddle.

Later during the day I observed Emma Lauder hanging her freshly washed laundry out for drying. How quickly I discovered the uniquely pleasing effect that such simple everyday household chores could make upon the spirit. For at times like these, with the wonderful vision of the often vigorous wind blowing the snow-white sheets and pillowcases out like so many billowing sails of a ship, and with the accompanying "snapping" sound the clean cotton fabric would naturally make as it was furled in and then out time and again, somehow all seemed incredibly right with the world.

During late spring the robust forsythia hedge was already growing chest-high all around the porch area of the Lauder home. When it finally came into full blossom, somehow a sweet canary-yellow richness managed to contrast itself against the gray weathered boards of their abode....

In due time, as well, a multitude of tiny clumps of "February Gold" miniature daffodils were already colorfully dotting the various flower beds throughout their entire yard. All the rest of what had been so thoughtfully planted by the previous owners of that wonderful farmstead either lay still sleeping underneath the cold earth, or were already well-established shrubs which had not as yet made their traditionally festive appearance.

Every now and then, usually just before suppertime, I would frequently spy several of the older boys tossing a well-worn football, or a baseball, amongst themselves. Also in a mood of equally good-natured fun several of the younger children would eagerly vie for a chance to emulate the actions of these older sports enthusiasts.

When the real season of spring was in full gear, I watched as the family next door began sowing seeds for a vegetable garden. A perfect location had been selected on one far sunny side of the barn. Several days after this particular project was completed, Felix Lauder took the trouble to claim for himself a small parcel of land not too far from this other place and began busying himself by planting a strawberry patch.

It should be remembered that because of my friend's unruly diabetic condition all the truly marvelous sweets and sinfully rich pastries which his talented wife was so skilled in making would naturally be soundly denied him. As a sort of consolation prize when his insulin intake was properly managed, Felix found great pleasure in eating fresh fruit—and strawberries, those luscious, ripe, sun-blessed strawberries, remained his all-time favorite treat.

In time Felix Lauder's precious strawberry patch reminded me of an amazing nursery where a multitude of tiny vulnerable infant plants required the utmost solicitous care and pampering. Every aspect of the project was being watched over by this most attentive gardener. On many an early morning, in fact, long before the fragile daylight made its welcome appearance upon the distant horizon of the east, I would often spot my future friend sitting upon a small chair out back, all bundled up to help ward off the cool dampness of those early hours….

Since hungry little rabbits possess a notorious fondness for such delicacies as strawberry plants, at one point it became quite a common occurrence to witness my neighbor standing watch over his special garden. Indeed, as those vulnerable shoots of baby green slowly grew and matured, Felix took to packing an unfriendly looking pellet-gun that he was not at all afraid to discharge when necessary.

Towards the end of that particular springtime when the weather now was more or less predictable—and when the nagging fear of being surprised by a sudden drop in temperature that would surely burn and kill the more fragile foliage was no longer an issue, something truly momentous occurred next door. I clearly remember that it was on one especially early Saturday morning that Felix and two of his older sons claimed both the automobile and the truck and promptly disappeared for the better part of that day.

Upon their arrival home sometime during the late afternoon hours I watched again as both vehicles slowly made their way up the driveway, heavily laden this time with no less than ten fully-grown oleander trees. All their tender flowering branches had been prudently trimmed back during the previous autumn and were at the moment expertly wrapped with a white gauzy material to protect them no doubt from the trials and tribulations of being moved from their former home back in Chicago, there to the family's newest residence.

Those amazing trees were Emma Lauder's pride and joy. They remained a living tribute, in essence, to her expertise as an excellent gardener in her own right for it was undeniably unusual to find such exotic beauty flourishing in a climate that could often, and would often, be so alien and inhospitable. The cultivated trees were poignant reminders of the family's formerly much happier early times when they first resided in Mexico.

Over the many years to come I would watch this lady tend to her special on-going exercise in uncompromising dedication. She seemed compelled to lavish the same genuine loving care upon these same fortunate objects as she naturally did upon the many members of her own precious family. Consequently the great happiness and joy, which certainly came to her when she achieved this level of gardening expertise, naturally also tended to benefit the rest of the family too. From my point of view, at least, this worthwhile endeavor of hers was really no different from the acute satisfaction and sincere pleasure that her dear husband habitually received from his immeasurable love of painting, and music, and philosophy....

Each one of the truly exceptional trees arrived already well-established within its immense deep clay pot. Only after Mrs. Lauder cheerfully made her appearance from within the house that day, where she must have been eagerly awaiting the safe return of her men, did the critically important decision of where to place each object finally begin in earnest.

From the kitchen window of my father's house I eagerly watched as eventually each cumbersome and exceedingly heavy container finally came to rest along either side of the long driveway. Five trees were being artistically arranged along one side, while the remaining five were being staggered along the other, with each now residing at a respectable distance of several dozen or so feet from one another.

After the protective gauze fabric was carefully removed from each new arrival, a mass of newly flowering stems of pure white blossoms now freely cascaded down around the smooth top of each clay container. Like so many steadfast soldiers-at-arms these lovely additions to our lives were destined to remain confidently poised exactly where they were thoughtfully placed on that very day—silently, and faithfully, guarding the entrance to the Lauder home.

Looking back I remind myself how one could always set one's internal "seasonal clock" by the events which naturally transpired relative to those beautiful trees. Each late autumn, during exactly the same time every year, the lush foliage of these resplendent treasures would be severely trimmed back and then painstakingly loaded onto a flat-bed little wagon which was built expressly for this purpose by Felix. With several people laboring exhaustively towards the same end, the oleanders would be slowly wheeled up the gravel driveway, one by one, towards the side door of the back porch. This is how those marvelous trees would be temporarily placed within the house in order to spend the next several months of winter, happily hibernating within the peaceful security and semi-warmth of this glassed-in storm-shuttered enclosed area, until their ever predictable re-emergence the following spring. Then come late April—or early May, the entire process would occur all over again, only this time in reverse.

During many a hostile wintry evening after I officially become part of this amazing family, there I would frequently remain all curled up in one well-worn wing chair and enviably wrapped from neck to toe within the generous warmth of a hand-knit afghan... Usually I was reading during these special times, but every now and then I would purposely pause to listen with genuine fascination to the insistent wind outside as it literally howled like some wild, half-mad creature in pain....

Without abating in the least this same zealous banshee would continue to cunningly encircle our fortress home, and then to sporadically barrage us from every conceivable angle with her ever fervent hope of gaining entry into this sacred sanctuary of ours, but always to no avail.... There by the soft golden light being reflected through the well-worn yellow shade of the antique table lamp nearby, those same fortunate trees and I would secretly acknowledge that we were all sharing this favorable refuge. Indeed, it was as though I had the excellent benefit of my very own arboretum. From here I could observe and enjoy the sleeping oleanders at my leisure. Quite naturally with the above described circumstances a magical wonderland was somehow being created for me that pleased me far more than any words can possibly tell.

For ages now—even back when the family resided in Mexico, Emma Lauder became firmly convinced that rain water was far superior to well water where the routine care of her dear trees were concerned. And so it was, after that first year when the overall amount of rainfall had been so pitifully meager, that an oversized cistern was readily constructed by Felix in order to solve such problems in the future.

Unbeknownst to me at the time—actually, unbeknownst to anyone at the time—these innocent trees were to unwittingly become the focal point of intense interest for others within our community. Specifically speaking, it would prove to be Cornelia Grimsley, herself, who would in fact grow to covet them, ultimately causing a chain of life-altering events that drastically impacted several good people including the Lauder family and me. From that deplorable time forward, needless to say, the bittersweet presence of those poor objects would forever recall this fact to my mind.

Summer that year was unusually hot and muggy. The heavily oppressive heat with its ever-present humidity would just hang around in the air for weeks on end, without giving us even a moment's relief. Hourly promises of benevolent rain remained abundant but unfulfilled for the most part. Likewise, restful slumber of any sort and during any given night became nearly impossible to come by, as the tireless mosquitoes and eagerly biting gnats became noticeably more and more troublesome.

It seemed that just enough moisture fell in order to tease the insects. This in turn whipped them into a continuous frenzy of motion. To gain any sort of a brief respite from the gross discomfort of my father's insufferable house, eventually I took to sleeping on the front porch again. During all this time, too, I was obliged to remember not to light the little lamp, for that solitary beacon served only to call forth those awful hordes of bloodthirsty pests which naturally tended to make life even more miserable for me.

Without the necessary blessing of life-sustaining rain for Emma Lauder's oleander trees, as well as for the family's vastly important vegetable garden—and lest we forget, for the near-sacred strawberry patch, too, Felix was forced to water everything manually. He used a hose as well as a five gallon watering can for those areas which simply could not be reached any other way.

Later that summer when the succulent red fruit finally came to be, I found myself secretly but whole-heartily congratulating our new neighbor on behalf of all his efforts. After those weeks of exemplary dedication and near backbreaking labor, not to mention the ongoing feud which was predictably still occurring quite regularly now between he and the rabbits, it seemed only right that such a spectacular victory should be his at last.

At one point during what I suppose must have been midsummer by then, there hung over the distant horizon for two or three days in succession a growing darkness which began to speak quite earnestly of our much-needed rain. Towards the last day, in fact, a healthy wind began to pick up, profoundly bolstering our hopes in the process. Within hours after the first strong rumblings of thunder first appeared and slowly fanned out to loudly echo across the lush fields of well-established grain that was growing all around us, we finally became more than certain that the merciful rain was really on its way this time and our spirits literally soared with gladness.

So it happened on this very day, when the strawberry season was more or less winding down, that I remained quietly kneeling in our yard becoming deeply engrossed in studying a small land tortoise that I spotted ambling along through the dense weeds. Obviously the little fellow was not used to being held for he writhed and struggled endlessly in a valiant attempt to free himself from my very able grasp. Completely lost in the magic of the moment I continued to carefully inspect each aspect of the little visitor's scaly skin, as well as the interesting markings of its decorative shell, when upon hearing an unusual clinking sound of metal upon metal I quickly glanced up. Passing along the top of our truly motheaten and terribly neglected hedge of pine trees which barely managed to separate our property from our new neighbor's I suddenly spied a suspicious-looking straw hat slowly bobbing towards me, all along the boundary's entire top surface.

Shortly thereafter I came to notice, with a sense of marked relief, that the hat was not traveling alone.... Now along the bottom portion of this same line of sad looking foliage, every now and then I would catch the flash of a pair of work boots moving more or less in time with the hat above it.... While I hung fairly spellbound, at this point, the vision of the man who was living next door to my father and me came into full view, just as he was presently passing a large opening in our hedge. And since we both managed to catch each other's eye at nearly that precise moment, I observed the visitor's forward momentum halt immediately. Quickly turning back around he came at last to stand there at the entrance of this narrow hiatus, not more than thirty feet or so from where I continued to stand avidly marking his progress all the while.

Because I had had no intention of keeping the small unhappy tortoise, the grateful creature was finally reinstated within our deplorable yard, pretty much where I originally found it. Having done this, I then felt obliged to wander over to where this gentleman continued to stand. As I cautiously approached our good neighbor, he in turn remained momentarily occupied in removing a smaller tin bucket which up to this point in time had remained well hidden within the larger one he was carrying....

It was the clanking sound made by these two empty objects, as they hit upon each other while the man walked along, that first captured my attention on that early afternoon. Then as Felix Lauder and I stood silently regarding each other for the very first time, his initial words to me on that memorable day of days were, quite simply, "Would you be able to help me, I wonder?" With this he turned to nod in the general direction of the dark threatening clouds that were already forming rather magnificently upon the horizon, and added with a note of concern in his voice, "Everyone else in our family happens to be away for the afternoon.... As you may see for yourself, there's a great storm approaching, and I would so like to save the remainder of my strawberry crop! Naturally I shall easily be able to manage this, if only you would consent to help me. "

The hauntingly rich sound of this man's voice with its unusual intonation of speech, coupled even further with the casual formality of his carefully selected words, had a rare and hypnotic quality that was such sweet music to my ears. Indeed, his marvelous Magyar accent had already thoroughly captivated my imagination whenever I chanced to hear him speak to one of his many children when they were out and about their yard as they so often were—or to his dear wife, whenever they were both out in their garden working together.

However, like an incommunicative child who was either deaf or mute—or both, for that matter, I remained literally planted where I was soundlessly taking in the complete picture of the man who was standing only a mere arms length from me. He, on the other hand, was politely waiting for some sort of positive response from me with regard to the worthy case he was pleading for my assistance. The narrow cotton strings from the comfortable-looking loosely-woven straw hat that he was wearing were tied securely under his chin, properly frustrating the playful wind's continuous attempt at stealing the item away from him.

While my charmingly courteous neighbor remained patiently holding out the smaller bucket for me to claim, I, in turn, was becoming helplessly lost in the glorious light which was pouring forth from the depths of his utterly kind and exceptionally intelligent eyes. Quite inexplicably those expressively beautiful eyes possessed the unique power to slowly and quite painlessly draw me ever inward, and ever onward, towards their dazzling center....

Although I instinctively sensed the rare profundity of the moment, because of my overall innocence and total lack of sophistication with regard to the great mysteries of life, as well as to life's equally great miracles, I certainly should have found myself at a loss to properly describe this happening in terms of words or phrases had I been pressed to do so on that day. It would be many years later upon my having become far older and wiser that I was destined to fully grasp the real significance invoked by those wonderful moments of our first meeting.... In time I would come to gratefully acknowledge the reality that Felix Lauder frequently made a habit of actually blessing me, in the truest sense, with that amazing grace whose source stemmed from his overwhelming sense of humanity.

Needless to say, I remained powerless to deny him his simple request that afternoon. While I finally reached for the small lightweight tin container which he had been patiently offering me all this while, rather spontaneously I was thinking to myself: Here, at last, is a person in whom I may believe.... Here, indeed, is a man who would never betray me in the slightest manner. With my keen instinctual belief in Felix's unequivocal goodness, which had come literally spilling out of his eyes and into my heart from that very first second, I also realized with a certain humility that I should always feel compelled to follow him anywhere; absolutely anywhere—even to hell and back, should he ever require it.

No sooner had I taken possession of the smaller of the two metal buckets when without so much as another word my future friend and most excellent mentor turned abruptly to stride back with me into his own yard. Side by side, now, we proudly walked together and quickly headed in the general direction of the strawberry patch which had grown so remarkably important to my new acquaintance.

Finally watching him kneel there in the rich earth to gently lift one flawless velvet leaf of a dark emerald-green strawberry plant, the fairly astonishing sight of a large luscious red strawberry was finally being revealed to both of us. Soon I heard him enthusiastically declare, "See for yourself how the fruit will hide under the leaves. Although most of the crop has already been harvested, if we were to leave behind these remaining few to be brutalized by the coming storm it would be such a shame—don't you agree?"

Knowing first-hand how diligently Felix had toiled for this garden of his, I nodded in complete agreement, as I passionately offered, "I'll be happy to help you pick what's left!"

Our entire exercise of quickly retrieving the remainder of the fruit became an enormous game in the end. To finally discover the where-abouts of those elusive treats as they continued to hide in amongst the lush foliage was challenging work, especially since both of us were laboring against the clock. Hurriedly crawling around in the dirt, up and down each row as I was doing, I would now and then feel inspired to happily call out, to no one in particular, "Here's a really ripe one!" or "Gosh! This must certainly be the biggest, and best, one yet!"

With Nature's swiftly approaching display of fireworks nearly upon us, at the moment, I began to notice that the baby-fine hairs upon my arms were actually standing on end now, as the ever-present electrical currents continued to actively play within the turbulent air all about Felix and me. To properly insure our safety it was my wise companion who finally had the presence of mind to end the strawberry hunt. Eventually I observed him hurry over to where I was still kneeling in the soil, fervently clutching the smaller pail to my chest and all the while continuing to gather what remaining berries I could find. Practically shouting in order to be able to communicate with me over the coming storm, Felix was telling me, "It's growing far too dangerous for us to remain outside like this!"

Now as we huddled together with each of us cradling our container of highly prized fruit my splendid neighbor was quickly putting forth his hand in the rather long-overdue ceremony of formally introducing himself, as he no less than shouted at me with a fine smile, "I'm Felix

Lauder! Tell me, please, with whom do I have the great pleasure of working side by side in order to save my wonderful strawberries?!"

I always liked the special way Felix had of phrasing things. And as
I gently placed my small free hand into his much larger one that day,
eagerly returning his smile with my own, without the slightest sense
of fear, or embarrassment, or shame, I found myself shouting back in
return, "My name is Adam Bodray!"

"I'm very happy to be making your acquaintance, Adam.... Thank
you for aiding me in my heroic effort this afternoon! I should have been
unable to accomplish the task, without your much-needed help...."

His kind words of praise were causing my small chest to expand with
immense pride. While he held steady the rim of my little pail with the
index finger of his free hand, as if to further protect it from the prank-
ish trickery of the wind, I watched with astonishment as this charming
individual began so generously to add to the meager amount of plump
berries I had heretofore managed to collect on my own. Eventually he
topped off my container to near brimming with the rich bounty of what
was previously stored in his own bucket.

With an undisguised touch of pride in his voice, this good man went
on to further exclaim, "Here, then, is my small reward for your very
able help today. You must sample for yourself the sweet rewards of our
labor!" Then just as the much-welcomed rain began to fall rather gently,
at this point, and, too, just as an extremely healthy bolt of lightning managed to hit something far too close to us now for our mutual comfort,
Felix Lauder quickly added, "Do hurry home, my young friend.... And,
once again, many thanks for your time and effort on my behalf!"

Upon hastily entering my father's dilapidated house by way of the
back porch that day, it was as though some sort of a silent signal had been
given. Merely seconds later the heavens were literally cleaved in two
causing the ensuing rain to fall so heavily that the sound of it all became
fairly deafening. With a new-found reverence I carefully placed the small
bucket of fruit upon the counter near the kitchen sink and then took a
long moment to critically contemplate the lovely vision before me.

The already powerful wind was beginning to strengthen quite noticeably outside, promoting the rather strange phenomenon of an odd
sort of interior moaning sound.... This remarkably haunting music was
being orchestrated in and out and all about the countless hollow places
located everywhere within the aged structure of our shameful abode.
With the benevolent rain which was now quite firmly blessing us at long
last, I finally consented to reach for one of the large red strawberries...

I instinctively felt that to touch it, and then to finally be able to taste it, would prove beyond any reasonable doubt that the highly unusual episode which had just occurred next door was not a mere figment of my imagination after all. While I slowly began to revel in the fruit's sweet succulent goodness, I also became poignantly aware that somehow some sort of amazing transformation had recently taken place within me, but I still remained at a substantial loss to name exactly what it was.

9.

MY POOR FATHER was slowly but surely going mad. His chronic alcoholism finally reached a critical stage where he was unable to keep down the precious booze which had long become the entire focal point of his day-to-day existence. Because of his desperately weakened physical condition, he was also no longer able to rise from his bed as before.

Naturally I continued to faithfully look after his basic needs by emptying the obligatory bedpan, as well as by washing his soiled bed linen and personal clothing, too, whenever he vomited some recently consumed drink in which he still insisted upon indulging, and which now frequently bore telltale traces of bile mixed with blood. This sort of demeaning behavior occurred several times a day. Somehow, through it all, I found that I was still able to manage. What began to distress me far more than these on-going cleanup operations, however, was the immense sense of personal guilt which began to firmly take command of me; that same overwhelming culpability which endlessly plagued me with the disquieting realization that I had for a long time already become an active accomplice in helping this sorry man end his life, as he definitely was in the process of doing.

Even though common sense should have indicated to my father that he was far too sick to continue downing the awful stuff, regrettably I was still summoned on a regular basis to make the usual trip to that same establishment of ill-repute in order to purchase more of what was slowly poisoning him to death. Because of the disquieting fact that his entire system had come to depend upon the consumption of significant amounts of alcohol, yet could no longer tolerate it, my father began to manifest signs of extreme dementia. During any given hour, and without any apparent outside stimulus of any kind, he would take to literally ranting and raving over terrible visions which he alone would be able to see there within his room....

Certainly on more than one occasion this hopelessly apathetic individual frantically insisted that a multitude of snakes were actually slithering all about his room, posing a terrible threat to him. Of course it became evident to me that these terrible phantom serpents dwelled only within his sick and confused mind. Like the small frightened child that he sometimes appeared to be, I watched with a sense of growing horror as he would curl up into a more compact mass of yellow skin, and long fragile bones, and badly matted dank hair. Many times I would find him laying in a more extreme fetal position there upon the bed, openly weeping and bombastically cursing with extreme fright. Meanwhile, during these same miserable episodes of his, I was being forced to do battle with a growing sense of utter despair which was quickly beginning to take over my own life.

Realizing that I was totally inept at dealing with the immensity of this problem, with each of these horrific tempests that occurred my trusty friend Jake and I would make haste to find our safe refuge there upon the back porch. Usually we cleverly hid between one portion of the sturdy railing and what remained of a once impressive pile of firewood, tightly covering our ears with our hands and ritualistically rocking back and forth in an ongoing attempt to hold counsel with one another—at least until the current ever-frightening episode with my father finally subsided....

It came to pass early one morning that from my usual perch at the kitchen window I witnessed "Doc" Owens' ancient automobile sitting idly in the driveway next door. That summer an epidemic of measles visited itself upon our community, and several of the younger Lauder children had contracted the acutely infectious disease. Our good friend was prudently summoned by Felix. With "Doc's" characteristically ever-dependable care, this visit would prove to be the first of many.

On that particular day, however, after I watched the two men leave the Lauder home together by way of the rear door, they stood for a few moments in the driveway near the old car to speak with each other. Sometime during this shared discourse of theirs I distinctly observed Felix Lauder nod in the direction of our home. After the two gentlemen shook hands and parted, I further observed with a growing sense of panic that instead of climbing back into his compact little automobile to drive off somewhere, "Doc" Owens was actually making his way through our old hedge and heading directly onward to the front porch of our house.

Good God! In a terrible state of heightened emotional turmoil many things flashed through my mind as I eventually heard this unexpected visitor's firm knock upon the wooden casement of the door out front. Naturally my deepest wish would have been to rush to the foyer and welcome this gifted man into our lives. I instinctively felt that he might be the only person in the world who could conceivably help my poor father stand down from the increasingly self-destructive path he had willfully chosen to tread.

But I also realized that in doing this I would be unforgivably betraying my father's trust. I would surely be betraying that staunch edict of his which precluded his desire to have any sort of contact with other people. As the more sensitive reader can certainly imagine, it continued to be these two diametrically opposed courses of action with which I was agonizingly obliged to weigh with such care that was currently troubling me so. As a second series of even louder knocks could be heard from my hiding place there in the kitchen behind the door, I soon heard "Doc's" now rather familiar voice loudly calling out, "Hello! Is anyone about the place?"

Holding my breath and tightly closing my eyes, I continued to suffer over this dilemma of mine. What should I do? There I remained, standing with my warm moist forehead pressed against the cooler boards of the wooden door which served rather well to protect me from being discovered by our visitor. With all my heart I was hoping beyond all hope for this kind man's much-needed intervention, while at the very same time I was also praying with all my might that he would not just enter our home, as he still might, and make his way upstairs to surprise my father.

By this time, having been denied any sort of a reply at all after his persistent inquiry, I eventually heard "Doc" slowly make his way down those precarious steps out front and then finally walk away from our house, thereby somewhat relieving me from having to wrestle with any more decision making. Without my bothering to go to the kitchen window to observe his departure, I still easily recognized the noisy racket that this good man's faithful little automobile was making as it was in the process of being cranked up. Soon the inevitable sound of his predictable leave-taking was being orchestrated, and I listened with mixed emotions as that already familiar sound of those extremely well-worn tires went crunching along, all the way down the loose gravel of the driveway next door....

Late that evening, shortly after my father's return from one of his more turbulent excursions into that unforgiving realm of madness, I dutifully went upstairs to look after him. Since such violent internal turmoil always left him absolutely spent in every respect, I had little cause to fear him at the moment. Customarily I would find him lying motionless upon the bed and staring sightlessly and soundlessly into space with a thoroughly glazed over and nonthreatening sort of look within his eyes....

However on that particularly unforgettable late night, by the more softly diffused light of the kerosene lamp which I placed upon the floor nearby, I diligently labored to clean up the mess that he just made all over the floor near his bed. Believing him to be incommunicado, as he usually was under such circumstances, I remained kneeling near his cot with my head bowed, totally engrossed in completing this necessary task of mine. Suddenly I felt the modest pressure of someone's finger lightly pushing down upon my right shoulder. Immediately glancing up I was absolutely dumbfounded to behold the intense stare of my father's eyes, as if he were being earnestly compelled to try and tell me something of very great importance.

Somehow those normally lifeless-looking windows of his soul had become the eyes of someone with whom I was completely unfamiliar, since they seemed so incredibly clear and so totally focused for a change. Indeed, their powerful intensity was such that they seemed to be attempting to bore a hole into my head, as well as into my heart. As our eyes continued to hold each other and in a well-modulated loud whisper my father was passionately declaring, "You cannot save me! You cannot save me.... But you must try, somehow, to save yourself!"

With these few cryptic sentiments of his, as if this most meager offering was meant to sum up his all-encompassing responsibility as a parent, he proceeded to turn his face away from me and just as quickly lapsed into a deep sleep. For quite some time after that I continued to kneel there, silently and pensively regarding the back of my father's head as he lay resting where he was. Holding the tattered remnants of that old cotton shirt from my former life which was presently being used as a wash cloth; and, likewise, with the small tin pail once belonging to Felix Lauder currently filled with the putrid water from the recent clean-up project which I had yet to finish, I found myself deeply contemplating these last words which my father would ever speak to me....

Had this strange, distant, self-absorbed man who once sired me ever truly loved me? Had it been within his power to truly love anyone? Was he soon to leave this life—and me, far behind him, thereby sentencing me to forever grapple with the endless questions concerning all the important personal issues which had thus far remained frustratingly unresolved between us? And what exactly was the true meaning of his last words to me anyway?!

In time Felix Lauder would eventually be shedding the long-sought-after light of truth and understanding upon these shameful and highly puzzling questions of mine. It would be this good man's love for a truly needy child—who was not even his own—that eventually inspired the necessary trust in order for me to one day open up and share the intense pain which my father's sin of omission had gravely inflicted upon his only son; that same nearly unforgivable sin of deeply-felt emotional neglect with which I was branded by him for life.

Not until I became a middle-aged man would I be able to weep at all for the father I never knew; for that same distant father who never took the necessary time to know me. Since "bitterness only pollutes life," as my adopted father so often contended, with the overwhelming love and compassion which Felix would be showering upon me from the very start, I would in time learn to forgive my own father. By finally bestowing this long-awaited absolution upon him, I would also inevitably be bestowing upon myself that elusive sense of peace for which my soul had yearned for such a long, long while....

That night I slept fitfully. Tossing and turning, I suffered through a nightmare that would continue to mercilessly visit itself upon me in various forms way into the future. In this highly disturbing dream of mine I would unexpectedly come upon a huge transparent glass container standing completely alone within an immense open field.... The colossal magnum was filled to the top with a clear liquid, and floating there towards the bottom—completely submerged in this dense amniotic-like fluid, was my father. Each time I beheld him, his highly-distorted face would be mashed against the glass. And those disturbingly defiant eyes of his would stare at me as if he and I were strangers. Indeed, he looked at me in such a manner that it was as though he and I had never met.

As this unusual dream of mine continued to unfold, I soon discovered myself carrying a long sturdy rope that was coiled upon my shoulder. Then as I proceeded to struggle with considerable difficulty to climb a high ladder that was leaning precariously against this same vessel, after eventually reaching the top I would frantically lower the rope into the bottle's wide mouth, until the far end of this cord dangled there, just within reach of my father's hands. Slowly glancing up, at long last, and having spotted the worthy device with which I was attempting so desperately to save him, he merely stared at the rope and stubbornly ignored any inclination to reach for it. In doing so he was also soundly negating this valiant endeavor by his only son who longed—

more than anything else—to save him from drowning within that thick all-encompassing mucus of life.

Sometime during that same hellish night, while I was attempting to secure even a fraction of much-needed rest for myself there upon the front porch, I was abruptly summoned from this illusionary world of mine by the sound of my father loudly calling out to someone. Since both the front and back doors of our starveling little dwelling were consistently being left open these days to inspire whatever fragile cross-breeze might be snared within these stiflingly hot summer nights, the sounds my father was making naturally came to me rather clearly.

Actually I was growing rather used to these sudden outbursts of his which happened rather randomly throughout any given day or night. But it was not until I finally sat up upon my mattress and attempted to try and discover whether the recent phenomenon was part of my dream, or not, that for a second time I distinctly heard his plaintive voice loudly calling forth with overwhelming clarity. With what may only be properly described as heart-wrenching emotional pain, I distinctly heard him very plainly yell out, "Dealya!" Following this, before I was even able to get to my feet to further investigate the trouble, I heard a terrible bumping and thumping noise which lasted for several long seconds only. After that there was nothing more to hear but an ominous silence which permeated everything—everything, including the very core of my being....

The continuous rain of those previous days and nights finally brought with it an unusually clear night sky which was presently filled with an abundance of all the twinkling stars I loved so well.... Likewise, the moon's creamy white face was so spectacular in every way that it managed to generously spread its soft clean light everywhere, creating a magical feeling that although it was already at some undetermined hour in the very early morning, it appeared somehow to be much later on in the day.

Naturally the odd commotion which had just occurred inspired me to spontaneously rouse myself from my bed and to quickly make my way to the open front door. Gazing directly before me now, there, by the bright night light of heaven's immense eye, I witnessed my father eerily sprawled across the mid-portion of several of those badly broken wooden stairs. Motionlessly he hung where he was. I could clearly see that his right leg was firmly entrenched up to its hip within the badly rotted remnants of the seventh step, while the rest of him remained suspended upside down and face up with his arms fully extended from his sides, like an inverted Christ upon His cross.

Much as if I were sleepwalking I slowly passed through the warped door frame of our front entrance, in order to move closer to this macabre vision.... Like a powerful magnet this unfortunate sight was helplessly drawing me towards it. And as I stepped aside, further allowing my father's corpse to be fully bathed in the gentle moonlight that was presently pouring through our front door, I could now better behold his countenance which was imprinted with a look of mild surprise. At the same time his lifeless eyes—those endlessly haunting eyes of a mortally wounded sparrow, remained blindly transfixed upon some point on the floor very near to where I remained standing....

Studying this heartbreaking scene in minute detail and having fully committed it to memory for all time, as I was compelled to do, I noted that before my father took that tragic plunge down those faulty steps to his death, he had chosen to don his huge green coat once more. Underneath this dusty and exceptionally well-worn outer gear, as well, I caught a glimpse of a portion of his dusty old uniform and one tattered old boot that remained poignant tokens of the soldier he once had been. Previously these items laid untouched for so many weeks, there beneath one side of his cot upstairs. How odd that he should choose to wear such heavy cumbersome garb in the heat of summer like this. And yet, in all the years to come, whenever I have summoned forth the tragic memory of my father, I have endlessly recalled him dressed exactly like this—pretty much as I first saw him on that unforgettable night within the train station in Chicago.

Although my father's end came abruptly enough, I sincerely believe that he actually had been in the process of dying for many years already. I remember thinking, at some point after this deeply traumatic event occurred, that my parents had been little more than two spawning fish in the vast ocean of life.... With their momentary union I was eventually conceived and born into this world. Later with my birth the three of us simply parted to go our separate ways, much like fish tend to do, without any sort of emotional bond or sensitive familial connection at all.

Nothing speaks so compassionately to the hungry or battered soul like music or poetry. Consequently, as the venerable old man that I have finally become, I often feel compelled to freely associate this profoundly dramatic occurrence of my father's death in terms of Vaughan Williams', *"Dona Nobis Pacem"*—and, more specifically, the moving lyrics to the chorus' fourth movement entitled: *Dirge for Two Veterans*, which is a poem composed by Walt Whitman that states so poignantly as follows:

The last sunbeam
Lightly falls from the finished Sabbath,
On the pavement here, and there beyond it is looking
Down a new-made double grave.

Lo, the moon ascending,
Up from the east the silvery round moon,
Beautiful over the house-tops, ghastly, phantom moon,
Immense and silent moon.

I see a sad procession,
And I hear the sound of coming full-keyed bugles,
All the channels of the city streets they're flooding
As with voices and with tears.

I hear the great drums pounding,
And the small drums steady whirring,
And every blow of the great convulsive drums
Strikes me through and through.

For the son is brought with the father,
In the foremost ranks of the fierce assault they fell,
Two veterans, son and father, dropped together,
And the double grave awaits them.

Now nearer blow the bugles,
And the drums strike more convulsive,
And the daylight o'er the pavement quite has faded,
And the strong dead-march enwraps me.

In the eastern sky up-buoying,
The sorrowful vast phantom moves illumined,
'Tis some mother's large transparent face,
In heaven brighter growing.

O strong dead-march you please me!
O moon immense with your silvery face you soothe me!

O my soldiers twain! O my veterans passing to burial!
What I have I also give you.

The moon gives you light,
And the bugles and the drums give you music,
And my heart, O my soldiers, my veterans,
My heart gives you love....

Becoming steeped more and more within a state of complete and ut-ter shock, my mind vaguely recalled my having climbed upon the porch swing—there, just outside the front door, while my father's tragically emaciated body remained grotesquely suspended where it was. I should still remain at a significant loss to properly describe the overwhelming sense of desperate loneliness which now quietly descended upon my being... Truly, it was as if I were alone in the universe; really and truly alone, and aimlessly floating about without any sort of an anchor, or compass, or kindly star by which to travel. My senses seemed as if they were being tightly bundled together into some sort of thick restrictive fabric, no doubt to protect my psyche at this point.... In essence, I was being held captive in an emotional "cocoon," unable to move, or to even think at all about anything in any normal manner....

God knows how long I remained sitting where I was. At some point, however, I must have made my way down the front steps of our house and then across our weed-infested moonlit yard, for it was as though some enormously powerful force was instinctively propelling me to-wards the farmhouse next door; guiding me there, in a real sense, as if my overall salvation greatly depended upon it. Although I remember relatively little of what transpired during that entire trip, it occurs to me that I surely must have knocked upon the back porch door of this warm and welcoming home, because even in my state of extreme muddled confusion I do believe I remember that the overhead glass globe there in the Lauder's kitchen was finally lighted, and very soon after this the screen door was opened to me as I eventually beheld the reassuring face and form of Felix Lauder....

While this special individual attempted to better focus upon me, himself very much like someone who had just been rudely awakened from a deep and restful slumber, I remember him asking me something. Even though I observed his lips moving, I was still mentally unable to focus upon what he was actually saying to me at this point. Only after I felt my protector's strong hands soundly grasp my small thin shoulders;

and after he knelt before me, with his deeply-concerned face now level with my own, did I finally hear him slowly and deliberately ask, "What's troubling you, Adam?!"

My voice had simply deserted me. Slowly concentrating upon this kind man's concerned eyes, and, too, the many details of his noble-looking face, I attempted to speak but found that I could not. Soon, from somewhere within the interior of this home appeared the lady of the house and several of the couple's older children who were at present solicitously gathering around me.... Without asking me anything more, I vaguely heard Felix instruct his wife to take me inside, while he, in turn, proceeded to head in the direction of the front entrance to my father's house.

After I was promptly seated at the small painted wooden table, there in the cheerful kitchen, a generous glass of milk and a thick piece of buttered bread miraculously appeared before me. With the loving care that was being currently administered to me by these genuinely concerned people who had subsequently formed a semicircle around me, and who each in turn was gently touching my shoulder every now and then to help reassure me that I was now safe from whatever harm had unexpectedly propelled me into their lives, I slowly began to awaken to those more familiar twinges of reality that were softly telling me that I had finally arrived at this particular haven where I would indeed remain free from harm—and, too, free from want. Something deep within me was attempting to assure me that, after all these lonely years of wandering from place to place, this young sojourner had finally arrived home.

In what seemed like a matter of moments only, Felix Lauder re-entered his home. Without saying anything to anyone he walked directly to the phone box which hung in the short hallway located just off the kitchen. Distinctly I remember that it was with a sense of rather great composure that my new host placed the necessary end of this apparatus to his ear, while with his other hand he cranked up the phone by using a small handle which protruded from its side.

Soon he was leaning forward to speak into the phone's mouthpiece, as his family and I heard him say, "My apologies for waking you, Miss. Dooley.... This is Felix Lauder, over on Highway "D." Please understand that it's most urgent that I contact Sheriff Parker." And then, as if the operator might be challenging the validity of his request in some annoying fashion, he went on to firmly state, "Yes! I am absolutely prepared to accept full responsibility for waking him, Madam.... Now, do please ring him for me—it's extremely urgent!"

After a brief silence where one could have actually heard a pin drop within the confines of that small immaculately-kept kitchen, all of us eventually heard Felix say to Sheriff Parker, "Good morning, Sheriff Parker... This is Felix Lauder, over at the Turbin's old place on Highway "D". I sincerely regret having to awaken you like this, but there's been a dreadful accident.... Could you please meet me here at my home, as soon as possible?!"

10.

LAUGHTER IS THE SOUL AT PLAY. Not the sort of rude laughter, mind you, that is hatched from those nefarious traits of maliciousness, or cruelty, or cowardice—but, rather, the truly blessed kind which young children are capable of thoroughly experiencing, as well as those special adults who remember to continuously honor the young child within themselves. By allowing those cheerfully contagious and honestly beautiful notes to bubble forth from a light and happy heart, such fortunate people as these learn to properly celebrate in a nearly religious sense the profound art of living.

Genuine laughter, as I was soon to discover myself, has the amazing ability to neutralize our tears. Whether this blessed phenomenon is consciously instigated by us on a daily basis, or whether it is merely enjoyed every now and then from the sidelines of our ongoing travels throughout life, this ever important experience has the benevolent power to graciously buffer those necessary droplets of benign saline solution which might otherwise turn to acid and eventually erode the relatively smooth complexion of our lives....

Basically, during those first eight years of my existence, I failed miserably in learning to laugh. This honest revelation might astound the reader but, as everyone knows, so often the simplest truths have the ability to do just that. Although laughter is such a natural thing, and is so often taken for granted by most people, in time it would be my beloved George who would finally begin the process of tearing down those wretched barriers which I had purposely erected for my survival.

Indeed, it would be none other than my dear friend who would time and time again therapeutically expose me to what remains the glorious birthright of every human being. Of course this invaluable gift proved to be just one of the many memorable tokens of friendship which George would be bestowing upon me during those few short months we were destined to know each other. Yes, that splendid gift of laughter would remain just one of the many remarkable keepsakes that so justly inspired my unending love for him.

Three days after his death, my father was finally buried in a small cemetery located on the far outskirts of town. As the young child I was at the time, I had little reason to delve into the exact reason for this, but I do recall initially thinking that it would have seemed far more logical to have him interred in the convenient cemetery there across the way.

Many years later, however, as an adult I came to fully comprehend that this important decision must have been carefully weighed and then strategically implemented by Felix, expressly with my overall welfare in mind. With the tragic circumstances of what had recently transpired concerning my father's demise, this wise and sensitive soul wished me a new beginning—a speedy psychological and spiritual healing, in other words, which might have otherwise been thwarted on a daily basis by this powerful visual stigma connected with my very painful and not so distant past.

My father's cemetery plot itself, along with a new black suit and a modest casket, were all paid for in full by the money which remained behind in the ancient tin coffee can. A few days after the funeral, which the older members of the Lauder family, "Doc" Owens, and my good friend Harry Hopkins respectfully attended, the ramshackle house in which my father and I had dwelled together for those brief months was completely leveled.

On one clear hot sunny morning in the latter part of July—promptly after breakfast it was, two burly volunteers arrived to enthusiastically dismember it. From within the security of the side porch area of the Lauder home, I remember that Felix and Emma Lauder, several of their children, and I watched with considerable awe as amidst the mighty noise and clatter of the heavy bulldozing equipment, and in what seemed like little more than a few inspirational moments only, everything was reduced to a mere pile of rubble.

Later that same day more men returned with a large dump truck and an equally impressive-looking crane to haul away the debris. Shortly after this it was Felix himself who boarded the family tractor to unceremoniously move next door and promptly begin to thoroughly plow under the old moth-eaten hedge, along with all those wretched weeds which were still continuing to proliferate all around the now otherwise empty lot....

When his considerable effort was successfully completed, miraculously not a single trace of what had once existed was left behind. In time, too, with the faithful passing of the seasons, the healthy robust carpet of grass which my new family took such pride in grooming on a regular basis within the boundaries of their own yard eventually took to wandering and spreading next door, to a point where everything seemed to be reborn anew in the form of a marvelous playground which all of us would take great pleasure in using for many years to come.

This dramatic event was, needless to say, the precursor of what would also be heralding many dramatic new changes within me. In time the deep wounds which life had inflicted upon me as a young child would slowly be healing, just as those ensuing scars which are a natural result of that indisputably positive process would ultimately serve as the strong foundation upon which the proud new structure of my new life would be built.

I remember so well that during that same early morning of the day my father died, there in the well-lit cheerful kitchen of the Lauder home, while Felix and Sheriff Parker waited next door for the coroner to arrive, it was George who immediately took me under his wing, as if this significant gesture was quite simply destined to be. I was deeply affected, too, by how Emma Lauder had understandably felt herself responsible for deciding upon my "temporary sleeping arrangements," as she had so matter-of-factly put it.... From this rather emotionless comment of hers, I was immediately left wondering whether this meant that my presence within their lives was going to be temporary; or, rather, whether where I was destined to bed for a while was the temporary aspect to which she was alluding.

During this same early morning she, like the rest of the family, was naturally still dressed in her sleeping clothes and robe. Emma Lauder's obviously long and healthy-looking dark chestnut-color hair, which otherwise would have been swept up sensibly in the back during the day, was now plaited with ribbons and hung down her back in a manner that would eventually become quite familiar to me as an adopted member of this fine family.

This unusually thick rope of her glorious tresses was modestly streaked with tiny silver threads and would every now and then swing from side to side, like the pendulum of a clock, as she remained momentarily absorbed in the process of making up the sofa in the parlor. Suddenly George, who was standing to one side of his mother at the moment and patiently holding the neatly folded bed linen in an attempt at helping her, seemed prompted to respectfully counter this arrangement with an interesting idea of his own where I would be moved upstairs to share the bedroom which he already shared with his brother Eddie....

"What nonsense, George!" Mrs. Lauder was saying in a mild manner of irritability. "I simply won't hear of it. That space that you share with your brother is no larger than a postage stamp. How can you possibly think of putting anyone else in there with you?" Dramatically fluffing up a feather pillow which was waiting upon a nearby chair, she seemed pleased to be finalizing this brief conversation of theirs and thoughtfully took to adding, "This is where our new guest will be more comfortable—so, naturally, this is where our new guest will be sleeping!"

Having become the unwitting center of this mild controversy between mother and son, at the moment, I was slowly becoming somewhat embarrassed. While this minor exchange of theirs was taking place, I remained uncomfortably standing in the open doorway which separated the dining room area from the parlor, nervously shifting my weight from one foot to the other. The last thing in the entire world I felt I ever wished to do was to cause any member of this good family any sort of trouble.

What occurred next was a perfect example of how George's charm and diplomacy, as well as his unequaled self-assurance, would usually win the upper hand in many such debates. This, of course, applied not only to his strong-willed mother, but to friend and foe alike. Despite my great weariness I watched with growing interest as I saw my new champion slowly and deliberately put down the extra folded sheet he was holding. As he moved closer to his dear mother and proceeded to gently wrap one strong arm around her shoulders, he quickly whisked her around—actually before she could even protest at all, to say to me with a wonderful smile, "Please do excuse my mother and me for just a little bit, won't you, Adam?"

To tell the truth, my mind was still feeling unusually sluggish. Before I could collect my thoughts to even utter some sort of an appropriate response, I watched as both people waltzed straight out onto the long "L"-shaped porch. Next I observed them more casually walking side by side with their heads bent together, sharing what appeared to be some sort of meaningful dialogue being initiated by George....

After mother and son traveled together like this, up and down the entire length of that room, they came at last to rest near the entrance to the porch door directly across from where I still remained dutifully waiting for them. I saw George graciously gesturing with his free hand in what I was soon to learn was already a habit of his whenever he became engrossed in trying to make an important point about one thing or another.

Having eventually turned around to stand directly in front of his mother, as if impatiently attempting to better elicit some sort of an important decision from her, I could see that this special son was a good head taller than this lady. In profile, at least, one could readily capture the more than slight resemblance between them. From my distinct place of advantage, too, I also witnessed that my new friend was smiling down at his dear companion with what may only be described as undisguised affection, much as if this sort of special interaction between the two of them was not at all unusual.

Indeed, I warmly recall that there was an almost enviable bond between these two strong and dynamic personalities. To better illustrate this important point I know that for many years Emma Lauder made a habit of keeping a small intricately carved wooden box there upon the tall polished mahogany bureau of the downstairs bedroom which she and Felix shared as a couple. Within this same small treasure trove, tucked safely away inside one of its several drawers, were a number of small personal keepsakes from her many children. Mostly these special objects consisted of handmade cards and other such trinkets which had been painstakingly collected over a period of many years already.

Perhaps the greater portion of this same remarkable memorabilia ended up being those simple little hand-decorated notes from George, since it was he who had taken so naturally to writing from the very start. This second son's innocent declarations of filial devotion were faithfully composed over a period of many years, beginning when he was a young child of five or six.... Quite naturally the authorship spoke of this special son's deep respect and glowing admiration for that special woman who continued to remain such an important part of his life.

Consistent with the charming rules of this rather unique game for two, after young George would lovingly pen a wee meaningful message upon some small scrap of paper with a colorful crayon, he then took to hiding his gift somewhere where Mrs. Lauder was sure to eventually find it. For example, two of his more favorite places might be within the bottom portion of her well-used sewing basket, or cleverly wedged behind a neatly stacked pile of fresh clean towels within the family's linen closet. Apparently their mutual interest in this ongoing and quite marvelous game of hide and seek between themselves, although far less frequently played as the years progressed, still managed to linger even after George grew to young adulthood.

Presently, however, as I continued to observe this current interaction between mother and son which was prompted by George entirely on my behalf, with marked relief I noted that Mrs. Lauder had actually softened her formerly more rigid stance and was seemingly in the process of bowing a bit more to her son's wishes. With a small playful frown that I immediately interpreted as signaling her acquiescence, she finally nodded in consent to whatever it was that George was saying to her. Then as if to seal a bargain between them, I was pleasantly astounded to see my young friend react in a thoroughly impulsive manner by giving his mother a huge hug which managed to lift her entirely inches off the ground and at the same time seemed somewhat to embarrass her too.

Within seconds these two good people re-entered the parlor, only to stand before me. Although I could clearly see that Emma Lauder was wearing a pensive look, George on the other hand greeted me with a cheerful smile—and a wink. Very soon the lady of the house was telling me, with the slightest hint of an apology hanging amongst all her carefully chosen words, "Perhaps it would have been far more polite of me to ask which arrangement you might prefer, Adam.... Would you prefer our sofa here, which could naturally afford you far more privacy in the end; or would you be more inclined to share a more cramped but undoubtedly far more friendly atmosphere upstairs with two of our sons?"

How could this lady have guessed that there was no contest, after all? No lengthy decision to be made on my part. I was already so acutely soul-weary of being alone. And, too, with the recent horrible events of the past few hours, I was still feeling indescribably vulnerable and so wretchedly needy.... Owing to this reality, with marked gratitude I answered in response to her kind inquiry by respectfully stating, "Upstairs will be just fine, thank you very much!"

Upstairs my new sleeping quarters were far more generous than what I was led to imagine. On the far right side of the room, positioned against the wall and located underneath one of the long dormer windows, was a day-bed where young Eddie lay comfortably curled up and sound asleep. Surprisingly enough, he had managed to sleep on through the entire ordeal of that night.

With the bright moonlight continuing to pour in through the open window, as it was, there was no need to turn on a light to disturb him. Confidently taking me by my hand, George tip-toed over to the other bed which seemed somewhat different from his brother's. Leaning down, he surprised me by pulling out from beneath this piece of furniture another bed which was built on casters and which had been hiding there all along.

Attempting to be as quiet as a couple of mice, my considerate host began to slowly open the top drawer within a nearby chest, causing this simple action to produce an unpleasant reaction. Since the normally smooth wood of this same piece of heavy furniture had most probably become swollen with the summer's heat and humidity, an annoying high-pitched squeaking noise was momentarily disrupting the other-wise silent atmosphere within the comfortable little room. Soon, though, in no time at all my great new friend was randomly selecting sleeping clothes from inside the deep drawer.... Then, as he turned to hand them to me, he mentioned in a whisper, "You'll be able to change in the bath-room across the way!" After this, with each of us comfortably tucked into our own bed for the duration of what remained of that momentous night, by the ever-compassionate light of the all-seeing moon, I observed my young mentor's kindly face unexpectedly peering down at me from over the edge of his own mattress... As he warmly smiled at me, he cheerfully said, "Good-night, sport!"

This, of course, was to become George's special nickname for me. "Good-night, sport!" I answered very tiredly in return, while I spontane-ously reached up to clasp the strong hand which was being extended down my way. As we participated in what was to become our regular good-night ritual of friendship from that time onward, my friend was still smiling down at me as he gave off a short charming chuckle.

Being very nearly asleep at one point, I did just manage to hear him whisper, "Are you a fisherman, Adam?"

"Don't know..." I barely recall answering. Then, in order to make myself better understood, I must have added as I slowly felt myself sink-ing into oblivion, "Never fished before...."

George's last comment to me on that particular night was, "Well, my young friend, early tomorrow afternoon you and I are going to change all that!"

Naturally with the abundance of wide-mouthed bass that habitually stocked the cold glacier waters of our lovely lake, the same fish, I might add, that were also keenly prized by all the other fishermen who ever challenged their expertise there, and which George and I would nor-mally almost always bring home from those numerous fishing expedi-tions of our own, Emma Lauder would usually create one of my all-time favorite meals. This virtual feast was a thick, stick-to-your-ribs fish stew, incorporating generous amounts of potato and leek that were simmered at length in a rich base of fish stock with quarts of fresh sweet cream added later. Just about an hour or so before this fragrant and spectacular tasting treat was served, a bevy of fresh parsley and other herbs would be added as a final touch....

Fondly I recall that whenever the large elegant Meissen soup tureen was ceremoniously presented at our crowded supper table, now liter-ally brimming to the near spilling point with its luscious creamy-white contents, George and I would always catch each other's eye and smile with an unbridled sense of mutual pride at having been able to play such a significant role in making it all possible. That same much-prized porcelain work of art which usually held part of our supper and which also so beautifully set off the entire meal in such a civilized fashion was a much-belated wedding gift from Felix to his young wife several years after they were actually married.

But, much to our mutual chagrin, on what was to have been George's and my very first trip to the lake which the two of us had so enthusiastically planned together for that next afternoon, never actually materialized. Instead both of us remained in the process of being punished by Mrs. Lauder who understandably had not at all taken very kindly to the infamous "pissing contest" which George had impetuously instigated between himself, several of his many brothers, and me....

In retrospect I suppose that that late morning's entire fiasco most probably could and should be blamed upon poor little Herman Redding, Carl Redding's five-year-old grandson. It became the child's unintended participation in this impromptu game the Lauder boys would occasionally play that was the real reason why things ended up as they did. Any thoroughly open-minded reader might aptly appreciate the fact that such unsophisticated games were the result of a mere moment's flash of inspiration, where such creative young souls were concerned.... Using the God-given equipment with which we were naturally born, my new friends and I enthusiastically chose to re-implement this familiar contest as a sort of initiation for me. Basically it was intended as a more "down-to-earth" welcoming into the fold, so to speak, which called for a certain amount of grave concentration and practiced "know-how" on the part of each one of the participants....

The rules to this "male-only shooting contest" were relatively straight forward and pretty much required the seven of us at the time— that is, George, five of his nine brothers, and me—to stand behind a thin line which was drawn in the dirt out behind the far side of the barn area. Directing the steady stream of one's urine flow towards an old metal bucket, which was purposely positioned some ten feet or so in front of us, the first contender to soundly strike the bucket would naturally be the lucky person accorded the title of winner.

On this highly memorable hot and windy late summer morning, however, with most of the family's chores around the farm having already been completed by now, no one noticed little Herman walk up behind us to take his place at one far end of the long line, pull down his pants, and begin to emulate what he was seeing all the rest of us doing.... Most of all, no one had had the time to carefully explain one of the game's preeminent rules to him, which was never to turn one's healthy stream windward. Naturally the happy child was no longer very happy when he had inadvertently chosen to do this very thing, causing the front of his shirt, and knickers, as well as the top portion of his shoes to become wet with his own urine.

Quite naturally, too, it was this youngster's frightful wailing and endless carrying on, which none of the other boys nor I could contain in the least, that eventually brought Emma Lauder hurrying our way that morning. Having instantly sized up the situation, as most mother's tend to be rather good at doing, George would be the one to bear the brunt of her substantial wrath since obviously it was he who was the eldest member among the group, and, consequently, as she more than once reminded him, he was the person who "certainly should have known better!"

I remember Mrs. Lauder firmly telling him—and rather justifiably, I suppose, while at the same time shaking her finger at him all the while she spoke, "Sometimes, George, your actions mystify me.... Although you already have the physique of a grown man, you still insist upon playing such childish games!" George, at this point, having made a rather feeble attempt at explaining to her the circumstances of the situation from his worthy perspective, was soundly neutralized on the spot... Waved off, in effect, as his mother continued on to angrily say, "Now, there'll be no fishing today—none of the usual personal time-off for any of you after lunch this afternoon—do you understand me?! There's always far too much to do around this farm, without having all of you make more needless work for me! Since you can't seem to find something more productive to do yourselves, I shall be quite thrilled to find more challenging work around here for all of you to do myself!"

And so she did. Emma Lauder kept her unwavering promise that day by loading me down with a large bucket that contained soapy water in one hand, while in the other I was obliged to carry along a large assortment of soft dry cleaning cloths. In no time at all I was promptly relegated to the upstairs bedrooms for several hours to expertly wash down and then polish dry the many baseboards there, as well as the window sills of each area.... While she managed to find equally stimulating work for all the offenders—minus young Herman, naturally, who was lent clean clothing belonging to one of the Lauder's younger sons and promptly sent home with a freshly baked cookie—as well as a note to the boy's mother, it was George who was placed in charge of tackling the extremely daunting mountain of family laundry that day, including the few articles of soiled clothing belonging to our neighbor's grandson.

From one of the tall dormer windows within the small room which I was privileged to be sharing with George and Eddie, and while I dutifully busied myself carefully washing and then drying the window sill exactly the way that I was firmly instructed to do, I glanced down in the yard below… My timing was such that I just happened to catch George standing there near the pump house. At the moment he was submerged practically waist-high amongst the dozen or so formidable-looking piles of that week's unwashed bed linen, and assorted pieces of grimy work clothing, with the large ever-faithful tin laundry basin and scrub board to one side of him and the sturdy washing machine with wringer to the other....

Catching my eye, this charming mischief-maker smiled broadly from ear to ear and, after what appeared to be a mere second's worth of deliberation only, for some unknown reason immediately became comically inspired to dance around the piles of soiled linen with both hands firmly clenched over his head, very much in the manner of a victorious prizefighter. He had, after all, won the "pissing contest" that day, and although the price we were forced to pay had been far dearer than either of us would have wished, I took his optimistic lead that hour by managing to make a game out of what we were now being forced to do.

With these priceless antics of George's, which he took to openly displaying with his characteristically exuberant abandon, something truly wonderful began to happen to me that day.... While I stood happily enraptured in observing my young friend's every motion, the gentle ripples of a heretofore inexperienced sense of great spiritual mirth began to well up from somewhere within the depths of my young soul. As if originating within that same fathomless subterranean spring, these heady impulses began at first to slowly and rather tentatively gush forth—not unlike the gentle flutterings of a tiny hummingbird's wings deep, deep within me, only to quickly grow, and then to helplessly expand. Ultimately what became the rather amazing finale to this entire process quickly erupted into a continuous barrage of spontaneous laughter, which my clever friend was purposely trying to elicit from me all along and which could no longer be contained.

That initial crystal-clear sound of my very own light and happy laughter momentarily stunned me, not unlike a small puppy might feel when being startled at the sound of its own voice when it inadvertently barks for the very first time. Naturally, upon acknowledging this wonderful sound, I went on to passionately abandon myself to those ongoing peals of mirth, which were now coming forth quite uncontrollably at this point, causing that impish rapscallion below to make it his business to make me laugh all the more.... Having by now expertly adopted the exquisite manner of Charley Chaplin's character of the "Little Tramp," George took to exuberantly swinging his imaginary cane and also tipping his imaginary little bowler hat as a greeting to me, all the while hurriedly walking that famous little walk whose signature shall forever belong to this much-beloved character of silent films.

At one point I was laughing so hard at this marvelous impersonation of his that my stomach actually began to ache. Wordlessly begging for mercy, I leaned against the frame of the window to steady myself, all the while continuing to hold my sides as I was. Shortly, precious tears that were being invoked by a tremendous sense of great emotional release were just beginning to run down both sides of my smiling and aching face. Perhaps it should also be declared that, even with the passing of all these many years of my long life, whenever I chance to think back upon this same momentous occasion which occurred at a time when I undoubtedly needed it most, the story's endless details have prevailed and have always managed to bring a smile to my grateful heart.

During those few short weeks of our immensely important friendship, which all too soon would be shattered by his untimely death, George patiently taught me to read and to write. Needless to say these highly esteemed offerings of his radically changed my world forever. Besides opening all those wondrous new doors of learning, which naturally began with my patiently sounding out the vowels and consonants in preparation for all that lay ahead, this important milestone also ultimately helped to promote the necessary confidence that would allow the young child I was to actually enjoy attending school one day.

However, as I am now quite honestly prepared to admit for the record, although reading and writing have long been a pleasure for me, no matter how hard I have striven over the years my ongoing attempt to become a truly worthy fisherman has always left something to be desired. Even now, after so many years have come and gone, I still find that I am unable to thoroughly master those finite techniques which George possessed so naturally—those same laudable qualities which helped to make him the consummate fisherman that he just naturally tended to be.

11.

WHAT DOES IT PROFIT ANY MAN if he lives to gain the world, only to suffer the loss of his immortal soul? For some reason these poignant words from the Good Book always come floating forth to flood my consciousness, whenever I recall the unfortunate person of Burtram Elsworth Parker.

The man was a true "character" in every sense of the word. Over the years I was to know him this real-life, flesh and blood, figment of the imagination might have easily figured into the highly entertaining literary masterpiece of the great Miguel de Cervantes, but only in some more or less inconsequential fashion. Or on a far less artistic scale he might surely have played some minor role in one of those similarly entertaining laugh-a-minute slapstick comedies of a "Laurel and Hardy" film. Indeed, from our very first encounter which occurred during those early morning hours of the day my father died, his overall demeanor was instantly imprinted upon my brain as that belonging to a serious-minded clown who was forever being inspired to play the part of a "dandy."

Being the highly impressionable youngster that I naturally was, I became particularly challenged in my on-going attempt to more securely place Burtram Parker within some proper sort of category relative to the many facets inherent in human nature. Actually this pint-sized so called "minor pillar of local society" believed himself to be quite the "ladies man." He would always be spotted—as well as heard, traveling about the countryside all the while driving his immaculately kept paddy wagon with its horribly rude siren being used far more often than was felt necessary by most of us. No doubt this unusual behavior of his was meant to better instill within the collective hearts of his local constituency the reassuring feeling that, as far as our general welfare was concerned, all of us remained quite safely resting within his very capable hands.

For ages it was politely whispered around the community that because of his rather diminutive physical proportions it was necessary for him to hide a copy of the formidable-looking Chicago telephone directory underneath the driver's side seat of his vehicle. Obviously this was done in order to allow him the ability to rise to the occasion, as it were, and to better be able to see out the windshield whenever he was driving. I well recall that with his usual air of "spit and polish" this rather absurd individual always chose to make a rather contradictory statement; contradictory, at least from my child's point of view, by wearing a colorful posy of some sort fitted snugly into the little top buttonhole located in the left breast pocket of his uniform, directly above the silver badge of honor that signified his chosen field of endeavor.... Because of what I automatically perceived as misplaced behavior on his part, try as I may I simply could not make myself imagine one of J. Edgar Hoover's well-trained agents, for example, behaving in a similarly ridiculous manner.

Having now only briefly alluded to this far more renowned individual who lived and worked in our nation's capital, just about everyone within our modest little community readily came to acknowledge the sobering fact that those far more interesting, as well as far more dangerous, professional assignments that might normally have come our little sheriff's way were being usurped on a regular basis by those far better trained government agents. These same dedicated F.B.I. officials were sworn to uphold the cause of "law and order" and so were prudently given far-reaching latitude where such things concerning the swift apprehension of bootleggers, bank robbers, kidnappers, murderers, and other such similar dregs of society were concerned. Basically the ongoing daily implementation of their critical work which extended far and wide from the hub of the populated metropolis of Chicago, and outward like so many spokes of a wheel to eventually touch upon all the smaller neighboring farming communities like our own, could never be overestimated nor over-appreciated.

As the local "grapevine" would have it, and for the greater part of the previous twenty-five years, Sheriff Parker had been semi-faithfully courting one Miss Edwina Dooley who was our local switchboard operator. Although there had been a lengthy string of promises made during all this time, which naturally included marriage sometime in their future, his all-time favorite passtime within the community seemed to be faithfully aiding much younger ladies in distress. For the most part these heroics usually translated into plucking a wayward kitten from its owner's nearby tree or promptly locating a troublesome cow or lamb which had willfully transgressed the boundaries of its owner's property line.

Miss Dooley, on the other hand, had her own lengthy list of priorities which included the unsavory habit of eavesdropping upon the day-to-day private telephone conversations of others whenever she was obliged to service their needs. Since Cornelia Grimsley, Sheriff Parker, and Miss Edwina Dooley remained "thick as thieves" with regard to the clique that was firmly established between the three of them within our small community—like it, or not, everyone in the community seemed to be forced into becoming part of this "one big happy family" of theirs, in a certain manner of speaking.

It would also be fair to state that soon after Felix and his family moved to the Lake Geneva area, my highly astute friend was able to properly discern the true nature of these unpleasant people. Although it was necessary for families in such remote areas as ours to share a phone line with at least one other family in town, because the Lauders shared a line with an elderly widower who remained extremely hard of hearing, this same neighbor never could have been accused of listening in upon any of the Lauder's daily interaction with others.

So quite naturally through the simple process of elimination, and for a duration of quite a few years, each time one of our family members was prompted to use the phone for any reason, more often than not causing us to become suspicious of another's presence on the open line, we just automatically assumed that Miss Dooley was listening in on us as usual. Sometimes with regard to this offensive and highly immature behavior of hers we felt inspired to initiate a bit of harmless interplay by making it an ongoing habit to overtly greet "Miss Edwina" with some polite and cheerful phrase, thereby allowing her to know that we all knew she was there.… Of course, having realized that we were "on to her," right away one would distinctly hear a discreet little click on her end of the line.

With astounding clarity I recall that Burtram Parker remained a man who passionately coveted his appointed position as local constable above all else. Sometime shortly after my arrival to the Lake Geneva area regional elections were taking place. Although I could not read, as yet, it was not very difficult to notice photo upon photo plastered everywhere around town, heralding all the various participants who were either running for re-election or seeking some sort of official public office for the first time. Since it always remained the mayor's important responsibility; or more correctly, in this particular case, the mayor's wife's responsibility to assure the uncontested and unbroken continuation of this particular man's professional tenure, our illustrious peacekeeper naturally felt that he owed a certain glowing allegiance to Cornelia Grimsley for this seemingly endless vote of confidence on her part.

To my frequently unerring perception where the basic nature of others is concerned, even back then when I was a mere child, there was something mildly disturbing about Burtram Parker's overall character that at the time I was far too inept to properly decipher. Although he possessed all the infallible instincts of a true politician and would go through any amount of trouble to curry favor with man and beast alike, I simply could not seem to shake my particularly strong feeling that he was definitely what Felix Lauder used to refer to as a "fence-sitter." In other words he remained someone who really did not enjoy being challenged whenever it came time to taking a firm stance on some important issue.

Instead this rather spiritually impoverished individual seemed far more comfortable in remaining fully clothed, as he always was, in his mediocrity. Likewise I came to sincerely believe that if he were ever challenged in some meaningful manner and had to stand tall to naturally expound upon those strong convictions inherent in any worthwhile community leader, he was surely destined to fail miserably.... Yes. Beyond any doubt, and just as surely as night follows day, Burtram Parker was destined to fail. In time he would not only be failing himself, but he would also be miserably failing a number of other people who had mistakenly placed their basic trust in him.

Over the years I have wisely concluded that to be a friend to every man is really to be a friend to no man. For as this long established rule of thumb forever dictates, it is in one's highly discriminating choice of any friend that remains the clearest indication of one's own moral character, or one's lack of it. With regard to such critical issues as moral strength and spiritual integrity, it naturally becomes impossible for anyone worth his or her salt as a human being to be able to casually put on, and then to take off, these things—much as if this predictable "barometer of the soul" were nothing more than some arbitrary article of clothing.

In complete fairness to Sheriff Parker one could never really find much fault with the man's basic overall gregarious nature. After all, he worked hard at being everyone's "good buddy." Occasionally, however, his language—especially whenever he became particularly angry, would often become more than a little "colorful." And lest I forget, he also had an annoying habit of sharing little jingles with the Lauder children and me over the years which were destined to stick in our highly impressionable minds like so many sheets of sticky fly paper.

To properly illustrate this point, one early spring afternoon when I was about ten or eleven years old, I was returning home from school. As I slowly meandered up the long gravel driveway towards the farmhouse that day, right away I could hear some sort of commotion coming from around the far side of the porch area. Just as I visually cleared a certain area of our home, I happened to notice the good Sheriff's truck parked nearby. Not long after this I more or less became astounded to hear this same colorful individual actually shouting rather angrily in his familiar falsetto voice, as he said, "Hell and damnation, Felix Lauder! You and your damn brats are gonna make me the laughing stock of every community from here to Chicago, if you keep this up!"

That long cigar which was nearly always present there at the corner of our wee visitor's mouth was now being considerably manipulated from one side of his small face to the other, obviously in keeping time with the speaker's abundant agitation. Right away I observed that our uninvited guest remained firmly planted where he was, a mere three or four feet in front of Felix, at the moment, with both his arms folded across his chest in a basic confrontational manner.

Furthermore, firmly clenched within one of his small fists I could also see that he was holding a rolled up newspaper. Although several of the younger Lauder children were standing silently behind their father at the moment, no doubt for better protection, Felix had taken hold of one of young Fritz's hand. Having instantly sized up the situation and even without having yet become familiar with all the facts, from the pathetic look on this seven-year-old youngster's face he was most probably the prime suspect figuring in this most recent family catastrophe.

What had happened the previous evening was fairly typical of what happened on a more or less weekly basis there at the busy Lauder home. To be more specific in my worthy attempt at placing matters into their more proper perspective, and naturally in order that the understanding reader might be more sympathetic to everyone concerned here, I should be forced to state that life within this amazing household quite simply proved to be a never-ending circus.... Without seeking to bore anyone with those never ending details regarding all the bothersome trials and tribulations invoked by the perpetual pranks conceived within all those healthy and creative young Lauder minds, suffice it to say that life remained anything but humdrum.

Gus Twilley was Sheriff Parker's loyal deputy of many years. That day he continued to sit where he could usually be found, which was on the passenger side seat of the paddy wagon. Looking relatively uninspired by the current situation at the moment, instead he remained thoroughly engrossed in licking clean the fingers of his right hand after having finally polished off something formerly located in a somewhat greasy-looking brown paper bag that was situated on the seat nearby.

Unlike his pint-sized mentor he was a heavy-set clumsy lad who always remained far less tidy in his overall professional presentation of himself.

For example, Bertram Parker was forever reminding his sidekick to tuck in the shirttail to his uniform's blouse, or repetitively asking him to wipe away the various foodstuff from the corners of his mouth. This, of course, happened quite a lot, since the more than robust fellow seemed to be eating all the time. In actual fact, the front of Twilley's uniform shirt would often double as a sort of overt "testimonial" where what he had consumed on any given day could be readily detected by anyone with whom he eventually came into contact.

Naturally very much like Bertram Parker, Gus Twilley was an unforgettable character in his own right. Possessing a bevy of colorful idiosyncrasies which included at the top of the list a thoroughly disruptive sort of laughter which mimicked the loud harsh cry of the kookaburra, or Australian king fisher, this odd fellow remained a continuous source of wonder to me. There would be times when this highly distinctive sound that he made could be heard nearly anytime, and anywhere, annoyingly competing with the caustic siren of the paddy wagon as the unusual duo went traveling about the countryside faithfully taking care of their usual appointed business.

Burtram Parker, I recall, remained a master at stating the obvious. For instance, whenever he glanced up at the storm clouds that were collecting on the distant horizon, with the annoying sagacity of some enlightened soothsayer he would predictably state: "Sure does look like rain, today!" With this remark his ever dependable sidekick would invariably be there to parrot this identical phrase, exactly like an echo, as if to openly punctuate everything that was uttered by his boss in this way was just something that he always felt compelled to do.

"Now, Mr. Parker, there's no need to carry on this way," Felix was saying in a calm and soothing voice, undoubtedly attempting to diplomatically defuse the potentially ugly situation. Soon he continued on to say, "Even though your present anger is naturally somewhat justified, I take exception to the language you've chosen to use in referring to my children!"

"Look," Burtram Parker was angrily announcing in order to better make his point, "why don't you just save us all a hell of a lot of time and trouble by just building an addition on to your house where I might live from day to day.... Or, better yet, maybe we could build a small place on a modest piece of land—say, over there, for example, which I might eventually call my own! That way I won't have to travel clear across town each and every day to settle these endless episodes of trouble that are beginning to really annoy me at this point!"

No one could possibly have missed the symphony of sarcasm being delivered with these words of his. To tell the truth, what had occurred the previous day was far more significant than anyone might have guessed at first, and so the reader will eventually learn after this interesting tale is told in its entirety. In actual fact this very same incident might have ultimately become responsible for great loss of property, as well as possible loss of life, too, for that matter. I recall that after things eventually settled down within the Lauder household, it was Felix who patiently pointed out this sobering reality to all of his children—even to those of us who had not been technically involved.

Placing world politics aside, weeks earlier young Fritz with the expert help of his older brother, Eddie, had labored at length to design and build an exact replica of Baron von Richthofen's famous red triplane.... This beloved mutual hobby of theirs usually came into play during those more restful and quiet Sunday evenings while the adult's conversation abounded somewhere nearby; and, too, when several of the other Lauder brothers busied themselves with their stamp and coin collections; and young Maria Christina and Anna Allegra took to carefully cutting out the paper dolls which Felix had quickly sketched for both of them upon the fragile newsprint of his artist's sketch pad; and while I, similarly, proceeded to attempt to defend my already badly tarnished sense of honor there upon the chessboard after always being challenged by either Willy or Charley, that the faintly pungent but still pleasant scent of a particular lubricating material would slowly waft through the air....

Enthusiastically collaborating together within the confines of the large enclosed porch area of the farmhouse, Fritz and Eddie could always be found working together from atop a roomy old desk. Generous sheets of absorbent newspaper religiously covered this entire area in order to protect the furniture from the sticky droplets of the "dope" which were being used to waterproof and strengthen the special paper that would be covering the light balsa-wood frame of the aircraft's fuselage, and wings, and tail section. I recall that this talented duo worked with remarkable precision and patience until their project was finally completed.

Once when Felix wandered over to that same well-used work table of theirs to critically inspect for himself this on-going project of theirs, after stooping low to observe the unfinished aircraft from several different angles, he impulsively took to quoting the words of Agur from the Book of Proverbs.... This charming intellectual offering was written some two thousand years ago and alludes to man's age-old yearning for adventure in the skies. In the true manner of a gifted orator everyone within ear shot eventually heard our wonderful patriarch openly declare: "There are three things that are too amazing for me to contemplate; four that I do not understand.... The way of an eagle in the skies; the way of a snake upon a rock; the way of a ship upon the oceans—and, naturally, the way of a man with a maiden!"

Days later, after the unusually large model aircraft was completed to absolute perfection by finally receiving its last coat of rich red paint, young Fritz enlisted the assistance of several of his school chums so that he might carry the project to Mrs. Turner's class for what amounted to her customary "show and tell" period. During this thoroughly enjoyable educational session which took place there at our small one-room school house, and which all the younger Lauder children and I also attended, with great pride Fritz Lauder detailed his personal account of each step of the project's progress from start to finish. While Fritz and his friends proceeded to head home that day, some sort of brash instinct to be able to witness this precision-crafted machine take off from a high place, and then fly around just like a real airplane might do, seemed far too tempting to pass up.

Pretty much out of the clear blue, really, everyone enthusiastically decided to hitch a ride together to William's Bay. Consequently their small entourage arrived at the local water tower sometime around dusk with the fairly cumbersome model airplane in tow. After painstakingly scaling the formidable-looking edifice which was located only a short distance from the lake, Fritz Lauder ceremoniously lit his marvelous aircraft on fire and then promptly sailed it forth from this high precipice on which he and his young comrades all stood, out in the direction towards the lake, and on what would surely prove to be both its first and final glorious voyage....

But as fate would have it, instead of ultimately crashing and then disappearing into the ice-cold waters of our lake as was originally planned, the ever-buoyant currents of swiftly moving air fooled everyone concerned and immediately changed course to eventually carry the fiery craft helplessly inland towards several unsuspecting farmhouses with their acres of dry autumn weeds and grasses. Sometime later, after having sheepishly confessed these facts to his father, as well as to Sheriff Parker, young Fritz declared that even as he and his friends watched with fascination as the airplane hit the ground hundreds of yards from the tower and instantly burst into a mighty crescendo of flames—even then, none of them actually recognized the potential hazards of their actions.... Eventually though, with a growing sense of panic, they were forced to watch as the arid grasses all around the area acted as a superb kindling for the fire, causing the blaze which they initiated to grow and then to begin to spread rapidly in every direction.

Since it remains perfectly understandable that any person's more normal perspective of the situation might have become far more distorted than usual, during this particular time of the day one poor highly-panicked elderly eyewitness upon seeing the blazing model airplane gliding stealthily over head in the dim light of the coming evening and then soundlessly crash into the distance in what must have been an impressive all-consuming ball of fire immediately imagined that Fritz's craft was the real thing. In a terrible state of genuine panic this same responsible individual hastened to contact the local volunteer fire brigade, as well as "Doc" Owens and our good Sheriff Parker who, in turn, promptly contacted his ever-dependable intermediary, Miss Edwina Dooley.... In the end the facts proved that it was none other than our own perky little law enforcement official who quickly dispatched a telephone call to the local newspaper editor, just in case this person might wish to become a "johnny on the spot," as the good sheriff used to quip, and not miss a moment of this first-hand excitement.

"Well, young man, what do you finally have to say for yourself!?" Burtram Parker was asking poor unhappy little Fritz, as all of us stood outside the Lauder's farmhouse that very next afternoon. While he was speaking these words in his usually insensitive manner, he took to dramatically waving a copy of the folded local newspaper that he had been holding all this while, and which now was helplessly flailing about in the air all around the top of his own head. He was angrily referring, no doubt, to the splendidly written article there on its front page; that same full page, photo-ladened, awe-inspiring story, mind you, which mentioned in great detail everyone's part in the previous evening's stimulating "doings." Then, even before the humiliated child had had a chance to properly formulate an answer to the first question, Sheriff Parker bombarded him with, "Tell me, do you really feel that the entire experience of last evening was worth even a fraction of all the damn trouble it's managed to create for everyone?!"

With a little friendly coaxing from his father Fritz Lauder finally found the courage to announce, in a noticeably touching mood of genuine contrition, "I'm really sorry, Mr. Parker...." However, not having had the ingenious foresight to stop with this solitary comment of his, instead the frustrated child chose to go on in his modest attempt to somewhat hedge this long overdue explanation and apology of his, by quickly adding, "But..."—only to be rudely shot down in midair, so to speak, by Sheriff Parker's forthcoming homespun philosophy in the form of a modest little jingle which each one of the Lauder children and I had already heard many times before this, and which by now we had all committed to memory: "Please! Please!", the good sheriff was impatiently telling Fritz, "If you don't mind! There'll be absolutely no more of your excuses—no more 'ifs' or 'buts,' especially.... Besides as you already know: If 'ifs' and 'buts' were 'candy' and 'nuts'—come December, we'd all sure as hell be having a more than merry Christmas!"

This is just the sort of inspirational jargon that this rather entertaining character would opt to use on a moment's notice. Once on a cold and snowy afternoon in midwinter, when I was visiting the Grimsley's general store to purchase a spool of navy thread for Mrs. Lauder, I observed Sheriff Parker gingerly making his way across the thin layer of ice and snow that still covered most of the wide wooden boardwalk out front. More or less out of a basic consideration for others, before he actually entered the building he took great pains to noisily stamp his feet several times and then to vigorously brush off his official-looking cap, in order to free these articles from the wet slush which formerly clung so obstinately to them.

Upon entering the warm and fragrant room, I further observed that he took to stamping his already fairly clean boots upon the wooden flooring again, mostly for effect and in order to immediately solicit the attention of others within the place.... Finally in a loud voice he enthusiastically quipped: "By God, it's damn near cold as a witch's teat out there!" Needless to say, such colorful comments as these managed to endlessly conjure up all sorts of possibilities within my fertile young mind, as I deeply contemplated how any one might come upon such interesting knowledge as this.

Meanwhile, at the moment, as the small band of us remained gathered where we were, I was occupied in thinking how like certain adults it was to ask a child a serious question, only to knock them flat in the emotional sense by not even giving them the basic courtesy to answer the question. Just as Felix Lauder looked as though he might be getting ready to say something rather important to Burtram Parker, a fairly new-looking automobile could be seen stopping in a noticeably tentative fashion at the entrance to the Lauder's long driveway, very much as if its driver was not exactly sure of where he was going. Shortly after this, however, after the vehicle's operator decided to park his automobile to one far side of the blacktopped country road out front and then to extract himself from behind the wheel to quickly, and rather purposefully, hurry our way, all the members of our small group chose to turn in unison to acknowledge this stranger's arrival and then silently pause to eventually hear what he had to say....

This obviously eager young man was wearing an eye-catching red, and yellow, and green, plaid suit which immediately seemed indicative of a robust personality that was clearly extroverted in nature. Carrying a large note pad and pencil in his left hand, he cheerfully greeted us by politely tipping his hat with the one that remained free.... Speaking in a noticeably well-modulated business tone, with a sense of considerable professionalism about him, he took to extending his right hand in friendship as he began to enthusiastically shake the hands of Felix Lauder and Sheriff Parker. Promptly after that he went on to inform us, "Good afternoon, folks, my name is Howard Setland. I'm a junior editorial reporter for the Chicago Tribune, and, needless to say, I've traveled quite some distance today in order to be able to interview all the important players connected with the near disaster of last evening!"

Brother. I shall never forget the look on Burtram Parker's face that very second, as he remained frozen in place, avidly taking in every aspect of this friendly soul's appearance. And, while this spunky young reporter continued to patiently await some sort of response from anyone, at this point, pencil and pad poised in obvious readiness, all the color slowly drained from Sheriff Parker's shocked-looking countenance... I sincerely believe that had he not finally bit down hard upon his ever-faithful cigar, which now lay rather limp and motionless there to one side of his sorry-looking face, the trusty appendage might certainly have fallen to the ground.

Turning slowly towards Felix, now, to address him in what may only be described as a certain air of defeat, our badly embarrassed constable angrily quipped—this time practically under his breath, "Someday, mister, you and your damn family will prove to be my ruination!"

With this, and without addressing our new visitor in any appropriate manner, Burtram Parker purposefully strolled directly to his paddy wagon, no doubt in order to make his escape. Before he and his loyal deputy drove away, however, he did turn to finally regard Felix and then to loudly state in a mood steeped in a more dignified resolve, "Seems to me you can handle 'this baby' yourself, Mr. Lauder.... After all, the entire problem actually begins and ends right here on your doorstep!"

"Right here on your doorstep!" quipped Gus Twilley. Then as predictable as ever, with the exquisite timing of some gifted impresario, and no doubt to effectively punctuate the reality of the moment, the clumsy lad spontaneously laughed out loud.

Each member of our small group, including the somewhat puzzled young visitor from Chicago, paused a long moment to reflect upon the little paddy wagon as it made its way hastily down the long gravel driveway, kicking up a modest cloud of dust in the process. Finally as the vehicle listed out onto the blacktopped road, heading now in the direction of Lake Geneva, the annoying sound of Gus Twilley's outrageous laughter could be heard faithfully trailing along after them.

12.

G EORGE WAS IN LOVE. Thoroughly, and quite hopelessly, in love.... Having finally been forced to accept this most unhappy truth of the situation, my own protective heart literally trembled for him.

By now, it was already the latter part of September. For quite some time his family and I helplessly watched as he took to riding a particularly demanding emotional roller coaster. One minute he was climbing the summit of some breathtaking peak to bask quite shamelessly within that brand new sensation of radiant joy that he was experiencing, all the while allowing some splendid melody of that same sacred song of life which was automatically being orchestrated deep within his young and innocent heart, to pour forth so openly for all of us to witness.... Next and totally without warning, sometimes occurring within a matter of only a few hours, this same unpredictable ride would just as quickly become responsible for dashing him into the depths of near panic and despair, causing him to obviously suffer beyond belief.

Because my dear friend had already come to mean so much to me, naturally I suffered along with him through all those numerous ups and downs. Even though I had never personally become involved in anything of such a powerful nature myself, from these ongoing spiritual ordeals of continuous extremes with which he and I were being forced to contend these days, at the tender age of eight-and-a-half I impetuously felt a real need to embrace the vow of celibacy. I foolishly promised myself, then and there, that no woman was ever going to be allowed to do this same unfortunate thing to me. After all, how could anyone in their right mind ever intentionally choose to be a part of this same maddening force called "love," when the nature of the beast obviously invoked such radically hopeless extremes of emotions?

The rare object of George's sincere and ever-growing devotion was a young woman named Cecilia Von Szeplak whom he met earlier that summer while working part-time as a lifeguard down by the lake. Baron Peter Von Szeplak, Cecilia's father, was a distinguished member

of Europe's more recent nobility, as well as a well-renowned international business tycoon. One could often find father and daughter's
striking likenesses conspicuously displayed across the various pages of
Chicago's society sections where these same publications meticulously
chronicled every aspect of the seasonal doings of the rich and famous,
and where this more modest branch of the Von Szeplak family lived for
the greater part of the year. Having very briefly been introduced to her
on one solitary occasion by George, himself, I came to think that these
same black and white photographs never quite did justice to the real
physically beautiful person she was.

These days, emotionally speaking, George reminded me of a child's
bright and shiny top which was wound to the maximum. Although
my dear friend was able to maintain an exhausting weekly schedule
which included his numerous chores around the farm that began each
and every day just before the crack of dawn, and likewise his guard
duties down by the lake, not to mention his attending a perfunctory
course several evenings a week that was intended to prepare him for
his application for a scholarship to Northwestern University that coming January, he still managed to make time for me and naturally for our
beloved fishing trips.

George was by everyone's reckoning an exceptional student. Since
attending college any other way remained prohibitive during those financially difficult times, the scholarship program eventually became his
highly-prized ticket towards a bright new future. Beginning sometime
during his earliest childhood, so I was told, creative writing had greatly
sparked his interest. Consequently, as far as scholastic pursuits were concerned, it seemed perfectly logical to his family and me that Journalism
should have inevitably become his choice of professions.

With this challenging schedule of his, I shall never know how he
managed to find any free time to visit Cecilia Von Szeplak at her palatial
summer home across the lake, but he did. Each moment that was not
consumed with these other priorities, including far less frequently our
wonderful two or three hours of fishing on the weekend, was dedicated
exclusively to her and with all the grand passion of any new and hopeful young lover.

Quite naturally, too, because I was seeing George significantly less
and less these days, I began to harbor a real grudge against this same
stranger whom I instinctively believed was responsible for usurping the
precious time and affection that I was certain belonged to me. Being the
sympathetic and highly sensitive soul that my friend was he began to

sense the problem that was developing within me—the prickly jealousy that was the result of my lopsided perception that, little by little, I was somehow losing this special friendship of ours which I had already grown to treasure more than anything else in the world. One day as the two of us were sitting by the lake—comfortably dangling our feet in the water and waiting patiently for a fish to bite, I found myself in a tortured mood where I greatly needed to address the entire situation concerning the two of us. In my characteristically up-front manner, I matter-of-factly inquired, "So, are you planning to marry that lady, any time soon?"

George turned to regard me with a puzzled look, and then, realizing to whom I was referring, he smiled as he answered in a completely non-disparaging tone, "You really are a smart little guy, you know that?! How in the world did you ever come to such a grown up conclusion, regarding my friendship with Cecilia?"

Picking up a small moss-covered pebble from the shallow waters nearby, and then hurling it out as far as I could into the glorious dark emerald green waters of our lake, without returning his gaze for fear he might see all the various destructive emotions that were welling up within me, at that precise moment, I casually answered, "Actually, it was pretty easy! These past few weeks you just haven't seemed like the same old George we all knew and loved.... In fact you've been changing a whole lot—changing right before our eyes!"

I vaguely hoped that the substantial anger I felt burning within me at the moment had not come through in these words of mine. After all, I was not angry at George.... I could never be angry with him. That unsavory emotion with which I was currently dealing was really being directed towards Miss Cecilia Von Szeplak. After my friend took the trouble to wedge the handle portion of his fishing pole deep within the wet earth of our little beach in order to properly secure it, he came to sit by my side. Placing one of his strong arms securely about my thin shoulders, while at the same time attempting to make contact with my eyes, he said with such warmth and understanding, "No one will ever be able to steal the special place I shall always hold for you, here in my heart, Adam.... No one! Do you understand what I'm saying?"

With me still refusing to look at him, George paused to gently turn my face in his direction until our eyes were forced to finally meet, and with marked emphasis he repeated his question, "Do you understand what I'm telling you?"

My poor heart was aching, but I could not let on. Finally in mock understanding I acknowledged what he was telling me by merely nodding my head.

With an unmistakable touch of awe, my dear friend went on to say, "Although I'm hardly an expert on the subject, Adam, I'm quickly discovering that love is such an amazing gift! Did you know, for example, that food actually tastes better than ever, when one is in love? Oddly enough, too, music even sounds better! Did you ever suspect this? And those occasionally drab hues of this often tired old world of ours seem miraculously renewed with such vibrant color and clarity, when one's heart sings with this rare enchantment called love!

Now George was laughing the familiar laugh I knew and loved so well—laughing as though his mirth were being directed towards himself, as he offered with a bit of good-natured embarrassment, "Guess I'm what the experts might call 'a hard case,' Sport ... a hopeless romantic, just like my father! But, as sure as I'm sitting here next to you, one day you'll come to understand what it means to find someone to love in the truest sense. And when this miracle finally does occur, you'll also find that your entire world has become transformed for the better."

"How will you ever be able to support a wife on a lifeguard's salary?" I was thoughtfully interjecting, with the fervent hope of introducing a bit of sobering logic into this fine picture he was happily painting for the two of us at the moment. "Women eat a lot—or so I'm told.... I just wonder whether or not you ever gave the whole situation much thought?!"

George was smiling at me now with undisguised affection. If he had correctly perceived the childish tactics being used by me at the moment in my rather aggressive attempt to sabotage the possibility of any permanent relationship between Cecilia Von Szeplak and himself, he never let on. Instead he was slowly and thoughtfully preparing to make my worst fears come true, as he very seriously began to state: "Someday, Adam, I'll prove to the entire world that I can be as good a provider as my father continues to try to be.... In fact, all my future energies shall be directed to this very end!"

After pausing a long moment where he seemed lost in a deep sense of personal reflection, my friend eventually continued on to say as if within his own mind he had long ago firmly established this personal criteria by which he sought to live, "You know, my family hasn't always lived as we are now. For as long as I'm able to recall, we lived in a large home where my mother never had to cook, or clean, or bother doing those mountains of laundry for so many people, each and every day. I shall never forget that it was with my father's truly amazing daily fortitude and endless hard work for many years that all of us eventually came to share in his immense prosperity. Financially speaking, since we've known both the best of years, as well as these currently far more difficult times, in my own mind, especially, the comparison between the two situations is such that I intend never to remain as we are forever. Although being poor is never a crime, as my father has always contended, still I've become thoroughly convinced that remaining so isn't for me. One day with proper schooling, and years of dedication and hard work, I shall finally be able to rise out of these difficult circumstances, all the while aiding and abetting each of my beloved family members in the process!"

As he spoke these words to me, his eyes literally burned hot with a deep sense of permanent resolve. Then in a more noticeably chaste and far more subdued mood George went on to further state, "When I decide to marry, as I shall inevitably choose to do one day, I shall forever cherish the special woman I eventually select for my wife—just as Father has always cherished Mother. This rare love for one another will grow to enrich both of us over the years. Of course, I should naturally feel obliged to protect this person I vowed to love forever, and yet I would never wish to overly protect her for fear that she'd fail in the end to become her own person!" After a brief pause, as though he had finally chosen to add something significantly important, he quickly said, "Of course, we'd certainly have children together—several bright, and happy, and well-contented children, who'd grow up knowing without any doubt that both their parents lived for them, just as they lived for each other!"

Looking out now at some distant point there across the lake, my dear friend went on to conclude by saying, "And if God so wills it, after a long and fulfilling lifetime together, I should eventually choose to have us buried side by side, thereby allowing our souls to wander off together, through time and space—for always!"

I well remember how these passionate words of George's profoundly humbled me that day. Judging from these deeply-felt sentiments of his I surely had not taken into consideration the depth, nor the breadth, of his feelings for Cecilia Von Szeplak. Finally, after a few moments of silence on both our parts, and very much as though he had been struck by a splendid idea, my friend quickly turned towards me to inquire with considerable enthusiasm, "Would you like to meet my Cecilia sometime, Sport!? Would you like to meet the incredible woman who will one day become my wife?!"

Being sincerely touched by the thought that my opinion mattered to him in the least—and, particularly, with regard to the subject of this special lady of his, I found that I was being forced to lie a little. Indeed, with quite some difficulty I finally managed to conjure up a wee smile as I politely answered, "Sure. I'd like that a lot."

Much to my everlasting chagrin, however, for me this more or less dreaded event came to pass much faster than I would have ever imagined. As the two of us collected the half dozen pan fish we caught that afternoon, as well as all the other paraphernalia which we were always required to bring along each time we traveled to the lake like this, George was the first one up the small incline behind us. Quickly turning to take my hand as he always did in order to properly hoist me up upon the grassy embankment where he already stood waiting, I temporarily resisted his help for a few seconds, as our hands remained firmly clasped together.... Then desperately holding his gaze, as I was, I finally felt compelled to ask, "Shall we always remain friends, George? Shall you and I remain friends for life?"

With one quick masterful tug from my strong friend, I landed soundly in front of him, splashing a bit of the lake water we earlier placed in the bucket for our fish. Meeting my hopeful stare with his deeply sincere and unusually penetrating gaze, George was firmly assuring me, "Yes! Yes, we shall.... You and I shall always remain friends!"

After all our equipment was carefully loaded into the back of the old family truck, and after the modest container which held our catch of the day was placed securely between us upon the floor of the vehicle for safekeeping, we decided to take the short way home that afternoon which just happened to take us by a place called "Shorty's."

This comfortably intimate albeit extremely low-key "barbecue joint," as it was commonly known, was a friendly hangout for all the young adults in town. This of course included both the numerous summer residents who lived around the lake during only part of the year, as well as the local folks. As George and I finally came upon the little hideaway that was located directly upon the lake and not so very far from where we had been fishing, my friend slowed down the progress of the truck's movement in order to quickly peruse the parking lot that was located there to one side of the small cabin. Right away I heard his happy sounding, "Looks like we're in luck, Sport! Cecilia's car is here." No sooner had this been said when we immediately drove into the small courtyard and parked directly next to a brand-new, thoroughly expensive-looking, shiny black Rolls Royce, as George thoughtfully added, "We'll just stop here for a few minutes so you can meet my special girl!"

As the two of us entered the modest-looking smoke-filled little pub, in a mere blink of an eye George professionally scanned the entire area of the room. Apparently failing to discover the special person whom he was so avidly seeking, we eventually strolled past the dozen or so people seated at the bar in order to finally make our way onto the porch area out back.

Already the giant orange and yellow orb of the warm September sun was slowly beginning to settle down into the horizon, there across the wonderful still waters of our lake. Likewise that afternoon's soft breeze continued to ebb and flow all around us, and I could not help noticing that this more tentative movement of air was causing the draped oilcloth material of several of the cheerful red and white tablecloths that were decorating this outside area to wave a little in response.

In no time at all, George and I eventually crossed the decking together to finally arrive to stand beside a handful of pleasantly talkative people who were all seated together at one far-removed table, there to our right. Languishing at the moment at the very center of this modest gathering was the young woman whose photograph from the newspaper I recognized right away....

As George dutifully made his rounds to enthusiastically introduce me to each one of these same outgoing individuals, all whom seemed genuinely pleased to see him there, in the end this same spontaneous cordiality led us to pause before one of the loveliest young women I had ever seen. With a radiant glow of extreme pleasure pooling there within the depths of his excited-looking eyes, as well as floating quite buoyantly atop his ever-confident voice, I was carefully observing George as he said with the utmost respect, "And finally, Adam, here is my dear friend, Cecilia Von Szeplak!"

Immediately I judged this rare object of George's extreme affection to be around the same age as he. Besides the young woman's obvious physical charms, which I became instantly inspired to liken in great part to the aristocratic lineage of some well-bred and highly prized Arabian steed, right away it was the young woman's unusual eyes with which I became thoroughly transfixed. For those few brief seconds, at least, I became quite lost in their exquisite color.... Even after all these years I should be tempted to liken them to the identical coolness and extreme passivity of the most rare and expensive aquamarine jewels that were each being dramatically framed within their thick chestnut-colored eyelashes.

Among my initial instincts regarding this fair young creature was the uncanny feeling that she really was not of this world. It seemed, rather, as though she belonged reposing somewhere all alone and more or less showcased upon some heavy marble pedestal within some well-manicured garden... Or, still, perhaps residing within some as yet undiscovered but soon to be highly acclaimed portraiture belonging to one of history's well-renowned masters.

As I proceeded to shake the smooth and graceful hand which this young elegant woman was slowly extending towards me, naturally in polite reaction to the introduction which George was presently making, I was unfavorably struck by the uncomfortably limp sensation her hand was initiating as she and I briefly made contact that day. After two additional chairs were brought to the table for us by the thoughtful man who earlier was working behind the bar, George and I ordered a couple of ice-cold chocolate sodas. When the treats finally arrived, I sat back quietly in my little corner to unobtrusively observe the interaction of all the people I had just met....

Critically analyzing Cecilia Von Szeplak, as I presently felt obliged to do, it was slowly becoming uncomfortably clear to me that despite her somewhat enviable gifts of great physical beauty, and social privilege, as well as obvious wealth, she nevertheless appeared to be a person much bereft of spirit. Because I intuitively felt that she and I were kindred spirits in at least one respect, primarily with regard to this same complex subject of spiritual bereavement, I also realized with considerable gratitude that there remained highly significant differences between us as well.

Attempting to observe this person every chance I could without calling undue attention to myself in any overt manner, my strong impression was that George's new friend was a person who was easily and quite unmistakably bored with her surroundings. Bored, for example, with the drink she was drinking; bored, too, with the splendidly well-cut clothing she was wearing; and most probably bored, as well, with the grand automobile which remained parked at the moment near our old battered truck out within the small confines of the parking lot. But certainly most disturbing of all this curious young individual seemed irreconcilably bored with those intelligent and highly good-natured people who were presently seated all around her at our table, innocently occupied in gregariously exchanging friendly banter relating to one subject or other. This fact, naturally, included my poor George who did not seem in the least little way to be aware of any of this, since he remained totally lost in his own world of great affection for her.

To my relentlessly probing manner of thinking, here was a young woman who seemed to have everything going for her and yet seemed completely untouched by any of it, almost entirely as if she were sleep-walking through life... Thoughtfully observing her, I found myself wondering what it might finally take to make someone like this happy. Oddly enough, too, I found myself feeling genuinely sorry for her. But more than anything else I was beginning to feel so wretchedly sorry for George.

How in the world could such an intelligent, sensitive, passionate, fun-loving young soul as he ever be attracted to someone who was so profoundly lifeless? So utterly needy in so many essential ways? If I were to openly challenge him with all these earnestly felt objections of mine with regard to this critical choice he was making concerning a lifelong partner, would he become cognizant of the dangers being perceived by me on his behalf? Or would he merely chalk up this highly negative attitude of mine towards Cecilia Von Szeplak as part and parcel of my previously felt childish jealousy?

With an overwhelming sense of honest to goodness panic slowly beginning to ferment deep within the pit of my stomach that day, I was being forced to concede that my dearest friend in all the world was now flying far too dangerously high over those jagged mountain peaks of deep purple and crimson splendor. Oh, yes! There off upon the not-so-distant horizon, George was willfully and so carelessly frolicking as he traveled in and out and all about those hallowed halls of heaven, so to speak.... He remained soaring so foolishly high inside his single engine craft, in the emotionally vulnerable sense, that he obviously failed to give even the slightest thought to any personal peril at all. Deep within my mind's eye, and much to my overwhelming consternation, I could read-ily see that because George remained so overtly confident in his abilities as an aviator that he had not even bothered to don a parachute.... And now, because of this apparent reality, I instinctively began to tremble for him....

Meanwhile, life around the busy Lauder home continued on as usual for the rest of us. Fritz, for example, was in trouble again. This time, however, although the family fracas dealt once again with this particular Lauder member's passion for flying, quite mercifully it had not included Sheriff Parker at all.

As it happened, every now and then, Mrs. Lauder would take in sewing for several of the wealthy families living there around the lake, including Rebecca Franklin who was reputedly the wealthy widow of one of Wall Street's former financial wizards. Mostly it was Felix or George who would customarily drive Fritz and me over to the Franklin home, during those occasions when Mrs. Franklin found a need to summon us in order to pick up the few articles of clothing which needed buttons replaced, or perhaps a hem of a skirt or a dress taken up or let down a fraction… Sometimes, too, with Emma Lauder being the consummate muse of that ancient goddess "Minerva" where the art of crocheting or petit point was concerned, Mrs. Lauder would ever so patiently appliqué some sort of unique handwork upon a sheet or pillowcase, more or less to the basic whim of such people. These endeavors of hers always afforded the family a little extra spending money, just as it gave Fritz's mother a sense of pride at being able to personally contribute to the family income in this manner.

Rumor had it that Mrs. Franklin remained financially solvent despite the shocking circumstances which were recently thrust upon the rest of the world as a whole with the unhappy stock market crash many months earlier. Perhaps out of a much-calculated eagerness to protect her current financial status, if such gossip were true, it sometimes became her habit to reimburse Emma Lauder's considerable time and effort in a most unusual way. In other words, instead of putting forth the seventy-five cents or so that was usually due upon receipt of the frequently tedious work which the widow had commissioned, she would surreptitiously place the equivalent amount in three-cent postage stamps within a small white envelope, seal it, and then hand it to poor little Fritz to take home.

Naturally since this dutiful youngster was never allowed to open these envelopes, just as his mother always requested, what would eventually be discovered therein upon his ultimate return home was almost always a surprise to everyone. So it was, on that particular day…. After I happily volunteered to accompany the boy to the Franklin home that Wednesday afternoon, carrying the obligatory bundle of dry goods to be returned to Mrs. Franklin which had previously received hour upon hour of exquisite embroidery work, Fritz and I decided to depart from the usual proposed schedule of returning home by car. In lieu of this, we talked Felix into allowing us to walk home from that point, just as we had both done before on similar occasions.

These trips of ours by foot normally took us a couple of hours, at the most. That marvelous freedom, above all, always proved an excellent experience for the two of us to bond more as brothers. This time we had the foresight to take along a small pickling jar which we hoped to utilize to collect tadpoles from a small pond we always passed along the way. With Felix's special request that we come directly home that afternoon, without any major "dilly dallying" as he liked to put it, the two of us were fairly overcome by a keen sense of real exuberance from that simple adventure we calculated waited for us on this special day.

I remember that after Mrs. Franklin handed Fritz the small envelope, Fritz in turn politely thanked her and took a moment to carefully wedge the article within one pocket of his knickers. Then with our light and exceedingly happy hearts we promptly started off towards home, with Fritz carrying the jar that was intended to eventually hold our cache of immature frogs, and with me carrying a small hand-held net to help facilitate their capture.

As fate would have it, though, a man named Sharp O'Reiley owned a crop-dusting operation in a neighboring county. Whenever he was not busy doing this sort of work, he would ambitiously take to making an extra bit of spending money by giving rides to interested people who lived within many of the surrounding communities. On our way home on that clear and balmy September afternoon, it was with an overwhelming sense of boundless joy that Fritz and I quickly spotted his brightly-painted yellow, circa 1916 Curtiss "Jenny," long before it came sputtering over a corn field to land not far from the country lane we were both traveling together.

This handsome early model aircraft was an American design which had been specifically built in a relatively small quantity for the Signal Corps, not long before the first great war. Basically it was the nearest thing to a combat aircraft that the U.S. Army owned at the time. However, in the end the plane proved sadly inadequate for the task of supporting this country's ground operations during what became known as the Mexican Punitive Expedition.

In this same conflict Pancho Villa and Emiliano Zapata's ongoing regional threat eventually widened, causing the emboldened Villa to lead his infamous and somewhat successful raids across the border and into our United States. Judging from the hefty collection of notches which the plane's various pilots had earlier taken to scratch along one portion of the aircraft's instrument panel, indicating most probably their ongoing tabulation of concurrent flights during this time, O'Reiley would always be proud as punch to happily point this fact out to anyone who might wish to hear the telling of the tale. Originally someone dubbed the old girl "Glades"—a name which was also still printed along one front exterior panel of the aircraft's fuselage, and by which young O'Reiley still chose to refer to her....

Although O'Reiley's vintage "Jenny" had undoubtedly once seen her fair share of exciting action along the "international front," sometime after she was officially retired from military service this same noble little craft was reduced to being refurbished instead to do battle here on the home front. With the various yearly infestations of destructive parasites that continuously preyed upon our local fields of grain, and vegetables, as well as the region's countless miles of orchards, this still quite spunky old girl could usually be seen as she went about faithfully vanquishing those seasonal hordes of pests.

The approach of this ever-exuberant man and his highly prized flying machine was far too marvelous to pass up for either of us, so Fritz and I hurried over to the wood and wire fence which continued to only momentarily separate us from this amazing aerodyne. Now, as we watched with nothing less than sheer delight, the wonderful double-winged phenomenon finally came to roll to an abrupt stop in an adjacent pasture. After its engine was finally silenced, we also observed with equally great interest its obviously bold young pilot agilely climb out of the airplane's rear cockpit, jump to the ground from off the lower edge of one wing, and then confidently stride around to the rear section of the craft, as he proceeded to adjust something there near the stabilizer. Keenly enthralled with this man's every movement my companion and I by now had managed to climb over the fence and to deposit ourselves upon the dense carpet of robust weeds and colorful wildflowers, not far from where the plane was parked. Having eventually spotted us sitting there, O'Reiley enthusiastically waved us over to where he was standing....

Naturally, not having to be summoned twice, together my young friend and I raced over to where the man stood dressed to the hilt in his well-worn leather jacket, dust-covered high leather boots, with a long white silk scarf casually tied around his neck for effect, I imagined. Our impressive visitor also wore a tight-fitting leather cap whose chin strap and ear flaps had been temporarily loosened while he was working. I noticed that his flying goggles, too, were resting comfortably there on the top of his hat.

Without a doubt this same intriguing young person reminded me of some romantic leading character in an adventure-laden silent film. And, as young Fritz and I approached to stand by his aircraft, he coughed and then expertly spat into the grass nearby as he finally said to both of us, "Well, kids, how about a short ride in my airplane here?! For a mere twenty-five cents, I promise to change both your lives forever! I'll actually fly ya over the lake and back, what'll ya say?"

Since I had no money at all, I immediately discounted any possibility of taking the man up on his generous offer. However, I was carefully watching Fritz Lauder at the moment, and I could not help becoming affected by his extremely excited countenance. His eyes, especially, were literally aglow as his intense gaze slowly traveled from the friendly face of this young entrepreneur who had just made this astounding offer to us, back over to lock firmly upon the fairly rickety-looking dream of an airplane which was parked a mere arm's length from the three of us at the moment.

Again Fritz's attention returned to the pilot and he looked very much as though he might have been struck by a lightning bolt. With warm brown eyes which by now had grown quite immense from the unequaled thrill of this rare prospect of actually being able to fly for the first time, and with every bit of hard-won self-composure resounding in his quivering young voice, I heard him patiently ask, "Would that, sir, be twenty-five cents for the both of us?!"

"No siree!" Sharp O'Reiley was immediately telling us. "Can't afford to give away these rides, ya know! Got to figure in the cost of gasoline and oil, as well as the normal wear-and-tear on this old girl here," he was currently assuring us, as he loudly patted the hollow-sounding fuselage of his aircraft. "Just had her painted last month, and that cost me a pretty bundle, believe you me!"

Continuing to watch Fritz, as Fritz continued all along to carefully study Mr. O'Reiley, my young friend seemed to be aggressively wrestling with something important within his mind. Finally, without a moment's more hesitation, I saw him reach into his pocket and pull out the envelope Mrs. Franklin had given us to give to Fritz's mother. Then, to my utter astonishment, I further watched him eagerly tear into the paper wrapper.... Quickly peering within, he immediately began to frown with a sense of overwhelming disgust and indignation, as he looked squarely at me and said, "By God, she's gone and done it to us again! Mrs. Franklin's paid us in postage stamps—once again!"

Even Sharp O'Reiley could not possibly have missed the bitter defeat so apparent upon Fritz's poor face and also within his angry voice. But being the realistic businessman that he apparently seemed to be, soon we were hearing him say in a somewhat conciliatory mood, "Look, fellas, maybe next time, okay? After all, I travel around these parts quite a lot, and if the three of us ever meet up again—and ya happen to have the necessary funds, then we'll naturally be able to do business at that time— what do ya say?"

With these words O'Reiley walked to the front of his well-maintained craft to jump start its propeller. Gingerly stepping back as the plane's sharp blades instantaneously began to whirl, he quickly rounded one slanted wing to expertly mount the superb craft from behind. Soon enough our adventurous friend was finally climbing into the small rear cockpit once more. With a sense of tremendous envy, Fritz and I watched him take a moment more to secure the harness that he was obliged to wear, snap on the chin strap of his leather flying cap, and finally pull his goggles down over his eyes....

Thoroughly encased as he was with all that impressive leather clothing, not to mention the marvelous airplane wrapped all about him, as it was, it surely seemed as though both man and craft were one. Indeed, Sharp O'Reiley reminded me of a knight of old making ready to do battle. As he smiled at us now with his wide band of snow-white teeth flashing there beneath his thick black mustache, he simultaneously raised the clenched fist of his right hand high in the air, with his thumb up, of course, in a pilot's traditional salute signifying his readiness to begin taking off. After this, with the engine loudly humming along, he enthusiastically waved us away from the biplane, as he yelled over the noise, "Now, why don't ya just move on back away from the airplane, so ya won't get hurt, okay?!"

At that precise moment, Fritz Lauder looked exactly like some poor soul might appear had he been unjustly denied entrance into heaven on some mere technicality. I could not help but feel his overwhelming disappointment.... Even though his great sadness touched me, I quickly took up his hand and faithfully led him away from the plane that was obviously preparing to turn some one hundred and eighty degrees to the right, with the idea of taxiing back down that block or so of long narrow pasture land and then to finally lift off and head back in the very direction from whence it had originally come. The two of us were standing side by side some fifty feet or so away from the bright yellow craft, waiting to see the young pilot engage the engine, pick up speed, lift off, and finally disappear into the bright blue cloudless sky, when something truly miraculous happened....

Much to our overwhelming surprise on that remarkable day—and most probably much to his own surprise, as well, I might add, at the very last moment Sharp O'Reiley seemed to have had a change of heart, for Fritz and I watched him quickly un-harness himself to hurriedly climb back out of his little yellow airplane. Standing there by its side, he gave one giant wave of his arm, impatiently motioning us back towards the aircraft once more. After we arrived he scratched his head almost as if he, himself, really could not believe what he was about to do and proceeded to shout at the top of his voice, "Why don't ya let me see those stamps, again.... After all, seems like I might be able to see my way through to making an exception for two young fellas like yourselves who seem so genuinely interested in flying!"

Fritz and I literally held our breaths as our kindhearted benefactor dutifully confiscated the small white envelope that Mrs. Franklin had given us earlier. Without even bothering to count the stamps, we watched as Mr. O'Reiley matter-of-factly tucked the modest little packet into the interior vest of his leather jacket. Then with a huge smile that seemed to exactly match the size of his huge heart, he loudly called out to us over the steady hum of his magnificent aircraft's engine, "Well, are you both ready for an experience of a lifetime?!?"

Before Fritz and I even realized it, we were being securely harnessed into the front cockpit. "Don't do anything that might release this metal lock," Sharp O'Reiley was shouting to us over the music of the plane's noisy engine, as he gave one last serious tug on the leather straps.... "Wouldn't want ya to fall out, once we get going—or anything like that!"

Although the two of us, Fritz and I, that is, were unable to see out of the front portion of our snug little compartment due to our sitting so low in the seat in the first place, we did however have a wonderfully unimpeded view from either side of us… While we waited a few moments longer, presumably for our pilot to safely harness himself back into his own cockpit, Fritz nudged me with one elbow. Just then I turned to look in his direction and observed him smile one of the most enchanting smiles that I have ever witnessed, as he took to mimicking Mr. O'Reiley by giving the pilot's "thumbs up" signal.

My young friend was quite clearly a natural-born pilot, if ever there was one. Truly, it would most probably be with the help of this amazing experience which the two of us were about to share with Sharp O'Reiley that would undoubtedly become the catalyst to solidify Fritz's love for flying. In my worthy estimation those few postage stamps could not possibly have been put to better use than they were on that unforgettable day.

Shortly, now, with the bright afternoon sun directly overhead, the small aircraft carrying the three of us began bumping and thumping down the uneven pockmarked pasture land, until we reached a point where we were traveling at an unbelievable speed. Finally, with the gentle gracefulness of some powerful bird, we effortlessly left the ground and began to slowly climb towards heaven....

All this while there were butterflies in my stomach. My hungry young spirit, too, was literally soaring—soaring long before the little double-winged craft actually left the ground. In perfect time to every little movement the airplane was making, I quickly discovered that this combination of rare sensations was not unpleasant in the least. And everything became even more highly magnified whenever our worthy pilot decided to bank or to roll the craft in one direction, then the another.

Below us we could see such incredible sights.... Our huge lake, for instance, with all its many contours looked very much like a small mirrored pond. Likewise those numerous grand estates which were all nestled so comfortably there along its irregular shoreline looked to be nothing more than some fortunate child's many ornate doll houses.... The tiny cluster of homes and shops, too, which made up the small town of William's Bay, also became readily apparent as soon as we spotted its familiar little water tower down below us. And only inches away was our famous observatory....

How wonderful! Oh, how indescribably wonderful it all was. Soon we three adventurers were flying over the larger town of Lake Geneva. All the tiny people there—whether on foot, or whether driving around inside their toy automobiles and toy trucks—were reminiscent of the tiny souls that figured so importantly in the amazing stories of Jonathan Swift's *Gulliver's Travels*.

What a glorious gift this maiden flight of ours proved to be. There was something so memorably innocent and pure about the entire experience, just as it always seems to be whenever one is honestly responding to something truly monumental for the very first time. We were effortlessly cavorting among the buoyant currents of air, only to climb so amazingly high one moment—so incredibly high, in fact, that I half expected to be able to reach out and gently touch the smiling face of God. Then a moment later and without the slightest warning, the three of us were arching over head to gently travel down, and further down still, only to pull up at the last moment before we actually grazed the emerald green waters of the lake itself.

Traveling so magnificently like this, as my worthy comrades and I continued to weave, and glide, and roll along, this brand new world of high physical and emotional intensity which we were currently experiencing somehow seemed far more desirable than the world we had just left behind. To me it seemed very much as if all of humanity's pain and sorrow, along with all of its inexplicable cruelty and injustice, were briefly discarded and intentionally left miles and miles behind us there upon the ground.... For me there was no concept of time—much as if this magical moment managed to completely obliterate any knowledge of such unimportant things. Indeed, much as if those vague lines previously delineating my past from my present and my future were all expertly blended together, creating an acute awareness of a different sort which would continue to live on within me forever.

Orville and Wilbur Wright's dauntless vision had already changed people's lives in so many incredible ways. Furthermore, had some gifted visionary pointed out what unimaginable wonders still lay ahead of us in the field of aerodynamics—and, quite specifically, what lay ahead in the coming age of space exploration—I should have been hard-pressed to envision any of it that day as young Fritz Lauder, Sharp O'Reiley, and I floated without the slightest care at all above the vastness of this ever-complex world that would never again look quite the same to me.

Upon our pilot's eventual retreat from his repetitive zigzagging motion above the smooth mirrored surface of the lake, we traveled inland, more in a northerly direction at the moment. Soon, off in the distance, Fritz and I managed to spot the ever-familiar steeple of our small Gothic-style chapel. With marked anticipation and utter exuberance—much like bold Ulysses in the extreme, we frantically motioned for Sharp O'Reiley to continue heading on in that general direction....

In a matter of a heartbeat, we found ourselves flying high over the Lauder's farmhouse as my young partner-in-crime and I eventually spotted far below us the little family toy truck parked at the end of our long oleander-lined driveway. Although there did not appear to be anyone about the place, at the moment, the clean bright laundry was still hanging there upon the back line. Somehow, too, those freshly washed work clothes seemed to be gently waving their enthusiastic greeting to us, firmly reassuring Fritz and me that all was well with our private and happy world there on the ground.

After O'Reiley finally landed his craft in the same field where we met him earlier that afternoon, he jauntily helped us climb from the plane. Even before any of us could even utter a solitary word or phrase, young Fritz Lauder—no doubt having become emotionally overtaken from the sheer joy of our recent experience, spontaneously hugged our fairly surprised pilot and said with marked feeling, "It's been absolutely the best day of my whole entire life, Mr. O'Reiley... Thank you! Thank you, so very much!"

Bidding Sharp O'Reiley good-bye, Fritz and I scurried on home to arrive in the kitchen just as the rest of the family members were washing up for supper. Not long after the blessing was offered, and while Fritz was busying himself by eagerly placing a generous forkful of mashed potatoes and gravy within his mouth, Emma Lauder was currently dabbing at one corner of her mouth with the linen napkin she was holding, only to pointedly inquire, "By the way, Fritz, where's the envelope Mrs. Franklin gave you this afternoon?"

Shooting a quick look at me which seemed to tell me that, although the two of us had shared equally in the rare excitement of this most remarkable of days, it was nonetheless going to be his responsibility to take any heat for the grave disappointment which his previous actions would undoubtedly be causing his family. Within seconds after this initial inquiry was made by his mother, but just prior to Fritz's having finished chewing and then properly swallowing the food in order that he might explain all he had to explain, sensing all this while that something might be wrong, Mrs. Lauder impatiently inquired once more, "Where's the money which was entrusted to you, Fritz?!"

After this exceedingly brave and thoroughly truthful young member of the family delivered his basic synopsis of the events which recently transpired, having finally come to the story's end, Fritz naturally remained seated where he was, with downcast eyes, staring absentmindedly at his unfinished supper and no doubt patiently awaiting his inevitable fate.... Meanwhile within my own mind I was desperately grappling for something helpful to offer in my young friend's defense when Emma Lauder sat back in her chair with a noticeably stunned expression on her face, and said in an incredulous voice that pretty much matched her surprised countenance, "How can this possibly be so?!"

Owing to this rather vague entreaty of hers, I was not exactly sure which part of the story she was finding hard to understand.... Was it the disappointing fact that Mrs. Franklin paid for all her time and trouble in stamps once again? Or was it, perhaps, the reality that Fritz had broken one of his mother's important rules by taking it upon himself to actually open the envelope; and then, of course, as if to further add insult to injury, to use those same stamps as the necessary collateral to buy us the airplane ride? Or was Mrs. Lauder seeing the bigger picture here and wondering how the two of us had had the nerve to embark upon such a reckless adventure, thoughtlessly putting our mutual lives at considerable risk, without having even bothered to obtain permission from either her or Fritz's father?

Except for young Lewis, each member of the Lauder family was present at the supper table that evening—including George, whose regular evening classes were canceled at the last moment making it possible for him to join us in the end. So, with Fritz's honest revelations concerning what had pretty much transpired earlier that day, everyone to the last man sat quite motionless, as well as speechless. After several long tense moments where Emma Lauder had currently taken to fix her attention upon her husband, she eventually saw fit to call forth in what I may only properly describe as a fairly hysterical entreaty, "Felix Lauder, don't just sit there! Say something to this child of ours!"

It might prove extremely helpful to the reader, at this point in the story, to understand that one of the major precepts which strictly governed the Lauder household had been for many long years already indelibly written in stone.... This important rule, as was patiently explained to me by George on that very next day after my initial arrival within their lives, dealt exclusively with Felix Lauder's staunch edict that each and every family meal was to remain "wholly civilized," as he chose to put it. This held with regard to any discussions, as well as each member's overall behavior at the dining room table. Anyone having anything unpleasant to discuss, or argue about, would be promptly removed from the room—quite naturally, to be dealt with later.

Any offensive behavior, whether willful or otherwise, would characteristically be subject to a hasty response from Felix. Usually in answer to such unpleasant things, the head of this remarkable family was prompted to rise to his feet and continuing to stand at attention there at his place at our crowded table—much like an experienced general commanding his troops, all that would be required for him to do was merely nod once to the guilty party, as he then correspondingly pointed towards the door... Following this, and in a controlled and remarkably calm voice he would always speak the words: "Leave us, this minute!" Normally if further punishment were warranted, not only would these rather rare albeit highly memorable theatrics clearly signal his definite disapproval, but the object or objects of his scorn were also expected to forfeit any uneaten portion of their meal for the rest of that day.

According to George, this important rule was necessarily implemented due to his father's frequently stressful business life, especially during all those former early years. Felix always had an urgent need to try and control the nagging indigestion which continuously plagued him and which remained part and parcel of his more delicate health issues.

Needless to say, because it was impossible to properly govern the ungovernable with respect to those outside influences upon his life, in order to be able to take control of the situation at all, this gentle man naturally wished to inspire a happier and more calming environment at home. Basically he perceived this far more civilized interaction between all of us as a near sacred daily responsibility, leaving no room whatsoever for even the slightest dissention of any kind.

This same laudable philosophy of his was appropriately summed up—and rather nicely, too, I might add, there upon a small hand-carved plaque which unpretentiously greeted each and every visitor whenever anyone entered the small home by way of the front door. In that same unmistakably clean and easy-to-read inscription that sounded more like a lovely prayer, the object read: "God bless this home; our haven from the madness of the world."

Naturally Emma Lauder was well-acquainted with this important rule of civility, as well as were all their children. With the present "ticklish" situation which loomed there in the dining room on that particular evening, suppertime had had the potential of escalating into a full blown "incident." At the moment, all eyes—all eyes except those of poor Fritz's, of course, remained riveted upon the figure who was still the indisputable head of this amazing family, since it was Felix who now was expected to pass his inevitable judgment upon the youthful "defendant."

Felix Lauder's role as disciplinarian, whether initially sought by him from the beginning or whether merely predictably evolving his way over the course of the years, never became a "bone of contention" where he and his wife were concerned. Actually, Emma Lauder always seemed quite comfortable in deferring to her husband whenever these more serious matters arose. From my perspective as an adopted member of the family, Felix seemed born to the position, since he always remained ever patient, and thoughtful, and fair, in his overall evaluation and criticism of every situation.

Furthermore George indicated to me during one of our more candid conversations dealing with the subject of their more intimate family life that none of the Lauder children had ever been spanked nor manhandled by either parent, whenever one or more of them was guilty of some transgression. Basically their parents sincerely believed that it remained unacceptable for any adult to ever treat a child in this way.

For the Lauders, in fact, it never became an issue of "spare the rod, and spoil the child." Rather, because of the innate respect and overwhelming affection each of the children automatically received from the parents—to be sure, the parents naturally expected and received this same sort of healthy treatment in return. This far more desirable interaction tended to far outweigh any other sort of destructive philosophy that might be founded upon basic fear and mistrust.

Due to this critically established factor, I remember so well that whenever one of the Lauder children fractured some rule or another—and, understandably, with so many healthy and curious natures abounding within one family alone, and with these more or less minor events occurring on a fairly regular basis, it therefore came to pass that that particular child's breach of trust and the ensuing guilt which followed eventually constituted the real punishment for that child, or children, in the end. Essentially the invaluable lesson inevitably became: By disappointing in some manner those who love and trust us, we naturally come to greatly disappoint ourselves as well.... Needless to say, this reality is precisely the sort of just punishment from which there is no escape. Therefore it remained this same unwritten civilized code of highly ethical and moral behavior which was the primary key to the overall success which the Lauder family unit always enjoyed.

Everyone continued to watch with abiding interest that evening as poor young Fritz dutifully raised his soulful eyes to finally meet the powerful gaze of his father. During this tense time, no one at the table had had the courage to speak—nor to move, either, for that matter.... Fritz's ultimate fate, it surely seemed, rested now in the hands of this special man who had become quite famous within the Lauder clan for his absolute fairness where such things were concerned. So, after taking a moment more to thoughtfully contemplate the facts—not unlike the wise Solomon himself, Felix looked first to his wife to politely but quite firmly state, "I believe that from now on, my dear, we should not consent to do business with Mrs. Franklin—seeing that she consistently refuses to meet her responsibilities by properly paying you for your considerable time and energy!"

Even though Emma Lauder's dark brown eyes were still blazing quite unnaturally from the challenge she just issued to her husband regarding the subject of their wayward young son, seemingly undaunted by her outburst Felix continued to patiently meet her gaze. Soon, however, probably coming to understand that her husband was correct in his thinking; and that, furthermore, this direct pronouncement of his was long overdue, she finally acquiesced by donning a far more dignified and noticeably less caustic expression.

Over the years, and actually from the very beginning of my relationship with the various members of the Lauder family, I came to carefully observe that there were moments similar to these within the day-to-day interaction between this husband and wife that gave one the distinct impression that if one were inclined to dig a little deeper into any situation, one would be likely to find that the apparent stimulus responsible for any angry outburst, such as this, was frequently being fueled by something other than what it seemed. In other words, whenever some sort of an event occurred which tended to disturb the more tranquil demeanor of the basic rapport they shared, one was prompted to consider that that vague but nagging discontentment—which seemed to linger just below the surface of their lives, and which now and then would be so openly exhibited by one or the other partner, was being prompted by something much deeper, and far more serious, in the final analysis. It was almost as if some previously inflicted wound that was received in a former conjugal battle of some sort had not been properly exorcised, thereby causing the misdirected anger and frustration from this former offense to reappear thinly veiled behind a more minor offense.... In this particular case it seemed to me that although Mrs. Lauder was quite justified in being very unhappy with their young son's behavior—and mine, too, for that matter—it surely seemed that the momentary anger which all of us witnessed springing forth from her highly expressive eyes that particular evening perhaps was not really being directed towards two small boys after all, but more towards Felix for some unknown reason.

However, with that indisputably sound advice which Felix had just offered to his wife, "our good judge" turned his attention next to his hopeful young son who had obviously remained all this while in a continuous emotional state of suspended animation, waiting patiently for his father's words to descend upon him in a similar fashion. Soon enough, and in a pensive mood very much as if Felix instinctively sensed the vulnerability of this particular child's worthy dreams, Fritz's father cleared his throat to finally ask with unfeigned dignity, "Please do tell us, Fritz, exactly how our little homestead looks from so high up in the sky...."

With what amounted to an unexpected reprieve from his very gracious father, Fritz spontaneously jumped up from his chair and quickly rounded the large table to finally wrap his small arms around Felix's neck. With his son's head resting comfortably upon Felix's chest, I distinctly heard Fritz whisper, "Even in a million, billion years, Father, you couldn't possibly imagine how wonderful it all was!" Then, respectfully stepping back with noticeable tears of gratitude swimming in his much-relieved eyes and without bothering to take his seat again, my young friend proceeded to go into great detail this time concerning the truly miraculous event which the two of us had shared earlier that day.

While Fritz Lauder enthusiastically began sharing our exciting tale with his family members that evening, I, in turn, took some moments to thoughtfully study the individual faces of everyone present—including

Emma Lauder, who was slowly and quite helplessly becoming caught up in the many exciting details of her son's lovely story. Suddenly the small room which we were all occupying at the moment became the wide open sky once more—just as the family's ornately-carved dining room table and many chairs became Sharp O'Reiley's magnificent little yellow flying machine.... And soon, with my young friend's own colorfully poignant version of what it truly felt like to fly for the very first time, we were all currently being lifted out of our more normal pattern of living to vicariously soar upon those ever-glorious currents of pristine air, all the while breathlessly leaving all that we ever knew, and all that we ever thought we understood, far, far behind us.

13.

FELIX LAUDER THEORIZED that it really is not sex or money that make the world go around. It remains, more precisely, that remarkably universal subject called gossip which somehow always manages to achieve this same end. Naturally, since most gossip concerns itself with those ever-fascinating subjects of sex, and money—and certainly politics, as well—the dependable "grease" which manages to "push things along," as it were, still remains gossip just the same.

With reference to this ongoing issue of certain people who traffic in rumor, be it groundless or otherwise, whenever the subject made its unwelcome appearance within our lives in some form or another, my dear friend would go on to tell his children and me that, "Gossips are frequently unkind souls. By their very nature they remain perpetual busybodies who far too often fail to properly discriminate between fact and fiction, thereby causing unnecessary difficulty for others in the end. So it has always been—and, most probably, so it shall undoubtedly continue to always be!"

However for the sake of our story here, it really is not this highly popular yet lesser sort of more benign exchange which concerns us at present. I, like my good friend and mentor, have lived long enough and well enough by now to have finally learned that within the larger scope of things there is yet another kind of negative interplay which is far too often indulged in by far too many within our society, and which remains undeniably far more subversive in its ability to mercilessly strike down and then eventually eliminate the life-force of another....

Fundamentally speaking, malicious gossip is nothing more than a cold-blooded activity cunningly designed to murder the good character of an often unsuspecting victim. This same unconscionable behavior endeavors to willfully dishonor the sacredness of that life by reducing it to the grand farce of some badly-written soap opera or play. When any evil perpetrator seeks with impunity to wantonly destroy that which remains the essence of another, are they not robbing that person of everything that is truly valuable and worthwhile in this life? In the end, what is a man or a woman without the supreme comfort of their good name?

As it happened, if one were inclined to place one's faith in the tales of the local gossipmongers, there was an exceedingly ugly incident which occurred within our small community of Peck's Station many years before the Lauder family and I actually arrived to live in the Lake Geneva area. Apparently this same sad tale was not allowed to wither and die away, as such things tend to do with the passing of time. Since the story's indecent details continued to endlessly intrigue and titillate the public in general, they naturally continued to be flagrantly whispered about for practically as many more years after I had actually grown up and eventually left the area.

The incident, I well recall, dealt with a young Swedish family named Andersson who arrived in America from their former home near Stockholm to live, and to work, and to raise their young son together there within our small normally friendly community. Although the head of this little household was a carpenter by trade, he and his wife managed instead to purchase an old farm on the outskirts of town and to eventually try their hand at the rather unfamiliar albeit highly demanding endeavor of dairy farming....

Their fragile business enterprise began with half a dozen cows that first year. However, sometime during the second year there occurred an epidemic of a particularly fatal disease which literally wiped out much of the county's livestock, causing this poor family to lose their initial investment. Having nothing else to fall back upon, in the financial sense, Mr. Andersson hired himself out once again as a carpenter. Eventually, in order to find the necessary employment that would continue to support his young family in the most modest way, he was often forced to travel to other counties and occasionally to the large cities like Chicago and Milwaukee.

It became well-known within our community that Mrs. Andersson neither spoke nor understood much English, just as she had not learned how to drive a car. Needless to say these things tended to make her life rather difficult by greatly isolating her there on the farm. Perhaps even more important than this, these drawbacks prevented her from freely associating with others in order to be able to make friends in the most ordinary and healthy manner.

Whenever Mr. Andersson knew he was going away for any length of time, he thoughtfully made provisions for his family's comfort by having an elderly widower by the name of Ludlow drive his wife and child into town whenever it became necessary to do so.... This same genuinely kind individual was one of their neighbors who owned substantial acreage that bordered along one side of their own. Basically, whenever Mrs. Andersson required those everyday items which every good homemaker so readily depends upon, she happily learned to call upon this same fine man. And so it became those wholly innocent occasions which ultimately became responsible for allowing this young woman and her lovely son to escape the confines of their frequently lonely farm life. Indeed, it remained these few isolated occasions that always offered all three of these good people a chance to mingle with the many strangers that frequented the Grimsley's General Store....

Although no one seemed to be able to remember just when the nasty rumors first began to circulate about Mrs. Andersson, within a matter of several weeks nearly everyone in town was privately speculating upon this young attractive woman's wicked infidelity with that equally lonely much older man who served as her driver. However, it was also eventually noted by someone much later on—and naturally some time after the needless tragedy occurred—that every time a handful of shoppers congregated there within the Grimsley's store, Cornelia Grimsley became the highly enthusiastic devotee who always had the most recent details of gossip to share concerning this sordid behavior which was now being attributed exclusively to Mrs. Andersson. Being ever religious to her unsavory nature, she wasted no time at all in faithfully spreading these cunning falsehoods all around the community like so many truckloads of manure.

After once hearing someone's version of this same sad story, I speculated that between the likes of Cornelia Grimsley, Bertram Parker, and Edwina Dooley—who remained truly nasty-hearted and supportive cohorts in every sense, that poor young family never had a chance. Unfortunately the grievous fact remains that there are people in this world who make exhilarating sport out of hurting others.... With what amounts to a personal campaign of blood-lust, which they randomly entertain whenever the occasion suits them, their utter cruelty seems to know no boundaries.

As one might imagine, when these unkind rumors eventually found their way to Mr. Andersson, as they were most probably intended to do, in a state of genuine mortification the poor humiliated man eventually took the couple's child and left the community—thereby completely abandoning his wife in the end. Given the inevitable passing of time, and having become pathologically steeped within her overwhelming sense of substantial loneliness and despair at being unable to adequately fight these unfounded allegations raised against her; not only by the community, but primarily by her formerly loving husband as well, the young woman chose to end her life....

Upon one extremely cold and gray wintry day, so the story goes, Mrs. Andersson simply placed a rope around her neck and then proceeded to hang herself from the rafters within the family's barn. With the passing of several days, it was the pathetic sound of the family's poor dog's continuous wailing that finally alerted and summoned their kindly neighbor to the Anderson home, that one last time....

During the official interrogation which followed, as this same good man openly relayed to the judge under oath his wholly innocent part in the tragic event, the poor emotionally distraught neighbor testified that no such improper liaison ever existed between himself and Mrs. Andersson. Additionally, he could not even imagine how such awful business ever got started. As soon as the entire nastiness first came to light, and naturally upon the good woman's own request, he had also sworn this same truth to her uncompromising husband—but to no avail. It was rumored, too, that as a last act of kindness towards the memory of the dead woman, the large sweet-natured dog which had belonged to the family was promptly adopted and loyally cared for until its own passing by the man who continued so fervently to denounce the horrible lies which rendered such hideousness upon one unsuspecting, and wholly undeserving, family.

Looking back with considerably critical hindsight, as I am, the thought has occurred to me that human society throughout human history has always grossly discriminated against women and in a particularly significant manner. Perhaps this behavior lies at the root of all the other major discrimination which is generally heaped upon these special members of society that are usually referred to as the "weaker sex." Because this same disingenuous behavior remains an ongoing phenomenon and is prevalent throughout every corner of the globe, it is rarely questioned—thereby assuring its endless proliferation and continuation ad infinitum.

A woman's indisputably influential sexuality remains both a blessing, as well as a curse. Although the honor so often paid to her as a woman is timeless, so is the hatred that is born with the accompanying fear and misunderstanding of her. Man continuously worships at the temple of her body, not always with respect, but more or less to satisfy the powerful carnal cravings that are born within all of us.

Was it not Freud, after all, who first raised the revolutionary concept of the "Madonna-Whore" syndrome? That more rarefied thinking
where on the one hand an individual, as well as a society, greatly es-
teems woman with the fervent zeal of some religious convert for all her
more genteel qualities embodied within that timeless reality of wife and
mother; while at the very same time, and with the relentless passion of
some irrational schizoid, both the individual as well as society greatly
disdain a woman's display of any overt sexuality whenever the least
possibility of not being able to maintain a distinct separation between
these two roles comes into play....

It remains far more than mere simple conjecture, too, that most
people frequently come to fear that which they fail to easily understand.
Consider, for instance, those perpetually unadulterated fears with regard to such critical issues as negative programming and subsequently
negative reinforcement that deal primarily with human sexuality, and
racial matters—and religious bias, too, for that matter, that endlessly
continue to promote such a profound sense of ignorance that eventually
leads to such gross intolerance and hatred in the end.

It is no secret that woman remains universally enigmatic for man.
The mere idea of one's sexuality, as well as its reality, is often used as a
weapon by both sexes. Without any doubt, the legendary timelessness
of man's brutality towards that object which he professes to need and to
revere, all the while continuing to choose to condemn because of the considerable power it continuously elicits over him, is still openly chronicled
within our daily lives. Whenever a woman—anytime and anywhere, is
beaten, or raped, or murdered, essentially womanhood as a whole feels
each and every blow. Indeed, each woman ultimately suffers this same
fate, albeit on a much wider scale....

Because the plight of women throughout human history has always
been so troubling; because, both literally and figuratively speaking,
women have had to claw their way free from the deep pit of ignorance
and despair which traditionally has become their birthright, it naturally
becomes particularly pathetic whenever an instance arises where one
woman seeks to grievously wound another by using this age-old tool of
their common heritage. What hope is there, in the end, that this world
of men shall ever become sufficiently educated towards a more perfect
understanding and appreciation of womankind, when these same her-
etics refuse to close ranks, so to speak, and at times willfully and quite
zealously betray their own gender?

Long have I suspected that there is often far too much emphasis
placed upon the sexual aspect of human nature. After all, is not each

and every man, as well as each and every woman, fundamentally the sum of all their parts? Are we not profoundly so much more than just the sum of our genitalia?

Are not each of us, rather, the glorious sum of all our experiences, as well as all those well-incorporated genetic particulars which are passed down to us by others who came before us? Are we not wholly unique specimens in every sense, which amount to nothing less than the amazing combination of mind, heart, body, and soul? Complex universes to be discovered and appreciated? With these critical things foremost in mind, let us not fail to mention society's habitually reckless attempt at sectioning out and then systematically isolating one particular group from the rest, referring now to the age-old subject of homosexuality, does not society become profoundly guilty of perpetrating a grave injustice not only towards these persons being so unkindly treated, but also ultimately towards itself in the end?

And yet, truly, this most ardent of storytellers would be the last person in the entire universe to ever attempt to disparage in the slightest sense the indisputable power of sex, as well as the incredible magnificence of human sexuality. For I, as with the majority of all the other members of humankind, have always enthusiastically worshipped at that very altar, becoming unceasingly humbled each and every time by the experience....

Within Nature's entire spectrum of overwhelming beauty is it not this unique dynamism—this critical driving urge to "procreate," which ultimately becomes responsible for bringing forth "beautiful new life"? Might we, then, not wisely compare this same primal intensity normally associated with the sex drive to every grand artist's natural impetus to create? Without this vital passion being intrinsic within every grand life force, would there have ever occurred the indisputable miracles that are Mozart, Beethoven, or Bach? Michelangelo or Leonardo da Vinci? Tennessee Williams? Not to mention that remarkable host of countless others, regarding human history's ongoing centuries of superb creative achievement?!

Without the essential motivation of one's sexuality, which forever remains the proud fountainhead of every creative endeavor, each of us would be the poorer for it. Each of us would become a far more insipid version of what we could, and should, be, and not a vibrant soul capable of creating, and inspiring, and living life to its fullest.

Sex, that incredibly powerful little three-letter word—even set apart unto itself—is so breathtakingly beautiful. Proof, indeed, that divine Eros lives.... Proof, certainly, that this same ageless "pleasure principle," this amazing gift, in essence, shall never go out of style.

Even as wonderfully exhilarating as healthy sex can be, genuine love-making remains far more than even this.... That ultra-dynamic combination of both the physical and the spiritual union joining two intelligent, and sensitive, and mutually committed individuals becomes that profoundly emotional statement which is tantamount to nothing less than "Communion" in the totally religious sense. Here, at last, is a worldwide religion that even the most pious atheist may fearlessly embrace.... Here, at last, is a ritualistic and thoroughly grand "rebirth of the spirit," in the truest measure—each and every time.

And yet, too, for the sake of dutifully covering the entire spectrum of such vitally important issues as these, what shall one say of Platonic love? Who will speak in favor of that noble Greek's philosophical ideal and state conclusively upon which of the seven rungs of spiritual discipline it rests? Or, lest one forget, what of the valid and uncompromising vision of the true ascetic's endless search? Where, then, upon that long and winding road leading towards a more perfect state of peace and enlightenment, may the weary traveler find these more rarefied and far less appreciated forms of love?

Taking everything into account, perhaps it is that far more prudent balance which should be striven for by everyone in the end. Perhaps every society, as well as each individual within each society, should learn to bow to the overall human integrity present within each individual among us. This, after all, would seem to be the golden key.... For with this applied new philosophy it could well be that in time the resulting new-found tolerance and compassion would naturally be generated towards every detail of life—and, likewise, towards all living things, and would ultimately become responsible for lifting our imperfect world onto a higher plateau, thereby greatly enriching mankind in the process.

Once, when I was older and had had the opportunity to reiterate this same unhappy tale concerning the Andersson family to Felix, quite pointedly I asked him whether he had heard the story. And if he had, whether or not be believed it to be true.... As was his nature, my dear friend carefully weighed what I had asked. Then, obviously not wishing to become even in the slightest measure responsible for the ongoing force necessary to further ensure the sad story's immortality, he chose simply to answer my question, by saying, "Your question, Adam, calls to mind a particularly interesting proverb which someone has attributed, either correctly or incorrectly, to the German people. In point of fact, and certainly during moments such as these, I remain sorely tempted to place my faith in that same sweet wisdom readily embraced by many a confirmed skeptic when they passionately assert: 'Believe nothing that you hear, and only half of what you see!'

"In other words, question the legitimacy of everything. Truth is often so very difficult to find…. However, while the truth of any situation begs to be discovered, when it finally is—no matter how unpleasant or shocking it might prove to be—civilized behavior demands one's ever quiet devotion to respect, to absolute respect towards the details of the story, as well as to those individuals involved. To mindlessly climb aboard some public bandwagon which consistently goes about disregarding this most basic of philosophies is to place oneself within the company of brutes and louses…. For me, the Eleventh Commandment has always been: 'Thou shalt not gossip!'"

To this very day it remains my unshakably strong personal contention that Felix had at some point become the involuntary recipient of those incredibly sad details relating to this same tragic event, and had undoubtedly been just as greatly moved by all of it as I was…. And even though I never knew him to ever refer to it in any manner—to anyone, really—nonetheless I have long speculated that the story became one of the primary reasons why over the years he always insisted upon having as little as possible to do with Cornelia Grimsley.

14.

FOR BETTER OR FOR WORSE it remains Fate which ultimately chooses the circumstances of a man's birth. Each man, in turn, becomes solely responsible for what he ultimately makes of his life, just as he remains ever free to discriminate in the careful choosing of his friends. Somehow the glorious sweetness of this latter reality helps in great part to temper the frequent injustice of that former truth. After all, is it not the most fortunate individuals among us who are able to live long and fulfilling lives and in the end are able to honestly tally up the number of these same memorable acquaintances upon two or three fingers of one hand? With respect to my own long life, I have learned that of all the truly exceptional treasures of this life that are worthy of being possessed, the greatest of these is genuine friendship and love.

Love is the great force that tempers. It remains the cool and refreshing drink for which every feverish soul endlessly yearns. This uniquely rare "pearl of life," once discovered and endlessly explored, has the wondrous ability to maintain its integrity and inestimable worth with the passing of the years—and manages to add such untold richness and meaning to what would otherwise remain an unbearably empty existence.

Is it not odd how, when one is truly unhappy, time barely creeps along.... Contrarily, when life finally blesses one with this much-required richness and stability which is naturally engendered within the purest concepts of friendship and love, the months and years become such a hopelessly fleeting thing. Certainly for the many special members of the Lauder family and me, especially during those particularly buoyant days when I first became such a happy and grateful new addition to their group, time became unforgivably guilty of moving far too quickly along....

It was already the middle of October. For several weeks now Felix had been avidly searching for a singularly memorable way in which to show his gratitude to "Doc" Owens, in light of all the wonderful care this fine physician always so generously bestowed upon his children. Most recently two of the older members of the group were only just now fully recuperating from a case of the mumps.

I honestly believe, however, that even if there had been adequate funds available to pay the medical bills—which, incidentally, never arrived in any form—knowing my friend as I did, he still would have felt bound to express his special gratitude in some far more personal way. After all, this was his nature. And, most assuredly, there are just some sacred things in life that naturally refuse to be reduced to the frequently pallid terms of mere dollars and cents....

Even those late evening meals and occasional lunches, too, which the Lauder family members always happily insisted upon sharing with our good doctor—whenever he would stop by to check upon the progress of his young patients—never quite seemed to be able to do real justice to the overall issue at hand. Then, during one particularly memorable Saturday morning, just before lunch, it was, upon receiving a long-awaited telephone call from a gentleman who owned and managed a small shop in the town of Lake Geneva which specialized in various editions of used books, a simple situation presented itself that promised to eventually solve this minor dilemma.

As was always the case whenever summer officially ended, there was far less hope of Felix being able to sell any more of his oil paintings and charcoal sketches, since the majority of his seasonal clients had already left the area. These same people reminded me of our migratory birds by dependably traveling elsewhere for the winter and eventually returning again sometime during the following year. With this in mind, a mutually satisfying agreement was eventually made with the elderly Englishman at the tiny book store where several pieces of Felix's more recent work had been taken in on a consignment basis.

So it was, on that highly fortuitous day, that several of the younger children—which naturally included little Maria Christina, Charlie, Stephen, Willy, and me, were invited to accompany Felix into Lake Geneva. Our mission was to finally retrieve some modest sum of money which had finally come about when some lingering "browser" from the Chicago area visited the tiny book store. Perhaps merely upon some whim that person so wisely decided not only to purchase a volume on Ancient History but also one small beautifully framed oil painting of Felix's as well.

With much anticipation, needless to say, the other children and I found ourselves looking forward to the very real possibility of being treated to a dish of wonderful homemade ice cream that was made right down the road at the Redding's own dairy. Those delicious mounds of vanilla ice-cream, which we all relished smothering in spoonfuls of chocolate "jimmies," were unequaled in their richness—just like the famous cheese for which Wisconsin is so well known. I recall that even during those decidedly far more rare times of that past summer, whenever a sale of his was similarly made, all of us were spoiled a bit in this way by Felix, undoubtedly as a special means of celebrating with us his own good fortune.

The morning was marvelously chilly and sunny. We used to call such glorious days "sweater weather." For several late afternoons during that past week, the family and I were dutifully occupied in raking leaves into large neat piles all around the lawn in order that we might later collect everything for our important mulch-pile. Naturally, right on schedule, too, the splendid oleander trees were carefully pruned back and then ceremoniously placed within the porch area of the farmhouse to patiently await the coming wintry weather that we reckoned was just around the corner.

As Felix and our impressive little entourage happily traveled down the road together, bumping along in the Lauder's large sedan with the car's windows rolled fully open, it was with a sense of unequaled ardor—albeit in a somewhat less than harmonizing fashion, that all of us became inspired to sing the long popular song from an earlier time called: "Yes We Have No Bananas."... Shortly, as we slowed down and were about to turn off the main road into the parking lot of the interesting little book store, we actually passed "Doc" Owens as he was in the process of leaving the place. With this our mutual friend jauntily waved to us, just as Felix tooted the car's horn in immediate response.... Certainly not wishing to be left out of this grand manner of friend greeting friend, the other children and I took to eagerly waving in unison, just as we all leaned out of the windows of the car together to exuberantly bid that excellent man "hello" in our cheerful chorus of highly enthusiastic children's voices....

While Felix was in the process of collecting what he originally came for, his children and I waited patiently for him just inside the door. Before he began to gather his things to leave, however, he took a moment more to browse several shelves that were located nearby. Whenever we frequented this charming place, I remember quite well that there was a significantly friendly odor that gently hung about all the many shelves of interesting books.... Basically the scent was a haunting mixture of the rich smell of old quality leather, mingled through and through with the distinct sweetness of some sort of light musky oil used for polishing.

Finally returning to the counter to collect his hat, but just prior to our actual leave-taking, Felix inadvertently spotted a rather tattered old volume of verse sitting upon the far side of the counter which immediately seemed to pique his interest. As he politely reached for it and began to slowly thumb through its pages, the owner of the store said apologetically, "Oh, I'm so sorry, Mr. Lauder. That particular volume is being set aside for someone who promised to come and collect it one day in the future.... He's a gentleman who really seems to appreciate poetry, you know—and just exactly the sort of person I always love to welcome into my place! Since he hadn't sufficient funds this day to make the purchase, I naturally felt I could do him the small favor of putting it aside for him. I feel certain that you must know the man.... His name is Chester Owens—Doctor Chester Owens...." As an after-thought, the talkative and exceedingly helpful gentleman concluded with, "He comes in here quite frequently—mostly to browse, you understand!"

While I was carefully observing Felix, he in turn was politely hanging upon every word the proprietor was speaking. From the fairly unusual expression that was now gleaming there in the depths of my friend's eyes, I guessed that he had just recently come to some sort of conclusion regarding something rather important.

This special 1914 volume which my friend was presently holding within his hands, the very book, mind you, which both he and the good doctor had admired separately and which each had wished to own privately, contained some of the earlier poetic works of William Carlos Williams. Although the modest-looking book's exterior had been badly abused over the years, the owner of the store further assured us that none of its pages were missing. Seemingly very preoccupied at the moment, as Felix took the time to reverently scan through the many pages of the small needy book, the other children and I finally heard him inquire, "How much are you asking for the book, Mr. Whittle?"

"Two dollars," the store's owner promptly answered, without flinching. "Naturally that would be the discounted price already, due to the fact that the book's cover is so badly damaged."

Continuing to hold the little book of poetry in one hand, Felix came over to where his children and I were waiting for him... Since it was I who was standing nearer to him at present, he gently placed his free hand upon one of my shoulders and in a low voice went on to politely ask, "Charley! Adam! I wonder if you would both do me the great favor by returning to the car.... There, in the trunk, you will find my portfolio of drawings which I find that I need at the moment."

As quickly as we could Charley Lauder and I returned to the shop carrying the heavy leather binder and promptly presented it to Felix. Soon Felix was slowly untying the long sturdy cotton ribbons which held the item's twin panels together and then promptly set about carefully spreading open this same protective covering there upon the empty counter in front of all of us....

After some moments where he remained occupied in thoughtfully rummaging through several pieces of his work—apparently in an attempt to locate something specific, he eventually extracted a lovely sketch of a sailing ship at sea—a square-rigger, it was, and then said to the store's owner, "Mr. Whittle, I wonder if I might be able to interest you in this fine little drawing, naturally in exchange for this equally fine book of poetry? As you have already indicated, the book's exterior requires considerable work which I am prepared to do myself before I eventually present it as a gift to our mutual friend, Dr. Chester Owens!"

"Yours is an interesting proposition," the distinguished-looking elderly gentleman was saying with a warm smile as he received back the thin tattered volume which Felix was handing to him from across the tall table. For a brief moment or two more, this same businessman remained occupied in judiciously contemplating Felix's interesting offer, all the while slowly turning the hapless item over and over again within his hands.... Then, momentarily placing the book upon the counter once more, and seemingly having become fairly overcome by curiosity at this point, he eventually inquired in a somewhat sheepish manner whether Felix minded if he looked at the rest of what remained in the portfolio which still lay prostrate between them....

I remember how all of us watched that day, and with a rather keen sense of growing delight, too, I might add, as Mr. Whittle eventually became completely intrigued by a much older sketch of a farm scene. One far more elegant building—located there off in the distance, contrasted greatly with the small thatched cottage that remained in the foreground of the picture. Actually, to be perfectly honest, everything depicted within that interesting work looked amazingly different, and not only with regard to the basic architecture of the buildings, but as far as the trees and various other foliage were concerned. Above all, the more our silent little group studied the rendering, the more it became quite clear to each of us that what we were witnessing at the moment bore absolutely no resemblance to anything that any of us had ever seen before, causing the man to mention this fact to Felix.

"Yes," Felix was musing, "the somewhat unfamiliar quaintness of the sketch's subject matter comes from the fact that it hails from another time—and another place. The scene, actually, was taken from memory.... It is one of my more favorite studies of a particularly special farmstead that was located in northern Hungary which became especially well-known to me during my earliest childhood and youth."

"Might you be inclined to part with it, Mr. Lauder?" the nice man was earnestly inquiring. "I mean, instead of the other sketch which you showed me previously? Please don't misunderstand.... Although the scene of the sailing vessel is quite good in every respect, I'm more inclined to fancy this one instead, for I instinctively feel that it is really something rather unique!" Then, as an after thought, the man quickly added as a means of further explaining his particular stance on the current situation, "I'd gratefully accept it in equal exchange for the volume of poetry—naturally!"

After the two well-satisfied men shook hands to solidify the bargain that had just been concluded, the small book which had obviously known such hard times in the past was carefully wrapped in plain brown paper and then promptly handed to Felix, as the store's owner cheerfully stated, "Once again it's been a real pleasure doing business with you, Mr. Lauder.... I haven't the slightest doubt that Dr. Owens will be as happy to receive your wonderful gift, as you apparently seem to be in being able to make it all possible!"

Within one darkened corner of the Lauder's farmhouse attic, beneath the slanted and badly weathered eaves of the old roof, sat a huge and enormously interesting leather steamer trunk. During the day the filtered light from a solitary air-vent shed itself nearly exclusively upon this "treasure chest" which, from the very first instant I was introduced to it by Felix, had had the power to captivate me. There was also a small overhead bulb that hung from the ceiling nearby and which naturally always provided the means to readily find what we required, especially during any given evening whenever we were obliged to make a necessary trip to that part of the dwelling.

I recall with much fondness, too, that easy access to this wonderful chest was never restricted in any manner. Its rather unusual twin leather and brass studded straps were obviously designed to properly secure the cumbersome object during transit and presently remained draped loosely over its top. Although the intricately-carved brass key always rested there within its heavy brass lock, this delightfully ornate travel-ing case was forever approachable in every sense—very much like its owner. Its entire interior, which included the single shelf that rested just within the top and acted as a spacer to divide the excessively heavy item into two nearly equal parts, top and bottom, was elaborately covered in a rich wine-colored silk brocade, lending a genuinely regal quality to its overall presence.

Residing within the top compartment of the chest one could nearly always find several neatly arranged stacks of private papers, belong-ing exclusively to Felix, with each firmly secured by a length of black ribbon.... Within the bottom section of this unusual trunk, once the top was carefully lifted out, was located a generous vial of a particular type of glue, as well as several thick rolls of exquisite Italian leather whose exact color matched that of rich dark coffee after it is lightly laced with heavy milk or cream. Such leather, in fact, after being properly cut and hand-sewn, was used on a regular basis during those former times to help create the luxurious head-bands for the inside of the elegant hats which once were so proudly manufactured by Felix's company there in Chicago.

Within the various other corners of the small attic many other inter-esting things quietly resided too. I remember quite well that there was a dress form which Emma Lauder would frequently consult during those exceptionally rare times when she found that she was obliged to create a costume for herself. This handy contraption, which was an exact replica of her own shapely torso, could be adjusted according to her changing body measurements over the years and further allowed her to pin and perfect whatever she was tailoring, instead of relying upon someone else for assistance.

Nearby, one sturdy wooden crate containing two dozen or more handmade wigs must have conjured up many a bittersweet memory for Felix, since they naturally alluded to one of his former lives.... Indeed, this same small collection of individually wrapped pieces of exquisite craftsmanship was only a small fragment of its original cargo sent long ago to a buyer in New York, who later reneged at the last moment on their agreement by refusing to pay for the merchandise. In order to forego the considerable time and expense it naturally would have taken to return the heavy box by ship to Mexico City, Felix had it sent instead to be temporarily stored at the home of a colleague there in Chicago.

In addition to a long mauve-colored silk shawl which Emma Lauder habitually insisted upon using to cover her dress form, no doubt for the sake of propriety, one or more of the younger Lauder children had taken to playfully adorn their mother's superb physical likeness with one of the wigs, lending an uncanny life-like quality to this comely apparition. The wig itself was cleverly secured from underneath by a large rubber ball, intended of course to signify the human head. For further effect, upon the front portion of this spherical toy some equally impish soul had penciled in a pair of smiling lips, a slightly comical nose, and two large round eyes, each fringed with an abundance of tiny little eyelashes....

So it was to this special place that Felix, Charley, Eddie, and I finally came to claim a single roll of the marvelous feeling and equally marvelous smelling leather which, when the entire project was completed, would appropriately become the grand new cover for the book of poetry that we happily intended as a special gift of thanks for "Doc" Owens.... With young Charley carrying the leather and Felix naturally taking charge of the heavy bottle of glue, the four of us headed down to the small anteroom off the barn which initially had been commandeered by my friend for use as his private artist's studio, as well as his private workshop where various repairs on "this and that" were always being made.

For several evenings following this time, Felix meticulously labored over this special project of his. I recall that the first step was to carefully remove the old tattered facade of the book. Gently, then, like some gifted surgeon with scalpel in hand, I watched him go about accomplishing this very thing. In time my friend was finally able to spread open this worn-out old "skin" there upon the small work bench and to further use it as a necessary pattern from which he would eventually cut the beautiful new leather covering. Next, after painstakingly stretching the rich pliable material as tightly as any well-made glove might be fitted, Felix went ahead and glued the new backing to the book's flaps using several small metal vice-grips to properly secure all the edges together until the glue finally dried.

Days later, while Felix sat at the dining room table that occasionally served as his official writing desk, he shared with his wife and their many children and me the fairly astonishing fruits of his considerable time and energy. Quite remarkably enough, this splendidly new-looking old book—this true labor of love, essentially, which had undergone such a complete metamorphosis, now bore not the slightest resemblance to what it once had been.

I noted, with pure pleasure, too, that in the future the little object would be able to hold its own anywhere. It would surely be able to stand proud from now on and take its more rightful place upon any bookshelf as a worthy tribute to the marvelous poet, who, like our own dear "Doc"

Owens, had also been an excellent physician in his own right. And there, upon one blank interior page located at the front of this same little book, each of us watched with great satisfaction as Felix took up his fountain pen and began to meticulously inscribe the words of his personal tribute, which read: *"For our greatly esteemed friend, Dr. Chester Owens—with the Lauder family's most sincere appreciation for all his wonderful kindness."*

That following Sunday evening, after yet another one of Emma Lauder's spectacular meals, as an enthusiastic and happy group we finally presented Felix's surprise gift to our mutual friend. Perhaps it should also be noted that whenever this same kindly soul became emotionally overcome in some manner, it was usually his habit to become quite speechless. Occasionally removing his handkerchief from one pocket of his trousers, "Doc" would quickly dab at his eyes to remove the excess moisture which had rather rapidly collected there, just as he also might be prompted to blow his nose, and lastly begin to shake his head slowly from side to side in a manner of disbelief.... That special occasion, in fact, elicited precisely this same response when young Maria Christina volunteered to present our collective offering to him, while she cheerfully announced for all to hear, "This gift is from all of us, Doctor Owens.... But mostly it's from Father!"

With all of us jubilantly gathered around the good doctor, at the moment, we eventually watched him take a deep breath just as he retrieved the small beautifully covered book of poetry from its crisp encasement of brown paper and twine. While he paused to thoughtfully scan its pages, he began to slowly move his head from side to side, as he was declaring, "My, my, my! How on earth did ya all know I had so wished to own this special little book!?" After taking the necessary time to carefully read what Felix had inscribed, this fine man eventually looked up to fix his rather keen attention upon Felix and to declare with unabashed emotion so readily imprinted within his voice, and likewise upon his entire countenance, as he softly said, "...and what are poets for in such destitute times?!"

The profundity of this timely quote from Holderlin's beautiful elegy entitled "Bread and Wine" was instantly grasped by Felix. Without missing so much as a beat, while the two soul-mates stood openly admiring each other, now, Felix answered his already excellent friend by quoting back from the same work: "But they are, you say, like the wine-god's holy priests, Who fared from land to land in holy night...."

Shortly, with mutual pride resounding in their combined voices, and as if each were helplessly acquiescing to this same unscripted dance of the spirit, both friends finally finished the poem together by stating,

"One thing stands firm: whether it be near noon Or close to midnight, a measure ever endures, Common to all; yet to each his own is allotted, too, Each of us goes toward and reaches the place that he can!"

Looking back with a particular clarity that often only comes with the hindsight derived from the passing of the years, I maintain that this was the precise moment when this already rare friendship of theirs was firmly and finally grounded. Indeed, that sincerely beautiful moment in time became for both of them a highly enviable marker where a sincere commitment was being established that mutually incorporated mind, and heart—and soul—and which would inevitably stand the harsh scrutiny of time by growing a bit stronger with each passing day, to ultimately bring them both such comfort and joy. It remains a poignant fact, too, that this same remarkable little book of poetry was never to leave "Doc" Owens' side. From that point in time, onward until his death, the ever comforting words of William Carlos Williams—along with the bright and shining memory of that unique evening at the Lauder home, traveled with him everywhere he went.

Felix likened the human heart to an uniquely-designed chamber possessing a single door that consistently begs to be left ajar.... Essentially this vital organ is capable of expanding many times over with the continuous addition of honest experiences faithfully collected over a lifetime where one's dear friends and other loved ones, especially, are welcome to come and go at will, helplessly claiming for themselves a significant portion of that heart in the end, just as they are forever required to leave behind a meaningful part of themselves in the process.... This ageless truth remains, quite simply, one of Life's unscripted rules; indeed, one of the uncontested laws governing the many joys, as well as the unavoidable sorrows, inherent within the miraculous gift called Love.

15.

FELIX'S STRANGE BEHAVIOR was beginning to worry me. Recently he had done something that was really quite odd—quite odd, to say the least, and I felt a pressing need to consult him about the matter at the very earliest available opportunity.

The incident in question occurred one early weekday morning, during that final week of October. As usual it became necessary for me to rise at the crack of dawn. But on this particular day, before bathing and then scampering off to school as I might otherwise have done, I was obliged instead to head off to the barn in order to meet my temporary responsibility of mucking out Old Zech's stall. Normally this powerful and moody fellow was left outside to continuously graze the surrounding pasture land.... Lately, however, several of the Reddings' cows had come into season, and, just as one might easily imagine, he was making a big-time nuisance of himself.

In a valiant attempt to keep peace in the neighborhood, when the heifers were out grazing during the day, our "Romeo" was unhappily sequestered there within our barn, all the while making the most outlandish rumpus imaginable in his worthy attempt at trying to solicit a bit of sympathy. Naturally when the "ladies" were later reclaimed from the pasture at the end of every day and taken back to the shed for their second round of milking, the poor frustrated beast would finally be given his temporary freedom to aimlessly roam about outside as before....

What happened on this day at issue, just as I was taking a brief respite from shoveling those healthy piles of manure into a large metal bucket, was that I heard someone quickly enter the barn from the far end of the building. This happened right after I stooped down to hurriedly tie up one renegade shoestring, there upon my left boot, which had been dragging in the dirt while I worked.

When I eventually stood up, but before I could even let this visitor know that I was momentarily loitering nearby, I witnessed Felix hurriedly open a container and then place a scoop-full of something within the confines of his clean linen handkerchief which was now spread open upon a nearby work counter. As I watched further he promptly gathered together each corner of the cloth to fold it and eventually place the item deep within his pocket, just as if this same little routine had already become fairly familiar to him. After securing the lid of the tall canister and quickly returning this medium sized object to one particular shelf within a nearby cupboard, my friend abruptly turned to leave the area. Making his way to the family's truck that was parked nearby, I soon observed him quickly drive off down the gravel driveway....

What was I to make of it all, I ask the reader? Naturally, quite severely overcome by curiosity at this point, I quickly wiped my hands clean and went directly over to investigate the matter.... I surely needed to see for myself what was residing within that suspicious-looking container.

Carefully prying off the receptacle's stubborn lid and then partially extracting a small heavy bag, I took a moment more to sound out the two words that were printed in large black letters across its front, just exactly the way George was teaching me to do. In no time at all, and to my utter amazement as well, I soon discovered that they spelled out: D.O.G ... F.O.O.D. Totally baffled at the moment and standing there for several awkward moments, as I was, the overwhelming discrepancy here, at least as I was seeing it, was quite simply that we did not even own a dog....

Although it was a common practice for Felix to take along a bit of food and even a tiny amount of sweets wherever he went to help regulate his erratic daily insulin level, I should still have never imagined that he had developed a penchant for such an eccentric delicacy as this. Still, giving my friend the benefit of the doubt, I finally decided that perhaps somehow he had very cleverly discovered the secret that these rather unconventional rations contained the proper balance of nutrients, and so forth, to aid him in his supremely difficult and never-ending battle.

That very evening after supper, when everyone else in the household was occupied in some other way, Felix remained conspicuously working at the large round dining room table, patiently going over the family's monthly accounts, when I politely approached him to discuss the matter of the dog food. "What may I do for you, my young friend!" he asked with his usual warm smile, when I finally made my presence known to him.

Taking a seat very near to where he was presently sitting, I watched him as he became engrossed once more in tallying up several columns of figures. As soon as he finished, however, I found myself whispering, "So, how does it taste?"

With my typical forthright inquiry, Felix glanced over at me with a slightly perplexed and totally innocent expression, to ask in return, "How does what taste, Adam?!"

"You know..." I continued to whisper, as I nodded in the general direction of the barn. Finally seeing that I was not getting through to him; seeing that Felix was not grasping, in the least, what I was trying to impart to him, I finally broke down to say with a touch of exasperation, "You remember ... the stuff in the barn? The dog food?!"

Having merely gone into the preliminary details of what had transpired much earlier that day—and with this, naturally, my mounting worries concerning the whole affair, Felix slowly began to smile from ear to ear. I watched further as he quickly removed his glasses and covered his mouth with the back of this same hand in an obvious effort to keep from laughing out loud. With his eyes closed, at the moment, his shoulders began to move in time to the substantial mirth which had obviously taken hold of him at this point.... In a moment or two, after regaining his composure, his trusty bifocals were promptly returned to their usual place there upon the bridge of his fine straight nose. Laying one hand now across my shoulders and with a far more serious expression, he proceeded to whisper, "Are you any good at keeping secrets?!"

Without so much as batting an eye, I responded in kind by enthusiastically whispering back, "Of course I am!"

"Tomorrow, then, after school, I'll meet you back here at the house.... After that we'll go for a little ride. Quite happily I promise to share something with you which will surely vindicate me in the long run by placing this seemingly odd behavior of mine into a far better light. But remember," he was cautioning me, "it's a huge secret!"

Practically all through that entire night I tossed and turned with the rare excitement that our little conspiracy invoked, believing that the morning would never arrive. Truly, I had considerable difficulty sleeping, for in my active mind I was attempting to correctly guess about that big secret Felix would be sharing with me. Needless to say, too, the hours there at school that next day dragged on far more slowly than normal. And after class was dismissed, I practically ran all the way home, only to find my dear friend already waiting there for me.

I remember, however, that our first order of business that early afternoon was to stop by the Hopkins' place. It was as if, with his innate sensitivity, Felix automatically sensed what I had originally surmised about Harry Hopkins early on in my relationship with him, that, fundamentally, this kindly man desperately needed the company of others. So, more or less under the pretext of going to visit our friend with the idea of dropping off a handful of stamps for Harry's prized collection, Felix and I were soon on our way....

Since Felix Lauder had within the not-so-distant past mastered such a lucrative business enterprise for so many years, it was not unusual for him to continue to receive letters or parcels from many exciting cities around the world. Naturally several of his own children, who were only just now beginning to develop a rather keen interest in this same hobby of stamp-collecting, usually got "first pick" of what always managed to find its way to the Lauder home. But it is also my vivid recollection that whenever something truly meaningful arrived—in other words, some sort of postage which was far more rare, and, consequently, craved to be appreciated by someone with a much better understanding of its true value, Felix dutifully put it aside for this fine neighbor of ours instead.

With the three of us huddled closely together around the small rickety outdoor table there in the Hopkins' back yard, I remained happily nursing my cup of warm tea and milk which Harry prepared for each of us in honor of our visit. That late autumn afternoon was brisk but sunny and so my steamy beverage was more than appreciated. I well recall, too, that the badly weathered piece of furniture which presently held our cups and saucers and teapot had one leg that was just a hair shorter than the rest, causing it to remain off-balance and to wobble a bit whenever contact was made with it in any manner.

As I sat quietly contemplating this, a splendid-looking and very amicable old tomcat silently ventured forth from his lair of leafless bushes nearby and proceeded to weave in and out of our own collection of human legs assembled there under that rusted table top. This exceptional-looking old fellow was a Russian blue—a magnificent specimen of its noble breed, and as I reached down to acknowledge his presence he immediately sauntered over in my direction to sit at my feet, all the while purring rather loudly with the pleasure that our mutual contact was creating.

Slowly running my agile fingers through the cat's amazingly thick blue-gray fur, at the moment, whenever I stopped stroking him my new-found friend would look up at me with his deeply penetrating gaze.... His mesmerizing light green eyes were confidently mirroring the uncanny wisdom of his more than five-thousand-year heritage, and within seconds thereafter, he took to gently swatting me with his right front paw as a somewhat impertinent signal that he was not finished being petted. Each time he behaved this way, I had to laugh a little. With this open expression of my utter delight, Harry finally looked my way to say, "Th-th-that's my old 'T-t-thomas'—my very l-l-loyal fr-fr-friend and c-c-companion!" After a few moments more, as our genial host continued to take in my interaction with this special cat of his, he soon added, "D-d-don't know wh-wh-what I'd ever d-d-do w-w-without h-h-him!"

Shortly after this he and Felix took to resuming their discussion. While I listened rather absentmindedly to Felix's dissertation on the fundamentals of repairing a piece of heavy farming equipment, the bulk of my attention was slowly becoming fixed upon Ugenia Hopkins. As always, she continued to make notably slow progress on those endless excursions of hers back and forth across the outer perimeter of the same yard. Trailing after her was that ever-present and badly rusted little wagon, which never ceased making that awful high-pitched squeaking noise as it traveled on, and on, and on....

Eventually it was Felix who paused from his ongoing discussion with Harry Hopkins. He seemed just as annoyed as I was, at this point, with that continuous assault of needless racket. Thoughtfully gazing out into the yard, now, to intently focus upon the culprit from whence the sound was radiating, in what I deemed a noteworthy effort on his part at attempting to remedy the on-going nuisance in the future, Felix patiently offered, "Next time I come to visit, Harry, I'll be certain to remember to bring along my oil can.... Then we should be able to quickly dispense with that ongoing noise your wife's little wagon is making."

Harry Hopkins seemed rather nonplused concerning this logical solution which our friend was agreeably prescribing. In fact, he was concentrating so much on what the two of them were formerly discussing that it was only at Felix's insistence that he paused to actually allow his senses to adequately zero in on that same vexing sound to which he had apparently long ago become more than accustomed. Then, oddly enough, as if the entire matter were being rendered a non-issue from his worthy perspective at least, this dear man cheerfully answered by insisting, "Ohhh...! C-c-couldn't do th-th-that.... G-g-got to always b-b-be able to f-f-find m-m-my l-l-lady! Y-y-you see, the n-n-noise always l-l-lets me kn-kn-know e-e-exactly where sh-sh-she is!"

As much as Felix and I hated to admit it, there was a certain undeniable logic in this man's thinking. Why we had not grasped it on our own, I shall never know. After Harry patiently enlightened both of us, as he did, I was struck by the notion that perhaps it was this similarly clever reasoning which first prompted the Swiss to place those little bells around the necks of their livestock, in order to be able to keep tabs on them... All in all, such predictable sounds, when heard often enough, inevitably cease to prey upon the conscious mind.

Needless to say, there were quite a few other questions I had wished to ask our host concerning this unusual behavior of his wife. I correctly imagined, too, that Felix Lauder's own thoughts were following along this same avenue, since he resisted going back and picking up the thread of their previous conversation. Finally, both of us could not help becoming thoroughly caught up in carefully appraising this pathological behavior of Ugenia Hopkins as she continued to mindlessly amble about, seemingly obsessed to accomplish what she was always doing. Realizing this, Harry Hopkins finally consented to lapse into a fairly in-depth explanation concerning the many facts of the great tragedy which had utterly shattered their formerly happy life all those many years ago....

Much as if our kindly host almost seemed grateful for a chance to share with us this extreme heartache of his—this unreasonably heavy burden of great personal sadness which had been his constant companion for far too long, he soon began to share his tale of woe by assuring us that the strangely behaving woman we were all observing at the moment had not always conducted herself in this way. Indeed, before the influenza epidemic of 1917–1918, where well over a quarter of a million men, women, and children in America alone perished, his wife had been an emotionally healthy, intellectually vibrant, and exceptionally loving human being....

As it happened, Harry and Ugenia Hopkins were married late in life. From the time they finally exchanged vows onward for many years after that, they shared their mutually overwhelming sorrow of remaining childless. More than anything else they had longed to be able to bring a child of their own into the world, but as every year came and went the unavoidable reality that this would never be the case eventually became apparent to them both. In order to fill the terrible void which this intrinsic injustice bequeathed to them, and, equally important, in order to find a more dependable way to channel the considerable life-force within his dear wife which was naturally becoming greatly thwarted with this unwelcome knowledge of theirs, Harry began to encourage Ugenia to involve herself in community projects of every sort.

According to her husband Ugenia's energy level was legendary. Not only had she continued to teach piano on a regular basis at the various homes of several young students who resided within our community, she became responsible, as well, for organizing a church chorus that became quite well known and respected. So much so, in fact, that folks traveled from neighboring communities to attend religious services there at the local Lutheran Church, and perhaps more than anything else to be able to enjoy the splendid musical and vocal accompaniment which tended to add so much to everyone's Sunday.

During every annual county fair, too, residents from as far away as Chicago and Milwaukee would always flock to the small booth which Ugenia Hopkins and her sister Maggey consistently took to manning each summer. There, upon the various clothes-lines assembled to adequately display the hand-crafted artifacts which the two spent the entire previous year creating for just this occasion, hung a multitude of awe-inspiring quilts, and beautifully knitted sweaters, and colorful hooked rugs of various sizes and configurations. And when the funds from the combined efforts of these two good women were finally tallied at the end of that particular busy weekend, a substantial portion of their profits would always be relegated to a fledgling project which was established by Ugenia and Harry Hopkins early on....

Basically this same selfless and energy-consuming crusade of theirs, which had become especially dear to Mrs. Hopkins from the beginning, consisted of properly educating other volunteer midwives like herself. In turn, these dedicated women would eventually instruct other women of childbearing age who lived throughout several local counties about the overwhelming importance of maintaining excellent hygiene, proper nutrition, and so forth—before, during, and after the birthing process. Because the infant mortality rate tended to remain fairly high and young mothers themselves far too often died in giving birth to their children, it was eventually felt by a growing number of sufficiently concerned individuals that something significant must be done relevant to the widespread ignorance that sadly contributed to this awful reality.

It was no secret around town, either, that "Doc" Owens found it impossible to adequately cover all of the bases himself, concerning such similar medical emergencies. This disturbing fact remained such that he, along with several locally elected public health officials, as well as concerned citizens like Ugenia and Harry, were beginning to take notice and to try their best to make amends for this former shortcoming. Predictably, with the slow rise of public awareness compounded in great part by the revolutionary momentum being established during these same years by the pioneering spirit of Margaret Sanger's own movement, badly-needed measures were presently being established and implemented to help shore up every young woman's control of this vital aspect of her life.

Then, quite amazingly enough, sometime during Ugenia Hopkins' forty-sixth year of living, a genuine miracle finally occurred. At long last it seemed that Fate chose to smile upon her and her husband by allowing them to realize that special dream which had previously eluded them.... For, in the spring of 1912, Mrs. Hopkins herself very proudly gave birth to twin sons, profoundly enriching their lives many times over.

While sitting where we were on that late October afternoon, several brightly colored delinquent leaves were caught up by the healthy breeze.... After being rescued from their former home in some nearby tree, they freely floated about for a few seconds only to land quite soundlessly there upon our table. Soon Harry began reminiscing about that particularly wondrous time in their lives, and in a thoroughly enchanting manner he compared his beloved wife to a late-blooming rose, as he mused, "J-j-just when I th-th-thought my G-g-genny c-c-couldn't possibly b-b-be more b-b-beautiful than sh-sh-she already w-w-was, m-m-motherhood made m-m-me see the er-er-error of m-m-my th-th-thinking!" Then a dark shadow seemed to slowly pass across his eyes, and he went on to sadly state: "B-b-but our splendid h-h-happiness wasn't m-m-meant to l-l-last!"

The dear man went on to confide to Felix and me that both their sons eventually contracted the dreaded influenza. This was during the latter part of 1917, and within only a matter of three days from the onset of their initial fever, both children died two days apart from one another. Needless to say, Ugenia was irreconcilable. The cold motionless bodies of their beloved children, in fact, had had to be literally pried from the woman's strong grasp by her husband, one after the other, in order to relinquish them to the undertaker.

With the subsequent emotional breakdown which she suffered immediately thereafter, her mental faculties remained gravely impaired, leaving her to wander across the back area of their property line day after day and forever pulling the small red wagon which once belonged to their children while they lived. Harry, too, had not gone unscathed in the emotional sense either.... During that same overwhelmingly difficult time, something involuntary occurred within his own mind which left him with his unshakable stutter.

Presently we watched as Harry stood up from his place at our table and proceeded to slowly make his way across the lawn towards his wife. Not long after this, with his large hand firmly grasping the upper portion of one of Ugenia's fragile arms in order to properly steady her, both of them were now shuffling along together as they continued to trail the small noisy wagon behind them. After they eventually returned to our table Ugenia was carefully seated in the place which her husband had just vacated. Felix and I continued to observe as Harry proceeded to lift a child's dolly from the interior of the deep wagon bed... Obviously it was a well-worn facsimile of a living sleeping infant that was wrapped in an old faded worn-out blanket which our dutiful host was gently placing within the outstretched and noticeably eager arms of his dear wife.

Immediately after Harry accomplished this small familiar act of kindness, it became necessary for him to return to the house to fetch a bit of supper for his child-like spouse. Felix and I promised to remain behind to attend to Ugenia until his return. As we waited, the elderly woman with the flat lifeless-looking stare and flyaway snow-white hair peeking out in a helter-skelter fashion from underneath the woolen sleeping bonnet she always wore, never acknowledged our presence in any manner.... Instead, clasping the doll close to her heart she began to slowly rock back and forth from the waist up, humming some little tune very softly to herself. Then, abruptly ceasing this behavior, she began to methodically unfasten several of the covered buttons located there at the front of the warm thick woolen robe that she was wearing. Having briefly exposed one sagging withered breast which had also undoubtedly suckled her own infant sons all those many years ago, she went about attempting to recreate the same effect with the imaginary infant she was now holding....

I shall never forget the sight. That rare moment, with its guileless authenticity, profoundly touched my mind and my heart that day. It soon became clear to me that that fiercely innate instinct to nurture and protect her progeny remained the last vestige of dignity which this poor woman possessed. Quite literally it was this deeply ingrained behavior of Ugenia's which remained the very last light of animated principle that ultimately would be extinguished only by her own death one day.

Watching her now, as she continued to go through these fundamental motions that are such a natural part of the beauty of motherhood, Felix and I began to comprehend how lonely and how difficult Harry Hopkins' life must have been. And yet, remaining true to himself, as well as remaining true to the woman whom he had promised to love and honor "in sickness, and in health—until death us do part," tremendous credit was due our friend, to say the least. Instead of relinquishing his unending responsibilities as a loving and caring husband, as he surely might have done under the circumstances by institutionalizing his wife and therefore placing her in the professional care of often uncaring strangers, this kindly and thoroughly patient man opted for the more difficult role....

I remember thinking that there was something truly remarkable about that entire picture. I was beginning to understand that the words of any vow sincerely made are deemed sacred; sacred in the most profound sense, even from the very first instant that they are uttered. Moreover, with the predictable passing of time, such promises that one continually chooses to honor actually develop the power to take on a life of their own by building tremendous character in the process, as well as inducing a distinctive feeling of genuine self-worth. Inevitably the true measure of every individual is predicated upon how true he or she is able to remain to this basic sense of personal integrity....

After Felix and I thanked our gracious host for his fine company, we naturally promised to visit him again in the future. With Harry sitting at the small table patiently feeding Ugenia her supper of warm vegetable soup, Felix and I quietly took our leave.

Merely seconds after we reached the truck, though, I remembered something important that I had forgotten to say to Harry. So, cheerfully sprinting back to the place that I had just left, past the now dormant dahlia garden where this same good man and I first met a little more than a year ago, I respectfully walked up to the table....

With Harry glancing up to acknowledge my presence, I stood openly appraising this unusually good man as I confidently said without faltering in the least, "Mr. Hopkins, thank you for that amazing box of clothing that you left for me last year.... Thank you, too, for the sunflower seeds, and all the firewood—and also for having finally fixed my father's broken down front door the way you did!" Then, pretty much as an afterthought really, which contained far more truth than I was ever likely to adequately express to anyone, I quickly added, "Your wonderful gifts actually saved my life!"

It became nothing less than the logical process of elimination which ultimately brought me to this important truth in the end, many months, in fact, before I was privileged to learn the astounding truth of my benefactor's life which he chose to share so openly with Felix and me on that day. And it became this critical sharing on Harry's part that finally furnished me with those important missing pieces to the puzzle that might have otherwise eluded me. I realized with great satisfaction that I had guessed correctly in believing that Harry Hopkins was my faithful guardian angel all along. Without having known the entire truth back then, the wonderful clothing in which I was in such desperate need had actually once belonged to his own beloved sons, and, as I stood there waiting for some sort of response from him, my heart was brimming with far-greater warmth for him than ever before.

Having just finished coaxing a bit of warm soup into his wife's mouth, and after taking a few seconds more to dab away a single wayward drop of rich broth which proceeded to run down her chin, Harry Hopkins finally took to resting the small spoon inside the large bowl that was sitting there upon the wobbly table.... Now he was thoughtfully studying me and in no time at all, with considerable emotion readily apparent within his own eyes, as well as within his quivering voice, he finally went on to tell me, "C-c-couldn't think of a-a-anyone that I would r-r-rather have g-g-given those articles of clothing t-t-to, than y-y-you, Adam!"

In response to this, and quite impetuously, too, I found myself doing something that was quite extraordinary—at least from my perspective, way back then.... After taking the necessary two or three steps towards this kindly soul, I instinctively placed my arms about his neck, just as if it were the most natural thing in the world to do, and quickly hugged him. With a touch of self-inflicted embarrassment and before either one of us could respond again in any manner, I jauntily trotted back to the Lauder's truck where Felix remained patiently waiting for me.

Shortly thereafter, the old truck in which we were traveling quickly traversed those uneven train tracks of the now hopelessly defunct Eagle Line Branch; the same familiar and thoroughly dilapidated corduroy way which I had so eagerly explored during my initial trip to Peck's Station all those months ago. Seconds later Felix and I turned right onto a road which ran parallel to these tracks. Bumping along this unpaved thoroughfare for a quarter of a mile or so, we finally came to stop by the side of this road, not far from an exceptionally large oak tree....

The ancient sentinel surely must have been the "great-granddaddy" of all giant oak trees. I judged at first glance that it most probably would have taken three or four grown men with their hands clasped firmly together to form a ring in order to be able to circle the entire girth of its massive trunk. Because of the prevailing winds which for countless years had obviously been blowing more from one direction than from any other, this hardy deciduous was leaning noticeably towards its southern exposure, pretty much confirming this fact in my mind.

I thoughtfully contemplated as well that its proud leafless headdress of thick limbs which were characteristically stretching out, and up, and all about the place, incorporated within the tree's stunning network of lesser branches and twigs the admirable ability to transform itself into an immense shade umbrella, no doubt, during the greater part of each year. Had it been possible for this silent old survivor to give a detailed histori-cal account of everything it had chanced to witness during its evolution from tiny acorn to adult tree, what amazing stories it might have told.

Felix had a particular fondness for such trees. Many of his pencil sketches or studies in charcoal—done quickly and quite often on a mere moment's notice, ultimately resulted in being effectively incorporated within one of his completed compositions done in oil, or watercolor, sometime later on. My friend used to say that for him a leafless tree was by far the more interesting study, since its true character could always be more readily discerned and, therefore, more immensely appreciated—much like the preferred open and honest individual, without mask or any other visible contrivance with which to hide behind.

While my friend dutifully turned off the vehicle's ignition, I quickly glanced around to observe nothing more than many miles of open fields. This erudite "tree of knowledge," in effect, with a great portion of its far-reaching latticework of gnarled superficial roots resting there upon the ground, and besprinkled at the moment with a thick patchwork blanket of lovely colorful leaves which had been recently shed, remained the only point of interest for a radius of some considerable distance.... Perplexed a bit, at this point, I addressed Felix by respectfully asking, "Is this the place where we'll find the surprise you promised?!"

Felix had already opened the door to his side of the vehicle, and as he made ready to step out onto the shoulder of the road where we were parked, he turned now to glance my way, as he said with a charming smile, "This is the place!"

My friend's present behavior was somewhat mystifying, to say the least. Here we were out in the middle of nowhere, without a soul in sight—without anything in sight, for that matter, except for that amaz-ing old tree, and I could not fathom in the least why we had come to stop where we had. Soon, however, from within one deep pocket of his work trousers, I watched as Felix carefully extracted the modest little bundle of dry dog food which was being secretly stowed inside the clean handkerchief he always carried. As I stepped from the truck myself and quickly made my way around the vehicle to stand by his side, I heard him whistle once—only once, and immediately following this signal he enthusiastically called forth the words, "Here, boy!"

All this while the small dog was actually sitting there cradled within one giant snakelike portion of root, very close to the base of the tree, no doubt watching Felix and me from the second we first arrived... His own variegated coloring was such that he blended quite expertly into the shading of the tree's multicolored bark, and so, naturally, had gone unnoticed by me in the beginning. The little animal was a mixed terrier breed of some sort, and although I could readily see that he was no longer a puppy, I surmised that he was not exactly an old dog either.

Literally spellbound, I continued to watch as Felix stooped down in the softer less compact dirt that bordered the road. As he opened the handkerchief which now exposed the small offering he was carrying, with marked feeling he repeated the exact words he had spoken only seconds before. Finally leaving the confines of the protective niche in which he was comfortably sitting the shy animal eventually came as far as he dared, before rolling over in what was a basic gesture of submission. Seeing that the dog was not going to travel any further in our direction, Felix finally stood up and proceeded to carefully approach him. Kneeling over him, at the moment, and gently patting his exposed belly, my dear friend began to softly speak to the little guy, as he said, "Hello again! As you see, we've brought you something more to eat!"

"To whom does he belong?" I asked.

"Can't say..." Felix responded. "George and I spotted him three weeks ago, just sitting here by the side of the road." After that initial greeting finally stopped, and after the little dog stood up to acknowledge the food Felix was offering him, without glancing my way again Felix proceeded to hand-feed the gentle creature.

After a few moments more, however, he decided to enlighten me with what he speculated might have happened, as I heard him further state, "I imagine that some summer visitor living around the lake must have just dropped him off here, and then left him to fend for himself.... Mr. Hopkins assures me that such unfortunate things happen quite frequently around these parts when irresponsible and uncaring owners abandon their domesticated dogs and cats, merely upon some whim, obligating the poor animals to try and survive as best they can where previously they were able to depend upon the more or less arbitrary kindness of their owners!"

I did not have to ask why such things happened. The way I saw it, at least, was that if certain people could find it in their hearts to abandon a child, how hard would it be to forsake an animal? Watching Felix continue to bond with the amiable little beast I noticed that the dog had no collar. However from where I continued to stand, I could readily see that he possessed a really sweet little face and bright intelligent eyes that occasionally wandered over to where I stood watching. He was carefully appraising me in return, all the while he was in the process of slowly consuming his meal.... Soon, with the bevy of questions the current situation just naturally invoked, I found myself inquiring, "Exactly how long have you and George been looking after him, like this?"

Glancing up to meet my eyes, all the while the dog was finishing his food, Felix answered, "From the very beginning, which was nearly three weeks ago, when George and I first spotted him sitting here. One of us always makes a point to stop by at least once a day, in order to feed him and to check up on him.... There is a small pond just beyond that ridge over there that provides the necessary drinking water he always needs. I confess that each time I drive over this way, I half expect to find the little orphan gone—but each time, so far, he manages to pleasantly fool me!"

"Couldn't we just take him home with us, instead?" I asked. This simple logic, after all, seemed to make the most sense.

"Early in our relationship with the dog, George and I attempted to do that very thing. However, I had not gone more than a half block in the truck with him, when the dog bolted past George's grasp, jumped through the open window, and scurried back to this exact spot—undoubtedly to wait here by the side of the road for the master that he still believes will eventually be coming back for him."

Carefully contemplating the remarkable little canine, as I listened to what Felix was telling me, I marveled at his obvious sense of fidelity and promptly said to my friend, "He's a very loyal dog!"

Without meeting my gaze, Felix continued to gently stroke the dog which had eventually come to place its little head upon one of my friend's dusty boots. In answer to what I had stated, he mused, "To be sure.... It would certainly seem that he is a far more loyal friend to his former master, than apparently his former master will ever be to him!"

"What will he do, when the snows finally come?" I asked, for I knew full well how terribly treacherous the winter months could be. Living out in the open like this was certainly no place for a small short-haired dog... Like Felix, I was already becoming awfully attached to the wee fellow.

"There's some unused wood in the barn," Felix was saying, "mostly odd pieces, some of which I thought might be utilized to build a simple dog house. Nothing complicated, just something that will help keep our little fellow from the wind and the snow. Perhaps you'd like to help me accomplish this task? After we finish, either George or Eddie will assist us in loading it onto the truck, and then we'll deliver it out here to our little dependant." After a moment or two of silence, as he finally nodded in the direction of the great tree, he went on to add, "I've further contemplated that if we were to set his new living quarters, just so—under that portion of the tree over there, facing the base of the tree, the dog would be well served by this in the end."

On our way home on that early evening, silently steeped as we both were within the growing dusk, Felix finally broke the silence and surprised me a good deal by quietly stating, "My own father once gave me a dog.... Actually, it was during that special time of my life when I wasn't much older than you are now!"

Although I was the most recent addition to the Lauder household—and presumably only a terribly grateful guest, at this point, I had already discovered that Felix was an extraordinarily open person in his interaction with others. Still, in all those years I would be privileged to know him in the future, from those first tentative weeks onward and up until the time of his death, it would prove to be an extremely rare occasion when he consented to share with me even the smallest detail relating to the subject of his own childhood. Most probably, too, because I had discovered little more than a mere pittance regarding my own father's past, which naturally included his childhood, I greatly welcomed the chance to view this amazing new friend of mine in terms of that more familiar perspective to which I could so easily relate.

Throughout my long life I have consistently discovered that those special people who are really worth knowing rarely reveal the many provocative details of their lives right away. It is only with a certain amount of trust that naturally comes with time and patience that one can ever hope to reap the benefits relevant to such things. For, much like the various layers of the many petals that comprise the vulnerable center of any lovely flower, those similarly sacred events and details of such a person's life will eventually be allowed to unfold to finally reveal the hidden treasures within.

At the moment my ever-acute senses were becoming fully alerted. Generally speaking my innately spiritual sonar missed very little of life's various stimuli and was presently standing at full attention—military style, so to speak, patiently awaiting these forthcoming impressions of a deeply personal nature. Something important was slowly beginning to unfold here.... I could just feel it. However, not wishing to ruin in the least little way that rare and wonderful spirit of trust which this small confidence was justly inspiring, I purposely chose to remain silent all the while sincerely hoping that Felix would continue on by elaborating upon this fascinating comment of his....

And so he did. As the headlights of our vehicle were eventually turned on, illuminating our pathway the entire distance home, in an unmistakably tentative fashion almost as if this most excellent of men were already acknowledging the fact that this brief voyage back into time might prove to be somewhat emotionally demanding in some particular way for him, Felix proceeded to confide to me, "Geza was my dog's name.... Being an only child, and, consequently, always being rather lonely, I had come to depend upon the daily companionship of this very loyal friend of mine!"

After yet another brief pause which perhaps was prompting him to attempt to gauge for himself what would be appropriate for him to share with me, at this point, at least, he soon continued on to say, "I grew to love that wonderful dog! From the time he was an eight-week-old puppy, in fact, he slept with me—and bathed with me in the marvelous lake located not far from the house...." With the slow surfacing of these fonder remembrances, Felix became inspired to thoughtfully add, "He became my shadow—my faithful shadow, quite literally, and followed me everywhere I went!"

Once again this exceptionally interesting man, after having lapsed into yet another few moments of silence—recalling, no doubt, highly significant happenings of long ago and perhaps even forgetting for a portion of this time that he was not alone after all, he finally bestowed upon me yet another coveted piece of that marvelously salient puzzle of his earlier life, as he went on to inform me, "Upon my father's immense summer estate which was located many miles from the city of Budapest—where he normally lived for the greater part of every year—there, just behind the stables, was constructed a series of buildings used to house his prized peregrine falcons; and, nearby, his considerable collection of geese and ducklings, as well as several noisy but resplendently colored peacocks which were cultivated merely for their beauty on a regular basis by our loyal grounds-keeper, Zapola....

"Often this same good man's wife, Gabriela—who was, likewise, part of my father's extensive staff, and who had been initially employed as head cook when my father, himself, was but a small boy, would expertly prepare the various types of domesticated fowl. These same succulent geese or ducklings were our chief source of food that were not obtained through the more traditional manner of hunting. Eventually such things, along with various other types of wild game, were proudly served to family members and guests alike during those few precious weeks in late summer when my father once again had returned to his estate.

"So it happened sometime during the late August of my ninth year—naturally after my beloved Geza had long grown from puppyhood into the magnificent animal he eventually came to be, that the productive hutches of these same treasures belonging to my father were being raided on a regular basis by a fox.... There was absolutely no question about this fact, for Zapola—even though he was already quite aged, by now, and undeniably impaired in his night vision, especially, almost always found the telltale tracks which the notably crafty animal would invariably leave behind during those highly successful pilfering escapades of his!

"Several days hence, sometime in the early morning hours while I lay fast asleep in my warm and comfortable bed, I was startled awake by the cruel sound of a gun being fired. Instinctively looking about for my dog, who had never once strayed from my side during any night, I found him missing... Hurriedly pulling on my clothing, I then quickly made my way towards the aviaries which were located quite some distance away. Having nearly arrived close to the place from whence the rude and unfriendly sound had emanated, through the rather dense ground fog I could just barely make out the vision of a lone figure, as it, in turn, was slowly making its way towards me....

Finally, from no more than a dozen paces away, I came to readily recognize that it was our excellent Zapola, and that, furthermore, he was carrying something large and rather cumbersome within his still powerful arms.... To my utter dismay, I soon discovered that he was openly weeping, as he tentatively approached me to stand merely an arms-length away, now helplessly cradling the limp and lifeless body of my dearest Geza...."

"Forgive me! Forgive me, my young master!" I barely remembered the old man pleading. It was a terrible blunder on my part, he confessed. But with the fog and with my faulty eyesight—and, naturally, with the great disturbance being made in the aviary as Geza himself was in the amazing process of challenging the fox on his own terms, I mistakenly took him for my target! Please forgive me!"

Having taken the pitiful story this far, Felix immediately fell into a deeply pensive silence. As for me, needless to say, I had already become emotionally overwhelmed at this point and did not know what on earth to say to him. This vivid recounting of that undeniably tragic event in my dear friend's early life had momentarily shaken me, just as it surely must have greatly distressed Felix when it originally happened. Presently I found that I could actually feel the pain from his loss of long ago as it proceeded to tug so relentlessly at my own heart.

"As it proved to be, Geza's death was my inescapable introduction to the great pain that comes with losing something—or someone, that I

loved...." To properly conclude this uniquely special dissertation of sharing with which he chose to so greatly honor me, Felix quietly confessed,
"I can't really explain to you, Adam, why these potent bittersweet memories of long ago have come flooding back into my consciousness, as they
just have... Most probably it must have something to do with our earlier
visit to our new little friend that was responsible for it all!"

During those several concentrated hours of work that it took to
build the dog house for our sweet needy little acquaintance, which
had been necessarily spread over three or four late evenings, Felix and
I never once missed going out to see the small dog—nor, of course, to
take him his food. Without further ado, either, the late autumn weather
finally turned rather bleak and bitter. Not only did the outside temperature drop significantly, but the steady wind bore with it traces of snow
flurries that would surely prove to be the trusty harbinger of that far
worse winter weather that lay ahead. Consequently, I imagined that
Felix was becoming just as worried as I was, with regard to the wee
dog's welfare. Hurrying to finish this comfy lodging, as we were, soon
became a race against time.

The very day that the project was completed, Felix, George and I
quickly drove it out to that lonely country road. We carefully placed it
under the protection of the great and wise oak tree. I remember how
we took extra-special care to thoroughly pad the entire interior of the
new kennel with what remained of a sumptuous old blanket. After the
animal was well-fed that day, the three of us climbed back into the truck
and made ready to head back to the much welcomed warmth of our
own home.

Initially the dog responded quite well to our enthusiastically coaxing
it into its special-built shelter. But, for some reason or another, a bit later
it chose not to remain there at all. As Felix put the truck into gear and
proceeded to cautiously drive out onto the road in our overdue effort to
out-race the coming storm, George and I glanced back through the small
rear window of the vehicle to check on our little ward and found him
standing there in the middle of the road. Looking pathetically confused
at the moment, as if he were struggling to decide something important
within his own mind, the small dog would take a step or two in our direction, only to hesitate, stop, and then look back towards the place where
he had been forced to wait so patiently all those many lonely weeks for
his owner to return to him....

Apparently from the side-view mirror Felix was intently watching all
this happen as well, for he promptly slowed down the forward progress
of the truck. Soon it was brought to a complete standstill, there in the

middle of the road, about a hundred feet or so from where the dog was still waiting and obviously still wrestling with some sort of major inner-dialogue of the heart.

What happened next was truly amazing, indeed. After a few seconds of deliberation only on Felix's part, Felix wisely opened his door and climbed out of our vehicle to stand near the truck. As he did this, the dog in turn responded to this action by striking an impressive pose of complete readiness.... I further declare that had the little runt been able to express himself in words, as people do, at that precise moment he might have openly lamented: Look, I'm getting awfully tired of living out here all by myself! If there's the slightest chance at all that you might need me just as much as I need you—won't you please give me some small sign!

We must surely have all been on the same wavelength. With the animal's telling body language, Felix merely whistled once—just once, and the pure honest quality of that unforgettable sound caused the wee dog to bound forward immediately. With such remarkable energy and enthusiasm and in no time at all, he landed inside the cab of our truck—upon George's lap, mostly, wagging his tail to beat the band and licking my dear friend's face all over as well as mine.

Heading home that evening with the newly-built unused dog house securely wedged in the rear section of the truck once more, and with a slight dusting of dry powered snow temporarily covering the windshield, at this point, all of our hearts were incredibly light and happy. Upon Felix's gentle command, however, our slightly rambunctious passenger finally quieted down for the ride and managed to make himself as comfortable as he possibly could under the crowded circumstances by laying across George's lap. Soon, however, I watched with growing affection as the little imp managed to slowly inch his way from where he was, across my lap, now, in an overt attempt to reach Felix.... Having eventually succeeded in this, he placed his small head upon Felix's lap and soon fell fast asleep.

I well recall that Emma Lauder's originally misguided philosophy concerning animals and their place in the world differed considerably from the rest of us. Upon our significantly late arrival home that day, with both the fortunate dog, as well as the well-constructed dog house in tow, she remained thoroughly implacable in her firm resolve that the dog remain outside.

Despite the predictable approach of the coming snow storm, in fact, she wasted no time at all in firmly laying down the law. Having rather brashly expressed her uncompromising logic sometime immediately after George and his father had so hopefully expressed otherwise, we were all finally forced to hear her say: "Have the dog live inside our home?! What utter nonsense! I simply won't hear of it, Felix! Everyone knows that animals are basically dirty creatures and should always live outdoors. That's just the way it is! And, furthermore, there's simply nothing more to discuss about the matter!" While she spoke these same disheartening words of hers, I remember that she remained standing guard at the rear of the house with both of her hands resting comfortably there upon her hips in that familiar yet quite formidable pose of readiness to back up her words should this prove to be necessary.

Obviously not having wished to push the point, which most certainly would have caused far too much unnecessary trouble in the long run, Felix and George—as well as all the rest of the Lauder children, and I, finally admitted defeat. Unhappily we went about placing the dog house in an out-of-the-way place within the confines of the barn instead. One of the younger children, having become totally delighted over the adoption of our new little friend, took to repeatedly climbing in and out of the sturdy kennel in a playfully helpful attempt to show the dog what was expected of him.

Over what amounted to our late supper that evening, while the foundling stubbornly remained curled into a neat compact little mound outside upon the top step of the several stairs leading up into the antiroom just off our kitchen—shivering all the while from the wicked cold, the family discussion inevitably came around to selecting a name for the gentle beast. After considerable thought was given to the matter by each of us, actually, it was George who finally said quite cheerfully, "Let's call him 'Here boy'! After all, this is just how Father and I have been referring to him all along."

So it was unanimously decided. And by more or less slurring the two words together, as we all eventually came to do rather naturally because they were used so often each day, our little dog's name finally evolved into the single word: "Hereboy."

By Thanksgiving of that same special year this newest addition to the Lauder household had somehow managed to worm his way into sleeping within the kitchen's far warmer anteroom, curled up quite comfortably there amongst the vast collection of shoes and boots. Then about two or three weeks later, during those wonderfully happy evenings just prior to that same marvelous first Christmas that we were all to share together as a family, somehow the little "con artist" managed to continue to work that same sort of magic of his.... Contrary to what she had originally deplored, Emma Lauder did not fight the idea of the dog sleeping within the warmth of the kitchen itself. There one could generally find him happily situated atop a small cushioned pallet that was thoughtfully arranged upon the polished floor, between the coziness of the wood-burning stove and the inner door leading to the alcove outside....

One quiet evening, maybe a day or so before young Lewis' homecoming, while each family member remained occupied with some sort of personal project in or about the parlor area, I was desperately trying to uphold any sense of personal dignity in what would become a fairly short game of chess instigated early on by my dear mentor, George. In time my attention wandered to the dog sitting in the doorway of the kitchen, very patiently and equally politely observing each and every movement that any of us were making. Smart little fellow that he was, he knew exactly where the boundaries lay for him, just as he instinctively sensed who it was that held his ultimate fate in her hands. Like an exceptionally gifted baseball player who was attempting to steal his way around all the bases, and to finally arrive home, so to speak, he always seemed to be able to properly gauge for himself exactly how far he dared to go with respect to running the risk of annoying the lady of the house; and, consequently, perhaps in the worse case scenario, ultimately suffering the disgrace of being thrown out of the game for good.

The inevitable "coup d'etat" occurred during that very evening, with Emma Lauder sitting in her chair diligently applying the finishing touches to a long woolen scarf that she was knitting for Lewis. Upon her lap lay a generous ball of bright cherry-red woolen yarn. As she momentarily shifted her position in the wing chair to make herself more comfortable, the cheerfully colored sphere of virgin wool promptly rolled off her lap and then bounced onto the floor to eventually roll towards the center of the room.

Meanwhile, with George keeping his long-awaited promise to me by patiently teaching me the various preliminary moves on the chess board, the two of us had recently embarked upon playing our very first game together. Having become momentarily distracted, however, by what just transpired there in the room, I quickly tapped my beloved instructor's forearm in an attempt to arrest his rather keen attention away from what we were doing and nodded in the direction where all this equally important action was currently taking place.

No sooner had my friend glanced up, when quick as a wink—even before Mrs. Lauder or anyone else could make their move to retrieve the object, we observed "Hereboy" leave the place where earlier he was firmly instructed to remain. He trotted ever so confidently over to retrieve the soft red ball. Following this more simple feat, he stunned everyone even more by automatically sprinting over to Emma Lauder with the wool sphere gripped firmly within his little mouth, just as if this were the most natural thing in the world to be doing. Then, sitting up upon his haunches, he properly charmed every last one of us as he finally presented the indispensable item to his new mistress with a precious turn of his sweet little head for further effect.

What a dog! From the very beginning of this charming and highly instructive display, Felix and the rest of us were silently involved in every aspect of its marvelous interaction between proud woman and headstrong little beast, but wisely chose to utter nary a sound with respect to what just occurred.... After all, true kindness—not to mention a goodly amount of pure and prudent common sense as well, strictly forbade any of us to make it an issue of "we told you so." Even after Mrs. Lauder slowly took the wool from "Hereboy," all the while wearing an absolutely unforgettable expression that most probably should have been captured on film for all time, she took a few long moments more to thoughtfully study this wee terrier that, more than likely, was really a "gilded retriever" in disguise. Having eventually returned to her knitting, every now and then she would pause from her work to look once more upon the dog that had decided on its own not to return to the doorway as before, but, rather, had decided to remain laying there at her feet.

After a respectable while, however—after carefully bidding his time, no doubt, I watched with considerable interest as "Hereboy" discreetly made his way over to where Felix was reading his newspaper, there in his favorite over-stuffed wing chair located next to our family library. Without the least bit of fanfare the little elfin further proceeded to promptly take his worthy place by his new master's feet, which in retrospect is exactly where he had carefully planned to end up all along. Soon the happy and well-contented fellow placed his sweet head upon one of Felix's soft well-worn leather slippers, just as was already his habit—and with a small sigh, he closed his eyes and fell sound asleep.

This, dear reader, is exactly how our wee foundling actually stole home. This, in effect, is the story of how the Lauder family and I acquired our very special mascot. Likewise the truth also bids me add, as well, that although "Hereboy" grew to love each of us—just as each of us grew to love him in return, by everyone's faithful account, he really remained Felix's devoted little shadow.... Yes, indeed. Without a doubt, and quite understandably, too, he remained Felix's wonderful dog—both body and soul.

16.

Within Aniela Jaffe's biography of Carl Gustav Jung, which is very aptly entitled: *Memories, Dreams, Reflections*, Jung is quoted as saying: "The life of man is a dubious experiment.... It is a tremendous phenomenon only in numerical terms. Individually, it is so fleeting, so insufficient, that it is literally a miracle that anything can exist and develop at all. Life has always seemed to me like a plant that lives on its rhizome. Its true life is invisible, hidden within that part of itself.... The part that appears above ground lasts only a summer. Then it withers away—an ephemeral apparition. When we think of the unending growth and decay of life and civilizations, we cannot escape the impression of absolute nullity. Yet I have never lost a sense of something that lives and endures underneath the eternal flux. What we see is the blossom, which passes. It is the rhizome which remains."

During these many years of my own already long life, whenever I consciously reflect upon the extreme pain that always comes with losing someone that I have loved, I am able to also rediscover the fascinating truth that no two people ever mourn in exactly the same way. I believe that the degree of one's personal agony, relative to one's loss, remains directly proportional to the degree of the deep regard that was established. And so with George Lauder's untimely death, in that early January of 1931, I initially came to believe that the bright warm sunshine which he became responsible for introducing into my desperately needy world would never again shine within my young life.

By mid-September of that previous year, immediately after Cecilia Von Szeplak and her family finally closed up their splendid summer residence to return posthaste to their other busy life in Chicago, she undoubtedly had not properly reckoned with George Lauder's sincere and ever-passionate regard for her. Apparently during this particular time in her life, she had already evolved into a fully self-absorbed young woman who had not as yet learned to fully appreciate the fact that genuine love and absolute fidelity remain that dual spiritual phenomenon that is, and has always been, quite rare. But this, of course, was exactly the sort of deep regard that my dear friend obviously felt for her. Because of this George was about to receive a sobering introduction into both the positive and negative aspects of personal intimate relationships, as well as the indisputably cruel reality that deceit and treachery are quite often part of the nature of others....

As it happened, the members of the Von Szeplak family were obliged to travel to Europe in October, planning all the while to return to our part of the world sometime soon after the New Year. Although George and Cecilia would not be seeing each other during all those many weeks which ensued, somehow my dear friend found a bit of required solace in faithfully burning the midnight oil long into many a night, in order to pen long detailed letters to her. These letters happily recounted the promises the young lovers made to each other that summer, especially with regard to their mutual plans for a long and meaningful future together. Usually on these same occasions several lines of wonderful poetry which my special friend became inspired to compose in her honor were read aloud to me, much as if I were George's trusted and ever-dependable sounding board. Emotionally speaking, although he strove heroically to remain on an even keel with respect to Cecilia's going away for such a long period of time, he naturally was plagued from the start with much acute loneliness.

As time slowly passed, and with Miss Von Szeplak's own rather sporadic and sketchy letters back to George, what he alone perceived as their once mutually strong relationship was now entering into some sort of negative phase. It obviously became this desperately helpless feeling—which all the physical distance between them obviously only helped to magnify, that seemed to push him to a point that bordered on near despair.... I could actually feel his growing restlessness—his misery of the soul which was intensifying.

Eventually this young woman's trite and passionless correspondence ceased coming altogether. Even with this thoroughly unkind behavior of hers towards George, his overwhelming confidence in the great power of love never wavered. Consequently he tended to rationalize the situation by taking the stance that the reason for this apparent emotional distance on her part was due to the fact that his "lady love" was constantly in transit, hopping from glamorous city to glamorous city, making it impossible for her letters to come to him in a timely fashion.

But, as I feel obliged to further confide to the reader, I was not fooled for a moment. Naturally because I loved George, as I did, and had wished more than anything else in the world to be able to protect him from the approach of any harm, I tended to embrace a far wider and far more honest perspective with regard to the present situation. Frustratingly enough, even though I was merely a child, I began to see quite clearly with that nearly infallible inner eye that is so often possessed by children. Indeed, against my most fervent wishes, I began to develop a highly disquieting premonition of impending doom long before George ever did.

Furthermore, I seriously contemplated that because George had not as yet been exposed to the emotionally devastating reality of rejection in any form, really—a rudimentary fact which remains incontestably part and parcel of life itself—it obviously was utterly inconceivable to him that this young woman could not love him as deeply, nor as well, as he loved her. Simply put, he never learned to play any sort of unkind games with the hearts and the minds of others. This highly unsavory practice remained totally foreign to his considerable intellect. Not only was my great friend completely honest and honorable in his every interaction with others, he so often also wore his heart vulnerably exposed there upon his open sleeve for all the world to see....

To my critical way of thinking, George just had not been given the necessary time to develop that thicker protective hide which loving and losing forever demand from those more gentle hearts among us. Looking back, as I sometimes still do, I sincerely believe that I could not have saved him from this life-defining experience—or rather, in his case, this life-ending experience, even though in my own childish way I once attempted to do that very thing.... Ultimately, with the combination of those various other circumstances which were to prevail, and which would ultimately become responsible for his inevitable passing, those of us who truly loved him so very much were eventually forced to bow low to Fate's wholly uncompromising decree.

Despite these ongoing day-to-day personal disappointments of George's, concerning Cecelia and their problematic relationship, there still remained those undeniably grand moments when the old George we all knew and loved would still occasionally delight us by making his welcomed appearance. There were still those special moments when he managed to rise to the occasion by playing the part of a clown as he forever loved to do. He made us all laugh, in spite of the unhappy personal situation in which he found himself immersed—like, for example, when he attempted to calm the unruly atmosphere there at our supper table on that particularly unforgettable evening only days before that special

Christmas of 1930, when Felix Lauder's well-intended "haircutting episode" eventually caused an upheaval within our ranks that bordered upon near anarchy....

Presently, as well, I find myself recalling a little saying of Felix's which both George and young Lewis were fond of quoting every now and then. George even once referred to it during these same more difficult weeks when he was left to deal with the heavy heart that was presented to him, care of Cecilia Von Szeplak. This bit of playful albeit slightly irreverent nonsense was highly indicative of the family's basic optimistic outlook on life. It also caused me to speculate upon the stimuli that might have prompted Felix's original attraction to the phrases. I finally came to suspect that the basic philosophy inherent within those underlying sentiments of the saying's rather dismal pronouncement was somehow invoked by the unavoidable dangers which once lurked in the mercurial-like business world for our beloved patriarch, especially there in Chicago with Al Capone and his highly unsavory group, as well as much earlier on during that terrifying time in Mexico through which he and his young family barely managed to live....

As I recall the little ditty, which I was told was a rough translation from Hungarian, went something like this: "A true optimist is a person who will enthusiastically assure you that it is a good day, indeed, if no one is shooting at you! Furthermore, even if someone is shooting at you, but fails to hit you—then, naturally, it remains a good day, too.... Likewise, and God forbid, even if you are shot, but are merely wounded, then it goes without saying that it certainly continues to remain a good day! And, whether on purpose—or whether quite accidentally, if someone should eventually shoot at you, and manage to hit you, causing you to die from your wounds in the end—well then, it hardly matters at all whether it's a good day or not!"

"Felix! Please promise me that you won't forget to keep the appointment that I made last week with Mr. Balducci to have the children's hair trimmed," Emma Lauder was hurriedly saying to Felix, as she took a moment more to glance into the hallway mirror downstairs to properly secure the long sharp hat pin that was tentatively being negotiated into the thick fabric of her dark green felt hat....

If my memory serves me well, Mrs. Lauder was in the process of making ready to be driven into the city by George. After all, she had had a doctor's appointment—something to do with "female trouble," as George matter-of-factly informed me. Judging from the way all the other children whispered this news around between themselves, being the wise and keenly sensitive child that I was, I instinctively felt that it might prove to be far more prudent for me to abstain from any further inquiries regarding the meaning of this strangely oxymoronic term. Just prior to her having made this simple request, Felix was involved in carefully counting out a handful of coins, as well as tallying up a few meager bills of limp paper money which beforehand were neatly rolled together and properly secured with a rubber band. Usually all of this booty was carefully stowed away within an unused cigar box, that, in turn, was always kept in one roomy drawer there within the wooden hutch located in our kitchen.

Also sitting there upon the kitchen table that day—opened once again to page "thirty-eight"—was the most recent copy of the Montgomery Ward catalog through which this good man had been browsing off and on for several weeks now. As it happened, Felix was in real need of new work boots.... Since he always seemed to feel somewhat guilty about purchasing anything at all for himself these days, with such a large and needy family to look after, he was still wrestling with the idea of which pair would prove to be the more economical choice in the long run....

Since the latter part of August, actually, I would inadvertently catch him slipping pieces of folded-over newspaper into the bottom front portion of his old worn-out footwear, in a worthy attempt to cover over those large deep holes which had formed within each leather sole. Although during the hot summer months this sort of temporary solution of his seemed perfectly acceptable, all of us understood that he could not possibly keep entertaining the use of this highly inventive method of prolonging the affair, since already the bitter-cold wet weather was officially upon us. This ongoing behavior of his was certainly apt to cause him to become quite ill, should his feet be allowed to remain vulnerable like that whenever he worked outside. Up to now, he was able to successfully postpone the inevitable. But it was already well into the month of December and it had become an inescapable probability, at this point, that those valuable funds which he so coveted would have to be doled out sooner or later in order to finally purchase these important items.

While Charlie, Robert, and I were finishing our appointed task of washing and drying the soup dishes from lunch, through the sparkling-clean kitchen window where there was an unimpeded view of one side of the house, as well as the courtyard area of the driveway, I observed Felix walk his wife and son to the family car. Remaining behind in the driveway, as was his custom whenever similar circumstances prevailed, he waited to cheerfully wave his good-byes to Emma Lauder and George, until the car finally disappeared down the driveway. Soon after that, my friend re-entered the house to sit for a few moments more at the seat he had vacated. I watched as he continued to study the thick and rather engaging book—the "wishing book," as it was generally referred to around the Lauder household, most probably realizing that time was running out and the moment for some sort of concrete action on his part, regarding the matter at hand, was imminent.

In order to properly calculate a bit more of the math necessary for this forthcoming long-overdue purchase of his, he proceeded to rummage around inside one of the deep kitchen drawers that held pads of writing paper and pencils and the like, when he apparently took notice of a pair of his wife's scissors idly laying there at the bottom of this same place.... Shortly after this occurred, I could not help noticing that for some odd reason he seemed to become greatly inspired....

The next thing I remember hearing was Felix confidently cranking up the phone box to ask Miss Edwina Dooley to direct his call to Angelo Balducci.... Following this, the short conversation went something like this: "Good afternoon, Mr. Balducci, this is Felix Lauder... Angelo—yes, of course. I'm very well, thank you! I sincerely hope that you and your family are the same.... Ah! That's wonderful! Yes ... Merry Christmas to you, as well! I'm sorry to be giving you such short notice, like this, naturally regarding the haircut appointments for our sons which my dear wife made with you days ago, but I find that I'm being forced to cancel everything for today. No ... No! Please allow me to assure you that there's nothing wrong.... Yes, indeed, we'll certainly be contacting you some time in the future, to re-schedule!"

Was I merely imagining it, or was there really an impressive glimmer of great personal satisfaction shining forth from the depths of Felix's wonderfully expressive eyes? What happened next was interesting enough.... While Charlie and Robert fortuitously escaped the area in order to attend to other matters, I foolishly remained behind watching Felix carefully laying out the scissors, a medium-size ceramic bowl, a single folded clean flat bed-sheet, and a large tortoise-shell comb—precisely in this order—upon the freshly scrubbed kitchen table with the precision of some master chef who was about to painstakingly create a soufflé for the very first time....

Now that these preliminaries were out of the way, with an unmistakable flourish my ever-confident friend picked up the sheet and flicked it open with a single movement of one hand. Next, standing there comfortably enveloped within what may only be described as a keen sense of anticipation, Felix quickly glanced around the room to find everyone gone but me. Smiling warmly at me now, he good-naturedly invited me to sit upon the high wooden stool nearby, after which he carefully tied the fresh-smelling cloth about my neck only to properly secure it in the back with a large safety-pin.... Right away, before I could even utter a word, the flawlessly smooth yet somewhat predictably cumbersome soup bowl was placed directly upon my head, as Felix wasted little time in taking up the pair of scissors. Then, in what amounted to little more than "two shakes of a lamb's tail," he began to trim around the bowl in his own particularly inventive method of giving a haircut....

Good Lord! I must honestly admit that many disturbing thoughts began to swirl around inside my brain, at the moment, as I remained dutifully sitting where I had been instructed to sit, now in a mood of mild shock, actually. For instance, although there had been absolutely no doubt in my mind whatsoever that my special mentor was an expert doghouse-builder, when it came to giving haircuts I was not at all certain just exactly how much practice he previously might have had with those scissors that he was presently wielding.

While Felix concentrated upon the back of my head, I managed to glance down every now and then to observe with growing interest the many semi-long strands of dark red hair which were now beginning to decorate the once immaculate kitchen floor. Nearby, taking everything in as well, sat our newly acquired mascot, "Hereboy." Every few seconds or so—every time a large section of my tresses fell soundlessly to the ground—the smart little guy would actually look at the hair and then promptly gaze up at Felix and me with a noticeably puzzled look that to my already worried mind spoke volumes.

As Angelo Balducci's "heir apparent" continued to cut away at my poor hair, he slowly eased his way around me much as if I were the stationary fixture of a Maypole and he one of the gay revelers traveling around me in a modest little circle.... Not wishing to distract him in the least from what seemed to me to be a most sensitive endeavor, requiring nothing less than a great amount of know-how and attentiveness, I patiently waited for him to finish before I finally initiated, "I know you're awfully good at building dog houses, Mr. Lauder—I just hadn't any idea that you were also an expert at cutting hair...."

Removing the slightly heavy bowl from my head, now, and promptly stepping back to critically gauge for himself just how well he was doing, my friend began to frown in a particular manner that immediately caused my heart to sink rapidly into my shoes. As he placed the scissors upon the table, continuing all the while to silently critique his work, he finally said with a slightly conciliatory edge to his voice, "Well, my young friend, it's really not all that bad—considering that it's my very first attempt at this sort of thing!"

While I stood before the tiny mirror located in the nearby hallway, quietly lamenting the depressing vision that was greeting me there, Fritz Lauder innocently wandered into the kitchen for something to drink. Soon I was hearing his father say quite cheerfully, "Fritz, my boy! Hop up here upon this little stool, and I'll trim your hair for you, just the way I've just trimmed Adam's!

Poor kid! Poor Charlie and Albert, too.... Most probably the secret to Felix's growing success rate where these awful haircuts were concerned seemed to be in his uncanny ability to pick us off, one by one, before the more than disconcerting news of what was actually happening managed to finally make itself known to the entire Lauder group. But the buck, as they say, stopped with Eddie, since apparently he was to be next in line for shearing—the next victim, essentially. Because he had not as yet seen any of his father's handiwork, and naturally before he would consent to undergo this same "stimulating" process himself, he actually had the presence of mind to demand to see those of us who were already placed upon the list of the "walking wounded."

Needless to say, the real fireworks began as soon as Emma Lauder and George returned home that day. Figuratively speaking, Felix soon found himself in the proverbial "doghouse."… I further imagined that, had "Hereboy's" excellently constructed little abode been a bit more accommodating relative to size, this former fact might well have become a reality.

I reckoned that it took about an hour or so for the initial shock concerning Felix's highly innovative haircuts to eventually dissipate a bit. Of course after the loud pandemonium of wailing and crying from nearly everyone concerned finally subsided, with a look of utter disbelief that caused her large fiery eyes to seem a great deal more prominent than usual, Emma Lauder plaintively accosted her highly subdued husband by demanding, "What on earth could have ever possessed you to do such a thing, Felix!? What about the usual appointment for the children that I made with Angelo Balducci?!"

Immediately following the traditional prayer that was offered at the supper table that evening, and undoubtedly because of the highly oppressive mood of complete unfriendliness which continued to permeate the air, due exclusively to Felix's highly unorthodox creativity, no one was speaking, and few of us were eating. In fact, poor Charlie was so miserable at this point that he literally had to be coaxed by George into coming to the table at all. When he finally arrived to take his customary place, he had taken to hide the overall damage underneath a baseball cap.

Had I been asked to objectively describe the overall effect that those unique haircuts inspired, as I silently looked around our table that night, I should honestly have to say that the three Lauder brothers and I greatly resembled several dedicated members of some curious monastic brotherhood which normally dwelled somewhere, naturally, off to themselves in some remote region of Europe—possibly in some cloister in northern Italy or Austria. All we seemed to be missing was the small medallion-size bald spot, usually placed smack in the center of the crown of one's head....

During this time I well remember that Emma Lauder was not smiling at all, even when she began to pass around the sumptuous containers of food to the various members of our unusually silent group. Before she actually took her own place there at the table, she lingered a moment more to thoughtfully study the four badly sheared "innocents," as she took to referring to her sons and me. Right after this, she could not seem to resist shooting us each a look of real understanding and deep compassion, only to briefly glance in Felix's direction to say with considerable authority, "I suppose that from now on I'll be obliged to take the scissors with me wherever I go!"

"Sure wish you'd thought of that earlier today, Mother!" Charlie piped in, as he, too, glanced over at his father, wearing an immense frown. Felix, however, remained slowly and silently occupied in finishing the meal's first course. Although he undoubtedly heard what was being said at the table mostly for his benefit, because he was obviously already feeling considerable contrition over the current situation, he had not bothered to look up at all at this point.... Shortly, pretty much as an after thought, Charlie went on to openly lament, "Mother, how in the world will we ever be able to return to school, looking like we do!?"

"With the holiday vacation being here at present, the four of you should be well on your way to looking the way you once did by the time classes begin anew in several days time."

These prudent and timely words of Mrs. Lauder seemed to have a calming effect upon all of us. Soon, however, after yet another long pause where one could only hear the more familiarly intimate sounds that come from eating, it was Fritz who finally commented, "You know, I bet this is how 'night school' was actually invented!"

"What do you mean, Fritz?" George finally asked, since no one else chose to respond to his kid brother's interesting comment.

"Well, the way I see it, night school probably came about because some poor kid's father decided to cut his son's hair—even when he didn't know how in the first place!" Thoughtfully having just finished chewing a small piece of bread which he had earlier placed in his mouth, Fritz went on to further enlighten our subdued group with his somewhat rational theory, as he continued on to say, "And, because the haircut turned out really, really awful, like ours—and, most of all, because it was too embarrassing to go outside during the day, night school was finally invented!"

Fritz's charming observation did manage to cause some of us to smile a bit—except for poor dear Felix, of course. What started out as a particularly noteworthy attempt on his part to save a little money, in order that he might finally be able to purchase the better pair of work-boots for himself, ended up with several members of his large tribe becoming bitterly unhappy with him. But, in spite of the fact that I was the first to be wronged in this relatively minor way, I still understood and appreciated why it had happened. Furthermore, and perhaps out of everyone else at the table that evening—except for George, naturally—I was the one who ended up feeling far more sorry for my dear friend than I really ever did for myself.

Moments later I watched as George rose from the table and rather unceremoniously went to help his mother remove the first course of dirty dishes. While Mrs. Lauder remained in the kitchen preparing for the main course of the evening, we all heard him politely excuse himself from returning to the table immediately after that. Naturally my thought was that he had gone to use the toilet. So after the lady of the house finally returned to take her rightful place at our table once more, we were rather awkwardly obliged to wait until his return before we could all resume dining together. After what seemed like an unusually long time had passed, George eventually did reappear—only this time cheerfully whistling a catchy little tune by Mozart and wearing, of all things, a long un-cropped black wig whose unruly bangs descended down low upon his forehead, nearly hiding his exceptionally playful eyes....

Very matter-of-factly, my comic friend promptly slid back into his customary place at the table, there to his father's immediate right. Choosing not to give even the slightest hint as to why he was behaving in this perfectly ridiculous manner, with a sense of great panache George quickly took up his napkin and placed it across his lap as before.... Then, while Albert remained patiently holding out the immense ceramic bowl which held that evening's creamed spinach, everyone continued to watch in silence as our family clown began to busy himself by spooning generous amounts of the vegetable onto his formerly empty plate.

Before anyone found the courage to speak, from somewhere within that amazing group of people there came a fairly hesitant twittering of nervous laughter. However, eventually speaking on behalf of our entire group, it was Felix who dutifully cleared his throat and addressed this much-loved son of theirs in a completely composed and rather forthright manner by firmly stating, "I can only suppose, George, that there's some good reason for this present behavior of yours...."

Openly studying his father with a thoroughly engaging manifestation of absolute kindness that was shining forth from within the depths of his wonderful eyes, at the moment George reminded me of a young and slightly uncouth Sir Lancelot. Being so consumed in his effort to save one particular lady in distress during all these past many months, it was as if our brave knight had not actually found any time at all to contemplate a badly needed haircut for himself.

Confidently returning his father's gaze, our irrepressible hero went on to cheerfully assure him, "As you see, Father, I've just stumbled upon the perfect answer to our current dilemma!" Quickly glancing around at the rest of us, who were at this same moment slowly becoming caught up in whatever he was playfully hatching there within his highly inventive mind, he went on to further explain as he seriously offered, "Don't you all see, hiding in that huge box in the attic are enough wigs for all of us! I've thoughtfully calculated that if each of us were to wear this same interesting look, as far as our hair is concerned, nobody would ever suspect that father has given several of you such dreadful haircuts.... In other words, wearing this marvelous theatrical prop would enable us to adequately hide this unavoidably scary fact—and, at the very same time, allow all of us to remind the entire world of the important reality that we are each part of this same terrific family!"

After a moment or two of complete silence where each one of us remained more or less toying with this unconventional rationale of his, it was Charlie again who finally piped in with an incredulously shocked sounding edge to his already unhappy demeanor, as he indicated in no uncertain terms, "What in the world makes you think that I'd ever want anyone to know that I belong to this crazy family of ours?! In fact, I'm actually planning to tell the entire town that I'm adopted!" His words were so passionate—so wholly intense, that I could not help covering the lower portion of my face with my linen napkin to quickly hide the smile that was helplessly spreading there. My fear was that Charlie might imagine that I was unappreciative of the currently serious situation.

As if to add her two-cents worth of commentary, Maria Christina quickly jumped into the fracas and promptly burst her brother's fine bubble by stating in a somewhat objective manner, "You know that your silly plan won't work, Charlie.... After all, you look far too much like Father—even with your new haircut, to ever think of fooling anyone like that!"

"Charlie, dear brother!" George was saying, merely half attempting to hide his infectious mood of playfulness that seemed somehow to go along with this new revolutionary disguise of his. "Don't be so thin-skinned—so self-centered, either.... You know that Father didn't cause your present misery on purpose! All he ever wanted to do was to save a few dollars so that he would be able to justify buying those work boots which he needs so badly.... Certainly you're able to appreciate this fact."

At this point, although Charlie still remained noticeably red-faced from the extreme frustration he had just expressed, nevertheless he also seemed to be at a momentary loss for the words necessary to properly effect a counterattack regarding his older brother's totally objective logic. Soon everyone remained sitting very quietly, perhaps attempting to place all that had happened into its more proper perspective. George, on the other hand, went on to further help us do this very thing by compassionately placing his hand upon Felix's forearm, as he gently said to him, "Father, don't be feeling so bad about all this! After all, you didn't remove the boys' heads, only their hair.... Soon enough, everything will be back to normal—whatever normal is suppose to be around here!" With these undeniably kind and wholly welcome words of his, my truly generous friend took a few seconds more to smile at each one of us, as if to intentionally underscore the importance of what he had just uttered. Finally, as a means to close the subject once and for all, he further quipped, as he began to laugh a little himself, "I further speculate that even if the boys had lost their wonderful heads, instead of just their wonderful hair—as they obviously have—being the consummate gardeners that both you and Mother tend to be, in no time at all they'd most probably be growing back their heads as well!"

This highly unconventional mental picture which he chose to introduce to our predictably receptive minds caused everyone at the table to either laugh out loud, or merely to smile a lot. Even Felix could not refrain from smiling. Finally removing that clever prop from his head and placing it upon his lap, my truly remarkable friend went about slowly gathering his father's slightly smaller hand within the protective confines of his own larger one... With a hearty sense of conviction so readily apparent within his voice and within his beautiful eyes, in a far more somber tone George finally promised, "One day, dearest Father, you'll own a dozen pair of the best boots that money can buy! One day you'll not have to do without these basic things, in order to see to it that all the rest of us have what we require.... This, I promise you!"

In time, and just as this noble son and his wise mother had formerly predicted, our hair did eventually grow back. Likewise and not terribly long after this sorry hair-cutting incident occurred, Emma Lauder wasted little time in making her perfunctory rounds throughout the interior of the entire house, as well as the entire barn area, too, in order to faithfully collect each and every pair of scissors that could be found. Most probably she became prudently inspired with the even more sound idea of later hiding them where only she would be able to find them from that time forward.

Meanwhile, Lewis Lauder arrived home for the holidays on schedule. With his much-anticipated visit, the Lauder family became whole once more....

Three days after that, however, a surprise telegram arrived for George from Cecilia Von Szeplak, who was currently vacationing in Paris. Harry Hopkins, in his usual thoughtful manner, took the time and the trouble to drive out to the farm to deliver it as soon as it came across the wire. It read, quite simply: ARRIVING CHICAGO, JANUARY 10. MUST SEE YOU! CECILIA.

For our beloved George these few meager words of unexpected hope acted as life-sustaining plasma for a decidedly injured man. Suddenly his greatly subdued manner of those past many weeks miraculously lifted. Although I detected nothing substantially positive in the message at all, my dear friend immediately interpreted it as some sort of significant revelation. Once again he began walking on air, all the while lost in the bright and shining promise of what he believed lay ahead for him.

That very evening; that same evening of the day this telegram arrived, Felix and Lewis managed to corral this high-flying soul of ours into the snugly enclosed porch area of the house. There, situated among the marvelous sleeping oleander trees, their mutual plan was to speak to George about similar worries they must have also had regarding his unrealistic expectations of Cecilia. Father and brother obviously conspired together in an attempt to add some necessary ballast to George's runaway balloon. That timely meeting, in fact, began shortly after supper and lasted for many hours long into the night.

Although no one else in the family was invited to take part in what inevitably became a fairly heated discussion from time to time, when I snuck downstairs on one occasion to more or less retrieve a glass of milk sometime in the earliest morning hours, I observed Lewis restlessly pacing back and forth in front of George and their father—much like a wild caged animal might behave…. While this eldest brother continued to do this, George, in an obvious attempt to defend himself, verbally speaking, from something which must have been said earlier on for his benefit, presently began to rally on his own behalf. Soon I heard him say with an unmistakable touch of desperation resounding in his voice, "But I tell you both that it doesn't matter that we're no longer rich…. My Cecilia really isn't interested in such things! What you're not comprehending, Lew, is the fact she really needs me…. In spite of all her impressive worldly trappings, she's an incredibly needy person! Trust me, when I tell you this…. Naturally because I love her, as I do, I plan to make a great deal of difference in the overall quality of her life—for the better, of course, which goes without saying!"

Finally opting to stand still, at least for the moment, young Lewis turned to face his brother. In a noticeably tired and petulant mood, he was responding in kind to what George had so naively initiated by attempting to make an important point of his own, "Look, George … you're apparently so hopelessly besotted by this young woman that you're failing to see the light! Besides, how can you possibly think of saving someone when that person's probably not even aware that they need saving in the first place!"

Apparently to take a moment to collect his thoughts and to better check his emotions, Lewis went on to more calmly add, "Please don't be fooled by the undeniably captivating exterior of the gift, George…. Damn it all! Try and get a grip on your emotions, and take some critically valuable time to objectively look inside the box! And when you do, I'm quite certain that you'll find it sadly lacking in all the crucially important ways! What I'm trying so lovingly to tell you is…. What it all boils down to, essentially, is the unmistakable fact that you're the one who's much too good for Cecilia! Even with the rather sobering issue of our lack of wealth, and social standing, too, for that matter—even if the two of you were totally equal on these two major counts, even then Cecilia Von Szeplak would never be able to measure up to all that you are!"

Yes! Yes! A million times—yes, I was thinking. These well-expressed sentiments of George's older and much-respected brother were likewise coming from a loyal and truly caring heart. Indeed, Lewis' cogent thinking on this undeniably important subject was precisely my own. During that same late night, while I continued to sit undetected upon one top step of the stairway that led down into the living room and then subsequently out onto the porch area where these three people were gathered, I had been absentmindedly nursing my ice-cold glass of milk. However, as soon as I heard those valid sentiments that were being expressed so well by Lewis, I wanted to stand up and shout: Yes! I couldn't have expressed it any better.... Hurrah! Hurrah, at last, for this bright and beautiful truth!

Actually hearing these triumphantly true statements being voiced out loud, like this, brought some measure of comfort to my own already profoundly worried mind. These two fine people who naturally loved George a great deal, too, were obviously also suffering from acute reservations regarding the worthiness of that Von Szeplak woman and her strong emotional hold over George. Returning to my bed that night, I recall hoping against hope that they might eventually make George see the light....

When the Lauder family originally moved to the Lake Geneva area from Chicago the previous year, they were obliged to leave behind several valuable yet cumbersome household items with the new owners there on Wilson Street. Naturally this was done with the express understanding that these same objects would be collected when time and circumstances permitted.

The short inventory included, for the most part: a fine carpet, two lamps, two small night stands, as well as a large ornate heirloom mantel clock which was purchased long ago during one of the Lauder family's formerly prosperous lives. Exactly a day after Cecilia arrived home from Europe, she telephoned George. Right away she invited him to her family's home in the city for what George now ecstatically imagined was to be their happy reunion. Around this time, too, George's mother immediately reckoned that it might be a perfect opportunity to recall some of those household treasures of theirs.

Since gasoline was rather costly to the average family during those economically difficult years, in order to better justify his necessary two-hour trip into Chicago, as well as the two hours back, George promised his parents that he would stop by their former residence and retrieve at least a portion of those items that would fit comfortably into the car. Mrs. Lauder had already prepared herself for the inevitable fact that this particular trip of his would undoubtedly prove to be the first of at least one or two other such unavoidable junkets.

Is it not remarkable how one may remember the smallest details relating to one's countless day-to-day experiences, as if that corpulent organ of the human heart were nothing less than a dependable camera's highly discerning eye? During those exceptionally cold and clear midmorning hours of that very next day, sometime just prior to George's departure for Chicago, I recall so well how he was personally preparing for this long-awaited reunion with Cecilia Von Szeplak. Since he wished to present himself to her and to her family in the best possible form, I recall what extreme care he took in his personal grooming. In any case, when the time came to retrieve his only suit from the downstairs closet for pressing; the same well-cut suit which he had not worn in at least a couple of years, he found to his overwhelming consternation that it was far too small to wear at all.

Hurriedly trying the clothing on for his parent's general approval, as well as for the rest of us who eventually all gathered together in the small kitchen that morning, my friend was forced to objectively admit that he resembled a poor country bumpkin. Those darn sleeves of the suit's jacket rose three inches above the place where they should have been, and the dark brown woolen slacks that were a perfect match to the jacket might nearly have passed for uncommonly long knickers instead.... Quite clearly not only had my dear friend grown inches taller, but obviously he had filled out in the shoulder and chest area during this time as well. Deeply pondering this inescapable fact as a family group, we unanimously decided that there simply was no way at all that he could get away with wearing the outfit.

Since it has always remained my fervent contention that mere clothing never makes the man, nevertheless, rest assured that no one understood better than I just how unpleasantly inadequate such situations could make one feel. Lovingly studying my dear highly-motivated young friend, as I was, I could see that George was being forced to unhappily concede that in lieu of the present situation he would be forced to wear merely a warm bulky sweater, along with his only other good pair of woolen slacks. He must have further rationalized that since the interior of the family car would remain somewhat more dependably warm, and that he did not expect to be staying out in the frosty winter weather very much at all, this decision seemed to be the only other solution available to him.

Just as all of us had come to finally accept this less than perfect solution, Lewis happened into the kitchen to say good morning, and to claim for himself a much-required cup of hot coffee.... This strong breakfast brew was undoubtedly expected to help him shake off his present physical and mental fuzziness which obviously still lingered from the considerable lack of sleep he was experiencing due to his all-night powwow with George and their father. Eventually glancing around to observe the pensive and far less than happy countenances upon most of our faces, he felt obliged to inquire, "Is there something important going on here that I'm missing?!"

Rather wistfully it was Emma Lauder who answered her son's question, perhaps more to herself at this point than to Lewis, as she said, "How I've often wished that clothing were made to grow with a person.... Just think of all the money, and all the time and trouble, people would be able to save if only such a thing were possible!" Then, quickly freeing herself from this brief tangential mental wandering of hers, she eventually answered her first born by matter-of-factly stating, "As you see, Lew, our George has finally out grown his only suit!"

Placing the rich-smelling beverage that he had just briefly tasted upon the cluttered sideboard of the sink area, Lewis promptly went over to his brother to more closely examine the situation for himself. Soon he was saying, "Sure isn't a very good time to discover such disappointing news, is it?!" After a mere moment's contemplation, however, after which he playfully hugged George in that more familiar "headlock" maneuver that remains synonymous with professional wrestling, Lewis was spontaneously offering in his personal effort to help out, "Well, little brother, I think I might be able to offer you a simple solution to your problem here.... Perhaps in the end you'll graciously accept this gesture as my own special 'peace offering' to you, since I wish to try and make amends for the very rough time I gave you last night regarding your new girl...."

Having promptly excused himself, at this point, our entire group could hear this born diplomat quickly making his way up the stairs, two at a time as always seemed to be his habit. In no time at all we also heard him as he came bouncing back down again, carrying a smart-looking worsted-wool sports jacket with contrasting slacks of the same marvelous fabric which were now both being casually displayed over one of his arms. "Since we're both about the same size, try these on," he was enthusiastically urging George, as he opened the flawlessly constructed dark navy-blue blazer to further help his younger brother glide into it.

George's face lit up, like magic. Standing tall and proud, now, with the unanimous approval of our entire group, he happily walked around the small room to expertly model this excellent new find. Slipping into the slacks, as well, he soon looked like a million dollars—needless to say.

In the end, to better see for himself how he truly appeared, George cheerfully strutted out into the hallway to critically study his reflection in the short mirror. "Picked those things up in L.A. last month when I was out there visiting one of our air bases," Lewis was calling out to him. "Sure looks like they were made for you!" With George re-emerging into the kitchen to thank his brother with an immense bear-hug, Lewis was finally saying to him, "Consider it a small gift from the heart, George—something special to bring you much-deserved luck in the future!"

As my best friend prepared to depart for Chicago a little later on that morning, the more tentative January sun was mischievously playing upon that season's most recent patches of frozen slush which were gathered here and there all about the surrounding yard. The bitter arctic wind, too, was blowing noticeably hard all around the exterior of our comfy little home. The temperature reading on the outside thermometer, I noticed, read well below zero... Br-r-r-r-r!

Having previously cleared the windshield of the family car by repetitively brushing off several pesky wet leaves and dry frozen twigs, George presently remained more comfortably seated behind the wheel, trying hard to coax the car's stubborn engine into doing what it was supposed to do. With the remaining family members and me now huddled together within the far warmer anteroom off the kitchen, each of us struggled independently to be able to successfully peer out at our beloved traveler through the slightly fogged-up glass of the porch's several long casement windows....

How we all cheered when my friend was finally able to inspire the old car into service that morning. Enthusiastically waving our collective good-byes, we observed him further put the vehicle into gear as nearly within the same motion he leaned out his window to jauntily wave good-bye to all of us in return. Within seconds George proceeded down our long driveway and finally disappeared from view.

That night I remember lying in bed, restlessly listening to the sound of the wall clock downstairs as it softly struck midnight. Across the way Eddie was fast asleep in his own bed.... Although there had been no word from George the entire day, I promised myself that I was going to stand vigil and to wait for his inevitable return, no matter how long it took. Sometime after that, however, I eventually must have deserted my post. The next thing I recall is being awakened by the sound of muffled voices coming from downstairs—or, at least, so I believed.... Specifically it was the sound of Emma and Felix Lauder loudly whispering something to someone whose own voice in return vaguely resembled George's....

Quickly rousing myself from my warm bed I tiptoed to the top of the stairs. My initial thought was to make my descent into the hallway below to investigate the curious disturbance.... Soon, however, I unexpectedly discovered that the muted rumpus was really coming from the upstairs bathroom located across the way.

As I stood there tentatively holding the doorknob and preparing to boldly knock upon the closed door in order to obtain permission to enter, I distinctly heard Mrs. Lauder say with an emotional sounding edge to her voice, "Why in heaven's name didn't you listen to your father and me, George?! Why are you so hardheaded, sometimes?! There was absolutely no need for you to try and bring all those household objects home in one trip ... no need, at all! And as far as your having consumed so much alcohol is concerned—as you've obviously done, I suppose there's no need for me to even venture forth on that sorry subject, being as unhappy with you as I presently am!"

Trying to muster the courage to knock softly upon the door, I soon became more than surprised when the door was finally opened upon me, even without my having knocked at all. Suddenly I was being confronted by Mrs. Lauder who seemed slightly annoyed to see me. "Is George all right?" I recall shyly mumbling to her.... After all, my dear friend had been on my mind the entire day long, as well as a good deal of the night, and I sincerely hoped that his inevitable reunion with Cecilia Von Szeplak had gone well for him....

"Go back to bed, Adam!" the lady of the house impatiently snapped at me. Judging from her obviously uncompromising demeanor, at the moment, I instinctively sensed that it might prove unwise for me to go against her wishes. Indeed, before I could even begin to offer anything in my defense, she quickly added, "You'll eventually be able to speak with George later on in the morning." Then as an afterthought, while she turned to look back at Felix to finally offer something more to him, she said in a loud whisper, "I'll go downstairs and make up the hot-water bottle—and some hot tea, as well.... Do bring him downstairs after you and Lewis manage to get him warmed up, won't you, Felix?! We'll put him in our bed for the duration of the night, naturally to monitor his chills and fever."

Having firmly issued this edict of hers like some gravely concerned "sergeant at arms," but just before she actually brushed passed me to quickly close the bathroom door behind her, there just beyond her right shoulder I chanced to spy Felix and Lewis somberly sitting around the deeply contoured antique-style bathtub.... Both of them were wearing similar expressions of an unmistakably serious nature that were clearly indicating extreme worry on their parts. Apparently they were holding consul with George who was presently sitting there in a fairly listless state nearly completely submerged within the hot steamy water from his bath....

After Mrs. Lauder disappeared downstairs to attend to George's future needs, I reluctantly returned to my bed as I was ordered to do. However, while doing this very thing I also firmly resolved to make the only possible concession that remained available to me and that was by keeping my bedroom door ajar in case anyone should wish to summon me. As I stubbornly remained sitting Indian-style there upon the tangled mound of unmade bed sheets and blankets, by the dim light being thrown my way from the hall lamp nearby I noticed "Hereboy" as he briefly appeared at the bathroom door.... And since no one bothered to admit the poor little guy, either, even after he whimpered softly once or twice, he finally caught sight of me and quickly trotted over to comfort me by silently taking his place upon the floor right next to my bed.

Sitting where I was ordered to remain and in a state of growing frustration, I could just barely make out the strangely muffled speaking sounds that were obviously coming from those same three people who continued to remain sequestered just beyond the wooden barrier in front of me. Naturally becoming terribly restless, at this point, and greatly worrying about George, I defiantly tip-toed back to the bathroom door to attempt to listen to what was being said. With my hand tentatively resting upon the cold glass doorknob and with one ear pressed against the cool smooth wood of the door, I distinctly heard the sound of George weeping....

No doubt because of this, he soon began to cough rather violently, too. With Felix and Lewis obviously trying to soothe and comfort him, after all this subsided I eventually heard George say in a choking voice filled with deep pain and regret, "You were both right, after all! Cecilia never loved me.... She planned from the very beginning to marry someone else!" And, with these weighty words, I heard the sound of his heartbreaking sobbing begin all over again. Soon enough, though, after the prolonged crying and coughing ceased once more, George went on to tell his father and brother, "After things went so badly yesterday, naturally I decided to bring everything home in one trip—against Mother's wishes, of course, since I don't plan to ever return to Chicago again!"

Suddenly I was forming a mental picture of the family sedan packed to the hilt with the items Emma Lauder had wished returned to the family—those same bulky and cumbersome objects which I later discovered had indeed taken up so much room in the front and back seats, as well as the trunk area of the car.... So much so was the reality that George was forced to travel all the way home in the subzero weather with all the windows of the car rolled fully opened, in order to be able to adequately accommodate the load. Because of this unnecessary foolishness on his part, he obviously become ill in the physical sense, not to mention emotionally sick from his once beautiful dreams which Cecilia Von Szeplak managed to break into a thousand pieces, and then heartlessly throw back into his face... Being forced to so unfairly remain where I was, far too far away from my grievously wounded friend at the moment, then and there I made a sincere vow that I should hate Cecilia Von Szeplak forever.

In between several more bouts of ungovernable coughing, I listened, totally wretched of heart, as George continued to openly confide to his father and older brother, "Do you know what Cecilia actually said to me? After allowing me no more than ten or fifteen minutes of her precious time, where she insisted that I remain standing outside the front door rather than being invited into the warmth of her home, she matter-of-factly delivered the words that I most dreaded.... In that frequently detached and totally carefree manner of hers, she actually told me that only a fool would ever take a simple summer romance so seriously! And then she went on to finally assure me that such uncomplicated friendships as ours really tended to be quite normal—even preferable, when one came right down to it, compared to any long-term 'entanglements'! Basically what I alone was perceiving as our incredibly special weeks together were being ruthlessly reduced to nothing more than an opportune moment for her to have a little harmless fun!"

During those next several days that were to follow, George and I would be severely cheated of any chance to speak with each other again, just as Mrs. Lauder previously promised. Nor would cruel Fate acquiesce in the slightest manner by compassionately allowing me, at the very least, to look upon my friend one last time before he died. Soon after those first dreadful hours which immediately followed George's hot bath, where he was dutifully placed within his parents' large four-poster bed downstairs so that he might be more closely monitored by them, his already dangerously high fever rose still higher, causing him to be propelled into an irrevocable state of delirium which rendered him totally incoherent from that time forward....

Hour upon dreadful hour the Lauder family, "Doc" Owens, and I, kept our ever-faithful vigil, but there was no improvement at all. George merely lay there, either quietly moaning to himself, or loudly calling forth in wild senseless phrases, never again to regain total consciousness. Death, I heartbreakingly speculated, had already been stalking my dear friend long before he actually arrived home from the city on that first early morning.

With the arrival of the meek and more tentative light of that first early dawn, when George's parents originally began to suspect the seriousness of the entire weighty situation with regard to their beloved son, I well recall Felix's desperate-sounding voice as he telephoned "Doc" Owens, literally begging for his help. And without fail it would be this same good man along with George's gravely concerned parents who would continue to sit by his bedside, all the while taking turns in keeping their continuous round-the-clock vigil. Even though I made it my business to slowly wander past that master bedroom no less than a thousand times each day, hoping that someone might eventually leave the door even slightly ajar so that the other children and I might learn what was happening, this small favor was not granted to us.

During those following next four days, although I remained physically present within the crowded little classroom there at our school which the younger Lauder children and I were still obliged to attend even against our most fervent wishes, I may just as well have stayed at home, for this was where both my mind and my heart always remained. Being a child and having had relatively little to do with death up to that point, I erroneously imagined that such a thing claimed only the old and the infirm. However, as one eventually learns, this is not the case at all. My father, as I sensed from the beginning, had reached a point of no return in his much-squandered lifetime where he actually longed for death; while our dearest George, who was filled with such life, and promise, and so much love to give the world, was surely destined to live to become a very, very old man....

Most regrettably, though, neither Time nor Fate chose to embrace this same belief of mine. Because of the maddening fact that antibiotics had not as yet become a reality, my dear friend quickly succumbed to the pneumonia which he was battling so ferociously. Greedy Death could not be dissuaded to relinquish its hold upon George, and it ultimately became the victor, thereby heartlessly robbing the Lauder family and me of the physical presence of this vital life-force.

Many years after George's passing, I had had an opportunity to travel to London on business. Somehow I managed to steal a tiny bit of much-needed personal time for myself, which I promptly decided to put to good use by visiting the Tate Gallery. There, quite unexpectedly, on that cold and rainy afternoon, I came upon the remarkable painting by Sir Luke Fildes entitled: *THE DOCTOR*.... With that amazing artist's totally sensitive rendering of his own uniquely intimate portrayal of a learned physician solicitously caring for a gravely sick child amid the obvious background of extreme poverty, as that child's loving mother and father looked on with their mutual anguish so clearly etched upon their haggard faces, against my will I was violently transported back to those same days when Felix and Emma Lauder, "Doc" Owens, and all the rest of us waited in vain for George to rise victorious from what would ultimately become his deathbed....

Oddly enough, even the sobering jolt of George's inevitable funeral could not seem to bring forth the true reality of his leave-taking. My tender psyche, or so it seemed, became literally obsessed in fighting the truth of it all. During those horrible nights, especially, I endlessly tossed and turned within my bed beneath the very place that my great friend once occupied.

Each and every day, too, like some lost soul in purgatory who was condemned to aimlessly wander about the acreage of the Lauder farm, I naturally found myself expecting to soon happen upon this ever-cheerful individual. It was as if my poor mind kept assuring me that George was only playing another childish prank of his by cleverly yet cruelly hiding himself from his family and me. In the beginning, with this same ongoing dilemma of mine, where I could not or would not emotionally come to terms with what had recently occurred, as time predictably began to pass away, my battered psyche also began to feel my resolve-to-ignore-the-truth slowly begin to erode and then to finally pass away....

Those thick fortress walls of dedicated resolve, which I instinctively erected for my protection, began to slowly crumble until they eventually came tumbling down altogether. By choice, in a fervent attempt to better gain my equilibrium and to better make some sense out of what was happening to me, I spent a great deal of time down by the lake. Needless to say, this familiar place became my ultimate refuge. Eventually, little by little, the pain of the unavoidable truth of it all did finally descend upon me in full measure. No longer was I able to remain in denial....

I learned that no one can ever outrun this sort of pain, nor, for that matter, can one hide anywhere from it either. From this poignant life-lesson I would also come to learn, as well, that the human spirit remains a gloriously resilient entity and that no one's badly bruised heart is ever condemned to wander in the wilderness forever. With the blessing of time, quite mercifully, and certainly just as every wise sage already knows, the process of the heart's healing slowly but surely begins....

Several weeks after George's death, I was presented with the most astounding gift imaginable. In fact to relive the moment, as I have so often done throughout all these many years of my substantially long life, is to re-connect with that marvelous treasure again and again.

Much as Felix was later destined to share with me on that particularly significant day, four years after George's death; indeed, on that same memorable day when he and I sat huddled together upon the roof of the farmhouse, I was to learn firsthand that love really is stronger than death. Exactly as Felix would come to propose, I also came to understand that genuine love has the ability to transcend death by reaching through that heavy curtain of space and time, to lovingly soothe and calm the spirit in pain.

Several weeks after my dear friend's departure, George finally came to say good-bye to me in a dream. Although initially the dream's overwhelming intensity greatly disturbed me, at the very same time this much-coveted experience also brought with it a profound feeling of such immense joy and peace....

In my exquisite dream George and I were once again happily fishing down by our lake.... Suddenly all around us there appeared upon the emerald-green waters, and in all the surrounding branches of the many trees, and likewise within the dark blue sky above us, too, a vast multitude of tiny bright lights....

To properly describe this marvelously unfathomable phenomenon, I should be inspired to say that that infinite number of buoyantly dancing nebulae resembled miniaturized suns—exact replicas, in fact, of our own immense life-sustaining daystar. And more than usual that day, it seemed to me that my dear friend remained particularly solicitous of how I was feeling, as well as being somewhat casually mindful that he remained under some sort of important time constraint.

As was George's habit whenever he and I eventually left our special spot by the lake to return home, he always held out his strong hand for me to grasp so that I could make it up the steep embankment, just exactly as he also did in this particular dream.... Once again, as he jauntily hoisted me up upon the grassy knoll, I felt compelled to ask him, "George, shall you and I remain friends for life?"

Soon, as a most enthralling answer from him, and with a gentle and truly loving look that nearly took my breath away, I found that his radiantly shining eyes were actually rivaling the bright lights that were floating all around us at the moment. And within their depths I could readily see that it was as if there was an immense secret which George longed to share with me, but could not.... Finally, after having securely clasped the small hand which was being so fearlessly entrusted to him, my dearest friend in all the world swore me an exquisite oath as he firmly but ever so gently stated, "Not only shall we remain the most excellent of friends throughout this lifetime, my dearest Adam ... please believe with all your heart, and with all your mind, and with all your soul, that you and I shall also continue to always remain the very best of friends throughout our many lifetimes to come!"

17.

WITH OUR GEORGE'S RECENT PHYSICAL PASSING, with his formerly youthful and robust body now having been finally laid to rest there within the frozen and unyielding earth, it would come to pass that his father's ultimate salvation would eventually be brought about through the compassionate benevolence of music. Speaking more specifically, any sense of relief from Felix's personal agony was eventually brought about by the hauntingly sad refrain that is continuously woven throughout Rachmaninov's *"Trio Elegiaque."*... After all, Life makes a habit of endlessly challenging us in so many different ways. What living never quite prepares one for, however, is the death of one's children. Somehow a grave intrinsic injustice is being perpetrated, whenever one is forced to outlive one's offspring....

During those dark and indescribably depressing weeks Felix suffered doubly with the sorrow that was currently present within all our lives. Because of this high level of emotional trauma, his own physical health began to slowly deteriorate, causing him to fight on two fronts—both at the same time.

Before my friend actually managed to gain the upper hand in this ongoing daily offensive, he was unable to take his prescribed nourishment at regular intervals. From the beginning of that substantially personal war of his, it was clear that he simply had no appetite. This, of course, caused his insulin level to go haywire, rendering him far too ill for several weeks on end to even rise from his bed at all. So, naturally, in order to rally in favor of our fallen general, while our own ever-faithful "Doc" Owens looked in on his patient each and every day without fail, it was Emma Lauder, the other children, and I, who initially doubled up on the numerous chores around the farm.

When our dear patriarch's health situation improved, even in the most moderate sense, it proved to be his beloved music which slowly began to help repair the grave physical and spiritual malaise from which he was truly suffering. How well I recall that hauntingly bittersweet melody which wove itself throughout this same somber piece, and end-lessly ministered to Felix hour upon hour as he offered himself up to its healing power.

Invariably our family phonograph, which was normally located in one corner of the parlor, played on and on throughout most of every day, as well as a good portion of each early evening—nonstop for sev-eral weeks. So much so, in fact, that this particular work by that same renowned composer involuntarily became part and parcel of my own existence, in spite of myself.

Quite often without my realizing it, I would helplessly slide into humming some aspect of the music's refrain whenever I was out and about attempting to complete my daily farm chores... Then, whenever I could find a bit of that more rare and quiet time for myself, I would subsequently make my way down towards the lake to at least partially escape my own tremendous unhappiness. Uninvited, of course, there that familiar music would inevitably be, faithfully trailing along after me only to begin playing over and over again within my own mind....

Speaking rather candidly, although to my thinking the powerful music had the tendency to depress one even more than usual due to the fact that its overall feeling of grave pathos was undeniable, for some rea-son Felix seemed incurably drawn to it, and obviously derived a certain sense of spiritual comfort from it. And certainly as it would eventually come to pass, several years hence, I would be learning the exact reason for this particularly fascinating happenstance....

During the year of 1877—the very year, in fact, of Felix Lauder's birth, the notable German author Hermann Hesse, as well as the mar-velous Hungarian pianist and composer Ernst Von Dohnanyi, were also both born there in the heart of Europe. Around this same time, too, Queen Victoria was proclaimed Empress of India, and that very same year, as well, Ibsen finished writing his special work entitled: *"The Pillars of Society."* Furthermore, while Brahms concentrated on presenting the ever-hungry music world with his now familiar masterpiece: *Symphony No. 2, Op. 75,* our very own Thomas Edison went about changing the entire world landscape in his own indubitable manner, right back here in America, by proudly inventing the phonograph.

As another point of interest, just prior to Rachmaninov's own thir-teenth birthday in March 1886, the initial performance of one of his first pieces of original music was a piano duet transcription of Tchaikovsky's *Manfred Symphony,* which he attended in Moscow, and where he was a student at the Conservatory there. In January 1892, this gifted young virtuoso composed his first *"Trio Elegiaque,"* which was a short one-movement work for violin, cello, and piano that already gave listeners hints into the young man's impressive personality.

Following Tchaikovsky's death a year later, the young composer proceeded to plunge into the strict discipline necessary to create the second *"Elegiac Trio,"* which was dedicated to the memory of his patron and friend, and whose opening bars are laden with such undisguised sadness and grief. The third movement of the piece, although short in duration, repeats the sublime message of the first movement and further succeeds in helping to distinguish Rachmaninov's lifelong intensity and passion.... Several years later, around 1907, after the composer revised the entire work with a far more seasoned and mature hand, the music would undergo yet one last "polishing" in 1917, before the master would decide that it was finally finished.

After I became a young adult, I recall that Felix Lauder once confessed to me that Mahler's music was also especially appealing to him, since those mysterious light and dark places within the complex terrain of the composer's soul seemed to very similarly match his own in so many ways. On the other hand, and quite understandably, as a very young child myself I had gained absolutely no knowledge of music in any form. This fact seems most regrettable, too, since music can be such nourishing food for one's spirit.

What brief unsolicited encounters with music that had visited themselves upon me included those formal church hymns from my highly oppressive years with Reverend Pouley, not to mention the occasional "honky-tonk" melodies that I barely noticed in passing while I traveled from foster family to foster family. I can honestly say that these things made not the slightest impression upon me whatsoever. In a manner of speaking, I remained a blank canvas waiting for someone's ever-patient instruction to help me begin exploring, and thereby more greatly defining, the richness inherent within my own interior.... By learning to appreciate fine music, which remains nothing less than the spiritual fingerprints of the ever-sensitive and ever-imaginative soul of another, I inevitably learned to thoroughly appreciate one of life's greatest joys.

My first introduction to serious music of any kind was the specific sort which appealed solely to my dear friend. And what ended up being a clandestine meeting of ours actually came about before Felix Lauder and I ever officially met.... During that first springtime right after the Lauder family moved into their place next door, and, too, while I more or less remained emotionally chronicling every movement that was being made by each member of their clan on a fairly regular basis, inexplicably I observed one of the older boys under Felix's careful direction awkwardly carrying the cumbersome phonograph out the back door of their house, across the wide span of courtyard, and then mysteriously off towards one side of the barn area....

Needless to say, over time this fairly benign little routine of theirs became somewhat of a predictable ritual. Finally allowing my curiosity to get the best of me, one relatively late evening immediately after that most recent transporting incident of the large phonograph occurred and with the rest of the Lauder household busy within the house itself, once again I could hear the distinct sound of some sort of enchanting music emanating from some undetermined spot across the way.... Having mustered the necessary courage to tiptoe through that raggedy hedge of ours and then to cautiously make my way around the barn towards the exact spot from whence the sound of the music was being initiated, my nocturnal wandering eventually led me to stand in the shadow of one particular area of the barn structure where I was privileged to observe Felix working in his small tidy workshop....

Although at that point I was unable to thoroughly appreciate the various complex musical plateaus abounding within this particular piece that was being played at the moment, I would however eventually come to know this masterpiece very well in the future. With the grand-looking phonograph presently playing the fourth movement of *Mahler's Symphony No. 5*—music so incredibly lovely that it has never lost the power to overwhelm me each and every time I hear it, that evening the young and wholly unsuspecting child soon began to be hopelessly drawn into its glowing "circle of light." Within each note of this truly wondrous music, what the listener is actually able to feel is a continuous ebb and flow of such incredible spiritual longing, as it weaves itself throughout the entire movement....

During that already amazing evening I continued to silently observe everything through the spotlessly clean windows of Felix's small art studio. My future friend was slowly cleaning several long paint brushes, with himself seemingly totally engrossed in listening to this same marvelous piece. What happened next enthralled me nearly as much as the sound of this heavenly music. Up to that point in time, I never guessed that it was possible that beauty such as this could actually cause the muscles of one's heart to contract with pain.... Felix, too, must have been moved in this similar manner. Suddenly, while the small boy watched from the security of the shadow of the building, the highly uninhibited gentleman bowed to the moment. Holding one long thick paint brush in his right hand—exactly as some gifted maestro might also hold his baton, Felix proceeded to brilliantly conduct his imaginary orchestra. There by the soft light of a desk lamp, and with undisguised passion for the music, I lovingly watched as my future father soon became lost to his silent and spellbound audience which consisted of so many bottles filled with turpentine, linseed oil, paint, and glue; a bevy of various sized canvases that had been carefully stretched upon their wooden frames—and me.

Later, and on more than one occasion after I became a happy part of this dear family, I would hear Felix remark when the phonograph in the little parlor was loudly playing Sarasate's lively *"Zigeunerweisen,"* or *"Gypsy Airs"*—or perhaps during the second movement of Beethoven's *"Eroica Symphony"* that, "If one were to even lightly scratch a true Hungarian somewhere there upon their person, what would surely appear on the surface of the skin would never be the usual droplets of blood at all, but rather musical notes instead!" With a marvelous laugh, my friend would add, "You see, either fortunately or unfortunately, people like me are born with music in our blood!"

Naturally this sort of playful remark came about during far happier times when several of his youngest children and I would occasionally stand about in the downstairs hallway, intently watching our dear patriarch as he expertly applied a brush filled with rich shaving lather onto his face.… Much to our ongoing delight he would then cunningly mold an exaggerated goatee upon his chin. When this was done to absolute perfection, from there our gifted impresario always turned around to face us all, as he proceeded to take up his imaginary violin. With a definitely impish sparkle dancing within his playful eyes, we would all clap in time to that equally flamboyant background music as Felix pretended to passionately accompany it as well, just as if to illustrate his former point.

Without a doubt George managed to enrich my life many times over by infusing my days with laughter, and by having just as thoughtfully taught me to finally read and write. His dearest father would one day also be significantly touching my life in a similar manner by teaching me to profoundly love music such as this—and to love art, as well.

I recall that when Felix eventually became strong enough from his terrible ordeal of losing George, and could finally be helped to a sitting position there within his favorite chair in the parlor, I would often times watch him completely abandon himself to Rachmaninov's musical therapy.… So much so, in fact, that quite frequently he seemed oblivious to others who might be nearby.

Once when I was making my way through that area of the house which he tended the most to occupy during those days, I paused in order to observe him resting. His feet were poised on the edge of the chair's ottoman, as usual, while his proud gnome-like head was restfully reclining against the back of the wing chair.... As I respectfully approached, our wee dog was the only one to acknowledge my presence, for his tail enthusiastically wagged from side to side, just as his ears were tucked back against his small head in this familiar and happy manner of greeting.

Still slowly recuperating as Felix was, my dear friend looked like a beautiful statue carved from Tuscany's rarest Carrara marble. With the cruel demands placed upon him from that recent emotional and physical trauma, his already thin form had lost even more weight causing him to look pathetically delicate and childlike. As I stood silently by to study him in profile, at the moment, I longed more than anything else to place my arms around his shoulders, and then to lay my head against his heart, in order to tell him so sympathetically how well I understood his misery and pain. Partially, too, I became inspired to do this to assure myself that this good man was still breathing—still living, in fact, for in this unusually inanimate state of his which was becoming all too familiar to his family and me these days, the pale and totally lifeless features of his fragile-looking countenance were truly reminiscent of a death-mask....

Without exaggeration, Felix was quite hopelessly living within himself these days. Indeed, he seemed to have found a dependable way of escaping this often painfully brutal world of ours by mentally encapsulating himself within that benevolent vehicle of divine music to briefly transcend this more common worldly realm of men. By allowing the sublime music to become his sacred key, he was able to finally unlock the thick and oppressive door where utter misery was keeping him its prisoner....

Now, merely at will, it was as though he would pass through the music's malleable membrane of therapeutic cleansing, to arrive at some hallowed place on the other side where no one could reach him. Rachmaninov's *"Elegiac" Piano Trios* , in effect, became that solitary haven which continually ministered to him—and for his survival, in the truest sense, he would often travel to that most private place of places where even I could no longer follow after him.

While Felix was slowly recovering his strength, Emma Lauder remained a study in continuous motion. Husband and wife evolved into opposites, in a real sense—with one member of the team not being well enough to move about very much at all, and with the other refusing to remain still for any normal length of time. I well recall that from the morning of George's funeral, until the second or third week in August of that same year, this painfully odd behavior of Mrs. Lauder's never once abated.

With that unnatural routine of hers this normally healthy and robust woman also lost a significant amount of weight. Her clothing began to hang loosely upon her frame, clearly indicating this very fact. Those dark circles underneath her now rather flat-looking and obviously very tired eyes were growing more and more pronounced. And, although I might have only imagined it, it certainly seemed to me that her once luxuriant chestnut-colored hair was streaked even more heavily with those silvery threads of gray.

Whenever I made my way into a particular room of the house where Emma remained in the process of thoroughly cleaning and polishing even the most trivial item located there, sometimes I would catch her momentarily resting upright against a door or wall for support. With my unexpected interruption she would become quite literally stunned into a more alert and wakeful mode, almost as if she were being caught red-handed at perpetrating some sort of crime. Then, rather quickly, she would insist upon automatically propelling herself full force into her perpetual cycle of motion all over again.... To describe the effect that this highly unnatural behavior of hers was having upon Felix and the rest of us, I should say, at the very least, that it was becoming extremely worrisome.

These days with the family's inescapable collective pain, our small farmhouse was slowly evolving into a mausoleum of sorts. Although taking food together as a family was formerly such a pleasurable experience, no longer did we live to eat as before, when two or three times a day Emma Lauder amazed us all with her considerable culinary talents. Instead, during this utterly sad time, for the most part the other children and I were obliged to pretty much scratch about the pantry and cupboards, searching for the basic sustenance merely to keep us going.

The perennial vase which habitually decorated our kitchen table and which was nearly always filled with such lovely seasonal wildflowers, or cultured blooms from Emma Lauder's wonderful flower garden, eventually ceased beautifying our dwelling altogether. Little by little, each of us seemed to be slowly and quite helplessly dying from the day-to-day suffering that came with George's own death....

With this profoundly painful discrepancy between our past and present lives, the remaining Lauder children and I soon felt condemned to a vastly different lifestyle where we were slowly becoming emotionally detached from one another, just as we were led to feel totally cut away from the much-needed healthy interaction with the parents. What naturally compounded this dangerous problem was the thoroughly depressing fact that there did not appear to be any viable solution at all in being able to aid Felix and Emma Lauder, who had themselves always been the indisputable nucleus of our heretofore close and supremely happy group.

These two normally responsible people had temporarily forgotten to remain united upon one common front, so to speak, as they were each compelled to wage their considerable up-hill battle on behalf of not only their own individual sanity, but for the overall emotional well-being of their many children as well. During this family's darkest hours, the frightening possibility that our eventual redemption from this ongoing misery might never come to pass left me with a grave feeling that bordered on profound despair.

Even after my dear friend and teacher became well enough and strong enough during the latter part of February to begin tentatively resuming the daily challenges of running the farm, I recall him fiercely urging his dear wife to cut herself a bit of slack as far as that unrelenting treadmill of hers was concerned; this same uncompromising pathway upon which she had either voluntarily or involuntarily placed herself. However, by this time it was as if this same physically brutal and emotionally unhealthy routine of hers had already become a necessary habit.

Truly, it seemed to me as if Emma Lauder was terrified to slow down at all, most probably because of her extreme fear that she would be forced to face the truth. In other words, it was as if this very strong and very proud woman pledged to outrun the agony that came from the overwhelming loss of their beloved son which continued to relentlessly pursue her. None of us could have imagined how all this would finally end one day....

Remembering back to this time I recall with a particularly virulent poignancy how remarkably beautiful the oleander trees were when they finally blossomed during that early summer. Naturally, had matters been left solely to Emma Lauder, the trees might well have remained unjustly tucked away within the protective area of the porch for that whole entire year, never to have known the sun's highly beneficial rays. The poor woman seemed to take so little interest in her usual passion for their welfare. Felix, therefore, was the one who took the necessary time and trouble to release them to the freedom they deserved.

Perhaps in some small way this was just another conscious attempt on my dear friend's part to help re-ignite some interest in living for his wife, especially after the healthy potted plants were dutifully replaced in their prescribed positions along the long winding driveway once again. Speaking for myself, with this much-welcomed beauty where the lovely flowers finally burst forth in all their lavish splendor and each delicate branch displayed overabundant clumps of silky white sprays, the unexpected result of Felix's actions seemed to be the only tangible celebration of life that could be found about the farmstead these days.

I was convinced that those lovely trees, which continuously spread their light-headed canopies over green lawn and gravel driveway alike, were blooming for our George.... Because of our collective and ever-pervasive grief no one found the necessary courage to visit his presently unmarked grave, which, up to that point, also remained undecorated with even as much as a solitary flower. Yes ... I remain quite certain that during that particular season of what amounted to our collective personal agony, Emma Lauder's trees, even for all the many seasons to come, would never appear lovelier than they did at the moment because they were blooming expressly for our dearest George.

Shortly, though, something totally unprecedented was about to occur that would finally shatter our deep collective mood of grief. Amazingly, too, it was as if this long-awaited miracle finally occurred exactly as if George himself had orchestrated it; much as if my friend took a very personal hand in finally bringing about this efficacious moment which we as a family so desperately needed.

Just as my ever-solicitous friend had been so generous in life, so was he also to prove incredibly generous in death. During this acutely painful time not only had he initiated the healing process within me, by fortuitously appearing to me in my truly magnificent dream; but, as well, he was about to be stripping away the hard protective shell which his beloved mother had so carefully constructed all around her heart. By doing this seemingly heartless thing, he would actually be initiating a similar healing process within her which might otherwise have never occurred....

On that unforgettable day I distinctly recall that the morning misleadingly began in the usual manner, with all of us busying ourselves with our many chores. However, soon enough Felix made a simple request that the older children and I remain behind to care for the younger family members—seeing that, basically, Emma Lauder was not behaving like herself these days.

Early on Felix promised Harry Hopkins that he would stop by his place to finally retrieve a bushel of the last of the season's fresh peaches which Harry was so kindly holding for us down in his root cellar. With Felix readily assuring all of us that he would not be gone very long, I eventually observed him quickly drive away in order to attend to this business of his.

On that hot and humid August afternoon, I was resting within the old worn canvas hammock which had been recently repaired and consequently re-strung between two large maple trees on one far side of the house. This of course was serving as my temporary lookout post. Languishing there, as I was, I was also loyally baby-sitting young Anna who was in the process of silently entertaining herself by attempting to place several wooden clothes pins within a brightly colored metal container. Mentally I was beginning to slowly drift off, as I thoughtfully took to contemplating the interesting cloud shapes overhead. Naturally with me doing my part for Felix, and with the other Lauder children up and about the farm, their mother—at least the last time I checked—was busy somewhere in the house....

Shortly, though, the next thing I heard was the sound of the back door slamming. Merely glancing in the direction from whence this rude sound originated, I caught sight of Emma Lauder hurrying from the house, much as if the devil himself were chasing after her. With a certain helpless fascination I was compelled to watch further as she quickly ran across the courtyard and finally entered the barn area.... I found myself speculating that for a woman who was so physically and emotionally exhausted, and was growing more and more so with every passing day, I thought it truly remarkable that she could muster so much stamina to move as quickly as she was.

No sooner had this worthy impression formed within my mind when next I observed her hurry out from the opposite end of the barn, wielding a long razor-edged machete. This, in itself, was not really very odd at all, since in her weekly gardening efforts the lady of the house had become quite proficient in the expert use of this fairly common tool.

But what instantly began to sound the alarm for me was the undeniable fact that as she returned from the tool shed carrying this substantial weapon, she was also wearing a terribly determined look of what truly may only be described as near madness painted all across her face at the moment. Naturally this behavior of hers shocked me into action and caused me to quickly rouse myself from my comfortable position there in the hammock. Dutifully taking Anna up in my arms, I walked as quickly as I could around to the other side of the house to see just what Mrs. Lauder might be up too....

And there, dear God Almighty—as my young charge and I stood at a relatively safe distance away, I immediately became even more thoroughly shocked to observe this generally benign soul literally hacking to bits the lovely trees which she so treasured.... Her own beautiful oleander trees! Like some crazed Amazon warrior of folklore, she was actually moving from one tree to the next, wildly wielding this considerably impressive weapon with both hands; first cruelly cutting down those larger sections of the plants, and then significantly bashing to bits everything that now lay helplessly upon the ground—practically everything, mind you, but the more solid ceramic pots themselves!

In time, with each carefully calculated thrust that she made, this overall viciousness naturally caused her lungs to emit primitive animal sounds which certainly appeared to accurately mirror her wild and frenzied mood. After Emma Lauder bitterly massacred the last stalk of the last tree, she stood there trembling.... Indeed, she was actually shaking rather violently from the extreme physical exertion this demented behavior of hers had demanded, all the while becoming literally drenched in heavy perspiration that now not only soaked her clothing, but was running down her face, and neck, and arms....

What in God's name could have possessed this poor woman to do such a horrible thing?! How could anyone so thoroughly and so callously destroy that which they obviously loved so much? Finally, in my own darkening mood of considerable emotional turmoil, I continued to watch as this same lady began walking towards me. I well recall that she was still red-faced from her immense exertion. She was also wearing a look of some undetermined purpose that was clearly pooling deep within her far from peaceful eyes. While Emma Lauder limply toted the dangerous-looking blade by her side, with noticeable difficulty she slowly began climbing the back steps that led into the house. Never even once did she glance my way to acknowledge my presence, nor the presence of her young daughter, either—nor, for that matter, the considerable havoc which her recent insane actions had purposely wrought all along the long curvature of our driveway....

While I continued to stand where I was for some moments more, totally speechless and feeling quite sick to my stomach, I tried hard to fathom the exact reason for this shocking display of hers. I was also obliged to attempt to comfort little Anna who had been crying all along. Desperately groping about in my confused mind for those critical answers to my equally important questions, several of the other Lauder children who by now apparently had also had the same great misfortune of witnessing this same morosely frightening spectacle, came to stand by my side.... Each of us, to say the least, remained at a momentary loss for words while I bravely contemplated making my way into the kitchen in an attempt to try to reach Felix by phone.

Finally Eddie and Charley, who were the eldest members of our small dismayed group, began vying for the chance to speak, when Eddie eventually won out and said with marked solemnity, "Look, all of you wait here while I go indoors to check on Mother.... If I'm not back in a few moments, run down to old man Reading's place and call for help!"

Having rather hesitantly strode up the stairs and into the house Eddie disappeared for a little while, only to reappear again in a noticeably dejected mood. Taking a moment to sit upon the top step, he somberly announced to all of us, "Mother's in their bedroom—and the door's locked!"

Before we actually found time to formulate some sort of secondary plan, the immensely comforting sound of Felix's truck was heard tentatively making its way up the driveway. Even before the automobile reached its usual parking place, there within the cul-de-sac of the courtyard, the Lauder children and I watched as their father literally sprang from his truck to run our way. Looking extremely pale with eyes that were wild with worry, all he could manage to ask after he swiftly made a head-count of the other children and me was, "Where's Mother!?"

None of us had had the slightest opportunity to answer his question, when he bolted up the steps and promptly entered the ante-room that led into the kitchen. Feeling much relieved to have him home, at last, we quickly followed suit and one-by-one silently filed into the house to finally post ourselves in one area of the kitchen where each person, more or less, had their individual bird's-eye view of the master bedroom door.

After Felix tried the door and found it locked, he initially knocked rather softly in order to gain entrance, but received no response. Following this, with growing panic spreading across his features, my friend called out, "Emma!" and then began literally pounding upon the door, but still Emma Lauder refused to unlock the door. Suddenly remembering a sharp object that he habitually kept on his key chain, my unhappy friend knelt down and proceeded to jimmy the lock until he eventually tried the door and pushed it open.

From where the other children and I were presently standing, we could just barely see Emma Lauder sitting upon a high-back chair in one far corner of their bedroom. Her rough and badly chapped hands were solemnly folded within her lap, and her fine head with its still remark-ably wet and wildly disheveled hair was resting peacefully back against the top of that same piece of furniture. We noticed, as well, that her eyes remained closed.... Actually her overall appearance seemed so radically composed at the moment that it might have misleadingly suggested, especially to any innocent observer, that that recent and thoroughly dreadful episode never actually happened....

But there upon the floor, right near this quietly resting lady's shoes—as if to prove otherwise, lay the now benign-looking machete which had certainly helped to murder the oleander trees. As our poor worried Felix knelt before his dear wife, the others and I watched as he gently took up her hands within his own. Soon all of us finally caught sight of Uncle Rudy's special carafe of extremely rare cognac that was now sitting all by itself, there upon a small round table next to Mrs. Lauder's chair.

None of us, either, could have possibly missed the fact that nearly a third of the exquisite bottle's rich amber contents were gone. Since Emma Lauder was never known to indulge in such things, I well imag-ined that it probably took very little of that strong stuff to properly numb her troubled soul. Felix, however, graciously tended to overlook this significant fact as his children and I heard him whisper with such heartbreaking sadness in his voice, "Liebling, ich verstehe nicht!... Dar-ling, I don't understand!"

Since German remained the couple's more preferred common lan-guage, especially on such rare and intimate occasions as these, they often tended to automatically lapse into its use. With my friend's very worried entreaty, when his greatly troubled wife eventually opened her eyes to look upon him, as she eventually did, she might well have been looking upon some total stranger.

This more than pathologically detached behavior of his wife surely must have wounded Felix. Not long after this, and with pronounced difficulty, all of us continued to watch as Emma Lauder barely managed to stand upon her feet and then begin to slowly make her way into the kitchen.... From that point she silently swayed past the other children and me, only to finally make her way out the back door of the house once more. During all this time she consented to speak nary a word to anyone, and as we helplessly watched her teeter—ever so slightly, there upon the small back porch—she eventually made it down the steps and then safely across the wide courtyard without too much difficulty, to finally disappear within the tall green and gold curtain of late summer corn which by now was towering way above her head.

Naturally our highly sensitive "Hereboy" was also a much surprised witness to all of this troubling action. Presently, as he looked eagerly from Felix towards the back door, he seemed to be asking permission to head out through the thickness of the surrounding acres of field in search of his mistress. After a round of somewhat hurried questioning, where Felix became obsessed to learn anything that any of us might know regarding what had earlier triggered this frightening episode, each of us readily assured him that no one among us had the slightest inkling as to what had set her off like that.

Next, precisely like the personification of that famous character in Sir Arthur Conan Doyle's ever-keen sleuth novels, Felix proceeded to make his rounds of the interior of each downstairs room, all the while carefully searching for some badly needed clue that would shed a bit of intelligent light upon this entire maddening event. As for me, personally, while my friend was taking the necessary time to accomplish this, I was becoming increasingly worried about Emma Lauder who was at the moment off somewhere roaming about.... To make matters worse she no doubt remained mentally dazed from the strong drink in which she had recently indulged, and all this while might possibly become permanently lost within that daunting maze of hundreds of acres of near-ripe corn.

Felix, however, must have sensed that she was in little danger. When he finally re-entered the pristine little kitchen area it was quite obvious that he still had not found that for which he was searching. Standing there in the middle of the polished floor and thoughtfully holding his chin, my friend was still wearing a slightly quizzical look upon his features, as I continued to observe him very methodically begin to scan the interior of this particular room. Naturally, nothing escaped his careful examination.

Very critically he searched everything; everything from floor to ceiling, and from wall to wall, until he finally spied the pantry door that had been left slightly ajar.... For some unexplainable reason, too, the ceiling light was also left burning. With a sense of renewed vigor, as if he might finally have stumbled upon something significant, Felix went to that near-sacred vault, opened its door wide, and walked inside.

As if choosing to act at last as Felix's silent and unobtrusive assistants, at least during this particularly fortuitous moment, the Lauder children and I quickly gathered about the entranceway to the deep pantry area, in order to carefully observe what Felix might eventually find there. But we did not have to look very long, nor very hard, either—for there upon the once immaculately-kept rustic flooring, right next to a pair of scissors and a thick roll of brand new shelf-paper, lay splattered literally dozen upon dozen of broken jars of various colored fruit jam whose ruthlessly disconcerting mayhem of contents were indiscriminately spread out across the smooth floor boards, like some pertinent psychological rendering of one of Rorschach's inkblot tests....

With Felix having entered this special room where the abundance of all the family's healthy provisions of food were always stored, I observed him kneel by the mess. Painstakingly studying the pattern that was sprawled upon the floor, he eventually reached for a tiny fragment of pure white paper which was barely sticking out from one corner of that great mangled mass of sweet sticky substance. This tiny item was practically lost amongst those various sizes of shards of sharp glass.... Carefully extracting the small note so that he would not run the risk of impaling himself upon any of the splinters of the broken material, he promptly carried it over to the sink where he allowed the water from the faucet to cleanse it well enough so that he would be able to make some sense of it.

Solicitously blotting the fragile folded paper until it was fairly dry, my friend ever-so-carefully opened it, and then began to read the message.... Having soon finished this simple task, he took a moment more to remove his glasses, and, still holding both the note and his glasses within his hand, he covered his eyes to stand there as if he were being instantaneously required to come to terms with certain substantially powerful emotions which surely had not been solicited on his part at all, but with which he was being compelled to deal nonetheless.

Finally looking upon his many children and me, it was quite obvious that Felix was currently struggling to keep from openly weeping. That overwhelming sadness within his eyes, at that very moment, was unmistakable and managed to greatly wound me as well. Soon, obviously choosing to take command of the situation as he always tended to do in difficult situations like this, he proceeded to focus our behavior in a more positive direction for the rest of that afternoon, while he, instead, went out to finally reclaim his dear wife.

Quite simply we were all being expected to take up the slack as far as the afternoon and evening chores were concerned. Usually this translated into Mrs. Lauder making the necessary preparations for our modest evening meal, as well as seeing to it that all the younger children were bathed and then dressed for bed. Now, however, the others and I would be expected to look after things, at least until Felix and Emma's inevitable return.

Confidently reaching for his faithful straw work hat that was always waiting for him there upon one wall peg within the kitchen's anteroom, Felix merely whistled once for "Hereboy." Instantly his alacritous little deputy was up to the task at hand.... Our wee terrier was ready to spring into action, quite literally, as his emotionally subdued master firmly announced, "Come, boy, let's go find Mother!"

Even before our keen little dog and Felix became thoroughly enveloped within that thick high wall of grain which began at one far end of the yard where Emma Lauder, herself, had some time ago already disappeared, the Lauder children and I ceremoniously gathered about the kitchen table to properly examine for ourselves that same solitary piece of paper which surely must have been the chief culprit responsible for all this recent family turmoil. With Eddie taking up the message and slowly opening it, instead of reading its contents out loud he chose instead to politely display it fully opened upon the small table in front of all of us, so that we might each read it for ourselves at the same time. Eagerly gazing past his right shoulder, now, where I had been standing all along, I looked down to carefully decipher the brief note.... Obviously written in red crayon, as well as in George's unmistakably adult hand, the tiny note read exactly like this: *Hugs and kisses for my beautiful mother.... Love forever, George!*

Over the years I have come to appreciate that so often miracles happen just when we need them the most. Indeed, they occur in their various shapes and in their various sizes—very much the way our special miracle happened on that unforgettable day when our dear George once again reached back through that thick curtain of death to softly stroke the soul of his dearest mother who was still in such excruciating pain....

Although as a family we were not yet seeing this hallowed truth of it all, just the same George was presenting us all with a wondrous gift. He understood that without finding the courage to face the miserable veracity of his death, his mother's heart would never be able to properly mend itself. And by unequivocally denying the required healing process, as she was so stubbornly attempting to do, her life as well as our family life would have continued to suffer and to have inevitably become gravely distorted over the coming years. In the end the happy family life which George particularly prized so much would have most definitely been destroyed.

Everything, it seemed, was riding upon Emma Lauder's wellness of spirit. After all, she remained the key to our stable life, the strong and dependable glue, in essence, that kept everyone and everything together. Needless to say with the supreme shock of finding that timely note, which I have always contended was purposely left behind by our George for her to eventually find on this particular day, the thick wall of unrelenting resistance which up to that point served so well as her only subterfuge was instantly seized and ruthlessly torn asunder to cruelly expose the entire naked truth from which she could no longer run.

When Mrs. Lauder so willfully and so ruthlessly sought to ravage that which she so loved—namely her beloved oleander trees, was she not in effect symbolically rending her garments in the age-old manner of openly grieving? Consequently, and just as surely as day follows night, with that moment's worth of cold and pitiless shock which naturally acted to open the flood gates of this good mother's grievously battered spirit, thereby finally exposing her extreme innermost suffering for all that it was—with the benevolent kindness that gentle Time so often brings—our family life would eventually become well and whole again.

One day all of us would be learning to laugh once more. One day, too, although the oleander trees miraculously managed to live throughout many more summers to come, I sensed that never again would they grow or eventually bloom to become quite as lovely as they had been just prior to that unforgettable afternoon when that visceral tempest, out of sheer necessity, visited itself upon our lives....

Sometime after sundown our emotionally-drained couple finally returned home. It was the unmistakable sound of our faithful dog's barking that enthusiastically heralded their arrival. With "Hereboy" proudly leading the way, the children and I observed Felix and Emma walking arm in arm towards us.... When they finally did come inside, within the soft glow of a nearby kitchen lamp, none of us could possibly avoid noticing that both of them now possessed eyes that were quite red and swollen from crying.

After declining something to eat, instead Felix accompanied his dear wife into their room. Since Emma chose not to offer the slightest resistance, he began to slowly minister to her by first sitting her upon one side of their bed, and then by gently removing her work shoes which she had been wearing all along. Finally, the others and I continued to solemnly watch from the doorway as this good man carefully helped place his dear wife comfortably on top of their bed.... With it still being such a warm evening, both windows were left fully opened so as to allow Emma Lauder the slightest benefit from the rare cross-breeze that consented, every now and then, to gently waft through the room.

After bending down to kiss her forehead, Felix tip-toed from their bedroom, softly closing the door behind him. Returning to the small kitchen he chose to sit with us for a while at the table, as Eddie felt obliged to ask, "Will Mother be all right now, Father?"

Reaching out to several of us now with his hands, Felix began gently stroking the sides of our faces, as he reassuringly told us, "With a great deal of rest, and just as much love and patience from all of us, Mother should be getting well again one day soon."

Since Felix was incapable of making a promise that could not be kept, I remember that a noticeable sigh of great relief from each of us seemed to pass around the small warm room that night. Then as if to take us into his most strict confidence, he leaned forward to say, "Next week your Mother and I shall be going away for a couple of days.... It's to be a surprise for her so I'm depending upon the group of you much more than usual to remain behind to look after each other's needs, just as if Mother and I were still home with you. Naturally, I plan to alert Mr. Hopkins—and 'Doc' Owens, too, in case there should be any problems. But, all in all, I feel extremely confident that you'll be up to what's expected of you!"

There was an obviously stunned look of real surprise, now, written all across the Lauder children's faces. Soon it was young Robert who seemed to be voicing the overall opinion of most of our group when he just could not seem to contain himself any longer, and quickly piped up to ask with a tinge of undisguised indignation readily apparent in his voice, "Where are the two of you planning to go, without the rest of us—may I ask?!"

Although Felix must have been incredibly tired at the moment, he smiled with much understanding at this special son of theirs whose particular temperament frequently led him to challenge his father like this. To answer him as pleasantly as possible, Felix responded, "I'm planning a long-overdue surprise for your mother, Robbie.... You see, every now and then mothers and fathers require a little private time together— quality time away from the usual cares of their daily life. Please try to understand, won't you?"

With this entreaty, which was really a pronouncement, Felix rose to go to the hallway phone nearby. With all of us contemplating these future plans of his, we heard him promptly place a telephone call to Chicago. As if to soundly frustrate Miss Edwina Dooley, who was undoubtedly planning to listen in on the forthcoming conversation as usual, everyone eventually heard my friend lapse into his native Hungarian tongue, as he went about rather enthusiastically making plans for the following week with someone he already seemed to know rather well there on the other end of the phone line.

On Friday afternoon of that following week, Felix kept the pledge he made to himself. I remember that after all the chores were completed that day, he cheerfully bounded into the house to shower and to shave, and then to carefully press a suit for himself which most of the younger children and I had never seen him wear before. During those several days which immediately followed that highly infamous afternoon that was responsible for bringing everything to a head, Emma Lauder was relegated to staying in bed to rest. Felix, I remember, had been quite adamant about this.

With the other children and me quietly mulling about the kitchen, eagerly awaiting the appearance of their mother and father, Felix and Emma remained in their room undoubtedly preparing themselves for their forthcoming trip to Chicago. How delighted our little group became when Mrs. Lauder eventually appeared from their downstairs bedroom dressed in her best linen suit. Naturally because of all that had recently transpired, emotionally speaking, she still remained in a fairly subdued mood. Nonetheless, I recall that she consented to don a small chic straw hat, and, as she patiently waited for Felix to join her, she began to slowly pull on a pair of her tiny white gloves....

Before Felix returned to the kitchen, however, I witnessed him surreptitiously enter the parlor by way of the other end of the short hallway where previously he stood straightening his tie. Not long after this the unexpected sound of gay and exceedingly happy music from the old phonograph began to fill the house. In no time at all, and with a sense of unequaled enthusiasm, indeed, it was with the charming air of some confident young lover that Felix returned to unexpectedly take his wife's hand. Gallantly bowing to her, at the moment, while all this was being performed in nearly the same smooth gesture, he seemed to barely brush his lips against her small gloved hand in a traditional kiss that was the usual custom from the land from whence he had originally come... Soon our beloved patriarch was politely addressing his sweet wife, as he lovingly requested, "Will you honor me with this dance, my dear lady?!"

On both continents—there in Europe, as well as here in America, for quite a few seasons already—Fritz Kreisler's fanciful "*Schon Rosmarin*" was literally the rage of the old and young alike. This romantic little tune was evocative of those never-to-return times; those "golden days" of a distinctly "golden era," as they were often called, just prior to the First World War when beautiful and happy couples of all ages frequented the summer gardens, and the more-than-pleasant cafes there in charming Vienna, or Prague, or Budapest, to dance away the late afternoon and evening hours....

This, then, was the special selection Felix thoughtfully chose that day when he gently enfolded his wife within his arms to the overwhelming astonishment and hearty approval of his many children and me. Before the far more reserved Emma Lauder could muster any objections whatsoever, with the supreme air of a most polished dancer, our excellent father began to twirl her about the kitchen, and then out into the dining area and parlor of the house, causing them both to eventually lose themselves to those far happier memories of days gone by.

What enchantment! What utter enchantment.... While our charming couple danced on and on, I recall so well how they moved as one. They simply glided around the entire downstairs area of our little home, superbly melded together with their two pairs of active little feet barely even touching the ground. Now and then, as I glanced around at the other children, I could not help but notice that they were becoming equally as lost as I was within this never-to-be-forgotten moment in time, as they continued to actively contemplate this strangely marvelous interaction between their normally far more sedate mother and father.

Undeniably, too, this same magical music was greatly inspiring our charming couple, causing them to momentarily forget that they were the responsible middle-aged parents of so many needy children. They were momentarily forgetting, as well, the highly challenging times through which we were all attempting to live. Here and now, for those few precious stolen moments, at least, they were once again dancing in the public square, there in the center of wonderful Vienna, not far from where the two of them had originally met and then fell in love for the first time....

That special moment touched me so. I simply had not conceived that it was possible for a husband and wife to behave in such a thoroughly magical manner as this—especially two people who had been together for as long as they. Later, as the other children and I finally walked Felix and Emma Lauder to their waiting automobile, which Eddie and Charley and I earlier volunteered to wash and polish for this grand occasion, soon the others and I were wishing them well as we enthusiastically waved our collective good-bye. In a matter of mere moments only our romantic couple finally disappeared down the long gravel driveway and then out onto the open road on their well-deserved way to Chicago.

Their inevitable return to us two days later, just as they promised, was to temporarily herald a new and far happier chapter in our lives. Emma Lauder's considerable emotional burden had, quite understandably, caused her to stumble and then to fall beneath its enormously heavy weight which she had insisted upon carrying all by herself.... But Felix was once again there to support her, and this made all the difference in the world. Consequently, dedicated husband and wife chose to take a little necessary time to selfishly re-commit to one another. By doing this critical thing, not only would their marriage benefit from this important sabbatical, but so would their many children and I.

Every now and then, over a several week period, right after their much-needed trip to the city occurred, I chanced to observe Felix openly becoming quite entranced by his wife.... More than once he would take to thoughtfully studying her as she went about accomplishing her many normal everyday chores around the farm.

For instance, when Mrs. Lauder was busy hanging several pieces of clean laundry upon the clothesline, all the while Felix and I were necessarily occupied in the dirty business of changing the oil in the family tractor, my friend became unwittingly distracted by her, and soon stood fondly observing her every movement with a look that could only be adequately described as "warm reverence." Glancing up to wipe away several wisps of her long hair which had carelessly fallen across her smooth forehead while she worked, Emma Lauder finally caught sight of her husband as he remained intently watching her like this....

After some moments where they seemed to be communicating with each other in a special silent language all their own, it would finally be she who would take the initiative to look away. With what often appeared to be a tinge of embarrassment on her part, Mrs. Lauder would quickly retreat into the sanctity of their home from whence she had recently appeared.

That particular season, just like all those other previous seasons before it, eventually came and went—and just as before there would be no new work boots for Felix. After all, those special funds which he previously coveted in order to be able to make their purchase had already been used for far more important things. Once again the ever-familiar Montgomery Ward catalog, which still stubbornly held that same small blank piece of paper which always purposefully marked a certain page therein, would be put away until some future time. And yet again, my dear friend would be obliged to patiently fold modest pieces of old newspaper and to snugly wedge each deep within the front interior portion of both of his scruffy old boots to help mollify those large and by now very familiar holes....

But Life is forever testing us. Like those awe-inspiring circadian rhythms of one's daily existence, our genuinely happy moments—which tend to come too few and far between—are forever interlaced amongst all our many heartaches and sorrows. It remains ever true that nothing lasts forever; neither one's joy, nor one's sorrow.... Consequently, it becomes each person's unique everyday "pluses and minuses" that tend to bestow their special meaning to whatever allotted time one has been given upon this earth.

Verily, just as the Good Book always tells us: The Lord giveth, and the Lord taketh away. As it happened nearly two years to the day, and around nearly that very same time of the year, an official government vehicle could be seen slowly winding its way up the long curved gravel driveway towards our farmstead.... Shortly two young and noticeably serious-looking uniformed men, who were both actually flyers in Lewis Lauder's same squadron, undoubtedly out of a sense of deep regard for Lewis as well as for his loving family, had volunteered for the painful but necessary duty of courteously delivering an official document to Felix and Emma Lauder. Respectfully and succinctly the paperwork stated that Lieutenant Lewis Lauder, their much-beloved first born son, had been killed on a training mission only two days before....

Alas! Once again those heavy iron doors of the cemetery gate would be opening wide—very much like the strong and familiar arms of a loved one, to protectingly embrace yet another child of theirs. Soon young Lewis would be joining his younger brother, George "...so that our George won't be alone anymore," as young Anna Lauder so sadly, and yet so perceptively, was to remark one day in the future. During Lewis' funeral, I found myself silently wondering whether it was a distinct possibility that such unrelenting and overwhelming grief—such gross unfairness that far too often travels hand-in-hand with true living and true loving—might eventually have the power to drive the remaining members of this special family permanently mad.

18.

FELIX LAUDER WAS A JEW. It was his wife who initially shared this important truth with me. Vividly I recall how she so matter-of-factly uttered those very words, just as if she were simply stating: The sky is blue—or the grass is green.

On that particular early spring Saturday afternoon both she and I were busy mulching the flower beds around the main part of the house when I foolishly became inspired to try to enter into a meaningful conversation with her. This more recent incident was being predicated upon a former happening where Eddie rather uncharacteristically passed along a bit of gossip concerning Cornelia Grimsley. Upon hearing this beastly woman's name, I instantly become "all ears," as they say.

During our conversation Eddie alluded to the fact that the Grimsley family faithfully attended church services each and every Sunday without fail. Mainly because of their own perceived important social standing within our tiny local community, one front pew within that same meetinghouse was habitually reserved for them alone.

Of course most old-timers who had lived in these parts most of their lives were well-acquainted with this rather selfish phenomenon of theirs and would never think of challenging the issue. Sometimes, though, especially during the seasonal months of vacation-time, innocent folks would visit our small hamlet who naturally had no way of knowing about how things stood with regards to this particular family's ongoing pettiness.

According to Eddie's story, one such poor unsuspecting soul showed up for services at the same church which the Grimsleys frequented. Having harmlessly taken their seat in the family's front pew, when Cornelia finally arrived with her small entourage of husband and children in tow to find what had occurred, with her characteristic bossiness and unspeakably bad manners she literally stood there rudely staring the visitor down. Eventually that unfortunate person became so embarrassed that they not only quickly vacated the pew, but without even staying for the start of that Sunday's service, they finally decided to vacate the premises too.

Upon hearing this story I did not find it hard to believe at all. In fact, with one colorful mental picture leading to the next, I tried to imagine what Felix might have done under similar circumstances had he been exposed to Mrs. Grimsley's overt rudeness in this same manner. I also tried to imagine the sight of the entire Lauder family as it might surely have appeared with our many members taking up the entire length of that pew, undoubtedly from one end to the other. With this, of course, my natural train of thought eventually led me to inquire of Eddie just why it was that none of the Lauder's ever attended church. I remember that it was with a modest shrug of his shoulders and a rather wry smile, too, which inspired this adopted brother of mine to instantly retort, "Go ask my mother why we never go to church!"

So naturally, at the more or less tender age of twelve, being very curious to know why all this was so, I did foolishly take my young friend's advice. One day I went searching for Mrs. Lauder, specifically to pose my question outright. This event, in fact, occurred on that very same Saturday afternoon in April when she and I were working the flowerbeds. Her answer to me that Felix was a Jew somehow left me with far more intriguing questions than answers....

For example, with her undeniably curt answer that day which afforded me little more than extra food for thought, my second and third question surely might have been—had I even been allowed any more questions at all: What does it mean to be a Jew? And then, don't Jews ever go to church?

However, as was so often her habit, Emma Lauder consented to speak not a word to me in return as I continued to serve in my more or less perfunctory role by helping to spread the moist-feeling and rather robust-smelling fertilizer all throughout her brand-new beds of peony plants. Momentarily remembering something important that she must have forgotten inside the house, and instead of taking a fraction of a moment to enlighten me in some meaningful manner about what I had asked, she silently passed me by, instead, to enter the house by way of the back door, just as if I had not addressed the subject to her at all.

Speaking quite candidly, of course, of all Emma Lauder's occasionally questionable habits, this sort of thing was exactly what always irritated me the most. In this important way she remained the total opposite of Felix. During all the years I was privileged to share in the Lauder family's life, I could never avoid noticing that George's mother also frequently treated Felix in this same way—and, occasionally, the other children, too, for that matter, so it was not as if she had some sort of a personal vendetta against me, or anything like that.

In total fairness to this very decent soul, if one thoughtfully considers the underlying ramifications of all the tremendous responsibilities that are inherent within the married life—and within motherhood, particularly, one might more readily see why this often undesirable behavior of hers really was not at all that unreasonable in the end. After all, with an ever-inquiring husband, not to mention so many all-inquiring children who quite conceivably might each ask a dozen or more random questions of her on a daily basis, this highly significant total sum of queries probably amounted to something in the neighborhood of one hundred and twenty questions per day. This simple fact becomes extremely daunting, to say the least. Perhaps in a fervent attempt to maintain a bit of personal sanity, early on Mrs. Lauder must have formed the habit of instinctively "weeding out" what she perceived were those less important questions from others she felt might be a bit more substantial and therefore worthy of being answered.

Because of this and also because I increasingly sensed that this "no-nonsense" lady ultimately held the key to my future, which lately seemed to be dangling ever so precariously within her hands, I chose not to push the issue at all.... Instead, with the ever-dependable logic of a highly intuitive child, I finally surmised on my own that whatever it meant to be a Jew must be a wonderful thing, for without the slightest doubt Felix Lauder was truly a wonderful man.

Often, and perhaps without intentionally meaning too, Emma Lauder made me feel like the proverbial "fifth wheel," with respect to my place in the family unit. From the first instant that I was invited to share in their lives, she gave me a sense that I was only temporarily visiting. This reality became especially so after George's passing, where up to that point my dear friend had pretty much become my ever-faithful protector. The growing perception of mine that one day I would be unable to stave off Mrs. Lauder's decision to eventually send me away to another foster home naturally brought with it much intense anxiety that, quite frankly, bordered on deep spiritual pain.

Much as if George originally sensed the precariousness of my personal situation, especially during those first critical weeks, he attempted to teach me to make myself indispensable to his mother. My always helping her as I did in absolutely any way that I possibly could was not really a calculated method to gain "brownie points" at all, but rather a natural method which allowed me to feel needed as part of their group. However, not long after Lewis' death it became crystal clear to me that a certain mental and emotional unpredictability had permanently descended upon Emma Lauder's soul, and that perhaps with only a mere moment's notice I might one day find myself unhappily packing up to leave the life-sustaining comfort of this haven behind, in dire pronouncement of life upon the open river once again.

What also continuously acted upon me as a subtle method of ongoing torture was the reality that every now and then, since my very first week with the family, Emma Lauder would insist that Felix research the possibility of locating some other relative of mine who might finally accept responsibility for me. There my excellent friend would sit—after being endlessly prodded by his wife, with fountain pen dutifully poised in the air while he attempted to compose the necessary query regarding this same important matter. Sometime later I would helplessly observe him place each letter within its envelope and then seal its back flap with a modest dab of hot red wax.… After this was done the warm wax itself was quickly imbedded by a weighty brass seal whose face would be carefully pushed into the smooth cooling substance and which always left behind an interesting impression of Felix's initials.

These more formal and businesslike solicitations of his, at least in the beginning, happened on far more rare occasions. But lately, in the present mood Emma Lauder was in, she seemed committed to making this request of her husband more and more frequently. With this I would quite literally die a little, especially whenever the mailman delivered our mail. I greatly feared that there might be some sort of positive response from someone—some heretofore unheard of stranger who might be subsequently paid a little money in order to be willing to accept me into their life.

From my worthy perspective Emma Lauder's seemingly obsessive wishes concerning the matter of this outgoing correspondence on my behalf tended lately to border on nagging Felix. I further sensed that in order to keep some semblance of peace and tranquility within our daily lives, my friend just found it far easier to do as his wife always requested.

After Emma Lauder and I finished our gardening on that afternoon, and with what I interpreted as her overt coolness towards me based pretty much upon her not having answered my important question relative to the family's stance on going to church, I began to experience a wholly familiar sadness that quickly began to spread throughout my heart. Instinctively, in order to be able to temporarily remedy this unhappy situation, I proceeded to search for Felix. Soon I located him working in his studio.

Respectfully knocking upon the door, I waited a second or two for a response. Then upon hearing my dependable friend's familiar, "Enter, please!" I did that very thing and found him pleasantly absorbed in working upon a medium-sized oil painting.

How I adored all those marvelous smells, as well as all those various earthy textures of the artist's enviable life. These same glorious things always tended to abound within this sacred retreat of his.... Standing silently beside the master, at the moment, as he remained comfortably standing before his canvas that was perched securely upon its wooden easel, I remember becoming thoroughly entranced in observing the manner in which Felix held his well-worn paint palette. At the same time he continued to make those firm and confident brush strokes which painstakingly imbued everything his sable brush touched with color, and depth, and meaning....

This particularly intriguing and perhaps most meaningful of all of Felix's works inevitably became a profound statement about his honest perspective of his own life—and, too, his own future death.... As the unschooled youngster I was at the time, however, the work's overall starkness hid the more meaningful philosophical beauty which I would ultimately learn to appreciate when I became much older.

Felix proudly referred to this unique interpretation of his as: "The Last Hill."... Its inspiration, he readily admitted, was borrowed from that of another artist's much more famous painting. In a way the overall work became reminiscent of one of the highly instructive medieval tales found in the collection of manuscripts known as the *Gesta Romanorum*, or *Geste Francor*, to be more precise. The famous *Song of Roland*, for example, where the tale intentionally hides its far more poignant story within a story, the theme of the work alludes to that timeless paradigm expiating a sin of birth.... The uncluttered freshness of Felix's personal interpretation, where the painting was concerned, aptly highlighted the lone figure of an obviously elderly gentleman. Seemingly this fascinating figure had taken a moment to remove himself from a well-worn pathway nearby—and to rest for a while upon the side of a steep incline, before making what appeared to be his final ascent up and over the summit of the hill in the background....

One could not help but notice that the old traveler was dressed in some unfamiliar garb which was also noticeably dusty and worn. At the same time strapped across his slightly stooped shoulders he was wearing an unusually large and very heavy-looking basket. As I further contemplated the subject matter of the painting, I could readily see that both of the subject's hands were noticeably wrinkled and gnarled and were comfortably grasping the top of his sturdy walking stick which was planted squarely in front of him, now, and which rested at an equally comfortable angle upon the ground. Although this ancient traveler's pensive and rather fixed stare was being directed outward at the surrounding and somewhat featureless winter landscape, he seemed instead to be deeply reflecting more upon the innermost terrain of his being with an unmistakable aura of peaceful resignation readily apparent upon the aged features of his weary-looking countenance....

This splendid—albeit unfinished—painting was already very powerful. Continuing to silently study its many subtle details, after a while I felt compelled to ask, "What does it all mean, Felix? Why is the old man dressed in such unusual clothing—and why does he have the huge basket strapped to his back, like that?!"

My dear friend and teacher seemed quite pleased that I had taken an interest in his work, which he obviously so loved. As incomprehensible as it always was to me, no one else in the family ever commented either positively or negatively upon whatever Felix accomplished with respect to being an artist. Nor did anyone show even the least bit of curiosity with regard to the often subliminal messages woven throughout much of everything he ever created. Returning very briefly to a previously discussed theme, perhaps his family tended to take such amazing things for granted.

With my eagerness to learn the exact meaning behind the symbolism of what I was seeing, Felix proceeded to enlighten me as he gently began to explain, "Years ago in my native Hungary, and long before I was even born, young men were commonly enlisted to travel from village to village carrying the mail like this man is doing in my painting. However, as you see, the tired traveler is no longer young anymore.... Throughout much of his long lifetime, and in dedicated service to others, he has diligently carried many baskets filled with letters and certainly packages, too, up and down many hills during all those years.... Observe, if you will, his worn-out shoes. And, too, the undeniable weariness readily apparent upon the pensive-looking features of his kindly face...."

After Felix finished this brief explanation of his, for a few more moments he remained silently transfixed—as if becoming lost in critically gauging for himself the progress he was making upon his work. Then as if releasing himself from these more private thoughts, I watched him turn to a side bench where he took to carefully placing this valuable tool he was holding. Shortly he began to squeeze a touch more of the raw umber-colored paint from its tube onto the palette's colorfully uneven patchwork surface, right next to an already generous glob of titanium white. Following this, I recall, he began to thin the too-thick medium with the appropriate amount of linseed oil, just as I already remember him doing on countless other occasions. All the while he remained occupied in this manner, I, in turn, remained thoughtfully studying the features of his own wonderful face, as well as every tiny movement his busy hands were making....

Soon, however, and much to my surprise, I presently observed Felix take a raw egg which was sitting nearby thoroughly camouflaged within a vast collection of odds and ends. After he expertly cracked its fragile shell upon the edge of his work bench, he paused further to very gingerly separate the yolk from its white outer liquid. Having managed to successful accomplish this task without making a mess at all, he then dropped the tiny egg yolk into a shallow dish to swiftly and thoroughly beat it, until its original firmness finally became liquid-like. Incredibly fascinated at what my dear friend was doing, I finally watched him incorporate some of this new substance into the waiting paint and linseed oil, after which he promptly went about creaming everything together, like some master pastry chef might blend together several sinfully rich ingredients to eventually form a taste-tempting icing for a delicious torte.

Turning to look at me, now, my favorite artist was smiling warmly at me, no doubt in response to what surely must have been my rather perplexed expression. With what amounted next to my basic initiation into the lifelong educational process of becoming a fairly accomplished artist in my own right, Felix went on to shed some light upon this recent behavior of his, as he told me, "As you may imagine, Adam, oil paints are very costly these days. So, in order to prudently extend my ever-dwindling supply, I have learned to add certain proportions of linseed oil in order to help achieve this end.... Similarly I have also come to learn throughout my years of experimentation that that wonderfully translucent effect required for the flesh tones of the human face and hands often relies upon the able assistance of one of nature's more profound gifts—namely, in the deceptively simple-looking egg yolk! When used in this particular manner, this marvelous additive seems to make all the difference...." Shortly, as Felix again began to gather his faithful palette into his very able hands, without missing so much as a beat, I heard him enthusiastically inquire of me, "Adam, do you think you might enjoy learning to draw and paint?"

This totally unexpected invitation of his left me literally thunderstruck. To have been able to arouse an equally salient response in me, Felix might well have offered instead: Do you think you might enjoy accompanying me while I swim across the Atlantic Ocean—from New York City to Lisbon, Portugal?!

Then as if the master guessed exactly what I was thinking, he sought to alleviate my initial foreboding by ever-so-gently reminding me, "My dear young friend, learning to draw and to paint is really no different than learning to read and to write! Everything we live to accomplish in this life begins as a process; a form of personal discipline, essentially, which we slowly learn to build upon, day, after day, after day!"

Instead of resuming his painting, as he might have done, in a charming mood of sheer inspiration once again Felix returned the paint palette he was holding to the nearby counter. Gently taking up my hand, together we walked over to the high wooden hutch in one corner of the crowded little room. And there, as my friend moved aside a tall canister filled with an odd assortment of sable brushes of various sizes that was obviously hiding what he now wished to show me, he nodded at something, as he smiled and said with a noticeable sense of wonder, "Look, Adam.... Look! See how even this small speck of a spider is also an amazing artist in her own right....

"I suppose one might more accurately refer to her as an architect and engineer of the first order. See for yourself how intricately fine and equally resilient her marvelous construction project has become...." Glancing at me for a few seconds, Felix soon asked with just as much enthusiasm, "Have you ever considered the fact that no two spider webs are truly identical in design? Is that not marvelous?! I suppose this reality is a bit like the very personal aspects of one's human fingerprints— would you not agree?!"

As he turned back to further speculate upon the spider, while she, in turn, seemed committed to shoring up one particular area of her spectacular structure of connecting silken filaments, I heard Felix softly confess with near adoration, "This spider's miniature masterpiece was discovered last week when I began dusting and cleaning up my studio. Since I was in such a great haste to finish what I was doing, I almost committed the unpardonable sin of nearly demolishing all that she has worked so hard to achieve by thoughtlessly whisking everything away with my hand broom.... And, truly, what a shame that would have been for both of us!"

After this I watched with growing admiration as my friend randomly began to search through several of the wide deep drawers located there within the tall nearby chest. He was swiftly opening and closing each in the process, only to finally open the last one at the bottom, as he proceeded to so generously inform me, "Here, then! Let's properly start you off by giving you a drawer of your very own where you'll be able to keep everything you do from now on here in this special place!"

From there my generous new instructor quickly stood up to reach overhead, as he began to selectively rummage through a pile of odd-sized blank pieces of newsprint. Finally having selected several from out of the group, he also took up a soft charcoal pencil as he continued on by saying, "Let us pull this high stool over here near the window, so you will have the benefit of the afternoon light which, at the moment, I am sorry to say, is slowly waning."

And so, during that unforgettable early spring of 1934, at the intellectually famished age of nearly thirteen, thus began my critical lifelong apprenticeship with art. I recall that the renowned artist Pablo Picasso is credited with having uttered: "Every child is a born artist. The problem is how to remain an artist once one grows up!"

Thinking back upon that special moment with Felix there within his marvelous retreat, I had already begun to thoroughly appreciate my overwhelming good fortune in having him for my tutor, not to mention having him for my incredibly special friend. With respect to this most worthy endeavor of art, and, too, those countless other positive aspects of living to which he was already in the process of so generously introducing me, I sensed that it was his nature to always remember to honor the child within himself, just as he surely remained disposed to habitually teaching me to do the same.

Much later that same day, not long after the Lauder children and I had gone off to bed, something significant finally transpired which would become responsible for setting a series of important events into motion; powerful events that would ultimately help clarify my heretofore uncertain future within the Lauder family. As it happened during that particular night, I was momentarily awakened from a relatively restless slumber by the sound of Emma Lauder's unnaturally shrill voice, as I heard her angrily say, "Look, he's just one more mouth to feed, Felix.... You know very well what's to be done about this already long overdue situation of ours!"

With this seemingly impromptu and disconcertingly belligerent outburst of hers, I noted that the rest of the couple's conversation quickly became comparatively low-key, and then eventually was reduced even more to its inaudible stage. Still, I declare that these harsh words acted as a sharp dagger might when plunged into the center of my heart. For months now, my escalating uneasiness about my future with this special family had become a highly ominous presence within my moment to moment existence.

In fact on two previous occasions I resolved to take matters into my own hands by finally packing up my few possessions, and dutifully penning a brief note naturally explaining the reason for my subsequent departure, and then quickly leaving behind all that I had grown to love so much during those past many months. Indeed, before I was forced to endure the excruciatingly painful process of having Felix or his wife actually send me away, I would somehow find the strength to force myself to do what would surely prove to be one of the most difficult challenges of my young life thus far.

Several days hence, upon the very evening when I vowed to myself that I would be leaving the Lauder household forever—that very night when I planned to force myself to run away, I caught Felix intently studying me at the supper table.... During these current indescribably dark days and nights having him regard me thusly, with what I mistakenly imagined might be his forthcoming prelude to preparing me for my inevitable forced leave-taking, I discovered that I had no appetite for the generous amount of food which Emma Lauder had just placed before me.

Immediately after dessert was enjoyed by everyone else, and while I excused myself to begin helping the others to wash and dry the supper dishes as usual, Felix approached me and said, "Adam, do please leave tonight's kitchen work for the others, and come along with me now. Naturally, there is something important that I feel we need to discuss."

While I was slowly following my friend out the back door of the farmhouse, and then across the gravel courtyard to finally arrive within the protective haven of Felix's little studio once more, my poor heart was slowly breaking with every single step that I took. After the small desk lamp was engaged, Felix reached for my hand and quietly led me nearer to the light as he told me with a sense of genuine concern readily apparent upon his face, as well as in his voice, "Lately, Adam, you have not been thriving as you should be.... For the last several weeks or so, I have been watching you actually lose weight, just as I have also observed those dark circles form beneath your eyes. Do please lift up your shirt for me, so that I might see for myself all these things which should not be so!"

Having dutifully removed my shirt, I reluctantly exposed the top portion of my torso for my trusted friend to examine. Felix immediately proceeded to run his fingers gently along either side of my nearly flesh-less rib cage. Pausing to turn my averted face towards him, which I now purposely took great pains to hide from his relentless gaze so that he might not be able to behold my genuinely sorrowful eyes, he asked in a fairly incredulous voice, all the while his deeply probing eyes contin-ued to openly seek my own, "Aren't we feeding you well enough, these days? It's obvious to me that you're losing weight, instead of gaining it the way you're supposed to be." Then, after he requested that I put on my shirt again, he was saying more to himself than to me, "I'll give "Doc" Owens a call first thing tomorrow morning, in order that he may evaluate you for himself."

Normally Felix would have been the easiest person in the world in which to confide. But on this particular evening, with my heart fraught with such heaviness and pain, I could not seem to find the words neces-sary to tell him what I longed to say. After all, how could I ever actually bring myself to say good-bye to someone who had already become the loving father I would have otherwise never known?! Someone who, for these last few incredibly fulfilling years, had provided me with the most wonderful and healthy environment which was also the only loving home I had ever known.

As I continued silently struggling with this inner dialogue of mine, I heard Felix say, "For quite some time, now, I've suspected that there might be something bothering you. Whatever it is, Adam, won't you please share it with me, so that I'll be able to help you overcome the turmoil you've obviously been carrying around all by yourself?!"

Having finished tucking in my heavy cotton shirt, I was literally cringing inside from the proverbial ax which I believed would be falling upon my young life any minute now. That inevitable pronouncement of Felix's promised to irreparably shatter me to bits. While contemplating these moribund thoughts, I chose to step back away from my friend—just a bit, in a conscious effort to begin physically and emotionally distancing myself from him. In this way what would soon be occurring might become a little easier to bear in the end. But as if instinctively sens-ing this negative game of mine, which was definitely not to his liking at all, Felix just as quickly retaliated by reaching out to me with his palm up in a silent and powerful gesture that was, in essence, a personal entreaty for me not to evade either him or the issue at hand.

His soul's energy was undeniably potent. With what had already become for me a rather familiar body language particular to him and which also so easily translated into a spiritual language for two, against my better judgment I finally found myself loudly whispering with heart-wrenching difficulty, just as I consented at the last moment to place my vulnerable young hand within his, "Why are you sending me away?!"

These words of mine proved far more painful to speak than they had ever been to only privately contemplate. And quite obviously what I had just asked momentarily stunned this good man, for in no time at all I heard him quickly respond in a nearly angry mood, as he said in defense of himself, "What are you talking about, Adam?! What nonsense is this?!"

Without holding back in any sense, I now began mentioning my litany of painful observations which included, for starters, the half-dozen written queries that began being sent out upon my initial arrival into their lives all those many months ago—and which, all along, I naturally interpreted as manifest proof of the ongoing effort by the Lauder family to rid themselves of me.... Then, of course, there was that no less hurtful and most recent event where Emma Lauder in a moment of obvious frustration managed to blurt out the truth of the situation, at least as far as she was concerned. Now at last having been allowed to purge myself in a certain sense by verbalizing exactly what was causing this ongoing trauma of mine, which perpetually kept me living within an emotionally helpless state of limbo, I waited patiently for Felix to speak.

In a truly somber mood of what may be properly described as devout contrition on his part, my dear friend chose to clasp both of my small hands within his, much as if we were both praying to the same God.... I continued to carefully observe as his eyes began to shine like brightly radiating coals of light that were only now ever-so-gently beginning to shed a ray of much-needed luminosity into the darkness of my vulnerable young spirit. With considerable emotion of his own, he quietly informed me, "There's so much that we must now speak about, my dear young friend.... There are so many important matters which I should have thought to address openly, and long before now!"

Slowly releasing my hands Felix firmly but gently placed his own upon the sides of my gaunt shoulders, instead, as he respectfully told me, "Adam, each small letter I wrote—especially that first one, was being sent forth into this huge world of ours with the slight hope that I might one day be able to locate your mother. Originally my wife and I deeply felt that we owed you this! Loving all our children as much as we do, we naturally imagined that, due to the past difficult circumstances of your life, Fate had so unkindly prevented you and your parents from being together as a family. So after your father's death, it was out of a sense of moral duty to both you and to your missing mother that we diligently began to try and locate her.... Can you possibly understand, now, what our feelings must have been back then?!"

Although I chose not to speak, I did manage to nod my head in answer to the seriousness of what my friend was telling me. Felix continued on, as he softly confided to me, "As far as my wife is concerned, Adam, surely you understand that she hasn't been herself since the death of our sons.... Neither of us have, actually. And because I believe that she hasn't as yet come to terms with all that she invariably must, this same highly caustic internal turmoil is causing her to react to those around her in an often negative manner. She's still in a great deal of pain, after all.... But time, I feel, may eventually make the difference. With patience and understanding, and a great deal of kindness on all our parts, we shall not only manage to avoid aggravating the presently difficult situation, but we should also be able to help expedite the process of eventually helping her regain her more dependable equilibrium—at least, this is my profound hope!

"Adam, when we found each other all those many months ago, not only did I consciously invite you into my home, but I lovingly invited you into my heart! Your living here with us as you've been doing has added greatly to the richness of all our lives. Not only did our George grow to love you, as you well know, but so have I! And, for that matter, so have the other children too.... Although my dear wife may not always show her affection towards you as openly as the rest of us, please believe me when I tell you that in her own special way she also cares a great deal for you, too.

I could feel that Felix's fingers were closing more tightly around my small shoulders, at the moment, no doubt to help emphasize what he was about to say. Very shortly I finally heard him promise, "From this day forward, there'll be no more letters! Realizing that you wish to remain here with us, just as much as I wish you to stay, makes all the difference in the world. Please know that from now on I should fight for the privilege of keeping you with us—but only for as long as you wish to stay!"

These gentle words of such unexpected kindness were beginning to act upon my tortured young spirit as potent medicine works upon a sickly body. Unable to control the overwhelming emotional release inspired now by all that I had previously kept locked away inside of me for such a long long while, I quickly covered my face with my hands and began to sob out loud. I remember briefly thinking that even with Reverend

Pouley's unspeakable cruelty, I still had managed all that while to successfully thwart his ability to make me openly weep like this.... But now, with Felix Lauder's tender words of genuine kindness—and love, above all else, I grew helpless to avoid the inevitable. As the sturdy floodgates of my battered young spirit were opening wide for the second time in my life, I was finally consenting to weep in front of someone else.

To further comfort and assure me, my adopted father gently pulled me to his chest, and held me tightly against his heart, just as the racking sounds of my healthy and much-delayed sobbing filled the hallowed stillness of our small studio, promptly drowning out those more familiar night sounds of the early summer crickets.... I recall how the scent of Felix's immaculate clothing and the clean scent of his person, too, smelled so reassuringly of the wonderful godliness of heavenly fresh soap. Finally, I began to believe that I was home.... Dear God! At long last, the small vulnerable leaf had been consciously plucked from its long unsettling journey down that turbulent and ever-dangerous river of life—to be solicitously patted dry, and then lovingly placed next to this remarkable man's ever-benevolent heart for safekeeping.

Much later on, after I frivolously spent every last drop of my great reservoir of tears, and after Felix helped me dry my eyes and blow my runny nose—as well as polish off a tall glass of water that was retrieved from the nearby sink in order to eventually help quell my seemingly endless bouts of hiccupping—arm-in-arm the two of us went out into the clear cool dry evening to sit together underneath the stars.

In point of fact, this most recent tempest of the spirit had finally passed. In its wake, at the moment, I remained emotionally spent and totally immersed in a heretofore unfamiliar numbness of body and soul that was not unpleasant in the least.

Sitting next to Felix upon the high slanted wooden box which he originally built to house Emma Lauder's smaller gardening tools and which was attached to one outside area of the old barn, I silently raised my eyes to stare into the never-ending heavens above, attempting to visually locate the various astronomic phenomena for which George had had such a penchant. Shortly, though, as if still desperately requiring more tangible proof of Felix's love and loyalty, as well as to more firmly secure a finite closure to those dreadfully painful years of my earlier childhood, I asked with some hesitation, "Do you ever imagine that there might come a time when you'd consider adopting me—in the legal sense, I mean?"

For me to truly belong to someone else, and to have them also truly belong to me—in the filial sense—had always been my lifelong dream.

With my friend's subsequently long silence, however, where he seemed to be carefully weighing what I had so impetuously asked, my buoyant heart began to sink rapidly. In its place a far more familiar anxiety was telling me that I might well have overstepped the boundaries of acceptable propriety by requesting far more than my friend was willing to give.

But my foolish fears were soon to be calmed as I finally heard this genuinely kind man say, "One day in the future, Adam, if you still feel as you do at this moment, then we shall certainly speak in far more detail about this important possibility. However for now, at least, while you're still relatively young and somewhat inexperienced about several critically important aspects of life, I should never want to run the risk of robbing you of your birthright!"

My immediate internal response to this unusual innuendo of Felix's was one of high negativity, since I felt quite certain that neither of my parents had left me anything of value to call my own. But at the same time, knowing that my friend never entered into important conversations of this nature without being able to support each and every detail of the interesting ideas he introduced, while I momentarily floundered about attempting to grasp the exact meaning of what he was suggesting, I was soon forced to indicate my ineptness, as I said, "I don't understand what you mean, when you say 'my birthright.'"

Moving closer to me, now, and securely linking his arm through mine—as was so often his habit, Felix began intently studying me, just as he began to smile his happy and ever-comforting smile.... In a moment or so, he finally continued on to inquire, "Do you know how amazingly similar we are as people—you and I?!"

This unexpected yet highly intriguing question, which initially seemed to indicate that we had somehow strayed from our previous subject, managed to catch me off guard so I spontaneously answered, "Are we?"

"Yes, quite so! You see, not only are we both very special people who continue to need others, but, just as importantly, we are people who shall undoubtedly always need to be needed by others!"

How I adored conversations such as these. While I silently returned my friend's undeniably radiant smile with my own, I patiently waited for him to continue on as with a slightly more serious expression he eventually said, "I sincerely believe that you are also a wonderful teacher, Adam. After all, you've already so wisely taught me that a man need not sire a child in order to grow to love that child as his own!"

Fully comprehending the supreme compliment that this excellent man was now graciously bestowing upon me, his words were once again tugging at the strings of my heart. No one—not a solitary person in my entire life, other than he and George, of course—had ever referred to me as being special. Quite unable to respond at this point with any appropriate words of my own, my silence allowed my friend to continue on to express several more important sentiments that would be radically changing the manner in which I presently viewed my place in the world.

With his characteristic wisdom and compassion, Felix proceeded on to indicate with pronounced sensitivity, "With all the difficulty which you managed to survive thus far within your relatively short life span, Adam, it is absolutely natural that you would wish to distance yourself further and further from your past. Indeed, the emotionally complex as well as the physically battered individual whom you only briefly knew as your father had eventually become a mere shell of a man.... Yet, I am willing to faithfully conclude that not so terribly long ago he was a fine boy very similar to you—a young man, no doubt, with a needy heart and a hungry mind filled with countless hopes and dreams of his own.

"Who can say for certain what led him down that highly destructive path he inevitably chose to tread? Furthermore, how could I ever in good conscience stand in judgment of him, not fully comprehending all the circumstances of his life? Still, being denied this, I am free to pity him.... I shall particularly pity the fact that he never lived to know, nor lived to thoroughly appreciate, the wonderful son who was part of him!"

Felix paused a moment as if to punctuate this remark, before he went on to tell me, "But there remains one thing of which I am absolutely certain, Adam.... Understanding something of life, as I do, as surely as you and I are sitting here together this evening—underneath the ever-watchful eyes of our loving and compassionate God, I am absolutely certain that either both of your parents, or just one of them, must have been incredibly special in their own right, otherwise they would never have been able to produce a child as special as you!"

Once again that single most meaningful word "special," which was being directly applied to me at the moment, fell upon my needy spirit as reverently as soothing raindrops might finally fall upon the parched and badly cracked earth of a dry riverbed—bestowing upon me the ongoing promise of a joyous new life for the future.... Soon I was hearing Felix say, "Because of the innate respect which I instinctively feel for your family history, notwithstanding the sketchiness of its more recent dark and painful past, I fear that if my wife and I consented to allow you to arbitrarily change your name; in other words, if we were to engage in the necessary paperwork to legally allow you to become a member of a family to which you already belong in every other way, than we would surely be robbing you of something truly significant! In effect, we would be cheating you of your natural birthright—your true history. Quite understandably because of your current youthfulness and inexperience concerning these critical matters, I feel that you might be unable to adequately appreciate the fact that Emma and I would be allowing ourselves to take advantage of the situation, as grown-ups sometimes tend to do—even well intending grown-ups, thereby soundly perpetrating a grave injustice towards you in the end!

"It remains my fervent belief that one day you shall live to bring honor to your family name, where your father failed to do so. After all, in my worthy opinion, you have already begun to accomplish this very thing! Someday you may well become responsible for initiating a stronger and far more viable family dynasty of your own—one that shall begin with you, and then shall be proudly built upon by you ... day after day, and year after year, all the while you remain reverently cognizant of the humbling reality that any such future edifice erected as a tribute to your years upon this earth was initially structured upon the sacred rubble of your parent's own failures and despair.

"My dearest Adam, never forget that Truth is everything! Never stray, even for a single moment, from questing for it.... Never cease from thirsting and hungering for it! For to deny even the smallest truth, is to lend a certain distortion to one's life!"

That night, there under the glorious stars with my beloved friend, I had come of age. Quietly, and with a certain newfound courage, I consciously chose to celebrate my having stepped from the passing world of my very difficult childhood—forward, into this next far brighter phase of my existence. Likewise, and for the entire rest of my life, I would never cease to remember the important things which Felix had so generously shared with me. Needless to say, for me he remained my special "man for all seasons."

Yes. He was my great teacher.... Next to George, he was also my dearest friend in all the world. And thanks to Divine Providence; thanks, indeed, to those indisputably benevolent powers that endlessly dwell within our never-ending Universe, persistently guiding and protecting innocent young children, he just naturally became the wonderful father I would have otherwise never known.

19.

THROUGHOUT EUROPE'S SIGNIFICANTLY LONG HISTORY, up to and including World War I, a number of the various countries there were proudly able to maintain their formidable aristocratic bloodlines—their impressive pedigree, so to speak. In bold contrast, however, America was from the very start a feisty and rebellious mongrel pup, continuously being suckled from the vast reservoir of the blood, sweat, and tears shed by all those who migrated from other lands, avidly searching for religious and political freedom, sweet-tasting justice, and a dependably better way of life for themselves and for their children.

With each passing year thereafter, as if to remain venerably mindful of its no less important history which has traditionally honored its "melting pot" persona, those countless others who continue to arrive upon our ever-promising shores continue to be generously greeted by our "open door policy" that has never wavered. Since the bloody days of the Revolutionary War, which was fiercely fought and finally won at great cost and where we finally achieved our status as a free nation, generation upon generation of noble citizens have never ceased reaching out to welcome those other visionaries from other places all around the world.

Once, however, when referring to his fellow "noble citizens," I remember that Felix Lauder somberly indicated to me with a nearly tangible sense of bitter conviction resounding in his normally pleasant voice, that: The immigrant's various manner of speaking—his accent, in other words, does not in any way denote an impairment in the mental processes, as so many of the sons and daughters of former immigrants have eventually come to choose to believe.... On the contrary, these same strong people often come to the shores of this truly remarkable land of opportunity having already proven themselves successful in the highly demanding arenas of business in some fashion or another, as well as in the professional endeavors of Medicine, and Law, and Education elsewhere, only to be unjustly set upon here by this strongly negative and thoroughly unprincipled philosophy.

My friend continued on to say: Many of the descendants of the children, grandchildren, and great-grandchildren of those originally adopted citizens of ours began with so little, and sacrificed so much, in order to be able to slowly inch their way up the proverbial "ladder of success." Their fervent dream was to inevitably secure for themselves their well-earned rewards of prosperity and, likewise, to eventually be able to pass these things along to their descendants.... But somehow along the way many of these same generations of fortune's children have forgotten what it means to be new to this country. They conveniently overlook how terrifying it is to face a new world where one cannot speak the language properly, and where the simple day-to-day transactions of daily life alone frequently pose a tremendous challenge.

Hence, these same rather unkind souls often help to continually propagate the erroneous belief that visitors from other lands who naturally speak differently, and who often dress differently, and who must work very hard at those more menial jobs at first in order to be able to procure even their most financially meager rewards, are basically ignorant people. What amounts to little more than a needless irrational victimization by those who should remember better, automatically casts the newcomer into an unfair category which only aids in further burdening their life.

Rudely thwarting others at every turn, in their endless desire to rise to their desired place in this traditionally rich society of ours, causes former victims to make victims of others. And, as if this were not already enough to discourage the heartiest spirit, the unsuspecting immigrant far too frequently becomes the target of those more unscrupulous members of our society, from greedy slum lords and shopkeepers to nefarious public officials; as well as to those far more educated professionals who behave as ruthless piranha among us, even after having sworn an oath before God and man to forever honor the sanctity of their distinguished vocation which is to faithfully assure that injustice and chaos within this society is kept at bay....

Although my friend and I never actually spoke of it, I came to believe that this same sort of intrinsic injustice to which he was alluding, the exact sort of problematic behavior which is founded primarily on extreme callousness and illiberality, may well have been responsible for him and his wife having early on decided not to pass along to their many children their considerable collective knowledge of the Hungarian, Czech, German, and Spanish languages. Most probably, as well, in matters such as these that pertain to other visitors from other lands who have lived on to eventually become naturalized citizens of this great country of ours, this same practice might have once held true and for the same reason. In a sincere attempt for loving parents everywhere to better be able to insure their children's timely assimilation into their new life and culture and, quite understandably, to be able to have them forego any repetition of those same painful insults which the parents had had to endure early on, the English language inevitably became the focal point of interest for everyone… It became a vital tool, in essence, which ultimately helped rescue them from the often deep and thoroughly confining pit of frustration and despair.

"Sinners beware! Make peace with your God, while you can! The world is ending.... The world is ending!" Standing at the moment upon the corner of one of Chicago's busiest and most prestigious streets, Felix and I quickly spied the dazed-looking middle-aged man, dressed from head to toe in dirty tattered old rags, who was responsible for loudly yelling out these disconcerting words over and over again.

Perhaps this unusual sight tended not to be so unusual for the average passerby, owing to the fact that no one within the huge crowd of city pedestrians, not another solitary soul, in fact, within that hustling and bustling mass of humanity, seemed to be paying this poor harbinger of doom the least bit of attention. However, having become as fascinated by the entire scene as I was, I found that I could not resist turning to my wise companion to openly declare, as soon as the two of us finally passed by this rowdy stranger, "That poor man speaks as if he truly believes what he's saying!"

I well recall that all this excitement happened on one early Saturday afternoon several weeks after Felix and I had had our very enlightening conversation which already began to change my life. An hour or so earlier Felix and I had left Eddie back at the dentist's office that was located in the Lauder family's old neighborhood on Wilson Street. Felix was assured that the wait to see the physician would prove to be a long one, and so my friend took me along to conclude some important personal business he had had at one of the local office buildings nearby.

But before we were due back to fetch our brave patient and then return to Lake Geneva from there, Felix and I impetuously decided to make the most of the warm breezy day. With the two of us presently heading up Michigan Avenue, we decided to travel in the general direction of the Tribune Tower. Without even hesitating in his forward movement nor missing as much as a single step in his smooth and elegant gait, my excellent companion finally acknowledged my comment with a brief smile, as I heard him answer in his typical good-natured manner, "Yes, indeed! Do you suppose, my dear young friend, that he knows something that we do not?!"

Every now and then it was Felix's marvelous habit to independently single out one of his many children or me to be able to share a little "one on one" quality time together. With all the endless activity around the farm, not to mention within our collective personal lives on any given day as well, such times became more and more rare and therefore more and more treasured.

Felix instinctively realized that this more personal attention which he sought to give each of us allowed for a special interaction that was emotionally and intellectually stimulating in a particularly unique way that was not possible to achieve as a group. As far as looking after everyone's ongoing needs was concerned, especially with respect to this rather unique philosophy of his, how he managed to keep the fragile scales of fairness on an even keel I shall never know—but he did. With his many children continuously vying for his attention this never-ending contest sometimes evolved into a sort of tug-of-war, thereby pretty much leaving me respectfully upon the sidelines…. But still I always secretly hoped all the while that I might eventually be factored into the equation, in good time.

What a beautiful day it turned out to be. The early September sun felt warm against my smiling face, just as the strong continuous breeze from the choppy waters off the nearby lake brought with it the opposite cooling sensation. I was truly in love with life! My unexpected holiday with Felix and Eddie that day, which took us to this fascinating city of Chicago, was won by default, in a manner of speaking. Much earlier that day when Felix initially invited Charley Lauder along to accompany Eddie and himself, with Charley uncharacteristically declining the gift and with me somehow just happening to be next in the line of succession, I was invited to take his place, which, of course, pleased me very much indeed.

During those nearly five years since I arrived to live in this part of the world, I really never had any occasion to return to the city. My arrival at the train station all those many months ago now somehow seemed more like a very distant bad dream. Likewise, since the three of us traveled into the city by car, instead of by bus or train, there was really little need for me to fear that those unhappier memories of mine—

which by now had to a great extent so benevolently receded into my past, would be playing any part in ruining these presently incredible happy hours for me.

Our compulsory trip into town that fine day initially obliged us to travel along beautiful Lakeshore Drive where I was astounded to observe that Lake Michigan looked more like some vast ocean, rather than anything else. Eddie was feeling poorly due to a nagging toothache which he had been nursing for some time, and which was becoming decidedly worse with each passing day. Rather than more practically soliciting the professional assistance of our local dental authority in Lake Geneva whose notorious method for always dealing with such things, no matter what the circumstances might otherwise prove to be, was to extract the tooth, Felix was naturally opting for a more comprehensive evaluation that might possibly lead to a far more positive outcome. Leaving our Eddie temporarily behind in the doctor's unusually crowded waiting room, with an ice-cold compress resting upon that one side of his slightly swollen face, Felix and I proceeded on with the business at hand, faithfully promising to return as quickly as we could before it was his turn to be seen.

Felix seemed to know this interesting city the way he knew the various contours of his own interesting face. After we parked down by the old Water Tower and Pump House, which remain the well-known landmarks that survived the devastating fire of 1871, we proceeded onwards those several blocks towards the river. Being rushed for time as we were, we could not justify the necessary hour or so required to tour the Tribune Building as we would have liked. Instead and unbeknownst to me at that precise moment, as we proceeded to diagonally cross the busy street in front of us and walk together in the direction of the famous Wrigley Building, my friend was essentially returning to the scene of an unforgettable crime....

Standing side by side, now, and having silently contemplated for several long moments the rococo "Wedding Cake" architecture of the huge snow white marble edifice standing before us, Felix just as quickly seemed to dismiss it from his mind, as I heard him rather pensively state, "When I first arrived here with my dear wife, not so long after the start of the new century, the city looked far different than it does now, Adam...." Pausing to gaze across the narrow river, and then up and down the street to our left as if recalling significant details from those days gone by, he continued on to further tell me, "Back then, horses and buggies were quite a common sight, you know! And although my very young wife and

I had only a few dollars to our name at that time, I vowed, nonetheless, to take this city by storm one day. I promised Emma, especially, on that memorable day in May as we both stood upon this very same spot, that I would never disappoint her in the future, and that someday she would have the sort of life that I felt she always deserved."

With this brief and relatively painless excursion of Felix's back into time, several obviously strong memories of a darker sort were slowly being resurrected in the process, causing a faint albeit highly distinct cloudiness to pass across the current seriousness of my friend's face.... I noticed, too, that his jaw seemed to lock more firmly into place, and in time he went on to add, "But life does not always fully cooperate with those well-intended promises that a young man makes, even in the best of faith!"

Perhaps weighing in his mind whether or not he wished to continue on with something that really needed to be openly addressed—not unlike a troublesome boil, in the emotional sense, that requires lancing in order for the sufferer to obtain some modest form of relief—he turned to look once more at the building in front of us. Soon he proceeded to enlighten me further, as he offered, "After several years of great personal sacrifice and seemingly endless hard work, my wife and I finally reached a point were we felt we had attained the noteworthy success for which we had striven so hard....

"Therefore, to more prudently insure the safety of my family's financial future, I wisely decided to invest a hefty sum of what I had earned and saved over the course of those former years in what appeared to be a rather sound speculative venture which basically translated into the timely purchase of a truly spectacular parcel of highly desirable land, here in the heart of the city. During those early years, as well, being fully aware that my finite knowledge of English was never as polished as it should have been, and perhaps more importantly because I did not completely trust myself to negotiate on my own behalf the considerable daunting legalities involved in making such an important deal, after many sleepless nights I eventually chose to rely upon the professional decency of a man whom I greatly trusted. This savvy individual was not only a highly astute legal mind, but my relatively longtime friend as well.

"This same person who frequently dined at my table over the years, and who just as often would sit upon the lush carpet within our comfortable salon to cheerfully entertain young Lewis and George while they played—indeed, this same trusted agent of the law who also pretended to love me as a brother, one day without the slightest hint of betrayal on his part proceeded to underbid me behind my back.... Yes! At the appropriate moment he became guilty of doing that very thing to finally secure this same parcel of land for himself! Believe it or not, that remarkably valuable land of which I speak is located here, Adam—here beneath this immense, white, innocent-looking building, which we now see before us!"

Over the years I was to know Felix, I came to better understand that this unfortunate incident in his earlier life would live on to become his proverbial "Achilles' heel," so to speak. In this respect he reminded me of a study in remarkable contrasts. For example, although he was an indisputably discerning artist whose painstakingly intimate relationship with brush and canvas was founded exclusively upon all the positive and negative aspects of life, my dear friend never balked for a second in his ongoing effort to borrow from the entire spectrum of life's provocative color chart, including all its more somber shades of gray, and brown, and black....

Conversely, however, in my humble opinion it seemed to me that whenever it came to acknowledging and accepting the numerous frailties and imperfections of others, particularly as these various subjects related to himself on some extraordinarily personal level, Felix failed miserably in remembering to condemn only those individuals directly responsible for some grave offense, rather than devaluing an entire body of individuals. I sincerely came to believe that because he was a rare man who supremely valued integrity—above all else, with respect to those profoundly sobering lessons regarding the inequality of human beings—he was occasionally left both emotionally and intellectually smarting.

It would also be fair to state that during most of Felix Lauder's lifetime, and certainly up to the moment he died, he detested not only the abuse of power—but certainly the abuse of friendship, as well. That wholly unsavory betrayal by this one corrupt lawyer alone never again allowed him to place his once considerable faith in the sacred precepts of our truly laudable albeit still imperfect system of law. Because of the uncharacteristically narrow vision which he continued to embrace after that particular hurtful incident occurred, and which automatically translated into a somewhat unfair appraisal of the entire legal profession as a whole, he inevitably would be causing himself and his family even more needless difficulties in the future. Quite simply put, he remained a remarkably near-perfect individual who was living in a manifestly imperfect world.

Once, when my dear mentor took the occasion to touch upon this same thought-provoking subject with our own wonderful "Doc" Owens concerning the rampant abuse of power within the legal profession, I recall how the good doctor chose to make his own noteworthy comparison that day between this age-old issue, and also the relative importance that women tend to play within any man's life, as he said with a wry little smile: "Oh, yes! As far as lawyers and women are concerned, one can neither live comfortably with them—or without them!"

Also, as a point in fact, Felix Lauder's highly negative feelings towards the Catholic Church had spontaneously erupted during one such similarly salient point early on in his life. According to his own faithful account which would finally be shared with me in great detail not long before his death, those same uncompromising sensibilities of his were grievously wounded during a thoroughly distasteful incident which occurred sometime during the latter half of the 19th century.... Within this same contentious period, a handful of Hungary's more powerful members of her Roman Catholic clergy became unjustly inspired to intervene in a time of acute personal crisis for my friend, and then unanimously voted against any sense of basic decency relative to the youthful Felix, thereby profoundly cheating this worthy individual of what had been legally bequeathed to him by his father.

Naturally, because of this landmark incident, he lived forevermore to harbor intense disdain towards this same formidable body. And so, just as with the significant betrayal of the unscrupulous lawyer years after that time, and here in this other part of the world, my friend promptly and forevermore cut whatever ties he might otherwise have had to this other great bastion of considerable power, never to forgive the injustice while he lived. But then the reader must forgive me for getting ahead of myself in my humble storytelling.... This, of course, would be neither fair to the integrity of this tale, nor to the faithful reader either.

Meanwhile back at Peck's Station, several days after our business in the city was successfully concluded, Harry Hopkins unhappily announced to Felix and the rest of us that his beloved cat was missing. Knowing how much this good man cared for old Thomas, and knowing, indeed, how much he depended upon the soothing companionship of this loyal four-legged friend of his, the Lauder children and I quickly rallied to the cause by making up a dozen colorful posters soliciting the badly needed help of others within our small community....

With a handful of freshly painted notices tucked securely under one of my arms, I was in the process of making my way into Otto Grimsley's general store. My objective was to obtain the necessary permission to post one or more of the signs somewhere conspicuously about the premises where daily patrons both coming and going would see the information and hopefully be able to shed a bit of much-needed light onto the presently frustrating situation. More than a week had already passed from the time we originally mounted our search effort to assist Mr. Hopkins. Everyone connected with the investigation was beginning to suspect that the dear old cat might have ended up having an unfortunate run-in with a fox, or wolf, or an ill-tempered badger, that were well known to frequently leave the confines of the more densely forested areas nearby, in order to raid our local farms.... But, even with this terrible possibility looming there within the back of our minds, we still could not bring ourselves to forsake our search effort—at least, not yet.

As I wandered into the busy place on that early Saturday afternoon, I headed straight for the small group of amiable individuals who were seated at the modest wooden table over by the wide oversized window. This same cheerful spot was habitually utilized on a more or less on-going basis by several of the local shopkeepers, as well as certain longtime patrons, too, who would generally meet there for a little while to brush up on their checker game.

Sheriff Parker forever frequented the place, too. I well recall that in all sorts of weather folks were routinely drawn to this spot, much like the predictable wildebeests that are drawn to a particular watering hole. Basically people enjoyed sharing a bit of harmless gossip while they tried to establish their personal winning streak there on the black and red game board.

During the colder and far more inclement weather, those same visitors would huddle together around the welcomed warmth of the potbellied stove, nursing their hot drinks and smoking their smokes.... In the late spring, as well as all through the summer months and into early autumn, everyone took to moving out onto the front porch area, with the faithful old checkerboard and pieces in tow, to casually sit and rock upon the several comfortable old chairs placed there for precisely this purpose.

Needless to say, this particular cool autumn day proved to be no different than all the rest, as I cheerfully greeted Angelo Balducci who was intently observing this same competitive game being played at the moment between Harry Hopkins and Otto Grimsley. Standing respectfully near this small gathering, I took a few seconds to study the move that was presently being initiated by the owner of the store. Soon "Doc" Owens approached our thoughtful little group, carefully balancing a cup of hot coffee. He finally claimed the last available spot at the well-worn oak table, as he gently patted me across the shoulders to enthusiastically inquire, "Any luck so far, Adam, in locating 'Old Thomas'...?"

"No, sir..." I responded, feeling very disappointed in being forced to admit the unhappy truth of the situation. Addressing the owner of the missing animal, I felt obliged to add, "I'm beginning to think the worst though, Mr. Hopkins, realizing that your special cat never wanders, and also knowing full well that the raccoons, fox, and badgers would naturally prove quite formidable—even to a large old boy like Thomas!"

Hating so much to be the one to point out this negative possibility to my dear friend I felt honor-bound to temper this highly distressing theory of mine with my on-going pledge that I had not as yet given up the search. In a somewhat soothing mood, more for Harry's benefit than for anyone else's at the table that day, I quickly added, "But we mustn't give up, just yet! After all, miracles happen when we least expect them.... Actually, Eddie Lauder feels that maybe one of the local female cats has come into season, and 'Old Thomas' has just naturally decided to go 'courtin,' as they say. Sooner or later, he's bound to come home!"

"S-s-ure a-a-appreciate all y-y-your h-h-elp, Adam..." Harry Hopkins was saying, as he took a brief respite from the game he was playing to sit back in his chair and to gaze at me with noticeable sadness within his eyes. "G-g-guess its j-j-just the not kn-kn-knowing for s-s-sure what h-h-happened to h-h-im th-th-that hurts the m-m-most!"

I recall that not terribly long after Felix Lauder and his family moved into the area, "Doc" Owens and Angelo Balducci tried without much success to draw my mentor into this modest social circle of theirs. The group had been formed several years before that time there at the Grimsley's store. Aside from those decidedly more rare visits which Felix would be prompted to make in order to procure such important items as construction materials for repair work around the farmstead, his only occasional presence there amongst these other fine men always left something to be desired on everybody's part.

Since my dear friend truly enjoyed the company of others, I naturally came to speculate that this unusual standoffishness of his was directly related to Felix's basic displeasure at being forced to endure the company of Otto Grimsley's offensive wife. Although Felix was too much of a gentleman to ever put these particularly strong sentiments of his into so many words, I understood far better than anyone the extreme negativity that woman's presence always invoked.

After Mr. Grimsley so generously promised to display one of my colorful posters within one front window of his store, I promptly left to scour the area for another equally perfect place to plant this same vital information of mine which avidly promised a meager reward for the return of old Thomas. Unbeknownst to me that day, with what remained of my collection of posters neatly secured under one arm, and with my mind thoroughly engrossed upon the important job at hand, suffice it to say that I was not at all prepared for what was about to happen next. Not in a million years would anyone have been able to prepare me for my forthcoming second major run-in with that terribly dreaded fellow Shamus Grimsley....

Years before that particular moment, when I had again visited the Grimsley's place of business with George, my fearless young champion and I were understandably still quite ignorant of the overall meanness of this unforgettable member of that particularly unforgettable family. I well recall, however, that it was after living with the Lauders for only a short while that my friend and I were in the process of entering the store for the things we required for our first fishing expedition. While my excellent sporting companion went inside the building, I became instantly captivated at observing this huge brute, Shamus, squatting upon his powerful haunches there in the middle of the wooden boardwalk. Obviously relishing the moment, the nasty fellow was in the process of bombarding a multitude of tiny helpless ants with drops of what looked to be scalding hot water....

Needless to say, the strange sight of this more than pathologically odd behavior of his was quickly absorbed into my mind. As the young boy I was at the time I struggled hard to fathom the reason why anyone would behave in this obviously cruel manner. With George having so unwisely left me behind on my own like that, the ugly perpetrator of this unnecessary crime against the poor ants eventually looked up and angrily glared at me. Then, as if desiring to frighten me even more, he finally stood tall as he literally towered over me. Slurred among his angry succession of rude epitaphs, he shouted, "How'd ya like it if I dropped some of this scalding hot water all over your stupid-looking face!?!"

Before me stood the evil person whom I just naturally came to believe would ultimately be responsible for my own untimely death one day in the future. Shamus Grimsley's splotchy pox-marked face always wore a pronounced sneer, just as his sparse and thoroughly wild configuration of kinky brown hair, centered more upon the crown of his immense head, seemed to highlight the unpredictable wildness of his totally unsympathetic eyes. Yes, indeed! There simply was no doubt about it.... From that moment in time, onward, I came to fear this truly fearsome fellow since for me he became the epitome of the dreaded "boogeyman" who so cruelly haunts the dreams of innocent young children.

The more than sobering reality that this awful man dwelled within the same community as I instinctively made me ever-vigilant whenever I traveled anywhere—especially when I was alone. Normally, too, Shamus was hardly ever seen without his reliable shotgun which he claimed to be a "bona fide expert" at using. Along with this dangerous weapon that he used to indiscriminately terrorize the countryside—dependably intimidating both man and beast alike—he habitually carried a large leather pouch tied to the front of his wide belt which held no less than a pound or more of those raw peanuts from his parent's store, and which he always seemed to relish eating from morning to night....

With regard to the subject of the peanuts, Shamus Grimsley had for a long time already acquired a decidedly unique and rather telling habit. I do recall quite exceptionally well that this same trustworthy propensity of his for leaving behind the shells of those edible kernels, subsequently caused the trail of debris to act as his own personal calling card. So, in a particularly salient manner, this odd behavior of his tended to represent, naturally to my ever-fertile mind, a current new slant on the familiar Hans Christian Andersen tale of "Hansel and Gretel."

Sometimes I would catch Shamus popping several of those unshelled nuts into his cavernous mouth. Early on I learned to prudently observe this maneuver of his at a relatively safe distance. With this food source being unattractively pulpified as it soon was, this first son of the Grimsleys' had likewise acquired the interesting ability to separate the more desirable food stuff from its individual outer covering and would eventually go about rudely propelling this masticated refuse from his mouth, onto the floor, or ground.... Occasionally, believe it or not, he also became somewhat notorious for liberally spewing out that same ungodly mess into the abnormally shocked faces of others, just to further intimidate them.

It was no secret, either, that this unfortunate individual eventually grew to covet "Doc" Owen's little traveling companion, Zelda. Whenever the good doctor found a moment to stop by the Grimsley's general store, often to warm himself a bit by the stove, or to brush up on his checker game with friends before he finally left behind the general hospitality of the place in order to continue on with his busy day, there one would usually find Shamus—slowly circling around the familiar old automobile parked out front....

All the while that big oaf continued to eagerly contemplate our innocent little bird, she in turn remained quite carelessly perched somewhere
atop the roof or the hood of the car, and so both mentally and emotionally I had absolutely no trouble in being able to momentarily place myself
in the poor creature's same unenviable position. On at least one such
occasion, I watched with considerable dread as this horrible antagonist
of ours proceeded to slowly move around the entire circumference of
"Doc's" little car....

Usually choosing to sporadically hum a few bars from Stephen
Foster's "Camptown Races," Shamus inevitably came to that specific
part in the song only to loudly call forth: "Doo Dah ... Doo Dah!" as
if mindlessly attempting to punctuate the frightening prospect of the
wee bird's ultimate demise. And surely as God remains my ever-loyal
witness, unmistakably lurking there within his cruel eyes one could not
possibly miss the wholly indecent gleam that surely seemed to signify—
particularly to this conscientious onlooker—that within Shamus Grimsley's badly twisted mind there danced that mouth-watering vision of
a baked chicken supper, along with perhaps a side order of dumplings
and gravy....

Anyway, it was my beloved George who managed to finally rescue
me during that first unforgettable experience when I had had the misfortune of originally making the acquaintance of this awful tyrant. As
the big bully proceeded to come at me in a totally threatening mood,
still holding within his oversized paw the cup of steaming hot water
which he was maliciously using to slowly maim and then kill off the ants,
George must have been witnessing these actions of his from inside the
store. In a heartbeat my vigilant friend arrived through the front door
of the general store to stand directly between Shamus Grimsley and
me. With my worried heart still pounding away inside the confines of
my small chest that day, I gratefully observed my special protector look
into those dull yet thoroughly disturbing eyes of that brute to say with
marked confidence, "Shamus! Isn't that your unhappy mother that I
hear calling for you from somewhere out back?!"

George's brilliantly impromptu ploy worked wonders for both of
us that day. Being very much afraid of his mother, at the mere mention
of her name Shamus quickly lost the threatening demeanor which had
up to that point taken such a toll on me. And before George could even
utter anything else, donning a far more sympathetic countenance the
big brute soon went lumbering across the front porch area of the store

and quickly disappeared around the building in avid search of Cornelia Grimsley.

However, George would not always be around to help me like that. Very soon I was about to suffer yet another unavoidable run-in with this same ruthless character. Indeed, as I crossed the narrow dirt road that ran out in front of the series of buildings which basically made up the commercial sector of the small hamlet of "Peck's Station," and headed over towards the abandoned railway station hut to dutifully attach one of my larger posters to the front door, I was humming a little tune of my own to cheerfully entertain myself.

Underneath my light coat I was wearing a modified version of Felix's own carpenter's apron where a small hammer and a handful of stubby modest-grade nails were being stowed in order to allow me to properly be able to secure the posters I made. While I dutifully knelt before the locked door of the station-master's hut, momentarily wrestling to retrieve one of the notices from the modest grouping which I had just placed upon the ground, I heard a grating noise coming from somewhere nearby.... Just about the same time my acutely sensitive sense of smell finally picked up a truly horrid scent of something indescribably awful....

Slipping my hammer back into place, at least for the moment, I ventured forth to investigate. When I finally rounded the west side of the long-abandoned building I was forced to look with absolute horror upon what was being displayed before me, there upon the outside wall of that relatively minor edifice. Nailed to the weathered wooden boards was a malodorous collection of unspeakably brutalized bits and pieces of what surely must have once been different types of small living animals. Everything was haphazardly placed here and there, pretty much covering the entire area and where those telltale vestiges of these very things were now in their various stages of decomposition....

Dear Lord! It was as if I had accidentally stumbled into the secret lair of some particularly fiendish wild beast. Without a doubt, it was surely as if some thoroughly mad individual was seeking to make unkind sport of the sacredness of life by so openly displaying their profane handiwork like this.... I was struggling hard to overcome my strong urge to vomit, due in great part to the foulest sort of stench which was accosting me full force by now, and far more noteworthy because of my formidable sense of growing terror relative to what this senseless mosaic of brutalized dead animal flesh truly represented. Very slowly my stunned mind began to focus upon one particular area of bloodied fur which somehow seemed different from all the rest.... Then totally dumbfounded, while at last I was able to finally make some sense out of that same unique blue-gray fur which, in retrospect, was already all too familiar to me, I quickly gazed up at the top of this vast collection of grotesque ghoulishness to finally spy what had once been the noble looking head of our poor dear old Thomas!

Who or what, in God's name, could have possibly been responsible for this hellish atrocity?! Words alone could not possibly describe what was currently coursing through the badly muddled labyrinth of my dazed mind. Presently, however, because of my rather rudely compromised emotional state, I was desiring more than anything else to quickly collect my belongings and to make my hasty escape. Clinging dearly to this worthwhile thought, I began absentmindedly backing my way around the far side of the building, instead of returning the way I originally arrived. With this unwise maneuver of mine I soon came to very nearly step upon the brute, Shamus, as he continued to sit cross-legged upon the ground, all the while carefully cleaning both barrels of his infamous shotgun....

"You, again—ya' little weasel!" this terrible young man shouted at me, as the upper portion of his huge body instinctively lunged my way, and his oversized paw attempted to grab my ankle. "Have a real hankerin' to hang your wretched hide in my wonderful collection of things, back there on the wall!"

Nothing else had had to be said to me—rest assured. With these uncommon words of such a grossly threatening nature, a surge of priceless adrenaline literally shot through my brain, causing me to turn on a dime, thereby just barely remaining free from Shamus Grimsley's bloodstained hands.... Not bothering in the least about my own collection of things, which continued to lay haplessly sprawled upon the ground by the front door of this same building, I quite literally began to run for my life....

Why I had not thought to cross that relatively short distance and head directly back towards the Grimsley's general store for help, I shall never know. But very much like a badly frightened rabbit, I intuitively headed out into the wide open fields that encircled us, somehow believing that my ultimate salvation lay in my being able to outrun my daunting pursuer. I well recall, too, that even though Shamus Grimsley outweighed me by a hundred and fifty pounds, or so, this dangerous mountain-of-a-man moved with the speed and forward momentum of some wild and totally out-of-control buffalo who had by now whole-heartedly involved himself in a relentless stampede designed for one.

Later that evening, it was none other than our dear "Doc" Owens who would be recounting to Felix his poignant version of what transpired next.... From the wide picture-window which was fortuitously located there within one particular wall of the general store, where "Doc" and those other good souls remained peacefully enjoying the more civilized society of one another, kind Fate eventually allowed the good doctor to glance outside just in nick of time to see me frantically dashing across the neighboring field, with mad Shamus slowly closing in upon me....

Hearing my doomsday melody loudly being orchestrated by Shamus Grimsley, all the while his heavy boots pounded closer and even closer upon the firm ground that lay directly between us now, I properly reckoned that this dedicated pursuer of mine was significantly closing the distance. In desperation I reached deep within myself for that last amount of firm resolve to be able to pull ahead of him, and to hopefully be able to remain out of his reach, but failed miserably.

The next thing I remember is being soundly grabbed from behind, there at the back portion of the collar area of my lightweight coat, and pitilessly dashed to the ground. I recall landing with such force that the breath was soundly knocked out of me. While I fought to replenish my needy lungs with blessed oxygen, Shamus made haste to place one of his huge knees upon my small chest, and in so doing chose to bear down on me with all his might....

Those were the very last impressions of which I remained barely cognizant. Such excruciating pain was now radiating outward from my entire being, all the while the wholly unwelcome sight of my tormentor's ugly face loomed close before me. There was also the unforgettable stench of his foul breath that was being hopelessly mingled with the indescribably disgusting scent of raw peanuts in which Shamus had no doubt recently been indulging. Just as my tender young life seemed to be slowly ebbing away, right before my eyes, the faintly distinct sound of "Doc" Owens car horn could be heard barking its ever-familiar: A-ooo-gah! A-ooo-gah!, somewhere way off in the distance, as the interesting and ever-challenging world I had only briefly come to know finally turned to the uncompromising blackness of complete and total unconsciousness....

But, as the conscientious reader has already surmised, I was not meant to die on that particular day—nor in that particularly wretched manner. With our ever-faithful "Doc" wasting little time jumping into his faithful antique automobile to promptly initiate my rescue, our ever-loyal Harry Hopkins volunteered to "ride shotgun" during the process. And I can only imagine how poor little Zelda must have fared as she went floundering about rather harshly, there in the rear seat of the car, with every rut that the well-worn tires of the car was being forced to negotiate.... According to several eye witness accounts, "Doc" had quite literally jammed the "pedal to the metal" the entire way.

With me still lying inert upon the ground where Shamus Grimsley must have so reluctantly left me, the next thing I recalled was the intensely acrid smell of strong ammonia which began emanating from the tiny amulet that "Doc" Owens snapped open and just as quickly placed under my nose to abruptly awaken me. After passionately waving away the indisputably helpful item that ultimately revived my senses, and also mercifully proved beyond any doubt that I could still be counted among the living, I eventually opened my eyes wide to look upon the gloriously friendly faces of my two dear friends. With the beautiful pale blue sky above, which was superbly framing their wonderful features, I well recall that at that precise moment I had considerable trouble deciding whether I wished to laugh or to cry.

Sometime during my desperate attempt to escape my supreme antagonist, I managed to hopelessly soil myself. Therefore, as a necessary prelude before actually taking me home to the Lauder farm, my twin guardian angels assisted me into "Doc" Owens little car as the three of us eventually proceeded on from there to Harry Hopkins' place—first to clean me up, and then to allow our good doctor to thoroughly examine me as he naturally insisted upon doing.

On that unforgettable day, although my basic dignity had been undeniably "beat about" by Shamus Grimsley's gross assault upon my person, this relatively minor scathing was not something that was going to be life-lasting. While "Doc" Owens sedulously listened to my heart with his familiar-looking stethoscope, and had me breathe in and out several times, he finally pronounced that, although I apparently suffered two broken ribs, neither of my lungs had been punctured by my recent ordeal. This, he went on to readily assure me with considerable conviction, was very good news indeed.

Next, to intentionally render me as immobile as possible during the next couple of weeks, or so; and, too, for the express purpose of having my badly bruised sternum, as well as the acute tenderness around my rib cage, heal themselves in a timely fashion, my kind and learned friend proceeded to bind up my chest with long lengths of snow-white bandages. Naturally it still pained me to breathe, but, all things considered, I was a very lucky fellow.

While I continued to be looked after by these good men, in turn I began considering my impending responsibility of having to finally share the terrible truth regarding Harry Hopkins' beloved old Thomas. The entire matter proved to be one of the most difficult duties of my young life thus far. How well I recall that after having wordlessly received the incredibly sad news from me that day, my valuable friend took a few quiet moments to honor the heartache which my carefully chosen words had understandably inspired. In time, Harry's own characteristically generous response to me was, "N-n-naturally I'll c-c-continue to m-m-iss my Th-th-thomas ... b-b-but had anything h-h-happened to y-y-you, A-a-adam, I s-s-should have r-r-remained forever u-u-unconsolable!"

After "Doc" and I bid Harry Hopkins farewell, we traveled home to the Lauder farm where Felix and "Doc" Owens immediately lodged a strong formal complaint with Sheriff Parker regarding this recent trouble with Shamus Grimsley. After all, it was fairly clear that had not the good doctor and Mr. Hopkins jumped into the car when they did to travel posthaste down the modest embankment which bordered the Grimsley's store, and then out across the open fields in hot pursuit of you know who, this story might well have been written by someone else.

That same night, just before "Doc" consented to stay for supper, and while all of us patiently waited for Emma Lauder to place the finishing touches upon the fine meal she was in the process of preparing, our cheerful visitor decided to entertain the family with a new trick "Zelda" had recently learned.

With Charlie kindly retrieving his large second-hand radio from his room upstairs and placing it safely upon one top step of the back porch area of the house so that its fairly short cord could be plugged into the appropriate wall socket there in the anteroom just above, "Doc" momentarily fiddled around with the dial of this electronic marvel, apparently trying to locate a particular station. Finally having properly honed in upon the channel of his choice, a notably rousing display of gospel music was presently flowing forth into the stillness of the heretofore peaceful evening. No sooner had the music come to be—with its marvelous hand-clapping and equally contagious foot-stomping rhythms, when that amazing little "Zelda's" much more nonchalant demeanor radically changed to where she began to actually strut around near where the antique car was parked below, much to the collective enthrallment of our happy group....

To prove a point, some moments later "Doc" just as quickly turned off the radio and with this unexpected behavior of his "Zelda" instantly ceased her dancing to fly up the three steps of the back porch and begin wildly pecking at the top of the radio's sturdy metallic covering.... With this relentless attack of hers, where she would stop at modest intervals just long enough to turn her head in "chicken-fashion" to stare at the now silent object, one could only presume that she was thoroughly put off by this rudeness on our part and was insisting that the music promptly reappear. To finally conclude what he had been telling us all along about his remarkably talented bird, "Doc" swiftly reached over to turn on the "music box" and with this welcomed motion his little clown—or his "holy chicken," as we decided to affectionately dub that wee traveling companion of his—went about fervently replicating her dance movements all over again.

How we all laughed that night.... Speaking for myself, especially, how wonderful it was to be able to laugh at all.

After supper was over, both Felix and Emma Lauder, several of their children, and I cheerfully walked "Doc" Owens to his automobile. Before I had a chance to thank him again for all that he had obviously done for me on that miraculous day, as if reading my mind the good doctor gently placed one of his arms around my shoulders to say with pronounced sobriety, "From now on, Adam, please stay away from that troublemaker, Shamus Grimsley. Some day that exceedingly sociopathic individual is bound to come to some serious no-good!"

Alas! Little did any of us understand just how prophetic that somber pronouncement of our excellent friend would prove to be. Never could "Doc" Owens and the rest of us have possibly guessed what unbelievable heartache Fate ultimately had in store for us.

20.

W**HAT IS MAN?** Is there a God? If not—if humanity's time-honored concept that a Supreme Being does exist is willfully negated, what are the overwhelming personal and collective ramifications of atheism? What, too, is the acceptable relationship between man towards his fellow man? Men towards women? Parents towards children? Likewise, how does the essential ethos inherent in a strong family life directly reflect upon a person's role in society? Upon human society as a whole? These are several of the deeply-rooted and highly provocative questions which have so often been posed by the more sensitive and imaginative minds within every culture, and throughout each and every succeeding generation of human history—and, more notably, during those often critical periods which are plagued with their seemingly endless turmoil and strife.

Indeed, these same alluring questions are also ultimately postulated by the great Tolstoy, himself, within the many chapters of his literary masterpiece, *Anna Karenina.* This thought-provoking historical and philosophical perspective of nineteenth-century Russian mores, remains nothing less than a substantially poignant venue of the more universally held aspects of the "human condition"—both past, and present. This highly laudable work of fiction finally came to be around the time of Russia's Emancipation of the Serfs, occurring in 1861. Perhaps not inconsequentially, either, just around this same time Tsarist Russia was becoming hopelessly embroiled within its staggering political, economic, and social turmoil that was to eventually spawn her infamous revolution.

It should also be remembered that during these very years Russia's social structure was fundamentally half-feudal and half-capitalist, an interesting albeit unstable condition which prompted an even greater state of flux where intense struggle and subsequent changes in thinking began to take root. The educated masses, for example, were beginning to quickly absorb the more notable works from our Western culture which naturally included ideas relevant to French literature, as well as German philosophy. This same intellectually hungry group of people also developed a penchant for what America had to offer, namely in the passionately altruistic writings of Abraham Lincoln.

Tolstoy's own considerably creative insight intended that his tragic character of Anna Karenina be the symbolic representation of humanity. Succeeding generations of eager readers who embark upon their own private excursions into this particular work's significance have been quickly introduced to the story's more adroit theme, and by the author's honest pronouncement, that abruptly states in the first line of the first chapter: "Happy families are all alike; every unhappy family is unhappy in its own way." Focusing upon this worthy idea, at the moment, and choosing to further expand upon it in a certain sense, this humble storyteller feels compelled to contribute a thought or two of his own relevant to this same rather intriguing edict by also confidently stating: By its very nature, which remains ever-fluid, and, therefore, ever-challenging, even the happiest of families may be deemed dysfunctional in some respect. Whether that greatly esteemed Russian sage might readily agree with me, or not, what it all really boils down to is merely a matter of degree....

Maintaining healthy and viable human relationships, even on the most basic level, is often very hard work. This fact tends to be significantly more magnified by that curiously innate and characteristically detrimental attitude which, for lack of a more substantial expression, this storyteller chooses to refer to as "the avoidance factor." Within the normal day-to-day interpersonal dynamics of any family, this same "abstract interaction" frequently inspires the group's various components to sadly neglect meeting both the large, as well as the small, issues head on.

To be able to "cut to the chase," as it were, has long been considered an art with respect to any worthwhile endeavor. This remains true whether one is speaking in the personal sense, or in the professional. Quite simply put: to be able to consistently, and to concisely, and to honestly, be able to say what one means, and also to faithfully mean what one says, often becomes a genuinely rare experience—not unlike discovering row upon row of little pearly-white teeth inside the beak of a canary.

By consciously or unconsciously perpetrating some gingerly intellectual dance configuration which generally leads one over, and around, and between any worthwhile matter up for discussion, what often happens and usually with a marvelous sense of adeptness is that one or more individuals are able to purposely avoid satisfactorily addressing a particular issue at all. Sadly, too, with this undesirable behavior, is it any wonder that people are given to misunderstanding one another, and on a regular basis? Is it any wonder, given the reality than none of us are mind-readers, that there are not more self-imposed stumbling blocks found along that frequently difficult road to a more perfect understanding with regard to decent human interaction and all that this naturally engenders?

Fundamentally speaking it remains no accident, either, that marriage remains the most challenging relationship of all. In fact, this sacred union is frequently compared to "a trial by fire." My dear mentor used to believe that because there are no perfect people there are understandably no perfect marriages, merely strong people who somehow manage to endure....

Having already learned a good deal myself concerning those valuable intricacies of living and loving, it has finally occurred to me that my friend's overall perspective regarding these same superlative subjects was not one steeped in the vagaries of self-pity, nor in any sort of bitterness, either.... Rather, his thinking evolved into a laudable philosophical outlook that was basically straightforward and totally honest in every sense.

With this in mind, lest the more untutored student of Life be led to erroneously believe that the relatively tranquil atmosphere within the Lauder household remained unburdened in this respect, it now becomes the sole responsibility of this more astute and highly sympathetic witness to state the basic truth of the situation, without any attempt at all to cruelly embarrass anyone concerned. Remembering as I always do that Felix Lauder greatly respected the truth of any situation, naturally I take heart in believing that he would have generously urged me to speak about these same personal incidents which had once so unavoidably, and so significantly, impacted upon our family life.... Surely by openly sharing such experiences with others, regarding those occasionally violent eruptions which tended to help define the true nature of this particular family—in other words, by sensitively probing those inescapable ups and downs inherent within the powerful human dynamics of living and loving, an enriching sort of kinship is bound to evolve between reader and writer.

Since the mere concept of strong familial ties, as well as its far more desirable reality, remain profoundly sacred, one might realistically compare the family unit to a small sovereign country which must always be defended at any cost. Likewise, it becomes imperative that the "constitutional laws" governing any small "country" should be firmly established from the beginning. Ideally these same laws should always be based upon nothing less than a dependable code of ethics faithfully implemented by the governing body referred to, in most cases, as the parents. This strong covenant, moreover, is intended to help guide and protect the integrity of the unit and to further assure its continuing survival.

Over the years it has been my rather keen observation—and, I might add, with very little exception—that within nearly every family where there are several children one will almost always find a particular member that is far needier than all the rest.... And so, within that remarkable Lauder clan, this particular child happened to be Albert Lauder.

Whenever I think back upon this special member of that special family—for, truly, each and every person became just that to me, I recall a sympathetic youth, as well as an even more complex young man, who was often so reserved and at times so emotionally withdrawn that one barely knew he was present among us. Quite naturally in a fervent attempt to keep this particular son of theirs within the fold, so to speak, Felix would often go out of his way to help initiate various interactions with this son, no doubt hoping to entice his interest in the group's day-to-day life.

My basic impression of Albert—or "Berty," as his brothers and sisters and I liked to refer to him—was of his being a truly sensitive person who only wished to establish for himself a modest niche of some sort which on the one hand allowed him to remain slightly apart from the family, without being totally free of the body's somewhat pervasive demands on the other. In many ways this obstinate son eventually evolved into a "loner" by choice. This standoffish behavior of his eventually became a real source of emotional pain for his parents, particularly for his father.

Although I remain at a loss to completely understand the complex mechanism that obviously triggered this ongoing behavior on "Berty's" part, in time I began to speculate that some of it might have been due to an unconscious effort to obtain the substantial love and attention that he naturally craved from his parents by actually promoting this less than desirable interaction—much as if he were "hell-bent" upon testing their allegiance to him every chance he could. I developed a real sense, too, that because of an innate feeling of inadequacy on his part, this particular son feared being placed in the "limelight" where he would be obliged to compete on a more or less daily basis with all his other siblings for the admiration and respect of the parents.... Perhaps he believed that in the end he might somehow fail to measure up to those other dynamic personalities, and to what he surely must have perceived as their already impressive list of amazing accomplishments.

But to my dependably honest way of thinking "Bashful Berty," as everyone took to lovingly nickname him, possessed his own "spiritual aura"—his own more gentle talents, too. This slightly "wayward son" continues to live on in my mind as being an immensely kind and generous soul by nature, consequently eliciting my unending admiration for precisely these reasons. Actually, when one comes right down to it, there simply was not a single rotten apple to be found within the entire Lauder bunch.

During those earlier years of mine when I stopped by the filling station where Berty worked, I would usually be in the company of one or more of the other younger children. With him realizing that all of us would eventually be showing up to casually sit around for a brief while and to happily observe him tend to his normal business, almost always this thoughtful young man would save the bulk of the sugar cookies or pound cake which Emma Lauder habitually incorporated within his metal lunch box each day to later be teasingly passed around to each of us. This was just the sort of predictably pleasant game that all of us liked to play. I suppose the basic concept behind this charming give and take was Pavlovian in nature....

As the frequently rambunctious group that the others and I could be, we quickly discovered that we could invariably depend upon a nickel's worth of free "petro"—as gasoline was sometimes called, for the spunky little go-cart Berty constructed for all of us as a surprise one summer. Of course there were also those near religious moments, too, when a dime would never be denied to some lone panhandler who somehow always found his way to the tempting little convenience that was located on the corner of that busy country thoroughfare, as if that same downtrodden individual instinctively sensed that here was a truly sympathetic soul. Actually, the then familiar phrase: "Buddy, can you spare a dime?" became just as well-known in our neck of the woods as it surely was in all the big cities.

With a sense of genuine fondness I still recall that it was often Felix Lauder's habit to walk to the end of our long driveway, with his faithful "Hereboy" forever tagging along at his heels, to wait for this "prodigal son's" dependable return home on many an early evening. Then together they would walk side by side, with Felix predictably linking one of his arms through one of Berty's; and with Berty casually swinging his now empty lunch pail there by his free side. How it warmed my heart to see father and son slowly meandering up the winding passageway, with both sets of feet making their familiar crunching sounds upon the loose stones as the two of them became interested in discussing the happenings of the day.... But, as I was to sadly learn, no matter how emotionally needy one particular member of this family might prove to be, nor for that matter how much these exceptionally fine parents truly loved each and every one of their children, the sacred covenant governing the welfare of the entire body was destined to be staunchly upheld. Eventually, with his characteristic style, Berty would one day seek to challenge this important rule which his father and mother had firmly established early on—just as a family group we would all be made to suffer his cruel fate, on this same account.

Nearly without exception, I suspect, each and every family eventually comes to jealously covet its various "little secrets"—its own uniquely personal chemistry which becomes responsible for promoting its many joys, as well as its sometimes staggering heartaches, reminiscent at times of those similarly complex dilemmas powerfully illustrated within Ingmar Bergman's poignant work entitled: *Cries and Whispers*. This, I have come to respectfully understand and to thoroughly appreciate, is the overall nature of all families.... It becomes Life's necessary light contrasted against Life's unavoidable darkness, with this never-ending process eventually coloring all our years....

"Boy! Oh boy! Is poor Berty ever going to catch 'hell' from Father, when Father finally finds out what our brother's been up too!" This rather intriguing lamentation, of course, is what I was clearly hearing as Eddie Lauder was passionately addressing his brother Charlie. Both of them were just now passing below the open windows of the porch area of our house, on their usual way around to the back steps. I, on the other hand, at least up to this critical juncture in time, had been innocently and quite pleasurably immersed within the many pages of my most interesting new book.

To be more precise, I had just begun delving into Felix's newly acquired prize of a 1926 edition of Langston Hughes' poetry entitled: *The Weary Blues*, which, I suspect, he rather fortuitously left sitting there for me upon the small table near the door. Naturally this unguarded statement of Eddie's, during that peaceful Saturday afternoon in the early spring of 1938, had instantly compromised me by more or less having unwittingly forced me into becoming even the smallest part of their "terrible secret."

While I was about to turn seventeen that year, Berty was already twenty-one years of age—and, as the story goes, had managed to romantically involve himself with a woman who possessed a "strikingly

colorful background," as those far more outspoken members of our local community eventually came to refer to it. Needless to say when the
shocking details of the whole business finally came to light, at least as
far as Felix was concerned, all sorts of troubling things began to happen
there within the Lauder household....

Ruby Fabriano, the focal point of all this trouble, was reputed to have
been the longtime mistress of one of Al Capone's famous lieutenants,
beginning at a time when she was a remarkably young woman. Actually,
if the truth be properly told, over the years she had had a string of live-in-
lovers who for the most part were all members of that same notoriously
ruthless pack of jackals. With her indiscriminately intimate involvement
with these various men, in time she eventually produced a half dozen
children whose paternal ties remained indisputably vague.

Thinking back, it occurs to me that Emma Lauder may well have
known of these rumors concerning Berty and this particular woman
long before Felix ever got wind of them. Just the same, it was never
really a case of her having a "laissez-faire" attitude concerning this
important matter. No, indeed. She did, however, seem to be immersed
in a peculiarly strong state of denial, pretty much playing a rather reckless game-for-one called "see no evil, hear no evil, speak no evil," since
she knew very well how her husband would take to the inflammatory
news that one of their sons had recently formed an inappropriate liaison with this person of dubious character, and who, in turn, had strong
ties to the very scum our dear patriarch had spent a good portion of his
life trying so hard to avoid.

I suspect, as well, that Mrs. Lauder remained painfully mindful of
the more tenuous aspects of the challenging relationship between Felix
and this particularly difficult child of theirs. No doubt she greatly feared
the possibility that any sort of major upheaval, like this current one looming there upon the horizon, would eventually lead to a grand display of
early fireworks that year, thereby promoting some form of painful emotional estrangement between the two of them in the future. I knew only
too well how terribly forceful both of these strong personalities could
be—referring, of course, to Felix and Berty—especially whenever push
came to shove regarding some crucial principle. When matters finally
did come to a head, as they always would, powerful negative energy often resulted from some challenge that had been sincerely issued by that
predictable opposing force, and then subsequently taken on by Felix as
part and parcel of his obligatory parental decision-making. Naturally the
unspoken governing rule was to always weigh as judiciously as possible

on behalf of one or more of their many children, whenever the necessity arose, without forsaking his and Emma's mutual sense of unrelenting parental loyalty to the family unit as a whole.... So, as the reader can readily see, Mrs. Lauder's position was already a highly sympathetic one, to say the least.

"Miss Ruby"—or "Roamin' Ruby," as several of the more unkind locals usually referred to her, was a genuine "head-turner" as far as her looks were concerned. Back then, I guessed her to be in her late twenties. As an extremely healthy young man myself, even at that point, who never could or would plead guilty to being lax whenever it came to appreciating beauty in any form, on the two brief occasions only when our paths happen to cross, I quickly came to surmise that Miss Fabriano was someone who was not at all shy when it came to living life.... No, sir! In fact, she gave one the definite impression that, although she could never have claimed the lion's share of credit for having so beautifully written that amazing book called "Life"—still, it was fairly clear to me at least that she may well have partially edited several of its more interesting chapters.

Fundamentally speaking, Berty's striking new acquaintance seemed to be the sort of free-spirited individual who, both consciously as well as unconsciously, reveled quite shamelessly in that innately primitive sexuality of hers. This same powerful inspiration tended to honestly motivate many a virile man, and of every age, too, into taking a deep breath whenever she entered a room, and then swallow hard before instinctively moving to straighten his tie. It was this identical stimulus, I might add, which nearly always prompted the opposite response in most women, namely in causing nervous wives and mothers everywhere to seriously contemplate locking away those more frisky husbands and sons of theirs for safekeeping.

From the way Miss Ruby dressed and moved, at least, she reminded me of one of those notably "healthy-looking" women who posed so naturally for the various photographs that were always rather boldly displayed on the dozen pages of an annual publication of a certain calendar which Angelo Balducci habitually kept tacked up in the back room of his barber shop. With a smile I now recall that at the very beginning of every new month, without fail for at least a couple of years, or so, several of the Lauder boys and I would high-tail it down to Peck's Station, and then—not unlike the faithful swallows returning to Capistrano, we would creatively invent some sort of flimsy excuse to visit that same back room, more or less under the more noble pretext of taking an accurate reading on just how the truly marvelous art of photography was advancing on a month-to-month basis.

One exceedingly pleasant day, when I was in the process of making an impromptu stop at the busy little gas station where Berty was employed to return a special wrench he so kindly loaned me, I observed "Miss Ruby" saunter out of the office, and then slowly and rather seductively climb behind the wheel of her old jalopy of a car.... Before she actually drove away, I watched further as she confidently turned to wave at Berty who was presently standing in one of the empty garage stalls, at the moment, absentmindedly wiping motor oil off his grimy hands, all the while wearing a look of rather intense interest with respect to the person who was just leaving.

"Who's that?" I impetuously asked, as I dutifully placed the item I borrowed upon the work bench where it was always kept. At this point Berty had not bothered answering me, which was sort of strange since he usually did not behave in this way. Soon, however, I promptly decided to take a seat nearby, thinking that maybe if I gave him a few extra moments that he might reconsider and eventually consent to shed a bit of much-desired light onto this obviously intriguing new situation.

"Can't talk to you now, Adam," he finally said.... "Got to hurry and close up the shop early today, so that I won't be late for an important appointment!"

Naturally this modest exchange which Berty and I shared that afternoon, several days in fact before I chanced to hear Eddie's offhanded remark to Charley, left me with an unshakably uneasy feeling that I might somehow be standing upon the threshold of something truly significant; something, surely, that might be more wisely left alone all together.... Returning home later on I purposely resisted sharing the incident with anyone for fear that I might be overstepping my bounds and inadvertently causing problems in some manner for that one especially vulnerable someone there within the Lauder clan.

How Felix came to hear of the news of Berty's extracurricular activities, I never really learned. Suffice it to say, however, that not terribly long after that particular day occurred at the filling station, those more astute members within our family who chanced to witness Felix as he negotiated his way up the long driveway as usual and then hurriedly step from the old sedan he was driving, could not possibly have helped but notice the incredibly stern look upon his face. I, for one, was absolutely positive that I had never seen this sort of expression on my friend before—and, furthermore, I was quite certain that I never wished to see it again. Instinctively all of us braced ourselves as our obviously much-troubled patriarch swiftly made his way into the house, loudly calling forth: "Emma! Emma, where are you?! It seems that you and I must speak with Albert, as soon as he arrives home!"

On that unforgettable day, Felix waited rather impatiently for our unsuspecting Berty to return home. Instead of walking arm and arm up the driveway as they usually did, this time they merely walked side by side with both of them remaining relatively quiet and reflective after their initial greeting was proffered. Not having entered the house to wash up for supper, as they were expected to do, upon Felix's insistence the two of them chose to pass by the back steps as they traveled on to head directly out into the wide open fields behind the house. Watching this simple prelude to what would soon prove to be a lesson in high drama as everything continued to quietly unfold there before my eyes, I thoughtfully put aside the book I was reading and promptly made my way into the kitchen to see if I might be of some assistance to Emma Lauder who was still in the midst of preparing our family supper. In no time at all I discovered her slowly pacing back and forth across the freshly polished kitchen floor....

There, too, so thinly veiled within this proud matriarch's not-so-peaceful eyes I was also seeing an unmistakable look of genuine grief. Soon Mrs. Lauder took to absentmindedly wringing her hands, as she continued her restless movement to and fro within that small cluttered chamber. Every now and then she would change course to travel a few extra paces towards the first of two windows which afforded her the best view of the surrounding fields. Then at one point, having spied neither Felix or Berty, I watched as she spontaneously made the sign of the cross and then continued on to behave as she was doing all along. Not wishing to interrupt her rather intense train of thought, nor her prayers, either, for that matter, I went about meticulously setting the table as quietly and as unobtrusively as I possibly could. Perhaps this minor action represented my humble penance for not having been able to contribute to the presently precarious situation in some sort of a far more positive fashion.

Lord! Upon the not-so-distant horizon of our collective lives, a fairly substantial storm was slowly brewing. I could just feel it.... Yes, indeed. There was no denying it, since the truth of the unhappy situation fairly hung about ever so threateningly, noticeably tainting the surrounding air we all breathed.

Feeling totally helpless to stave off the inevitable, I sought refuge in my ever-reassuring conviction that Felix was a wise and patient man who would somehow be able to defuse the presently volatile situation by eventually managing to find some sort of an appropriate solution or middle ground for everyone concerned. But naturally, too, at the very same time that nagging and conflicting little voice that lived somewhere deep within the center of my brain was also firmly reminding me that, with Berty being a significant part of the presently troublesome equation, there would be no telling what the actual outcome from all this adversity might be....

Father and son remained conspicuously absent from the supper table that evening. When they did choose to return home, they arrived independent of one another, with our flushed-faced Berty being the first to angrily appear within one doorway of the parlor. Wordlessly passing through this room on his way to the staircase that led to the second floor, and while the rest of the family members and I continued quietly sitting about attempting to entertain ourselves as best we could, he began to dash upstairs with a grave sort of purpose written all over him....

In no time at all this terribly upset young man reappeared, toting a large military-style duffle bag which originally belonged to young Lewis. As Felix was just now entering the same room, obviously in a similarly shaken albeit doggedly pensive mood himself, without looking at his father at all, Berty quickly hugged his mother and then somewhat calmly informed her, "You'll be able to reach me at the garage, should you need me at all in the future, Mother...." Apparently unable to contend with Emma Lauder's genuinely sorrowful expression which these words of his had automatically elicited from the loving woman who had borne and raised him during all those previous years, he passionately added with a voice that had finally reached its breaking point, "I'm sorry! I'm sorry, but I just can't live here any more! It seems that I've chosen a life for myself that doesn't seem to meet with Father's approval.... And since he's never been able to understand me ... since he's never understood the basic reality that I'm not at all like the rest of his children, our rather enlightening conversation this evening has left me with no other recourse!"

Such hurtful things were being said, at the moment. Just before Berty left the kitchen to actually head down the oleander-lined driveway on his way towards this "new life" which he was apparently choosing for himself, an indescribably abyssmal silence quickly permeated the sanctity of our small farmhouse. That wholly unnatural feeling was as hopelessly thick, and as damnably dark, in fact, as any sticky molasses could ever be.

Whether to intentionally lighten this somber mood of ours with a millisecond's worth of comedic relief, or whether, instead, to merely express a more rare personal sentiment of his own which subsequently had not been shared with any of us before this time, but which was nevertheless also being deeply felt at the moment, eleven-year-old Stephen quickly spoke up to plaintively address his beloved older brother, as he bravely implored, "Berty, may I go with you?!" Only to passionately assert, immediately after this, "God knows that nobody around here ever understands me very much, either!"

With Berty having firmly resolved to live alone within the one-room apartment located above the little garage where he worked, none of us saw a great deal of him after that, except of course for Emma Lauder who insisted upon baking bread or sweets for him on a regular weekly basis. With this marvelous-smelling booty of hers still warm from the oven, one of us would generally volunteer to drive her over to the busy little garage, so she might personally deliver these small tokens of her undying affection to this inordinately stubborn son of theirs. Perhaps far more importantly, she might faithfully observe for herself exactly how he was faring in body and spirit.

Then, approximately two-and-a-half months after that terrible blowup occurred at the house—pretty much out of the clear blue, it was, Berty decided to pay us all a visit one Sunday afternoon. Politely phoning ahead to simply say that he wished to come home for a brief visit, somehow his family and I impulsively interpreted this as a thoroughly generous overture on his part that might conceivably lead to some sort of mutually-coveted reconciliation as far as father and son were concerned.... However, just as if he purposely chose to sabotage the moment, something outrageously foolish actually prompted him to bring along Miss Ruby and several of her children.

Whether this basically insensitive behavior of Berty's was consciously calculated to rub salt into our collective wounds, I sincerely doubt. After all, it really was not his nature to ever behave in such an overtly cruel manner as this. Instead, however, it remains my own personal theory that this desperate young man had chosen to "storm the castle," in a real manner of speaking, thereby attempting to gain entrance to a more neutral place beyond those thick and well-protected fortress walls of our fair city....

Perhaps it was his dearest hope, no less, of being able to stake his familial coat of arms there at his proud sovereign's firmly-planted feet, somehow imagining that this brave endeavor of his might shine forth and eventually force his inflexible father into softening his heart. Not unlike the exceptionally intuitive Cervantes, I have also come to understand, where human nature is concerned, that there are certain men who walk among us that are essentially far too gentle and far too naive for this world....

These same kindhearted "dreamers" often travel through life somewhat gracelessly, as well as quite unrealistically, attempting to risk all in their fervent endeavor to surmount the more common banality of things. Within their uniquely-wired romantic minds they continue to do battle with those opposing forces, somehow eventually managing to transform the everyday sordidness of persons and places into rare objects of shining beauty which, of course, only they are able to see.... Indeed, if this rather insane plan was truly at the bottom of this more problematic logic of Berty's, he had certainly miscalculated once again.

The heavy misting of warm spring rain which fell continuously throughout that entire Sunday morning eventually ceased altogether, just as the early afternoon officially made its appearance. Not long before Berty was due to arrive for his much-anticipated visit, the more tenuous rays of our usually bold sun began to initiate a familiar game of "hide and seek" within the less thick grayness of the cloud cover, causing me to optimistically speculate upon the possibility that all this might surely be a good omen for our Berty.

Long before the break of dawn Felix, Eddie, Charley, and I began diligently working the acres of empty fields closest to the house. As usual we were in the process of faithfully clearing and then rigorously refining the formerly sleepy winter landscape, hoping all the while to be able to remain in step with what amounted to our near religious covenant with nature.

If all went as carefully planned, several days worth of concentrated seeding would finally follow directly after that stage. This particular weekend our more regular plan of attack, as far as our collective work schedule was concerned, was slightly altered with Berty in mind. Normally Felix would have begun relentlessly assaulting the back acreage first, just exactly the way he had always done for so many years already. But on this special day it seemed that he genuinely wished to be near at hand, in order to personally be able to welcome home this often challenging son of his whom he truly loved.

I recall that the hour was just slightly past noon when Felix and the rest of us broke early for lunch. As we joined forces in the kitchen to dutifully wash up for the occasion, naturally with the happy thought of having Berty join us at the bountiful table which Emma Lauder began enthusiastically preparing for everyone's benefit immediately after breakfast that day, someone heard the sound of a car slowly making its way up our driveway....

While several of the now rather grown-up Lauder children and I continued to playfully jostle each other at the sink, Felix already ventured out into the anteroom porch ahead of everyone else. Not long after this I watched him eagerly make his way out the back door and then down those few steps, before anyone could snap their fingers. Candidly painted across this dear father's highly expectant face, I recall with tender poignancy, was a perfectly bright and happy smile.

In the past it became Berty's habit to occasionally drive one of his clients' cars home, but only whenever he was in one of the various stages of expertly tuning the vehicle's engine. Because he was usually required to take the auto out for its customary "road test" after the work was completed anyway, on certain days he consented to ride a little ways further just to be able to stop by the house for lunch. So, as one might imagine, hearing the sound of some unfamiliar vehicle making its way towards the house never really seemed that unusual to any of us.

As a mere side note to this family saga of ours, I particularly remember that several of the Lauder sons developed a real passion for jazz, beginning actually when they were all quite young.... Looking back I feel quite certain that it must have been Lewis and George who may well have had a hand in this, by pretty much leading the way in that wonderful direction themselves. Consequently, throughout those meaningful years when I was privileged to be a part of their extraordinary family life, I too became equally fond of this highly expressive form of music.

Without having meant the slightest disrespect I recall that young Eddie once proffered the interesting notion that his father, being an émigré to this marvelous country of ours, was more or less destined to remain a "hybrid American" by virtue of this very fact. In other words, because of Felix's personal history he was to remain a man hopelessly straddling the Atlantic with one foot tentatively poised within the country of his birth, while the other remained firmly planted within this new land which he came to so passionately call his own.

Felix and Emma Lauder's many children, on the other hand, all of whom had pretty much been raised entirely within this unique culture of ours, naturally felt compelled to enthusiastically focus upon the endless new stimuli that continuously came their way. From the very beginning this similar yet far more modern and highly energizing principle seemed to induce each of the youngsters to learn to stand proudly upon both their feet which unmistakenly remained firmly planted in this inspiring land of their birth. Perhaps this was exactly the reason why jazz was so appealing to them. After all, the music itself was like no other that anyone had ever heard.... Indeed, those uniquely wild and wholly untamed sounds of this grand new music came to represent the wild and youthful spirit of America itself.

Understandably, too, with each of the children having been religiously fed a steady diet of classical music from the time they existed "in utero," somewhere within their hungry and highly experimental young minds this ever-familiar idiom eventually came to signify their father's wholly distant and unfamiliar past. As a result, and opting to be thoroughly American in every sense of the word, they therefore sought to add to their noticeably lopsided repertoire by striking out upon their own and eagerly embracing these fantastic new sounds which boldly epitomize that same contagious spiritual energy that was, and still is, truly American.

So, having been helplessly drawn to this modern idiom, as all of us were, what had previously occurred with our faithful day-to-day instruction by Felix regarding his beloved classical music—or "serious music," as my dear friend always staunchly contended—somehow seemed to fall by the wayside especially during those teenage years of ours. More or less in deference to their father's more rigid stance on the subject of this "new-age music," whenever Felix would be out and about the farmstead—usually working in his beloved strawberry patch, for example, or simply taking those long pleasurable strolls of his out miles past our property line on some late Sunday afternoon—whenever one of us discovered that the coast was clear, then "all hell would break loose." With the knob that controlled the volume on our faithful old phonograph literally turned to the "max," those unequaled and totally blissful sounds of the great Louie Armstrong, and Bix Beiderbecke, as well as those really "scorching" numbers by Benny Goodman, Duke Ellington, and Count Basie, could be heard reverberating throughout our old farmhouse, as well as around the entire perimeter of the place, just celebrating life in general....

Our Berty, on the other hand, maintained a genuine lifelong love affair with the "Blues." Consequently, and always with his father being temporarily absent from the house for any length of time, those same lonely earthy melodies and accompanying lyrics from the then highly popular songs being sung by the incomparable Bessie Smith, Billie Holiday, and Dinah Washington would speak so convincingly to a listener's needy soul with their explicit messages that dealt so honestly with the basic human problems concerning love and sex, as well as poverty, and death.

And so it was none other than that hauntingly fleshy vocal prowess of Bessie Smith, herself, which was currently being broadcast from a

Chicago-based radio station—and subsequently being piped in through the car radio of a brand-new automobile belonging to one of Berty's many "well-heeled" clients which he briefly borrowed to return home. Yes! Quite unmistakably Bessie Smith's memorable vocal sounds were presently wafting up the tree-lined avenue of our long gravel driveway, loudly and fortuitously heralding what was to have been Berty's happy homecoming.

Felix had already made his way jauntily toward the cul-de-sac where family members and visitors alike were always obliged to park. Soon, however, I watched my dear friend swiftly halt in his tracks, right there at the end of the short sidewalk, just as our "knight-errant" was opening the passenger-side door of the car he had been driving.... In no time at all Berty Lauder was in the process of politely assisting his fair "Dulcinea" step from the car, as she in turn was in the process of so brazenly making her brief appearance within our lives....

With Emma Lauder and the rest of us silently gathered together upon the tiny enclosed back porch, we soon became quite literally thunderstruck at the unprecedented sight of what was happening outside. No one seemed to find the necessary courage to join Felix as he stood there all alone. For precisely now, as our proud patriarch was also wordlessly acknowledging the arrival of these same visitors, his ramrod-straight back was eminently reminiscent of a rigid and fairly unflappable sentry who was obviously vowing all along to never waiver in some forthcoming and emotionally demanding task.

From the sound of the continuous commotion which we were only at this second being able to more easily define, particularly after the blaring radio was finally turned off, one could only imagine that there must have been at least three or possibly four small children sitting somewhere in the back seat of the car... Of course with the bright glare of the midday sun's rays shining full force upon the clean windshield, thereby gravely distorting any possibility of being able to clearly view whatever was taking place inside the vehicle, all that could be properly discerned in the acoustical sense was a sort of collective yet overlapping wailing sound which was now freely emanating from each open window, much as though these same young vocalists were competing with each other in every possible sense.

Then, apparently without the least sense of embarrassment to herself, the Lauder family and I observed this physically attractive woman who was presently traveling with our Berty turn swiftly to address this phantom group of noise-makers. In what surely struck me as having already become a well-practiced response to this same sort of thing, she loudly shouted back at her unruly brood in her own unique method of reprimanding them: "Now, shut up! Do ya hear me...?! Or am I goin' ta have ta smack ya ta kingdom come!"

With what amounted next to merely a few seconds only of greatly contrasting silence—naturally only after this less-than-dignified mother had delivered this indisputably rude ultimatum of hers, she promptly turned back around to face her stunned audience.... All this while she proceeded to pull a bit frantically at the waist of the too-tight dress she was wearing, before finally standing there to mutely appraise Felix, just as if this moment's worth of ugly tirade had never actually happened.

Needless to say, with this excruciatingly tawdry theater that was being so openly exhibited at the moment, my originally tolerant and far too generous open-mindedness concerning Ruby Fabriano was fast slipping into oblivion. With every passing second it was growing more apparent to me that her overtly bad manners towards what I imagined must have been her own poor children certainly did not even remotely match her substantially healthy and vigorous good looks.... Deep down within her very soul there obviously existed something significantly shoddy and offensive.

After being treated to this rather impromptu eye-opening introduction to Berty's new friend, Berty chose to move away from the car. Taking several steps in Felix's direction, he quickly paused as he half-hesitatingly offered, "Hello, Dad...."

As I continued to carefully observe Felix, who was standing more in profile at the moment, I could readily see that he was no longer smiling. Very soon the many members of his highly distressed family and I were hearing him say, as he solemnly beseeched his son, "What is the meaning of all this, Albert?!"

Oh, Berty! Berty... For goodness sake! What in the world could you possibly be thinking?! What have you gone and gotten yourself into—anyway? And why, oh why, do you insist upon breaking the hearts of the mother and father who love you so much?! These, naturally, were some of the worrisome thoughts which sprung to the forefront of my mind as I remained standing a mere fifty feet or so away, all the while continuing to observe this very sad spectacle.

Without looking away from his father, Berty bravely but so foolishly answered by saying, "I felt that if you actually had a chance to meet Ruby and her children, you'd surely be able to understand—certainly far better than you once did—I mean, you'd know why her friendship has become so important to me!"

Emma Lauder, who at this point was clearly unable to bear anymore of the grave disappointment which Berty was inflicting upon all of us at present, hurriedly left our rather cramped little quarters. Not very long after that, from somewhere within that "sanctum sanctorium" of her small tidy kitchen—which, of course, had long become our very own pantry closet, her other children and I could clearly hear the sound of her weeping. With Eddie finally going to comfort her, I remained rooted to where I was standing all along, praying hard that something good might still come of all this.

Implacably stationed where he was from the beginning, in order to zealously guard the home which was nothing less than profoundly sacred to each of us, in response to what Berty had so naively just offered—and still without having addressed Ruby Fabriano in any overt manner either, Felix wasted little time in firmly reminding this obstinate son of his: "Although this woman and her children shall never be welcomed here within our home, Albert—and you certainly cannot deny that I have made you well aware of my sincere feelings on this very subject already—you on the other hand shall forevermore remain free to come home, but only so long as you see fit to observe my wishes!"

No doubt this brevity of words from his father's highly appropriate edict fell upon my young friend's heart, just as surely as any heavy hammer might also have struck some vulnerable sweet-spot there upon his undeniably hard head. Soon enough, with this rugged standoff between proud father and equally proud son looking like it was not going anywhere at the moment, Ruby Fabriano finally shattered the disquieting silence. Not so much for Berty's benefit, but apparently more for Felix's, she cooingly addressed our poor Berty, only to rather engagingly proclaim, "Look, baby, let's get outa' here! It's clear as hell that your old man ain't gona' change his mind about me and my brats, here ... no way! After all, once an asshole, always an asshole—that's what I always say!"

With these shocking and extremely rude sentiments of hers having been so openly expressed in front of the entire family, like this, even our wholly naïve Berty seemed quite stunned. Instantly swinging around to face the speaker as if instinctively wishing to state for the record his own particularly strong feelings regarding what this same churlish woman had just uttered, all of which was destined to actually bring some small measure of comfort to my already aching heart, Berty properly addressed this new friend of his by angrily retorting, "Don't ever speak about my father like that again, do you understand me, Ruby!?" Then almost in that same breath, and pretty much as an afterthought, I suspect, this good son went on to quickly add with a great deal of unnatural passion quivering within his young voice, "For that matter, don't ever speak to anyone I love, as you just did!"

With this somewhat unexpected angry pronouncement of his, Miss Ruby merely shrugged her shoulders and then turned to silently climb back into the waiting car. Moments later, she, and her children, and naturally our poor dear Berty, as well, could be seen slowly departing down the long winding driveway, only to eventually disappear from view. My heart felt incredibly heavy that afternoon, as I remained observing the lone figure of the man I had also come to love and to admire so much, just as he in turn remained silently transfixed upon that same tiny point in the far distance.... Both of us continued to watch as the automobile Berty was driving rounded a distant bend and eventually disappeared from view.

After Felix stood for some moments more, apparently lost in his own private thoughts, the once formidable spell which had originally grounded him where he stood was finally broken. As if to place matters into their proper perspective, he abruptly turned to purposefully walk towards the barn. A short while later the familiar hum of the family tractor was heard coming from somewhere just beyond that point, and eventually I watched long enough to see my special friend proceed out in the direction towards where the boundaries of his furthermost acreage began.... After all, that season's far more difficult work was still waiting there for him.

On numerous occasions right after that incredibly sad day, and mostly during many a late evening hour, I would invariably discover Felix sitting pensively there within the enclosure of our mutually favorite reading spot, staring down the long gravel driveway which ran along that side of the house. Usually at times like these a favorite book might be laying open across his lap, but he never seemed to have reading on his mind. Instead, I knew that he must be thinking of Berty—thinking of this hard-to-reach son of his who had not yet decided to return to the fold.... Consequently, the touching sight of it all never failed to cause my heart to hurt a little....

One particular evening when I happened to come upon my dear friend—resting just so, I quietly took a seat not far away mostly just to be near him. With both of us having put in such a demanding day around the farm, I speculated that neither of us really had much to say. However, finding me like that, Felix predictably reached out his hand to take mine, and quickly bid me sit more comfortably there upon the well-worn ottoman by his feet. Somehow a solitary wayward moth found its way into our sacred domain and proceeded to make tiny pinging noises as it continued over and over again to faithfully dart at the soft golden glow of the reading lamp nearby, naturally hitting the tantalizing torch's well-worn shade instead.

For several consecutive evenings, now, I could not help but notice that that same thin but exquisitely-bound book habitually graced my friend's lap. As a matter of fact, this much-prized work was a rare collector's edition of a translation of Turgenev's play entitled: *A Month in the Country*, which Felix had managed to happily secure for his own, back during those far more prosperous times when he lived and worked in Mexico City.

George once indicated to me that his father had paid a substantial amount of money for the distinct privilege of owning this small treasure. Really excellent books, after all, were one of Felix's consummate weaknesses. Although I imagined that this particular work's proud owner certainly had re-discovered its engaging lines time and time again throughout these many passing years and, consequently, had probably already committed the story line to mind and heart long before now, still on occasion I would observe our erudite professor pluck this special volume from its time-honored place within the family library and soon begin to pour over its contents yet once more....

That evening, too, upon the well-used turntable of our ever-dependable old phonograph, the indisputably beautiful notes of Bach's *"Arioso"* (*Sinfonia from Cantata #156*) were blessing the interior of our small abode. In the process this lovely music was justly ministering to my dear friend's greatly troubled spirit. Yes.... Very soon this same splendid therapy began to gently soothe both of our heavy hearts, as eventually I came to ask, "Do you think that Berty will ever be coming home again to stay, Felix?" After all, this basically honest and open inquiry of mine remained the primary subject that usually occupied most of the Lauder minds these days.

As our wee aerial acrobat continued to hopelessly fly at the lamp's enchanting light, all the while creating its own distinct brand of rather desperate-sounding auditory phenomenon, Felix sighed and I eventually heard him softly whisper, "At this point, I cannot say.... Still, all of us may continue to hope that this mutual dream of ours shall one day be coming true!"

Ultimately, however, the many members of the Lauder family and I would be learning one of Life's more painfully poignant lessons, in that it is quite possible to lose a child—not only to death, as was already clearly the case, but to that maddening spiritual distance which tends to be irrevocably established whenever two living people insist upon embracing such radically different mind-sets, only to finally fail to meet in the end. Much to our overwhelming collective regret, our Berty was never again to return to live under his father's roof. As it happened by the end of that same summer of 1938, one day Ruby Fabriano just up and ran off with a traveling salesman from New York. Up to that point, apparently, she had been living with her several young children off somewhere on the distant outskirts of town, like some cunning feline who instinctively takes to hiding her young and vulnerable kittens. When Berty finally figured out that his lady love was no longer part of his life, he properly assumed that, although she rather impetuously absconded with that stranger, she had also just naturally taken her children along with the two of them....

Shockingly enough, though, this did not prove to be the case at all. Several days after that sad and embarrassing event shattered our young hero's life—while at the same time the negative experience also eventually brought him more to his senses, some anonymous individual staying out at that same flea-bitten motel where Ruby and her family once temporarily resided dutifully reported the regular sightings of several very young children raiding a nearby garbage dump. Apparently these unfortunate youngsters became obliged to "pretty much scavenge around for sustenance in order to keep themselves from starving," was what our local newspaper's account eventually printed.

When "Doc" Owens was finally summoned by Bertram Parker and the other local authorities and taken out to witness for himself what was afoot, he found to his great dismay, as well as to his overwhelming sorrow, those same six small children once belonging to Ruby Fabriano whom she now had abandoned upon some mere totally irresponsible whim. According to "Doc" the youngest children were twin boys who were not any older than two, with the oldest of the group probably being somewhere around eight years of age. Seemingly even before their abandonment these youngsters lived for some while within their filthy lice-infested surroundings, and in each case, judging from their ill-clad and undernourished state, in time they might well have perished had help not arrived when it did.

A remarkably compassionate and kindhearted Catholic priest by the name of Brannigan, I seem to recall, who had long resided in a neighboring community and who was well-acquainted with several caring board members belonging to an organization which oversaw the running of a home for underprivileged children, finally accepted the responsibility for the quality care of these same poor little waifs. In time the children were all placed within respectable foster homes, thanks in great part to this same good man's considerable personal efforts. However, as far as our Berty was concerned, it would be taking him a mighty long time to even modestly recover from the unhappy experience of all this—for, not only had he come to genuinely care for that feckless woman, he had also become emotionally attached to her many children as well.

Eventually our badly wounded young hero was destined to properly heal from this life-defining experience of his. Likewise, in time kind Fate would be justly smiling upon him by finally introducing him to a thoroughly decent young woman whom he eventually married, and with whom he would be responsibly raising his own special family. However, during all those many years to come, in a certain real sense he would continue to remain a stranger to our lives. All too rarely would he be finding an opportunity to return home to the Lauder farm, even though I suspect that Felix never gave up hoping that ultimately things might one day be different. Basically, at least from my worthy perspective, I came to believe that in Berty's heart of hearts this particularly elusive son of Emma and Felix Lauder remained unable to forgive his father for having been right about Ruby Fabriano—and subsequently, because of this obliquely disingenuous behavior on his part, all of us remained the poorer for it.

With respect to these unavoidable emotional "ups and downs" inherent within our family life, it would also be fair to state that such extreme events as this gratefully remained few and far between. Mostly our day-to-day interaction with one another might be appropriately described as a sort of ongoing "balancing act." With so many robust personalities as ours being of various ages, as well as often unique inclinations towards one thing or another, we continued to faithfully love and respect one another, all the while fully acknowledging the undeniable fact that all parents make mistakes, as well as all children.

Without a doubt, too, each and every vulnerable young fledgling bird must inevitably try its wings and learn to fly away, just as each human child must appropriately mature to a point where they feel confident enough to eventually abandon the protective nest of the home and make their own way within this large and ever-challenging world of ours.... But unlike innocent little birds, precocious young children are usually able and willing—as well as frequently encouraged by their parents, to return to the comfort of the family nest, particularly whenever they discover that their precise time for soaring has not yet arrived.

Thinking back upon this particular time, I well recall that at the age of fourteen or so, young Robert Lauder reached a point where he became more than a little disagreeable as far as his relationship with his parents and siblings were concerned. Actually, though, in utter fairness to this fine young person, besides the substantial challenges that almost always go hand-in-hand with adolescence, young Robbie had the dubious distinction of being the only child of the Lauders to inherit Felix's propensity for having acquired diabetes. Because of this substantial ongoing problem, and therefore those relentless attempts by Felix and Emma—as well as our own dear "Doc" Owens—to be able to keep the youngster's blood sugar levels where they needed to be, Robbie's interaction with others frequently became a bit difficult.... Truly, sometimes the general atmosphere around the house ultimately became so testy, especially between father and son, that one suspected in many ways the younger tended to blame the elder for having been so unjustly branded by him with that same physically debilitating disease.

Once, in a notably difficult mood that managed to greatly upset the entire household, young Robbie Lauder became violently defiant with regard to taking his crucial insulin injections. He rebelled even further by angrily announcing to his father that he was going to "run away from home at the earliest opportunity." Of course with Felix's consummate wisdom that so easily understood this particular child's great burden, as well as the boy's critical need to one day discover himself—and perhaps to also rediscover within that same important process what it meant to be an integral part of his thoroughly loving home, Felix became inspired to meet his unhappy young son half way by eventually striking a bargain that would necessarily involve the help of their indispensable friend and neighbor Carl Reading.

With timing being all that it is in life, especially as it pertains to the fortuitousness of everyday events, one man's loss often becomes another man's gain. As it happened around this same time Mr. Reading somewhat inadvertently shared with Felix the disappointing news that he recently suffered the considerable loss of his fine young helper, Hector, who had been working there at the Reading's busy dairy for the previous three years.

Thank goodness that this bit of problematic information relating specifically to this endlessly accommodating friend of ours was carefully filed away somewhere in the back of Felix's well-organized mind. For soon the no doubt intriguing memory of their brief encounter of sharing was duly preempted to move ever-so-swiftly from the shadows, where it had been more or less peacefully hibernating, onwards and upwards to travel posthaste to the forefront of my dear friend's thinking. Eventually this same noteworthy idea became responsible for initiating a quick visit by Felix to the Reading place. It was during that same afternoon on the very day when all the terrible trouble finally erupted concerning Robbie's more acute frustrations, which by now were surely pushing the needle of the family's personal "Richter scale" to the unmanageable point, that our diligent patriarch returned from our good neighbor's place wearing a wholly confident expression.

Basically the ultimatum that was being presented to Robbie by his clever father amounted to Robbie living and working there at the dairy with Mr. Reading six days out of every seven. He was expected to labor substantially, both before and after school, for the then historically decent sum of five dollars a week. Consequently, as these relatively strict rules comprising Felix's "new deal" were being carefully spelled out by our illustrious patriarch, the critical point which was being continually stressed over and over again for the thorough understanding of our now far more subdued young man, was the vastly important issue that he must always take his insulin without fail.

Mr. Reading also faithfully assured Felix—no doubt sometime during the course of their initial agreement, that he would be keeping a careful eye on his new ward, especially as far as those important measures to help insure Robbie's continuing more stable health were concerned. It was also acknowledged by all the parties involved that should there be any problems whatsoever, as far as this somewhat "green" and untried worker cutting himself any needless slack with respect to his fair share of all the demanding work involved in the dairy business, then the entire deal would be rendered "null and void."

Until further notice, too, Emma Lauder staunchly forswore that Sundays belonged exclusively to her, as far as Robbie was concerned.... Indeed, before this verbal contract between Felix and Robbie and Carl Reading actually received its final blessing, our dignified matriarch promptly put forth this very edict which stipulated, in no uncertain terms, that this particular son of theirs would be spending his only free day there at home with the family, naturally resting up and dining on her wonderful home-cooked meals in what would surely prove to be an indispensable respite from the rigors of his ongoing day-to-day responsibilities.

In many ways what began easily enough as a rather desperate family experiment soon rivaled what is commonly known as "boot camp"—or a long stint in some daunting military school, although young Fritz enjoyed reminding us that such places as these rarely ever dealt with cow manure on a moment-to-moment basis. Actually, if the truth be properly told, the whole experience was absolutely the best thing that could have possibly happened, not only to our large family as a whole, but for Robbie most of all. Perhaps in his ever-abiding wisdom this is what Felix had intended all along.

During that entire long year when this Lauder son remained living away from home, as he did, and working extremely hard to save what he had earned all the while, a truly amazing transformation took place within him. Robbie seemed to recognize that the substantial faith his parents were investing in him was meant to test him, and ultimately caused him to rise to the occasion. By so doing, not only had he won a new self-respect which surely was not there before, but with this newly acquired emotional growth-spurt of his he was developing a far more cognizant attitude relative to his special place within our wonderful family, not to mention a far more realistic and lasting perspective relative to his ultimate place in the world.... In other words, our dear Robbie had come of age. Not only would he finally be returning to the fold, as he was surely expected to do, but he would be doing so very willingly and quite happily.

At long last a far more familiar feeling of genuine peace properly descended upon the Lauder home shortly after Robbie's return in that spring of 1939. There, newly planted at the base of this same pleasant sensation, was the wonderful reality that our young man no longer blamed his father for the undeniably difficult physical and emotional burden which he had inherited. With new-found insight and far more dependable emotional maturity, it was as though Robbie were finally acknowledging the keenly insightful fact that he and his father were nothing less than brave "comrades in arms," both diligently fighting the same up-hill battle in order to gain better footing against the day-to-day onslaught of their mutually dreaded enemy....

But this marvelously secure family feeling was not destined to last.... With early summer's arrival during that same year, daunting swarms of hungry locusts descended upon the region and quickly managed to devour everything within their path. Quite vividly I recall that these giant insects came shortly after the rigors of planting season were over—during that numinous time when those small vulnerable shoots of vegetables and flowers had just barely established themselves, before they were literally cut down and totally destroyed by those relentless invaders.

Because of this genuine tragedy there would be no cash crop for market that year—nor, for that matter, extra money of any kind. Certainly just as emotionally hard to take, along with the badly blighted fields which had not been allowed to produce a single mature plant, there would naturally be no usual harvest of fruits and vegetables for our family's pantry either.

Friend and neighbor all pretty much found themselves vigorously "bailing" together, so to speak, within that same leaky boat. Consequently, Emma Lauder would once again be expected to work her magic by carefully "hyper-extending" what was left of last year's bountiful harvest. Needless to say, at this point there were noticeably far fewer glass jars sitting upon those many shelves within her kitchen pantry, since she had already generously fed her large family throughout all the previous long cold seasons of late autumn, and winter, and spring.

The very second those dreadful grasshoppers arrived "en masse," I very vividly recall that one simply could not step anywhere without actually crushing a dozen or more of them at a time. They were, in every respect, horrific nuisances.

True to form, however, our little "Hereboy" soon developed the rather imaginative sport of collecting these highly animated creatures, just for the great fun it provided him. Soon it became his habit to secretly ferry these disgusting insects into our house, sometimes two or more at a time, to be promptly deposited within his ongoing treasury which he took to establishing early on directly behind Felix's favorite wing chair in the parlor. Had he consented to bring those highly energetic specimens of his into the house already dead, all of us would have been far more appreciative than we were. But for some reason this more sensible idea never seemed to occur to our spunky little dog, as the Lauder family and I were forced to do battle with those awful unwelcome pests—both inside and outside the house.

For some unknown reason that year, practically as if Divine Providence had had a say in the matter, Emma Lauder was shamefully late in preparing her potted treasures for display. Solely because of this I have since come to speculate that, very much like little children, even beautiful oleander trees have guardian angels....

Basically it proved to be nothing less than this highly unusual departure from her normally careful observation of the calendar which ultimately kept all those glorious specimens from perishing. Continuing, as they were, to peacefully reside all huddled together within the wonderful protective porch when late spring and early summer did finally arrive that year, there the fortunate trees remained still completely safe from the hoards of munching grasshoppers and the unspeakable carnage that was taking place moment to moment everywhere else outside....

During that particularly unforgettable early summer, too, Willy Lauder and I both graduated from our local high school there in Williams Bay. However, with the atrocious things that were taking place in and around the community, the special significance of that singular moment for us somehow managed to get lost in the mayhem.

This exceptionally difficult year would eventually be remembered for a series of "earth-shaking" events that further tested our endurance as a family. Most distressing of all, Emma and Felix Lauder's marriage would be placed for a brief while squarely upon that proverbial line, so to speak, for with the beautiful and totally innocent oleander trees acting as bait, an evil presence soon found its way into the sacredness of our home.... Totally unbeknownst to any of us, this same ominous force would also be sowing her evil seeds of a highly destructive nature which would eventually be maturing in the months to come, and to finally live on to indirectly inflict its terrible bounty of ruthlessness and revenge, culminating in an unspeakably cruel event that would literally be shattering many lives within our small community.

Was it not, after all, the seductive beauty of a solitary tree growing within the flawlessly beautiful Garden of Eden that tempted man's Fate, and in the end opened those damnable doors on to what has become humanity's endless legacy of struggle, and strife, and unbearable suffering? So, too, and more or less in the Biblical sense, it surely was no secret to any of us that Cornelia Grimsley openly coveted Emma Lauder's splendid trees....

With God as my witness, from the time that these same well-established beauties were thoughtfully placed where they were destined to remain for ages to come, one would now and then glimpse the frightening sight of Mrs. Grimsley's car sitting at the end of the Lauder's long gravel driveway. After significantly loitering for a few protracted moments more, no doubt in order to carefully study every aspect of the gorgeous trees, this cunning woman would eventually take her leave. While George lived, in fact, he and I had an ongoing bet as to how long it might reasonably take before the proprietress of the local general store actually developed the nerve to approach our house, knock upon either the front or back door, and then guilefully inquire about those special trees.

In order for the dedicated reader to ultimately be able to ascertain a far better understanding of how and why the ensuing chain of consecutive events transpired as they did, it might be fair to begin with a slightly in-depth perspective of Emma Lauder herself. Understandably what I am about to share is merely an overlay, in many respects, for it is my own sincere feeling that guarded people such as she are rather innately difficult to know on a truly personal level. And so my humble offering with respect to her more basic history was originally shared with me by her beloved son, George....

According to George, his mother was the second child and the only daughter of respectable middle-class Catholic parents who lived during the time of Emma's birth somewhere in the small town called Miku-lov.... This particular spot is located on the border that joins the countries of Austria, as well as what was formerly referred to by the world back then as Czechoslovakia. During Emma Porkorney's sixteenth year, she and her parents, along with her dearest brother, Rudolph, moved to Vienna—and there, within the immense shadow of St. Stephen's Cathedral, in what has continued to remain a rather upscale shopping district, they purchased and then faithfully ran a tiny elegant flower shop.

As the story goes, even from her earliest childhood young Emma embraced a rare passion for all of nature's exquisite flowers. Often she and her own mother would frequently enter local contests which displayed what they had carefully cultivated, causing them on more than one occasion to proudly walk away with either first or second prize in the process. George once confided to me that his father originally spotted his glorious young wife-to-be working quite diligently amongst several resplendent bouquets of pale yellow roses whose individual mammoth containers practically took up the entire front area of their modest-sized family-owned business....

Because Felix had only recently arrived in Vienna from Budapest, and had rather fortuitously found part-time employment as a modest clerk in some local business establishment nearby, with his having so little money to spare, buying flowers for himself—or, for that matter, anyone else, tended to remain out of the question. However, being the terribly awestruck young twenty-five-year-old that he instantly became—naturally with respect to young Fraulein Porkorney, in order to be able to continuously fan those healthy flames of growing interest which must certainly have already been present within him, all he could do at this point was to simply "browse about" quite endlessly within the family's newly acquired shop....

With Felix's ever-growing intensely keen interest in this beautiful young woman, he would sometimes show up several times a week to accomplish this very thing, causing Emma to eventually become thoroughly embarrassed with these overtly forward overtures of his. Actually this same predictable ritual of Felix's reached a point where, whenever Emma would see her star-crossed admirer confidently striding her way through those sparkling clean windows of her parent's charming little business, she quickly absconded by way of the back door, only to return sometime much later on when she was certain that the coast might finally be clear.

Regarding this sublime preludial "first movement" of one of Life's sweetest symphonies—especially where a passionate young man's heart is worn so openly upon his sleeve, like this, and where he is obliged to remain faithful to the integrity of those uniquely-inspired notes being played upon his heart-strings, one may easily imagine that Felix was not going to be discouraged, in the least, by this initially disappointing behavior of Emma's.... It is said that when one is young and fairly innocent in love, there is something incredibly "stimulating" in the "hunt" itself. It would seem that the more of a challenge that it becomes to obtain the object of one's desire, the more attention one naturally applies to the task at hand....

Having been only temporarily stymied by this present predicament of his, Felix planned a bold new strategy. Quite simply put, he would go out of his way to befriend Rudolph Porkorney, naturally with the fervent hope of being able to enlist the considerable help of this fine young chap who was in turn expected to plead Felix's worthy case before the young woman whom they both held in such high esteem. In the end this plan proved extremely providential to everyone concerned, since not only would Felix ultimately be marrying this exceptionally strong-willed young woman, but in the bargain he would also be gaining a lifelong friend in her wonderful brother.

George, I recall, always kept a particularly special photo of his mother tucked away within one secret compartment of his wallet. This fetching likeness of her was taken by his Uncle Rudy during this same romantic time of long ago when his daring young father first spotted the woman of his dreams, and had so impetuously fallen head over heels in love with her.... Now and then my dear friend would take to carefully extracting this small snapshot, there from its safe retreat, and then proudly share it with me.

Gazing at length at what George offered me, and with a good deal of real pleasure, too, I must admit, I would thoughtfully study the likeness of the striking young woman with her subtle hourglass figure which was bound up quite demurely in the fashion of the day. In this treasured photograph the very young Emma was wearing a high-neck dress and long sleeves that tapered noticeably towards her tiny wrists, and which eventually exposed merely her slim flawless hands with their unusually long and graceful fingers....

Since this mere wisp of a schoolgirl was not yet qualified to be placed within the far more reserved category of "matron," she was naturally free to wear her long thick dark curls cleverly gathered at the crown of her head, with the remaining sumptuous tresses cascading down over her shoulders, just as was exemplified in the photo. Although this telling picture of that once extraordinary beauty was done to perfection in the photographer's more preferred muted sepia and cream colors of the age, the soon-to-be Frau Lauder's sparkling and highly playful eyes literally jumped out at the viewer—not so gently whispering of a rare hidden passion for life which undoubtedly had not gone unnoticed by the young Felix Lauder either.

"Mother, please tell us again how you and father met," would be the familiar phrase that one or more of the Lauder children generally spoke every now and then over the years I was to share in their lives.... And if one just happened to catch Emma Lauder at precisely the right moment, frequently with a modest little smile she would patiently reiterate this same ancient tale, yet one more time, punctuating the ending with her customary, "Your father was the most obstinate young man I had ever met! The word 'no' simply was not printed anywhere within his personal dictionary. Finally, in complete desperation—if only to gain a moment's respite from his profusely romantic energy, I realized that I would have to marry him, after all!"

"Did you love him, then, as much as he seemed to love you?" was the pointed question Anna Allegra once just blurted out with an adolescent's perfect understanding that her mother would naturally continue on to so graciously enlighten our small spellbound audience with her own personal version of these things which surely must have remained close to her heart. Far more characteristically, however, with a certain profundity as if she were posting notice that this rare moment of sharing was abruptly concluding, that particular day was no different as Emma ended the charming tale of hers by quite matter-of-factly stating with a tinge of something which seemed akin to bitterness, "What could a sixteen-year-old girl possibly know about love...? What could she really know about anything, for that matter?!"

Eventually it was Rudolph Porkorney who graciously loaned his beloved sister and her new husband the funds to travel to America. After having eventually established themselves there in Chicago, in time Emma Lauder would be hopelessly attracted to the local garden society. Here interested women of all ages, and from all backgrounds, gathered together on a prescribed basis to share what they knew concerning the cultivation and appreciation of lovely flowers.

After the family took up residence in Mexico City, it was Emma who helped organize a chapter there. One imagines that within that amazingly lush semitropical region of the world, this lady's special passion for such indigenous vegetation as orchid, cacti, bougainvillea, hibiscus, and oleander soon began to firmly take root.... Furthermore, I suspect that this same love remained flourishing deep within her soul for the rest of her life.

With the comparatively rich social life which Emma Lauder must have known for so many years, she remained far more free to continuously interact with other women. In so doing not only did she greatly enrich their lives with her consummate knowledge of these same splendid hobbies, but she also enriched her own life with the decent fellowship of others. These critical factors become essential in order to insure one's continuing emotional good health. With this in mind, it certainly came as no surprise to me that the frequently lonely existence which tends to be such a great part of farm life in general had already taken its toll on her.... Undoubtedly because of all of this, a fertile environment had already been created that refused to recognize real trouble when it arrived in the future, especially when Cornelia Grimsley finally began making her long-overdue overtures of friendship towards this good woman.

With a sense of tremendous empathy I am also forced to state that within this more or less impenetrable aura of latent loneliness and frustration which had by now become fairly familiar companions to Emma Lauder, as the many years passed she inadvertently became lulled into being a somewhat willing prisoner in a certain respect. Because of the ever-demanding yet socially sterile life which she and Felix were required to establish early on for the general welfare of their family, how could she ever have been expected to properly weigh those more critical facts relative to the danger to which she was unwittingly exposing all of us, naturally in connection with her forthcoming positive response to Mrs. Grimsley's tantalizing offer? For, as everyone well knows, there was a meddlesome snake already present in the "garden," waiting to work her great mischief....

Chronic spiritual isolation ultimately becomes responsible for slowly effacing one's sacred life-force. Nevertheless—and speaking now within a far more sympathetic reality, depending of course upon one's innate predilection towards the omniscience of Life, this same miserable fact tends to carry with it a certain minor comfort which very nearly borders on the positive. Frequently traveling hand-in-hand with this rather rare and insightful wisdom comes the hard-won knowledge that within each of us a tiny seed of profound longing establishes itself from that divine moment of conception onward.... And true to the nature of all living things, with time that tenacious little kernel slowly begins to germinate, and eventually to grow and mature, until it is finally transformed into one's lifelong companion that all too frequently chafes the tender spirit as it faithfully accompanies us upon our entire journey from cradle to grave....

Few souls are ever spared this timeless and ignominious journey. Imperious Fate decries, equally, that this inescapable lesson embrace prince and pauper alike. Certainly, too, the inflexible rule which faithfully governs this entire process tends to be: The more intelligent and sensitive an organism—relative to its innate spirituality, naturally the more acutely shall it become destined to suffer in the end. Yet, paradoxically, one's inevitable salvation is eventually gleaned from the modest comfort of realizing the substantive truth in all of this... With the profound reverence that this rather sound philosophy generally inspires, one eventually becomes cognizant of the reality that one is intimately connected not only to one's fellow man—but, unyieldingly, to the even greater picture of existing as one does within this never-ending and thoroughly awe-inspiring universe.

Mankind's perpetual legacy of spiritual hunger may be likened to a thin golden thread that pierces each gentle soul through and through upon his or her entrance into this world. The soul remains ever-fixed by this strong and resilient cord to the earth's umbilicus. In turn, and in time, this vulnerable force takes on a life of its own. By becoming powerfully energized and therefore substantially elongated, what has finally grown into a thoroughly unique entity begins to weave itself through other sensitive spirits—those who presently share this planet with us, the countless multitudes of righteous individuals who previously existed in the past, as well as those incalculable masses of humanity destined to ever share our world in the future, regardless of color, or creed, or other finite particulars of any sort, naturally causing all of us to remain irrevocably bound together as kindred spirits of the highest order. It really never becomes an issue of "misery loving company" at all. Instead the timeless process produces a sense of tremendous emotional comfort which is eventually derived from accepting this uncommon truth. In the end, perhaps it remains this same compassionate philosophical treaty which ultimately becomes responsible for promoting everyone's natural redemption.

With regard to our continuing story, since there is generally some sort of a prelude to every major event, one day that initial volley came flying over our family's net, so to speak, in the wholly unwelcome form of Burtram Parker. This sorry individual's brief visit to our home subsequently set into motion that forthcoming and entirely unsavory game.

Thinking back, I remember that our illustrious "peace-keeper" often acted as Cornelia Grimsley's personal "mouthpiece," or "lackey," for one reason or another.... One afternoon right after Felix nearly ran into Parker's familiar paddy wagon, just as our good sheriff and Gus Twilley were leaving our driveway, my friend came into the kitchen where Emma Lauder was dutifully peeling a small mountain of potatoes, and pointedly asked, "Why was Burtram Parker here, Emma? What in the world could be wrong, this time?!"

Glancing up from this rather uninspiring job of hers, Mrs. Lauder seemed to be taking a moment to focus upon what her husband had just asked, when she finally offered as an answer, "Why must you always assume that something must be 'wrong'?"

At the moment Felix was obviously not in the mood for this sort of simpleminded banter. There was a frown upon his face, but at this precise juncture in time I simply could not tell whether it was due to the subject of Sheriff Parker having recently visited the house, or whether this present mood of his was a reflection of the far more important matters with which he was being forced to contend these days—and sometimes on an hour-to-hour basis.

With the disturbing reality of our failed crops already weighing heavily upon his mind, and likewise most recently with the advent of the highly disturbing news from Carl Reading that initially indicated to everyone concerned that our usual supplementary purchase of hay and grain might be abruptly curtailed—due exclusively to the probability that it was hopelessly tainted with some form of dangerous fungus, it was not surprising that my friend would be mentally preoccupied and perhaps even a little ill-tempered at the moment.

Days later our worst fears came true. With the dire pronouncement that all the corrupted fodder and hay—both at the Reading's barn, as well as everything within their three enormous silos, were most certainly being rendered worthless, a general state of real panic momentarily took hold of us. Poor Mr. Reading, himself, was in even more desperate straits than we were, since it was fast becoming very clear to all of us that he would no longer be able to feed his own substantial herd of one hundred and fifty head of prized dairy cows.

Knowing Felix Lauder, as I did, no doubt there would be a number of wholly wretched nights where he also would be getting little or no quality rest, until such a time when either he or our friend could come up with a proper solution that would adequately lay to rest this mutually threatening problem of theirs. So, quite understandably, our dear patriarch was hardly focusing on this lesser conversation between he and his wife at present.... Soon, however, as he approached the sink to wash his hands, he merely called over his shoulder as a sort of afterthought, "When has Burtram Parker ever taken to call upon us, socially speaking?!"

During this terribly worrisome time for everyone, both Willy Lauder and I found ourselves immersed within our own personal state of "limbo."... Although for several years we were faithfully employed by Mr. Dunbar and the Chicago Tribune on a part-time basis only—beginning early on during our grade-school days and leading up to and including the current time when high school officially ended for both of us, I supposed that with our daily work schedules having finally evolved into a far more predictably permanent status which would also be promising much better pay in the future, there was a certain amount of pride and comfort that went along with all of this.

Our ultimate goal was to be able to attend college one day. But at the moment, with neither of us having the necessary funds to begin to even seriously contemplate the preliminaries of such a big step, we pledged nonetheless to work hard for a year or two and to save the greater portion of what we earned in order to be able to help insure an even brighter future for ourselves. Faithfully adding every extra penny to what we each already put aside over the years had practically become second nature to both of us by now.

For as long as Willy and I could remember, every second Friday of each month was payday. That particular Friday—that same Friday, in fact, during which this same dialogue between Felix and Emma Lauder was taking place, had been no exception. So there the two of us sat, comfortably situated at the kitchen table, quietly and methodically tallying up our most recently acquired funds to eventually be added to all the rest of what we saved.

Merely seconds later, however, after Felix made this undeniably true albeit uncharacteristically curt remark concerning Burtram Parker, I glanced up just in time to witness Emma Lauder virtually slamming down the vegetable peeler which she was using all along, thereby causing several thin strands of rather limp potato peel to go flying off in a number of different directions....

Slowly drawing herself up, with what may only be properly described as a heroic sense of pride—not unlike some highly sympathetic character in an operetta by Offenbach, perhaps, this spiritually-wounded lady finally caught and then quite firmly held her husband's surprised attention, only to forcefully state, "And I suppose that it never occurs to you that I might well possess other stimulating talents—other than peeling potatoes, washing clothes, cleaning house, and bringing our numerous children into this world!" Obviously fighting to control her considerable anger, at this point—but probably not enough to actually allow herself to substantially weaken this more optimum stance of hers thereby risking the possibility of breaking into tears any minute now—while steadying herself upon the closest edge of the little table, Emma Lauder went on to inform everyone within earshot that: "For your information, Burtram Parker was making his usual rounds in the community when he stopped by to so kindly inform those of us who might be interested that several of the local women were getting together to establish a gardener's club.... Furthermore, this thoughtful man also indicated that I might seriously consider contributing to this same group, in a rather special way, actually, by sharing with all the others what I've learned about my prize oleander trees over all these many years!"

The overtly passionate delivery of these highly unexpected words of hers momentarily stunned us all. In a way, they were being delivered just as an excited child might deliver them, with a certain amount of breathless excitement. Presently, while Felix remained anchored to that same spot over by the sink, and with the clean hand-towel he was formerly using up to that point in time being held in a state of suspended animation, Willy and I continued to sit where we were deeply pondering these obviously near-sacred sentiments of Emma Lauder's which had so violently erupted upon the heretofore quiet scene.

There was something else, too. Warily my ever-dependable anten-
nae were beginning to pick up disturbing signals similar in effect to what
I could only imagine were the ominous vibrations one might normally
feel whenever two massive subterranean plates begin slowly inching
their way beneath the surface of the earth, thereby moving hopelessly
towards an unavoidable collision with one another.

Certainly the age-old reality that men and women are "wired differently," and therefore tend to communicate in totally different ways from
one another, comes as no great revelation to the reader.... Long have I
speculated that the Gods in their supreme wisdom—and perhaps as well
with their slightly sadistic humor, have decreed this to be so. Case in
point: Had that far more well-known Adam from Biblical lore emphatically yet quite illogically commanded his Eve to partake of the forbidden
fruit which was growing within that same splendid Garden of Eden, instead of following the letter of the law as prescribed, would the inevitable
outcome of human history have possibly been any different?

Men are by nature logical problem-solvers. They tend to be at their
very best when systematically presented with a series of details to some
difficult situation, naturally with the idea of solving that particular quan-
dary posthaste. And it certainly goes without saying, too, that this manifestly intrinsic skill of theirs becomes undeniably invaluable, since living
day-to-day in this complex world of ours is an ongoing process that is
endlessly fraught with one stimulating challenge after another....

Women, on the other hand, are notoriously blessed from birth with
complex skills of their own. One particularly noteworthy communication technique includes a masterfully coded language which often
eludes the more perfect understanding of the average man. Indeed, this
same impressive cognitive power is based on a legendary intuitive prowess with which only the female of the species seems to be so incredibly
well endowed. Therefore it becomes perfectly understandable why the
average man might become rather testy when a woman characteristically expects him to not only properly guess what remains lurking at the
bottom of some random difficulty, but sequentially proceed forward at
that point to attempt to find a viable solution to the problem.

This timeless gift of woman which seems utterly fraught with ambi-
guity is no accident either, since the use of its powerful properties remain
critical to insuring the protection, as well as the overall continuation, of
the species.... Having stated these important truths, one comes to ultimately acknowledge as well that all women, like all men, are not created
equal. The reality has long been established that within the hands of any
noble-hearted individual, regardless of gender, these individual modes

of communication have the ability to enrich the lives of others, just as, contrarily, within the hands of some cunning evildoer, innocent people in general may be made to suffer greatly.

As a youngster, and youth, and young adult, I had long observed how considerably gifted Felix Lauder was—particularly in being able to understand and appreciate others. That fact seemed to especially apply in his interaction with women and children. This rather rare ability alone placed him upon a very special plateau of immense relevance, especially for me, making him a true man among men. Perhaps his uncanny grasp of that complex dialect which women tend to prefer using was, likewise, basically innate within himself and no less part and parcel of those truly unique gifts generally imparted to the worthiest of philosophers, and artists, and the like, when they make a habit of staying in touch with the feminine side of their natures.

Within Emma Lauder's highly expressive eyes, at the moment, one could not have possibly missed finding a wildly volatile mixture of acute disappointment, mingled with substantial amounts of frustration and pain. After all, here was a fifty-one-year-old woman who knew what it meant to endlessly sacrifice for those she loved.... Quite remarkably, too, not once in all the years that I was to know her had I ever heard her complain, in any sense, about her life.

In my warranted opinion Felix Lauder certainly could not have wished for a stronger, nor a more resilient, partner than she. Naturally meant in the most loving sense, husband and wife subsequently reminded me of a couple of well-paired horses that were both bound inextricably together by a mutually deep sense of love and loyalty—with both obliged to faithfully pull the same heavy load, year after year, as they continued to travel down that long and winding pathway of life together....

Although it was undeniably true that this fine lady was no longer the sprightly young beauty of George's favorite photograph, still hers had become a mature womanliness whose comfortable well-rounded good looks continued to speak volumes with regard to the totality of childbearing, as well as to a particular Rubenesque sensuality that could very well have inspired many a great artist and poet—both past and present. Yes ... looking back, although I was a bit too young at the time to ever really be able to appreciate the total picture, Emma Lauder had evolved into a lovely rose in full bloom. Hers was an earthy sumptuousness. This remarkable quality, I have learned, frequently compliments the unique wisdom that only experience and one's acquiescence to the unrelenting forces that mold our individual lives choose to bestow upon highly responsible wives and mothers, particularly, who themselves have been tested so often and usually over such a long period of time.

At the moment, as if instinctively changing gears in the emotional sense, Felix went quickly to his wife's side. After having rather ardently clasped her to himself—and before she could resist, naturally, as she might otherwise have done, Willy and I heard his father eagerly confessing over and over again as he forced his lips against Emma's right ear, "Emma, I know how difficult—and how lonely, this life has been for you! I know ... I know ... I know!"

With this, Willy Lauder quickly exited the room. I watched as he eventually wandered out onto the porch area next door, probably in order to be by himself during this more difficult time. Avidly contemplating my own need to follow his impromptu lead and to allow this husband and wife these more intimate moments alone, I respectfully stood to do that very thing and began to quietly travel across the room. Just before I managed to make my way into the anteroom off the kitchen with the thought of going outside, I distinctly heard Felix say to Emma in a loving manner that was not the least bit patronizing, "You know, my dear, a 'gardener's club' would be a marvelous idea! Why you had not contemplated this sooner, I shall never know...." Immediately after stating this, and as if to lighten those previously more harsh moments with a tiny bit of humor, he quickly added, "But it does also readily occur to me that those other members who will be attending the meeting with you should certainly be advised to bring along reams of paper, as well as several well-sharpened pencils, owing to the fact that you have become a true expert in everything there is to know with respect to gardening!"

That following day all the contaminated silage for the animals belonging both to Mr. Reading and to the Lauders was properly discarded and then burned. Following this Carl Reading and Felix, along with the rest of us, spent several labor-intensive days washing everything down and attempting to further purge the immense silos with gallons of a properly diluted antiseptic solution to kill what harmful bacteria remained behind from the former process. After all, we could not risk having other stores of precious grain ruined in the future.

Sometime during this extremely hectic time for us, Cornelia Grimsley initiated her second move. Rather cleverly she had her dependable little cohort Edwina Dooley telephone Emma Lauder to propose that everyone interested in helping to lay the groundwork for the community's upcoming gardener's club meet three weeks hence at Mrs. Grimsley's own home. These rather loose details concerning that first meeting came to light when Eddie happened to be in the kitchen on this same day and chanced to overhear the one-sided conversation taking place between the two women....

Meanwhile, as good fortune would have it, Carl Reading's wife claimed a distant family relation living in Libertyville, Illinois. Since the epidemic of locusts had not reached down into this area of the country to work its powerful destruction that year, a heroic plan to save the dairy was promptly initiated. It eventually required the dedicated assistance of many generous-hearted individuals living in our community. During those first days when both of our families joined together to frantically pursue the necessary "clean-up operation," several genuinely empathetic neighbors took it upon themselves to make a number of timely contributions from their own healthy granaries so that the Reading family would be able to make it through those first desperate two weeks. What happened next, chiefly due to the considerable efforts of these same excellent people, was really quite remarkable....

As always, the key to any future success proved to be teamwork. Every available neighbor in the Peck's Station area offered their assistance and a substantial convoy of trucks and wagons of every conceivable size and shape were promptly inducted into service. With the Reading's three huge empty silos now waiting to be filled, Willy Lauder and I happily made our own substantial contribution to the cause by agreeing to loan Carl Reading the twenty-eight hundred dollars which both of us had saved for college.

A portion of this money would be spent up front to provide the gasoline for all the vehicles that were traveling south to secure these desperately-needed provisions of ours, as well as payment for the tons of untainted fodder which were going to be very favorably sold to us at cost. Although Willy and I would not be directly involved in all this forthcoming "hand's on" action regarding the huge transporting operation, due primary to the fact that we were now being expected to help run things on the Lauder farm, we still felt a sense of immense pride at being able to help fund this important cause as we were now both doing.

During that early pre-dawn morning of the day the convoy was scheduled to leave, Felix was in the kitchen hurriedly polishing off his breakfast when Carl Reading made his scheduled appearance in our driveway, enthusiastically manning his own truck and double set of wagons that were going to be used in this great effort of ours. With well over a dozen trucks waiting to join together to form the major portion of the impressive team, there at some pre-arranged spot on the outskirts of town, Emma Lauder was handing her husband a large sack which contained his medicine and enough food and snacks for the long trip. Felix responded by kissing her on the cheek, as I heard him cheerfully say, "Good luck on the speech you will be giving at the first meeting of your new gardener's club!" Then momentarily focusing upon the process of putting on his lightweight sweater, he absentmindedly thought to inquire, just as he took a moment more to begin tying up the loose laces on one of his work-boots, "By the way, where is this meeting going to take place, Emma?"

With what may only be described as an unmistakable sense of timid reluctance on her part, Emma Lauder hesitated before answering her husband that morning. After all, perhaps better than anyone else except me, of course, she understood full well her husband's strong aversion to Cornelia Grimsley. Soon, as Felix, several of the Lauder children, and I, watched Mrs. Lauder stand tall and take a deep breath, no doubt in anticipation for the reaction her words would naturally be causing, she finally offered nothing but the truth, as she bravely blurted out, "Edwina Dooley telephoned the other day to inform me that our first gardener's club meeting would be hosted by Mrs. Grimsley—there at the Grimsley's own home early this afternoon...."

Quite predictably, the mention of this awful woman's name brought Felix Lauder to an immediate standstill in his shoe-tying effort. Finally finishing this simple task of his, all the while staring at his wife with a look of total disbelief that managed to speak volumes, my friend's previously calm demeanor presently took on a far more rigid tone, as he asked in an obviously stunned voice, "Are you telling me, now, that this woman is to be involved in this new project of yours?!" Before Mrs. Lauder could even utter a single word in response, and while my friend remained adamantly shaking his head in angry disbelief, Felix hurriedly went on to add, "By God, Emma! You know very well that in the past there simply has not been anything that I have ever denied you.... But now—and certainly for the very best of reasons, despite your great need to belong to this new organization, I caution you to seriously consider the unsavory folly of this idea! Beyond any doubt Cornelia Grimsley remains someone with whom we must never seek to cultivate any sort of a relationship—even indirectly!"

Rarely had I ever seen my friend being more explicit than this in his request of anything. Emma Lauder, on the other hand, in a natural spontaneous response to this undoubtedly overwhelming disappointment of hers, was obviously fighting back the tears which were beginning to form there within her unhappy-looking eyes. And, as I have already attempted to convincingly indicate to the reader, it certainly took a great deal to actually bring this unusually strong and resilient woman to this point....

I was recalling, too, with a twinge of sadness that morning that throughout those many previous days whenever Emma Lauder's normally busy schedule involving those more or less mundane household chores allowed her to do so, she would pleasantly occupy herself by painstakingly placing little finishing touches upon the extensive dissertation which she eagerly looked forward to presenting at what was to have been that forthcoming meeting of hers. But with Felix's unwaveringly strong disapproval of this much-anticipated future event in her life, and certainly more than anything else Cornelia Grimsley's part in any of it—no matter how insignificant it might have proven to be, ended up being the proverbial straw that finally broke the camel's back as far as Emma was concerned.

Soon, however, with Mrs. Lauder looking as though she was about to offer some sort of a modest rebuttal pertaining to this same touchy subject, her husband rather uncharacteristically cut her short and quickly followed up what he had been previously saying by reaffirming his strong edict—in case she had not fully understood the intrinsic importance of the whole matter from the start, "Emma! Do please oblige me in these very important wishes of mine! Although it literally pains me to require this of you, I am asking you to telephone Mrs. Grimsley and to politely inform her that you shall be unavailable to attend that meeting at her home!"

With the unexpected emotional duress that these harsh and sobering sentiments of his were obviously invoking within him, Felix quickly took up the packet his wife had so thoughtfully provided for him. Without saying another word to anyone he swiftly left the currently upsetting predicament which had really only just begun to brew there within our kitchen. Eventually the others and I could hear the long-familiar music that my friend's feet were making upon the loose gravel outside. He was obviously on his way to join Carl Reading who was still patiently waiting for him at the entrance to our long driveway. After the men took their leave together, I observed Emma Lauder quietly enter the couple's bedroom and then rather firmly close the door behind her. Erroneously believing that this was the end of the entire matter, Willy, and Eddie, and I went outside to busy ourselves with our numerous farm chores....

Sometime around mid-afternoon of that same day, however, as I was returning to the farmhouse by way of the barn, I remained deeply engrossed in my private thoughts.... Whistling a little upbeat tune to help carry me more easily throughout that portion of my demanding day, I was instantly obliged to halt in my tracks. Nearly within the same heartbeat this decidedly light-hearted music of mine, which was being so innocently projected out into the world, quickly died a rather painful death there upon my lips. In case the reader is unable to guess what awful stimulus might have prompted this involuntary behavior of mine, the more than shocking reason is quite simple.... There, right before my astonished eyes and parked in the cul-de-sac of our family driveway, was none other than the truly unwelcome vision of Cornelia Grimsley's own shiny black automobile. With my being utterly stunned beyond belief, at this point, it would be fair to admit that I felt instinctively compelled to go over the possible ramifications of this presently dangerous situation very carefully within my mind.

As it happened, not terribly long before this same rude discovery of mine occurred, Felix telephoned from somewhere just south of Chicago—pretty much to apologize to his wife for having begun their day on such a sour note. Although his sincere contrition was not negating in the least little bit his ever-fervent resolve concerning his overall sentiments regarding Cornelia Grimsley, still he must have felt terribly heavyhearted about what had transpired earlier in the kitchen. Furthermore, he felt obliged to mention that he and Carl Reading would not be returning home until late evening, and that we were not to consider holding supper for him. So what I was naturally thinking, as I cautiously approached the house that day and ever-so-quietly entered the kitchen by way of the back door, was what a good thing it was that our guests' visit would not, at least, be coinciding with Felix's own return home later on that same day.

My fine upbringing under normal circumstances would have dutifully inspired me to make at least a brief appearance, in order to politely greet Emma Lauder, Cornelia Grimsley, and Miss Edwina Dooley, as they were presently gathered together there in our family parlor.... But with the way I just naturally felt about Mrs. Grimsley I immediately decided that had I been given a choice between doing this, and having the dentist drill out a deep cavity in one of my molars—excluding any benefit of Novocaine—then without the slightest hesitation I should certainly have chosen the latter. Frankly, even just contemplating the physical presence of this wholly unsavory person as she remained presently sullying the overall sacredness of our special little abode made my stomach churn rather painfully. Likewise, I could feel those silky fine hairs at the back of my neck begin to stand out in bold relief against my normally smooth skin, as an inadvertently animalistic warning of impending danger.

After pouring myself a generous glass of ice-cold milk from the large clear-glass pitcher which was habitually kept in the refrigerator, I reached into the deep ceramic jar for an oatmeal cookie, all the while wondering how long these two visitors had been there. Far more significantly, I found myself wondering just how much longer they intended to stay. Like a little mouse that was presently being made to feel rather uncomfortable in its own domain, I thoughtfully munched upon my homemade treat, all the while stealthily negotiating my way towards a similarly covert spot within the kitchen where presently I was able to obtain an unimpeded view of Cornelia Grimsley and her irritating little cohort, Edwina Dooley, as they remained seated side-by-side upon the sofa barely feigning interest in what Emma Lauder was currently telling them....

At that precise moment Emma Lauder was rather passionately delivering a summary of her speech, as I heard her cheerfully state: "So now, to finally conclude what I've been saying all along, I wish to state that with reference to assuring the proper growth of any type of plant—and especially in the case of my prized oleander trees, I've consistently found that rain water is always far more superior to anything else!"

Apparently these important words of wisdom which were being so selectively and so proudly shared with the only other members, thus far, of the newly formed gardener's club, were sadly falling upon deaf ears at the moment. It was fairly obvious to me that our two unwelcome guests were avidly occupied instead in hungrily devouring the details of their current surroundings. With what I feel obliged to accurately describe as an overt and highly offensive rudeness towards their genial hostess, those twin pairs of deeply probing spectrometers became lost in blatantly wandering over every millimeter of the contents of our large bookcase, and each finite detail of Felix's many paintings, as well as all the other personal knickknacks and memorabilia which had been so lovingly collected over a very full lifetime already, causing neither of them to even notice when Emma Lauder concluded her speech. Consequently, this fine woman was left standing undeniably perplexed over this strange behavior of theirs, until the two offenders finally regained some modicum of sense regarding the primary focus of why they had originally come....

For the benefit of our story what had happened much earlier that day—about an hour or so after Felix's departure and apparently after Emma Lauder was in the process of coming to terms with her great personal disappointment, she dutifully telephoned Cornelia Grimsley to cancel their original appointment just as Felix had insisted. However, being the ruthlessly conniving soul that this odious woman tended to be, somehow Mrs. Grimsley managed to turn the tables on this naive and thoroughly unsuspecting lady by managing to manipulate her way into our home—which, in retrospect, is exactly what she intended all along.

Stationed where I was and critically gauging for myself all that was taking place within the next room, I became cognizant of an unusually palpable sense of growing irritation which was slowly beginning to foment within me. My fervent impulse was to unceremoniously escort both these nosy women back to their waiting car, after which I would have felt sorely tempted to go about diligently fumigating each of those poor hapless rooms which their mere presence had so badly befouled.

As I feel certain the reader already knows, even the most innocent and uncomplicated surprises have a way of backfiring upon any playful perpetrator.... With this in mind, and certainly just as Fate had also chosen to decree, with Felix's unscheduled arrival home hours ahead of schedule that evening, needless to say, he was the one who ended up being the most surprised. Apparently the trip to secure the necessary provisions in Illinois went far better than he and Carl Reading had ever planned. Without a glitch of any sort the tons of rich untainted fodder were quickly loaded into the numerous waiting vehicles and then brought directly back to Peck's Station, with the intent of finally unloading all this booty into the empty silos....

However, just before this important last leg of my friend's overall responsibility to Mr. Reading was to finally occur, for some reason Felix impetuously decided to take a few moments out of this planned schedule of theirs to happily surprise his family by arriving home in time to preside over supper as usual. But with the currently unpleasant and entirely unprecedented situation being what it was, by the time our hungry patriarch quietly stormed into our kitchen where I was still "holing up," so to speak, it was already well past seven-thirty in the evening.... And, if things were not already bad enough, because Cornelia Grimsley and her sly little sidekick continued to remain locked in that wholly inconsiderate process of theirs by continuing to monopolize every second of Emma Lauder's precious time with their ongoing trivial chitchat which had not subsided in the least since my own arrival, it was beginning to look more and more certain that the entire Lauder family and I might not be having supper at all that evening.

Currently, Felix Lauder's highly expressive face was properly mirroring my own feelings of anger and frustration, as I heard him say to me barely under his breath, "I can only presume, at this point, that there must be some sort of a plausible explanation for that woman's car being parked in our driveway, Adam...!" Then as he moved even closer to where I was standing and tentatively peeked around to one side of me, he managed to catch sight of both our visitors. With them now indulging in their umpteenth cup of coffee and similarly substantial amounts of lemon cake, which Emma Lauder must have baked for the occasion, my friend went on to ask with a fairly irritable-sounding edge to his voice, "How long have those two women been here?!"

After dutifully sharing with Felix all that I knew concerning this unsavory turn of events, he in turn began to slowly pace up and down within one small tightly confined area of the kitchen, very much like some terribly annoyed caged animal might also behave. Earlier on when he originally entered the house that evening, I noticed that he was carrying that day's newspaper. Although this particularly benign behavior was not odd in itself, while my sympathetic friend continued to move about in that thoroughly agitated manner, he took to more or less absent-mindedly rolling up this collection of numerous pages of printed matter until the oblong item which he eventually held greatly resembled a small compact club.... Then while he continued to fretfully pace back and forth, apparently deeply lost in his private thoughts, he kept in time to this marching rhythm of his by using this same paper baton with which to strike the palm of his free hand, creating a low and quite formidable thumping sound, slightly reminiscent of troops preparing to engage themselves in some rigorous form of military exercise....

Finally, without another moment's delay—as if Felix had arrived at an understanding within his own mind regarding something important, I further watched as this good man promptly walked past me. He strode directly into our normally cheerful and hospitable little parlor next door, much to the overwhelming shock and substantial chagrin of his wife. While I pledged to observe all the forthcoming action more or less from a safe distance there in the kitchen, the justly annoyed master of our home purposely planted himself quite near where Cornelia Grimsley and her little friend continued to sit, still unsuspectingly nursing their cups of hot coffee....

By now, with every bit of Mrs. Lauder's normally healthy coloring quickly draining from her rosy cheeks, and with her not knowing whether to greet her obviously upset husband at this point or not, both of us watched as Felix addressed the three women by saying, "Good evening, ladies! I trust that all of you have had a full and very meaningful day?!" Then turning to solely engage his formidable nemesis with a smile that was noticeably strained, to say the least, he went on to announce to Cornelia Grimsley, "Madam, your dear husband and children must be quite gloriously adept in the kitchen!"

With these undeniably intriguing albeit totally ambiguous words of his, Mrs. Grimsley's eyes instinctively narrowed to small glistening slits, there within her pale and pasty-faced countenance. For some seconds more she continued to silently appraise Felix. Undoubtedly not having been able to fully comprehend the exact meaning of his somewhat cryptic sentiment, she answered in kind as she said, "Why, whatever do you mean, Mr. Lauder?"

"Actually, it is quite simple," was Felix's curt reply. Immediately following this, and in order to patiently explain his precise meaning to this wholly unwelcome guest of ours, he continued on to say, "With the hour being so late and, naturally, with my own wife having been thus occupied in entertaining you and Miss Dooley for as long as she has obviously been doing already, I just could not avoid noticing that our family supper this evening has not yet been prepared.... Consequently, I further conclude that perhaps your own family is either suffering this same form of gross neglect, or, instead, that you may have prudently taken to instruct them over the years in how to fend for themselves whenever such similar meal times come and go so cruelly unheeded—just as this one is in the process of doing!"

Mercy! With these sharply pointed words of his which were so uncharacteristically steeped within complete and total rudeness, Emma Lauder's current expression was truly pitiful to behold. To know and to understand Felix Lauder, after all, was to know that this sort of thing was never allowed to happen.... Never. On the other hand, as his many family members and I were also very much aware, whenever he was made to go far too long in between taking his necessary nourishment which tended to drastically cause his blood-sugar levels to go haywire, one could predictably sense a certain uncontrollable irritability swiftly building within him—just as now.

Had this indeed been the case that particular evening the entire business was naturally even further magnified, in the acutely negative sense, by having Cornelia Grimsley's unprecedented presence there within my dear friend's home. Without a doubt here was a truly excellent gentleman who always took immense pride in being sincerely cordial to everyone he met. Even in those worst case scenarios, which tended to be few and far between, he always managed to at least conjure up a mood of basic civility in his interaction with others. In any event, what I have more or less described was under normal circumstances.... And, lest the more sanguine reader need reminding, this particular evening certainly did not fall into that category of "normal circumstances" at all.

Cornelia Grimsley, I noted, actually seemed to be enjoying this confrontational moment with Felix Lauder. Her thoroughly caustic spirit definitely seemed to be in its element when attempting to make trouble for others. As she purposely prolonged her initiative to return her coffee cup to its former place there upon the short rosewood table, which also held the modestly-designed silver coffee service, along with several used linen napkins—not to mention a frightfully empty-looking porcelain plate that some hours before must have proudly displayed Emma's sumptuous cake, but which was now embarrassingly naked save for a mere teaspoon worth of dry-looking yellow crumbs, this ever-so-cunning evildoer was actually silently mocking Felix with her nasty eyes, while in her usually challenging demeanor she rather forcefully yet foolishly announced, "Look here, mister ... I'll leave when I'm good and ready to do so, and not a moment sooner!"

What happened next might have hopelessly shocked even the most seasoned spectator. After my long-suffering friend began to energetically finger the tightly compacted roll of newspaper which was still being firmly held in his right hand, I watched him swiftly raise the object high in the air, as a sort of silent salute, in effect, much as if he were the ancient Norse god, Thor, armed with his magical hammer.... With everyone breathlessly waiting to see what would occur next, it was nearly within the same graceful movement that Felix proceeded to quickly stoop down upon the floor and just as urgently begin to wildly rap upon that same space with this ingeniously constructed club of his, over and over again—and more than once nearly swatting Mrs. Grimsley's black leather shoes in the process, as he began to confidently chant over and over again, "Go home, you thoughtless and meddlesome woman! Go home to your poor neglected husband and children.... I say, go home and quickly prepare that unforgivably late meal for which they must all still be waiting!"

With this amazingly creative initiative on his part, Miss Dooley instantly gave off a loud shriek and then continued to further overreact by running helter-skelter fashion from the parlor, through the kitchen without glancing back, no less, and soon out the back door.... This, of course, had not in the least deterred Felix's consummate thumping effort, nor, for that matter, even slowed him down an iota. Just as if with this comically depraved behavior of his he was avidly seeking to murder hordes of troublesome cockroaches, or the like, in time these same unusually menacing antics obviously began to frighten Cornelia Grimsley, too. With every succeeding blow that my dear friend continued to expertly inflict upon the presently crumb ladened floor, all the while predominantly focusing upon one specific area that presently surrounded our now indignant guest's feet, he wielded this most unusual weapon of his with a remarkably fierce sense of vengeance. He seemed to be intentionally moving closer and closer with it, in a slowly narrowing circle, most probably with the highly promising idea of inevitably reaching Cornelia Grimsley's large feet before it was all over....

Personally speaking, I must joyfully confess that I could not have imagined a more glorious use for that day's edition of the *Chicago Tribune*. My, oh my! As our last uninvited guest finally decided to throw her considerable pride to the wind, no doubt in order to assure her overall physical safety at this point, she literally jumped up to escape from the room. From the porch area of our small abode, I further watched with acute fascination as she rushed out the back door, and then down our short sidewalk, to where her automobile was parked—just as her little cohort had done a few anxious moments before her. Not long after this I was at the point of becoming heroically inspired myself as I watched Cornelia Grimsley inadvertently give a wee jump with each substantial smack from the noisy newspaper, all the while Felix continued to relentlessly trail after her, barely missing the back portion of a shoe each and every time his club made firm contact with the ground.

Never before and never since have I ever experienced anything quite that exhilarating! To tell the truth, the entire episode really did wonders for my spirit that day. Furthermore, had I had the insight and the courage to do this very thing myself—hours earlier, in fact, I might certainly have beaten Felix Lauder to this most remarkable initiative that eventually aided both of us in ridding ourselves of these two troublesome women, once and for all.

Standing well behind her open car door at the moment, undoubtedly for better protection against Felix Lauder, the still noticeably apprehensive Mrs. Grimsley was currently looking unusually flushed. However, in a worthy attempt to gain back at least a fragment of her usually robust dignity she soon began shouting at her playful antagonist, as she said without a trace of compunction, "Do you know what you are,

Felix Lauder!? Well, I'm about to tell you.... Not only are you a thoroughly depraved soul, but you're also a Godless heathen as well! Yes, you are! Nothing less than a Godless heathen—mark my words. One day you'll surely burn in Hell!"

With these powerfully angry sentiments of hers Cornelia Grimsley made ready to duck down to enter her car, but halted in the process. Standing fully erect once again and looking directly at my friend with a markedly savage sneer that made my blood run cold, she added to this string of unkind pronouncements by loudly stating for those of us close enough to hear, "Someday I shall get even with you for all this!" With this last substantial threat she proceeded to quickly jump behind the wheel of her large automobile, naturally before Felix could threaten her in any manner again. After that she wasted little time in loudly slamming the door shut behind her, and promptly locking it immediately thereafter.... Lastly, without a second's more delay, several members of the Lauder family and I watched her put the vehicle into gear and then to rather haphazardly back all the way down our long oleander-lined driveway. By sheer luck the woman made it safely out onto the open road that ran past our home without damaging a single tree or terra-cotta pot in the process, only to eventually disappear from view.

As the reader might well imagine the entire community of Peck's Station would very shortly be learning of the harrowing events of that evening, not from Felix, of course, but from the two terribly wronged parties themselves. Actually each and every astounding detail became the talk of the town for some years to come, with folks of all ages more or less becoming sympathetic to the party of their choosing—pretty much as in the case of every issue of political intrigue.

In any event, I fondly recall that years from that day, in fact, a year or two after Felix died, I rather fortuitously came across a wonderful cartoon that I assumed had been presented to my dear friend by "Doc" Owens sometime after this same amusing incident occurred. Indeed, during what amounted to merely a brief return to the farmstead, naturally to pay my respects to Mrs. Lauder, I came across that same small folded paper tucked away in a volume of Felix's favorite poetry. Since both men embraced such a special admiration for America's late and great Theodore Roosevelt, "Doc's" entertaining little sketch depicted a likeness of our famous president wearing Felix's face.... Behind this caricature's back, as well, was being hidden a substantially large club-like weapon. Carefully printed underneath the cartoon, and clearly in our dear doctor's own familiar handwriting, were the words: "Speak softly and carry a heavy rolled-up newspaper!" Needless to say the basic message made it abundantly clear, at least to me, upon which side of our community's political line of demarcation "Doc" Owens found himself.

During that same infamous night when Felix was in the process of giving Cornelia Grimsley his unique and highly memorable send off, Emma Lauder quickly retreated to her kitchen. Throughout the otherwise silent abode, he, the other children, and I, could hear the rather disturbing sound of pots and pans being noisily banged together in what we could only surmise was the matriarch's signal that she had also faithfully taken her husband's far less than subtle suggestion, and was at present in the midst of preparing supper for all of us.

A bit later during our family's excruciatingly awkward process of dining together that evening, not a single word was uttered by anyone all through that first course of soup. Even apart from this strained silence there was an indescribably unsettling feeling that insisted upon lingering about, indicating perhaps only to me that there was certainly to be much more trouble ahead. With the lovely porcelain tureen not having been removed as yet, the way it usually tended to be just before the second course was served, Mrs. Lauder went about wordlessly placing the roasted chicken and parsley potatoes upon each of our plates. Other than the usual polite "thank you" being heard all around the table as this was being dutifully accomplished, still no one bothered to speak.

Immediately after his wife took her place at the table, Felix proceeded to take up his knife and fork to begin to eagerly cut into the marvelous-looking breast of chicken which was modestly situated next to his small spoonful of that evening's vegetables.... After only a few seconds passed, however, I watched him just as quickly put down his utensils. Looking now with considerable frustration at Emma Lauder, who was presently busying herself with the contents of her own plate, he somewhat angrily informed her as he said with a sense of profound incredulity, "This piece of chicken is still raw, Emma! How in the world is a hungry man supposed to eat raw chicken?!"

Because of the many unfair properties relating to Felix Lauder's specific ill-health, my friend often suffered from gums and teeth that would become extremely sore, causing him at times to require food that was soft and malleable—or at the very least cooked to a wholesome point where it was no longer rare or bloody and therefore quite impossible to chew. Emma Lauder was well aware of this ongoing problem of his, but with the present angry mood she was in herself, I had trouble deciding whether this poorly cooked meat that evening had come about accidentally due exclusively to her haste in preparing supper, or whether instead this was her unique method of getting back at Felix for having so thoroughly embarrassed her in front of that profoundly annoying pinnacle of our local society....

Felix, along with the other children and I, were intently watching and waiting for Mrs. Lauder to address this unhappy state of affairs in some appropriate manner. We waited in vain, however, since she continued silently eating, just as before, all the while appearing not to have even heard the cranky words which were recently spoken for her benefit alone. With this obviously rude avoidance on her part, Felix stood up at his usual place at the table and continued to address his obstinate wife, as he called forth, "Emma! What is the meaning of all this?!"

After our proud but stubbornly silent matriarch took to rather dramatically dabbing at one corner of her mouth with the crisply-ironed pale yellow linen napkin she was holding with both hands, she eventually glared back over the table at her husband to openly declare with a touch of malice that must have somehow rubbed off from Cornelia Grimsley, "Well now, Felix, you'll just simply have to do the best you can with the food that I've prepared for you this evening!"

Well now, indeed! Between this angry husband and angry wife hot sparks began to fly across that wide span of table. Into the bargain as well and as incredible as it all still seems to me, undoubtedly as a sort of grand impromptu response to everything annoying that had transpired since his surprise arrival home that evening, Felix passionately grabbed the pale yellow linen tablecloth with his right fist and exactly like a well-trained magician might do, he spontaneously attempted to pull it out from underneath all the dishes.... Unfortunately, though, where the practiced magician usually manages to leave all the dishes exactly where they belong—fully intact upon the tabletop, Felix's unnatural act of frustration caused everything to go flying across the room and in every possible direction. This, of course, included the rare Meissen soup tureen which soon noisily hit one wall with a particularly unforgettable thud, instantly breaking into a dozen or more random size pieces.

Good gracious! Is there anything more difficult to bear than being made to witness some unusually brash behavior on the part of a truly noble spirit, as he literally goes about shattering one of his very own important edicts, naturally intended to properly inspire a more civilized way of family life?! Poor, poor Felix! Actually, for that matter, poor everyone else too that evening....

Having instantly realized what my dear friend had done, and no doubt instantly loathing himself for having done it, a heartbreaking look of genuine anguish came flooding across Felix's formerly aggressive-looking countenance. Right before the people he most loved—and, perhaps even worse than this, within his own stringent thinking where his day-to-day quest for personal excellence was concerned, he had committed one of those truly unpardonable sins. By losing control of his temper in this way that moment's worth of substantial rage aptly translated into his brief inability to maintain his much-prized mastery over himself. Understandably this rare moment in time was destined to live on for him as his very own highly significant punishment.

Before Felix promptly left the dining room table in a thoroughly dejected state, and headed out into the moonlit fields for an unusually long walk to more than likely contemplate his recent volatile actions which had so badly frightened the majority of people who looked to him for guidance and stability, each member of the Lauder clan and I heard him helplessly beseeching us, "Please forgive me.... Please forgive this unforgivable behavior of mine!" Then with these profoundly sincere and wholly contrite sentiments of his, he and our faithful little "Hereboy" were finally gone.

Eddie, Fritz, Charlie, Annie, and I stayed behind that evening to assist Emma Lauder in her substantial clean up effort. Felix's stormy theatrics had automatically produced quite a mess. With our working side by side as we were obliged to do, no one bothered to speak at all. There was an undeniable cloud of terrible gloominess that was hard to escape. And so, after we managed to wipe down the dining room walls and floor, as well as to carefully scrub clean the upholstery of several of the dining room chairs which clearly became the other luckless victims of that same unexpected barrage of food and drink, the five of us stood by sadly watching as Mrs. Lauder went about dully retrieving every last fragment of the costly porcelain ware which once had been her excep-tionally outstanding wedding gift from Felix....

Each of those shards of exquisite porcelain were lovingly reclaimed and then stoically placed within a large hat box to later be set atop one particular shelf of a rarely used closet upstairs. Why these telling objects were kept, none of us could say. But sometime long after the dust had finally settled from this entire incident, I remember that Felix unexpect-edly came upon that same box and, too, its painful-to-behold contents. Although he went about laboriously attempting to properly glue everything together, his considerable efforts were to no avail. Sadly, it was as if these poor inanimate objects somehow had conspired together with the basic intent of forever reminding us of that unhappy time in our lives.

Returning to the house after his long walk, sometime during the wee hours of that next morning, Felix must have found the bedding his wife conspicuously left for him upon the small sofa in the parlor. As if to confirm that she had not taken to forgive his churlish behavior quite yet, their bedroom door was also firmly locked against him too.

With my dear friend's sense of personal dignity having finally managed to return to him during those long private hours of his wandering all alone, I knew full well that Felix would never have consented to be made to sleep in this no less than insulting manner, there within his own home. So having retrieved the decretory sheets, and blanket, and pillow, he and our wee dog eventually wandered out into the barn where they felt obliged to make their temporary nest within the structure's dry and sweet-smelling hayloft....

How does that famous old saying go: 'To err is human; to forgive divine'? Well, it certainly seemed that Emma Lauder was not sufficiently moved in order to forgive Felix his recent transgressions. Basically this still considerably angry lady was not feeling "divine" in any sense of the word. In several significant ways her husband's outlandish behavior had wounded her deeply, causing her to lose considerable face within our indisputably close-knit community. And this, of course, was not to be taken lightly.

To further punish her counterpart, later after he eventually returned to their home to bathe and to secure a bite of breakfast for himself, neatly strung across the downstairs portion of our normally friendly communal living area—as if to add more insult to injury—one could not possibly overlook a substantially long length of cherry-red yarn.... Firmly anchored between two heavy pieces of furniture, which were located at opposite ends of the room, this blood-red symbol remained a rather pitiful warning to Felix and explicitly signified that some sort of "cold war" was continuing to be waged with respect to their relationship. Without question, here was tangible proof of their ongoing conflict's unavoidable line of demarcation....

What was being indicated, in such childish terms, was the reality that the living arrangements were being severely altered until further notice. Now, of course, with the line being absurdly drawn as it was, only part of the house remained his, while the other part was to become hers exclusively, with all the Lauder children and me still having the full run of the entire place as before, since no one was really angry with any of us at the moment.

How thought-provokingly odd that two such substantially grown-up individuals, as these two good people were, should behave in such a thoroughly infantile manner. Naturally the truly sympathetic reader will certainly be able to understand that such an unsatisfactory arrangement as this could not, and definitely would not, be tolerated by a man like Felix. In fact, no man worth his salt as a man would ever logically consent to being treated in this demeaning way for very long. So, after nearly a week of those very same "fun and games" where my dear friend continued to be treated so unkindly by his wife of so many years, upon that seventh day when Emma Lauder wandered into her kitchen to prepare the usual coffee, a small white envelope awaited her....

Being rather brief this personal message to her from her dear husband was written in German. Mrs. Lauder remained in a noticeably subdued frame of mind, at this point, as she slowly read and then reread the solitary page several times. Upon her children's aggressive insistence, she finally consented to share it with all of us. Slowly translating the note for our benefit, and more than likely editing it somewhat as well, with an unnaturally flat sounding voice she was advising us that Felix had decided to leave us for a while.

Within the letter's postscript this good man went on to implore his many children and me to make him proud of us by continuing to look after each other, just as we always did—and, of course, to especially look after their mother until his inevitable return home. The body of his correspondence had earlier explained that with the family's funds being so badly depleted, and with there being no crop at all upon which to financially rely during the many months to come, Felix vowed to scour the countryside looking for some sort of work—any work, whose modest wages would be able to help see us through this decidedly difficult episode in our lives. Before his departure our wise patriarch had taken to locking "Hereboy" on the porch. Knowing the little rascal, as he surely did, Felix knew for certain that his faithful mascot would go looking for him and most probably would become lost in the process.

As if our collective mood was not miserable enough, shortly after the letter's contents became known to each of us, Eddie finally exploded over breakfast that morning and angrily addressed his mother as he critically proclaimed, "Forgive me for pointing out this fact to you, Mother, but all of this is your fault! Your ongoing meanness to Father was far more than he ever deserved.... God forbid, should anything happen to him, the entire blame will ultimately be yours!"

These were strong words, indeed.... Now with the unavoidable reality of Felix being gone, a significant depression descended upon our home, as well as our hearts. During this difficult time I worried a great deal about my friend. We all worried about him. What would he be doing about his insulin, for example? Had he taken enough clothing—and enough food, when he left us? Most of all, when would he be safely returning to all the people who loved him so very much?!

That following Sunday evening after all of us spent the entire previous week pining over Felix's absence, and likewise greatly deploring the ridiculousness which had brought us all to this point in the first place, Felix finally telephoned us from some undisclosed place in order to assure us that he was well. Little more than this was shared with us, but as I chanced to observe Emma Lauder's demeanor while she spoke with her husband that night by phone, even though I had no knowledge of what they were saying in German, I could tell that the thick ice which had formerly encrusted her proud heart was surely melting little by little. This, of course, was an excellent sign. I found myself wondering, too, if this same significant reality was also being perceived by Felix, there on the other end of the line....

Exactly ten days after that evening, our beloved patriarch finally returned to us, although this major event in itself left a great deal to be desired. Up to that moment each time the telephone rang, or each time someone else's car could be heard coming up our long driveway, we would all spontaneously scurry about in response, hoping with all our hearts that it might really be Felix.

During that same highly momentous mid-August evening which was to herald Felix's much-anticipated homecoming, while the Lauder children and I were gathered together upon the porch attempting to busy ourselves in a wholly uninspiring manner, Emma Lauder remained off by herself heavily immersed in praying her rosary. Sometime later a light summer rain began to fall.... Eventually we would all be hearing the curious sound of a car slowly making its way up the driveway towards us, but it was really our "Hereboy" who first sensed that something was amiss....

Now with our little dog standing so rigidly at attention, his front paws up upon one arm of Felix's favorite reading chair located within the protective porch area itself, we watched as the animal began eagerly pushing his small nose against the screening of the adjacent window.... His ever-dependable ears, too, were fixed in their usual "tracking mode," as he began to spontaneously create that particular whimpering sound which he reserved exclusively for his master.

Merely seconds later, as the intensity of the cooling late summer rainfall began to increase, the twin headlights of an automobile could finally be detected as the vehicle made that familiar telltale crunching sound upon the stones of the driveway. With this, "Hereboy" jumped down and began to nervously pace about upon the smoothly-painted floor boards, not far from the chair he had formerly occupied.... He also began to bark rather incessantly, all the while wagging his stubby little tail to beat the band—precisely the way he always did when ever Felix returned home.

Continuing to eagerly glance out the window, as by now we all insisted upon doing, what we were presently witnessing was not Felix's car approaching after all, but "Doc" Owens' instead. Needless to say we remained slightly puzzled by all this, and immediately began to think that our usually dependable mascot must be losing his touch, in a manner of speaking, since he obviously mistook the good doctor's arrival for his master's. All in all, still being immensely pleased to see our excellent friend in spite of our initial collective disappointment, with the early evening rain falling as hard as it was Eddie and Charlie ventured outside carrying a huge oversized black umbrella to officially welcome our visitor into the ever-familiar comfort of our home.

While Emma Lauder and the rest of us continued now to observe these actions from our far more dry and comfy place within the anteroom off the kitchen, we spied "Doc" Owens as he first greeted the two brothers. Following this, and without further ado, we watched further as he hastened around from his driver's side of the car to the passenger side, where he began to carefully assist Felix in his own attempt to eventually emerge from the vehicle....

"Hereboy" had not been mistaken! His great affection and endless loyalty towards his beloved master automatically produced within him a truly uncanny ability to zero in upon those otherwise impossible-to-detect subtle sensory perceptions, by using that uniquely special "sonar" with which such amazing animals are blessed. Felix had returned to us! God, in His abundant goodness, had surely consented to hear our endless prayers after all....

Presently, though, with the distressing sight of seeing Felix resting the better portion of his weight upon his friend's arm for support, as he obviously was doing, and while both brothers continued shielding the duo as best they could with the immense umbrella, all of us watched with growing dismay as our seemingly wounded patriarch began limping up the short sidewalk towards us.... Merely moments later, there within the main part of the kitchen after both men dried themselves and then were presented with cups of much-appreciated hot vegetable broth, Felix's many anxious family members and I were only just now being able to more leisurely contemplate the large bandage across Felix's forehead, as well as the unusual reality that he was no longer wearing his bifocals.... In fact, there sat his poor glasses—plain as day, directly in front of him upon the kitchen table, with the right lens completely missing and the other lens badly cracked in several places. After resting for a while longer, and upon considerable coaxing from each member of his greatly-interested audience, this very weary man finally consented to share his recent tale of woe which included some fairly gruesome trouble which he had just managed to narrowly escape.

Purposely sparing his audience those far more ugly details as propriety demanded, especially with all the younger children present, we were still able to pretty much read between the lines and to eventually grasp the true nature of this recent trauma inspired by that former situation. According to Felix, it was a short and rather tantalizing notice posted in the *Tribune* which initially caught his eye two days or so before he actually left us. Sincerely believing that this same promise of rather sketchily-defined work upon some building project which was being partially subsidized by the government, ended up being the significant bait that really did the trick as far as managing to lure him away from the safety of our home was concerned.

What happened was that some well-known company was looking to hire two hundred men for various types of work connected with road building just north of the city of Chicago. Of course these days, with most folks still being so desperate for work, word about this major event quickly spread like wildfire.

Although the tiny and somewhat benign-looking newspaper advertisement seemed fairly lost among the larger and more important stories of the day, and ran for less than a week's time, the overall response had been absolutely staggering. Genuinely hopeful men of all ages, coming from several neighboring states, as well—practically twelve thousand of them, according to the follow-up newspaper article that so accurately chronicled the ensuing mayhem which was to ultimately transpire, became begrudgingly bitter over the entirely disappointing reality that most of them would soon be required to return home empty-handed. Furthermore, since it had not taken long at all for the bulk of this same restless crowd to feel a real need to vent its substantial rage over this negative turn of events, what soon happened was unimaginably frightening to say the least.

According to Felix's own personal account, when he finally did arrive at the makeshift encampment that was originally intended to act as a sort of staging area for the would-be building project, sentiments had already turned extremely ugly. To make matters worse, professional hecklers sent by unscrupulous members of the powerful labor unions—as well as a few notoriously troublesome elements from the mob, managed to further foment additional agitation. Shortly, and rather similar to what occurs when fire is added to a substantial mixture of gasoline, tempers eventually flared beyond control, causing one poor man to be killed right away in that hellish mayhem, while scores of others were severely injured.

Before my friend made it back to his car, no doubt desperately seeking to escape the ruthlessness of the situation, an impressive crowd of even more crazed individuals began brandishing clubs and hammers to systematically destroy everything within sight. Without any recourse whatsoever, Felix numbly watched as our faithful family automobile became a casualty of this relatively minor war.... Indeed, within mere seconds every window of the vehicle was cruelly smashed and all of its tires punctured. Ultimately with the frightening mob going absolutely berserk, the entire car was eventually pulverized to a point where it barely resembled what it once had been. Then the same ferocious mob became quickly inspired to begin setting fire to everything that remained in its path, subsequently lighting up the normally inky-black sky with torrid red and orange flames of glowing destruction....

Pausing only briefly to deeply contemplate this moment in time, Felix finally said with a somewhat amazed edge to his voice, "Until that particular moment in time—even after having considered our long-ago preemptive flight from Mexico, I never fully conceived of just how incredibly frightening the human face can become when the spirit of even a single individual is literally consumed with a primitive rage to invoke true evil.... Having become temporarily lost, as I was, within that vast sea of wild and turbulent eyes which continued to speak volumes concerning the depths of debasement into which these particular souls were willfully choosing to descend—for a short while, at least, I truly believed that I was in hell along with the rest of them!"

"How did you manage to save yourself, Father?!" was Maria Christina's first question, after this brief lull in the story-telling occurred.

Felix took a little while to rub his eyes which were presently looking incredibly tired and somewhat equally sad too.... Placing one arm around this elder daughter of his and instinctively hugging her to him, he went on to finish sharing the harrowing events of those past many hours, as he told us, "By sheer good fortune, actually, as the ruthless mob continued burning and pillaging everything, I managed to slip into a densely covered ravine located not far from where I originally parked the car upon my arrival there. With the superb cover of night I vowed to faithfully follow its gentle stream of bubbling water for quite some distance, until I could no longer hear the worrisome sound which that same highly agitated throng was currently making as it collectively yelled forth its endless profusion of wild obscenities, as well as continued to do horribly obscene things to everyone and everything within reach....

"After traveling this way for some undetermined amount of time, I eventually chose to finally leave behind my secret avenue of escape... Next, having walked for many miles along a well-paved but fairly deserted road, I was eventually aided by a kindly good Samaritan and his wife who took genuine pity upon me. Fortunately for me these same compassionate people were traveling by car from their home in Chicago, onwards to attend a family reunion in Racine. Naturally upon seeing my apparent distress, not to mention the gruesome-looking gash upon my forehead, they immediately volunteered to take me to a hospital. Indeed, this is exactly were the three of us were headed next, to the nearest medical facility which happened to be the tiny medical center located on the outskirts of Twin Lakes.... And just as kindly Fate would also have it, our own dear 'Doc' Owens was already there in that very same small emergency room, faithfully accomplishing what he always seems to do best—namely, in helping other people in distress!

"Having solicitously scrubbed my face clean with the idea of judging for himself what damage had been done, this excellent fellow here immediately stitched me up and just as quickly pronounced me 'good as new'!" With this mild attempt at a bit of humor, Felix also managed to conjure up a wee smile, as a couple of fingers from his right hand gingerly found their way to the bandage to tentatively explore it.

With a moment's worth of somber silence that quickly followed Felix finally adopted a far more serious demeanor. Slowly taking the necessary time to visually engage each one of us, as we in turn continued to gather more protectively around him, there within the small kitchen on that unforgettable late night in August, our grateful patriarch's loving gaze finally fell upon his wife. Soon we all heard him announce with considerable emotion apparent in his weary voice, "How can I possibly express to each and every one of you just how desperately wonderful it is to finally be home once more!?"

To the best of my knowledge, as well as to my everlasting relief, never again would my friend be made to sleep within the hayloft of any barn. That evening after the many members of the entire Lauder family and I finally walked "Doc" Owens to his little Ford, and after all of us thanked our friend rather profusely for all that he had done for us, we bade him good-night. Immediately following this the Lauder children and I soon took our own leave, as well, and promptly went off to bed.

Felix and Emma remained for a long while quietly seated at the small kitchen table holding counsel together. When the moment eventually arrived for them to follow suit, both of them could be heard entering their special sanctuary together located there on the ground floor of the house. After having respectfully closed and then locked the door behind them, they set forth leaving their past troubles far behind them....

With myself presently occupying the bed which once belonged to our dear George all those years ago, and of course with Eddie already fast asleep nearby, I listened with immeasurable comfort to the insistent rain drops as they continued to play against the glass of our bedroom windows. Although at the time I had scant knowledge of the true profundity associated with that amazing celebration of life which the Bible so aptly refers to as the *Song of Solomon*, still I believed that Felix was currently where he most longed to be.... There, within the strong protective arms of the good woman who obviously still loved him, he would soon be receiving that long overdue sacrament of absolution for his past sins.

There, too, as this special intimacy between husband and wife caused their conjugal bedsprings to softly moan under their combined weight—naturally in perfect tempo with the couple's passionate rhythm of love-making, I found myself hoping for the day when such sublime things would also be known to me. Meanwhile, as I made myself even more comfortable by turning on my right side and gently curling into a modified fetal position, which for as long as I can possibly recall has remained my favorite attitude for sleeping, I gratefully embraced that night's particularly peaceful slumber to the ever-gentle music of the falling rain.

21.

PROFOUND IGNORANCE regarding the innate sacredness of Life, is—and has always been—mankind's worst enemy. Since ignorance generally begets ignorance, this ongoing and highly unproductive phenomenon usually becomes the primary basis for intolerance. Historically speaking, with intolerance notoriously spawning such bitter hatred and malice towards others, what will it finally take to properly educate humanity towards a more perfect understanding and genuine reverence for all aspects of life and all living things—ending, once and for all, century upon century of anti-Semitism and its ugly twin of equally destructive racial prejudice?

I, myself, have endlessly dreamed of such a world: A wiser and far more compassionate place where each and every person's worth is judged solely upon the interior composition of their heart and soul; their ethical and moral manifesto, no less, rendering the more obvious packaging of the physical self either secondary, or perhaps, better yet, of little importance whatsoever. From that early September of 1940 onwards, the many members of the Lauder family and I were destined to learn a particularly unforgettable lesson regarding the innocent joys that naturally are associated with true friendship. We would also ultimately be experiencing the extreme shock and overwhelming sorrow that likewise accompanies any brutal act of hatred.... In other words, each of us would be made to heed the sobering reality that there are certain souls born into this world who remain far too gentle to live among the wolves....

John Brown Ketchum, according to his own reliable account, was the youngest son of former slaves. For generation upon generation his proud ancestors spent practically their entire lives working the cotton and tobacco fields of the deep south. Upon his birth, which he judged to have occurred sometime around 1880, he was appropriately named in honor of the ardent abolitionist of pre-Civil War's Harper Ferry fame. Furthermore, although he never learned to read nor write, as a very young man fortune smiled upon him just the same in the form of a kindly mentor who subsequently imparted to him the many important intricacies of the blacksmith trade. Naturally with these valuable tools of knowledge he managed to travel from place to place dutifully earning his living wheresoever he went.

On the other hand, his lovely partner-in-life, Bessy Ketchum, was a self-taught seamstress by trade and considerably younger than he. In fact, on the day the Lauder family and I were privileged to meet these two remarkable people, I incorrectly surmised that they were father and daughter, instead of husband and wife.

By some amazing turn of Fate, and not so terribly long after that thoroughly unforgettable succession of personal challenges visited themselves upon the Lauder household, it eventually became Anna Allegra's typical persistence in having her own way—not to mention the highly fortuitous timing related to a broken rear wagon-axle, that was ultimately responsible in the end for having quietly ushered the Ketchum family into our collective lives.

"Father! Mother.... Come and see for yourselves! There are two strangers sitting in an old mule-drawn wagon, out midway along the west side of our property!" With an unmistakably mystified ring to her already rather grown-up voice, this is what eleven-year-old Anna Lauder was declaring to her parents when she sought them out and soon found them both comfortably resting in their usual places, there within our long "L"-shaped sun porch during that warm and humid Sunday afternoon.

Soon enough, with Felix, Fritz, Charley, and me firmly in tow, despite our having initially been far less than eager to accompany Anna in the first place, this tall and lean wisp-of-a-girl seemed unusually insistent that we follow along in order to properly sort out the entire business. Basically this introductory episode which was the important prelude to all that lay ahead dealt with young Anna having just returned from attending her monthly Junior Girl Scout meeting at the local civic center. One of the other children's mothers thoughtfully telephoned ahead to volunteer to drive her home, thereby saving Emma and Felix the trouble. When this same small cheerful band of people finally rounded the usual bend in the narrow country road that happened to run past the Lauder family's back acreage, it was at this precise moment that the travelers unexpectedly spotted our two visitors....

"I don't know why you're making such a fuss, Anna!" I recall Charlie Lauder openly protesting to his kid-sister, as the three of us climbed into the rear section of the Lauder's pickup truck. With Felix sliding comfortably behind the wheel to drive, and with Fritz quickly jumping in next to him for company, very shortly we were off to investigate the current situation as Charlie added with a note of exasperation so readily apparent in his voice, "After all, those poor people you're talking about probably just decided to pull off the road to rest for a while from the heat of the day.... Now with our invading their privacy, as we're most certainly doing, how embarrassing it'll prove to be when they eventually tell us this very thing!"

"Charlie..." Anna Lauder was patiently telling her older brother in that particularly feisty way of hers, and pretty much as if she reckoned that he had not as yet been blessed with the same insightful reasoning as she, "as soon as I saw those people earlier today, I immediately got the feeling that somehow they might be needing our help in some way."

Much later on in a somewhat sketchy account of the history of their life together which, incidentally, John and Bessy Ketchum only consented to share with us little by little after they came to know us better, the two of them had originally moved from Creedmore, North Carolina, to Muskogee County, Oklahoma, soon after their marriage. Nearly two years after that major move, but still prior to the great difficulties that would naturally be intensifying with the coming Depression Years, signs of hard times were already slowly making themselves apparent to the average farmer. Back then when those several consecutive seasons of infamous drought began to literally decimate the soil, causing farming communities nearly everywhere in that region to eventually dry up and all but blow away in the years to come, the handwriting was clearly being written upon the wall. At least as far as John Ketchum was concerned, he instinctively sensed that the work which was normally reserved for a blacksmith would eventually no longer be available to him, so husband and wife were forced to travel elsewhere in order to survive.

Loading their few possessions onto their wagon, and with their faithful old mule Hannah leading the way, the couple spent many harrowing weeks slowly inching their way back across the country to finally arrive in what originally must have appeared to be a far more peaceful farming community located this time in West Frankfurt, Illinois. But this new place, too, would soon prove to be merely a brief respite from the traveling life with which they were both becoming so familiar.

After all that particular year was 1925—the same infamous year, in fact, when a deadly series of totally devastating tornadoes joined forces to snake their way across several adjoining states, destroying property and lives on an unprecedented scale. With respect to the ultimate fate of the Ketchums, very shortly the compassionate God in Whom they both so passionately believed would be miraculously sparing them from harm; while at the same time inflicting untold destruction everywhere, including abruptly ending many hundreds of lives in the process....

There remain various types of destructive forces with which one is often required to deal during one's lifetime. Some, as in this particular case, stem from the powerful savagery of nature; while other equally caustic barbarity is chronically brought about by those far baser intellectual forces that dwell among us, and which seek no less passionately to override any sense of righteous decorum in order to intimidate and destroy the human dignity of others.

Just as even the most modest history buff is surely already aware, during that same frenetic period which immediately followed the first great war, the organization still infamously known as the Ku Klux Klan gained a rather substantial re-emergence. Without bothering to ferret-out the dangerous underlying philosophy of bigotry and extreme hatred which was being systematically perpetrated by this same unsavory group towards not only African Americans, but also Catholics and Jews as well, this highly subversive yet superficially wholesome-appearing white supremacy group's enrollment grew by leaps and bounds, all across our land....

Each of us possesses an innate desire to belong to something truly meaningful within our day-to-day lives. However, during this specifically troubling time far too many naive men and women of all ages and from nearly every walk of life who originally imagined that they were joining an upstanding and law-abiding group, whose hyperbolized patriotic agenda seemed to measure up so significantly to all that they genuinely believed makes this country of ours so great, allowed themselves to become caught up in the follow-the-leader mentality, much like sheep instinctively do.... Without bothering to question the vital dogmas relevant to this seemingly attractive new religion of theirs, they blindly fell victim to that powerful and indisputably dangerous "herd mentality" and were consequently severely judged by history for the brutish company they so willingly sought to keep....

Indeed, how painful it still is to look back and to be made to admit to all the destructive thinking which had gone unchallenged until nearly the mid-portion of this most recently past century. How basically ignorant we were, as a people, to have tolerated in any sense whatsoever the terrible injustices of the past which were so commonplace, and therefore so readily accepted.

To honestly and to openly contemplate this former travesty in thinking which so many of our citizens never bothered to question—whether
it be as basic as that once truly unkind edict relevant to separate drinking fountains, and separate lavatories—should forevermore remain a
profound embarrassment to all of us. Looking back, now, upon that
long arduous road towards sanity and enlightenment which we as
citizens have been rightfully shamed into finally treading in the form
of the Civil Rights Movement, how far we have managed to come in
these few years.... And yet how much farther we must still contemplate
journeying, in order to reach what Martin Luther King referred to as the
"Promised Land." Any premeditated and systematic day-to-day denial
of even one person's civil rights amounts to nothing less than robbing
that individual of their subsequent human dignity, and further translates
into an insidiously poisonous atmosphere which robs us collectively as
a great nation.

My earliest impression of John Ketchum was that, like Felix, he was
no stranger to life, nor to life's endless struggles. I well recall that in the
back of his well-used old wagon, besides the necessary tools of his trade
that were habitually carried everywhere he traveled, one could also find
a pair of heavy iron shackles which had been worn by his paternal great-
grandfather upon being brought by slave ship to this new land.

These important things were powerful symbols that served to
remind John of who he was, and likewise who his "people" had been.
These items remained tangible evidence of an ongoing struggle for the
basic dignity for which every soul yearns—indeed, the fundamental dignity and respect that every soul deserves. I quickly discovered that the
same gentle strength and moral integrity inherent within this fine man
were the same wholesome attributes which Felix Lauder also possessed
in great measure. And if it is possible for one beautiful soul to instantly
recognize its own likeness in another, and to instinctively gravitate towards that light in a sort of unconscious celebration of this fact, then it
should also come as little surprise to the reader that these two excellent
men—even from the moment of their first meeting—were destined to
become genuine friends....

"Good-day to you both!" Felix was cheerfully saying, just as he
stepped from the truck he was driving and began to walk towards our
two visitors. Undoubtedly grasping the fact that the man and woman
were in need of some sort of assistance, just as young Anna had intuitively felt, he quickly went on to add, "What seems to be the trouble?"

With my dear friend's ever-abiding sensitivity and his abundance
of common sense relevant to any given situation, Felix purposely chose

to park our own vehicle several paces well behind the rear of the mule-drawn cart, on the opposite side of the road no less, in order not to initially startle either the animal nor its owners. Barely leaning out from my own self-designated post within the rear section of our faithful old truck, I observed a rather young woman standing to one side of this same wagon.... In her right hand she was holding an extremely well-worn parasol that was open at the moment and whose formerly numerous imperfections were now skillfully camouflaged underneath various size patches of brightly colored fabric. These cheerful cumulative little additions were carefully darned onto the item's convex surface, bestowing upon the valuable object a keen sense of uniqueness.

For me this beguiling and utterly tranquil scene was uncannily reminiscent of a masterwork by Seurat, with the aura of bright afternoon sunlight falling just so and softly bathing that particular stationary figure in a similar neo-impressionist manner.... While that same modest little convenience served to ably protect the lady from the strong rays of the still extremely warm sun, within her left hand and firmly cradled against her bosom she seemed to be protecting what appeared to be a large thick black book—a Bible, in effect, which in the numerous months to come I would rarely ever see her without.

Upon hearing Felix Lauder's friendly words, the elderly gentleman finally managed to carefully roll out from underneath his wagon where he had been during this time. Up to that point he was lying there face up upon a wide band of dried weeds and butter-colored dandelions, with only the hole-ridden soles of his badly worn shoes protruding outwards. As Felix just naturally reached out for the man's hand in order to help him to his feet, in a somewhat absentminded fashion our visitor went about solicitously brushing off the seat of his trousers, before staring rather forlornly at Felix to answer, "Dun gon and busted da rear axle of ma wagon!" Taking a moment more to look back at the wagon, and then almost as if he were thinking out loud, he added, "Shaw is a piece of bad luck dat has come ma way!"

"Mind if I take a look for myself?" Felix was saying.... Then before anything more could be said, my excellent friend was himself sliding underneath the bed of the wagon. While Felix was taking an accurate reading of the situation, I observed the man and woman quickly ex-changing glances with the young woman's overall deportment taking on a far more cautious tone as she chose to move a few inches closer to her companion.

By this time our Anna could no longer contain herself. Wasting not another second, she bolted from out of the back of our truck and then literally sprinted across the little country road to finally deposit herself fairly close to where the woman and man were now standing, themselves rather intently observing the boots on Felix's own feet as he proceeded to tinker around underneath their wagon. Soon the others and I heard Anna exclaim in her irrepressibly outspoken and thoroughly friendly manner, all the while extending her hand in politeness to say, "I guess it's a really good thing that we've come along as we have! My father can fix anything... Anything at all! By the way, my name is Anna Allegra Lauder... And my brothers Fritz, and Charley, and Adam, are over there in the truck!"

With this sort of backhanded introduction of hers, Felix promptly climbed out from underneath the rear portion of the Ketchum's wagon and cheerfully offered his hand as well, as he said in his characteristically good-natured manner, "My name is Felix Lauder.... And as you have undoubtedly already guessed by now, I am the father of this shy and highly reserved young woman here!"

Despite the troubling aspect of their present predicament, John and Bessy Ketchum both managed a smile in response to this candid remark. Next, pretty much as if the other boys and I were being shamed into leaving the place where we had been quietly sitting all this while, we quickly followed suit by walking the short distance across the road to shake the hands of the good folks whom Fate had ushered into our lives....

These same pleasant people who obviously had traveled so far only to end up stranded upon the Lauder family's doorstep like this, were dressed in clothing that seemed appropriate for attending church services on any given Sunday morning. Despite the still formidable September heat, not to mention the substantial dust and grime which they both had accumulated along the way, an undeniable sense of real pride in their own self-worth as people literally leaped out at the onlooker, causing one to ponder many things.

Without wishing to stare too openly at the person who was standing nearest to me, every now and then I would quickly cast a glance in Bessy Ketchum's direction and decided that she was a strikingly beautiful woman. Besides her apparently proud and elegant bearing, which modestly suggested a considerable inner resolve to meet any necessary challenge head-on, there was also a distinct counterpoint of feminine vulnerability which had earlier been demonstrated when she chose to move closer to her husband's side whose role she obviously must have felt was that of her protector.

Likewise, I recall thinking that this rare lady's facial features were quite flawless in every respect too, even with its substantial layer of undesirable dust and grime.... To my highly creative young mind she began to remind me of an ever-so-fair Nubian princess, who, for some unlikely reason had just recently consented to grace our simple lives with her lovely presence. Regarding her further I observed with some interest that even though her well-worn parasol provided the shade she required, she still took to wearing a simple straw hat that was completely unadorned and barely hinted at her shortly cropped black curly hair underneath whose wet shiny tendrils were now clinging rather tenaciously to the pronounced beads of perspiration there upon her forehead and neck....

Although John Ketchum was also wearing his Sunday best, it surely seemed to me that this same clothing, much like the times through which we were all currently living, had seen far better days. Moreover the highly enduring effect which the sight of this charming husband and wife team just naturally produced within me, as they stood together side by side on that day, was that of two animated figurines one might conceivably find atop a beautiful wedding cake. A little later on, however, as the tall and noticeably lean man took to moving to the other side of his lovely wife, for the first time I actually became aware that our visitor possessed a very pronounced limp.

Once, much later on when "Doc" Owens had also made this man's acquaintance and subsequently became his trusted friend, he was allowed to freely examine John's left hip, and leg, and foot. Purely out of professional interest our good doctor became greatly inspired by a rather ingenious idea that was naturally intended to help remedy the difficult situation of that one particular leg of John's being a little less than an inch shorter than his other. Felix and I eventually heard "Doc" candidly tell his new patient that with some time, and trouble, as well as a whole lot of ongoing devotion on both their parts, John's gait would eventually become vastly improved.

So, most probably out of a basic fear that he might offend our good doctor should he decline this rather unusual offer of his, Mr. Ketchum finally acquiesced and later allowed what would have normally become a fairly lengthy process to begin. With Felix's assistance the interesting plan of attack was to invent a sturdy metal brace for John's deficient leg, which when worn daily and then faithfully adjusted a fraction each week, or so, over the coming many months ahead would ultimately serve to rotate the hip into place. In conjunction with this seemingly cruel and decidedly painful methodology, a wooden lift would be placed within John Ketchum's boot or shoe, naturally allowing him to better disperse his body weight, instead of having him continue to favor his shorter leg as he was forever compelled to do.

However, after about two weeks of this well-intended "abuse" by the two men whom John already considered his friends, one afternoon John Ketchum was spotted hobbling along without either his brace, or his boot lift. When asked why he had abandoned that important experiment, John endearingly answered with a near Ciceronian eloquence, "Surely don't mean no disrespect.... But somehow it don't seem rite to go over da head of da good Lord! After all, dis is da way He made ol' John Ketchum." Finally, as if to make light of the entire situation with which he had obviously long ago come to terms, he good-naturedly added, "Ma Mamma used to say that God must ta been d'stracted when he put me together, 'cause he made my one leg a speck shorter den da other!"

Standing together by the wagon as we all were on that first day, when Bessy Ketchum finally took a moment to shift the heavy-looking book she was holding all this while, there from underneath her loosely fitted pale blue cotton dress one could not miss the fact that her normally firm belly was already heavily swollen with child. Suddenly this marvelous trio of visitors put me in mind of the faithful depiction of the Holy Family that is so often found within the pages of various books.... And since our Anna rarely missed anything, upon witnessing this same important detail which had also become apparent to me, she immediately inquired in her dependably open manner, "When is your baby going to be born, Mrs. Ketchum?"

"Anna! That will do," Felix was quickly interjecting, as he finally climbed out from underneath the Ketchum's wagon for the second time that day.

Removing his ever-present linen handkerchief from its usual compartment in that rear pocket of his worn work trousers and subsequently taking a well-deserved moment to wipe away the many beads of perspiration which had formed upon his brow and upper lip, as if attempting to speak above the never-ending humming sound being orchestrated by our late summer's hordes of insects, Felix confidently announced, "About the broken axle, Mr. Ketchum ... I believe that it can be properly fixed, and with relatively little trouble.... Actually, I have several lengths of iron pipe back at the barn and if you will allow me I shall help you fix your wagon, at least well enough to permit you to travel to wherever you're going." After a second of silence, my friend soon went on to inquire, "By the way, where are you both headed?"

Although Bessy Ketchum seemed noticeably reluctant to answer our question, her husband on the other hand was a bit more open with us as he finally confided to Felix, "C'aint rightly say! Spec the Lord God will provide for Bessy and me, dough—just like He's always dun in da past… Sure enough, some fine day we be findin' a special place dat is real peaceful—somewheres ta call home where the travelin' life be endin', once and fur all!"

It was obvious that our two visitors were exceedingly tired, and hot, and dirty, from their long journey. Old Hannah, too—if only she had possessed the gift of speech, might certainly have had much to say on this same subject. Briefly studying the Ketchum's faithful mule, as I was at the moment, she seemed far too lean for her own good, and presently was hanging her head in such a manner that it seemed as though she carried the weight of the world behind her.

"Charley, Fritz, Adam!" Felix was saying, as he instinctively placed one of his hands atop one of Fritz's shoulders, "Please unhitch the Ketchum's mule and slowly walk her back to the barn for me…. After that, wash her down. And after she has been properly cooled and watered, make her comfortable in one of the empty stalls. Then we shall feed her along with the other livestock at the usual time."

Emotionally speaking John Ketchum seemed to come a bit unhinged, at this point, with the thought of what Felix was planning to do. In somewhat of a rush to make himself clearly understood, and to certainly impress upon Felix one highly relevant point concerning his current financial situation, our visitor briefly fumbled around in a state of mild confusion for the appropriate words, as he soon managed to say with a touch of pronounced embarrassment, "Don't have no money to pay for such kindness to Ol' Hannah—nor to Bessy and me either, for dat matter!"

I recall that Felix was in the process of helping us free up the mule so that we might do as he initially requested. Hearing these no less than desperate-sounding words from John Ketchum, Felix handed the mule's dried and cracked leather reigns to Charlie and proceeded to walk towards the gentleman who had taken the necessary time to express his overwhelming worry at having no way to pay for what we were doing for him. Standing before John Ketchum, now, I watched and listened as I heard my friend quietly tell him, "I can certainly appreciate what you are telling me, Mr. Ketchum. After all, times are still terribly hard for everyone.... But please know that these small gestures of kindness, specifically towards you and your wife, are being given quite freely— and also quite happily!"

While these friends-to-be remained standing before each other like this, I chanced to observe a particularly poignant look as it slowly began to come to life within Mr. Ketchum's eyes. It seemed to be the identical feeling with which I was already quite familiar. Indeed, our newly-acquired acquaintance was openly contemplating Felix as if he were silently questioning the reality of what was happening to him; much as if he just could not really believe that such kindness, from this complete stranger, was being offered to him and to his wife seemingly without strings or attachments of any kind. My heart involuntarily smiled a bit, as Charlie and Fritz and I began to walk up the country road together, dutifully leading poor tired old Hannah away.... Certainly on more than one occasion over those past many years of my young life, I too used to find myself deeply pondering my own amazing good fortune in having finally found such a true and genuine friend in Felix.

By the time all of us arrived home as a group, and by the time the other boys and I properly looked after the Ketchum's mule, it was sundown. Felix and John Ketchum temporarily lost themselves in rummaging through a footlocker containing a multitude of various size pipes and other irregular pieces of metal from my friend's wide-ranging collection. After learning of Mr. Ketchum's expertise as a blacksmith, Felix was quite obviously delighted and said, "Between the two of us, Mr. Ketchum, we shall have your wagon fixed in no time at all!"

During this friendly banter of theirs, I observed that Mrs. Ketchum had taken a seat upon our sturdy tack box located in the breezeway of the open barn area. Sometime later on, no doubt upon having witnessed the slow migration of our hot, dusty, and rather ragtag group of people as we slowly plodded along up the long driveway towards the stables, Emma Lauder eventually emerged from the farmhouse with Maria Christina. Together both of them were obligingly balancing a huge pitcher of iced lemonade, along with numerous glasses atop a rather sumptuous-looking serving tray....

Initially, although Emma Lauder and Bessy Ketchum were noticeably standoffish towards each other, both women seemed to readily acknowledge the reality that their husbands already had much in common. No doubt with them silently bowing to this important fact, they apparently decided to let this new situation between their two families play itself out, probably never having suspected for a moment that one day in the not-too-distant future they would likewise be learning to greatly respect and appreciate one another as well.

"Looks like it might already be too late in the day to begin our task of setting up the fire and working the bellows in order to heat up and then re-form this length of pipe that we shall be needing to fix your wagon, Mr. Ketchum," Felix was enthusiastically saying. "But with the early morning light, and after my usual chores are completed, the repair of the wagon's axle will remain the first item on my list of things to accomplish."

With these fine words of comfort and hope, John Ketchum smiled gratefully. Then as if to conclude their personal business for that day, Felix went on to assure our visitors, "For the time being, at least, you are both more than welcome to sleep in the hay loft above the barn." Throwing a significant glance my way, and with a bit of amused chagrin my wonderful friend quickly added in his typical good-natured manner, "Actually, I have it from a highly reliable source that it really is not a bad place to spend a night—or two! Yes ... it's clean and dry and if one keeps both windows at either end of the large room fully opened, it remains possible to even stay a bit cooler with the cross-breeze which usually blows through the place." As a rather critical after-thought, just before my friend turned to leave, he remembered to quickly add, "I almost forgot to mention that on the far side of the outside of the barn you will both find a special stall reserved exclusively for washing. Later, after having sufficiently refreshed yourselves, my wife and I shall be bringing out a bit of supper for you."

This, then, is precisely how the Lauder family and I met the members of the Ketchum family. Life seemed exceedingly good for all of us during those days. So good.... Even our little "Hereboy" whom Felix and I strongly contended remained an excellent judge of character, upon having been introduced to these same fine people, took an instant liking to them.

With each passing day thereafter came the remarkable lesson that the simplest of life's pleasures remain the best. We learned, as well, as two separate families, that working together to improve each other's lives was such an effortless thing to do. We learned, most of all, that genuine kindness often becomes a two-way street; and just as the Good Book forever assures the reader, kindness remains its own reward.

That following morning, sometime around the crack of dawn, John Ketchum was already bathed and dressed and patiently waiting for Felix and the rest of us as he seemed most eager to be able to earn his way by actually assisting us in our usual daily chores. Much to my personal amazement, too, despite his substantial limp he proved to be no slouch at all when it came to getting any job done.

During that afternoon both men went about making preparations to fix the wagon's broken rear axle. I recall that after Mr. Ketchum set up his special tools, and naturally, after the robust fire he started within his special oven eventually began to burn white-hot, a specifically selected length of iron pipe was deeply scored lengthwise from end to end. After this was done the metal was slowly softened over the fire's considerable heat to properly encourage those twin pieces to open fully, and to eventually meet the exact dimensions required. In the end what the men were working upon was carefully fitted around the damaged axle, itself, in effect creating a strong brace which managed to shore up and significantly strengthen the entire length of the back wheel rod against future breakage.

After the measurements were calculated and then re-calculated in a necessary attempt to reach the exact specifications, John Ketchum began to use a pair of special heavy-looking tongs and an even heavier looking hammer to carefully manipulate and bend these objects. In what might be compared to a series of more brutal ballet movements, I watched as this obviously talented gentleman expertly wielded these tools of his trade which allowed him to adroitly work his magic. Finally, as if to signify the end of the show, he placed the red-hot pieces of iron into a caldron of cold water, subsequently causing an immense puff of snow-white steam to billow out into the surrounding area. This, of course, served to freeze and solidify what had previously been rather malleable metal.

"Looks like an excellent fit, John," Felix was remarking with pride, as the two men lay side by side upon the ground underneath the old wagon that was temporarily parked behind the barn.

After they reemerged from bolting the brackets into place, I heard our new family friend say to my already excellent friend, "Much obliged for all yur help!"

Somehow after that there did not seem to be any need for the Ketchums to leave.... It goes without saying that each and every member of the Lauder family, including myself, had already grown quite fond of having them around, while they, in turn, seemed to have finally found that peaceful life for which they were searching. It also became crystal clear that it would be impossible for them to continue residing in the loft of our barn. Naturally with winter coming, someone needed to come up with a better idea. In the end that person proved to be our faithful friend, "Doc" Owens.

Not long after John and Bessy quietly entered our lives, "Doc" stopped by the house to pay his respects and as usual stayed to enjoy a bit of supper with us. It was during this intimate little gathering which naturally included the Ketchums, and which we had all taken to enjoy around the kitchen table which had been impetuously moved outside for this purpose, that a marvelous solution to our collective dilemma managed to make itself known.

"Felix, isn't that abandoned old tobacco shed still viable? You remember—the modest little structure located out there on the far eastern portion of your property?" This offhanded comment of "Doc" Owens was what actually started the ball rolling as they say. Our exceptionally fine friend was just finishing off his second piece of Emma Lauder's marvelous cherry pie, the same amazing dessert which called for cup upon cup of those sweet ripe Door County cherries that she put up the previous season, when the seed of an important idea began to take root in the good doctor's mind, only to begin spontaneously growing and growing....

Not being able to immediately follow our friend's train of thought, Felix was assuring him, "Yes, I do remember. One day in the future I shall have to either dismantle it, or mend it… Every now and then I even entertain the thought of using it to store my smaller farm equipment."

"How's the roof?" "Doc" persisted.

"What are you thinking?" Felix asked.

"Well, since we've been avidly discussing our need for a place for the Ketchums to reside, temporarily speaking, until a far better place may eventually be built, I imagined that if that same little house is still in relatively good shape, then they might use it.... What do ya think?"

After considering "Doc's" idea for a moment, Felix seemed to dismiss the idea, as he offered, "With winter coming, the place would be far too cold and drafty for anyone to use as a home. Besides, I vaguely recollect that part of the roof leaks rather badly.… Frankly speaking, I have not been inside the place for years. Goodness knows in what overall shape it might really be!"

"Well…" "Doc" Owens was saying, as he smiled at Felix from across the small cozy table, "since when have you ever balked at fixing a roof?"

With this comment naturally Felix gave off a substantial chuckle. After a moment of silence our dear patriarch finally said with a bit of mixed enthusiasm, "I suppose the best thing to do would be to travel over there tomorrow and to have a look for ourselves." Then politely addressing the two people who surely would have the last say in the whole affair, Felix inquired, "Would this idea be agreeable to you, John? Bessy?"

Many years ago, as it happened—long before either the Lauder family or even my father and I had come to reside in the community of Peck's Station, some overtly optimistic soul from South Carolina took it upon himself to build the modest little structure with the specific intention of planting and growing prime tobacco. My guess was that it was meant to be used as a "curing shed." Apparently the reality of those intensely bitter Wisconsin winters had not initially been taken into account. After the first planting season took place, and with that particular year's many months of discouraging weather that followed, this same little residence—along with that man's ill-conceived dream, were finally abandoned. It was precisely this very same modest two-room cottage, in the end, which both "Doc" Owens and Felix Lauder were discussing on behalf of Bessy and John Ketchum....

The more labor intensive work on the family's new residence was mostly accomplished by the Ketchums themselves. In several weeks time this diminutive yet decidedly quaint abode was ready for occupation. Somehow "Doc" Owens managed the substantial miracle of securing a secondhand wood-burning stove which promised to do its job by keeping the new residents cozy and warm throughout the next several months of late autumn and winter.

Later on with the more tentative arrival of that following spring, an impressive new vegetable garden was already in the process of being thoughtfully planned out by our newest residents. All in all, everything seemed right with our little world. Now, not only did the Ketchum family have a far more respectable place in which to live while they both patiently waited for their first child to be born, but certainly, too, and very much as kind Fate had also so generously decried, the many members of the Lauder clan and I successfully managed to retain these same gentle souls as our good neighbors—and even more significantly as our welcome new friends.

Meanwhile, during the better part of that same summer and autumn of 1940, I began working part-time for a large commercial logging company located some miles north of Madison. Carefully calculating that if I sacrificed and saved hard enough, for long enough, then I would eventually find myself that much closer to being able to head off to college somewhere. Although I was as "green" as they come, relative to having any knowledge of the logging industry, still I learned quickly enough that it was not only physically demanding work, but significantly dangerous work as well.

Usually my normal game plan amounted to my hitching a ride north to work those three or four days a week. Then, in order to be able to share at least one long weekend each month with my family, I would eventually manage to hitch a ride with someone who might for one reason or another be heading south during this time. Since confession always seems to be good for the soul, I am unashamed to admit to the reader that my being away from the old homestead, as I was naturally obliged to be, inspired a continuous sense of genuine homesickness.

Indeed, during these notably difficult times for me, I greatly longed for the precious sights and sounds of my life on the Lauder farm which had become such a significantly stabilizing force within my presently well-established life.... With a sense of latent poignancy I can still actually recall counting those many empty hours until I would once again be happily reunited with those special people I loved; that same amazing group of very special individuals who also loved me.

Thinking back upon this valuable time in my life, I also recall that it was with a sense of enduring certitude that Felix used to compare life to a classroom, and the acute reality that so often those truly worthwhile lessons regarding one's living a decidedly full and respectable life are not always found within the pages of any book. In order to help properly illustrate this point, there occurred two separate but equally salient episodes within our day-to-day living as a family which more than aptly applied to this same eminent philosophy....

The first of these "life lessons" dealt with an issue which was specific to young Steve Lauder and his passion for the game of basketball. Even back during the time when Lewis and George Lauder were youngsters, Felix felt obliged to supplement his children's normal school lessons with hours of learning there at home. All the while I was privileged to remain part of this remarkable family, there was a wonderful game that was still being played within the Lauder home, albeit far less frequently.... This charmingly witty game was deceptively simple in its basic presentation, but also remained clever enough to inspire each participant to be caught up in searching out certain facts relevant to specific subjects and then dutifully sharing whatever was discovered with our entire group.

Basically the idea was for each of us to spin the marvelous globe of the world which Felix usually kept upon the top shelf of his bookcase in the parlor and, habitually relying upon the "honor system," each participant would be expected to close his or her eyes and then to finally allow one of their index fingers to land upon some random spot on the sphere.... With this initial task completed, we were subsequently expected to give a short dissertation regarding such essential knowledge pertaining to the topography, history, and the people of that specific region. However, if some previously unexplored place located upon that same familiar curvature of our world map was unknown to us, we were temporarily excused from delivering any data on the spot, but were given the following week to track down the necessary information to be delivered with a certain gusto the following weekend. Normally it was late Sunday afternoon or early Sunday evening which tended to remain our preferred hour of choice, relevant to these ongoing and thoroughly enjoyable bi-monthly family "learning events." These fun-loving sessions in which we were all encouraged to indulge were a relatively painless method for studying history and geography. Ultimately it became impossible for any of us not to learn something important about this truly amazing world in which we all live....

One particularly memorable early Sunday evening in mid-October, with my having happily returned for the weekend from working up north at the lumber mill, I was sitting peacefully in the parlor reading with several of the other family members when Felix pretty much out of the blue chose to initiate this "learning game" of his.... "Stephen, it has been such a long time since you spun the globe and played our game!" Felix was good-naturedly reminding his fourteen-year-old son. "Come, won't you, and try your luck this evening—naturally so that we might eventually see what we might all learn together."

Having just recently returned from a lengthy physical workout at the school gymnasium, where he, his coach, and their class basketball team had been faithfully practicing for a couple of hours, needless to say young Stephen Lauder was not particularly enthusiastic about what his father was presently proposing. However, with his more energetic siblings faithfully urging him onward to participate in this intriguing game, he soon took a seat upon the sofa... With the well-used globe sitting within his reach upon the small sturdy table in front of him, he finally closed his eyes and gave it a healthy spin as everyone gathered around to see where his index finger might land.

Recalling that this truly confident member of the Lauder clan was both an exceptional student, as well as an enviable athlete, he was equally well-admired by his teachers and peers alike. These days his family and I rarely found him out and about the house or farmstead. Also upon nearly every inch of wall space upstairs in his bedroom confirmation of his ongoing love-affair with nearly every sport was clearly exhibited, since for years he faithfully collected various posters and photographs of all the more well-known college and professional stars of baseball, basketball, football, and tennis. But clearly of all these various sports, basketball always held his rather keen respect from the very beginning. So much so, in fact, that even after participating in the normal schedule of practice sessions there at our local school, he took upon himself the considerable responsibility of bringing together other interested young-sters of compatible ages living within our community for the express purpose of promoting a growing interest in this same marvelous sport which he just loved to play....

That appointed evening after the colorful metal globe was placed into motion, and immediately after the tip of the index finger of Ste-phen's right hand landed squarely upon the precise spot known as the island of New Caledonia, our somewhat reluctant participant quickly announced this fact to everyone else in the room since many of us were not able to see for ourselves precisely how things stood. Finally, along with establishing this same topic for discussion, he wasted little time in honestly stating that he knew relatively little about this part of the world.... So true to the rules of the game, Felix made it known to him as well as to the rest of us that he expected a short albeit characteristically interesting report the following weekend.

Well, as one might expect, the busy weekdays ahead came and went very quickly for all the members of our family. Quite happily, too, with the approach of that momentous weekend I soon found myself at home once more. Remembering this marvelous game and Stephen's important role in all of it, which was to occur sometime during that fast approaching Sunday evening, by midday on Saturday I chanced to run into my young energetic friend as he was making haste to leave our home to meet with the other members of his newly formed basketball club... And so in passing I quickly mentioned to him that I was looking forward to his report.

With my offhanded comment, he actually seemed quite stunned as he retorted with a bit of annoyance, "Report? Gosh! I've forgotten all about it!" Then as he rather absentmindedly reached for a chocolate-chip cookie from the ceramic jar which was sitting nearby, he made ready to feast upon the treat, just as he flashed me a thoroughly engaging smile to finally insist, "Don't worry, Adam, I'll polish off something to pacify my Father—most probably before tomorrow evening.... Thanks for reminding me!"

But the necessary time required to produce any sort of a well-crafted report, just as Felix always demanded, never actually materialized. That next evening as Felix and Emma Lauder were gathered in the parlor with several of their younger children, patiently awaiting Stephen's inevitable descent from his room so that he might make good on his responsibility, I was still upstairs myself currently in the process of observing my young friend "fudging" the entire project.... I watched with noted interest as he went about quickly penning a few random lines which seemed to flow more from his imagination than from anything else.

While this decidedly brash young soul finally went about so shamelessly delivering those same ridiculous lines which he had only moments before put to paper, he never once allowed his eyes to meet those of his father. Naturally there was a good reason for all this.... With his present attempt at perpetrating his modest little hoax, thereby intentionally trying to hoodwink his father in the process, he could not possibly run the risk of betraying himself by allowing his father to eventually find the truth clandestinely hidden there within his eyes....

Listening to Stephen's "off-the-wall report" was, to say the least, a highly entertaining moment in time. For example, somewhere in his opening remarks he actually found the nerve to proffer the thoroughly ridiculous statement that this interesting South Pacific island located off the East coast of Australia was originally settled by a fierce tribe of Amazon women who frequently cannibalized men and boys of all ages, whenever one of them would be discovered there upon their island. From that point onward, as well, similar flights of fancy abounded, until in the end it was quite obvious to every listener among us—moreover especially to Felix, that the report was either far less or far more than it should have ever been, depending upon one's point of view. Finally finishing with a characteristically theatrical flourish, by now the other children were laughing quite heartily with genuine amusement at their brother's brave antics, as he eventually announced to everyone, "And there you have my report!"

Following this it must have been our athlete's intention to quickly leave the house to join his friends who were no doubt impatiently waiting for him on the basketball court there at school. But as young Stephen confidently folded the single piece of paper he was holding, that same rather commonplace material upon which those few unforgettable lines of true nonsense were illegibly inscribed, I feel certain that it was also his intention to quickly slip the thing into his pant's pocket and just as hurriedly allow this minor episode within his life to fade into inconsequential nothingness, until Felix promptly announced with a slightly disturbing edge to his normally calm voice, "Not so fast, young man!"

Halting in his tracks with that same bit of paper still poised in midair, Stephen paused and then glanced up to behold his father's undeniably challenging countenance, as we all finally heard Felix ask somewhat nonchalantly, "Have you not forgotten to mention something rather important, Stephen...? What about the famous 'tigers' of New Caledonia? Naturally within your incredibly brief yet indisputably entertaining report this evening, you never once bothered to mention the 'tigers'!"

Needless to say, there was an uncomfortable game afoot at present. Standing quite motionless and deeply contemplating these challenging words his father had just delivered, it was quite obvious that young Stephen was at a loss for words. Soon, though, still wearing that memorably puzzled countenance, he responded by saying, "Tigers? Did I actually hear you say 'tigers,' Father?!"

"Yes, Stephen," Felix was responding, without so much as a smile. "It was my sincere hope that you might enlighten our audience with a few well-chosen words about this fascinating subject."

Beginning to feel uncomfortably awkward concerning this continuing game which our young friend had originally instigated, but in which his father now quite obviously was gaining the upper-hand, Stephen proceeded to slowly dig away at the hole in which he was already standing, making it just a little bit deeper and roomier... Purposely glancing away from Felix, most probably with the intention of hedging his bet, he meekly offered without very much conviction at all, "Well, as every one certainly already knows, tigers are large and extremely menacing animals!"

With this line the other children began to laugh in response to this seemingly lighthearted and happily entertaining banter between father and son. Soon, however, with Felix staring rather disapprovingly at this son of his with a look now that proclaimed in no uncertain terms that their impromptu little game was over, Felix stood and firmly said, "I trust that you shall be much better prepared to give a far more honest report, next Sunday!" And with these somewhat dire-sounding words of his, Stephen's father left the room and slowly wandered out onto the porch to finish reading the Sunday paper.

It was around the latter part of the following week, when I just happened to be making my way into the tiny community library located in Williams Bay, that I chanced to spot my young friend sitting all alone behind a significant collection of various reference books.... Engrossed as he apparently was in his forthcoming project for Sunday, he never even bothered to glance up to acknowledge my presence until I finally spoke his name.

"Oh! Hi, Adam!" he said in his normal cheerful manner.

"So!" I said, marveling at this turn of events, "I see you're working on that report for Sunday...." Feeling somewhat obligated to shore up this more or less anemic remark of mine, I went on to further interject, as I politely inquired, "How's it going, anyway?"

Studying me with a determined look that practically made me smile, Stephen said in a thoroughly forceful manner, "This is going to be the best damn report my father has ever heard! I'm going to make sure of it...." Then promptly returning to his notes to critically mark through almost an entire paragraph of words with the broad-edged pencil he was holding, he glanced up at me for a second time to enthusiastically ask, "By the way, would you like to review what I've written so far?" Before I had time to adequately respond in any manner, he proceeded to slide this same collection of several pieces of handwritten notes my way, and went on to add, "I'd certainly appreciate it if you could give me a few pointers, in the process—should you feel so inclined!"

With this undeniably urbane entreaty of his, I immediately responded by sitting down and helping him rework a few minor details with respect to what I sincerely believed was already a remarkably good report—and I told him so. That late Sunday afternoon while dressed in his impeccably clean basketball uniform, and obviously ready to go out and practice as usual with his teammates, my noticeably confident young friend was the first person to arrive in the parlor, this time himself patiently awaiting the arrival of the other members of his family and me....

Possessing considerable composure, Stephen Lauder proudly stood and delivered one of the most interesting reports to date. In a clear and well-modulated voice he offered fact upon fact of interesting information, and when he finally arrived at the end of this highly favorable event everyone, everyone except Felix, that is, began to clap enthusiastically in obvious appreciation for what my young friend had just shared with us.

After this short-lived congratulatory mayhem was allowed to subside, however, and after the room had once again become silent, this same self-possessed individual took a moment to visually engage his father. In words which clearly suggested that he had learned far more in writing this second report than he initially ever expected he might, he went on to respectfully inform his father as he said without hesitation, "Just as a final point, Father, you might be interested to know that there aren't any tigers on the island of New Caledonia... For that matter, there never have been!"

Spontaneously taking up that same impromptu little personal game of theirs, Felix continued to faithfully hold his son's determined gaze, as he thoughtfully answered in mock surprise, "No tigers?!"

"Not a one!" Stephen was assuring his father in a special mood that was deeply insinuating far more important underlying matters than this simple banter of theirs could possibly indicate.

Presently I thought I detected a small flicker of pride and joy begin to play there within the depths of this loving father's eyes, as Felix continued on by urging this special son of his, "Please tell me what else you have learned, naturally with respect to all that has transpired during this past week."

Deeply pondering the question for a moment everyone in the room eventually heard Stephen speak up with a sense of truly amazing conviction, as he said, "Well, sir—with all due respect, I've learned first-hand that 'bullshit' takes one only so far in life!"

With our audience's critical gaze currently fastening itself exclusively upon Felix, at the moment, I thought I also detected a slight play of a smile at the very corners of our patriarch's finely-chiseled lips, as we all heard him go on to urge, "What else?"

Finally, with a sense of even greater persuasion, as if this valuable lesson his father had chosen to impart to him was being firmly taken to heart, and never to be forgotten in the future, young Stephen properly concluded by saying, "I've learned, too, that any job worth doing is a job that is worth doing to the very best of one's ability—naturally the first time around!"

"Yes, Stephen... My compliments to you on a job well done." This, of course, is what Felix was presently saying, as he stood and then walked over to hug this much relieved son of his. "Now you may go and join your friends for that game of basketball!"

This example of positive interaction between father and child was, more or less, fairly typical of how the Lauder children and I learned so many of Life's more important lessons. Felix remained a tough and thoroughly discerning task-master, to be sure. Never once did he ever waver from always remaining consistently true to himself, as well as being true to those of us whom he sought to instruct on a daily basis. And he never expected more from his students than he, as our very able teacher, was endlessly prepared to give.

Exactly two weeks after this memorable happening occurred, I was unexpectedly laid-off from my part-time work at the lumber mill. Naturally, with my being the last to be hired, I eventually became the first to be fired. In lieu of this fact, I began pouring my substantial energies back into those many daily chores of mine which continued to abound all around our busy farmstead, attempting to conscientiously take up the slack which had naturally coincided with my being away for so long.

One late November evening while I sat happily lost upon my favorite perch located in my special corner within our marvelous enclosed porch area, I remained fairly hidden amongst Emma Lauder's gloriously slumbering oleander trees... I had been quietly reading and thoroughly enjoying a truly marvelous quote from one of Rilke's personal letters which was written to a friend a year before the poet's death.... The lines read: *"To our grandparents, a 'house,' a 'well,' a familiar steeple, even their own clothes, their cloak still meant intimately more, were infinitely more intimate— almost everything a vessel in which they found something human already there, and added to its human store. Now there are intruding, from America, empty indifferent things, sham things, dummies of life.... A house, as the Americans understand it, an American apple or a winestock from over there, have nothing in common with the house, the fruit, the grape into which the hope and thoughtfulness of our forefathers had entered...."*

Contemplating this rather punctilious insight my eyes eventually fell upon Felix who recently succumbed to that tantalizing nether world called sleep. Earlier he and I had been happily engrossed in sharing our usual quality conversation relevant to various topics of mutual interest when he eventually left my side with the intention of returning to his well-stocked little library the small book he had also been enjoying. But before taking a second to officially bid me good-night, as he might surely have done under the circumstances, I watched him inadvertently discover yet another book which instantly captured and held his attention. Following this he seemed to feel a need to glance through it. However his only real folly connected with this worthy idea was in choosing to comfortably recline there within the generous embrace of that wonderful old wing chair of his, for it soon came to pass that instead of scanning the work which presently lay unattended upon his lap, he managed instead to fall fast asleep....

The hour was already quite late. Soon it would be necessary to rise from our warm beds as a family and to officially greet this new day as

we enthusiastically began our many chores all over again. Vaguely I recall hearing the clock that was strategically placed within our otherwise
silent abode begin to herald the reality that it was midnight. And since
I was feeling rather weary, too, at this point, I soon found myself avidly
contemplating going off to bed....

With this tempting plan floating lightly within my well-contented
mind, I reached over to click off the reading lamp. Despite a telling yawn,
I purposely sat a little while longer within the now darkened space to
think upon many things, all the while lovingly studying this same gracious soul there in the next room. Felix's facial features were presently
being bathed in the soft amber glow from the nearby lamp, bestowing
upon his face and neck a gentle halo of sorts.

Before I actually took the initiative to rise and then to head upstairs,
I chanced to witness young Anna Allegra stealthily tiptoeing down the
stairs. Not having wished to startle the young woman, nor her father,
either, for that matter, I continued to respectfully observe the two in
silence. At the very same time I was becoming aware of some slowly
impending special event which I sensed might otherwise have been
foiled, had I chosen to make my presence known to either of these two
good people.

While Felix's favorite daughter knelt there upon one generous
corner of the area carpet which protruded out from underneath her
father's favorite chair, she took some time to silently and thoughtfully
contemplate the many intimate details of his face. Meanwhile "Hereboy"
had merely glanced up from his nap to find Anna nearby and proceeded
to give a less than enthusiastic wag of his tail.

"I just knew that I'd still find you here in the library, Father..." Anna
was loudly whispering, as I watched her dutifully stoop lower to pet our
wee dog until he began to slowly settle back down as before. Standing
up to wrap her warm flannel nightgown and matching robe more tightly
around her lean torso, she began making herself quite comfortable upon
the wide seat of the chair right next to Felix.

With a heartfelt smile I could not help but notice that upon her feet
she was wearing her unusual large fluffy slippers, the same characteristically extroverted type that looked very much as if she were allowing a
pair of live overgrown rabbits to accompany her wherever she decided
to go.... Those same furry feet which might have otherwise just stuck
out in midair, due to the fact that our Anna was already a good head
taller than her father, were now being somewhat ceremoniously hoisted
up upon the broad ottoman right next to her father's and then neatly
crossed at the ankles.

Just as if this same orchestrated little number of movements which she seemed obliged to perform had not yet been concluded, she went on to matter-of-factly entwine one graceful arm through one of Felix's as she confidently hugged her weary companion to her.... In a moment more Anna turned to gaze rather steadfastly into our dear patriarch's sleepy eyes, as she seriously inquired, "Father, would you be completely honest with me if I asked you something truly, truly important?!"

Without missing a beat young Anna and I both heard Felix respond, by thoughtfully answering, "Anna, you already know that you may always count upon me to be exactly that in every situation."

With a somewhat pained expression clearly written across her pale and slightly furrowed brow, and with her thick sleep-tousled hair exquisitely framing her intelligent face, this delightful young woman soon went ahead to inquire with a note of genuine hopefulness, "Am I beautiful, Father? I mean, is there a chance that someday I'll become beautiful—if I wait long enough?!"

With this desperate sounding personal entreaty of hers, Felix frowned a little himself in response, as he looked squarely at Anna to say, "But you were born beautiful, Anna—both inside and out! Surely you already suspect as much...."

Gazing even more deeply into her father's eyes, at the moment, as if the elusive answer to her important query might somehow be more clearly defined there in their bathyal depths, she firmly stated without so much as a glimmer of humor, "But, don't you know...? All fathers are suppose to say such kind things about their own daughters, most probably whether they're true or not!"

"Oh, is that so!" my friend was saying in response, as he seemed to be trying hard not to smile.

"Do you know that I'm already the tallest girl in my class!?" Anna went on to unhappily lament. Then sticking one rabbit-covered foot into midair, in order that her father might critically examine it for himself, she went on to further state with considerable exasperation, "And look at this.... See how large my feet are! Why already they're even bigger than yours!"

By now Felix could no longer hide the smile he was openly smiling. Naturally as Anna caught sight of this fact, she placed her face close to his, as she overtly suggested in only a slightly playful mood, "This isn't the time to laugh at me, you know! After all, I'm a very sensitive person and I'm being as serious here as I possibly can be!"

"I know, my dear..." my friend was assuring his terribly vulnerable young daughter in a far more compassionate tone. Soon choosing to impart an appropriate analogy intended to help explain this often difficult and awkward stage in a person's life, Felix went on to confess, "However, my splendid Anna, what you do not as yet understand is that you have become temporarily lost in that 'great land of transition'—or perhaps it might be more appropriate for me to say, considering your point of view, naturally, that 'not-so-great land of transition.'... In other words, you are presently living as a young caterpillar might live, by dutifully following the prescribed edict of your sacred life-cycle and subsequently having gone and woven yourself into a somewhat uncomfortable and highly restrictive cocoon, so to speak.... One day for certain, though, continuing to be true to your nature you shall finally break free and spread your colorful wings to eventually bask in the glorious reality of being a lovely butterfly!"

Having been properly caught up in this visual imagery of his, Anna wasted little time as she asked, "How long does it usually take for a caterpillar to become a butterfly?"

"Not long..." my dear friend was whispering. As Felix continued to lovingly study the innocent face of the young daughter he so loved, all the while Anna continued to hopefully study his face in return, he went on to add with such tenderhearted conviction, as he announced with an obvious tinge of real sadness, "Not long, my dearest child—and yet, in so many important ways, not quite long enough!"

After several moments of silence passed, where neither father nor daughter chose to speak, Anna decided to slide a bit further down into the huge leather chair so that she could better be able to rest her head upon Felix's chest. While this father's strong arms protectively encircled his daughter's shoulders, both Anna and I heard him whisper just over her head as he mused, "You simply have no idea how many times I have contemplated the fortunate reality that Fate so generously allowed you to look like your mother, instead of like me... Imagine how awfully unattractive you would be with a balding head, and an ongoing need to shave your face each and every day!"

In response to this humorous remark, I watched as Anna immediately pulled away from her father and turned to meet his eyes while she passionately asserted, "Why, you're the most handsome man in the entire world, Father!"

Literally beaming at this point with a secret message of some sort, Felix responded in kind by good-naturedly exclaiming, "It does readily occur to me that loving daughters are forever obliged to say this sort of thing about their poor old fathers—naturally, whether the sentiment is true or not!"

"Touche!" Anna was exclaiming as both parties continued to snuggle together, as well as attempt to tone down their mutual laughter which this lovely game of theirs was currently inspiring.

Now with Anna's head more in profile, and with the left side of her face resting comfortably there upon her dear father's chest once more, Felix went on to initiate, "You know, Anna, I have long suspected that even the Gods are seduced by great physical beauty… Certainly when it comes to acknowledging this sort of earthly perfection, somehow it only seems normal that we mortals also respond in kind to this same overwhelming impulse…."

Taking a second or two to shift his weight just a fraction, thereby allowing himself to become more comfortably situated in the chair's wide seat, my dear friend eventually went on to add to these remarks, by thoughtfully saying, "As an artist, I have long been an ardent connoisseur of beauty in every imaginable form. I have come to appreciate, too, that even the most resplendent rose eventually loses its highly valued bloom with the inevitable passing of time…. But this in itself is not a great tragedy, since this normal process of evolution can never really compromise the overall integrity of the flower itself! And as far as people are concerned, if one chooses to dedicate one's life to the preeminent folly of focusing primarily upon one's exterior physical characteristics, quite often to the sad neglect of one's vastly more precious interior beauty, life becomes far less than it could and should be….

"If a person is blessed with great physical attractiveness, then all the better. Those more discerning Gods, as well as we mere mortals, shall continue to reap the overall enjoyment that such things just naturally engender. It does frequently seem to me, just the same, that such particulars of life remain the proverbial 'icing' on the cake—and certainly not the whole of the experience at all…."

With these unusual words of Felix's, Anna turned her face upwards to better study her father's weary-looking countenance while he spoke. As her silent attention focused entirely upon him in this way, he continued on to reveal to both of us, "For example, how could any sensitive soul possibly seek to live a healthy and robust existence, by dining exclusively upon that sweet icing alone? Surely there must always be a cake… Hopefully, too, a substantially durable and thoroughly nourishing cake—somewhere underneath all that sweet stuff!

"I suppose that what I am really attempting to impart to you, my dearest Anna, is my near religious belief that one should focus more keenly on becoming an interesting person. This, in the end, tends to serve one far better, since the natural benefits from this lifelong pursuit remain ongoing and constant. With this noble practice, whether one is blessed with physical good looks, or not, one's everyday life shall continue to become richer and far more fulfilling in ways that could never possibly be imagined otherwise....

"I have often reflected that interesting people generally become even more interesting with the predictable passing of time. As an added benefit, they seem to cultivate the art of attracting other such rare beings of a similarly intellectual and spiritual disposition. How terribly frustrating it has always been for me to be forced to acknowledge the unhappy reality that each of us would be required to live hundreds of consecutive lifetimes, just in order to even begin to grasp a mere fraction of all that there is to understand about this amazing universe in which we all live.... Do you realize how wretchedly humbling this severely sobering truth can be?!

"When one contemplates this relatively simple philosophy, one eventually comes to better understand that to focus strictly upon oneself in the purely narcissistic sense insures a deservedly boring and highly unfulfilling life, to be sure! A person eventually comes to understand the important nuances pertaining to their own unique interiors, only when they bother to passionately explore those interior spiritual reservoirs of others. By pledging to meet this challenge on an ongoing basis, one slowly comes to understand and appreciate one's own unique relationship to the divine miracle of it all.... Naturally, with this sound prescription for a far more quality life, how could anyone possibly consider living any other way?"

Anna finally broke her silence, to eagerly whisper, "How may I become truly interesting, Father?"

"By resolving in the core of your being that you shall maintain a genuine interest in other people, and places, as well as even the most seemingly trite events of day-to-day life which continue to occur all around us—taking extreme care, all the while, to never squander a single moment of any day that is yours!" With these revolutionary thoughts which Felix was proposing, I watched him take a second to pass his free hand lovingly across young Anna's face, in order to brush aside a solitary strand of renegade hair which had fallen carelessly across her cheek....

Then as if seeking to adequately sum up these rather grown-up ideas of his, Felix went on to recite what I still imagine was his own personal litany for living a life of quality. Shortly my friend went on to softly say to his beloved daughter, "Promise me, dearest daughter of mine, that you shall always remember to acknowledge that special beauty which already dwells within you, just as you shall instinctively feel compelled to endlessly search out and discover for yourself those similarly magnetic qualities which also dwell within the souls of certain other people too.... With this invaluable philosophy you are bound to learn the dazzling truth that for everyone of all ages happiness becomes the best cosmetic!

"Strive to know all that there is to know about yourself, and faithfully develop confidence in your abilities, for with these priceless tools you will never be poor. In essence, this same necessary confidence will better arm you against the everyday disappointments of living and loving.

"Furthermore, envy no one. This, too, shall become critically relevant to your future happiness. After all, each and every person's life becomes an inescapable kaleidoscope of infinite joys and sorrows.... And it remains no secret, either, that so many people merely play at life. For reasons either known or unknown to themselves, they choose to hide behind those carefully crafted disguises of their own unique design.... So in the end, with regard to this same unfortunate age-old game of 'human charades,' who may say for certain what is truly real and what truly isn't?!"

Soon after this Felix adopted a slightly mischievous smile as he went on to proclaim, "Never fear playing the fool, either, my Anna Banana! Personally speaking, I discovered long ago that unless this frequently embarrassing attitude is allowed to become chronic in nature, it remains perfectly natural to occasionally be humbled in this way.... As a rule people generally learn from their mistakes and frequently even find themselves in the enviable position of actually being a bit wiser when all is said and done!

"Finally, my dear, never take money, nor fame, nor power over others, for your God, inasmuch as these notoriously much-coveted gems of every human society tend to pale considerably in comparison to what is truly sacred. Seek, instead, to allow Truth and Justice to guide your travels. With these more than respectable attributes as your latitude and longitude, you shall never become lost. Strive ever more to live your life to its fullest since Life, by design, remains implacably tenuous.... And most of all, my beautiful, beautiful Anna, never forget for a single moment that your father loves you so dearly!"

Smiling up at Felix, now, with a truly breathtaking look of what may only be described as charmed wonderment, Anna finally confided to her father, in return, "I love you, too, Papa! I love you so very much....

Someday I'm going to marry a man who's exactly like you in every way!" Shortly, thereafter, with these sincerely expressed words of hers, arm in arm father and daughter headed off towards the staircase where they eventually parted to go their separate ways.

Presently, with my having remained behind to quietly ponder that entirely meaningful scenario which had just occurred between this special father and this equally special daughter, I was significantly struck by several important realities. For instance, although the powerful emotional connection between fathers and sons is legendary, quite frankly far too little consideration is given to the extremely vital role a father is destined to play in the life of his daughter.

With the potent "imprinting" which normally takes place within this far more neglected realm of relationships, the father inadvertently becomes the "first significant love object" of his daughter's world. With respect to this particular parent, the overall significance of this fact becomes enormous. For better or for worse, the girl-child often becomes psychologically compelled to systematically pattern all her future relationships, notwithstanding her future intimate partnerships with other men, based upon this solitary "hero-figure."...

Should any young girl happen to be consistently raised with a father as gentle protector and dependable provider, that fortunate child will more than likely grow to adulthood with a strong foundation of highly significant personal confidence which is firmly based upon being sincerely cherished and loved. Likewise, when such a child is reared by a man of dependable integrity who continuously treats her with ongoing respect and dignity, this adult is also ultimately impressing upon the child the absolutely critical reality that she has great innate value as a human being. In time the woman that the child eventually becomes will be able to confidently stand upon her own feet, making it possible for her throughout her lifetime to carve out a relatively safe place for herself in the world.

Conversely, if early in her life any female child is beset by ongoing physical or emotional abuse relative to this important parent figure, she is likely to become sentenced to travel through life expecting very little else from other men she comes across.... Should her own father either consciously or unconsciously place her upon this demeaning life-path, which is destined to be pockmarked with criminally inflicted feelings of little self-worth, what is usually being perpetrated for this unfortunate individual is a truly difficult future that is often burdened with similar kinds of abuses. And unless such a woman becomes wise enough and/

or lucky enough to somehow be able to defy this structured mold of betrayal which was established by that particular person whom she as a young child once instinctively trusted, history will oftentimes repeat itself in the lives of this woman's daughters and granddaughters, ultimately robbing more than one generation of people—as well as all of human society, in its attempt to significantly add to our world in the positive sense.

From my worthy perspective, and certainly just as Felix himself had also proclaimed, Anna Allegra Lauder was a genuinely beautiful person—both inside and out. Whenever I think back upon this adopted sister of mine, and upon my treasured relationship with her, I shall always remember an amazingly self-assured young child who found the courage to back me into a corner that day when I teasingly used the special nickname which her father had early on bestowed upon her, and which had been reserved for him alone. Likewise, and with just as much affection, I shall forevermore recall that much older Anna who, on that same memorable late evening, purposely sought out and subsequently found—there in our wonderful family library, a typical sampling of the ever-dependable wisdom and abundant love her father always reserved for all his children and me.

Years later, Anna's relatively short life would be filled with much joy, as well as much sorrow. One day she would marry. And with regard to this sacred union, two wonderful children would be born; a daughter and a son, both of whom would surely add to the sum of all our happiness as a family. But as so frequently happens, for one reason or another, in due course Anna's marriage would be ending.... With the sobering reality of her two small children to support, she would be readily accepting the challenge of returning to school with the primary intention of earning a degree in nursing in order to accomplish this end.

As it happened, though, during that infamous early summer of 1956, when Anna and her children and I returned independent of each other to stay there at the Lauder's farmstead, and moreover, to visit with Emma Lauder for a couple of weeks, something happened which would forever be altering our lives.... Having fortuitously left her infant son behind in the family's able care on that warm and exceptionally sunny Saturday morning, Anna and her lovely six-year-old daughter, Kathy, became inspired to take a ride into town with the thought of purchasing a small measure of colorful ribbon for the child's hair....

Alas, too, as unkind Fate would be dictating, on that very same morning after having only hours before acquired his learner's permit

to operate an automobile, some decidedly drunk and criminally irresponsible sixteen-year-old youngster was out joyriding with three of
his friends when he failed to heed a stop sign.... Plowing into the side of
Anna's car at an excessively high speed in which the group was traveling,
the subsequently violent impact sent the young woman's vehicle rolling
into a nearby ditch, instantly killing both mother and child.

Days later at their funeral as emotionally stunned family members
and dear friends, alike, once again solemnly gathered together at the
small cemetery upon the hill—there underneath the protective branches
of that now resplendent red maple tree, despite my own heart which
was badly breaking with such irreconcilable sadness, I did nevertheless
find a fragment of much-required consolation in the fact that Felix had
not lived to witness this same heart-wrenching event. Although the Lord
giveth and the Lord taketh away, as each of us is destined to eventually
learn, in His abundant mercy our compassionate and loving God had
taken pity upon this good father by not having inflicted this same overwhelming sorrow upon his spirit while he lived.

22.

"ADAM, PLEASE PROMISE ME that you will not attempt to make it home this evening.... With the snow storm intensifying as it has been for the past several hours, it would be foolish for you to try to negotiate those back roads! Just sit tight and wait out the storm. Tomorrow morning, if the weather cooperates, we'll find a way to solve the problem." Of course these were the worried sentiments which Felix was currently expressing on my behalf, as I respectfully listened to what he was telling me from my end of the telephone. My solicitous friend soon went on to quickly add, "Naturally we will be obliged to leave the truck where it is, and then dig it out sometime during the next couple of days or so."

This particular conversation of ours was taking place on the late afternoon of that highly eventful Christmas Eve of 1940. Much earlier that day, with the substantial threat of a genuine blizzard hanging over our community, I volunteered to drive a goodly portion of our holiday supper over to Harry Hopkins. Although our dear family friend was earlier invited to join us at our own holiday table, for deeply personal reasons of his own he chose to decline. With his beloved "Lady Genny" having died shortly before the Thanksgiving of that same year, he was forced to live alone. Without anyone to care for him—nor, too, without anyone for whom he might also care, the Lauder's and I naturally rallied to his cause. Customarily one or more of us would make the daily pilgrimage those eight miles to his home to take him a bit of homemade nourishment and to share, perhaps just as critically, too, an hour or so of much required human interaction.

Weeks before this normally far more happy time, it was our poor Harry who eventually discovered his wife lying motionless beside her little wagon. She had suffered a heart attack from which she did not recover.

Having faithfully traveled back and forth across their yard each and every day for all those many years in an ongoing attempt to endlessly follow her own compulsive needs, Ugenia Hopkins' once strong and loving heart eventually just stopped beating. Harry, quite predictably, took her loss extremely hard. Therefore, in a conscientious attempt on our part to comfort him, as well as inspire within him even a modest reason to continue living, we would cheerfully seek him out in order to attempt to bolster his ever-growing mood of darkening moroseness....

"Mr. Hopkins, do you think that you could possibly stand my company until sometime after breakfast tomorrow morning? As you see, the snow is really coming down quite hard, and it might certainly prove far more prudent for me to stay the night, if that's OK with you!" This is what I was presently suggesting to my faithful old friend as he sat quietly absorbed in his private thoughts, more or less absentmindedly watching the snow flurries as they continued to collect across the various gently-sloping elevations of the surrounding countryside, all the while slowly blanketing the many acres of his land in a thick layer of lovely pristine alabaster....

Before the telephone call arrived from Felix, Harry and I were attempting to finish a game of checkers which had been originally initiated several days before that time. However, with my friend's present inability to concentrate very long upon any one thing, the game pretty much became secondary for both of us. With my genuinely hopeful inquiry, he slowly looked up. Obviously grappling with his difficulty to mentally focus upon me, at this point, it became quite clear to me that he was beginning to feel somewhat defeated in his inability to properly come to terms with what I had just asked....

Upon his ancient old phonograph, which was sitting over in one far corner of the same room that we were occupying, the now scratchy sound of Rudy Valley's voice was crooning an old song which he helped make very popular in his day. Only after I took the initiative to sit by Harry's side and to ever-so-gently take up one of his hands did I slowly repeat my question. His noticeably swollen and misshapen fingers remained indicative of his years of suffering from the debilitating menace of rheumatoid arthritis. Shortly, with my success in visually engaging his attention, he answered me by matter-of-factly quipping, "R-r-real q-q-question, A-a-adam, s-s-seems to be whether y-you can p-p-put up with th-this old f-f-fart until t-t-tomorrow m-morning!"

This impromptu remark of his made me smile a little even though lately, with that predictably significant depression over his wife's death, he was becoming more and more down on himself. Understanding full well the mechanism which was prompting this highly uncharacteristic behavior, I felt obliged to deflect this self-effacing remark of his by countering with a sincerely-felt sentiment of my own, and quickly assured him, "Since I was a youngster, I've always greatly esteemed your very fine company, Mr. Hopkins.... And it certainly goes without saying, as well, that there aren't a whole lot of people who fit into this same very special category!"

With my enthusiastically delivered remark, Harry merely smiled somewhat wistfully at me. Soon, in silent acknowledgment of the compliment I had just paid him, he briefly patted that hand of mine which was still clinging to his own. In my valiant attempt to keep him mentally engaged, I went ahead to mention, "Mrs. Lauder sent along some of her marvelous holiday fare.... I'm willing to bet that if she's stayed her usual course, then she's sent along enough provisions to feed a small army! In which case, my dear friend, there will be enough goodies for both of us to share for our Christmas Eve supper later on this evening."

Since Ugenia Hopkins' death, Harry's usual solicitude in attending to his personal grooming was currently lagging a bit. This, quite understandably, remained an outward manifestation of his ever-present depression. Without anyone or anything for which to care these days, his more keen interest in the usual day-to-day business of life was definitely waning. Recalling how truly kind this good man always was to me— especially back when I was a young boy, and how he instinctively took me under his protective wing to become my very own private "guardian angel," now, of course, in a conscious effort to be able to return to him even a small measure of this same sort of kindness, I earnestly set about to try and better his presently difficult situation in the most ordinary of ways....

Realizing only too well how marvelously beneficial a hot bath can be, even under normal circumstances—and not only in the physical sense, but far more importantly in the emotional sense, I went ahead and filled the bathtub for this woefully neglected soul. Soon enough, while Harry soaked rather contentedly for quite some time there within his deep pool of soapy water, I further attended to his needs by dutifully shampooing his head. Lastly, as two important final gestures, I further went about trimming his rather unkempt hair and also shaving clean his pale face from its former thick snow-white stubble which had collected over time.

Unbeknownst to me, unbeknownst to anyone, for that matter, this was to be my dear friend's last Christmas with us. Because I have come to better understand the many underlying intricacies involved with loving in the deeply human sense, I have also come to know that whenever an individual suffers this sort of spiritual deprivation—as strongly as our poor Harry, their own life-force begins to hopelessly wane, eventually bringing them to a point where they no longer fear death but actually welcome it.... Perhaps this highly significant knowledge already dwelled somewhere deep within me, for I do believe that I instinctively sensed the truth of it all and therefore decided to honor the moment—as well as to honor this dear man, by going about ceremoniously attempting to make that evening we were both about to share as special as I possibly could....

After helping Harry dress warmly in a pair of thick corduroy slacks, and, too, an extremely well worn but thoroughly comfortable-looking green and red plaid heavy woolen shirt, I finally slipped upon his stocking feet those ever-present bedroom slippers of his which he was so extremely fond of wearing around the house. Next I struggled to slide one heavy low antique table over more towards the center of the huge picture-window in the living room where my companion normally enjoyed sitting all the year through. Following this, I proceeded to decorate that modestly-constructed dais with two cheerful holiday place-settings—along with a small white candle which I inadvertently found in one of the kitchen drawers.

In time I thoroughly rewarmed all the splendid food from Emma Lauder's magic kitchen. And, of course, after allowing a few seconds more to deferentially light the small luminant which I expressly chose to more perfectly symbolize this special event, happily I took my place across from my dear supper partner and remarked, "Thank you for allowing me to share this fine meal with you, Mr. Hopkins!"

Sometimes, just as the sensitive reader is also aware, there are those near-sacred moments in one's life when there does not seem to be any real need for speaking. To be more specific, there are those infinitely special times when mere silence alone has the unique ability to speak far more eloquently than any words possibly can. And so, with the true spirit of Christmas locked within my heart, there the two of us quietly sat—my faithful old friend and I, slowly and quite wordlessly enjoying our supper together....

There, indeed, by that solitary beacon of our small candle's softly flickering light, fleetingly I recalled one especially memorable line in the Good Book which alludes to Christ being "the light of the world"—mankind's much-needed salvation. During that same remarkably holy evening, too, not only was I consciously acknowledging the ever-reassuring thought of God's love for mankind—which is predicated upon genuine kindness in the truest sense, but I was also acknowledging the profound beauty of genuine friendship and love with respect to man towards his fellow man.

Warmly wrapped within these intensely comforting sentiments of mine, and at the same time bowing low to this splendid moment by consciously choosing to utter nary a sound, Harry Hopkins and I continued to be mesmerized by the powerful snow storm that was currently swirling all about his little home. With a sense of growing respect and humility, we watched while the fierce intensity of nature's fury caused that icy cold whiteness to completely obliterate any sense of color, as well as any dependable sense of perspective, too, there throughout that undeniably hostile world outside....

Upon waking during the following Christmas Day morning, what surely had occurred during the course of the previously stormy night to be ardently savored by the more discerning spectator, was a picture of unequaled contrast. Here and now with the bright sun presently shining upon the dense layer of newly fallen snow, and, likewise, with the unique splendor of all the thick ice-encrusted branches of the nearby trees and shrubs, it was as if God had gone about exquisitely decorating our small part of the world in joyful celebration of this fine day. Everything in sight seemed meticulously crafted by nothing less than the divine hand of a well-practiced artisan. Naturally using those unique tools of His splendid trade, an infinite multitude of tiny glittering diamonds abounded....

"Merry Christmas, Felix!" I was enthusiastically saying with a light and happy heart, as I was forced to practically yell into the mouthpiece of Harry Hopkins' wall-box phone. To further assure my adopted father that he need not worry about my current situation, I loudly added with the hope of making myself understood above the current static which was wildly dancing about within the phone line, "With our truck firmly buried in the snow as it is—and with the roads completely impassable as you previously predicted, Mr. Hopkins has very kindly consented to loan me his pair of old snowshoes which I intend to put to good use! After a quick bite to eat, I shall begin to make my way home."

Having shared a very substantial breakfast of eggs and toast with Harry, I finally bid him good-bye before securely tying upon my hefty winter boots that rarest pair of museum-quality snow shoes. Following this, as I mentally prepared myself for a healthy work-out, I cheerfully headed out into the cold clear morning with the positive notion of breaking some imaginary record for such challenging travel by foot.

As I set out for home on that wonderful morning, I quickly rediscovered the unusually stark and all-encompassing silence which usually accompanies such extreme samplings of winter's handiwork. Consequently, the only sounds to be heard besides the more familiar beating of my heart within my ears were those sporadic gusts of not-so-gentle wind. Those vigorous air currents were often ruthlessly competing with the measured puffing sounds my own breathing was making as I labored strenuously to make my way across the deep snow. Not so far in the distance, now, I could just barely see the wonderful sight of the long-familiar steeple of our tiny chapel, inspiring within me a genuine burst of energy as I continued to plow forward, on and on.... However, not less than three hundred yards or so from that same hallowed ground, the ragged old leather bindings of my left snowshoe finally gave way, causing me to spontaneously fall forward with a considerable thud, and then to further tumble headlong into a formidable-looking ice-encrusted snow bank....

I quickly noted with some relief that about the only real thing which had been even slightly injured was my pride. Eventually extracting myself from my self-made "nest" of tightly-packed snow, I was forced to promptly remove the other shoe, in order that I might make it the rest of the way towards the little church quite literally on foot. Opting to shorten the distance to our farmhouse as much as possible I decided to approach the cemetery grounds by way of my own private back entrance, with the idea of squeezing through that same narrow portion of iron fencing that remained missing several of its tall rods. After all, since my earliest boyhood this timesaving method of reaching home had already become quite familiar to me.

Being exceptionally winded from my recent physical exertion of snow-shoeing all those miles, not to mention becoming unnecessarily cold from my unexpected trounce in the deep snow bank, I casually glanced around and noticed that there was not another soul in sight. Of course with the recent blizzard—and given the fact that folks rarely made use of our tiny chapel anymore—this perfectly peaceful solitude which our small cemetery nearly always afforded seemed just as it should be.

Before I actually made my way over to the graves of George and Lewis, naturally to pay my respects on this particularly special day, I was overcome by an overwhelming need to quickly settle somewhere and to temporarily remove my heavy winter boots. An inordinate amount of ice-cold snow had managed to lodge itself deeply within each, and I found that I simply could not go another step farther without taking a moment to relieve this terribly unpleasant sensation.

Subsequently having spotted a long empty stone planter that was conveniently located directly at the rear of the chapel, I immediately established myself upon one corner of the object. Shortly, thereafter, while becoming typically engrossed in the process of accomplishing this relatively simple task of mine, my attention was instantly arrested by the totally unexpected sound of harmonica music as it slowly began to echo out across the silent whiteness of the surrounding fields, apparently pouring forth from its original source which seemed to be somewhere quite near to where I now sat....

Harmonica music—of all things! Heavenly harmonica music of the most endearingly superb quality, which up to that particular point in time I had actually only had the privilege of hearing George and his father play… Furthermore, how could anyone have possibly not recognized Bach's own *"Ave Maria,"* which was presently being so passionately brought forth by way of that small and frequently understated musical device, and just in time to firmly bless this already fine Christmas Day.

Once, in his characteristically generous mood of sharing, our George indicated to me that during his father's own childhood and youth back in Hungary, Felix had become quite adept at being able to play the violin. However, sometime years after he married George's mother—for some unexplainable reason, he took to putting the instrument aside, never to play upon it again....

When Lewis and George were youngsters, early on Felix began patiently teaching them to play mere fragments of several lively Hungarian folk songs there upon the harmonica. Presently, with myself concentrating on nothing else but this other magical music which continued to float all about our small cemetery grounds, as well as down and around the surrounding countryside to appropriately consecrate both of these places, I became cognizant of the fact that this simple little instrument was being expertly handled by someone who obviously understood music in the most intimate sense. I found myself secretly betting that it could only be Felix who had chosen to so greatly honor this day by playing this exquisite masterpiece by Bach....

Somewhat puzzled by this unusual turn of events, I continued to hold my remaining boot suspended there in midair.... With my initial surprise at hearing this wondrous music I had not even bothered taking the necessary time to put it back upon my foot right away.

My curiosity was intensifying with every second that passed, and I soon felt compelled to hop those mere three or four feet towards the back wall of the church to lean there upon that strong fortification for support. I proceeded next to eagerly peek around the corner of the building in order to finally discover for myself who might actually be responsible for creating this wholly enchanting phenomenon. Sure enough, there in one discernibly empty far corner of the cemetery grounds—more or less directly across from where the graves of George and Lewis could be found, Felix was standing all alone, apparently having wholly lost himself to this rare moment in time....

How perfectly odd this entire picture began to appear to me. As far as I knew—and I certainly felt that I knew every inch of this hallowed ground by now, there was not a grave of any sort located over where my dear friend was presently occupying himself in this highly mystifying manner.

With my vulnerable backside pressed against the ice-cold chapel wall for better support and balance, and all this while still having remained out of sight of Felix, I hurriedly put on my other boot. Hence, standing fully erect, I chose to remain leaning against the wall with my eyes closed, all the while deeply contemplating all the possibilities that might eventually explain this unusual behavior of my dear friend. Soon I was becoming just as hopelessly lost as Felix apparently was in that same glorious music he was making. Each perfect note wavered so clearly within that cold clean air, and it was as though I were being serenaded by the angels themselves....

As soon as the music ceased altogether, my first impulse was to hurry over to where Felix was standing and to happily greet him by wishing him a heartfelt Merry Christmas. But as I proceeded to round the corner of our little chapel with my mind firmly set upon doing this very thing, I was forced to come to an abrupt halt, just as I chanced to witness my great friend remove his handkerchief from his back pocket and seemingly begin to wipe away the tears from his eyes. Not long after this, he also took to blowing his nose with that same trusty linen cloth. Finally I watched further as he unknowingly turned his back towards me and began to slowly negotiate his way down the snow-laden hill of the cemetery grounds, clearly in an effort to make his way back home....

Indeed, what was I to make of it all? After having unwittingly stumbled upon this extraordinarily moving yet highly mysterious behavior on Felix's part, how should I have interpreted this most private moment of his? Was someone actually buried over in that more remote part of our cemetery? Someone whom he might have known in some special way?

A child, a woman, or a fellow man, perchance, whom he obviously still greatly esteemed? If so, whom might it be that even in death still held the power to so profoundly move this incredibly special human being into actually weeping on their behalf?

Very much like any solicitous detective might have behaved under similar circumstances, and before I actually wandered over to investigate the mysterious spot where Felix formerly stood, I went about carefully examining his many footsteps which upon his initial arrival made it quite clear to me that earlier he had gone first to the graves of his sons. For there, clear as day, the telltale trail of fresh imprints that his heavy work-boots made within the deep virgin snow remained exposed to view. Now, too, laying across both of those twin graves were identical bouquets of freshly-cut sprigs of Christmas holly.... As I reverently stood nearby, emotionally taking in this touching sight, an emboldened raven gently fluttered down to land upon George's wooden cross.

Glancing up, I observed its eager mate sitting upon one sturdy lower branch of our presently leafless maple tree. Naturally without my having moved at all, I represented little threat to them. Eventually calculating this same reality for themselves, the noisy companion responded by quickly descending to land at last upon the same grave. Then, undoubtedly without meaning the slightest disrespect at all, the two hungry thieves began to eagerly separate that sumptuous collection of abundant bright red berries from their resplendent absinthian-hued greenery.

Obsessed to finally investigate the identical place where Felix had formerly stood while he serenaded that early morning, I eventually discovered the precise spot. Kneeling upon the snowy ground I soon beheld a small wooden plaque which must have earlier also been sought out by my friend from underneath its deep blanket of pure white snow. For there, having obviously been wiped clean by either one of Felix's hands—or possibly even his clean handkerchief, for that matter—the tiny object mutely greeted me as I carefully continued to contemplate its lovely existence. While I took a moment more to reverently run my fingers over the interesting hand-carved marker, there within its center I could not miss seeing the modestly-inscribed initials: A. M. G. Likewise, beautifully decorating the entire border of this nearly flat and highly unobtrusive work of art was a continuous succession of hand-carved roses intermingled with various musical notes....

Over these many years of my relatively long life, I have finally evolved to a point where I am able to confidently embrace the pragmatic belief which states that it is truly impossible to know another person in the truly complete sense. Owing primarily to this same universally held conviction, it stands to reason that within each human soul there remains some fairly isolated inner-chamber which utterly defies the curious probing of others. Notwithstanding the overall complexities inherent within that vast and individually unique terrain known as the human spirit, mysteries abound—both great and small, very much like the ever-beguiling mysteries of our vast universe itself.

Perhaps in the end, if one is fortunate enough and truly dedicated enough in one's lifelong quest for truth and understanding, what is hopefully achieved is a more perfect understanding of oneself.... And, personally speaking, who among us would ever wish to alter this divine order of things? Who among us would not be pressed to sincerely acknowledge that there is something basically comforting with respect to the more stable nature of all this wisdom?

Already possessing an inkling concerning this same fundamental axiom of mine, I purposely dallied about a little while longer that morning, chiefly for the chance of attempting to divine the proper relevance of that small mysterious treasure which was hiding within the still relatively unspoiled snow. Now, not only was I marveling at the wondrous secrets which I somehow already suspected dwelled deep within the heart of my dear friend, but, likewise, I was also marveling greatly at the complexity of his powerful spirit, fully appreciating all the while that these same enigmatic qualities undoubtedly helped contribute to make him the vastly interesting man that he just naturally seemed to be.

Generally speaking, whenever it came to our more formal dining routine within the Lauder household, especially during those several important holidays throughout every year, it was the custom of the family's many members to gather together for the main meal around three or four o'clock in the afternoon. Therefore with respect to that particular Christmas Day afternoon I supposed that it was to be no different. When I finally arrived back at the farmhouse by faithfully following the telling trail which Felix had unknowingly left behind for me, I gratefully claimed for myself the necessary time to bathe and to dress in honor of the approaching celebration. After that I intentionally wandered down into the kitchen where I found Felix and Emma....

Since it would prove to be at least another couple of hours before we would feast upon yet another one of Emma Lauder's glorious home-cooked meals, Felix was currently indulging in his required snack of toast and tea. Upon my relatively exuberant entrance into that marvelously fragrant little place where the mouth-watering scent of baked duckling was unmistakably originating to mercilessly tease everyone's senses by spreading its glorious tidings throughout our happy dwelling, I watched as the lady of the house was characteristically bustling about in the process of seeing to all the small personal touches that she believed were necessary. As soon as I appeared in the doorway, Felix quickly stood up from his place at the table and promptly cleared away a modest spot for me amongst all the various jars of interesting spices and other secret potions his wife used for cooking. Next he graciously invited me to join him at the table for a piping hot cup of temptingly aromatic tea, which I gratefully accepted.

After the two of us went about amicably exchanging a bit of light-hearted banter relating to this minor subject and that, and, more importantly, after I took the obligatory time to advise both Felix and Emma on just how Harry Hopkins was faring, our rather spontaneous interaction eventually ceased altogether, as I observed Felix slowly withdrawing into himself. Although my friend continued to go through those somewhat mindless motions of sipping his tea, it was becoming quite clear to me that both mentally and emotionally he had already unwittingly left me far behind within the comforting atmosphere of our small kitchen, to travel rather innocuously on to some sacred other world. And all this while I was becoming acutely aware of my having been innocently afflicted by that more rarefied feeling of a rather familiar sort of frustration, since in this particular case I was being hindered from following in my dear companion's footsteps....

My thinking was that Felix's present mood of considerable introspection naturally stemmed from what had just recently transpired within the cemetery. Loving him as I did, and, too, deeply respecting him—which surely goes without saying—despite this nagging and undeniably virulent curiosity of mine I just could not bring myself to venture forth with even a single question regarding what I had so fortuitously chanced to witness earlier that day.

However, and as most gifted students of Life will undoubtedly concur, with extreme patience and a certain unmollified resolve—not to mention a tiny bit of unusually good luck thrown in for good measure, such initially evasive mysteries as these have a way of eventually finding their way into the light, thereby more agreeably defining themselves for the sake of posterity. One day in the future, and certainly just as I fervently hoped might eventually happen, as consummate proof that Felix loved and trusted in our special friendship just as I did, he would one day in the future consent to bestow upon me many of the intimate details of an amazing love story which would once again be greatly enhancing my already positive perspective of life. For, remaining consistently true to himself, as well as to me, I would ultimately become the welcome beneficiary of a rare glimpse into that far more guarded region of my dear friend's glorious soul—and, with this timely gift, I would also be reaping untold spiritual wealth of the precise sort which lasts a lifetime.

23.

JOHN-ABU JEREMIAH FELIX KETCHUM was born between two major snow storms, during that early pre-dawn morning of January 10, 1941. Upon his initially tentative entrance into this amazing world of ours—and, no doubt, to herald his long-awaited arrival by his parents and the rest of us, he became solely responsible for a series of highly disruptive lusty wails which were purely plaintive in nature. Only after his thoroughly exhausted—yet unmistakably happy—young mother took him eagerly to her full and rounded breast, did he finally consent to be calmed in any manner.

Much to his doting father's overwhelming sense of joy and profound relief, too, his already strong and active little legs were both quite obviously identical in length. Moreover, since he was being proudly named after a long succession of highly exceptional people which included his father, great-grandfather, maternal grandfather, as well as our beloved Felix, this same impressive albeit slightly cumbersome title of his seemed a bit daunting for such a wee baby boy, prompting Bessy and John days later to nickname him "Johnny."

Felix passionately asserted that the arrival of any vulnerable new soul into this often tired and spiritually jaded old world of ours was proof positive that hope reigned eternal. He likened such wholesome prismatic beauty to a new beginning—a new chance for humanity. In the creative sense, each new life represents a fresh canvas begging for the various definitive colors and textures with which the fingers of Being and Time inevitably imbue it, consequently arousing endless possibilities for that particular human being throughout their lifetime, as well as promoting that uniquely personal tally of all the pluses and minuses which each of us eventually becomes responsible for imparting to the world....

When Bessy Ketchum first began going into labor, "Doc" Owens was nowhere to be found. On account of those debilitating snow storms, both of which happened in rapid succession, the telephone service for miles around became temporarily disrupted. And as if this seemingly dire predicament in itself was not already challenging enough to panic even the most fundamentally stout-hearted individual, the roads throughout many a county, including our own, became totally impassable.

Thank God for Emma Lauder's cool head and her considerable knowledge when it came right down to such vital matters as bringing children into the world. I well recall that it was with a profound sense of urgency that John Ketchum eventually made his way to our farmhouse that day, riding upon the back of his faithful old Hannah.... He was noticeably ashen-faced and actually physically trembling from far more than just being cold.

The accumulation of newly fallen snow from both storms measured over knee-high. Nevertheless, with John relentlessly coaxing his obliging little beast, the animal managed to eventually forge her way across those several hundred yards of presently inhospitable terrain which comprised the better part of the Lauder's back acreage. Arriving at long last at the boundary of the far outer fringes of the family's courtyard, most likely erroneously assuming that she had already fully accomplished her required task, old Hannah promptly halted in her tracks and utterly refused to move another inch in any direction....

Caring deeply for his dear wife, as John Ketchum obviously did; and, likewise duly acknowledging his highly significant role in the beautiful and truly humbling drama which was about to occur, with his never having been exposed to the demanding emotional rigors of birthing before this, he was understandably at a complete loss to know how to attend to Bessy in her time of great need. After failing miserably in redeeming poor stubborn old Hannah so that we might shelter her from the unkind elements, John and I were eventually reduced to literally bribing the stoical animal with an armful of hay to finally achieve this normally simple routine.

While I busied myself with the important responsibility of placing her within a relatively warm and dry spot inside the barn, Felix and John wasted no time at all in hitching our wooden wagon to the far more dependable family tractor. Finally, with Emma Lauder scurrying about the house all this while and attempting to secure those necessary items upon which every competent midwife worth her credentials relies, she was soon bundling herself into her own warm outerwear after which she hastened to accompany both men to the small cabin where the Ketchums lived.

Man is miraculously born of woman. God, in His infinite wisdom, decrees that this should be so. Looking back and fondly recalling the day when little Johnny Ketchum was born into this world, something rather awe-inspiring also managed to unexpectedly transpire between Bessy Ketchum and Emma Lauder. As was earlier intimated, although from the very beginning of their relationship these equally strong and unquestionably resilient women had basically sought to remain merely polite to each other—in time, and with the two of them struggling mightily together to achieve their respective goals, a remarkable understanding and genuine admiration for one another slowly began to blossom forth.

That timeless and bittersweet struggle required to bring forth new life into the world soon allowed this new and inexperienced mother to fully appreciate the entire process. Quite understandably, too, through all of it Bessy came to greatly value that unwavering devotion which her fellow-sister was pleased to so compassionately bestow upon her.

Motherhood, by its very nature, remains an exclusive fellowship where the agony of childbirth imparts to every participant a certain unique wisdom which may only be gathered in this way. Each prospective mother is required to bravely surmount that ageless barrier of temporary pain and suffering. In the end the process becomes nothing less than a woman's ultimate triumph, owing to the inescapable reality that it is within this simultaneously shared introduction to Life's inescapable pain and suffering—by both the mother and the child—that traditionally becomes responsible for so fiercely bonding the two together for all time.

During one cool and unusually dry spring afternoon of that same year, before the planting season actually commenced in earnest, Felix and I happened to spy John Ketchum sitting underneath a large oak tree that was growing all alone not so far from his modest little cabin. Currently only one side of this still magnificent specimen was in the process of majestically bringing forth its multitudes of tightly rolled buds of pristine greenery, while the other side had long ago been severely charred by a bolt of lightning and therefore was rendered quite lifeless. Together both halves managed to create an unusual vision which was a marvelous study in contrasts. Sleeping peacefully nearby within a large roomy laundry basket that was being partially shaded by that vast intertwining network of thick limbs and lesser branches of the healthy side of this tree was the Ketchum's beautiful little son, Johnny....

When Felix and I initially began walking John's way to pay our respects, as well as to see for ourselves just how the child was thriving, John was duly engrossed with what appeared to be his wife's Bible. The substantially large book lay open there upon his lap. Respectfully approaching the spot were he and his infant son were resting we distinctly heard him reciting out loud these following words, as every now and then he'd pause to briefly consult the book's text: "We hold des Truths ta be self-evdent, dat all Men are creat'd equal, dat they are dowed by da Creator wit certain unailable Rights, dat among des are Life, Liberty, and da Pursuit of Happiness...."

After Felix and I greeted our friend, Felix inquired in an off-handed sort of manner, "Is that not the Bible you are holding, John?" Then pretty much thinking along the same lines as I was, he went on to add, "But the phrases you were just speaking a few moments ago are not from the Good Book at all, but rather from our own Declaration of Independence—from America's very own Constitution!"

"Yessr!" John was answering with an unmistakable sense of pride in being able to acknowledge this same fact. Holding our attention with a look which could only be described as pure joy, this good man went on to announce, "Mighty fine words, don't cha think!?" After only a brief second or two of introspection on his part, where he chose to gaze down upon this particularly special copy of the Bible, he went on to further muse out loud, "Yessr ... mighty fine words, fur sure!"

Being thoroughly perplexed over what I initially perceived as some sort of discrepancy with respect to John Ketchum's recitation from this magnum opus he was cradling within his lap—and, quite naturally, without having meant any disrespect, at all, I could not help going a bit farther to openly state for the record, "But, John, that passage from our Constitution's Preamble isn't found anywhere in the Bible.... Besides, I thought you told me that you couldn't read!"

At the moment John Ketchum was smiling good-naturedly at both of us, almost as if he were taking a child's delight in being able to mystify us, as he certainly was doing. Shortly, to properly enlighten us, he cheerfully proceeded to assure us, "C'aint read! Never learned...." Then holding the large heavy book up for Felix and me to examine for ourselves, the two of us quickly discovered an elegantly handwritten script which someone had painstakingly inscribed upon a piece of quality parchment. This same document had by now grown quite old, since its yellowed and badly worn edges bore testament to this very fact.

This touching keepsake—for certainly this is exactly what it was, had long ago been carefully glued into the front binding of the well-worn old book. Presently, as if relishing the idea of actually sharing its ongoing history with Felix and me, John proceeded to tell us a very interesting tale concerning "his people"—his family, in other words, as he always chose to refer to his ancestors.

Sometime back around what must have been the latter-portion of the eighteenth century, John Ketchum's great-grandfather, Abu, was brought to this land by slave ship. Not long after that an extremely prosperous old family from Virginia eventually purchased him, in order to have him work among the small army of similarly acquired laborers trained to run their immense plantation on an ongoing basis. At the time of this man's cruel abduction from the land of his birth, he had a young wife and three small children who—although originally kidnapped along with him and forcibly boarded all together for the duration of the long and horribly arduous voyage—were eventually separated from him, with John's great-grandmother and her little ones having been unconscionably sold off to some other bidding agent....

Although this middle-aged patriarch of John's now painfully fragmented family was an unusually handsome man in the physical sense, he was not particularly strong or able enough to labor sufficiently well on behalf of the abundant acres of tobacco and cotton fields. So in time the elderly mistress of the manor selected him to work exclusively within the "great house," as the main home of the plantation was often called, seeing to the many needs of her extended family's more intimate day-to-day life....

From the very beginning it was said that this same God-fearing woman came to favor John's great-grandfather with her loyal friendship, for sometime during their initial years together—and undoubtedly prompted very much out of a compelling devotion to a basic sense of true compassion and justice, with time and considerable expense the woman eventually managed to locate Abu's wife and children and subsequently had them reunited. Furthermore, with regard to her personal inclination towards this preferred filial continuum, within her Last Will and Testament provisions were also specifically made to further insure the retention of all the members of Abu's family, in order that they might never again be separated.

Thanks to the insightful planning on the woman's part, more than one generation of John's family was destined to be born and then to live out their relatively long lives together among those family members whom they knew and loved, and within that same highly unusual atmosphere of more dependable emotional tranquility. Even after our bitter Civil War was fought and finally won at considerable cost to both sides, and, at long last, after the unjust ownership of one human being by another was promptly curtailed and then duly abolished for all time—by then, and by choice, the many surviving descendants of Abu's family remained living and working as free men upon that same ever-fertile soil of Virginia....

Upon his mistress's deathbed, and undoubtedly as her special tribute to Abu for his many years of loyal friendship and service, the woman personally bequeathed her own Bible to him. For seemingly important reasons upon which one may only speculate, firmly nestled inside the protective front covering of this wonderful gift and exquisitely penned upon a sheet of beautiful English parchment—presumably in this lady's own refined hand—one could still find those poignant lines to our beloved Constitution's Preamble.

Was it purely coincidental that this highly significant passage from our own Declaration of Independence, whose undeniably progressive and nobly-expressed sentiments continue to this very day to so greatly impact upon the hearts and minds of all good people everywhere, was placed within that book? By chance had this extraordinarily kind and insightful woman been able to glance into the future and to have barely imagined those immensely positive intellectual changes that would in time be enveloping this country, relevant to that utter barbarity invoked by the willful subjugation of one man over another? And might it have also been her specific intention that these spiritually uplifting words by Thomas Jefferson—which to my mind remain on par with many of the similarly moving passages found in the Bible, continue to bring some small measure of consolation to Abu's family until then?

Many of the members of John Ketchum's long and illustrious line of ancestors never learned to read. However, one imagines that with those many years of faithfully repetitive open readings from the Bible, which most probably must have been initiated on a daily basis by its original owner for the consummate benefit of her family members, as well as Abu's, those truly worthwhile and ever-sustaining moral concepts—both from the Good Book as well as from our Constitution—were miraculously committed to memory and then carefully passed down to those various members of each succeeding generation. Consequently, not unlike the faithful troubadours throughout the ages, this is how those much-treasured spoken words ultimately managed to survive the passing of all the years.

On that same memorable afternoon, while Felix, and John, and I continued to sit together underneath that grand old survivor of a tree pleasantly attending to the sleeping child, I eventually asked John Ketchum, "John, how'd you like it if I taught you to read?!"

Our gentle friend was quite obviously much surprised by this im-promptu offer of mine, and soon responded by saying in a half-joking sort of way, "Don't spec ya can teach an ol' dog like me new tricks!" Then as an after-thought, really, he went on to more enthusiastically state, "I'd be much obliged, dough, if ya wur ta teach my boy here ta read some day! One day ma Johnny goin' to go to school.... One day he goin' be a better man den his ol' pappy!"

Without allowing a grain of dust to settle upon this statement which John Ketchum had just made, I well remember Felix glancing John's way—and then, as my dear friend took a moment to reach over to pull the light winter blanket up across one of the baby's hands which had freed itself from underneath the covering, he went on to remark in a manner that touched both John and me, "With the powerful winds of change that will one day be blowing across this land, I faithfully predict that your son shall one day be free to pursue any dream that he has the courage to dream, John!"

Rather effortlessly continuing to hold both John's attention and mine, Felix went on to say, "Indeed, there will be no limits to what he may one day achieve.... And regrettably, although you and I shall undoubt-edly not live to see this long overdue change ourselves, I shall further predict that someday there shall be an African-American man or woman popularly elected as President of these United States of America!" After a moment of silence Felix went on to state with notable conviction, "Yes ... powerful winds of change will eventually be blowing across this land!

"Those of us already privileged to ascertain these important future events must also remain ever-respectful of this approaching pheno-menon's profound significance. Within this same aura of divine light which is far too slowly approaching, let us always refer to it as nothing less than Mankind's long-overdue poetic justice! One day our young Johnny will certainly learn to read and write, just as one day he will also be free to attend any school of his choice in order to be able to firmly establish his lifetime priorities and goals. However, John, from my dis-cerning perspective, even after he works hard and diligently applies himself to proudly be able to achieve all these things, it will be impossible for him to ever become a better man than his father!"

Two days after this memorable episode occurred beneath the watch-ful eyes of that old veteran of a tree, Felix, Eddie and I once again became engrossed in the process of preparing the fields for planting. No sooner had we managed to finish barely one-third of this ever-demanding proj-ect, when our poor old family tractor finally suffered a heart attack and promptly passed on to wherever good old tractors eventually go.

The timing relevant to this great problem of ours could not have possibly been any worse. With there being insufficient funds in the family till to even consider making a down-payment upon some temptingly new yet prohibitively expensive machine; and, likewise, with the unlikelihood of Felix being able to sell off any of his marvelous paintings, since the summer vacationers would not be returning to live around the lake for another several weeks hence, my poor friend became fairly consumed with the challenge of how he was to solve his current dilemma....

In the end, it was John Ketchum's keen insightfulness that would be solving our frustrating problem. Having earlier taken up temporary residence within the hayloft of the Lauder's barn after he and Bessy initially arrived within our lives, John became inspired to remember the bits and pieces of an old hand-plow that for ages now was being openly displayed upon one wall in that upper portion of the building. For one reason or another, this genuine relic of former times was left behind by the previous owners and most certainly had not been used for many years prior to the Lauder's having purchased the farm. It occurred to me back then, as well, that Felix must surely have forgotten all about this rather antique item which was patiently waiting to be re-discovered.

Pretty much as a major surprise for Felix, Eddie, Maria-Christina, Anna Allegra, and I secretly helped John remove the interesting apparatus, piece by piece, from where its various metal parts remained slowly rusting away. With only a bit of minor trouble, really, we began to put it all back together again, very much like a jigsaw puzzle, but found a critical part of the main frame of the plow missing. Remaining fairly undaunted by this seemingly daunting reality, John immediately took the necessary time and trouble to recreate what we needed for the plow by smelting down a piece of flat metal which he found inside that special box within the barn. Then happily for us, while most likely not so happily for old Hannah, the sturdy old girl was promptly inducted into service to help finish preparing the remaining acreage for planting.

This, of course, was how our two families passed those ensuing weeks and months of our collective lives. Just as always we continued to labor without end in a frequently heroic effort to keep both farms going, all the while never failing to steal a bit of quality time together whenever we could. Looking back, it became these same particularly up lifting experiences of a distinctly personal nature which so greatly added to the overall texture and substance of our day-to-day living. It became that extremely vital human interaction for which all souls so readily yearn that summarily added to our lifelong store of personal wealth.

During that same unforgettable year, too, while Adolf Hitler continued to master his own uniquely personal version of Machiavellian politics, his dastardly and seemingly unconquerable war machine was confidently moving even more purposefully towards an even greater offensive.... In short, the world was slowly but quite indisputably going mad. Then, on December 7, 1941—as History shall undoubtedly forever recall, with the relentlessly shocking bombing of Pearl Harbor by Japan, America could no longer afford to safely stand upon the sidelines of this galvanic world conflict as a mere distant observer....

Very suddenly the overall situation became stunningly personal. With that solitary barbaric act which was so outrageously thrust upon the minds and hearts of all our citizens, courageous men and women everywhere would instinctively ally themselves with our ever-compassionate God to ultimately defeat Tyranny at its worst. With what surely became a highly significant pivotal moment in time, the future end-game of this horrific world struggle was about to be inevitably insured.

By mid-December of 1941, as the members of both the Lauder and Ketchum families faithfully gathered together around the radio each evening in order to hear for ourselves the critically important news of the day, little could we have imagined how significantly this war would be impacting upon our own lives. Days following that already extremely depressing Christmas, in a passionate effort to do his part for the war effort, Eddie finally volunteered for pilot's training. Although he had not harbored a second thought relative to what he instinctively believed was expected of him, nevertheless I watched him wrestle endlessly, in the emotional sense, with the dire implications brought into focus by this dramatic decision of his. Quite understandably, there at the forefront of his justifiably worried mind lay the extreme question of how his parents would ultimately be receiving this news....

"Adam, I don't suppose you could give me a few exclusive pointers about how I am to proceed with my father—naturally, with respect to the decision I've just made?" This, of course, is what young Edward was quietly asking me as he sat on the edge of his bed on that evening. Following this statement, and more or less as an indication that he was prudently building a case for himself with regard to defending his recent actions to his father, he went on to muse, "After all, it's no secret that I've always wanted to fly! Now with America obliged to do her part against the tyranny of Germany and Japan—as she surely must, it just seems like the absolutely right thing to do!"

With me sitting across from this special adopted brother of mine, I was carefully considering his open plea to me, and with some difficulty I managed to say, "Knowing your father as we both do, Eddie, my overall recommendation to you is that you remain totally open and honest with him... In other words, that you approach this difficult subject the way you've just shared these important thoughts with me. As much as I'd like to be the one to be able to spare you this unpleasant task, you're bound to agree that there are specific times in everyone's life when they're forced to go it alone!"

Not long after we finished this brief talk of ours, Eddie finally descended into the parlor with the primary intention of specifically seeking out his father in order to be able to share this major decision of his. And how I ached for him.... How I also ached for Felix and Emma, for I suspected that this currently worrisome news which they both were about to receive would naturally be causing those mutually substantial old wounds of theirs from the death of young Lewis, of course, and George, to cruelly manifest themselves all over again.

Eddie was gone for an inordinately long while, just as I anticipated. However, when he did finally return to his room, I poignantly recall that he was wearing a smile of telling gratitude, as well as a look of considerable relief written across his tear-stained face.... Sitting next to me there upon my own bed this time, he casually placed one arm around my shoulders to tell me in a wholly relieved albeit somewhat mystified manner, "You know, Adam, the older I get the more special my parents seem to become! Even though it must have been hard as hell for them to have to listen to what I was obliged to tell them this evening, in the end my father told me that he never wished to be responsible for standing in the way of what was clearly so important to me. Even though what I was forced to ask of him was one of the hardest things in the world for him to hear, he managed, nonetheless, to give me his blessing.... Can you possibly beat that?!"

Two weeks later, Eddie was on his way to Rhode Island for pilot training. Charley, on the other hand, no doubt becoming greatly inspired to actively promote that similarly spirited young Lauder vitality towards yet another branch of the service, promptly signed up with the Navy. And certainly not willing to be undone in the least by either of his older brothers—and subsequently left behind on the farm when all the other eager young men and women throughout this great land were going off to war, Willie decided to join the Army as a paratrooper. Young Fritz, on the other hand, was literally hell-bent upon fudging his age on the necessary paperwork that assured him at least the basic entrance exam for pilot training school. In a matter of only a few short weeks the Lauder household would be growing uncharacteristically far more quiet than it had ever been before.... Consequently, more and more of the farm chores were being left behind for Felix and me....

Sometime during those rather intense months ahead for Eddie, while he was in the process of being thoroughly schooled by our Army-Air Corps, he had the grand good fortune of meeting an extraordinary young woman from Watertown, Massachusetts. They both fell head-over-heels in love with each other and subsequently married in a short and much-rushed ceremony at the base chapel. It was the couple's intention all the while—and they indicated this to all the members of their new collective family, that upon Eddie's return from the conflict we would all be celebrating this happy occasion, and in a much more traditional manner, with a large family wedding there on the farm....

Three days before 2nd Lieutenant Edward Lauder and the other members of his 317th Fighter Squadron departed to destinations unknown to us, he was generously granted a twelve-hour pass and surprised everyone by returning to us for an impromptu visit. Although I did not witness the hired car arrive earlier to drop him off, when I was returning from the barn on that early afternoon to head back in the direction of the house, I distinctly heard the unmistakable sound of Billie Holiday's velvet-encrusted voice crooning a song entitled: "Them There Eyes," which I already knew was a longtime favorite of Eddie's, and which he teasingly used to sing to his sisters whenever the moment inspired him to do so.

Hurriedly entering the house by way of the back door that day, I instantly spotted my friend's over-stuffed flight bag sitting there upon the shiny kitchen floor, and my heart leapt with joy. There, too, as even more proof that Eddie had actually come home to us, was his warm military-style overcoat which was neatly folded and then casually placed across the back of one kitchen chair....

With me expectantly peeking around the corner of the room, but just prior to my actually having stepped into the parlor which was presently rocking with this loud and fairly lighthearted music, I observed the other family members gathered in a semicircle and enthusiastically clapping in time to this same welcome mayhem of good-natured fun... As this was happening Eddie was in the process of expertly mouthing the words to that marvelous song, all the while attempting to carefully negotiate his way around the cramped area of the little room, clutching young Anna firmly to him, while she, in turn, concentrated on remaining perched atop his shoeless feet....

Eventually spotting me leaning comfortably against the wall which separated the dining area from the parlor, these two charmers intentionally waltzed over towards where I was standing, as Eddie cheerfully called out above the music with a mischievous smile, "By God, Adam, you're next in line for a dance! Just think... How many people will actually be able to boast that they danced the night away with a future World War II flying ace!?"

There within our modest little parlor, as a brief but truly sacred respite from the terrible things that were occurring in so many other parts of the world, we remained feverishly celebrating the joys of living. Looking back, I wonder how many times such similar occurrences were being played out within other homes across the land—and within other hearts, as parents and their beloved children and dear friends, too, were finding it necessary to bid those they loved farewell and Godspeed.

The several brief notes which we would be receiving as a family from Eddie were obliged to pass through a clearing station in order to be properly censored by the military authorities. This, of course, was for our country's overall protection in case some homesick individual inadvertently gave away information that might aid the enemy in some manner. One such letter which I remember particularly well, and which had been originally addressed to Willie Lauder sometime shortly after he arrived within the European Theatre to join up with his fellow troops, would in time eventually find its way home to be shared with all of us. Judging from the nature of its overall script, it was easy to speculate that the note had been hurriedly penned and then posted some time on March 12, 1943. Underneath this date, the message bore the words, "Somewhere in Africa," and the letter's text read as follows:

Dear Willie,

Finally received your letter mailed to me from Europe, dated January 6th. I'm sure glad you're enjoying your outfit. Makes it a lot nicer, being where you naturally feel you belong....

Right now I'm Deputy Flight Leader, so instead of just looking out for myself, I've three more P-40s to watch over. It certainly is a great life though! Most of our work is knocking off enemy tanks and truck convoys.... Occasionally we fly over the Mediterranean Sea and escort some of our ship convoys to safety. It's pretty hard when we're forced into a scrap with these German pilots, though, since their planes are just so much more superior than the ones we fly. All we can do is to wait until they come down and jump us, since we remain at a distinct disadvantage of not being able to operate at those high altitudes like they do.... Lots of times we see them circling above us at about 20,000 feet, waiting patiently for one of us to lag behind so that they can break formation and come down at us like a bat out of hell! When this happens—if we're lucky enough to spot them first, we turn into them because it's certainly no secret around here that they're afraid of those extremely daunting six-fifty caliber guns we carry. However, the old timers assure us that it's the enemy plane we fail to see that will inevitably get us!

As a side note, really, last month I took a few days to visit Casablanca and Algiers.... Very interesting places, to be sure—just the sort of exotic scenery that would definitely inspire our father to paint! But, truthfully, even with all this I'll be mighty glad to finally get back home to the United States—and when I do, it will take an awful lot to get me to ever leave again!

Well, junior ... I've got to sign off for now. Please drop me a line or two when you can (And don't forget to change your underwear after every parachute jump!)

Your loving brother, Eddie

Exactly nine days after this letter was written and posted to Willie Lauder there in Europe, Eddie's P-40 was shot down.... According to official military data, which would eventually be shared with the family after the war officially ended, he was subsequently killed in that plane crash two miles south of Ain-El-Turck, Algeria. And, as cruel Fate would also have it—exactly six months after his death, his beloved wife gave birth to a beautiful son whom he would never have the pleasure of knowing; that same special son, indeed, who would also never be learning firsthand how incredibly special his father had been....

Poignantly I recall that it was five long years after Eddie's death before his body was finally returned to this land he so loved, in order that he might finally be laid to rest next to his older brothers George and Lewis. By then, of course, Felix was also buried there in that one special corner of the old German Settlement Cemetery.

Having been the designated "next of kin," it was Eddie's wife who ultimately received the small foot locker which contained her husband's few earthly possessions. Once, long after his death, I inadvertently came across the War Department's list of its meager contents. Carefully scanning that same official document, something deep within the core of me wanted to shout out to the world that there had been so much more to my friend than these mere pitiful personal trinkets which some kind soul had obligingly itemized, packed up, and eventually sent home to us....

Some thirty-five years after that moment in time, as amazing as it might seem, I was on assignment as a journalist for a well-known newspaper and began traveling extensively throughout Europe. In a hotel bar in London I was subsequently granted one of the richest emotional experiences by actually having come across a man who served in Eddie's flight squadron during the war. When I mentioned Eddie's name to this stranger and further explained my relationship to him, I went on to hopefully inquire whether or not he remembered him. Somehow it was intensely important to me that this individual recall someone who had made such an impression upon my own life. And with my deceptively simple-sounding entreaty, how it warmed my heart to see this former comrade's overall more casual demeanor change before my eyes....

With a truly stunned look which may only be properly described as the embodiment of blissful surprise, this same interesting man went on to declare, "By God, I most certainly do remember your brother, Eddie! Who could possibly forget such an outstanding young man?!" Then as if spontaneously taking a moment to recall certain personal memories of long ago, it was finally with a remarkable sense of acute nostalgia that Eddie's former friend returned from this rather brief impromptu journey of his to firmly focus upon me. Before he took the necessary time to share those vastly important memories with me, he proudly interjected with considerable conviction, "Please know that it was not only a genuine pleasure to know your brother—but it was also a distinct privilege for me to have served with him, as I did.... I'll always remember Eddie Lauder as being one hell of a fine fellow—one hell of a nice kid, without any doubt!"

24.

IN TERMS OF HUMANITY AS A WHOLE, and therefore each and every person's fleeting relevance within this undeniably complex world of ours, how shall one seek to ultimately measure one's self-worth? Which vital criteria should one use in order to adequately measure the basic worth of other individuals? Owing to mankind's perpetual pursuit of great power, and wealth, and fame—which to be sure remain highly revered prizes that so frequently are won at any price—does there exist perchance some special something of a far more substantial nature whose day-to-day quest might better mark a person's all too brief presence upon this earth?

Indeed, might there be some far more subtle something which shall eventually prove to be particularly more rewarding and beneficial to the individual entity, as well as to the world as a whole, than that far more common and relatively popular formula for success? During those inescapable moments of sobering contemplation when one's psyche is assailed by nagging fears of inadequacy and self-doubt—and when arm-in-arm the dreaded specter of one's inevitable mortality allies itself with the essence of Sacred Truth, thereby dutifully unmasking the vulnerable soul and bidding it reveal the deeds of a lifetime, which yardstick shall one be obliged to use?

America's spirited and wholly patriotic young men and women who were destined to go off to fight in that terrible world war would be leaving home as unseasoned youngsters for the most part. Conversely, and by the grace of God, those more fortunate individuals who were destined to be returning to their loved ones would often be doing so as emotionally scarred and battle-weary adults.... For this is what war has the ability to do to people. With the unavoidable graphic carnage which inevitably takes place during such times, one's youthful innocence is challenged, along with that formerly untarnished idealistic belief in the sanctity of all living things....

And yet, quite paradoxically, it seems that in losing our innocence in this most dreadful manner ultimately forces us all to view the darker sides of human nature and the world for what it frequently can become and tends to make life even more precious when so cruelly delineated against these great horrors of death and destruction. Basically it becomes the profound reality of that "gentle light" being unavoidably contrasted against the blackness of all that "ungodliness" which ultimately bestows upon all life and all living things its wondrously sacred meaning....

Days before Eddie, Charlie, Willie, and Fritz eventually left home to do their part for this country's war effort, together all of us formed a solemn pack where I faithfully promised that I would forego any future plans to leave the farmstead until at least one or more of them returned home to take my place. After all, Felix was not well during this time....

Anna Lauder would be thirteen that year. And eighteen-year-old Maria Christina recently married an earnest and hard-working young man from William's Bay. That same year Stephen Lauder turned sixteen and naturally was still in school. Robert, on the other hand, undaunted by the fact that his diabetes prevented him from serving in the military at all, promptly headed off to Washington in the hope of finding some sort of interesting work which would still allow him to make an honorable contribution on behalf of this country he loved so much.... Last of all, with our Berty whom few of us ever chanced to see any more, John Ketchum and I more or less evolved into the sturdy rocks upon which Felix and the entire group of family members could still steadfastly rely.

Because of the extreme circumstances so often brought about by the latter stages of diabetes, Felix was slowly losing his sight. On two occasions I accompanied him to an optometrist's office located in downtown Chicago for an extensive examination by a renowned specialist. My dear friend and I hoped that something might still be done to at least slow the progressive deterioration of his sight, but were told that he would inevitably become completely blind.

One seemingly fine afternoon in the early spring of 1944, with me dutifully chauffeuring Felix and John Ketchum to the Grimsley's General Store so that we might purchase some emergency plumbing supplies needed to repair the downstairs toilet, the three of us soon found the local convenience bustling with a handful of busy shoppers. Because of Felix's faulty eyesight and the fact that John never learned to drive a car, this fairly new role of mine soon became one of my established jobs. Since what we were being compelled to acquire for this impromptu project of ours was located out at the back of the store, this is where we ended up directly after we arrived—in avid search of Otto Grimsley....

Being the pleasant and helpful man that he always was, Mr. Grimsley went out of his way to assist us and all the while gave us tiny pointers on how to best achieve more lasting results with our repair efforts. When the four of us returned to the main part of the store to pay for what we selected, we found that we were further obliged to wait in line for two or three other patrons to be assisted before we could be aided in the same way.

During this time Burtram Parker wandered into the store. Right away I noticed that he went in search of Cornelia Grimsley who at this time was busy in another part of the place helping one of her assistants help a client. They were cutting a generous length of colorful cotton fabric from a substantially heavy-looking bolt which had been previously sitting high upon one shelf behind them. While I remained waiting, I impetuously decided to break ranks with the others and to claim for myself a penny's worth of lemon drops, more or less for old times' sake.

Generally speaking, whenever business within the store became unusually brisk, as now, the order of the day usually required people who suffered the pangs of a sweet tooth to help themselves to whatever tempting fare happened to appeal to them. So rather solicitously weighing up the tiny white bag as Cornelia Grimsley might have done under normal circumstances, and then dutifully leaving behind the required change upon the counter—right near the other register which was closed at the moment, I took a second more to spill out a couple of the almond-shaped confection into my hand, and to briefly study them before actually popping them into my mouth....

However, before I had a chance to accomplish this last step, my attention was immediately arrested by some sort of loud commotion which was beginning to take place back at the station that I had just vacated. Quickly returning to Felix and John to see for myself what unpleasantness was in the process of transpiring, I observed Cornelia Grimsley standing on the other side of the cluttered counter directly across from Felix and John.... Both of her unattractive stubby little hands were resting upon her ample hips in that unmistakably challenging manner of hers, while at the same time I could also readily see that glimmering deep within her unchaste eyes she was triumphantly promoting within the store a thoroughly negative atmosphere with which I was already overwhelmingly familiar....

"My husband and I refuse to serve 'his kind' here in our highly respectable store!" Mrs. Grimsley was openly declaring for everyone in the vicinity to overhear as she rudely gestured at John Ketchum with a cunning nastiness that had truly become second nature to her by now.

During this initial dissention my rather critical gaze instinctively touched upon every soul in that room. Otto Grimsley, for instance, whom I could not help but notice was standing only a few paces to one side of his wife when this insane outburst of hers occurred, had been in the relatively cheerful process of placing what Felix was purchasing into a brown paper bag for us. Now, however, his normally pale countenance had grown extremely more so and was currently expressing a dreadfully pained look of complete embarrassment. Truly, his overall demeanor was openly declaring to me that if the well-worn floorboards of his prosperous country store could have possibly opened up and swallowed him whole, certainly he would have remained eternally grateful to be able to escape this uniquely unkind interaction which his horrible wife took to initiate on both their behalfs.

Studying Burtram Parker, too, I vow I saw a sly smile creep across his small ruddy-colored face, and then quickly disappear.... Soon, as if suspecting that he was being observed by me, he chose to step back more into the surrounding shadows of the large room. John Ketchum, meanwhile, at whom this caustic behavior was being specifically directed, was silently staring down at his shoes with a sense of amazing fortitude and dignity which was telling me quite clearly that this sort of behavior towards him was not something new at all, but was something decidedly nasty which he and other black Americans were forced to endure on an ongoing basis.

The young and rather reserved woman who had been previously assisting Cornelia Grimsley in cutting the crisp new fabric was literally frozen into place—much like Lot's wife in the famous Biblical story, and all this while holding her pair of scissors quite motionlessly in midair. And as the evil perpetrator of this entirely unpleasant business finally switched her steadfast gaze from John Ketchum, only to fasten it now upon Felix, Felix remained silently and rather coolly appraising this nasty woman in return....

Honestly! One could have heard a pin drop at this point, since no one seemed to have the courage to make the next move. All the while I continued to watch my great friend to see how he was going to respond to this unsettling meanness, he in turn remained wordlessly studying his troublesome nemesis.... With both of them in profile, now, to my mind what I was actually witnessing was the flesh and blood personification of true goodness versus true evil.

Ultimately breaking that unholy spell which had managed to permeate and to befoul the entire room, Felix promptly set about to diplomatically purge the hot air from Cornelia Grimsley's overtly billowing sails. Intentionally ignoring the woman who alone was responsible for the present stench, he chose instead to politely address her mild-mannered husband by quietly stating, "On second thought, Otto, I find that I shan't be needing those items which we selected a little while ago.... Seeing that your wife's unforgivable discourtesy towards my good friend here has made all the difference in the world, naturally I feel obliged to take my business elsewhere! Please understand that I deeply regret this decision of mine—but only as far as you, yourself, are concerned."

As if taking his subtle cue from Felix, poor John Ketchum walked out the front door and headed in the direction of our truck. Likewise, that once smooth and dry candy which I was still holding within the palm of my now unusually moist hand had finally become unbelievably sticky and wholly unappealing. With me moving forward to instinctively follow after Felix on his relatively short trek across the large crowded room, I took a second more to quickly toss all the confection I recently purchased into a small trash can on the way.... But before Felix and I actually reached the exit to make our inevitable escape into the welcome daylight and that far more breathable air outside, from behind us we distinctly heard Cornelia Grimsley's unpleasant voice shout out to us, "Nigger lover!"

I well remember that her cruel words cut through that already foul air like a painfully dull serrated knife. My instantaneous response to this intentionally demeaning phrase which this awful woman had wantonly chosen to use was totally reflexive in nature, and acted upon my overall being much as if someone had taken their long jagged fingernails and slowly scrapped them down against the blackboard of my soul.... At the moment I was feeling such righteous indignation at this profoundly ig-norant and willfully hurtful statement which she had just uttered that all that I am as a human being instantly recoiled in absolute disgust. At the door Felix paused a moment with his back towards the crowd, probably fighting to control some strong urge to verbally cut this woman down to size, but admirably resisted nonetheless. Finally we both left together, walking side by side until we reached the welcome familiarity of our waiting vehicle....

Neither John, nor Felix, nor I, uttered a single word to each other for quite some time, even after we moved out onto the open road that day. Sometimes powerfully moving things occur within one's day-to-day living where there are simply no appropriate words to counter the miserable feeling with which one is left to deal. Eventually, however, Felix took to role down his window on the passenger side where he was presently sitting.... With John silently riding between us, and without having bothered to visually engage him at all, my pensive friend found the strength to finally say, "I am profoundly sorry for what just happened back at the store, John!"

In answer to this inadequate attempt by Felix to comfort our friend, and with what I shall forevermore remember as a truly remarkable sense of great composure and dignity on John's part, John finally remarked, "Don't never need to 'poligize for da bad behavur of udder foks—or yo be 'poligizing all da time! All ma life dis is how da white folk always be treatin da blacks.... Actually, sum times we be treated much worse den dis!" Then, after a modest pause, with words which were laced through and through with a particularly strong sort of emotion, this good man went on to conclude what he was saying by adding, "But yor family be different, somehaw.... Yo treats ol' John an Bessy like the Bible say—yo lives by da Good Book, and by da Const'tution, too. Swear to God, never met nobody like yo and yor family befor dis!"

Around supper time during that same late afternoon, it began to rain. When the three of us arrived at the Lauder home Bessy Ketchum was proudly putting the finishing touches on twin candied-yam pies whose secret longtime family recipe she graciously shared with Emma Lauder. Since it was too early in the year for either of their gardens to have produced the wondrous bounty which was required to render these same marvelous tasting treats, Emma opted to use several large jars of the sweet potatoes that she put up the previous autumn.

Rather unceremoniously entering the kitchen, Felix and John and I had beforehand established a pact between us where we would forego any reference to the recent trouble back at the Grimsley's store. After all, what would have been the sense of reliving all that unpleasantness? Instead, upon setting firm foot within the fragrant-smelling sanctity of the Lauder's small kitchen, Emma Lauder and the rest of us merely stood around becoming briefly mesmerized by Bessy's accomplished hand movements as she went about artistically decorating the top of her rich honey-colored pies with dozens of whole pieces of pecans.

Akin to the fair "Minerva," that ancient goddess of wisdom and the arts, this same talented lady was in the process of creating a wholly eatable mosaic-design upon the thick rich batter of unbaked yams, molasses, and spices… Happily playing underneath the wooden table upon which his lovely mother was so ably working was our three-year-old baby Johnny himself….

It would have been obvious to any onlooker that this bright handsome child remained his parents' pride and joy. At present, the well-mannered youngster seemed completely obsessed with the new wooden toy which Felix had created especially for him, and which earlier in the day had been presented to him with a sense of unmistakable pleasure.

I specifically recall that the small object was a hand-carving of a fat little duckling. Its streamlined base was carefully engineered so that when the toy was led about by a short length of red string, quite naturally to the utter enthrallment of my dear friend's special namesake, the ingenious little invention bobbed its head up and down, all the while making a particularly pleasing clicking sound as it faithfully followed its little owner wherever he went.

Sometime during that same fateful late night, although I was to initially misinterpret the whole affair as being part of my unusual dream, I heard the sound of "Doc" Owens antique car hurriedly making its way up the loose gravel of our driveway. I even seem to recall the vehicle's bright and uneven headlights briefly dancing upon the painted surface of my bedroom walls…. After this I vaguely remember the muted sound of people's voices anxiously whispering back and forth together downstairs before the car hastily departed, and then with me actually falling back into a deep slumber once more.

My not having dutifully roused myself from my bed, as I normally would have done to more appropriately challenge the moment, basically stemmed from the fact that hours before this unusual occurrence transpired Emma Lauder insisted upon preparing me a hot-toddy to help nurse the chest cold I was still battling…. This powerful drink was the very same ungodly concoction of hers which consisted of a little bit of this, and a little bit of that, and then was finished off with an overly generous jigger or two of 80-proof "spirits."

George, I well recall, when similarly accosted by his well-intending mother for the same reason, used to jokingly refer to this same homemade medicine of hers as "Mom's hair-remover." Naturally with my already having put in a full day of hard work around the farm, and after I was commanded to down that highly potent drink of Mrs. Lauder's, suffice it to say that that evening's uncommonly heavy sleep only complicated my overall mental fogginess. Upon inadvertently being awakened as I was with the good doctor's impromptu visit, it became maddeningly difficult for me at one point to properly decipher what had been real and what had not....

However, just prior to the more official dawning of that new day, once again the unmistakable sound of "Doc" Owen's little car could definitely be heard as it returned for a second visit within some as yet undetermined time frame. Fully awake, by now, I went bounding from my bed to the open window which was closest to me.... Quickly parting the light and airy curtains to one side and then eagerly glancing down into the cul-de-sac below, I observed Felix and our longtime family friend sitting together inside "Doc's" little automobile, obviously conversing with one another.

Needless to say, something just did not seem right to me. I could actually feel a growing sense of virulent foreboding as it began to settle within the marrow of my bones. Grabbing my robe I sprinted out of the bedroom and impulsively began taking the stairs two and three at a time. After I reached the kitchen I hurried ahead from there to the little vestibule that led outside where I eventually found Emma Lauder already waiting for Felix. Obviously she was in the process of observing the same things which I had just witnessed from my window above.

With only the solitary exterior porch light throwing its diffused rays out into the early morning rain, as well as into the small space which both Emma and I were presently sharing, I could now more clearly discern the unmistakable signs of worry and fear which were etched across my companion's features. Before I had a chance to address her in any manner, however, together we turned to silently observe Felix as he very slowly began extracting himself from "Doc" Owens little vehicle....

The three of us, in turn, waited as the good doctor finally drove away in the pouring rain. Even before Felix turned to walk slowly towards his wife and me, I felt a great heavy stone roll across the surface of my heart, only to remain there.... As Felix finally turned towards the house, he made no further movement to advance himself in our direction. Obviously being totally preoccupied in the mental and emotional sense, as he surely seemed to be, I felt certain that he did not even realize that his wife and I were there at all.

Instead of prudently entering the house as he should and would normally have done, so as to protect himself from becoming unnecessarily wet, Emma Lauder and I further witnessed Felix slowly remove his glasses and purposely just stand there within that swiftly growing downpour. We watched in dismay as he went about methodically opening his arms wide, exactly as if he were urgently petitioning God, Himself, in some inexplicable manner. Slowly dropping back his head to vainly search the still darkened cloud-covered heavens above, it was as if he were allowing the benevolent rain to wash away some terrible sorrow which had begun to permanently descend upon his soul.... Accompanying this movement, a heretofore wholly unforgettable primitive animal sound managed to finally escape from the confines of his open mouth, and went on from there to thoroughly permeate deep into the quiet stillness of that tragic morning....

Never shall I be able to forget that astonishingly wretched sound! Never. Instantly that unbelievably plaintive cry caused the muscles around my heart to involuntarily contract. Quickly glancing at the woman who remained standing beside me for some hint as to what we should do, I observed Emma Lauder's hands as they now covered the bottom portion of her face. In point of fact, within her own tortured eyes I watched as great tears began to pool in their depths and then slowly begin to melt down in between her long slender fingers....

Finally leaving the woman behind, I impetuously threw open the door to quickly descend the steps, and from there hasten over to my dear friend who was obviously suffering so much. As I reached Felix and called out his name, his overall demeanor never changed.... Only then by the rather scantily diffused light of the porch lamp could I finally see for myself the horrific sight of his blood soaked clothing. The cool spring rain was blending itself with this life-sustaining fluid, inevitably causing multiple rivulets of diluted pink-colored water to course down my dear friend's person, only to eventually sink into the already abundantly wet ground upon which we were now both standing....

Hatred is an unforgivably terrible thing. Hatred on any level.... And, owing to this more than shameful fact, the many bloodstained pages of our common human history shall forevermore attest to man's ongoing and unspeakable cruelty towards his fellow man.

Hours before all this happened—indeed, all the while I so innocently slept within my warm bed, it was in a state of profound shock that our poor "Doc" Owens arrived to frantically summon Felix to the Ketchum's residence.... Sometime after midnight when our dear doctor was initially returning from an emergency house call located somewhere across town, eventually he passed along the country road that bordered the Ketchum's little cabin, and this is when he detected a light pouring forth from the family's open front door. To his mild surprise, owing more to the reality that the morning hour remained still inhospitably cool from the rain, naturally "Doc" could not justify the reason for this being so.

Alerted by his instincts that something surely must be wrong, our friend went to investigate when to his horror he discovered the lifeless bodies of John Ketchum and young Johnny-Abu both lying in a wide pool of blood just inside the front door. They had been shot to death.... In a state of utter panic, he further searched the tiny abode for some sign of Bessy Ketchum and eventually found her laying dead outside upon the ground, not far from her discarded laundry basket which much earlier she must have taken up to collect that day's clean clothing from the line. Undoubtedly it was the startling sound of those previous gun shots being discharged when John Ketchum first opened the door to their home that quickly brought the panicked woman scurrying their way—and, like her husband and young son, also led to her own inevitable death....

Since the Ketchum's did not own a telephone, Felix and "Doc" were forced to alert Sheriff Parker by using the Lauder's phone in the kitchen. However, even after the ruthlessly battered bodies of our dear friends were removed by the county coroner, nothing official was being done in any manner as far as initiating a thorough investigation to find the murderer, or murderers. That next day, in fact, immediately after the bodies were discovered and removed for burial, Felix, "Doc" Owens, and I went to the crime scene to wait for Burtram Parker, but we found that we were obliged to wait in vain.

While staunchly committing ourselves to remain there at the crime scene—standing guard, in effect, we sought to make good use of our time by carefully scanning the premises and by personally taking note of several pertinent clues which certainly might have helped to solve the crime. For instance, located directly outside the front door and blatantly scattered now upon the rough-hewn wooden planks of the front porch area were several spent shot-gun shells, not to mention what would have amounted to several large fistfuls of empty peanut shells....

At that point, as the reader may well imagine, my normally hot blood immediately turned to ice on the spot... After all, who within our small community particularly favored using such a lethal weapon to terrorize others? Likewise, who else had the disgusting habit of always leaving behind that telltale trail of peanut-shell droppings wherever he went? While the three of us were duped into patiently waiting for Justice to be served, all the while speculating between ourselves what we already strongly believed were viable clues that might certainly have helped to solve the puzzle of who murdered the members of the Ketchum family in that particularly cold-blooded manner, all of us could not help but wonder what, in God's name, was keeping Burtram Parker anyway?!

In the end, after being bitterly forced to acknowledge that Parker was avoiding his professional responsibilities in the most overtly offensive manner, and, naturally, having also concluded why this was undoubtedly so, Felix had me drive him to a lonely pay phone there on the outskirts of town. Standing near the phone-box as I was obliged to do in order to assist my friend, since he could no longer read the pages of the directory well enough by himself, together we finally managed to locate the home telephone number of one particular longtime acquaintance of his in Chicago, who, as fate would have it, was connected in some minor capacity with the F.B.I.

What we both felt was definitely needed at that precise moment was the expedient and wholly unbiased reaction by trustworthy officials who might eventually be able to apprehend the perpetrators of this dastardly crime against our friends. Loyally stationed where I remained, I was carefully listening to Felix as he responsibly attempted to take charge of the situation by sharing this same information with the party on the other end of the line....

During that emotionally-turbulent night, as both Felix and I impatiently waited at home for those crucial reinforcements from Chicago to finally arrive, some worried someone who obviously had not wanted us to solve our profound dilemma saturated the Ketchum's cabin with kerosene and set the entire place ablaze. By the time those two professionals finally did arrive from the crime department in Chicago—pretty much as a favor to Felix Lauder really, there was nothing left to pick through except a modest number of thoroughly charred remnants of old weathered wood, the cast-iron stove which the Ketchums had used for cooking and heating, along with substantial piles of ghostly-white ashes....

Needless to say, when the authorities finally located Burtram Parker and subsequently barraged him with all the many pertinent questions relative to his so-called lack of interest in the entire matter of the Ketchum family murders, our good sheriff chose to eventually retaliate in the only way he could by saving a few angry words to be eventually directed at Felix. I recall that it had not been more than a few hours since those visiting agents finally took their leave and returned to Chicago, when a thoroughly angry Parker came storming around our community in avid search of my dear friend.

Felix and I eventually observed this gross offender's familiar paddy wagon as it came speeding up one particular country road heading in our direction. Then, like some badly written scene in a "B-movie," the angry driver of this official vehicle chose to pull in front of our truck, literally cutting us off at that point and thereby preventing us from continuing on our way. Already terribly red-faced from the extreme agitation with which he was obviously currently dealing, and chomping rather tellingly upon his ever-present cigar, no doubt to help alleviate his extreme discomfort, we watched as Burtram Parker wasted no time at all in jumping from his truck and then racing around to the passenger side of our vehicle where Felix was sitting to angrily state for the record, "I sure as hell didn't appreciate that visit from your important friends in Chicago, Mr. Lauder! You know damn well that they don't have any jurisdiction over what happens in this community!"

Barely catching his breath, this sorry excuse for a man went on to further inform my silent companion in a particularly distasteful manner as he shouted "Are three stupid 'niggers' really worth all this fucking trouble you've been creating?! I might have lost my job over this mess! Did that ever occur to you?! And believe me it would have been entirely your fault, if I had!"

In a nasty attempt to cap things off, and with a remarkably profane sort of sneer, Burtram Parker continued on to further prophesy, "You can't fool me with your 'holier than thou' attitude, either! I actually know something about people, too! With good jobs being hard as hen's teeth to find over these past several years, the plain truth happens to be that you're just jealous as hell that I'm still Sheriff! But you can't fool me—no siree! If our positions were ever reversed, I'd bet all I'm worth that you'd behave no differently than I've been all along!"

With this last highly volatile sentence he spoke, the little twerp turned, straightened his cap, and then proceeded to march back to the driver's side of his paddy wagon, obviously feeling somewhat relieved at this point to have been able to shed all those heavy things from off his indisputably diminutive little soul. With Parker finally stating all this for the record, never before had I seen Felix Lauder move as quickly as he eventually did....

I vow that before our sheriff's little rump actually touched the thick phone directory upon which he usually sat, Felix had already opened the truck door on his side of our vehicle, rounded the front of the paddy wagon, and finally stood upon the running board of that same vehicle to no doubt be able to make the necessary eye-contact with this pompous little "hit n' run" assailant of his. Before Parker ever knew what hit him, I watched Felix grab hold of the man's left forearm.... After intentionally moving his face far more intimately closer to the sheriff's, at this point,

from where I was sitting I could actually see that my dear friend's somewhat sightless eyes were presently glowing with a particularly unholy
light, as I heard him finally tell this disappointing individual, "Never
seek to measure me by that thoroughly inadequate yardstick you always
use to measure yourself, Burtram Parker! Never, never do that to me....
After all, I should never deserve such an unkind fate as this!"

As far as I know this was the last time Felix Lauder and Burtram
Parker were to ever meet. Actually, thinking back, that particular day
would be the last occasion where the majority of the folks living in or
around Peck's Station would be seeing my friend. With the utterly cruel
and totally wasteful demise of the members of the Ketchum family, Felix
would never again be quite the same person....

In the weeks to come I watched as my friend began to uncharacteristically shun the company of others. He chose instead to live more and
more within himself. So much so, in fact, I remember that whenever he
would be required to purchase something important from the store, he
always requested that I drive him to another township in order to be
able to conclude his business. In other cases, despite what he might be
needing, I speculated that he just simply managed to do without. Sadly
it became increasingly obvious to those of us who knew Felix best that
something vital in the very core of his being lay badly broken, never to
be mended again.... And it literally broke my poor heart to have been
a witness to it all.

Even with the deaths of several of his own beloved children, which
occurred over those many passing years of his life, Felix remained the
sort of rare individual who—with his ultimate understanding and true
compassion for every situation—even managed to forgive the Gods for
their cruelty. But with regard to this other unforgivable crime which had
been carefully calculated and then flawlessly executed by others of our
species, he was obliged to suffer without end as a direct result of this.

Up until Felix's own death I sincerely believe that it was on account
of what he must surely have perceived as his significant part in that
entirely horrible affair that continued to haunt him. Indeed, he came to
fully grasp the extraordinarily painful reality that it remained Cornelia
Grimsley's undeniably potent hatred towards him—and consequently
her consummate attempt to grievously wound him in the most effective way possible—that undoubtedly prompted her to play the pivotal
role she did in utterly destroying those three innocent lives. Therefore,
within my dear friend's own highly acrimonious judgment, he become
indirectly and irreconcilably responsible as well.

As it happened, about three or four years after Felix Lauder's death, I chanced to hear through the local grapevine that Shamus Grimsley was stabbed to death during a vicious brawl which he had initiated within some bar located there on the outskirts of town. Certainly of far greater interest to all of us who loved the members of the Ketchum family was what was inadvertently discovered among several of this derelict's personal effects.... Those more astute police authorities of Walworth County eventually located Shamus' purloined booty wrapped within an old painting tarp in the back of his pick-up truck, ultimately proving that it was he who had undoubtedly played the major role in the Ketchum family's cruel demise.

What was eventually found among the many boxes of a particular caliber of ammunition were the iron manacles once belonging to John Ketchum's great-grandfather Abu when he had been forcibly apprehended and eventually brought to this country to live out his life as a slave. Along with this valuable and highly incriminating evidence was also inadvertently discovered that same much-treasured family Bible which John and Bessy Ketchum so deeply revered. Indeed, there was absolutely no doubt that this telling article had surely belonged to them, for still glued within the book's front cover was that same highly personalized copy of the Preamble to our Constitution of the United States of America which these good people had formerly sought to always use as their own special guiding light in order to perfect their day-to-day living.

Looking back, as I am, I frequently speculate upon the uncanny wisdom Felix Lauder professed when he assured his many children and me that: Truth is a poor beggar, and Justice—if it can be found at all—often comes in unexpected forms." Why is it, though, that these relatively common truths fail to comfort me—even now, after all these years? Why am I still haunted by the tragic loss of those three fine people whose cruel destiny it eventually became to have so trustingly allowed their sacred lives to become entwined with our own? And why, above all, was it necessary for them to eventually pay the ultimate price for that mutual friendship of ours?

25.

WHAT WOULD LIFE BE LIKE, without being able to love? Without being loved in return? Which excessively haughty or sadly inexperienced individual among us could ever comfortably conceive of existing in such an inhospitable terrain as this for very long? Ever poignantly I am reminded that this was a favorite theme for Felix Lauder, both in our cherished discussions on this same topic which from my humble perspective were worthy of any great philosopher, and of course quite frequently with regard to his beloved art which remains a profound language all its own.

Speaking of language, and without seeking to disavow in any manner the obvious importance that clear and logical communication plays within one's more familiar day-to-day existence, long ago I discovered the critical benefit of always heeding that special language which only the human heart has the ability to speak. Typically this most tender and endearing of transference deals not with the more easily delineated words and phrases of common speech, but rather in those far more subtle nuances with which so many intelligent children—as well as great poets, and artists, and philosophers of all ages are born to use. This marvelously germane "language without words" is telepathic in nature and becomes nothing less than a spiritually enriching discourse between two or more uniquely sensitive souls where the normal concepts of time and place and distance rarely ever play a significant part....

"Felix, I sure miss you! How are you getting along these days?"

Unbeknownst to me on that unforgettable occasion of what was about to become my last meeting with my great friend and teacher, I was in the process of stealing a few precious moments in order to be able to telephone him there at home from one particularly crowded area of the normally busy Chicago airport. This was for me the more important part of a terribly hectic forty-five minute layover. Much earlier that day I was obliged to travel from my home base at the university I was presently attending in Los Angeles, onwards to New York for a seminar on journalism. Right away I was being forced to acknowledge to myself that there would not be enough time for me to hurry on to Lake Geneva and to share a few treasured hours with Felix and Emma, as I would have greatly preferred. In any event, I still harbored a real need to console myself by at least being able to hear the sound of this special man's voice, thereby allowing me to learn as best I could by phone just how he was faring in body and spirit.

Nietzsche, I recall, is credited with having once stated: "Those utterly demanding experiences of life which in the end do not bend and break us eventually serve to make us stronger." Remembering back to that late autumn of 1947, which was up to this point in time the undeniably rich culmination of all of Felix Lauder's many lifetime experiences, I have come to reverently contemplate the wisdom of this particular philosopher and, too, my sensitive perception that, despite my dear friend's vast array of frequently overwhelming personal trials and tribulations which often left him unquestionably bruised and battered, over those seventy years of living he nevertheless remained a man unbroken by Life.

Metaphorically speaking, during my childhood and youth especially, I often came to think of myself as being that light and airy leaf whose destiny it was to travel about upon the wide surface of the "Great River of Life."... Felix, on the other hand, was perceived by me as being a great Herculean rock which, during his early formative years was eventually hurled out into this vast world—actually spewed forth, in a real sense, from within the hot turbulent bowels of the earth itself, much as great rocks tend to be, in order to be made to slowly cool and then to more properly solidify with time. At this point, and not unlike an artist evaluating the clay with which he is expected to labor throughout his days, my friend naturally was required to truthfully acknowledge to himself those personal qualities of his which consisted of all the fascinatingly rough and irregular areas of his being, as well as those far more contrastingly smooth and angular planes, all of which quietly heralded that wonderful uniqueness that was he alone.

Since great rocks by their very nature do not easily move or float about, they inevitably prove to make perfect protective havens for tiny battered leaves. These far more delicate objects fight continuously to stay afloat during their randomly appointed travels down "The River," as they are frequently carried in some frighteningly helter-skelter fashion. But even rocks and stones are never free from being ravaged by nature's forces. The overall process remains no different than those consistently challenging and ever-changing forces of Life itself. One need only experience the ineffable grandeur of the Grand Canyon as a stunning case in point and to become appropriately humbled as in the end one is made to grasp the significance of these same amazing powers that be....

Yes, whether sitting completely submerged within some madly rushing current of water, year in and year out, or existing somewhere merely partially submerged in some deceptively lifeless-looking pond, even the most impressive rock is forced to bow to its ultimate fate by gradually becoming eroded with Time's patient and frequently indiscriminate hand. With those continuous forces of nature that are bound to act as superb polishing agents, and which may never be countered or denied in the least, all in all it becomes an absolute certainty that great rocks—like great men, eventually succumb to the overall process of it all, until at long last, as Felix himself used to say, in the physical sense they become polished out of existence.

Towards the conclusion of his truly heroic life, my great friend once dispassionately confided to me that basically it was the complete acceptance of this inescapable mandate for living which ultimately becomes the only worthwhile and comforting aspect about growing old. According to Felix each and every highly introspective individual is challenged to quietly acknowledge the sacred power of Life's ongoing process of endless change which amounts essentially to those inseparable twin legacies of active creation and ongoing destruction....

Before the final curtain is fully lowered and the near deafening roar of applause begins to fill every corner of the great "opera house" known as the Universe, those more powerful souls among us ultimately come to revere life in all its magnificent complexity. It remains the truly sensitive spirit that eventually learns to bestow upon that "Great River" their perfunctory and frequently long-overdue blessing, all the while remaining cognizant of the reality that this same amazing process remains part and parcel of the overall Divine Scheme of things.

"Adam ... how good it is to hear your voice! Where are you, at this moment?" Then before I could answer my wonderful friend, Felix went on to ask with an unusually weary, yet no less extremely hopeful sound to his voice, "Shall you be coming out to the farm, so that we might share a little quality time together? Naturally I would so enjoy it, if you could!"

After I explained my unhappy situation to Felix, all the while attempting to console both of us by promising to drive out to see him and Emma in two weeks time as part of my return trip, of course, I detected within the sound of his familiar voice what I may best describe as an unmistakable tinge of genuine sadness finely interwoven in between his carefully chosen words of acceptance, as he responded by promptly assuring me, "Ah, yes ... yes! With your very busy schedule this naturally will be the best option."

What was it about our meager little conversation, thus far, that began to trouble me so? What significant message was to be deciphered from within that maze of characteristically upbeat words of his, which seemed to me to be so inadequately masking some particularly virulent disappointment on his part? After all, with our souls being so inextricably connected as they surely were, what was my friend's heart attempting to impart to my own, perhaps without actually realizing it? Yes.... Something emotionally unsettling about our conversation had managed to touch me through and through, yet I remained at a loss to understand exactly why this should be so.

Having been born a creature of rare instincts, especially where my interaction with others is concerned, after I heard my forthcoming flight being announced for the second time over the loudspeaker and subsequently was required to hastily bid my best friend good-by, my already troubled spirit became even more so as I continued to sit within the glass enclosure of the narrow phone booth, deeply contemplating the thoughts and feelings which were barraging my mind and my heart at the moment.... Then, as is often my nature, having soon arrived at some important understanding involving this impromptu internal conflict of mine, without so much as a second thought I went quickly searching about through my pants pocket for some change....

After rearranging my travel schedule with only a minor bit of trouble really, I promptly telephoned my colleagues on both ends of the country to notify them of the necessary change in my plans. Doing this I rushed on to a ticket office located within another concourse of the building, to initiate the required marker for a similar flight which I was being assured would be leaving early that following morning. Not long after this, with a mind and heart that was noticeably lighter and far more care-free, I impetuously purchased a round-trip ticket by Greyhound Bus to travel on to Lake Geneva in order to surprise Felix.

With that early-afternoon bus being practically empty of passengers, and with no one choosing to sit next to me during this first leg of the nearly two-hour ride, I was quite contentedly being left to my thoughts. Eventually my mind began to wander back to the recent past and to the earth-shaking events which had managed to greatly impact not only upon the world as a whole, but to more intimately impact as well upon our individual lives as a family... Looking back, I was remembering that fateful day of August 6, 1945, when our country was forced to use the atomic bomb which so devastated Hiroshima; and three days after that, when a second bomb was dropped on Nagasaki. Following these most desperate of acts, Japan finally announced its surrender and formally signed documents to this effect aboard the U.S. battleship *Missouri* in Tokyo Bay on September 2, 1945....

With the inevitable capitulation by Germany and Japan, worldwide hostilities officially came to an end, although the globe was destined to remain politically unstable as it fought to slowly recover from the incalculable physical and moral trauma wrought by the largest and most costly war in human history. Both soldiers and civilians, alike, suffered from this unprecedented conflict which actually obliterated entire cities, as well as countless lives in the process. After this cruel madness was finally silenced, masses of suffering humanity were subsequently left homeless, and diseased, and starving.

With Hitler's systematic attempt to exterminate entire groups of people, unspeakable atrocities were ruthlessly inflicted upon millions of innocent men, women, and children.... Those far more fortunate individuals who somehow managed to miraculously survive this holocaust could from that point onwards be counted upon to remain an ever-active force on behalf of sanity and reason—a powerful force, indeed, to shame the entire world into endlessly grappling with all the profoundly disturbing questions regarding the various destructive tendencies inherent within the human animal.

During that particularly providential winter of 1945, too, Willy, Charley, and Fritz Lauder all safely returned home in time for Christmas.... But even with the joy of our much celebrated reunion, no one could possibly have overlooked the painfully empty seat at our crowded holiday table which once belonged exclusively to our Eddie. Certainly for all those many heroes who would also never be re-joining their loved ones, in this physical sense, ever again, there was destined to automatically be reserved within the minds and the hearts of all the living a holy place, a sacred reservoir, so to speak. Here, mingled together with our boundless joy at being alive, was also being honored an undeniable sadness that forced each of us to quietly acknowledge the terrible price the world had had to pay in order to finally be able to establish peace on earth once more.

In early January of the following year—on New Year's Day of 1946, to be more specific, our beloved family friend "Doc" Owens unceremoniously slipped out of this life, leaving those of us who had come to love him so much to become greatly bereaved with his passing. Poor Felix seemed to suffer this overwhelming loss most of all.

As it happened, one of "Doc's" longtime patients—a gentleman, in fact, who had himself been assisted into entering this world nearly four decades earlier by this same fine medical practitioner—eventually discovered our mutual friend's frozen body slumped behind his little antique automobile. Sometime earlier the car must have become stuck in a deep snow drift, off somewhere on the side of that lonely country road. Perhaps "Doc" initially pulled off this less-traveled thoroughfare with the intention of taking a brief nap, as was frequently his custom over the years....

If this more popular theory was true, one further imagines that upon eventually waking our old friend must have also discovered himself at a distinct disadvantage when the engine of his old relic of a car refused to turn over and start. Instead of waiting for someone to eventually come along to assist him, he probably took the unwise initiative and attempted to push his venerable old chariot out of its deep rut all by himself. Tragically, with his wonderful old heart being made to overwork itself with all that excessive exertion, "Doc" eventually suffered a massive heart-attack. According to the available medical data, he died very quickly.

If a trustworthy sign of any man's overall lifetime of positive achievements may be tangibly marked by the number of friends who attend his funeral, then it certainly goes without saying that Dr. Chester Owens was well loved by so many people. I clearly recall that during his memorial service, which was held within the newly constructed communal hall in William's Bay several weeks after his death, there was not even available what one commonly refers to as "standing-room only" for that impressive mass of genuinely bereaved individuals who had come from near and far to pay their last respects....

Not amazing to me in the least was the significant fact that those same people arrived driving vehicles of every size and description from as far away as Chicago, Milwaukee, New York State—and even West Virginia. With each person intent upon being there for the best of reasons, the overwhelming majority of that same significant throng was required to wait outside in the brittle cold of deepest winter to become at the very least even indirectly part of that solemn farewell service.

Someone in our community who was sensitive enough to properly understand and appreciate the rare friendship which Felix Lauder and "Doc" Owens enjoyed for so many rich years requested at the last moment that Felix offer a few words to honor the man who always gave so much of himself to so many others. This rather impromptu request, in turn, caused Felix to briefly search his memory for a particularly special poem by William Carlos Williams which became the necessary closure to what my sensitive friend had already shared with the congregation.

Of course Felix's ultimate choice was no mere accident, either. The attending members of the Lauder family and I distinctly remembered that this special poem ranked somewhere close to the top of a fairly substantial list of mutually admired poems of theirs, and remained appropriately documented within the expertly mended little book which "Doc" Owens had treasured so much. As a final and highly sentimental part of his personal tribute to the memory of his great friend, Felix openly shared with those of us present the words to this special poem entitled, "Pastoral":

> *When I was younger*
> *it was plain to me*
> *I must make something of myself.*
> *Older now*
> *I walk back streets*
> *admiring the houses*
> *of the very poor:*
> *roof out of line with sides*
> *the yard cluttered*
> *with old chicken wire, ashes,*
> *furniture gone wrong;*
> *the fences and outhouses*
> *built of barrel-staves*
> *and parts of boxes, all,*
> *if I am fortunate,*
> *smeared a bluish green*
> *that properly weathered*
> *pleases me best*
> *of all colors.*
> *No one*
> *will believe this*
> *of vast import to the nation.*

During his otherwise faultless delivery of this poem, Felix only briefly hesitated on one occasion. Right away I suspected that that momentary lapse was not because he had forgotten the words, at all, but rather from the fact that he had become somewhat overwhelmed with such strong emotion from the loss of his beloved friend.

While Felix took a moment to gain control of his feelings, Anna Allegra could be seen hurriedly elbowing her way to the front of the exceptionally crowded room. As if seeking to transfer the necessary strength from herself to her father, so that he might finally continue through to the end, she quickly laced her arm through one of his and gave him a noticeably substantial hug. With this gentle kindness on her part, Felix managed to finish this poetry recitation of which I fondly recall thinking "Doc" Owens would certainly have approved.

With the approach of that early spring the older Lauder boys, along with the thousands of other financially disadvantaged individuals like them who had recently returned from the war, decided to make good use of their allotted portion of the recently appropriated funds that became better known as the "G.I. Bill." With this timely and most welcome monetary assistance initiated by our government young men and women could subsequently reclaim their dreams for the future which they had had to put on hold during those grueling years of service to our country. Soon anyone desiring to attend college became free to do so.

With me finally being able to go off to school as well, I initially was required to work a couple of odd jobs to help fund this longtime dream of mine. Later by some stroke of genuine luck I fortuitously obtained a wonderful part-time job with a newsroom in Los Angeles. This eventually provided not only those same critical funds for my ongoing tuition and living expenses, but also provided an unexpected bonus in the form of on-the-job-training. Presently I was able to concentrate upon that important and highly exacting craft of journalism which my beloved George had originally inspired within me when I was still only a youngster. Naturally, with all the Lauder children and me required to be away from home these days, Felix and Emma Lauder were being left more and more alone....

Realizing the fact that Charley was off at this very moment studying marine biology at the University of California, and, too, with Willy having just enrolled at the University of Wisconsin at Madison to finally be able to pursue his long-sought-after dream, naturally pleased me very much. Lastly, but certainly not least of all, with Fritz continuing to serve in what was officially to become the United States Air Force—as a fighter pilot, of course, the family nest was slowly and quite predictably growing empty. Naturally this knowledge was prompting something substantially strong within me to want to pay tribute, in some small way, to the adopted parents whom I came to love as I did.

While the driver of our bus expertly maneuvered his vehicle along the many highways and byways which constituted our designated route, I finally remembered that it was Sunday... Hence, no longer steeped within those heavier thoughts of mine, I began to take proper notice of the fact that I was moving closer and closer to home. In doing this I began to marvel at the wondrous sight of all the glorious oak and maple trees which had just recently donned their traditionally brilliant autumn colors of dark magenta, and crimson, and okra yellow.

Lord, Almighty! How exquisite the trees were.... The cool crispness of the invigorating air, too, touched some primitive sacred cord within my deepest being. I was beginning to feel familiarly energized—completely whole once again.... Yes, without a doubt, of the four splendidly distinct seasons of the year, autumn has always remained my favorite time of all.

Almost as if that endless parade of breathtaking trees also wished to acknowledge this same truth, they continued to go about freeing up their more frivolous leaves, subsequently causing those bright flashes of wondrous color to wildly cavort about within the strong gusts of brisk late October wind, quite naturally in spontaneous rhythm to that timeless dance called "Life." Truly, along both sides of those softly undulating country roads upon which my fortunate companions and I were presently traveling, these same miniature "flying carpets" were so engagingly celebrating my homecoming.... And I took substantial joy in the wholesome knowledge that soon I would be arriving where I instinctively believed I was required to be.

Early in life I learned that that near consecrated reality of "home and hearth" becomes essential to one's emotional well-being. So much so, in fact, that I have often contemplated the possibility that the world's "first Adam"—in other words, that famous "Adam" to whom Genesis continuously refers, surely must have coined the phrase: "Home is where the heart is!"

Yea! Those foolish "non-believers" among us who often state with such conviction that people cannot possibly miss that which they have never before experienced, are denying one of the preeminent truths concerning the human psyche. What surely amounts to nothing less than an absolute hunger and overwhelming need to belong to others who instinctively love and accept us—no matter what—is an innate longing that remains as ancient as time itself....

It is the fortunate individual who is born into such an emotionally nurturing environment from the beginning, religiously returning to benefit from its healing powers on a regular basis whenever time and circumstances allow. In my particular case, it was ever-compassionate Fate that quietly took the hand of that desperately needy child I once had been and subsequently led me to that dependable haven for which I still endlessly yearn. On a far less comforting note, whether one is forever damned to go searching about throughout one's life for this same frequently elusive necessity of body and spirit, or not—all of us become pilgrims in the end, passionately searching out and hoping sometimes against all hope to eventually claim for ourselves that "hallowed Mecca" of our dreams. Most assuredly, home is where the heart is.... And presently, although not yet fully comprehending why it was so, some indisputably potent yet completely wordless language of the spirit was powerfully calling me home once again....

There at the tiny bus-stop at Delavan, which was merely a convenient sort of "lean-to" arrangement that basically kept a traveler somewhat protected from the more inclement weather, I quickly claimed my suitcase from the overhead rack of my transport. After politely tipping my hat to the bus driver, I began walking at a fairly healthy clip in the direction of home. When I had gone less than a quarter of a mile, or so, I was eventually stopped by a very pleasant couple who asked where I was headed.

Originally it seemed to me that these same fellow travelers might have planned to return directly to their own home, after having earlier attended church services and a church picnic.... But as chance would have it instead, and rather luckily for me, I might add, the church grounds just happened to be located directly across the street from the modest little bus station. Naturally having spotted me struggling along as I presently was with my heavy bag, all the while I was committed to making good time in the process, they no doubt became rather curious as the old car they were driving finally slowed down a bit, tentatively inching up behind that young determined stranger who remained lumbering along as he was upon the side of the road....

After I stated where I was going, it became the couple's mutual decision to travel with me that extra distance out of their way in order to see me on to Peck's Station. From that point, even though I explained that it was only a hop, skip, and a jump to the farmhouse from there, with a charming air of mild conspiracy, almost as if these "Good Samaritans" instinctively understood and appreciated my eagerness to make it home in a timely fashion, they surprised me even further by actually going the entire distance and finally depositing me at the bottom of the Lauder's driveway....

Throughout my endlessly interesting travels in life, so often I have had the ongoing opportunity to discover that within most of the people I chance to meet there tends to be far more good within them, than not.... Grateful, indeed, for the kindness shown to me by these brand-new acquaintances, I enthusiastically thanked them. Snatching up my traveling case from the back seat where I was temporarily sitting, I finally turned with a sense of great purpose and began eagerly making my way up that long, and wonderful, and ever-familiar, gravel road.

As it happened months earlier, with the Lauder sons and myself required to be away from home as we were, a long-time game-plan needed to be established in order to help Felix with the essentials of running the farm. Naturally with the depressing reality that my dear friend had grown completely blind by this time, Herman Redding—Carl's grown-up grandson, was to play the most vital role in effecting this desperately required help.

If I remember correctly, it was Mr. Redding's idea that dependable help for Felix and Emma be established on a faithful day-to-day basis. As payment for this valuable assistance the Redding family was granted full use of the Lauders back acreage for the express purpose of grazing their substantially large dairy herd. In the end what began merely as an honorable experiment in human relations, soon evolved into a familiar and far more comfortable way of life for everyone concerned in the matter.

Our little "Hereboy's" predictable rumpus, particularly whenever anyone even contemplated making their way up the long road towards the farmhouse, was now a thing of the past.... This truly marvelous family companion of ours died quietly in his sleep in the late summer of 1943. Felix and Herman Redding eventually found him curled up under the hammock where he usually preferred to go to lazily wile away the heat of each warm day.

This, of course, is what I was recalling as I made my way up the colorful leaf-covered pathway.... Soon I was passing by those ten familiarly empty spots where Emma Lauder's glorious oleander trees customarily rested within their deep clay containers during the better part of each year. Now, too, pouring forth from what had obviously become the far more winterized porch area of the house once again, I could distinctly hear the more-muffled sound of music. As if in anticipated celebration of my homecoming, from Felix's ancient old Gramophone the sweetest notes of the fourth movement of Dvorak's *New World Symphony* were wrestling to free themselves from the confines of the old house, naturally with the ever-exuberant hope of being allowed to buoyantly float out across the surrounding landscape of brilliantly beautiful autumn....

Those beguiling notes were helplessly calling forth such pleasurable mental impressions evocative of America's overall breathtaking scenic beauty.... Subtle hints incorporated within its strains of folk music, too, must have invoked for Felix incredibly nostalgic memories from a former life which ultimately was destined to remain part of a time forever past.

As I scampered up the back stairs leading to the tiny anteroom off the kitchen, the inspirational music naturally became more defined and more pronounced. Opening the outer door to enter the house, just as I had been privileged to do a thousand or more times before this, my heart began to spontaneously dance to the spiritually intoxicating rhythm of the moment....

Home! I had come home, again! This special place and these incredibly special people were the loving home and devoted family which I might otherwise have never known.... Quickly sliding my rather cumbersome bag close to one wall within the kitchen as soon I entered the place, I then playfully tossed my hat upon the kitchen table—mostly for dramatic effect. As I consciously took a moment to absorb all the familiar sights, and sounds, and scents of the place—just exactly the way I used to do as a child, I found myself eagerly calling forth over the last strains of the lovely music, "Felix! Emma! I'm home!"

Oddly enough I received no response from anyone. Meandering through the dining room and then on towards the parlor where that familiar musical apparatus had just finished playing Dvorak's famous piece, still I found no one about the place. Instead the now silent phonograph mutely greeted my presence, refusing to assist me in any manner with regard to this ongoing search of mine.... After having made short work of investigating the equally empty rooms upstairs, I eventually decided to head out towards the barn, thinking it odd that Felix would leave the music playing unattended the way he had.

Crossing the cul-de-sac of the courtyard with only one thought in mind, my feet were in the process of betraying what was to have been my secret arrival, since all the while they continued to make their familiar loud crunching sound upon the loose gravel of the driveway. Searching for some familiar signs of life all I could do at this point was to press onward and to follow my rather keen instincts which were now leading me towards the barn area of our dwelling....

In no time at all I discovered myself standing within the portal of the familiar doorway of Felix's small studio, and with marked relief I realized that my private game of hide-and-seek was over.... There at last was the welcome sight of my great friend and teacher, sitting all alone in the dimness of his former work space, wordlessly calling me to him....

Behind Felix at the moment, even within the far poorer late afternoon light which was being softly filtered in through the dusty glass of the room's two large windows, as it was, I could readily see that resting upon the wide secure lip of the master's well-used easel was the now completed painting of *"The Last Hill"*.... Without a doubt, this extraordinary piece of work was destined to symbolize this talented man's consummate maturity as an artist. Although the splendid oil had been technically finished for quite some months before my friend's sight finally failed him, oddly enough he never took the initiative to frame it nor to display it in any manner within any room of the house. Instead, here it peacefully sat in the exclusive company of its talented creator, faithfully and most befittingly commiserating with him whenever possible....

"Who is there?" Felix called forth in my direction. I noticed immediately that within his reticent-sounding speech there was also the slightly strained tonality reminiscent of someone who had already grown unaccustomed to speaking on an hour-to-hour basis.

With a heart that was brimming with a complex mixture of so many emotions, I responded in kind by enthusiastically assuring him, "It's Adam, Felix! It's me... I decided to come home for a visit, after all!"

"Adam..." I soon heard him repeat. Then after a few seconds of silence, my friend went on to inquire, "Is this foolish old man dreaming, without actually being asleep?! Or have you really come home as you say you have?"

"May I turn on the lamp, so that I might better be able to see you?" I was inquiring, all the while I began cautiously moving into the small crowded area.... Having accomplished this simple thing, I instinctively turned to happily behold my dear friend, only to become somewhat stunned to so unexpectedly observe the overall negative physical change which had taken place in him during those nearly seven previous months of our forced estrangement.

While I quickly moved to Felix's side, he in turn was in the process of very slowly coming to his feet, after which we finally hugged each other in greeting. Then to more or less uphold the more intimate behavior which had naturally evolved into a rather unique custom of his, particularly since his sightlessness became a reality, my adopted father once again took a few seconds longer and allowed the fingers of one of his hands to act in place of his eyes, as he slowly and quite deliberately went about tracing the already familiar features of my face. Shortly, with highly charged words of an extremely emotional nature which were being delivered just above a whisper, I heard him finally declare, "Thank you for coming home, as you have, Adam.... Your being here means more to me than I can possibly say!"

Sitting quietly together at the moment, Felix took a few seconds to rather absentmindedly fondle a medium-size sable brush which I used to watch him expertly manipulate whenever he chose to paint in the past. Formerly it had been sitting among a cache of other rather expensive brushes whose glass container was still located upon the work bench directly before him. Almost as if he guessed my thoughts, he went ahead to confirm them anyway, as he told me, "Sometimes I miss painting so much that just being able to come to my studio, like this, and to sit here for a time in order to smell the ever-familiar scent of pungent turpentine, or perhaps a smattering of that far more rich and subtle linseed oil, comforts my poor soul the way nothing else can!

I ached for him.... His words of such conspicuous honesty actually hurt my heart. After all, there seemed to be so little richness in his life these days. With "Doc" Owens gone there would be no one of such excellent quality to call upon him and consequently to allow him to share those vital thoughts and feelings which are normally responsible for keeping one's life on an even keel. Perhaps cruelest of all was this latent blindness which prevented him from accomplishing work that was also so critical to his emotional happiness and spiritual well-being.

Worrying about him, as I could not help but do, I respectfully ventured forth to state the obvious, as I said, "You've grown so much thinner since I last saw you, Felix...." Hoping that I would not be "pushing the envelope," as the saying goes, much more forcefully I went on from there to inquire, "When was the last time you saw our new doctor from Walworth County?"

Taking a second to gently grope about for the proper container in which the paint brush he was holding all this while could now be stowed, my friend patiently answered me with words which betrayed the fact that he must have already accepted certain aspects relating to his present situation. Furthermore it sounded as though he hoped that I might compassionately consider doing the same thing, as he went ahead to bravely tell me, "As you already know, as yet there is no cure for diabetes.... Nor for old age, either, for that matter! Consequently, ever-united as these same formidable opponents happen to be at present, they possess the astounding ability to slowly plunder one's life beyond belief!

"My dear Adam, you must not worry about me so much!" Felix was saying, most probably to comfort me. Then after a brief pause, I watched as my mentor stood and purposely walked over to the finished painting which was being displayed behind us. Once again in Braille-like fashion his nimble fingers began very slowly tracing along the various aspects of the lovely painting's dry surface, as if in this fascinatingly tactile manner of his the various pleasing properties of muted color, and exacting perspective, as well as those far more subtle textures once imparted by brush and knife, alike, could be mentally re-absorbed by him in this interesting way....

Borrowing from Shakespeare, by and by my friend went on to poignantly assure me, "You must not worry.... For now predictably weighing down upon my mind and heart is merely that sobering 'winter of my discontent'! It would seem—and pretty much upon a moment-to-moment basis, that my poor spirit is being plagued with a uniquely sublime and overriding restlessness whose precise equivalent I have not experienced since my youth. And either fortunately or unfortunately, whichever the case may be, it remains my sincere belief that there is no proper antidote for this troubling malaise which some months ago became my ever-faithful companion!"

These fateful words of his were beginning to greatly oppress me. That tiny crowded room, too, also began to seem unusually stuffy and woefully dark to boot.... In a desperate attempt to rescue both of us from this less desirable atmosphere, I became inspired to enthusiastically suggest, "The day is so lovely, Felix! Won't you consent to walk with me, just for a little while? I remember so very well how you always enjoyed taking your long walks out across the fields, and sometimes those much-treasured sojourns down by the lake, whenever the spirit moved you....

"In a short while the warm sun will be sinking down into the far horizon, just as nature forever demands of it.... Reliably, as well, the bright evening star—along with its ever-proud consort, the moon, shall once again be making its glorious appearance. Now, of course, would be the perfect time to seize the moment and to attempt to make the most of these few precious remaining hours of daylight which have been allotted to us!"

Outside, by the far more obtuse light of that late autumn afternoon, I could finally see far more clearly the unrelenting toll which years of illness had inflicted upon this good man. My dearest friend seemed to have grown noticeably shorter and was nearly waif-like with his current weight loss. Oddly enough, too, even though he could no longer see, he still chose to wear his ever-present glasses....

Perhaps most disturbing of all was the reality that the more translucent flesh of Felix's face, and neck, and hands, seemed slightly bloated, and possessed a significantly yellowish tinge which I was positive was an indication of some profoundly worrisome condition that was frequently connected with diabetes. Another insidious side-effect came in the form of vascular disease which often led to limbs being amputated, as well as even the smallest wounds being excessively difficult to heal— therefore raising the significant threat of infection eventually being spread throughout the body. Then, too, and specifically in the case of men, there remained the grievously troubling issue of sexual dysfunction which frequently evolves into permanent impotence....

But I chose not to address the prospect of these painful issues, at least for the moment. Instead, I hastily returned to the house to secure a much heavier sweater for my needy friend and far more substantial footwear, too, fearing that without all of it the chilly weather might certainly become responsible for adding to his health burden should he inadvertently catch cold.

In no time at all, as we began walking arm-in-arm down a well-traveled path that bordered along several acres of Felix's rich dark farmland, we found ourselves heading in a westerly direction, prompting my special companion to ask, "Please describe the sunset for me, Adam.... After all, like you, I can feel those weak yet gloriously revitalizing rays of sunshine as they play upon my face at this precise moment!"

With this simple request that would prove to be such an easy gift to procure for him, chiefly as one acknowledged artist to another, I proceeded to carefully describe in infinite detail my personal impressions of what Felix and I were presently feeling.... When I finally finished, I paused to gaze upon his radiantly smiling face and also chanced to glimpse the shining vision of all that I had just described reflected there within the depths of his sightless eyes.... Subsequently, in response to what I had so lovingly shared with him, he slowly nodded with pleasurable satisfaction, as he went on to assure me, "Yes! Yes.... This is how I am also seeing it!"

When we finally returned to the house, dusk had firmly descended upon our little world. Meanwhile Emma Lauder, who over the past several months since my departure had more and more begun to keep company with Aida Redding, Carl's fine wife, on a regular basis now, had apparently just recently come home herself to prepare a light supper. But as Felix and I entered the kitchen, I noticed that she barely looked up to greet us.

Prompted at the moment not merely out of an elementary sense of politeness towards this rather familiar-looking figure, but quite honestly more out of a genuine affection for all that she had come to mean to me over the years, I made a point to travel over to the sink where the lady of the house was currently slicing a generous handful of asparagus. Lightly touching Emma Lauder upon one shoulder, I cheerfully greeted her as I said, "Good evening, Emma! Please pardon me for not giving you any notice of my arrival earlier today.... You see my visit was basically unplanned and rather spontaneous, to say the least!"

"It's always good to have you here with us, Adam," Felix's wife was rather matter-of-factly assuring me with her characteristically reserved and sometimes slightly annoying manner. Truly, it almost seemed as though she were speaking to a casual new acquaintance, instead of someone who had already shared so many eventful years with her under the same roof. While she spoke these words, I noticed too that she never bothered to turn around to officially greet Felix as any loving wife might have done under the circumstances. And in all this while she had not missed a single beat in expertly slicing and dicing the pale green vegetables which I watched her earlier claim from one tall glass pickling jar that was also passively sitting nearby....

Continuing on to tell me, as if she were somehow being annoyingly distracted by her husband and me from being allowed to entertain thoughts of a more personally pleasing nature, I heard her add very much in the same emotionally detached manner, "Adam, would you please set the table for the three of us here in the kitchen? As you'll undoubtedly observe, many things have changed around here, now that Felix and I are living alone. For instance, whenever we dine, we always take our meals here in this part of the house...."

Certainly happy to help out in any way that I could, I cheerfully set about accomplishing what had already long ago become a rather familiar household routine for me. Finally, after the three of us sat down together to share the tasty fruits of this good woman's labor, and before anything else was proffered by either Felix or me, Emma Lauder charged ahead to firmly announce just as if under no possible circumstances would she ever be deterred in changing her plans, "I won't be able to stay behind to clean up this evening's dishes. Mrs. Redding is holding her customary bi-weekly sewing bee, and I've vowed to attend each and every session from now on.... Tonight, and hopefully for the rest of the time that you're with us, Adam, I trust you'll be able to help look after 'things' around here?!"

What was it about this woman's flagrantly cool and ruthlessly calm delivery of that undeniably placid message that began to unnerve me so? Where was that basic warmth and consideration for others which I remember would occasionally make its welcome appearance within our lives? Indeed, I felt that I was beginning to see the overall truth of the situation far more clearly at the moment....

Suddenly a cold and inhospitable current of raw air somehow managed to invade the sanctity of our little home. That same disturbing feeling went briskly coursing throughout the more normal physical warmth of the little kitchen, only to disappear as quickly as it came.... So, I was thinking, this is what Felix has had to contend with during these past several months! In effect, and in every sense, my dear friend remains truly alone. And yet knowing him as I surely did, I guessed that within his heart of hearts he already made concessions for his wife's presently indifferent behavior. With his bountiful wisdom and consummate understanding of the many facets of the "human condition," and despite his own presently restless state of mind, he was clearly accepting all that managed to come his way.

Immediately after supper was over, Emma Lauder kept her promise. Our good neighbor Herman Redding arrived to thoughtfully chauffeur her back to the Redding's place, and I took a brief moment to escort both of them to Herman's waiting truck the way Felix would certainly have done in the past. Emma was not going to be made late in pursuing those forthcoming hours of healthy social interaction with those several other women in town who obviously had welcomed her into their midst....

While I was in the process of seeing to all this, earlier I sent Felix into the parlor to rest for a while, naturally with the promise that I would be joining him immediately after I tidied up the kitchen. Eventually coming to find him where I just naturally thought he might be, instead I discovered him standing in the dining room with a box of Havana cigars sitting upon the bare table. Actually, as I continued to stand in the doorway, my genial host remained in the more challenging process of attempting to fill the first of two impressively well-crafted glasses with some sort of strong fruit-flavored aperitif....

Those same pungent-smelling cigars, especially when they were being smoked, brought back wonderful memories which were highly reminiscent of that remarkable friendship once enjoyed by Felix and "Doc" Owens. I remember that as a rule the two men would make a point of seeking each other out in the name of that glorious friendship so rare, and from that point onwards they generally ended up happily whiling away many an evening hour with discussions on countless fascinating subjects. Otherwise Felix rarely ever indulged in smoking or drinking at all. At the moment, thoughtfully observing my great friend as he went about inadvertently spilling far more of the rich amber liquid onto the table top than was originally intended to target both interiors of the crystal glasses, I rushed to offer my assistance as I boldly inquired with as much tact as I could possibly muster, "Will indulging in these rather sinful extravagances be good for you in the end, Felix?! After all, what would the new doctor say, in the event he learned the truth?"

Finally allowing me to rescue the bottle from him—owing exclusively to the benefit of my being able to see—with a remarkable flourish of my far more steady hand I quickly finished the job which my worthy companion had begun on his own. Felix's forthcoming response to my rather audacious yet still carefully measured playfulness was unexpectedly swift and no less astounding, as he declared rather forcefully, "To be expected to endlessly live within some relentlessly strict parameters of what others feel is good for one, and what isn't, would be hell on earth! Just stop for a moment, if you will, and really think about it…. If I consistently chose to live my life this way, my life would cease to belong to me! And as you surely must know by now, Adam, I shall always insist upon remaining 'captain of my ship'!"

With these words that definitely rang true in every respect, I could not help but smile to myself as arm-in-arm Felix and I both ventured into the parlor together. Shuffling along as we were, with my great friend absolutely insistent upon toting the slightly cumbersome box of cigars under his free arm, while at the same time I volunteered to attempt to carefully balance the twin glasses that were quite full at this point, we safely made it across the room to the wing chair and ottoman that were destined to become our comfortable "base" for the rest of the evening.

With what I instinctively felt would be an excellent background accompaniment intended to aptly coincide with our forthcoming "soiree for two" that even now promised to be yielding such untold spiritual wealth for me primarily, I intentionally selected a particularly special musical piece for the phonograph. Now, of course, with the superlative tones of Beethoven's *Violin Concerto in D Major* beginning to rise so magnificently, I watched with overwhelming affection as my great friend and teacher snipped off the ends of the twin cigars he was holding, thereby allowing me to eventually do my part by lighting both of them with the slightly exaggerated style of an accomplished "homme du monde" or "bon vivant." Restfully sitting together, as we were soon doing, and very much like two mischievous bachelors gone wild for the evening, we began forcefully drawing upon our sinfully smooth Havanas in an ongoing attempt to inspire them to life, all the while the ever-passionate music played on and on in the background.... Finally raising his glass in order to be able to make an appropriate toast to the moment, Felix was saying with a much welcomed smile, as well as with a truly charming sense of old world formality, "To your homecoming, Adam!"

"To your health," I foolishly blurted out in response, and the second those callously hurtful words left my mouth—naturally, never to be recalled again—I helplessly watched as that moment's worth of rare sunshine noticeably dimmed within Felix's face....

However, in response to this and as though to compassionately help extract me from this same thoroughly awkward situation of my own making, I heard him cheerfully admonish me as he insisted, "No! No.... We must not waste a perfectly good toast on such a dismal subject! Instead let us place our heads together so that we might eventually select something more meaningful that will allow us to truly celebrate this special moment in time!"

Pondering away as we both were obliged to do, Felix took to comfortably resting his head against the back of his favorite chair and quickly closed his eyes. At the same time, while I remained steadfastly perched upon the trusty ottoman nearby to seriously consider the challenge which my friend had recently initiated, I noticed that each of us was holding his venerable "crystal chalice" in a temporary state of suspended animation.... Not long after this, I became greatly inspired to venture forth with a poet's eagerness to report: "Shall we drink more appropriately, then, to the outstanding beauty of Life in all its forms—as well as to the frequently understated beauty of genuine friendship and love?!"

With this fairly buoyant and sincerely expressed sentiment of mine, my modestly wounded spirit began to calm itself for I happily watched as my excellent companion's face became instantly animated with genuine warmth and light once more. Shortly Felix was passionately declaring, "Ah, yes! Yes, indeed! I should swiftly raise my glass to honor these most critical factors—anytime and anywhere!" Just as we both agreed to acknowledge that fine moment in this outstanding manner, the exquisite clinking sound of rare crystal could be heard briefly weaving itself into Beethoven's masterful work, as around the same time Felix added with considerable feeling, "Welcome home, Adam!"

After several peaceful moments where neither of us chose to speak, Felix decided to take another long sip of that misleadingly innocent drink in which we were both indulging. Then as a proper sort of "chaser," in effect, I observed him take another substantially generous drag on that fragrant cigar he was holding. Next he began to delight me by creating small airy circlets of smoke that, one by one, began floating conspicuously towards the ceiling....

By and by my dear friend became greatly inspired to take that same wand of tightly rolled tobacco and with it begin to conduct the exquisite music we were both hearing. Literally abandoning himself to this worthy project for some moments, he took to actually humming along in time to the piece. Eventually, with a long pleasant sigh that seemed to signal that he was now a man well-contented, I heard him unexpectedly announce in a mood of real seriousness, "Have I ever told you, Adam, that Ludwig van Beethoven and Sigmund Freud are my patron saints?!"

Naturally with what struck me as a significantly humorous pronouncement, I just could not help laughing out loud. To my thinking this disarmingly engaging remark of his was a sure sign that, even with that relatively small amount of alcohol which he recently consumed with such amazing gusto, all of it might be beginning to have this delayed effect upon him.... Unusually piqued as I was by this unprecedented confession of his, I urged him to enlighten me further as I answered, "Actually, Felix, in all the years we've known each other, you've failed to mention this interesting fact!"

"Then, by all means, do allow me to apologize for this significant oversight on my part," he was saying in that familiarly charming manner which was undeniably characteristic of him. At the very same time I noticed that he was also purposely off-setting the entire effect of this initial remark of his with a disarmingly mischievous grin, as he went on to further assure me, "What I have just confided to you is perfectly true! Furthermore, and just as every outspoken religious zealot of the world would have us faithfully believe, those sublimely comforting gifts of this life which so frequently make us the happiest are often openly declared to be either sinfully fattening, and therefore bad for the health—or just plain sinful in the end!

"Lately I find myself perpetually contemplating the reality that if, indeed, the overt passion found in great music, and, similarly, the equally passionate fervor found in great sex—not to mention the more simple pleasures brought about by an excellent cigar and a generous glass of 'spirited' spirits every now and then—is a threat not only to one's body, but more importantly to one's immortal soul, then by all means let it be stated here and now for the record that I should ultimately choose to burn in hell—and for all eternity, rather than be forced to part with these naturally sublime gifts of life!"

How I loved this man... I recall that even as a young child I used to marvel at Felix's great moral strength—his utter goodness. Now with both of us being adults, I could more readily appreciate that incorporated within these same laudable traits was his immense sense of humanity. There was also a certain undeniable vulnerability about him, too, which really only made him more human and therefore more lovable within my eyes. Acting as a sort of dependable glue to hold the entirely attractive package together in such a splendid manner, somehow he managed to endlessly curry this same vital humor of his which always had the reassuring ability to help ease a person through their more difficult moments in life.

Sitting beside my great teacher and friend, as I was on that already remarkable evening, I became cognizant of the fact that there was so much I wished to ask him concerning those fascinating issues relative to what I long ago perceived as the great mysteries surrounding his past. Furthermore, unhappily obliged to acknowledge the unkind reality that Time was becoming our enemy, I respectfully ventured forth with an important question of my own, as I bravely initiated, "May I ask you something rather important, Felix?"

Perhaps it was something specific in the tone of my entreaty which immediately captured and held my companion's imagination. Although Felix was blind, as I was inclined to remind myself, it was as if his remaining senses had pulled together in a most impressive way to make up for this deficit. After all, he never for a second lost the astounding ability to properly gauge for himself all those infinitely subtle nuances concerning the in-depth interior workings of other people.... Now out of necessity those important elements of touch and sound merely became that much more expertly developed—thereby allowing the all-seeing eye within him to remain continuously attuned to his surroundings.

Carefully sliding his near-empty glass gently across the small side table to his right, he finally turned towards me once again as if he could actually see me in the real sense.... He began his uncanny process of mentally and emotionally zeroing in upon me. Shortly, in response to my simple query and also in the form of a question, he went on to inform me, "Do you not know, by now, that there is nothing that I would ever deny you—anything that I would not grant you, if it were in my power to do so?!"

Feeling the immense stature of the moment and Felix's obvious readiness to speak about many things, I respectfully began that evening's dialogue by asking, "Felix, how is it that you first came to me on that unforgettable afternoon which I've since chosen to refer to as 'the day of the strawberries and storm'? Without a doubt, your amazing presence within my life has remained so significant that I absolutely refuse to imagine that our coming together as we have was just an accident.... It's impossible for me to believe that this truly remarkable event was merely some random happening...."

After assisting my companion to safely place his lighted cigar in the small porcelain tray which was located on the nearby table, I watched him recline more comfortably in his chair. Taking a brief moment to more properly formulate his forthcoming response, as tended to be his habit whenever similar situations arose, he was soon admitting, "Our meeting all those years ago was not really an accident, Adam.... Although my keen sense of honor bids me admit that benevolent Fate was instrumental in laying the rudimentary ground work for this important event in both of our lives, I know for a fact that our meeting that day was slightly more than this...."

Practically hanging upon Felix's every word in my eagerness to hear his personal version of what had so miraculously transpired all those years ago, I found that I was obliged to shift my weight a bit in order to better deal with my present mood. Soon I was being told, "Not long after my family and I initially arrived in this community, I began hearing rumors that your father, although terribly unwell and also highly reclusive, had oddly enough taken to welcome a youngster into his life. Of course those same kindly souls managed to off-handily indicate to me that they were shocked by this highly unusual turn of events, given the fact that your father was not well enough to properly care for himself, let alone care for a young boy too.

"Shortly after this happened, your father and I actually had the unforgettable experience of briefly meeting. At least it remained so from my standpoint!

"That particular day I was driving home towards our farmhouse when in passing your property I happened to glance in the direction of your father's place and spied a man lying motionless, face-down, upon the ground.... Being understandably concerned, as anyone might be under the circumstances, I quickly drove into the yard and hurriedly made my way to your father's side to assist him in any way that I could. When I was finally able to rally his mental state to a point where we could interact with each other at all, I eventually managed to help him to his feet, and this is when I smelled the strong odor of alcohol upon his breath....

"When your father's senses seemed to clear even a tiny fraction more, he finally became acquainted with the reality that this stranger was attempting to aid him. At this point he suddenly became extremely violent towards me, swearing rather colorfully and threatening my life if I did not leave the premises right then and there!"

"Yes. That certainly sounds like something my father would have done," I was interjecting, as my mind traveled back in time to touch upon many painful things.

"Owing primarily to my substantial fears regarding what I instinctively perceived as your own personally perilous situation, throughout my future day-to-day life as your new neighbor, I consciously searched for significant little signs of life next door. Usually these things came in the form of a tattered upstairs window blind rustling nearly imperceptibly, as I poignantly imagined that you might be seeking to vicariously involve yourself in our far healthier family life. Occasionally, as well, I frequently supposed that I might have actually glimpsed the sight of your lone shadow quickly moving across the downstairs kitchen window, like some innocent soul obsessed with not being left out of those endlessly active goings-on next door....

"Perhaps the crowning experience that eventually lent such urgency to this ticklish situation involving your father was the preeminent fact that both 'Doc' Owens and Harry Hopkins—even though at the time I had only just recently met the two of them, confided to me their own significant worries about your welfare, too. Notwithstanding this unanimous feeling the three of us seemed to share, then and there I made a binding pledge to myself.... I promised that I would search for a way to meet you and then somehow sensitively begin to draw you out from those surly shadows in which you consistently dwelled, and eventually into the far more wholesome light of day! You see, Adam, even before we met as we inevitably did, I possessed the overwhelmingly potent ability to actually feel your terrible loneliness. Truly, I felt your bittersweet longing for a better life as surely as if that feeling had been my very own!"

Tears were beginning to well up in my eyes, and all I could manage to do was to whisper, "It's all true.... What you've just described about me and my awful life back then is true—in every respect!"

As if Felix understood what his words were doing to me, he confidently reached for my hand. I allowed my strong fingers to gently encircle those long and nearly fleshless fingers of his own far more fragile hand, as together we gently squeezed in silent mutual acknowledgment of the profundity of it all.

Soon my dear friend's favorite chair was slowly being transformed into the privileged navigator's seat within our own exclusive time-machine. I observed Felix slowly place both of his slender hands together in a posture reminiscent of pious meditation. It readily occurred to me, too, that perhaps he might be carefully weighing the cost of what our forthcoming excursion back into the past might eventually be exacting from the two of us—in the emotional sense. For as we both already knew, those undeniable experiences of joy and sorrow continue to remain the opposing sides of that same amazing coin of life, and naturally what possesses the power to gratify one's spirit on the one hand, also has the frightening ability to inflict a great deal of pain on the other....

Surrounded now by the spiritually moving sound of Beethoven's extraordinarily beautiful music as it continued to play on and on, together Felix and I set forth upon our unforgettable journey, as I heard him openly confess, "You have no idea, Adam, how much I adored my own father.... Indeed, while he lived, he became nothing less than the earth and the heavens to me! Although I am certain that he loved me in return, our life was such that rarely were we able to share much time together. So you see with my being an only child, just as you originally were, loneliness was no stranger to me....

"By all accounts, and in the truly classical sense, my father was an extremely well-educated man. Likewise during his entire life he remained both financially and politically well-connected. As was his custom whenever he was not living away from my mother and me, which was the greater part of each and every year there in his other home in Budapest, he would faithfully return to his splendid summer estate in Beled for those few remaining weeks of summer. Occasionally he consented to visit the cottage where I was born, and where my mother and I always lived and waited for his inevitable return."

Unable to postpone asking the obvious question, I soon interrupted Felix's narrative by spontaneously interposing, "Why is it that the three of you didn't choose to live together—both when your father went away to the city, and again when he returned to the country?"

"As a child this arranged life-style seemed perfectly normal to my mother and to me, and so this is how we lived until my father's death. If you recall, once I mentioned that my father retained in his employ a wonderful caretaker for his summer residence...."

Remembering every single word of that still much-prized albeit fairly one-sided conversation of Felix's, which occurred that day in the family truck, I went on to enthusiastically exclaim, "I do remember! As a matter of fact I believe that you told me the man's name was Zapola.... And his wife's name was Gabriela.... And, of course, the large dog that your father had given you sometime around your seventh birthday was named 'Geza'!"

"You never seem to forget anything!" Felix was presently admitting with a touch of real pleasure.

Soon my dear friend went on to tell me, "Poor old Zapola—good man that he was! Naturally I was far too young to ever have given him the proper credit he deserved for being my trusted guardian. You see, during those long and lonely months of every year when my father would again be obliged to be away in the city, it was this same dear old man who was given the lion's share of the considerable on-going responsibility of looking after me. Being a child, of course, I tended to be endlessly curious and therefore endlessly involving myself in situations which might have proven catastrophic had kindly Fate, as well as faithful old Zapola, not been on twenty-four hour alert!"

With the memories which were being invoked by these mental wanderings, Felix began to smile rather wistfully. Remembering a specific incident that perfectly illustrated his point, he went on to say, "As strange as it might seem, since my earliest childhood I have harbored an intense affection for great storms! This is true.... Great and powerful storms that generally possess the ability to strike genuine fear into the hearts of most other people! I especially recall that on one late spring afternoon weeks before my father actually returned to visit the country with his wife and three grown daughters, that there upon the distant horizon, and certainly without much warning at all, was manifest proof that a terrible tempest would soon be upon us....

"It was while that small army of obviously concerned members of the household staff went scurrying about my father's immense collection of grand rooms—in order to remain faithful to their individual positions of trust—that I was given my usual freedom to thoroughly explore the entire interior of the place which by the time I was five years old was as familiar to me as if my mother and I actually resided there on a permanent basis. With everyone rushing about frantically attempting to secure my father's property I became inspired to take advantage of the situation, erroneously believing that I would not be missed at all.

"Within my father's impressive library was a secret door which led up a short flight of steps to what I would correctly describe as a small hideaway.... Essentially this small multi-windowed circular enclosure was designed as an observation platform. By standing within this space and by slowly gazing all around one was easily captivated in being able to see across long distances and in every possible direction.

"Actually I feel obliged to confess that I had already visited this unique place on my own quite a number of times before that particularly memorable day of the storm.... Of all the spectacular rooms in my father's wonderful house, this was my favorite. So, while everyone else remained thoroughly occupied in more constructive ways—naturally on behalf of that fast-approaching tempest, I headed directly for a place where I was certain that I would have the best view of all!"

Felix smiled with delight and slowly began to shake his head from side to side, only to eventually say with such conviction, "Are not young children the most amazing of all God's creations?!" With this he paused to take another sip of his drink, and soon returned to our story to say, "On that unforgettable day I was not content with just staying indoors to watch the powerful gusts of wind blowing the huge branches of all the ancient trees, just as if they were mere playthings! No, indeed. As the fireworks began to light up the sky in the distance, followed by giant peals of earth-shaking thunder, nature seemed to be summoning forth something extraordinarily primitive deep within me....

"In no time at all I managed to open one of the long windows and then to gingerly step outside upon the narrow ledge which hung suspended up above that far more timid world below with which I was already much more familiar. Walking out along this dangerously high 'mini balcony,' in effect, I began to literally inch my way along the outer circumference of that wall of glass—ever mindful not to let the angry wind steal me away—until I found the precise view that I wished to have. From this new direction, as that same harsh wind now acted to more helpfully press my small body against the building, and with the prickly needles of cold spring rain beginning to come at me in an endlessly pounding assault, with a profound sense of abandonment I proceeded to yell forth into all that madness.... Attempting in vain to lift my child's voice above the deafening roar of brutal wind and frenzied assaults of lightning and thunder, it was as if I was attempting to pit my small vulnerable self against the substantial wrath of the Gods themselves!"

Felix began to laugh out loud, just as if he were obviously re-living the whole experience all over again. Soon he was assuring me, "Truly I was not the least bit fearful of that storm, Adam.... Nor, for that matter, have I ever since really feared any of Nature's subsequent tantrums, although I have endlessly managed to maintain a healthy respectful for such things.

"For me what usually transpires during these same wild expenditures of Nature's savage industry has the rare ability to greatly satisfy my restless soul.... More than likely this unusual reality may only be properly understood and thoroughly appreciated by others who have been similarly branded with the true nature of an artist, or poet, or philosopher! In a most unique sort of way powerful storms consistently act upon my restless spirit as an intense emotional release, thereby bringing unspeakable comfort in the process. It is exactly as if all that terrible energy present within the storm itself somehow manages to temporarily equalize those powerful passions long present within me!

"When my dear frantic old Zapola finally found me—none the worse for wear, really, just merely physically wet and cold and emotionally exhausted from my carefully calculated confrontation with those impressive Gods of wind, and rain, and thunder—naturally he felt that I had a great deal for which to account!

After the storm finally subsided, and Zapola and I were on our way back to the cottage where my mother was anxiously awaiting me, my exceedingly frustrated care-giver again severely admonished me for my foolishness. Of course, witnessing the aggrandizing effect which my former experiment had produced within that dear old fellow, I eventually became far more contrite for having obviously caused him so much emotional turmoil.

However, even after all those appropriate apologies of mine were sincerely proffered that day—both to Zapola and then more earnestly to my own dear mother, something highly significant was still left to be desired from my perspective. Indeed, forced to live as I always was with my own sense of incurable frustration which stemmed from my usual inability to adequately express to anyone the existence of these same relatively complex realities already present within me at birth, all I felt I could do in order to cope with this uncomfortable situation was of course to look forward to the future and quite naturally to that next display of Nature's therapeutic outbursts....

"Perhaps this is why I have come to believe that most adults rarely ever give credit to these near inspirational complexities which are inherent within the youngest child. Far too often these same highly beneficial gifts ultimately run the great risk of prematurely starving to death.... Because the rudimentary stimuli responsible for fostering the basic creative effort in every child's critically formative years is allowed to be slowly and subversively negated by the world's less sensitive parents, and teachers, and other adult care-givers, in most cases the end result ultimately produces an emotionally unsatisfied adult!

"In my particular case, it was my own excellent father who must be credited for having so sensitively inspired that endless tendency of mine towards creativity and towards that same innate longing for self-expression which remains such a vital part of every human soul. I well recall that just before my sixth birthday this incredibly discriminating and thoroughly generous man took a moment to directly inquire what I might wish most of all to have as my special birthday gift from him....

"With his sensitive inquiry I was prone to remember that locked away within the well-appointed music room of his summer residence there existed three immense glass and mahogany collector's cases. Each piece of furniture seemed to be a true work of art, in its own right.... And with the three of them sitting together in a row, they managed to substantially cover one entire wall of the room. Furthermore, proudly displayed within was my father's private treasury of various makes of violin—including the rare Stradivarius, and Amati, and Guarnerius! Consequently, from the very first moment I chanced to carefully study this spectacular vision, which occurred many months earlier, I began to secretly covet the idea of one day being able to play such an instrument.

"Chiefly as a result of that fairly unprecedented inquiry on my father's part, I immediately took advantage of the situation by boldly addressing the subject of my heart's desire. Three or four weeks later, much to my overwhelming surprise and equally boundless joy, my highly enthusiastic father ceremoniously presented me with a small violin which he had had designed especially for me.

"With immense fondness I also recollect how particularly pleased my mother was when this same good man finally brought his special gift to our cottage and proceeded to show me how the tiny bow and the finely-crafted little instrument should be held, and likewise how both should come together to be expertly played... Then, as if these wondrous gifts were not already enough, a fine music tutor was commissioned to come each and every week to our home to help me learn to emulate some of this life's most glorious sounds!

"Perhaps without his ever having fully realized the truth of it all, it was my own dear father who ultimately saved my life.... Certainly with him having initially introduced me to the consummate joy inherent in music, not to mention the sublime satisfaction received from ultimately creating works similar to his own personal artistic renderings in oil and watercolor, these highly pleasurable and far less risky outlets for my all-consuming passion eventually replaced my dangerous obsession to so overtly spar with those ever-powerful Gods!"

I took a moment to refresh both of our glasses from the bottle that was left behind on the dining room table and quickly returned to my mentor's side to once again present him with his glass. With my gentle urging he soon continued on with these more fond reminiscences of his, as he eventually began to tell me, "In celebration of my fourteenth birthday my father presented me with one of the greatest gifts of all. He arranged the grand miracle of our being able to spend that entire day together.

"After breakfast with mother, the two of us went riding out into the countryside.... Later on as we paused for a while to allow our horses to rest, from atop the pinnacle of a scenic hilltop we chanced to observe a small army of workers gathered below. They were all in the midst of preparing the fertile fields for planting. Becoming inspired to be a part of their truly laborious industry, my father and I galloped down the hill and headed directly on towards the small group of a dozen or more men and women who were cheerfully singing as they worked....

"Taking a few moments to cordially greet these friendly people who regularly toiled this fertile land belonging to my father, and who immediately already seemed to know who we both were, Father and I thoughtfully removed the cumbersome tack from our trusty steeds, naturally in order that these highly spirited horses might be able to move about more freely and then to graze at will while we worked. Ceremoniously rolling up the sleeves of our clean shirts with a sense of boundless enthusiasm we began to help clear away the long thick tufts of wild grasses which had begun to encroach upon the more cultivated areas of the vast terrain....

"I recall that one of the workers proudly handed my father a long sharp scythe. With this I quietly observed as this special man who sired me began to expertly wield this valuable instrument, very much as if he were born to this ever-demanding life of rugged physical labor. Indeed, completely enthralled as I was, my father began to slowly move forward using his arms and the top portion of his torso to begin widely swinging the curved blade he was holding out in front of him.... Following this, in utter compliance to this ongoing assault of that same smooth back and forth motion, large clumps of the long strands of bright green grass were forced to bow to the moment. Swiftly and quite soundlessly they fell to the ground, eventually allowing Father to pass unimpeded through their more tractable midst like a conquering hero!

"Since I had not as yet mastered the grandeur of that unique tool, I diligently began following not-too-closely behind in his wake to help the other workers gather up the loose grass which would eventually be dried and then fed to the farm animals. Overall that remarkable effect of my father's continuous display of high energy was such that he immediately put me in mind of a talented "figurant" who was smoothly engaged in a sort of ancient dance step.... Having lagged substantially behind in my duties, at one point, I was soon re-energized once again by this good-natured man who unexpectedly began to whistle the charming folk tune which the other workers were originally singing when we arrived. Obviously becoming more and more enamored by the sheer magic of the cheerful music, everyone involved in that day's work also began to whistle and sing along, making our physically demanding work far more enjoyable in the end....

"Much later on during the early afternoon, since we had not wisely planned in advance for the eventuality of needing to bring along food or drink for ourselves as the other workers had prudently done, on horseback once again Father led the way across several acres of rich hilly land until we arrived at the edge of a small lake where we promptly felt obliged to remove our footwear. Following this we proceeded to energetically wash ourselves and our soiled clothing as free as possible from the considerable sweat and grime that was collected over those past several hours.

"Lingering for a while upon the bank so that we might properly dry our feet before pulling on our tight-fitting riding boots, I watched with interest as my father reached deep into the soft obliging earth and in the process grasped for himself a generous fistful of the rich black dirt.... Holding this small treasure up between our faces, he soon exclaimed, 'Felix, next to the consummate joy that genuine friendship and love always bring, this sacred land of ours is the only valuable thing worth possessing! Always remember this.... This ancient land upon which our people have lived and toiled for generations remains a wondrous living thing that year after year is capable of yielding such beautiful life—not unlike a beautiful fertile woman.... Remember to endlessly honor and appreciate it. Know, too, that one day in the future much of what you see displayed before us now shall eventually belong to you!'

"Nearby an extended family of gypsies were camped along the same rustic body of water. As my father would soon be explaining to me, it was my father's grandfather who had originally invited these same fascinating people to use this particular spot over and over again during their predictable migration to and from the area. Having initially surprised the members of the seemingly industrious gathering, who themselves were now occupied in preparing their own midday meal, we rode up to their campsite with the intention of merely paying our respects. However, we were both greeted with such genuine enthusiasm by the majority of these same demonstratively friendly folk that I recall thinking at the time that one might easily have become predisposed into believing that my own father, himself, was a long-lost member of their tribe!"

"Were you and your father eventually invited to share in their meal?" I swiftly interjected, practically imagining myself part of this amazing story by this time.

"Oh, yes!" Felix responded, "After all, this sort of thing represented an integral part of their unwritten code of family honor, with respect to being a remarkably close-knit people possessing a historic way of life.... They naturally hold family and friendship in such high esteem that I have often heard it said that any member of the group would sooner cut off one of their hands, rather than run the risk of tarnishing or degrading this innately personal philosophy by which they have continued to live for centuries.

"I recall that my father seemed so much at home among these incredibly interesting individuals. Likewise, as I was eventually introduced to 'Zoltan,' the famous patriarch of this particular branch of the gypsy community, I was swiftly and quite soundly embraced by him just as if he and I were already excellent friends. This dignified and thoroughly likable individual, incidentally, had himself witnessed the predictable transformation of my father over those past fifty-seven years or so, while Father was in the process of growing from tiny boy to fully grown man. Taking a few moments to openly study me in a totally inoffensive manner, our genial and outspoken host finally declared that I was indeed my father's son since it was obvious to him that the two of us resembled each other in every possible way....

"Having dined with this exuberant group of perhaps twenty-five or thirty people, where during the course of the rather excellent meal our gracious host insisted that I be seated between my father and himself, afterwards I took note that three of the older women of the family promptly disappeared only to return again carrying several musical instruments, including a truly magnificent violin.... Well fed and immensely contented as we all eventually became, but presently wishing to seek a bit of relief from the summer's late afternoon heat, instinctively we took to gathering within the resplendent lushness of a nearby grove of enduring old oak trees. Soon one of Zoltan's younger granddaughters ceremoniously presented her amiable grandfather with the violin, and much as if my father and I were already considered an important component of this effusive congregation of extremely outgoing individuals, this obviously much-beloved leader of theirs began to play the most extraordinarily exuberant music that I had ever heard, as our entire audience happily lost itself to the moment....

"Eventually, and no doubt meant as a significant honor, the fine instrument was soon passed to my father who wasted little time in attempting to gratify the wishes of our charming host by effectively playing several passionate little Hungarian folk tunes of his own which quite conceivably were even older than the branches of the ancient trees that were presently sheltering us. This, then, is how father and son shared those treasured moments which have continued to live on with such vitality within my mind and my heart.... Although my father hailed from an age and from a dominant intellectual culture that basically frowned upon men speaking openly of love and affection towards their own children—and, likewise, either publicly or privately expressing such important things with even the simplest familial hug or kiss—nevertheless on that remarkably special day and without the benefit of so many words, nor any other overt demonstrations as proof of affection, I was left with the absolute certainty that my father did indeed love me!"

Something Felix stated earlier seemed to conflict with another statement he made in conjunction with the same subject. To properly clarify this minor inconsistency which I initially felt must surely have been an oversight on my part, I began to explain to my friend, "Felix, forgive me for interrupting your story, but I remain a bit perplexed about something.... Earlier you mentioned the fact that like me you were an only child, while later you went on to refer to your father's wife and three grown daughters. Naturally attempting to sort out this somewhat minor technicality within my own mind, I have come to finally speculate that your father must have been married twice, in which case these same three young women were essentially your half-sisters.... Am I correct in my thinking?"

Contemplating my words with the utmost care, Felix took a moment to reach for his drink. Then after I watched him empty the modest contents of the narrow crystal glass, he consented to answer me by saying, "Actually the truth surrounding my birth remains far more complicated—and much more controversial, than your guessing. Biologically speaking, my father's daughters were my half-sisters.... In other words, what I am attempting to impart to you—as delicately as possible—is the relatively simple truth that my mother and father were not married to each other...."

My great friend's rather courageous pronouncement came as somewhat of a surprise to me, for truthfully I had not even remotely considered this significant possibility. While I remained pondering these extremely personal things which Felix had just openly shared with me, I listened to him go on to elaborate in a manner which led me to erroneously conclude that he had long ago come to terms with all those particulars concerning his earlier life. Shortly he began to explain, "I shall always have the distinct honor of being my father's only son. No one can ever steal this reality from me.... But in the same instance, while I am obliged to duly acknowledge society's ever-precise and stringently unwavering rules and regulations, I also remain consummate proof of an un-sanctioned intimate liaison which eventually evolved between a very young woman and a much older man who from the very beginning were devoted to each other, just as later on they were also devoted to me!"

For some moments after these powerful statements were made, Felix remained in a state of silent immobility. Eventually, however, I watched as he slowly removed his glasses, the way I observed him do a thousand or more times since we met. He then more or less predictably lay them carefully within his lap, as with the fingers of one of his hands he began to gently rub his tired-looking eyes.... Almost as if he were seeking a brief but necessary reprieve for the spirit before being forced by our circumstances to continue on with this most personal of tales, he politely asked if once again I would crank up our faithful old phonograph, this time with the sole purpose of resurrecting Beethoven's *Moonlight Sonata*—which, needless to say, I was more than pleased to be able to do for both of us.

Once more he took up the fragile glass which earlier I refilled for the third time, and then returned to him—that same small chalice, in effect, which was resting so comfortably within the protective embrace of both of his cupped hands at the moment. Soon enough, and obviously no longer hesitant to continue on with our fractious travels, Felix finally inquired in what I instinctively recognized as the rhetorical sense, "Does any society, or any organized religion within any society, ever have the right to condemn an individual for the circumstances of his or her birth? Does one automatically become responsible for the so-called sins of one's father? Alas, would it not be far more just and noble for the world in general to hold every person accountable for what he or she ultimately chooses to make of their sacred God-given life?!"

Tightly interwoven between these impassioned sentiments of Felix's, I began to ascertain the uncomfortable presence of some age-old malady which presently seemed to be in the process of being resurrected by my friend's direct probing into his now distant past. Once again choosing to rest his weary head upon the top back portion of his chair, and with his eyes more comfortably closed, at the moment, he proceeded on to inform me, "My mother was also an only child.... She was the beloved daughter of a husband and wife of extremely modest means, both of whom for many years pursued the tailor's trade, and who happened to be devout Orthodox Jews as well. Lauder was their family name. On the other hand, both my father and his legitimate wife were the progeny of equally proud parents who had each descended from their own separate long lines of financially and socially privileged individuals belonging to the Christian faith—actually, belonging to the Roman Catholic faith, to be more precise!

"As a young and thoroughly innocent woman of sixteen my mother had originally sought, and was in time graciously granted, full-time employment as one of the many members of my father's substantially large household staff, there in Beled. Sometime later on, however, after the illicit union was formed between them and after I was subsequently conceived and eventually born into this world, with the tremendous shame that this furtive affair understandably produced for my maternal grandparents, not to mention for the local Jewish community, as a whole, my mother and I were completely disavowed by her parents from that time forward.... Consequently, from the time of my birth up until the tragically unhappy day of my father's death, Father became our solitary guardian and protector.

"Before death actually took my father from my mother and me, I lived a relatively sheltered and carefree existence. But after he died I summarily received a bitterly caustic lesson on just how cruel the outside world can be.... Equally sobering, I was to also learn the unjust reality that that dreaded and uncouth beast of anti-Semitism remains ever-alive and well, thriving on and on within the hearts of certain people.... I discovered that this same timeless and thoroughly wretched insidiousness tends to dwell just below the surface of respectability. Every now and then, it springs forth with the cold and calculated intention of hopelessly ensnaring some poor unsuspecting victim within its hideously sharp teeth—only to subsequently drag them down into its gloomy lair to be drowned and eventually to be shredded into bits in order to be devoured!"

"Throughout those eighteen years of my life, right up to the incredibly sad time of my father's passing, never once did I have a single occasion to meet any of the members of my father's 'other family.' This reality, of course, was soon destined to change.... And just as assuredly, my life would forever become drastically changed as well!

"In less than a week after my father was buried—and surely even before his poor body was allowed to grow cold from death's tenacious grip, my father's wife and her formidable entourage of very able lawyers wasted no time at all in summoning forth several members of the hierarchy of the Catholic Church. This last group included one high-ranking archbishop who was rumored to have been a distant relative of this same vindictive woman who from the very beginning seemed 'hell-bent' upon pitting her personal cause against my mother's and mine. And so it was to be, when this oppressive clique officially banded together in staunch support of their common goal—which, in effect, amounted to nothing less than annihilating any possible claim I might be entertaining with regard to my father's legacy, in time my mother and I were ordered to appear at that ensuing meeting which was to occur in Budapest....

"For me to properly lay the groundwork for what transpired during this time, it might also be helpful to state that within the everyday social and political landscape of Hungary for many centuries, and up to the time of Communism's birth, its citizens were never allowed to experience the more noble doctrine which promotes the necessary separation of church and state as we have come to know and appreciate here in this land of America.... On the contrary, for literally ages the Catholic Church wielded immense power and subsequently that often arbitrary line of 'Justice for All' remained merely an obscure dream for another time and another place!

"What ultimately acted as the supreme catalyst which became responsible for invoking the absolute rage of our intrepid band of worthy opponents was the reality that several months before my father left us, he had taken the unprecedented legal responsibility of actually claiming me as his own son... Before God, and also before the entire world, he finally claimed me as his own! Notwithstanding three generations of his truly shocked and mean-spirited surviving family members, it became wholly apparent—especially to my mother and me, as the two of us kept our appointment in the city that day—that both of us had long remained one of my father's best kept secrets!

"Naturally my illegitimacy was destined to become an immense 'bone of contention', particularly after it was discovered that properly documented within my father's *Last Will and Testament* he had indeed kept his promise to me by first of all bequeathing me a generous parcel of his most choice land. He also left my mother and me the small quaint cottage which the three of us had always referred to as 'home.'.... And lastly, there was to have been a substantial amount of cash, as well as a handful of other significant valuables which finally included an exotic-looking old chest that my own dear father always preferred to use whenever he went traveling....

"During this 'mock trial,' which is certainly what it was, it soon became crystal clear to me that even if my mother and I had had the substantial financial means to properly defend ourselves—which of course was not the case, with that unrelenting push by our cunning adversaries to literally deny us everything to which we lay claim, we were destined to ultimately remain on the short end of the stick.... Indeed, when that fateful pronouncement of considerable doom and gloom finally descended upon our hearts in full measure, and the head-conspirator in the unforgettable form of that dastardly two-faced prelate from Rome stood before the crowded court that day to so sanctimoniously read his unjust verdict out loud, truly—and for the first and only time in my life—I sincerely entertained the tempting possibility of actually murdering another human being!

"Although this awful unrelenting man alluded many times to the 'shameful circumstances' of my birth, and the fact that due to this same 'unholy situation' I should always remained damned before God, as well as damned before my fellow men, I should quite justifiably in the end be left with no rights whatsoever.... What he was also unmistakably stating, if one took the time to read between the lines, was his absolute view that my Jewish blood only helped to further seal my miserable fate!"

Quite obviously this highly disturbing part of Felix's story was beginning to deeply affect him. I witnessed his jaw inadvertently tighten in a wholly telling manner, just as a large vein at the side of his forehead began to protrude a bit from the substantial emotion that he must have been feeling. Not until I purposely reached out to gently touch his shoulder in my ever-so-humble attempt to remind him that I was nearby did his tightly-clenched fists begin to relax in any way that might signify a release from all this harmful negativity....

After a time and with a demeanor that seemed far more relaxed, Felix began to muse out loud, "Because the dead remain notoriously inept at looking after those critical interests which once occupied them during their lifetime, everything my father so lovingly bequeathed to me and to my dear mother was eventually stricken from the legal rosters and forever deemed 'null and void' by the Catholic Church. Even his personal wish that I finally be able to inherit his name was summarily denied me.... After my mother died from consumption some time later, I left Hungary for good, eventually making my way to Vienna where I hoped to begin a far more promising chapter in my life.

"And, alas! As patient Time would invariably be teaching me, acute bitterness has very little value in the overall scope of one's ongoing accumulation of the years, since more often than not it tends to pollute the basic sacredness of one's life. But it took me a long while before I came to this conclusion on my own.... Lately, particularly during this deep and relentlessly restless winter of my discontent, I have been thoughtfully considering the important reality that although so much was stolen from me during my youth, God in his abundant mercy never once abandoned me! When the Catholic Church in shameful league with those same corrupt legal minds of the day blatantly denied me my birthright, what they actually took from me at the time were merely those more tangible treasures. Whereas those highly invaluable remaining riches which no church, nor any mortal man, either, would ever have the power to steal from me remained properly safeguarded in here, and in here!"

With this last fairly emotional sentence, Felix intentionally pointed to his head and then to his heart. Soon he was finishing his story by telling me, "You see, Adam, my beloved father died a contented man, firmly resolute in his belief that he had responsibly provided so well for my mother and for me; just as when I finally leave this life, I shall also be leaving with a contented heart remembering that his greatest gift to me was his devotion and love for both of us. In his supreme generosity he also taught me to love music—and to love art! Naturally with these wondrous gifts to enjoy, I have always believed myself to be a truly wealthy man....

"Out of an enduring respect for the memory of my dearest mother, too, I have endlessly credited her for the rich Jewish blood which courses through my veins.... It is this ancient 'blood of Abraham' which has added greatly to the required tenaciousness of my nature! Most assuredly, it is this same life-sustaining fluid which I proudly bear in both their names that has managed to support me all the while I have traveled down those far more difficult pathways of my life....

Soon I found myself asking Felix, "Is it this great disdain of yours for the Catholic Church that has led to a certain amount of friction between you and your wife over the years?"

"My early past was never kept a secret from Emma. I would certainly never have been able to do that.... When the two of us met and subsequently decided to marry, I seriously advised her of my strong negative feelings towards the Church and, quite naturally, why this was so. Furthermore I stated in no uncertain terms the fact that should we ever have children—in deference to the rules of equanimity, they should be raised neither as Catholics nor as Jews. So important was this future covenant to my emotional and intellectual well-being that I remember painstakingly pointing out to my wife-to-be that, if this vital matter was something with which she could not live, then it would be best if we admitted utter defeat, then and there, before we ever took our marriage vows! The dreadful prospect of year upon year of agonizing push and pull between us, with sole regard to this formidable matter, left me recognizing that ultimately we might become doomed as a couple."

"But as is fairly characteristic of most women, somewhere there in the back of Emma's stubborn mind she confidently entertained the ongoing notion that with time and an endless amount of not-so-pleasant 'kibitzing' on her part, my irrefutable stance might eventually be altered to her complete satisfaction. I suppose she honestly believed that my extraordinary love for her, especially in the beginning, would possibly allow her the upper hand where she would ultimately be able to override my deeply felt wishes.... But, back then, she obviously had not known me!

"Looking back, as I tend to do on a regular basis these days, although at times our many years together have often proven inordinately difficult—due more or less to this same volatile bipolar stance of ours on the subject of religion—in retrospect I should still not have wished to alter anything that has occurred as far as our union is concerned. I suspect that over these past many years it has been that slow and inevitable process of dependable erosion which is forever created by the passing of Time that has finally made a difference....

"With life's infinite challenges having the tendency to wear away at us, certainly if one is patient enough—for long enough—one's resistance becomes restructured just as one's priorities also become reshuffled. I vow that in the end it has remained the birth of each one of our beloved children which has finally invoked the overall compassion to properly redeem both Emma and me.

"Although religion theoretically has the power to 'civilize' the masses, world history and I know only too well that it also has the ability to act as a cunning subterfuge that cleverly hides gross corruption on many levels.... Over the centuries how many unnecessary wars and how many other political intrigues of a diabolical nature have been spawned in the name of all the various major religions of the world? Surely God, in His consummate disappointment and robust nausea, must be tempted to openly puke in appropriate response to all this flagrantly subversive debauchery by Mankind!

"Regarding that important subject referred to as 'civilizing forces,' to my thinking it is always the ever-loving and ever-wise parent that should consistently seek to play this vital role in their child's development. It remains my consecrated belief that genuine kindness that is born from sound and unwavering moral principle, and likewise a keen dedication to one's equally strong foundation of ethical persuasion, is ultimately the purest religion of all!

"While all the great religions were basically founded upon these historically uncommon principles, and by those remarkably wise and thoroughly visionary prophets such as Buddha, and Mohammed, and Christ, certain people throughout our world forget to remember this critical sticking point. So much of the incredible brutality, and bloody horror, and damnable injustice, throughout the ages has been traditionally invoked in the name of God, leaving the world and its religions sadly lacking in the most profound sense!

"Perhaps it remains no secret that you and the other children have become what Emma and I treasure most in this world.... For this reason I alone just could not bring myself to sacrifice any of you upon that blood-stained altar of gross hypocrisy!"

After we both took a short break to visit the downstairs lavatory, and after I offered to make some toast and tea for Felix which he summarily declined as politely as ever, we soon returned to our prescribed seats and I ventured forth to inquire, "Does Emma leave you alone like this very often, Felix?"

Smiling good-naturedly my wise teacher glanced over towards the sound of my voice, as he enthusiastically answered, "Ah! But I am not alone this evening.... I have your excellent company to enjoy!" Fully aware that my question was of a more serious nature, Felix finally obliged me by generously stating, "You must not judge my dear wife too harshly in the end, Adam.... After all, it is a fairly well-known fact that healthy flowers are forever compelled to grow towards the light! Both God and

I know that Emma has earned the right to finally be able to go off and claim a little sanity for herself, naturally in the more wholesome company of her new friends!

"To tell the truth, I have not been especially good company these last few months. It would seem that more and more I have developed the overwhelming need to live within my own mind.... And since my diabetes has yet to so ruthlessly confiscate my hearing, naturally my glorious music remains a continuous source of soothing companionship for me!"

With these last words of his my friend reached for my hand and gently patted it, as if to personally assure me that what he was telling me was perfectly acceptable to him. With the gentle silence which began to envelop us Felix became more inspired to confide to me with an unmistakable note of chagrin stealing forth into his serious-sounding words, "Please understand, Adam, that Emma is not solely to blame for the frequently violent displays of 'fireworks' which have tended to plague our many years together."

My muteness which followed these words of his naturally seemed to give my friend the necessary push to continue on and to better elaborate upon the fairly intriguing theme he had just initiated. Shortly, as the antique clock in the downstairs hallway began sounding the hour of midnight, Felix confided to me with such earnestness, "Sometimes I imagine how difficult it must be for my dear wife to live with, and also to love, this rather complex man who possesses the turbulent soul of an artist....

"Quite frankly, the truth of the entire matter is that artists, and poets, and philosophers, all suffer from a peculiar sort of 'madness'! A divine madness, in most respects, whose never-ending impetus stems from a desperate need to live in a way that few outsiders can scarcely imagine. This great affliction, as one might imagine, often becomes responsible for making us unbearably moody and ill-tempered at times!

"For the sake of more clarity, this powerful intrinsic malady of the spirit is never contagious in the true medical sense. Rather its basis remains profoundly genetic in origin and therefore possesses no overt threat to the world as a whole!

"Being an artist yourself, Adam, you have already begun to appreciate the reality that when the moment is right, and when you are being utterly true to your nature, you have the uncanny ability to actually 'taste' colors! Likewise, those seemingly trite differentiations of mood that tend to occur within everyone's more mundane day-to-day existence—those same infinitesimally minute variations to which most people never even bother to take notice, become highly significant to people such as we....

"Essentially, my dear young soul-mate—like it or not, what you and I have been obliged to become are the 'human barometers' of our species.... On the one hand, we live without end to greedily absorb and then to faithfully store away all the tantalizing raw data that is freely offered to us by generous nature, and, too, by every other facet associated with the consummate art of living. In this legendary manner we feed the creative furnaces of our souls. Of course this double-edged reality remains both a welcome blessing, as well as a profound sort of curse! As one only has to imagine, with the smallest incentive that unavoidably wears upon our spirit—day after day, and year after year, towards the end of our life the entire ongoing process tends to exact an often hefty price....

"It is my unerring belief that God, Himself, willfully fashioned the artist, and poet, and composer of great and lasting music, in this discerning manner. Within milliseconds of our extraordinary conception within the never-ending womb of the Universe, we alone remain firmly attached at some ever-fixed point by a strong yet invisible umbilical cord.... From this time forward—and ever onward throughout the duration of our frequently too brief existence in this world, much like the essential pendulum of an amazingly accurate clock, our poor spirits are hopelessly destined to slowly swing back and forth—quite literally between life and death, and heaven and hell, until that sacred cord is finally severed and we are once again freely propelled out into the unknown world from whence we originally came.

"Naturally it goes without saying that a certain abiding sense of loneliness traditionally remains part and parcel of the human experience. This sort of thing only tends to help exacerbate that unique madness which is inherent within every true artist. Like a pitiful orphan, in the spiritual sense, one is relegated to spend the days of one's life searching for that significant counterpart whom one instinctively believes will help to validate one's existence—realistically accepting, all the while, that such excellent fortune rarely ever occurs during any lifetime!"

With this last pronouncement of his, Felix took a moment to reach for another cigar. This time, as I clipped the ends for him and then with one hand steadily held the small light in order to make it possible for him to smoke, he soon picked up where we left off earlier to quietly declare, "Throughout my life's interesting travels, I have consistently been drawn to visit some random graveyards located here and there along the way.... Somehow I become significantly comforted in a certain bittersweet melancholic sense by being able to sensitively investigate the various parameters of these same sacred plots of earth, as without fail I also feel obliged to take special note of the various names and dates of those strangers buried there. During these same 'holy sojourns' of mine, my spirit invariably becomes obsessed to speculate upon how many of those same individuals lived and died with their hearts and souls filled with all the glorious treasures which no one else bothered to seek out, and then to adequately explore....

"For any soul to be born into this world and then to be required to live all their days with the desperate hope of achieving this frequently elusive goal—only in the end to be forced to admit defeat, shall always remain for me the greatest of all human tragedies.... The best of what we are so frequently lies locked away in its own secret vault, there underneath a shallow layer of dry sand, patiently waiting for some inquisitive soul to open the box and to eventually behold all the significant treasure within!"

Taking a few moments to rest, Felix finally chose to tell me, "People make a habit of saying that opposites attract with regard to choosing one's partner in life. Perhaps there is a great deal of truth in all of this.... For instance, and for the sake of this very personal discussion of ours, consider the reality of Emma and me....

"When we met, I foolishly believed that I had enough energy and more than enough love to be able to conquer any obstacle that life might present to us as a couple. What living and loving failed to prepare me for was the actual prospect of having my soul locked away in some dark and airless place, and possibly suffocating to death in the most inhumane manner.... To be expected to live one's life according to the precise edicts of another eventually becomes hell on earth! I fear that there really is no other way to describe it. And with the absolutely criminal result of being placed in this deplorable situation for any excessive amount of time, one eventually runs the risk of losing one's overall perspective with respect to one's place in the world, as well as any concrete sense of one's identity....

"As difficult as it is for me to openly admit, it remains my lasting conviction that even from the beginning of our relationship Emma harbored an intense dislike for my beloved art and my music.... Yes, what I am telling you is the truth! And during those first two decades of our life together, this was particularly so. She seemed to fancy that I was wasting my time on 'nonsense'—and nothing I could ever do or ever say to make her see otherwise has ever occurred. I suppose the real trouble in our marriage began shortly after she decided to construct a tight little 'box' of her own unique design which was built expressly to sequester—and then ultimately to tame, the passionate and freedom-loving spirit with which I was just naturally born....

"When I categorically refused to live in this wholly infamous manner, which no longer allowed her to attempt to randomly shape and mold my psyche into something less threatening to her, I actually believe that she began to hate me for it. Truly, the more resolute I became in retaining my life-sustaining passion for painting and music, which is nothing less than the vital 'bread and wine' that feed my very soul, the more pronounced and indelibly written became those battle-lines for our ensuing and ongoing marital conflict.... Can you imagine how destructive it would be to love someone so much, and for so many years, all the while pledging to honor all that that person is—and all that that person might ever hope to become in the future, and not have them ever choose to honor you in this very same basic way?

"Quite honestly I feel compelled to confess to you that in all the years that the two of us have known each other, at no time has my dearest Emma ever chosen to take her hand and to gently brush away those few grains of sand which barely cover the surface of my soul, in order to discover for herself the small treasure case that remains the most significant part of me.... Dear God! Not once, in all these long lonely years, has she ever been curious enough—nor kind enough, to learn who I really am!"

No longer able to contain my overwhelming sense of curiosity, I finally found myself abruptly asking, "Felix, who's buried up in our family's graveyard—not so very far from George and Lewis? What special man, woman, or child, so touched your life that a significant part of you seems to lie buried within that same earth along side of them?"

After I took the necessary time to very sensitively explain to my dear friend exactly what had transpired on that special Christmas morning years before when I was involved in the totally innocent process of returning home from Harry Hopkins' place, I respectfully waited for Felix's inevitable response. With my characteristically honest inquiry I watched with growing interest as Felix finally covered his face with both of his hands, and in this precise manner just continued to sit there in silence....

Erroneously believing that my more than frank question might have been strictly out of line, and therefore had significantly offended this good man, I quickly stood and placed my arms about his fragile shoulders as I made haste to assure him, "Please don't feel that you're obliged to answer my intrusive question, if in any way you don't wish too, Felix! It's just that for some reason our current discussion somehow greatly inspired me to ask for the truth, that's all. Indeed, from the moment that that uniquely memorable episode transpired, I have endlessly attempted to arrive at some plausible explanation concerning what I've long referred to as one of the major mysteries of your life...."

Eventually removing his hands from his face, my friend soon lifted his head to gaze in my direction, and this is when I unexpectedly observed that he had been weeping. Beholding his sightless eyes that were presently moist from some great emotion which had obviously disturbed those relatively tranquil waters of his soul, I recall thinking that in all the years I had known him this was only the second time I ever witnessed him cry.

I was beginning to feel indescribably wretched for having managed to so callously reduce Felix to this heart-wrenching state. Silently lamenting this fact, I wasted little time in hastily reaching into my back pocket to promptly remove the clean linen handkerchief that I habitually kept there....

Pressing the item into one of Felix's hands, as a sort of inadequate peace-offering, I suppose, I continued to watch as he finally wiped his eyes dry and eventually answered me by saying, "The special person to whom you are referring, Adam, was Alexandra Maria Grassi... Furthermore, owing to the indisputable fact that genuine admiration remains one of this life's purest forms of love, from the second of our first and only meeting which occurred quite unexpectedly nearly a lifetime ago, she was—and has always continued to remain, my extraordinarily significant gift from God, Himself!"

Still clutching the small square of pure-white linen there within both his hands, I watched further as my dear friend and mentor once again took to reclining more comfortably within his old chair. Even though Felix might well have wished to personally lose himself to those forthcoming more intimate moments in the exclusive privacy of his own company—still, in time, and surely prompted by the supreme kindness he had always shown towards me in the past, he finally consented to break his silence as together we continued to venture forth on our incredibly interesting journey....

Presently I was hearing him tell me, "At the time of my momentous meeting with Madame Grassi, Emma and I were living in Mexico City.... Naturally young Lewis and George were with us as well. In fact it was during that eventful early summer of 1912 when my family and I finally relocated from our home in Chicago to live instead within a small well-appointed *hacienda* that was situated on a quiet cheerful street not so far from where I would be working. That same tedious trip became necessary for all of us in order that I might be able to more professionally attend to several overriding problems which had rather lamentably arisen within this newly established branch of my business empire.

"With respect to Madam Grassi, of whom I shall always speak with undying affection, it was through extensive training on her part that she ultimately became a talented musician in her own right. Her 'forte,' as a matter of fact, remained the concert piano. It was she and her father Pietro, as well as her only brother, Emile, who made up the well-renowned musical group referred to back then as the 'Trio Grassi' which continuously traveled from capitol to capitol, throughout the world, bringing great joy to music-lovers everywhere!

"I have often reflected how miraculously wonderful life can be.... How significant, too, become those tiny details of our day-to-day lives, if only we take the necessary time to notice and to acknowledge the fact!

"My great friend and I were destined to meet, of this reality I remain absolutely certain. I well recall that on that specific Friday morning of the day we were to become acquainted, the day began very much like any other.... However, as those hours slowly progressed, this reality would soon be changing to become one of the most memorable days of my entire life—just as this remarkably special person was to become the great love of my life!"

With these words, Felix paused. Observing him, now, more in profile, he seemed to be incredibly more relaxed at the moment. By the soft glow of the familiar old table lamp, too, he even seemed to have grown nearly youthful again. As a pleasant sort of smile began to spread across his features, I heard him tell me, "Whenever the weather was especially enticing, as it surely was on that remarkable day, I usually made a habit of walking those several blocks to my office....

That morning I was running a little behind schedule. Because of this fact, I decided to take a short cut through a side-street which, up to that point in time, I had not previously explored. Finally re-emerging from this minor thoroughfare into a much wider and busier one whose small but exceedingly well-kept row houses were each proudly displaying within their own personalized wrought iron balconies the traditional flower boxes filled to near bursting with their brightly colored booty of geraniums and bougainvillea, something on the wall directly in front of me immediately captured and held my attention. There, in fact, being openly displayed for the benefit of the public at large, and more or less being well-hidden amongst a dozen or more far gaudier notices which were exuberantly heralding the various dates and times and locations regarding several local bullfights, I was immediately drawn to the only one that stood out from all the rest, primarily because of its far more sedate and genteel qualities.... Even though I was rushed that morning, I still felt obliged to stand for a while and to pensively absorb each line of the interesting information being readily offered by this same forthright announcement....

"This less colorful and far more-diminutive sized poster was formally advising the public that the musical ensemble known worldwide as the 'Trio Grassi'—and of whom, incidentally, I had never before heard, was due to arrive in our great music-loving city to entertain those members of our more cultured populace who might wish to obtain a ticket. Checking the dates, I quickly realized that this was already the third day of the group's entire ten-day stay before the three musicians would undoubtedly be packing up and traveling on from there to another city.

"Absolutely adoring music, as I surely do, I became utterly inspired to do something which I would not have ordinarily ever thought of initiating under normal circumstances. Prompted solely by what I had just read, I rather impetuously proceeded to dash off down the crowded street towards the grand music hall located only a few extra blocks out of my way....

"Hurrying along, as I was, I attempted to mentally balance the more sobering idea of my not wishing to be too embarrassingly late for an important scheduled meeting back at the office, while, oddly enough, at the very same time I was becoming far more good-natured and emotionally focused at the excessively happy prospect of actually being able to obtain two tickets for one of these ongoing performances that were being advertised. After all, that uniquely designed marquee was promising that each of the future programs scheduled during the next seven consecutive evenings would be featuring several of those sublime works by Rachmaninov.... And quite naturally in order to properly feed my ever-hungry soul, I knew that I needed to be there for at least one of those performances!

"Never having imagined for a single second that the ten performances might actually have already been sold out, you can imagine how disappointed I was to finally learn that this was indeed the case. Terribly frustrated that I had so impetuously wasted my valuable time in pursuing something that obviously was not meant to be, I quickly hailed one of the horse-drawn carriages which were almost always available for hire throughout the city's numerous districts, and promptly putting the thought of my missed opportunity behind me, the driver of the small 'hack' wasted little time in finally delivering me to my office....

"Sometime during the course of that ensuing business gathering which I had taken the trouble of announcing to my staff the evening before, and which consisted primarily of my being required to interview several new prospects who were each vying for a managerial position there within my growing firm, not long after the meeting commenced did my already exceptionally talented business partner and friend, Ugo Madera, politely interrupt this somewhat informal 'tete-a-tete' of ours.... With this man quietly advising me that there were two other important visitors presently waiting in my private office to consult with me; and naturally given the fact that not only would it be unforgivably bad manners to keep others waiting in some needless fashion, but also remarkably bad business sense as well, I eventually excused myself from the company of the members of my presently affable group and went directly to see what I might do to assist these prospective new clients of mine!"

Felix paused briefly, as if recollecting significant details of the story. Then, of course, remembering that I was still there with him, and that he had so kindly involved me at least this far in this already extraordinary tale, he soon went on to say, "I remember that when I initially entered the large room which was to eventually become my official office in the future, that same modestly appointed enclave, I might add, which weeks earlier had been somewhat jealously commandeered by me as my necessary 'home away from home,' the first unusual thing that greeted my senses upon entering this cool and refreshing space was the exquisite fragrance of lush roses which had ever-so-gently managed to permeate the entire air that I was now breathing.... Furthermore, I readily surmised that because this newly coveted place of mine overlooked a small walled-in garden that was up to that moment still so pathetically devoid of any cultivated vegetation of any sort, I naturally came to realize that this rare and highly pleasing floral phenomenon which I was currently experiencing was coming from somewhere within that very room....

"As I further proceeded into this sunlit space, and finally moved close enough to dutifully greet each of the two women who were still seated upon a long padded divan located in one far corner of the room, I could not help but observe that the mysterious woman on the right was wrapped nearly entirely from head to toe within a light cape, and was quite undeniably the bearer of this exotic perfume which I was presently savoring with such delight! Her companion, or *'la duena,'* on the other hand, was far more simply dressed in the traditional costume of the *'mestiza'* class, which consisted of a colorful cotton skirt and blouse, with a black lace *'mantilla'* or *'chalina'* resting upon the young woman's head and shoulders. Peeking out from underneath the many gathered folds of her long skirt's loosely-woven fabric were a pair of small sun-tanned feet, each exquisitely encased within their handmade leather sandal. Without a doubt, I could readily see that it was the co-mingling of the rich blood of that once proud and mighty Aztec nation and that of the Spanish conquistadors which had naturally produced the lovely swarthy coloring of this young woman's eyes, and hair, and skin.... I felt quite certain that this particular visitor's stunningly angular face and high cheekbones would have greatly tempted any artist worth his or her salt into capturing with oil and brush upon canvas....

"'Good afternoon!' I said, feeling unusually cheerful. 'I am Felix Lauder, the proprietor of this fine firm...." Naturally choosing to address the woman in the cloak, I went on to ask, "How may I assist you, Madame?'

"'Good afternoon, Señor Lauder,' this more formally clad woman finally responded in a well-modulated voice from underneath the light fabric of the generously constructed hood which she was wearing, the same article of clothing, I might add, which was completely hiding the entire top portion of her head—including her eyes. Consequently, the only symbol of any real significance that was strongly hinting at this visitor's more privileged station in life, as well as her stature as an artist supreme, were her long and slender and absolutely flawless hands that lay so elegantly reposing within her lap at the moment. 'Sir,' she went on to say, 'I have it on the best authority that your fine company, as you say, has the outstanding reputation of being able to create the most extraordinary wigs.... Is this true? And, if it is so, would it be possible to have one custom-made for me in a little less than a week's time?'

"After we agreed that such a thing might be possible, I further assured my new client-to-be that it would be necessary for one of my technicians to measure her head as soon as possible. Likewise, someone else would further assist her in selecting an appropriate style and color which would best flatter her in every possible manner.

"Becoming mildly agitated over this normal request of mine, with measured hesitation the woman proceeded to confide to me, 'Please know that all of what you're asking will be truly difficult for me. You see, Señor Lauder, mine is a highly unusual case.... Since I have just recently recovered from a long illness which was originally accompanied by a high fever that caused me to lose most of my own hair, perhaps with your innate sensitivity you'll be able to appreciate why I tend to wish to hide myself from the openly intrusive stare of others.... To make matters ever worse, my professional duties are such that I'm forced to remain exposed to the general public on a more or less ongoing basis. Recently I've learned to find a small measure of solace in being able to cleverly don one of several of my makeshift turbans for what has become an unusually exotic look—yet which I assure you really isn't my nature at all, in order to gratefully be able to camouflage this very embarrassing personal dilemma of mine!'

"Suddenly, without being able to explain exactly why it was so, my heart began to be filled with such immeasurable warmth for this very interesting stranger. Her voice betrayed a slight accent which I guessed at the time most likely made her a citizen of either Italy, or possibly Switzerland.... And nearly imperceptibly woven throughout the words of this brief dialogue of hers, I was able to poignantly discern a considerable amount of genuine sadness whose haunting reality touched me in such a way that I was truly taken aback....

"In a conscious effort to hide these strong unsolicited feelings of mine, and, too, any trace of what might be misconstrued by either of the women as improper behavior on my part, I purposely donned a far more formal manner. Just as any trusted and well-respected physician was expected to behave in the professional sense, where one is frequently obliged to walk that fine line between being appropriately compassionate, without becoming too compassionate in an inappropriate sense, in order to finally distance myself from the present situation and quickly regain my equilibrium, from a nearby wardrobe cabinet I hastily retrieved one of my workman's smocks....

"Prompted by my solicitous concern for this woman's basic feelings as a needy human being, where quite understandably her present adversity was deeply offending her innate sense of feminine dignity, I managed to inquire, 'Dear lady, would you possibly consider trusting me enough in order to be able to place your presently troubling circumstances within my very competent hands? In other words, if you would consent to it, I would personally take responsibility for the necessary measuring and so on and so forth, in order to preclude the necessity of your being forced to interact on such a personally distressing basis with so many other people.'

"Having taken several moments to silently ponder what I had just initiated for her overall benefit, from underneath the security of her hooded cape this lady's companion and I heard the lady eventually say to me in response, 'What you're suggesting, sir, would indeed be a very great kindness to me!'

"After taking a moment to excuse myself from the company of my distinguished visitors, I saw to it that the rest of that afternoon's appointments were moved ahead. Shortly thereafter, I escorted both women to one pleasantly deserted work room upstairs that was located just above my office, and then closed the door behind us for privacy sake. Politely seating my new client at the ornately-carved workbench where over this same long sturdy table there hung a huge gilded antique mirror, I proposed that she now remove the substantial impediment which she was wearing, and which continued to prevent me from witnessing for myself the overall damage that she claimed existed....

"Nearly as if responding on cue and without looking into either the mirror, which was presently situated directly before her, or up at me, this interesting woman in the cape very slowly began revealing herself.... Finally when the generous folds of light green sateen cloth lay decorating her shoulders, as well as a major portion of the flooring all around her, my visitor remained sitting there as a young child might sit when forced to deal with some sort of major unpleasantness. Indeed, there my far too timid guest remained, with eyes that were presently downcast and a soul which was attempting to avoid any possibility of encountering either of our reflections in the mirror....

"This vulnerable middle-aged woman instantly reminded me of a fragile porcelain figurine, or doll, whose former glorious auburn tresses had been badly abused in some rather unpleasant manner. Truly, all that remained of her once long and undoubtedly sumptuously thick hair, now existed in the form of a few sporadic patches of dry hay-like matter which were protruding rather unattractively from the smooth and shiny bed of her totally bald scalp....

"Obviously in a rather desperate attempt to better tame these pathetic remnants of what once had been, their unhappy owner had taken to gathering up all the fragile strands as best she could and further sequester the meager lot at the back of her finely sculpted head with one slender hairpin. Naturally, the overall severity of this unusual look of total guileless vulnerability only tended to highlight the woman's facial features, thus making her seem unusually beautiful to me.... Her skin tone, too, was incredibly pale. And underneath those emotionally-wounded eyes of her averted glance, I was certain that I detected telltale signs of the recent physical struggle to which she had earlier alluded, that very same malady, I might also most gratefully add, which had just recently delivered her into my life!

"Deeply contemplating these intriguing exterior qualities of my special guest—naturally, with the discerning inner eye of some master craftsman—my initial impression was that other people might conceivably have found this woman plain-looking in the physical sense. However, for the sake of truth and beauty—truth and beauty, at least, from my own worthy prospective—long ago I discovered that there simply are no plain people. There are, instead, those non-visionaries among us who remain sadly untutored in the subtle techniques used by those of us who have more or less mastered the ability to search out, and then to thoroughly explore, those marvelous secret inner landscapes which remain virtually undetectable with the naked eye. With the wisdom of any true seer I have endlessly reveled in the unique joy that each of us remains a marvelous universe to be discovered, and so often with the most valuable terrain carefully hidden somewhere deep within the overall package itself… These, of course, were a few of the important thoughts that were foremost in my mind that day, as I vowed to immediately commit myself to my personal mission of avidly seeking out and eventually uncovering those remarkable treasures which this woman's more austere exterior tended at first to hide….

"Now in what surely became my spontaneous attempt to rally to the seemingly desperate cause of my obviously needy guest, I instinctively attempted to make her more comfortable in my presence. In the process, I hoped to be able to alleviate some small portion of her miserable embarrassment. First off, I chose to stoop down by her side. With this simple gesture of mine, I sought to make myself appear less formidable—less threatening to the unhappy woman, as I eventually said in a comforting tone, 'Quite truthfully, Madame, please know that this sort of thing is not at all unusual for me…. Actually, in the most strict confidence I shall further share with you the fact that both men and women alike have frequently come to me in the past with similar needs such as yours…. I have often come to think of myself, as well as the many members of my highly dedicated staff, as 'caring practitioners' in a real sense. Basically, at times like these, we feel extremely privileged to be given a significant hand in going about reconstructing the less than tranquil lives of our clients!'

"Having stated all this I rose to my feet and asked permission to touch the woman's hair with the solitary idea of determining its texture.

Right after this, I became inspired to tell her, 'If you would allow me a little constructive criticism—relevant to our future working relationship—I suggest right away that I be allowed to severely trim away these longer and far less resilient tresses of your hair in order that the wig I shall ultimately be creating for you will naturally fit better.'

"At last! With the woman finally having the courage to look up at me, our eyes met for the first time within the mirror, as my very interesting visitor took to informing me with a note of real gratitude, "I shall happily place my future within your able hands, sir.... Please do what you must!'

"After I borrowed a pair of my foreman's best cutting shears from within one top drawer of a tall cabinet nearby, I began dramatically trimming back those unruly and thoroughly pathetic excesses of drab hair which this poor woman's recent illness had so unkindly left behind as its calling card. While I was busy doing this, I also took note that my most recently acquired client was beginning to take an active interest in what my efforts were achieving, for she began critically studying her reflection in the mirror... Very shortly, after finishing this necessary task of mine, I passed a small hand-mirror to her so that she might be able to obtain an overall appreciation for the more civilized effect which had just been created—even now.

"In a mood of modest wonder, as beforehand she returned to me the object I had given her, both of the woman's long exquisitely-shaped hands were finally being raised to gently and quite thoroughly investigate her current situation, and she eventually declared, 'Now I look more like the brother that my only brother always wished he'd had!'

"Greatly impressed and therefore somewhat emboldened by this slight display of humor on her part, I quickly responded in kind by firmly proffering my own truthful sentiment, 'Rather a young and terribly courageous Joan of Arc, I should imagine!'

"With these heartfelt words of mine, my special visitor immediately turned away from her reflection in the mirror to gaze up at me in earnest. While she continued to openly study me in this fashion, I became aware that this was no plain human being in any remote sense of the word. Here, indeed, was an amazing person who was well worth knowing.... Holding each other's eyes for even those few brief moments, I became immensely humbled from the uncanny reality that presently I was staring at my soul's own reflection—there in the mysterious depths of this unusual woman's dark green and gold-flecked eyes, which, in effect, had become our common mirror!"

"To hide the overwhelming impression which this remarkable truth was helplessly inspiring within me, and the distressing fact that my poor heart was pounding nearly out of control at this point, for those next few moments, at least, any normal sense of time and place had suddenly lost their meaning for me, and I went hopelessly ambling around the confines of that small tidy room like a soul magically possessed.... I suppose that I was more or less absentmindedly searching out a small familiar leather binder which dutifully held the names and the various other important data from all my other clients.... Hoping that my strong emotions were not betraying me, and after I eventually discovered the whereabouts of this invaluable item, I finally began to take the important measurements that were required of the lady and judiciously jotted everything down upon one blank new page. Then after we consulted together as to which rich and luxurious shade of deep chestnut auburn most closely resembled the healthy and luxurious hair she once possessed, I also made a note of this information.

"Lastly, with my pen poised in the air, just as the awful embarrassing truth literally descended upon me that up to this point in time I had not as yet had the presence of mind, nor the good manners either, to even bother discovering the name of my amazing guest—without further ado I mustered the necessary fortitude to inquire, 'And now, Madame, if only you would generously consent to place aside my unforgivably bad manners and finally grant me the real pleasure of discovering whom I have been addressing.... Likewise, for the sake of our business transaction, to what address shall I ultimately be delivering the special merchandise which you have instructed me to create for your benefit?!'

"'First of all, Señor Lauder,' the woman responded, 'even though it may be of little consequence to the world in general, for critically important personal reasons of my own, I've never consented to marry.... Therefore, owing primarily to the various invasive labels which society so often insists upon imposing upon others, I suppose that my situation more correctly demands that this middle-aged woman be referred to as mademoiselle—or senorita! However, having prudently looked ahead in time—towards the not-so-distant future, and being forced to honestly admit that some day it shall undoubtedly become horribly ludicrous to actually hear others refer to this elderly spinster by either of those terms, perhaps the title of 'madame'—which you've already chosen to so wisely bestow upon me, all in all will prove to do very nicely!'

"My truly wondrous guest was smiling amiably at me, as she spoke these last words in a happily teasing sort of way. Then with a remarkably contrasting note of genuine sincerity, she went on to add, 'But please know that because of your uncommon gesture of true kindness towards me in my moment of great need, you actually managed from the start to put me more at ease during what I originally feared would be an unbearably difficult encounter for both of us! With this in mind, then, I should be most pleased if you would refer to me by my given name which is Alexandra ... Alexandra ... Maria ... Grassi....'

"With these refreshingly outspoken and innocently friendly sentiments of hers, I instinctively began to feel a renewed sense of comradeship towards my brand-new acquaintance. I felt utterly compelled to believe that here was a rare human being who was not afraid to say what she meant, nor to mean what she said either. Knowing what I know of life, and of people, certainly, this same unvarnished propensity to behave in that far more desirable manner where any potentially negative sort of human interaction is quickly defused and manages instead to leave all the parties concerned basically unscathed by it all, truly remains an example of refined diplomacy.

"No socially appeasing politeness nor irritatingly mindless 'chit-chat' for this rare lady, either, no doubt.... No, indeed! Even from the beginning it was my strong impression that, although Alexandra Grassi remained well aware of the many inadequacies of life and, too, the basic shortcomings relevant to those stolid non-visionaries among us, she strove to carefully cultivate a working philosophy very similar to my own where she good-naturedly took everything in stride, without flagrantly betraying her lifelong dedication to some higher ideal by which she avidly sought to live each and every day of her life....

"By now as I went about cheerfully and rather nonchalantly chronicling those three names of my guest, one after the other, upon that formerly pristine sheet of smooth vellum paper as she spoke them in a slightly hesitating manner—when the second finally arrived for me to aptly record her family name, I looked up with great surprise to say, 'Grassi ... Grassi! How odd that your name should already seem so familiar to me!' Of course, less than a moment later, with the jolting vision of that extraordinarily fine placard which was still being displayed not only upon that one particular stucco wall within our beautiful city, but still within my own mind and heart, as well, all I could do was sit there in stunned silence....

"Without having uttered a solitary word Alexandra Grassi responded to my overall amazement with mild surprise of her own and I felt obliged to attempt to explain my utter befuddlement, as in hurried detail I recounted the interesting episode of that morning. Listening most attentively to everything I told her, she finally confided to me with a truly uncanny understanding of the entire situation, 'Ah, yes! There have often been times in my own life when I've come to the inescapable conclusion that some miracles are just meant to be—just as it also becomes startlingly clear to me that certain special people are destined to meet!'

"Much later that same afternoon, after Madame Grassi and I had successfully concluded our business together and I was in the process of laying the fundamental groundwork for not only the truly handsome-looking wig whose overall design she had just chosen for herself, but one of my very own revolutionary design which was to ultimately become my special parting gift to her, a messenger came to my firm bearing an envelope.... Inside the thin packet was a note from this same intriguing individual, and quite amazingly enough two tickets for the "Trio Grassi's" last performance, which would be occurring exactly one week hence.

"I shall never forget, either, that beautifully penned upon that single sheet of quality paper which had previously cradled her supreme offering to me, and which, incidentally, bore the telltale fragrance of roses, were the words: 'It remains quite clear to me, now, that some things are just meant to be.... Please accept this humble offering as a symbol of my profound gratitude for your unexpected generosity and kindness! Alexandra.'

"Needless to say, in order to be able to complete the many hours of work necessary to create both the wigs—and within record-breaking time, no less, several of my finest artisans along with myself labored day and night to be able to meet the necessary timetable specified by Fate, and particularly by Alexandra Grassi, herself, before she was due to leave our fair city for destinations unknown to me....

"Well do I recall that during this specific era of history women of polite society generally chose to wear the more rigidly established style of clothing and accessories born within the Victorian and Edwardian mold. This long-accepted rule included undergarments, for example, that unnaturally pushed and pulled a woman's tender body in the most barbaric manner. Outerwear, too—dresses, and cloaks, and hats, and so on—were endlessly adorned with lace and rococo beading which was always considered 'high fashion' in any circle.

"When Madame Grassi unerringly selected a hairstyle for herself that was far more sleek in design, and therefore dramatically departed from the more familiar form of tiny ringlets and curls which other women generally preferred, this had not come as any real surprise to me. After all, is it not in tune with every true artist's nature to 'cut to the quick,' as the saying goes? To instinctively shun the superfluous? In other words, to characteristically wade through the often cumbersome and distracting minutia of one's day-to-day existence with the idea of arriving at what is far more honest, and therefore far more desirably beautiful and true?

"With this fascinating woman's preference for this same intrinsic philosophy by which we apparently both sought to live, I would be obliged to very tastefully create a more modern upswept look where the thick luxurious hair of my excellent wig could be fashioned into an elegant knot, or 'chignon.' This, of course, would ultimately be flattering to her on and off the stage....

"With even that very brief glimpse of mine into the attractive soul of this already dear lady, I became energetically inspired to take a chance by creating an alternative arrangement for her which I truly believed would ultimately highlight Alexandra's own sense of creative flare. Although the style of this second wig was really not new since, essentially, it dated from the time of those earliest dynasties of Egypt, just the same I actively speculated that it might seem to be so to most audiences who were long programmed into accepting what had sometime ago evolved into an old 'socially sacred' methodology.

"Happily working day and night as I was prepared to do in order to accomplish my goal, what I so proudly designed for my new friend was a slightly shorter than shoulder-length helmet of rich, thick, shiny hair which would actually move ever-so-slightly whenever Alexandra moved.... My conscious hope inevitably became that each time she consented to wear my splendid offering, it would gently cradle the crown of her finely-shaped head, as well as her pale flawless brow, just like the hands of any ardent lover might do.... Painstakingly constructed, as this second wig eventually was, to look as natural and as carefree as any child's head of hair, in time this 'diva supreme' would be bringing those discerning musical audiences to their knees long before she ever seated herself and began to play her beloved piano!

"On the morning of the last day that the *Trio Grassi* was scheduled to be performing in Mexico City, I personally delivered both wigs to the address which was given to me. Unhappily for me, though, Madame Grassi was not available to see me at this time.... Presently I was feeling cheated at being unable to see or to speak with her again. But because of my own terribly hectic schedule I was summarily being forced to leave behind my exquisite offerings for her, including a modestly detailed note carefully explaining how the wigs should be handled for the maximum amount of years of wear. I also penned a short postscript thanking her once again for the tickets to that evening's performance—and most of all for the extreme pleasure which I had gained from meeting her and from being allowed to assist her in her time of need.

"True to Emma's own nature—and, too, true to the destructive tendencies which plagued our relationship from the start, at the very last moment my young wife managed to bow out of her promise to attend the forthcoming musical concert with me. Even my fervent plea that those highly prized tickets of ours had been incredibly difficult to come by did not sway her determination to stay home. Painfully accepting what I could not change, but at the same time staunchly refusing to allow her characteristically stubborn standoffishness where music and art were concerned to dampen my spirit of vigorous anticipation, I dutifully bathed, and shaved, and then finally donned my impeccably-groomed formal evening attire to eventually leave the house by hired coach....

"Later at the concert hall when the house lights were properly dimmed and the heavy dark red velvet curtain slowly began to rise above the stage to signify the start of that evening's performance, a solitary shiny black grand piano mutely greeted the audience. Soon after this I watched with tremendous excitement and pride as Alexandra Maria Grassi began gracefully walking across that wide and starkly decorated platform, making her way towards that same magnificent instrument....

"I shall never be able to forget, either, that the very second this great artist made her appearance, one could actually hear the collective sound of hundreds of people taking life-sustaining oxygen into their lungs— as if on command, and at the very same moment! For there, in all her glory—and wearing the very revolutionary wig which I had so lovingly designed especially for her during those past few hectic days—stood the beautiful woman who had already changed my life!

"There she stood, that solitary and noticeably confident figure, completely unadorned except for the remarkably ultra-plain long taffeta gown she was wearing whose dark blue-gray color reminded me of the predictably moody North Atlantic Sea as it might surely appear on any blustery sunless afternoon in deepest winter.... There she stood, politely acknowledging the enthusiastic greeting of that grand room filled with ardent admirers—and not a solitary soul, other than she, of course, could have possibly guessed how pleased I was to even have been remotely part of that whole triumphant scene!

"Without further ado Alexandra promptly opened this musical celebration of ours by doing absolute justice to the first of the three movements of the second of Rachmaninoff's piano concertos. Similarly, her passionate fervor for the music never wavered, in the least, as she eventually completed the last two movements of this same very demanding piece. Her audience understandably—especially myself, became thoroughly enraptured from start to finish.... My God, how well she had mastered that marvelous instrument!

After a brief intermission Alexandra and her father, who would be accompanying her on the violin, and of course her beloved brother, who long before this moment in time had also mastered the cello, finally came together as a family to take divine possession of that small sacred space, there upon that otherwise empty stage. After a few necessary moments, which the energetic group dedicated to properly tuning their instruments, the incomparable Trio Grassi ventured forth to once again mentally and emotionally enchant their much appreciative audience—this time playing together as a group to expertly perform Rachmaninoff's unusually haunting "Trio Elegiaque"!

"At the end of this final portion of that evening's performance, the robust roar of the audience's approval was nearly deafening.... After several curtain calls, a highly enthusiastic young gentleman ventured forth from somewhere within those more obscure regions bordering the stage and eagerly presented Alexandra with a generous bouquet of pale yellow roses... Strangely enough, I found myself actually envying him! Indeed, if the truth be properly told, I envied even more those lovely flowers which lay passively cradled there within this lovely woman's obliging arms....

After that traditional gesture of appreciation was concluded, the now heavy and oppressive shade of voluminous scarlet fabric all too quickly descended once and for all upon the decorous festivities of the evening. Depressingly being impressed upon my mind was the unavoidable reality that all wonderful moments such as these must inevitably come to an end. I recall that for some time after that I remained seated where I had been sitting all along, spiritually spent in the most intensely passionate sense.

"Not wishing to lose the prospect of being able to personally compliment all three of that evening's unusually talented musicians, nor, even more desperately important to me at this point, the overriding hope of being able to see Madame Grassi one last time before she and her family departed the city, I waited patiently until the huge concert hall was fairly emptied of its former occupants.... Then respectfully wandering back stage, I eventually made my way to the place where Alexandra and her father and brother had already begun packing for their forthcoming trip to Paris....

"Being genuinely pleased to see me again, my great new friend wasted little time in exuberantly introducing me to her other family members. Later I helped carry several of their heavy traveling cases to the rear of the building where a driver had been contracted to take the valuable items on from there to the train station. Upon their most sincerely-delivered collective invitation, I finally consented to join this refreshingly upbeat group for a late supper in one of the city's loveliest spots.

"The four of us continued to happily dine and drink together, there in the quaint terrace garden of that same small but elegant restaurant.... After I faithfully promised to later on escort Alexandra back to the nearby hotel, where they as a family had all been residing during their stay in our fair city, Pietro and Emile Grassi cordially excused themselves from the table and promptly left Alexandra and me alone together to share what remained of the special gift which Fate was bequeathing to us....

"On that wondrous evening my charming new friend and I spoke of so many things that interested both of us. Indeed, those few amazing hours became a feast of sharing! Certainly too—and from the very beginning, Time became our dreaded enemy.... Eventually the two of us were forced to acknowledge, with mutual surprise, that that brand new dawn of a brand new day was just beginning to break upon the deep purple and scarlet hills beyond the city. How equally surprised we both were to learn that the similarity of our spirits was such that during those few sacred hours, at least, time and space and those other familiar realities of one's day-to-day existence had temporarily released us from their hold!

"Although Alexandra Grassi and I were destined to never meet again in the physical sense, still for those next three and a half critical years which followed, we eventually evolved into the most faithful of correspondents.... Initially, without even having realized what was happening, both of us willfully committed to this seemingly innocent and natural-feeling course of action. So much so, in fact, that I actually reached a point where I began to live for her letters! Each word she penned became food for my hungry spirit.... So often from some interesting or exotic place around the world, this great lady took the infinite time and trouble to share those long fascinating pages of written discourse with me, as she went about carefully highlighting her travels—and more importantly, too, her valuable descriptive impressions of all the many things which touched her in both the intellectual and spiritual sense.

"It was established sometime early on that it would be best if I posted my letters to her by way of a particular address located in Geneva which, for continuity sake, had already become the long-established Grassi family's 'base' or personal headquarters. But, after many months of faithful correspondence between us, one day her letters ceased to arrive.... For what already seemed to be an inordinately unbearable length of time, I was forced to impatiently wait for weeks longer but still no such-sought-after word from her came my way!

"Quite frankly with my having become literally obsessed by the worry that something serious must be wrong—but unable to know where Alexandra and her family might be performing at any given time so that I might promptly contact them and thereby be able to put my fears to rest, little by little my emotional turmoil only increased with the slow and excruciating passing of time.... Eventually though, and as if to prove my worst fears true, many months after I received her last letter a relatively small and nondescript parcel finally arrived at my Mexico City office from Switzerland. I could not fail but notice that it was addressed to me by someone whose script remained unfamiliar.... Upon opening the outer wrapping which protected the small compact box inside, it was with a sense of great foreboding that I soon discovered a modest-sized envelope which was bordered all around in black—a well-known symbol used by many countries throughout Europe to respectfully denote someone's death....

"The brief note, in fact, was written to me by Emile Grassi. His opening salutation more formally begged my forgiveness for his having waited so long to send word of his sister's death! And as my hands began to tremble quite unavoidably with every miserable word that I read, I could actually feel this good man's own pain as it came seeping up through the print to sacrilegiously accost me now in my own heart-wrenching state!"

Presently, with these emotionally charged words of Felix's, I witnessed that my friend could no longer ignore the pain which this unhappy remembrance was reawakening in him—even now after all these years. Once again quickly covering his eyes with the handkerchief that I earlier placed within his hands, he began to sob quite openly....

Being moved to tears myself, at this point, with this strong man's uncharacteristic display of such overwhelmingly genuine grief, all I could do was to allow this latent sadness he was expressing to spend itself in this undeniably therapeutic manner.... In time, when that fractious internal storm of his had eventually subsided, I was obliged to ask, "Felix, had Madame Grassi ever indicated to you in any of her letters that she was ill?"

"No! " Felix responded. "After all, this was not something that she would have ever done. Knowing her as I did, she undoubtedly did not wish to burden me in any sense with the troubling fact that for some months prior to her passing she was actively battling tuberculosis.... She died in a small sanitarium located on the outskirts of Geneva, with only her father and her brother in attendance.

"It remains my implacable belief that had I been made aware of her grave situation, at any time during the course of her illness, she likewise instinctively knew that I would be prompted to leave my family behind in order to be there at her side. Being the devout Catholic that she was, she no doubt also understood that this behavior would most surely have been interpreted by others as substantially shameful on both our parts— and this, of course, was something with which Alexandra would never have wished to contend.

"As the highly intuitive person that this good woman just naturally was, it most probably became obvious to her from the beginning that my marriage to Emma was far less than it could, and should, have been— even though we intentionally refrained from ever openly addressing the matter. With both of us being so similar in nature we managed to grasp the reality that our overriding sense of innate integrity would always have remained a considerable 'stumbling block,' naturally with regard to furthering our relationship in any physically intimate sense. We were destined by Fate to remain lovers but only in that most rare spiritual sense....

"One's ever-abiding conscience, I discovered long ago, notoriously forbids a truly responsible person from ever leaving behind their considerable sense of responsibility to others. For the two of us to have attempted to build any long-range happiness that was predicated upon the utter misery consciously inflicted upon others would have become ultimately self-defeating for everyone concerned in the end.

"Yes ... Alexandra Grassi already knew this. She knew that if I were even indirectly summoned to her side in what surely must have become her greatest time of need, without hesitation I would certainly have gone to her! So she chose not to burden me, nor to betray my family, either, with any sort of personal decision required on my part which ultimately may well have torn my already difficult marriage apart at the seams....

"With her fervent resolve to do the honorable thing, she decided to tempt neither Fate—nor me. And since there can be no genuine love without true respect for ourselves and for others, this is how she chose to respect me, as well as to also respect the difficult circumstances of my life. Naturally what amounted to a wholly unselfish decision on her part only caused me to love her all the more!"

Sitting there, as he was, my great friend and teacher continued to carefully dab away at the moisture from his eyes. Being greatly perplexed by something, I soon inquired, "Felix, how in the world did Madame Grassi ever come to be buried up in our cemetery?" This question seemed perfectly normal, given the extraordinary circumstances of the story which were just shared with me.

Reclining more peacefully, Felix soon assured me, "She is not buried in the cemetery across the way.... Instead what remains of her physical self lies reposing in her own family's graveyard, located outside Zurich, Switzerland.... That small hand-carved plaque which you found within the snow on that particular Christmas morning was basically created by me as a tribute to the memory of our special friendship. Upon Alexandra's death, and during every season of all the many years which have come and gone ever since, wherever life has taken me, there I have consistently honored her memory by erecting similar shrines.... This is the only way in which my troubled soul has managed to find even the smallest measure of comfort."

"Earlier you indicated that the letter from Emile Grassi was accompanied by something else—something in a package, I believe you stated...."

With my usual openness and characteristic curiosity, Felix closed his eyes and chose to rest silently for a few moments before answering my question. Shortly, however, remaining absolutely true to himself, as well as to me, he proceeded on with this incredibly personal tale of his, to finally declare, "Instinctively understanding that certain music possesses the unique power to speak so much more profoundly to the needy soul than any letter possibly could—in lieu of Alexandra Grassi's necessary words of farewell to me, which would never have sufficed for either of us, really, her parting gift to me remains instead that special recording which was made in Europe with the splendid accompaniment of her dear father and brother, some time before she became far too ill to participate.... Indeed, her gift remains none other than the Trio Grassi's own triumphant rendition of Rachmaninoff's 'Trio Elegiaque'!"

Now I understood. At that precise moment, not having initially anticipated this particular response from my dear friend, I became incredibly humbled by his revelation.... With regard to that same special recording, which I myself had long ago become most familiar, a far better appreciation of so many important things came literally flooding back into my consciousness....

"Never for even a single moment have I ever stopped loving her, Adam—just as she has never stopped loving me! During all the more difficult and trying times of my long life—when I felt certain that I might eventually buckle under the tremendous weight of some seemingly endless turmoil and pain—Alexandra Grassi has always been there to comfort me, and to gently minister to me through her beautiful music.

"Truly, during my darkest hours, it was as if the welcome essence of her magnificent soul consciously consented to slowly pass across my own—very much like the moon eclipsing the sun, to gently and faithfully remind me that she has never abandoned me.... You simply cannot imagine what immeasurable consolation has been brought to me by this same endearing process, each and every time it occurs!

"Through my beloved friend, I have learned that love is stronger than death.... Because of her genuinely true regard for me, in the end I know that I shall not be damned throughout eternity for having lived and died within this often callous world of ours with my heart and mind filled with all the wondrous treasures which no one else bothered to take the time to search out and find! This, of course, has ultimately remained her greatest gift to me. Likewise, there is the ever-redeeming knowledge that with all the many miracles that occur in this lifetime, there must surely be just as many more waiting to eventually be discovered beyond the grave!"

Throughout that entirely momentous night, we had managed to travel exceedingly well together—my own beloved friend and I. Soon, however, with the old rooster's predictable crowing, where that still spunky bird was responding to his unthwartable need to enthusiastically make welcome that brand new day, I stood and helped Felix to his feet, and together we spontaneously hugged each other for several long seconds without bothering to utter a single word....

Sometime after midnight Emma arrived home. And without much fanfare at all she promptly had gone off to bed leaving Felix and me to ourselves. Likewise, sometime after our clock in the downstairs hallway was in the process of sounding the hour of midnight, Herman Redding thoughtfully took the trouble to personally usher this lady to the front door where I was there to greet them both. Remembering that I would be requiring a way to ultimately return to Chicago, I requested the great favor of having this same good man later drive me to the bus stop in

Delavan where I would be able to keep my appointment with destiny and that Greyhound bus....

By six that same morning, after quickly washing up and changing my shirt, I went into the kitchen to help Emma prepare tea and toast for the three of us. Then, as she eventually proceeded to occupy herself by accomplishing those time-honored little odd jobs around the kitchen, I quickly finished packing my bag just in time to hear the sound of Herman Redding's truck making its way up the driveway to fetch me.

That particular early autumn morning was quite chilly. Quickly peering out through one kitchen window, I could see that a thin coat of frost was decorating the ground all around the farmhouse.... With Felix wishing to accompany me out the back door and down the wet steps towards the waiting vehicle, I finally managed to discourage him from doing this. Perhaps when he sought to return alone to the sanctity of the far warmer house, with his inability to be able to see he might somehow have slipped and fallen. Instead, I politely but quite firmly suggested that he wait upon the long porch as I inevitably made my departure....

With him graciously bowing to my solicitous wisdom, we hugged each other one last time. During that moment, while I continued to hold Felix's fragile presence briefly within my far stronger arms, I became overwhelming inspired to say, "Felix, I love you! How may I ever thank you enough for having taken me into your life—and for having taken me into your heart?!"

Never before this time had I spoken these important words to any-one—not even to my beloved George.... And so, with these poignantly expressed words of mine, I well recall that this very special man who had from the start so willingly become the loving and dependable father I so needed was returning my hug far more intensely than usual, in wordless acknowledgment of what I had just expressed....

With Herman Redding impatiently tooting his truck's horn to speed things along, I quickly added to what I just told my friend by actually pleading with him as I continued to make my way towards the back door, "Felix, please promise me that you'll make an appointment with that new doctor just as soon as possible.... Naturally, I'll telephone you by the end of the week to see how you and Emma are both doing!"

Almost as if he had not heard my earnest request, Felix responded by quietly stating, "You must hurry, now, or you'll miss the bus!"

Wasting little time I jumped into the passenger-side seat of Herman's old truck, and soon the two of us began slowly driving down the road towards the street below. When we neared the now enclosed porch area of the house, however, I had our thoughtful driver slow to a stop, just beneath the spot where I suspected that Felix would be standing....

Even though I knew that he could no longer see me, I took immense consolation in the reality that his hearing remained quite remarkable. Obviously listening for us, as he was, the familiar sound which the truck's tires were making upon the loose gravel of the road clearly advised him that we were waiting at a standstill nearby. Shortly, and very much as I had anticipated, with the ever-passionate sound of those first phenomenally intense notes from Beethoven's *Fifth Symphony* rising rather challengingly towards the heavens, and tentatively fanning out in every direction to greet that new day—there Felix stood, like any proud admiral might stand upon the bow of his ship....

Instantly that last incredible vision of him was indelibly etched into my memory for all time. That truly glorious combination of this particular scenario's visual and audible aspects has long represented to me that quintessential religious concept embodied in the "Trilogy," where God, and man, and artist remain one and inseparable....

Spontaneously reaching over to quickly give the truck's horn a playful blast, the special man I grew to love so much simply raised one hand in open acknowledgment of my farewell greeting to him, much as if he were bestowing his ultimate blessing upon me.... Then, as Herman Redding dutifully put his truck into gear, Fate decreed that loving father and son be finally separated from each other.

This was the last time I would ever see my great friend alive. Three days later while I was working in New York I received a telephone call from Anna.... In between her overwhelming sobs of genuine anguish and grief she barely managed to tell me that our father had just recently died from an overdose of insulin. While Emma was off visiting friends—and as usual with no one else being about the place, it was Emma who eventually returned home too late to be able to save him.... With this shocking news I remember numbly sitting upon the bed, there within that small room of the hotel, literally fighting to attempt to grasp what I had just been told. After all, I simply could not imagine life without Felix....

From that indescribably lonely moment, and throughout these many years of my own substantially long lifetime, I often find myself questioning the circumstances of Felix's passing. For instance, I have frequently pondered whether it takes as much courage to die as it surely does to live. Although Felix Lauder was a man who revered life in all its infinite forms, I know for a fact that he never feared death.... Indeed, on one specific and highly memorable occasion, he actually told me so.

For Felix—as the consummate artistic spirit that he was, life and death were the two contrasting sides of the same amazing coin of Life. Knowing and loving this outstanding individual, as I still do, I have always had difficulty in conceding to that more prosaic speculation that his death was an accident. Ever remaining a man of great depth and mystery, whatever the truth may actually be, I shall still cling to my personal belief that his end was not inspired by any sense of despair on his part, at all, but rather by a truly rational acceptance of the inevitability of what the future held in store for him....

Being a thoroughly dignified man, in every sense of the word, he had wished—above all else, to be able to pass from this life on his own terms. I surmise, as well, that he understood that any seriously protracted illness—along with its many frustrating and needlessly expensive complications—would ultimately have bankrupted Emma and their children in the end. Undoubtedly wishing to forgo this unacceptable conclusion to their lifelong struggles together, which had been basically held together by their many years of shared joys as well as their many shared sorrows, I believe that he may well have found the courage to take matters into his own hands....

Had my great teacher and friend finally found the courage to sever that sacred cord which bound him to this life? Did all that terrible restlessness from which his powerful spirit seemed to be so significantly suffering—especially towards the end, ultimately dictate his course of action?

Was it not his uncommon belief that from the very second of an artist's conception, onward throughout whatever time is allotted them upon this blessed earth, that that same critical factor of acute restlessness also acts as the significant substance by which the soul becomes more or less tentatively attached to the universal umbilical cord referred to as "humanity"? Being suspended as he was in this amazing fashion from that life-sustaining pendulum-like device of endless motion which continually sent him slowly gravitating back and forth between his own personal earthly reality of life and death—and heaven and hell, too—which person among us would actually ever have the audacity to pass judgment upon him in the negative sense?!

For, lo and behold! With that single snip of those proverbial scissors, does he not now travel out into that vast open universe—quietly alone, just as he once intimated that every creative spirit frequently longs to do, in order to eventually become truly free at last? Free at last from those tangible gravitational restraints, while at the very same time ever destined to remain anchored within the minds and the hearts of those who were privileged to know him and to love him?

Felix Lauder believed that salvation comes in various forms. Therefore it naturally stands to reason that such a portentous thing as this is not destined to become the same experience for everyone. Each of us in time is obliged to formulate our own personal concept of God—and with this our own ultimate reality of Life's awe-inspiring meaning. That tantalizing yet frequently elusive meaning of life which begs us to make as much sense out of all the interconnecting experiences of one's personal journey justifiably causes the process to evolve differently from person to person....

With these relatively sound ideas foremost within the reader's mind—and feeling substantially duty-bound as I am to actively plead this good man's case within the deeply philosophical sense, let us all respectfully bow to the perpetual knowledge that some "Higher Power" shall ultimately be judging each of us at the time of our own death. Rest assured, too—and quite likely without exception—that this Supreme Entity which endlessly embodies true clarity, and ultimate goodness, as well as an impeccably well-ordered Universe, shall one day faithfully be judging saint, and sinner, and madman alike....

Hence, in the true spirit of loving friendship, which to the critically discerning mind appropriately represents that significant fragment of true Godliness which may be found within most men, and which, without a doubt, tended to so readily exemplify Felix Lauder's own beautiful nature, I find myself openly beseeching the wise and compassionate reader to withhold judgment regarding my dear teacher and friend.... I ask that you join with me, instead, in belatedly wishing this good man a safe and meaningful journey as he continues to travel somewhere out there within that great mysterious world beyond.

EPILOGUE

W AS IT NOT CORNELIA GRIMSLEY who once mordaciously remarked to Felix Lauder that he was a "Godless heathen"? Embracing the significant reality that such a despicable person as she could never in a million years know and therefore genuinely appreciate the rare worth of such a man as this, I well recall that upon hearing this unkind and thoroughly impassioned pronouncement of hers I was instantly obliged to discount the validity of her words.

Knowing and loving my great friend, as I still do, I wish to openly state that he was the kindest and most sensitive man that I have ever known.... Even the smallest of life's joys which were generally bestowed upon other people he had known, as well as all the many unavoidable sorrows, too, were faithfully absorbed by him in order to make them his own. This, after all, was the true nature of the man. Not unlike the benevolent Christ, and Mohammed, and Buddha, who long ago consented to bless this sinful world of ours with their ever-remarkable presence, Felix Lauder remains for me the epitome of all that a truly religious man should be. In the most real sense the world became his cathedral, just as untainted goodness towards every living thing became the fervent creed by which he always sought to live....

How I miss the man. How significant has been his gentle yet far-reaching impression upon my already well-lived lifetime. Since his passing all those many years ago, not a single day has ever come, or gone, without my having quietly acknowledged something meaningful that he once said or did.

On the depressing day of Felix Lauder's funeral I am also unable to forget what a rumpus our young Anna Lauder made when her mother actually presumed to telephone a poor unsuspecting young priest from a neighboring community to summarily request that he come over to the house to baptize her recently deceased husband into the Catholic faith.... This happened no less than an hour or so before our dear patriarch was finally to be laid to rest across the street in the family's own section of the German Settlement Cemetery. How odd after all their many intimate years together as man and wife, and, too, with all that Emma Lauder surely should have understood about this fine man, that she still sought to go against his wishes. Basically, with his physical passing she was attempting to have the final say.

"Mother!" Anna angrily vowed, "If you so unjustly consent to do to my dear father in death, what he never would have tolerated from you while he lived, then please know that I shall actually pray that his justifiably vengeful spirit might haunt yours—not only throughout the rest of this lifetime, but throughout the next as well!"

So strong and so violent were our courageous Anna's cries of utter protest against what she instinctively perceived as unjust treatment towards her dead father that in the end it was a highly embarrassed Emma Lauder—not to mention a thoroughly red-faced young clergyman, too—who for the sake of a more peaceful family life in the future consented to finally drop the dangerous subject. And since those few special people whom Felix had referred to as his devoted friends while he lived had each, one by one, already passed from this life themselves, the only other truly caring people who solemnly attended his burial on that late morning were the members of our immediate family.

Afterwards, after our small band of emotionally subdued mourners returned together to the house, it was Anna who eventually pulled me aside to say, "Adam, before I forget to mention it, Father left a small packet for you.... For safekeeping, naturally, I placed it within the top section of his old trunk up in the attic!"

Not long after this brief conversation of ours took place, in order to be alone with my great sadness—and likewise being "egged-on," so to speak, by my growing sense of curiosity, I quietly and unobtrusively made my way up to the warm and cozy little room upstairs. Since it was still early in the day, what gentle sunlight there was outside now came filtering in through the vent in the overhead ceiling and proved more than adequate for my present needs....

Sitting respectfully before that immense trunk which I now strongly suspected must have belonged to Felix's own father, although in hindsight I was unforgivably remiss in not bothering to actually acquire the exact details of how the young Felix eventually came to take physical possession of it, I carefully lifted the ornately decorated lid.... There within an otherwise empty top drawer and nestled peacefully in one corner of the only slightly worn wine-colored fabric that covered it, I was pleasantly greeted by a small package which was carefully wrapped in the coarse brown paper from a shopping bag. Expertly tying everything together was a generous length of two-ply twine whose parent supply even now remained in the form of a perfectly rounded sphere that was still being kept in one special drawer of the tall chest that was located within my great friend's wonderful studio....

Slowly and somewhat ceremoniously reaching for the item, I noticed that penned across the top in Felix's own distinct script were the words: "For Adam, with love.".... Taking up his gift and quickly pressing it to my heart I began to weep softly from the significant emotion that this special moment was inspiring.

Having finally unwrapped the item, I discovered a thin packet of several letters which were being solicitously bound together by a black satin ribbon. Upon my ultra-critical inspection, even though the letters had been officially addressed to various places in Pittsburgh, as well as to other cities around the country, quite oddly enough none of them had actually ever been sent out into the world.... Further studying the details of this unusual find I turned each envelope over within my hands, only to discover the telltale mark of blood-red wax which was the more preferred practice of Felix's whenever he used to post important correspondence.

Carefully opening each one of those five individual pieces of correspondence I slowly began to visually scan the lines of the messages in order to attempt to decipher their reason for being, when the sudden impact of the shining truth of the entire situation finally descended upon my mind, and my heart, in full measure! Once again being unable to control my strong emotions, I began to openly weep....

Originally there had been six letters. Of this fact I remain quite certain. But remaining true to his promise in attempting to try and locate my mother not long after my father's untimely death, although Felix dutifully composed each letter just as Emma Lauder had always insisted he do, he must have posted only the first one. For there within my grateful hands I was actually holding the remainder of what he had once taken so much time and trouble to write, but purposely never bothered to mail....

Here at last was tangible proof that my beloved adopted father had always wanted me to stay within this special family from the very beginning. All my nagging uncertainty over my place within the family group, and likewise those numerous bouts of absolute anguish on my part where I imagined that I might be uprooted at any moment and then finally sent away from them, had not been necessary after all.

With the poignantly reassuring knowledge of all of this, I soon began to laugh out loud at the long-overdue joy which I was feeling—just as at the very same moment more tears of real understanding and gratitude continued to flow from my eyes and to run down my cheeks. I feel certain that this unusual and wholly spontaneous experience of mine could be likened to a rainy Summer's day when a bit of unexpected sunshine consents to break through the clouds, inevitably creating the effect of a beautiful rainbow across the heart....

Even in death this good man's kindness towards me had the ability to bring forth this same significant emotional release. In life, as well as in death, Felix's regard for me was such that it naturally inspired those truly blessed tears that always symbolized the mutual vulnerability which is born from complete trust. That same acute vulnerability of the spirit, I might add, which no amount of cruelty could ever exact from me in exactly the same manner.

While I sat quietly pondering so many important things, my attention was soon arrested by the sight of another piece of white paper which remained surreptitiously tucked away within the recently discarded brown paper covering that now lay crumpled at my feet.... Quickly rummaging through what I might have otherwise thrown away, I finally retrieved a solitary envelope and soon discovered within it the black and white photograph of my own father when he was a young man whose age I now was. Studying his only slightly familiar likeness, much as I had done on that evening when I was a mere boy of eight or so, the sight of him as he stood there—willfully choosing to remain apart from his comrades in his utter aloneness—I found that I could now face so many truths that without Felix's wisdom and love would not have been possible for me.

What was it that my great friend and teacher had particularly wished for me to remember? Ah, yes! Now I recall.... "To deny any truth is to lend a certain distortion to one's life!" And, "Upon the sacred rubble of my parents' lives I must find the courage to go forth and establish my own far more healthy existence—my own far more resilient dynasty!" Just as Felix did, in time I would come to better understand and appreciate the truth that no individual is ever responsible for the circumstances of his or her birth, but rather what they inevitably choose to make of their life....

In order to consciously honor this valuable truth, just as I have always sought to continually honor the special man who accepted me from the start as one of his own children, upon that very day I made a promise to both of us. Within the welcome privacy of that attic room, I took a solemn oath to forever attempt to make a success of my life.

That same night Felix came to say good-bye to me in an extraordinarily beautiful dream. Very much as George had also done so many years before that time, our beloved patriarch chose to bestow upon me an equally meaningful gift whose richness of prophetic meaning has never left me, yet continues to travel with me still.

In that marvelous reverie of mine, Felix and I were struggling to make our way up the long precarious ladder of the William's Bay water tower.... We climbed and climbed for what seemed to be an inordinate amount of time, not complaining in the least as we huffed and puffed along, but vigorously working together to achieve our worthy goal....

By the time he and I finally reached the top, we were both indescribably exhausted from our effort. Managing just enough strength to literally drag each other over to the more flat and safe pinnacle of the high tower, we laid back and finally closed our eyes as we instinctively reached for each other's hand.... For quite some time all that we could hear was the labored sounds that our mingled breathing made.

Eventually opening my eyes and glancing over at Felix, I realized with mild surprise that he was the same Felix I had met years ago; while I, in the same manner, had returned to my youth by once again becoming the young vulnerable child of seven or eight. With both of us spontaneously giving off a bit of heartfelt laughter, we began to help each other to our feet, as I managed to say, "Gosh, Felix! That has to be one of the longest climbs ever recorded!"

Placing his strong left arm firmly about my thin boyish shoulders, just as he always used to do in order to ground himself more firmly to this life, my excellent friend gently hugged me to him all the while smiling with such incredible warmth, as he answered, "Come, Adam.... Come! There is something significantly grand that I wish to share with you!"

Standing together at the very edge of the tower, as we were, from somewhere well beyond the white and downy puffs of clouds that were floating far far below us at the moment, we distinctly began to hear those undeniably optimistic notes from the first movement of Brahm's "Ein Deutsches Requiem" as they benevolently took to fanning out in every possible direction, profoundly blessing that remarkable moment in time.... With our standing proud and tall together, we both looked out into the distance to see what we could see....

There instead of the expected sight of our beautiful Lake Geneva to our immediate right—and to our left the miles of familiarly rich farmland which should have been spreading out as far as the eye could see—I was absolutely stunned by the fact that man and boy were standing at the top of the world. Indeed, beneath us at the moment and spreading out across the endless landscape were all the countless peopled cities, and towns, and villages of the world, along with its vast oceans and seas, as well as all the mountains and the deserts, too.

Not bothering to turn to look my way Felix lifted his free right arm nearly chest high and with the palm of his hand spread open towards heaven in the form of an open greeting to the same benevolent God in whom we both believed, he slowly began to pass that hand out across the wide panoramic view of all that we were now experiencing together.... Boldly reminiscent of the noble Job of ancient times, with both of these good men having certainly experienced their share of many joys and surely just as many overwhelming sorrows to last several full lifetimes, with true exaltation sounding within his very familiar voice my great friend finally exclaimed, "Look, Adam! See for yourself.... See how incredibly beautiful the world can be!"

His lovely words, along with all that he was showing me, literally took my breath away. Presently, with that endlessly inspirational chorus still accompanying the same wondrous music which I well-imagined must have comprised all the many hundreds of millions of righteous souls who once lived upon this amazing earth, as well as all the countless other wholly civilized beings destined to ever be born in the future, all were united en masse to sing forth their astounding words of praise....

From St. Matthew v. 4, they sang forth: "Blessed are they that mourn; for they shall be comforted"; and eventually continuing on from there, with the ever-reassuring words of the prophet Isaiah: "And the ransomed of the Lord shall return, and come to Zion with songs and everlasting joy upon their heads; they shall obtain joy and gladness, and sorrow and sighing shall all flee away!"

At last, with the two of us turning to acknowledge each other, I could readily see that Felix was smiling the smile I knew and loved so well.... There within his endlessly beautiful eyes I was re-discovering all the love that he still felt for me. Indeed, I was happily discovering all the wonderful love which would always be there for me....

Quite inexplicably, too, within the sublime aura of his indisputably powerful gaze, I was actually beginning to feel the incredible movement of his soul's powerful gravitational pull, as it gently but quite firmly took to engage me in order to more thoroughly interact with my own spirit. Very soon, and without the slightest resistance on my part, I allowed the unwavering trust which this dear man always inspired within me to finally release me from what had grown so familiar to me, and therefore seemed far more safe to me, in order to begin traveling towards the beautiful light that was glowing deep within his eyes.... Finally, beyond the only world which I was accustomed to experiencing, together Felix and I were presently journeying out past the sun and the moon, as well as past the endless succession of galaxies of brightly glowing stars, heading with boundless excitement towards the great open universe beyond....

Never shall I be able to forget that amazing dream, just as it would be quite impossible for me to ever forget that truly remarkable human being who so generously inspired it. With Felix Lauder's boundless patience and love I was diligently taught so many important truths regarding the great mysteries of living and loving.... For instance, I have learned first-hand that genuine love is stronger than death. Likewise, I have also always remained pleasurably mindful of the fact that even tiny spiders are consummate architects and engineers.

And thanks in great part to my dear friend, as well as to the daily practical knowledge one usually always acquires by traveling through the years, I have come to readily understand and appreciate the fact that each of us is ultimately defined by the unending collection of our every thought and deed. Each of us becomes more legibly circumscribed by the unique interior of those deepest regions of our soul....

In the end it becomes nothing less than that great moral imperative of true spiritual integrity which is really the only reliable yardstick by which we are obliged to measure ourselves, and also obliged to measure others. Without this superlative foundation or tool which in essence acts as a sojourner's trustworthy compass, and which unerringly coincides with one's insatiable hunger for Truth, and Justice, and Beauty—as well as with one's endless reverence for all living things, a soul is destined to remain utterly lost and hopelessly impoverished. With regard to this same monolithic consistency suffice it to say that elected leaders of any nation—nations both great and small—who are pathetically lacking in this priceless attribute of uncompromising integrity, eventually not only impoverish their own country, but also manage to eventually impoverish the rest of the world as well.

Finally—and remaining no less gloriously valuable to me than these other treasures have surely proven to be, in his boundless generosity Felix Lauder taught me to trust enough in order to be able to love in the truest sense. No less critically important he taught me that I was born a good person and worthy of being loved in return. And as the far more discerning reader has already learned so very well by now, these last two crucial things have made all the difference in the overall quality of my life.... All the difference in the world.

Beverly Horvath DiMare is an artist and
writer living in southern Florida.